UNBOUND ORDER

THE UNBINDING CHRONICLES: VOLUME II

J. NEFF

EDITORS: J. M. NEFF, MARIKO IRVING, SHANE POPE
COVER ART: EMILY VERKAMP

UNBOUND ORDER
THE UNBINDING CHRONICLES: VOLUME II

ISBN: 979-8-9911610-4-6

EireneBros Publishing LLC
4414 82nd St, Ste 212 – 318
Lubbock, TX 79424
www.eirenebrospublishing.com

Cover Art: Emily Verkamp
Illustrations: J. Neff, Aesthetically Inked

*This volume is dedicated to Ashley, Jené, Justin,
Katherine, and Niki*

West Espa
Farzg Estate
[The Lichwood]
Osgood
Osgood
[Draikin Peninsula]
The Astral Spire
[Mammoth Moors]
Tuzin Forest
Shester
North Timbyl
Alabaster
Eodan
[Zenith Plains]
Osfer
[Gulf of Nocturne]
Alabaster
THE SHINDOR OCEAN
[Ermen Moors]
Seltan Range
Thaliston
[Ezdell Hillcountry]
Argentum
Devitus
Claston
Claston
Lancethinas Estate
Nulodia
K'tal H'yuck
Ft. Cunningworth
Glern
Beriton
Acero
Mystalon
[The Tymbyrwylde]
Mt. Ember
Tanlin Falls
Carulus's Camp
Port Undine
Sea of Undine
N
Chyu'Taï Ocean
Tobit
Solar Sea
Cassack
Tibot
Ignia Sea
Scale: 100 Miles
[The Isles Known for Nothing]
Yendralia

Summer
Autumn
Winter
Spring
GROWING
REPLENISHING
EQUINOX
SOLSTICE
FLOURISHING
HARVESTING
EQUINOX
FESTIVAL
FALLOWING
SOLSTICE
RESTING
WARMING

Annual Cycle of Espa

Winter
101 Days – 3 Months

The Fallowing – 40 Days
Winter Solstice – 21 Days
The Resting – 40 Days

Vernum
103 Days – 3 Months

The Warming – 40 Days
Equinox – 23 Days
The Replenishing – 40 Days

Summer
101 Days – 3 Months

The Growing – 40 Days
Summer Solstice – 21 Days
The Flourishing – 40 Days

Autumn
103 Days – 3 Months

The Harvesting – 40 Days
Equinox – 23 Days
The Festival – 40 Days

Time and Specifics

1 Week = 5 Days

1 - Pri
2 - Seg
3 - Treg
4 - Quilli
5 - Paz

1 Day = 24 Hours

Content Warning:

This book contains some fantasy violence including death. Disturbing imagery may unsettle some readers. Please read with caution and self-care.

Illustrations by Aesthetically Inked

Miranda at the Battle of Beriton

Ezelbrecht

Foreward

The arrival of *Unbound Chaos* coincided with a time of significant mental and emotional changes in my life. It was the pinnacle of a chapter where dreams were coming true and life was finally as rewarding as it was challenging.

Little did I know those moments would coalesce into a bigger, faster paced, more exciting experience than I ever anticipated.

Unbound Order has challenged me to grow as a writer. The lessons learned through *Unbound Chaos* have been present in my mind for two years, and I hope those lessons have distilled into a more exciting, entertaining, and engaging reading experience.

While my core inspirations haven't changed, *Unbound Order* is definitely influenced by the ebb and flow of life over the last two years. My experiences with death, trauma, and suffering have been juxtaposed with the fight for what is right and good. Those words have come to life in a book I never expected to have the privilege to write.

To all of you who have given me a reason to write, I thank you from the bottom of my heart. There are no words to express how joyful it makes my soul that I can share Miranda's story with you. The girl from the frontier has a few more things to learn, and so do I.

J. Neff

TABLE OF CONTENTS

Chapter 1
A Discovery

"The eggs of the Old Ones are enigmatic, delicious, and unimaginably dangerous. Handle with caution and dine on the lifeforce of the universe." – Chef Tapato

igh Priest Thomas Selasine peered into a crate in disbelief. Inside was a single dragon egg, its shell a bright, bluish-green, indicating it was the egg of a sea dragon. The situation concerned him. Slavers expending the effort to acquire and transport dragon eggs defied normal criminal activity. Their value plummeted after The Unbinding, but they were still hard to locate and harder to steal. This was not the first confiscated egg, either. The Church of Invictus had intercepted at least two dozen in the last month. He wondered why Eldon Farzg's henchmen were so interested in them.

A voice grabbed his attention. "Nulestotejin, are you alright?" The elven word for brother-in-law indicated the speaker's identity just as clearly as the rich voice that spoke it. The high priest turned to see Pirate Lord Erilkaiden Lancethinas standing behind him. Most people called him Captain or Erk for short, but their relationship was complicated. Thomas was the High Priest of Nulodia in the Church of Invictus, a god dedicated to upholding order and justice. Erk was formerly a dread pirate who ruthlessly resisted the unjust rule of a usurper in his home kingdom of Claston. Though they walked different paths, their shared love of Erk's sister, Iria, gave them a close bond. Together, they had worked tirelessly to damage Farzg's slave trade, but dragon eggs were an increasingly common discovery during these raids. Erk approached as Thomas shook his head in response to the elf's question.

"Another egg," the high priest commented.

Erk's eyes widened a bit. "That's at least, what, seventeen? Eighteen?" the pirate replied, his voice inquisitive and calculating.

Thomas shook his head again. "Apologies, brother. Damil reported that Justin and August's crew found six more on a raid down in the Sea of Undine earlier this week," he explained. His former pupils had spent the last five months with a newly formed division of the church known as the Airborne Marines. Combining their budding experience in naval and aerial combat, the young paladins led efforts against Farzg in the Solar Sea and the Sea of Undine. Erk and his betrothed, Pirate Lady Naomi, employed their fleets to aid them in their mission. Selasine speculated, "I wager Farzg is working for a new, unknown client paying a hefty sum for dragon eggs."

Erk smiled. He was a handsome elf approaching middle age, but his participation in the Claston Civil War and his work as a pirate kept him muscular and fit. "No need to apologize." He gave Thomas an affirming nod. "We can't remember every detail when Farzg is moving this fast. What in the Infernia does he want with dragon eggs, though?"

The two stood in the cargo hold of a Death Pirate junk the same size as Erk's galleon, *The Nebula*. This deck was empty as the victims were freed once the church crew docked the junk in the port city of Nulodia. The coastal metropolis was massive and welcoming to refugees and otherwise displaced peoples. Naomi had built a network across the kingdoms of Alabaster and Claston to help kidnapping and trafficking victims find their way back home. This left High Priest Selasine and Pirate Lord Erk to confiscate the remaining cargo on the ship.

In Thomas's mind, that was the critical issue. Dragon eggs weren't illegal to transport. He struggled to imagine how they could be used for criminal means. Furthermore, dragon eggs were enigmatic. Legends described two gods, one of good and one of evil, creating dragons by shattering themselves into the flow of the arcane stream. Every dragon was considered an immortal entity made of magic, a shard of their respective deity come to life. They were complex and wielded incredible magic at one point in history. Thanks to The Unbinding, they were no more threatening than giant lizards with deadly talons and fangs. Selasine contemplated that information as he confessed, "I'm at a complete loss over the eggs.

Do you have any ideas?" Together, they looked in the crate. The egg was almost three feet in diameter. Its shell reflected its color despite the poor lighting of the cargo deck.

"I have the education of an adept wizard, but I haven't the slightest." He cleared his throat and suggested, "We should ask Miranda about this." As a dragon trapped in human form, Selasine's adoptive daughter was the closest entity they knew who might have an idea why Farzg would seek dragon eggs.

Selasine chuckled. "Her last letter came in the day before yesterday. She's still off in K'tal H'yuck with the draikin and those warriors from Mystalon. She said they discovered a way through the Dundoi Mountains up to Argentum. There's a lot of archaeological value up there, especially since it was the epicenter of The Unbinding." He always shared what he knew about his daughter's activities, which Erk cherished. Though the young woman loved the pirate dearly as a mentor, she only sent a weekly letter to Selasine. After the Battle of Beriton, she was adamant that her next adventures would be uniquely hers. They were worried current events would pull her back into the rage of a world-changing conflict. They wanted her to experience the joys of adventuring and helping people without the weight of her heritage hovering over her.

"The draikin are known to defend the eggs of the old ones," Erk commented, using a colloquial term for dragon.

"I'm sure they would share our concern, but Damil can't reach Miranda," Selasine lamented. Draikin were a humanoid race, but were closer to small dragon people than humans. They stood upright with large, reptilian heads. They were brilliant and dexterous but lacked the physical strength of the dragons who began their magical genetic line eons ago. The high priest continued, "He thinks it's because he only connected with her while she was under the usurper's curse. He can usually find a person after he's made contact once. He thinks her transformation changed her mind, too. Plus, her return trips to the city have been scarce and swift. They've not seen each other since she departed at the end of The Harvesting." The high priest chuckled. "For a retired guy, he sure manages to find a lot of work."

"We could send Evan. You know, he's dying to see her anyway," Erk teased, their voices bouncing with a faint echo in the empty cargo hold.

Selasine laughed. "Is he now?" he interrogated, putting pressure on Erk to reveal information.

He smirked. "Just as much as any of us, I'm sure," the pirate deflected.

Selasine narrowed his left eye, his right eye hidden underneath his eyepatch due to the injury given to him by Farzg twenty-five years ago. "Erilkaiden," he growled without malice, indicating he did not want to deal with the pirate's games. Selasine suspected something more than gratitude was stirring in the younger Lancethinas brother's feelings.

Erk sighed, but his lips twisted up into a smile. "Well, we all owe her a debt of thanks, but Evan especially. It's like he's still barely ninety years old, even though he's only ten years younger than my one hundred and forty. She didn't just heal his body. She gave him a second chance to live," he elaborated. "Thirty years of life is still a grand sum, even for an elf."

Selasine tilted his head a bit. His black hair was pulled into a tightly braided ponytail, a holdover from his service as a warpriest of Invictus. He did not change his style or manner after being promoted from bishop to high priest. He was heavily armored and rugged but approachable and serene. "Imagine what I could do with thirty years," he mumbled. He, Damil, Iriliandria, and a hellspawn named Haelia were once one of the church's most prolific crime-fighting teams. They pursued Farzg three decades prior. Their time together ended when they destroyed Farzg's smuggling ring and raided his estate far in the north. In the aftermath, they presumed Farzg was dead, but they were incorrect. Haelia perished, rescuing thousands of people from an icy fate. Losing Haelia broke Iria's spirit and sent Damil into reclusive service as a Pegasus Knight. Thomas was heartbroken by the loss of his friend and the departure of his love, but he understood. Damil cherished the three of them so much that he couldn't stand the thought of losing Thomas or Iria in addition to Haelia.

Erk watched Thomas's eye close as the priest scanned his memories. "Apologies, brother, I didn't mean to send your thoughts to the past," he explained. The elf knew he had to get Selasine's attention back on the present quickly. "Besides, Miranda is beautiful, loving, and incredibly brave. She and Evan, ah, well..." he trailed off, noticing that Selasine's attention had returned. "Evan said he can't get her out of his head. You know. How that goes," Erk finished, his pauses uncharacteristic.

Selasine smiled and let out a hearty laugh. "I know, nulestotejin. Damil doesn't have any more available contact points, though.

Severing one of his current connections could delay the relay of information that will save lives. It can take a couple of days for his mind to find someone again after he breaks away. We wouldn't have real-time communication with the troops in the east if he gave up a spot for Evan. Would Evan undertake a blind journey like that?"

Erk laughed, picking up the heavy lid to the crate with the dragon egg. "Well, let's get this back to the church, and we can discuss it during the debriefing." He closed the crate, and together they carried it off the junk and into port.

The next day, there was a meeting at noon in the high priest's study at the grand cathedral of Invictus in Nulodia. Thomas had modified his office to be reminiscent of a ship captain's private quarters. A long table sat in the center of the room. It was usually covered with tomes, scrolls, and paperwork. Thomas's church staff included a dozen clerics that would keep the information organized on the numerous bookshelves that lined the walls of the study. He also oversaw the penitence service of Gaius Carulus, the former high priest who lost himself to the madness of chaos during the conflict with the usurper in Claston. He was an impeccable bureaucrat, and with his two-fold clerical assistance, Selasine never had to do much paperwork. He was able to focus on taking action, while Carulus employed his uncanny magic to its fullest potential. He could increase his mental acuity while reading or writing, allowing him to process information at incredible speeds. For the first time in over twenty years, the high priest of Nulodia was an active symbol of justice for the people of the metropolitan city, something that Carulus and his predecessor were unable to be thanks to their dispositions.

Carulus had prepared the study for High Priest Selasine and his inner circle. The high priest called the meeting to address the increasing concern over dragon eggs being discovered in the possession of slavers. Carulus readied highlights from various texts discussing dragon eggs, and he included correspondence from adventuring paladins and priests describing encounters with dragons or their eggs. In his own mind, he only lamented that he would not be participating in the meeting.

Selasine stood with Erk at the head of the table, confirming their identification of the sea dragon's egg. Dozens of straw-filled crates had been stacked behind them, blocking some of the light from the stained-glass windows gracing the north side of the room. The entrance to the high priest's study was on the top floor of the cathedral's library in the northwestern wing of the complex. As they stood, peering over the documents in front of them, the latch on the door clicked. The two of them looked up to the southeastern side of the room as a blond elf slightly taller than Erk entered the room.

"Moshirote! Nulestotejin!" the elf greeted in formal elven.

"Evanthalus!" Erk called back.

Evan's gray eyes were somewhat warmer than Erk's, shimmering with mirth and excitement. He smiled at his brother and nodded, walking to the table in the center of the room. It was a circular room with two floors, the second accessible by several ladders leading up to a balcony wrapping around the room. Bookshelves towered along the walls and were built into the very architecture of the deep-purple stone cathedral. Though he had been here many times, Evan always felt excited to be with his brother and brother-in-law. He helped raid the junk that the Church of Invictus brought into port the previous day and was also concerned about the number of dragon eggs confiscated recently. "So, you found another one, Your Holiness?" Evan asked, using Selasine's formal title.

Selasine scowled, "Indeed, though I'm not sure what it portends."

Erk added, "If it's Farzg's handiwork, it isn't good."

Evan frowned at the mention of the slaver's name. "Without a doubt, brother," he spat, feeling his anger surge and relishing the sensation. While he was previously cursed, his physical body began to wither away. His uncanny magic could destroy the moisture in a large radius around himself, but the usurper tried to use that same power to kill him. While languishing in a desiccated state, Evan could feel nothing but an unquenchable thirst, not even emotions. After Miranda healed him of the curse, she also healed his body, restoring it to its condition from thirty years ago. However, as his soul returned to his body, he lost his connection to the arcane stream. Seeing his continued life as a gift, he took every emotion he felt and savored it as much as he could. He understood that life without those emotions was a fate worse than death.

Before anyone else could speak, the door creaked open again. In the doorway stood an imposing, beautiful woman with mostly elven facial features including longer, pointed ears. She towered at six feet and five inches, with her long silver hair pulled back into a ponytail. Her dark, brown skin shimmered in the well-lit study. She had a purple bandana tied around her hair and wore thick, magical leather armor, which enhanced her agility. She had numerous pistols on her belts, and four bandoliers full of finely crafted throwing daggers. A warm smile rested on her lips as she greeted the room, "Darlings, I've returned!" Her voice was deep and rich.

"Naomi, my dear!" Erk replied, looking back to the door where his betrothed stood.

"You might as well leave the door open for a bit Naomi, the others should be arriving soon," Selasine suggested.

With a smile, Naomi blinked. As she did, a nearby doorstop made of iron slid into place under the door. "As Your Holiness wishes," she teased. Selasine, Erk, and Evan laughed. Naomi was normally an informal person. It sounded comical to them when she used formal titles unironically.

"Holding the door for us, Pirate Lady Naomi? How sweet of you," a gruff voice piped from behind her. The three at the table tried to peer behind Naomi as she turned sideways in the doorway to glance behind her. There stood three young paladins, two human men and a human woman. The young man that spoke had brown hair and rugged features.

"August!" Naomi replied to the paladin that stood a step behind the other two. He was the tallest of the three, almost standing face to face with Naomi. The other man was shy of six feet tall, and his dirty blond hair was pulled into a tight ponytail braid behind him. He had a warm, tan complexion and a soft but handsome face. The woman was pretty, and her stern expression made her look scrutinous. In spite of her intensity, her brown eyes sparkled with excitement and friendliness. Her brown skin gave a pleasing contrast with her blond hair. The sides of her head were shaved, but the hair on top was pulled into a tight ponytail braid as well. Almost all of the clergy of Invictus with the exception of a few divisions of paladins kept their hair long and braided, using the metaphor of a strong, braided rope or thread as a symbol of strength and unity. "Valarie! Justin!" she added to greet the two who had said nothing up to this point.

Both Valarie and Justin had large tower shields strapped to their backs, indicating their continued service and training with the Shield Knight division of the Church of Invictus. They were dressed in field plate mail. Naomi towered above them. She was the grandchild of earth giant nobility. She was incredibly large for someone who was primarily elven. She embraced the smaller paladins.

Justin eventually pushed out of the hug, and he and Valarie stomped to attention and saluted in the way of the Path of the Sword of Justice. They put their shield hands to the hilts of their weapons and put their sword hands to their chest, their palms turned upward. "Pirate Lady Naomi, ma'am! Airborne Marines, reporting for duty!" Justin exclaimed in an authoritative voice. Their crew had captured dozens of Farzg's ships in the last five months. Justin's tone captured the confidence built through their achievements.

Naomi giggled a bit. "You aren't supposed to salute me, sweeties. I'm just a pirate!" she replied to their sudden formal stances.

Naomi and August locked eyes. She gave him a devious smile. When they first met, August was not sure how to handle Naomi's confidence and beauty. She had earned the nickname Succubus of the Seas for a reason. As August's own self-confidence grew through success in his actions, he finally understood the giantkin. He prompted the teasing this time. "What, no hug for me too?"

Naomi laughed and extended her arm. August took it, and Naomi pulled him in for a friendly embrace. Since August was a little taller than six feet, Naomi did not overwhelm him like she did Valarie and Justin. Instead, they looked like two family members who had not seen each other in a while.

A voice from inside the study rang out. "Naomi, dear, stop teasing the rookies," Erk prodded.

The four outside of the study shared another smile, entered the room, and approached the table.

"Are we all here, then?" Evan asked, considering everyone present.

"Damil is coordinating two battalions attacking a potential slave caravan in the western reaches of Claston," Selasine explained. That meant that Damil would not be present in person nor telepathically.

Erk replied, "That's good news. Evil never sleeps, and chaos gnaws at the heels of society. The righteous must be ever vigilant," he said, reciting a catechism of his chosen goddess, Lexcord the Silver Maiden. She was a goddess of truth, beauty, and goodness. She was said to be an elf that ascended to godhood during the Legion of Hoxark. After defeating the usurper, Erk had given more attention to the scriptures of Lexcord and Invictus, swearing to uphold their ideals of law and order. He and Evan began training again after Evan's curse was healed, and they used the most strenuous practices of Lexcord's elite troops known as The Harbingers.

"And may we serve the Sword of Justice and the Silver Maiden with humble hearts and actions worthy of praise," Selasine added, including the end of a catechism of Invictus that mirrored the recitation in Lexcord's folds. The god of justice, Invictus, and the goddess of righteousness, Lexcord, were considered siblings by the followers of their churches and often collaborated in their efforts against evil and lawlessness.

Evan nodded in agreement. "Very well, then. Dragon eggs. Right?"

Naomi tilted her head in the direction of the door as all seven of them gathered around the table. The doorstop jolted out of the way, and the door shut gently. "I also have something weird to report," she interjected as she turned her silver eyes back to the table after shutting the door. "The last ship that we raided on *The Violet Blur* not only had a dragon egg on board, but most of the captives were faekin, and I don't mean the big ones."

Everyone at the table looked at Naomi immediately. Erk blurted, "Faekin? Like pixies and leprechauns?"

Naomi tilted her head and frowned. "Darling, that's exactly what I meant by faekin. The slavers were equipped with brutal, magical cages powered by gemstones. I left the derelict ship a little out to sea." She shrugged.

Justin then said, "Two more eggs have been confirmed in the Sea of Undine. We returned only two days ago, and the evidence has been documented properly and stored with the rest of the confiscated eggs."

August added, "Perpetrators included the Death Pirates and Farzg's henchmen. It seems that Farzg is feeling the pinch and is seeking mercenaries."

Erk sneered at the mention of The Frozen Death's name. Farzg was ruthless and had earned himself a kill-on-sight warrant from The Council of Four, the heads of the Church of Invictus. Normally, Invictus himself would have to issue such a warrant, but with the overwhelming evidence and Farzg's refusal to stand before the court of the church, the Council deemed him worthy and voted unanimously to issue the warrant. "Like vermin, fleeing from the light," the pirate lord cursed. "We knew he'd eventually turn to the Death Pirates. Ba-le-ba-ne has been especially active recently since he was nearly obliterated in The Battle of Beriton," Erk explained, referencing their final confrontation with the usurper and his Death Pirate allies seven months ago.

Selasine listened. Evan looked anxious. Valarie continued the conversation. "High Paladin Aguila and Pirate Lord Ut'wah are both concerned with the increased Death Pirate activity. It's an indication that the forces of Hoxark are mobilized," she explained. "Cantalus has warned they have new allies inland. We need to be wary of the demons in league with the Death Pirates."

Evan shook his head. "None of it adds up, then. Dragon eggs, faekin, and Death Pirates. And to make matters worse, these are becoming common," he said, holding out an elaborate sword. It was made of advanced mechanical parts straight out of a clockmaker's dream. Gears churned within the inner workings of the sword. In the hilt, there was a strange pommel stone. It radiated a bright pink aura, and several, small wooden spikes were drilled into a pink gemstone which rested within. "These weapons are powered by an unusual substance, but it seems to be crystalized magic." Evan gave the sword a spin and then sheathed it. Since he had lost his uncanny magic, he had been training nonstop to develop his fighting skills. He enjoyed showing them off.

Naomi's eyes widened and she added, "Those are the same stones that powered the fae cages!"

Selasine shook his head, but then he started to nod. "It can't be helped, and I can't deny the evidence anymore. We need Miranda's thoughts. I know where she is and what she is working on in her adventures, but I have not disclosed the many perplexing details of our struggles against Farzg." Everyone agreed, knowing that Miranda would have been back three months ago if she had heard about the dragon eggs or the proliferation of strange equipment. Selasine had hoped not to call his adoptive daughter back to Nulodia so soon, but at this point, they needed to find answers. "Problem is, there's too much classified information to send by written message. We need somebody to go and consult with her. Damil has tried to reach out several times, but his mind cannot find hers. Nor can he spare any communication channels right now. The delay in restoring his connections to our current leadership could cost lives or operational success." He explained, matter of factly. Erk smiled, understanding the resolve and strength that his sister saw in the remarkable priest.

"I'll go get her!" Naomi inserted immediately. She was very protective of Miranda and had insisted for months that the young woman should join her crew as they hit slavers and rescued people.

Erk laughed. "But we have too many leads on Farzg that need to be checked out, my dear. We need The Blur and her beautiful captain doing what they do best," he continued, stepping close to his betrothed. He reached out and took her hand in his.

Selasine nodded in agreement. "And the Airborne Marines are required for a mission here in the city this week."

Everyone's eyes shifted to Evan. He blinked quickly and looked around. "Woah, I feel like somebody just made a decision, and I don't know if I like it yet."

The team laughed. Erk spoke, "Would you be so kind as to follow the intelligence we have and fetch Miranda? Or at least get a report to her. She will know what to do. She is wise."

Naomi rocked her shoulders with a teasing movement, "Hey, that's a great idea, send loverboy! You can journey day and night, crawl through the desert, find yourself at her feet and," she tossed her hand up to her forehead and made a caricatured swooning gesture, "and tell her how much you love her." She drew out the sound of the "o" for much longer than was comfortable.

Evan blushed, his fair complexion making it easy to see his embarrassment. "Hey, c'mon now Naomi, you're the only one who thinks that," he retorted.

Most everyone burst into laughter again at Evan's expense. On their last night at sea back in the late summer, Miranda and Evan had spent some time together thinking of the future. Miranda was the reason Evan had a future. It filled him with a whirlwind of emotions about her. He wasn't sure if it was love, admiration, or respect. Maybe it was all of them, and that's why the feeling was so overwhelming, he thought. He had disclosed those thoughts to his brother and Naomi, but Naomi missed the nuance.

Still, Evan considered the importance of finding Miranda and figuring out what to do. Though their overall mission was grim, the team in Nulodia managed to keep their camaraderie and morale high through their mutual love and friendship. Selasine interrupted, trying to compose himself. "Or we could just send him by pegasus, and he can talk to Miranda about the situation." He nodded with a warm, fatherly smile. They were bound together in a way that contrasted the chaotic state of magic in The Unbinding, and it made their efforts worthwhile.

Evan clenched his fists with building excitement in response to Selasine's suggestion. August saluted with his interruption. "One bird ready to fly at the high priest's orders," he said, smiling at Evan. They made an excellent duo fighting on pegasus in the Battle of Beriton. August had confidence in Evan's flying skills.

Evan shrugged. "Sounds like I've not got much of a choice, then, yeah?" he said with a chuckle. "My hands are tied." He held them up in a taunting gesture at Naomi.

Erk laughed louder than anyone. Naomi scowled and murmured,

"Yeah, well. I know what you sound like when you ask about her. That's all." She squeezed Erk's hand.

"Enough, enough," Selasine prompted, keeping his friends and family focused. "Please, Evan. Go to K'tal H'yuck and see what Miranda's thoughts are on these issues. I have my own suspicions, but if dragons are involved, she's definitely the one we need to consult."

Evan punched his right fist into his left hand. "I'll get some things ready for travel then. Meet me in the courtyard, Commander Burchard?" he asked, looking at August.

The paladin replied with a renewed salute. "Sir!" he commanded. Valarie and Justin also saluted.

Erk broke away from Naomi and approached his brother. He gave him a firm embrace, Evan's additional height creating a strange contrast as the younger brother was taller. Erk warned, "Don't be surprised if she insists on coming back with you, yeah?"

Evan patted his brother on the back with an affirming pop. "I know." As he pushed away, he looked around the room. "Finally, I get my own mission. Maybe one of you will figure out how to give me a cooler title than Drymouth. I really don't like that one. Never did," he finished with a laugh.

"Evan the Seeker," Justin piped.

"Evan, the lovesick puppy," Naomi insisted. Evan smiled, hearing the sincerity in Naomi's teasing. Nobody else laughed, fearing the pirate lady might push the joke past its appropriate limits.

Evan's smile widened. "Let's all agree there's more pressing issues, and we can make solutions from there. Savvy?" he asserted. He managed to say his goodbyes and depart the cathedral before the noon hour had ended.

After Evan's exit, the others split up to act on leads related to Farzg's operations within the city of Nulodia proper. Bureaucrat in penitence, Gaius Carulus, entered the study to organize the documentation he had researched for His Holiness. As he approached the table, tears welled in his eyes. "They didn't even touch the paperwork!" he bemoaned. "A high priest is only as good as his information!" he continued to lament.

He felt a voice stir within him. "So, stay vigilant and offer your voice when it's clear your counsel is needed, yes?"

Carulus closed his eyes and smiled, letting the lone tear that had formed run down his cheek. "As Invictus wills it, so shall it be," he prayed in thankfulness.

Yuvina stared out a boarded-up window. A narrow gap between the planks made it easy to see out during the late afternoon. She did not want to be surprised when her contact arrived. As a member of The Forgotten, a secret society of individuals without Unbinding powers, Yuvina had recently completed a significant mission. She fully documented the uncanny magic possessed by all of the guard staff for a merchant guild in Nulodia. Upon completion, her superiors in the organization recommended her to meet with an outside contact.

She waited, watching the foot traffic in the alley behind the building. At one point, it might have been a tavern, but it had been abandoned for years. Yuvina sighed. She really did not like meeting people she knew nothing about. She had been a reconnaissance officer for The Forgotten for almost a decade. She knew the information being traded through this contact would be safe with her, as were so many other secrets and plots.

Yuvina's thoughts were interrupted by the sound of a door opening and closing at the front of the abandoned tavern. She drew a dagger from inside the cloak she had pulled tight around her. The contact was not supposed to come in the front door. The activity seemed suspicious. She listened for footsteps or movement but heard nothing. She stayed near the window, unafraid of who or what it might have been. A few moments passed, and she began to relax. Perhaps somebody in the street in front of the building had opened the door by mistake or curiosity. After a few more moments, she could see someone in the alley.

The stranger looked to be an elf with wiry, white hair that stood out in every direction. He was dressed in a brown leather tunic and trousers. Yuvina knew this was the contact. Perhaps he checked the front for spies or eavesdroppers, something she had already done on her arrival. The Forgotten's work thrived in secrecy. They struggled against a society that discriminated against them for their lack of uncanny magic. Their deific patron, Pulhash, was a god that fought for people like The Forgotten. Yuvina despised her oppression and cursed the structures of law that continued to allow unlucky individuals to be cast aside by society. This information exchange was only a tiny step in a bigger plot to even the standing of members of The Forgotten.

The elf stopped directly outside the back door and opened it. Yuvina snapped her attention to the light now coming into the building from outside. A moment later, the stranger entered. He was average height for an elf at five feet tall, and he looked like he could have seen at least a century before The Unbinding. His eyes shimmered with a rainbow of colors, and his features were ragged and stressed. He locked his gaze with Yuvina's and smiled. He began to speak, "Starved of magic, drink from the fountain of Doctor One!"

Yuvina nodded. That was the code she expected, so she replied, "On behalf of The Forgotten, I am here to drink and to learn."

The strange elf began bouncing excitedly. "I'm so pleased with your superiors. They sent me a prime specimen! Your body is practically devoid of magic," he explained, reaching up to his monocle positioned in his left eye. Removing it, he peered at Yuvina for a moment. She was a kitsune of thirty years, her face stoic and reserved. Her orange and green eyes shimmered, vulpine pupils in the center narrowed as he spoke to her. She had a dagger in her paw. He replaced the monocle and nodded. "The stream doesn't flow through you fully. I want to know if I can make it do so."

Yuvina pulled her hood down. Her fur was dark gray with white accents. "My superiors didn't mention any of this to me," she replied, giving him a menacing glare. Her whiskers twitched at the end of her small snout.

The stranger sneered. "Do not worry, fox. I do not anticipate any harm will come to you. This is the information that The Forgotten's leaders promised me."

Yuvina blinked with an incredulous cadence. The message she had for him was very cryptic. It was mostly diagrams written in elven, which she did not know. She replied, "My mission was to deliver this to you." She withdrew an unsealed scroll she had reviewed several times. She offered it to the elf, and he snatched it. He unfurled it and skimmed over it briefly. As he looked up, she continued, "We graciously accept Doctor One's assistance in this matter."

A wicked smile crossed his lips. "Correct. I am Doctor One, and I can make the device pictured in this scroll. And that's when I need you."

She briefly shook her head, more in disbelief than disagreement. "I'm sorry, but I know nothing of this device."

Doctor One licked his lips with intensity. His mouth stayed drawn up into an excited smile that radiated genius and insanity. "I need to put the device in your skin! You might bleed, but it won't kill you. Afterward, I bet you'll have some powers! Isn't that what you want?"

Yuvina gulped. "You want to give me powers with this device?" she asked, her voice emotionless but high pitched.

The elf's wild hair shook up and down as he nodded. It looked dirty and stiff and made Yuvina uncomfortable. Doctor One continued his explanation, "You see, the device is an eolnut conduit. Are you familiar with eolnut trees, my child?"

Yuvina shook her head, her ears twitching slightly as her frustration built.

"They are one of the three sacred trees in the world of Espa. Their wood is very special. It transfers arcane energy into the mortal plane. You see, these are the diagrams to guide me in the creation of an eolnut injector. We can filter some crystallized magic through the device. The results can transform the recipient in various ways depending on the source of the magic." Doctor One sniffed and lost his smile for a moment. "Do you understand what I mean, forgotten one?" he tried to clarify.

Yuvina grumbled, "Not one damn bit. Just tell me what your device does before I agree to anything."

Doctor One inhaled and started to smile again. "We will insert this device into the skin of your legs, arms, and torso. We put a lacrima-deum in it, and it will dissolve into your body, filling you with arcane energy. If it goes well, it will bond the arcane stream to you and infuse you with power you've only dreamed about!"

The kitsune's stoic expression became skeptical and she tilted her head a bit. "What's a lacrima-deum?" she asked in reply.

"A tear of the gods, you might say. It's a stone filled to the brim with mana that has crystallized and become trapped in the mortal plane. It happens in a variety of ways, you know," he continued.

Yuvina really did not want a lecture, but she wanted a chance at acquiring magical powers of her own. This Doctor One might be the solution to building a more equitable society for The Forgotten, and she now understood her bosses' motivation. "Very well, I will accompany you," she interrupted him as he continued to explain how magic crystallizes into the lacrima-deum things.

He stopped mid-sentence, his smile broadening. "Wonderful, I believe these might be a cure to all of your ailments. If this works, I think you'll be put on the most rewarding mission of your life."

Yuvina finally smiled a bit, revealing her razor-sharp teeth. "Then I put my trust in you as my superiors have done, Doctor One. Help me acquire powers," she sincerely requested.

She followed him from the derelict tavern and across the city to a shack in the slummier area of Nulodia. The door was not locked. He opened it before turning to face her. "I hope you are not afraid of the sewer," he commented.

Her whiskers and ears twitched again. "Gross," she replied. "Whatever, I've been through worse."

Inside the shack, there was a trap door under an unassuming rug. Inside, a ladder descended, built firmly into the stone and earth below. The emptying delta and plentiful flow of the Starlock River provided Nulodia with unrivaled infrastructure for sewage and plumbing. Wastewater was diverted away from the Nulodian Sea with massive, underground stone pipes which had been crafted by incredible dwarven water engineers. The sewers were complex, and most people avoided them due to the smell and the fear of getting lost.

Doctor One descended the ladder first, and Yuvina followed, her vulpine grace making her agile and lithe. She scampered down as the elf below held up a stone that lit up the sewers around them. He led her through the waterways for half a mile when they came to the end of a pipe covered by a large metal grate. The pipe emptied outside into an aqueduct twenty feet below that would carry the water to ponds located in the Ermen Moors far to the north of the city. Yuvina saw a small boat tied below in the aqueduct. Doctor One opened a humanoid sized door built into the structure of the metal grate. He walked to the end of the pipe and stepped off without hesitating.

Yuvina shrieked with surprise and rushed to the end of the pipe as well, the stream of wastewater pouring into the aqueduct below. Instead of falling, he walked through the air as effortlessly as on the ground. The fresh air smelled amazing compared to the dingy sewers. She found a ladder built into the stone wall beside the pipe. The tide wall on the west side of the city was visible from the aqueduct, and the port glowed with activity. Yuvina's curiosity ran wild as she descended the ladder next to the pipe, and she stepped onto the aqueduct at the bottom. She approached the little boat where the strange elf was waiting. She was not expecting this part of her mission.

"Hurry, hurry," Doctor One insisted as she neared the bottom of the ladder.

"Why the rush?" she asked. He had untied the boat already, and she had to make a short leap from the aqueduct wall as the vessel started to drift.

"We don't want anyone to see us. This will take us to my estate outside of town with no record of our departure at the gates," he explained, his voice hushed and raspy. He began to pump the oars, helping them accelerate down the unmonitored aqueduct. Eventually, they passed under the small tunnel built through the city wall to let wastewater exit. Yuvina had to duck as the underpass was only four feet above the water. It was even a tight fit for the seated elf.

They floated out of the city for a couple of hours before the aqueduct emptied into a waste lake in the Ermen Moors, a desolate frontier north of Nulodia. The region was positioned just to the west of the Selian Range, the highest and most dense part of the Trollcrag Mountains. It was a temperate desert with very few inhabitants. They tied the boat to a tree near the lake and continued on foot for another hour into the barren moors. Darkness was descending across the landscape as the sun settled behind the horizon to the northwest. In the dusky light, Yuvina saw a building in the distance, but it did not look like an estate as Doctor One described.

As they arrived at the stone building, Yuvina smelled sulfur and another, unknown odor. It was a pleasant break from the stench of the moors. The building itself was larger up close than she realized from afar. There were numerous windows paned with darkened glass which made it impossible to see into the rooms of the complex. A single normal-sized door entered the building from the east side. Doctor One approached the door. He leaned down and whispered to the handle. After a moment, it opened on its own.

"That's a neat trick," Yuvina commented.

Doctor One smiled at her, the rainbows in his eyes swirling with excitement. "A trick that hopefully can be given to you, as well." His voice was erratic and overly enthusiastic.

Yuvina shivered. She had concerns about this strange elf's plans and powers. She had seen him walk on air and open a door with a word. The powers seemed unrelated, so she knew it was not an uncanny power. She cleared her throat before continuing, "So where are we?"

"Enter and see," he replied with an excited buzz in his voice.

Yuvina walked inside to see a large parlor open up before her. There were numerous doors on all sides of the room except the entrance. Doctor One had some sort of living space arranged in the center with sofas, tables, and chairs positioned neatly. Though the stone outside looked very plain, this room was an opulent contrast. A multicolored crystalline chandelier hung from the ceiling, lit by everburning candles. The doors surrounding the parlor were labeled in elven script. Her eyes narrowed as she looked around, scrutinizing.

"I should be able to craft the eolnut device through the night. Make yourself comfortable," Doctor One ordered, closing and locking the front door behind him. Yuvina felt trapped and uncomfortable, but she had faith in her leaders and Pulhash. "There are bedrooms of many styles down that hallway," he explained, gesturing toward the first door to the left of the entrance.

"How have you accumulated so much wealth?" she asked, a marveling high pitch in her voice.

He turned to her with his insane smile, "How, indeed. I am a genius, child. I was once a premier wizard with a promising path. The Unbinding took that from me, and now I have applied my intellect to correct what has gone wrong in the universe." His voice was grating and displeasing. He continued his bragging, "I have engineered a way to draw the magic out of lacrima-deum. You will be the first sentient, biological entity whom I will infuse with magical power."

Yuvina scowled, her black nose flaring with her words. "You mean to experiment on me with no understanding of the risks? That would be blasphemous even to Pulhash!" she objected.

Doctor One shook his head. "No, no! Come, have a look," he ordered, taking her to the second door on the right side from the entrance of the parlor. Inside was a large, well-manicured conservatory. The sound of birds echoed throughout the room. It looked like a jungle with trees and vines arched over a stone path forming a circle in the center of the room. Yuvina followed him into the center, noticing there were numerous cages made of a strange metal lining the circular path in the magnificent, indoor garden. Doctor One approached the cages, motioning for her to follow. "You see, they are proof that this will not cause you undue harm," he explained, gesturing toward the animals inside the cages.

Yuvina observed several small mammals of varying species. Many of them glowed with a seemingly magical light. "What have you done to them?" she asked, monotone.

"I've used a different style of infusing device to inject them with magical energy. I used shards of a light lacrima-deum to fill them with an arcane gift. They use their light as naturally as their eyes and their paws," he explained. He pointed as a mouse in a cage flashed its brilliance periodically.

Yuvina began to smile in excitement. "Why did the masters choose me and not take this opportunity for themselves?"

Doctor One's genius and insanity permeated his response. "Because, Yuvina, I've chosen you for a specific mission. The merchant guild you have been observing was a mission requested by me. Your work is worth more to me than infinite wealth."

The kitsune tilted her head. Her dark fur glistened in the conservatory's light. "And you plan to destroy the corrupt merchants?"

The elf nodded in reply. "There will be violence, undoubtedly, but they hold something I need desperately."

Yuvina's whiskers stood out. "What is that, then?"

Doctor One drew a hand up to his chin and smiled. "Dragon eggs. They have several stored there as merchandise. I need them to make more lacrima-deum." He pulled up his trousers a bit, showing Yuvina his boots, which were made of complex gears. "I was able to extract the power of flight from one egg, and it powers these shoes. And the lock?" he reminded her. "I built it using lacrima-deum from the egg of a shield dragon."

Yuvina's eyes widened with excitement. "And you think you can infuse me with power like you've done with these animals?" she replied, her voice perking up.

He nodded with enthusiasm, "The plans you've brought to me. They have been altered for the biology of a faekin such as yourself. That's another reason I selected you!" he explained, his tone growing more intense as he spoke. "I had to consult a former necromancer who is now a Forgotten. He will be richly rewarded, and you," his eyes narrowed, and his smile turned from enthusiastic to devious. "You will be the first of The Forgotten cured of their condition."

Yuvina's heart skipped a beat. Her dreams were coming true in real time, and she wondered if she would wake up soon.

Chapter 2
Argentum

*"On the day magic fell apart, Argentum was lost to history.
There were no survivors and no spectators, not even the gods.
The first knowledgeable entity to find this necropolis will likely
have the tools to control the world."* – Historian Oddawl,
Magical Calamities: Unbinding Edition

Miranda bent down to examine the marble tile that made up the flooring of the magnificent palace outbuildings. She was in the royal stronghold of Argentum, a once flourishing magical kingdom that relied on wizards and sorcerers for their way of life. The city once surrounded this palace but now lay in ruins. The Unbinding sparked an extremely violent civil war here. Miranda inhaled through her nose. The mana surged toward the palace in the center of the complex, and its density reminded her of the solisberry at the top of the Astral Spire.

A voice from behind Miranda interrupted her. "You're not afraid of the dark, too, are you?" it asked. Miranda's eyes narrowed, and she gave a playful smirk. She turned around to see one of her newest adventuring companions, Celyth Fernith, an elf with beautiful purple hair and green eyes. Her new companion continued, "I suppose not, otherwise you'd be carrying the torch." Her voice dripped with sarcasm, but the tone was playful and light.

Miranda shook her head. "I told you, I can see in the dark. Besides, I said I was afraid of small spaces, not caves, dungeons, or ruined palaces," she continued with a giggle.

Celyth's lips perched into a snide but cheeky smile. She was tall for an elf at a full five and a half feet. "Well with that shield on your back, I don't blame you for disliking small spaces."

Miranda blinked and then laughed. She was lucky she had friends in the Shield Knights. Over the last six months, she had been back to Nulodia a handful of times. During one of those trips, she spent a two-week training intensive with Justin and Valarie, and they insisted she learn how to use a tower shield. Justin told her that he fell in love with Valarie during their combat training, and Miranda understood why. Valarie was an incredible combat instructor, and her confidence and personality shone brightest while teaching. Miranda taunted Celyth, "We'll see who appreciates the shield if you need cover while bandits are raining arrows down on us."

Another voice piped up, "Would you two knock it off?" It was Arlindra Fernith, Celyth's cousin. Arlindra's hair and eyes were both a light shade of blue. The hair on the right side of her head had been shaved, leaving her with a wild hairstyle Miranda was jealous of. The haircut had a reason, however; both Arlindra and Celyth were elite elven archers. Celyth was trained in the way of the warrior, while Arlindra walked the path of a ranger. While warriors received training in all types of weapons, many of them chose a specialty weapon. Celyth selected the longbow, and Miranda had already seen the efficacy of her new friend's training. Rangers, on the other hand, pursued a balance with nature. Arlindra's proficiency with bows came from her extensive hunting experience. She was also the more serious of the two cousins.

Miranda glared through a smile, and her bright sapphire eyes shimmered in the torchlight. She replied, "Sorry, I was afraid of the dark." As she finished her sentence, she cast a devious grin in Celyth's direction. Both Celyth and Arlindra held a torch; Miranda discovered a way to use her draconic gift to grant her the ability to see in the dark at will. It had been approximately a year since Miranda even discovered that she had a gift, but it took another six months before anyone understood her situation. Even the gods lacked answers initially. Miranda was the daughter of Reshiria and Philotrax Hyacinth, two dragons that had been trapped in human form at The Unbinding. Though Miranda's exterior was permanently that of a human, the inner workings of her biology and magic were twisted between that of a human and dragon. She was a magical anomaly, and the mana of the arcane stream pooled within her. Miranda could draw on it to work miracles, but she lost a significant portion of her capabilities while defeating Gelidor the Usurper of Claston. These days, she found small, practical applications for her gift that would not exhaust her supply of mana.

Arlindra shook her head with exasperation, "You're still teasing her Cel?" The cousins looked at each other with sibling rivalry permeating their gazes. Arlindra's voice was serious and smooth.

Celyth pushed her hair up with her hands and let out a deep sigh. "I'm sorry, archaeology is just boring to me! Cut me some slack, Arli." Her tone made it clear that she was mostly joking. "I'd rather be fighting stuff," she continued and perched a hand on her hip.

Miranda interrupted the exchange, "The palace is in remarkable condition considering the stories about the violence that erupted here. The stone is immaculate." Her voice was floaty and musical, a contrast to the elf cousins' voices.

Arlindra tilted her head, "Wouldn't the stone be alright anyway? It's not like it was the target of the violence," she reasoned.

Celyth nodded in agreement, but Miranda explained, "Magical fire should have charred the stone. Magical electricity should have broken it if it was strong enough to harm people. Acid, ice, any magical element should have caused some damage."

Arlindra understood. If there was great conflict in Argentum, it either didn't happen in the palace, or it was wrought with metaphysical means. She then reflected on the information they had regarding The Unbinding, asking, "Didn't Tyrdrac's ritual happen in the heart of the palace?"

Miranda nodded. "That's what I need to know. Where did he conduct his ritual? The mana flows thick here, it's no wonder he chose this location." She peered down a hallway of the ruined structures around the palace complex. She could see massive tree roots had grown through and around the marble floors further down. The trees were likely eolnut, one of the three sacred trees of Espa. They responded to magical intensity by growing at an impossible rate. Natural trees would have taken centuries to grow through the marble. "I just want to know exactly where," she added absentmindedly, reaching out to touch the stone wall.

Celyth started down the hallway. The structures around the palace were massive, and they had only explored a small portion of them. Right now, they were in a corridor between two outer buildings. Miranda insisted they search every inch of the grounds, but Celyth suggested they start from the inside and work their way out. Still, though Celyth teased Miranda, she recognized the young woman was exceptionally wise for her age. Celyth spoke as she held her torch up, "More of the same down this way. Except for more trees. There's all kinds of roots again, and you already said that's not what we're looking for." Celyth spoke with optimistic derision.

Miranda nodded, her vision in the dark extending further than even the elves' incredible eyesight. The warpriest caught movement in the shadows apparent in her magical perception. "More than roots this time," she warned, drawing a beautiful, magical sword out of an ivory scabbard on her belt. As she armed herself, she also slid her shield from her back to her left arm. "In close, quick!"

Celyth carefully placed the torch on the ground and took several quick steps backward, her bow and an arrow in hand before she could identify any threat. Arlindra also readied her longbow, albeit a bit slower. Miranda slammed the tower shield down in front of her, and she prayed. "Invictus, with your wisdom and patience, you are like an unyielding rock in the tides of time. Surround us with your protection and ward away chaos." As she finished the recitation, a shimmering orb formed around the three of them. Not only would the prayer protect them from physical harm, but it would also nullify hostile magic affecting the area.

"What do you see, Miranda?" Arlindra asked.

"That!" she exclaimed as numerous tendrils made of shadows struck the barrier surrounding them.

"Sure seems like an Umbral," Celyth spat, recognizing this type of creature.

This was not the first Umbral that they encountered while investigating the city. After finding their way through the mountain between Argentum and K'tal H'yuck, they faced a group of humanoid shadows. Miranda expressed familiarity with creatures made of darkness, and she helped the elves make short work of the Umbrals with a small burst of intense, purple light. She needed to rest for almost four hours before they could continue their exploration, however.

"How about a little light?" Celyth growled as she knocked her arrow and fired into the darkness down the corridor.

The trio heard a splashing noise followed by rapid pops. A light emerged from down the hallway followed by an explosive blast. Celyth had fired an arrow with a magical supplement called a magitab attached. Magitabs were a special product of her homeland, Mystalon. They duplicated the effects of numerous spells. This one in particular would shatter on impact and create a bright aftershock.

The attack was especially effective against undead creatures, but it also worked against enigmatic enemies like Umbrals.

In the explosive light, Miranda, Celyth, and Arlindra could see the horrifying creature lashing out at them with dark appendages. It looked like a demon with dozens of tentacles, but its features were hidden by its shadowy form. The only indication it was a creature were two bright, red eyes in the center mass of its incorporeal body. It responded to the light from the arrow with anger and spite. In retaliation, the entity flailed its tendrils, smacking against Miranda's prayer with such force it began to crack. It was the next moment, however, that made the companions say a prayer of thanks to Invictus. Waves of electrical power filled the air around them and struck anything that could conduct it. Parts of the hallway shattered as energy found a way through the stone to the ground.

Arlindra hummed her own prayer to the earth mother, Gaiater. The ranger thought long about the spotted sabretooth and its incredible speed. With that aspect of the animal in her mind, she spun out from behind Miranda's shield and fired a volley of arrows as she sprinted down the hallway with unbelievable velocity.

Though the arrows did not explode with radiant bursts, they were powered by the alternative magic of Mystalon. Small blasts of magical fire exploded into the essence of the Umbral as Arlindra rushed past it, evading its tendrils with almost no effort.

The electricity in the air intensified again. It struck Arlindra with a large blast, and the shield surrounding Miranda and Celyth shattered from the impact. Arlindra made her move just a moment too soon, a painful miscalculation. Her body stiffened mid-stride and she found herself unable to move.

"Arli!" Celyth shouted as she dropped her bow and drew a short sword.

Miranda grimaced. "Sword of Justice, trade our fates," she whispered. An electrocuting blast wracked her body. Arlindra, however, found herself without pain or injury and resumed her sprint to take position behind the Umbral. The light from Celyth's flare arrow still burned bright enough to distinguish the creature from other, natural shadows.

Celyth rushed forward from behind Miranda's shield, charging at the Umbral with bloodlust in her eyes. As it whipped tendrils at her with blinding speed, she parried with her enchanted short sword. She did not wield a shield or a second weapon, but she was agile enough to parry attacks from a dozen tendrils with her single, small blade. "Is that the best you can do?" she taunted, not even knowing if the creature could communicate.

It became apparent, however, that it understood her chiding. The demon's arms of darkness reached a frenzy, and arcs of electricity began to jump from shadow to shadow as it prepared another charge. Celyth's eyes widened with realization, and she made a quick move forward to strike at the core of the monster.

Half of the tendrils stopped swiping at Celyth. After taking position behind the Umbral, Arlindra unleashed another volley of fire arrows into the creature's back. Arlindra found it odd that it still persisted after being hit by so many magic weapons. She shouldered her bow and drew a great sword from her back. Then, she activated her uncanny magic. She began to turn invisible rapidly, but in reality, her body and essence were phasing in and out of existence. While invisible, she would also be intangible to weapons and magic. She mustered a charge, causing the Umbral to divide its focus between the two of them.

Miranda clung to the shield, and the electrical burns throughout her body caused pain to radiate from her core to her extremities. "Restore to order what was damaged by chaos," she prayed, producing a white light to envelope her body. As the light dissipated, her injuries were no more. She gripped her shield and tilted it so she could observe the cousins as they closed in on the Umbral. She started to smile until she realized that the creature was preparing another dose of lethal electricity. Without enough time for a prayer, she called on the mana inside her to replicate a spell Erk had taught her.

This time, the light coming from Miranda was purple. In a flash, it beamed from Miranda to the Umbral, covering its tendrils in a purple haze. The electricity within was immediately nullified. The dispelling light required the equivalent amount of mana as the magic it canceled, and though this demon's attack was powerful, it did not utilize much mana. Still, she was grateful they were in Argentum. Here in the palace, the magic within her would be back at full capacity within minutes.

The creature made no sounds, but Miranda saw its eyes change from violence to fear. Her dispel had taken away its last line of defense, and within seconds, Celyth and Arlindra began to stab the Umbral's core with their swords. After a few clean blows, the shadow began to dissolve into a miasmic cloud of sparks floating through the air. It lingered in place, slowly wafting in swirls through the corridor.

Celyth and Arlindra exchanged glances with swords in hand. "I'm pretty sure I hit it four times in a single second," Celyth asserted, shaking her blade. Her uncanny magic allowed her to change relative time in a small aura around her. Though she seemed to move incredibly fast to those under its effects, it was only because her opponent had been slowed down. She used it to unleash attacks in rapid succession against compromised reaction times.

Arlindra continued to phase in and out of view for a moment before dismissing her uncanny magic. "You definitely had better form this time," she admitted.

They both turned to check on Miranda as the priestess shouldered her shield. Her red hair was braided toward the front of her head, a symbol of her status as a healer within the Church of Invictus. She was a couple of inches shy of six feet tall, and she wore the elven battlemail she inherited from her mother. It consisted of an ornate mithril breastplate, an adamant ringmail, and an adamant mesh long skirt. Miranda almost always seemed to be smiling or in awe of something, even after a dangerous encounter. This moment was different, however, and Miranda was perplexed.

Celyth detected Miranda's discomfort and asked, "What's wrong?" Her sarcasm was absent.

Miranda approached the two. "When I was at the Astral Spire, my companions fought a ton of shadows like these things you call Umbrals. But none of them had extraordinary attacks like this one. I feel like this Umbral was different." She knelt down, looking at the tile, now shattered by the intensity of the creature's electrical blasts. She began to whisper another prayer, "Sword of Justice, guide my eyes to the truth." Miranda searched for traces of Indervill, the god of madness and chaos. After a moment, she could feel the discernment of Invictus pouring into her mind. The miasma was still dissipating, and Miranda could not feel any trace of Indervill in it. She focused for another moment and did not detect any other gods.

Arlindra asked, "Any clues?"

Miranda shook her head. "It's not divine." As she spoke, she stepped into the miasma.

Celyth reached out to stop her a moment too late. "Miranda, what in the Infernia?" she snapped, worried.

As Miranda breathed, she could smell and taste the essence of the Umbral. She felt an unfamiliar energy alongside the particles of magic. She analyzed the concentration of ether, finding a prevalence of particles full of electrical energy. She spoke with a contemplative melody as she shared her conclusions with the cousins. "There's more than magic here, but I can't identify the other powers. It's similar to the Umbrals that welcomed us to Argentum, though."

Although they had no explanation for why the shadow creatures existed, they assumed it was connected to this location's proximity to The Unbinding. Arlindra nodded and speculated, "If these creatures were unique to Argentum, then I wouldn't worry so much. But we have had so many in Mystalon over the last three months. We were sent to find answers about the origins of the Umbrals." She smiled, a rare expression for her stoic demeanor. "Unfortunately, we're finding more questions as we go. That's why we're here." Her gaze shifted to Celyth. "If there are other energies within the Umbrals, we need to rethink our theories. I suspect the answers will be complicated. We are grateful for your assistance, Miranda."

Miranda gave a half smile. "Well, I'm afraid it's not so easy stumbling in the dark looking for answers to ever-changing questions. This super Umbral concerns me. If they vary in strength and power, I fear for Mystalon." Her music sounded somber as she spoke. Ordinary shadow creatures could be destroyed by magic weapons or simple, destructive spells. The demonic Umbral was much tougher, and it wielded devastating power. She murmured, "I think I need to seek out somebody more experienced in matters of magic."

Celyth and Arlindra traded glances. Celyth clarified, "Like your wizard friends back in Nulodia?"

Miranda nodded. "I was hoping for a simple answer. The unknown power concerns me, but the creature's attacks were definitely powered by mana. I know how bad lightning can hurt somebody. What if there's one that can use fire? Or worse?" She shuddered. "This is now official church business as it threatens to upset order."

Arlindra's eyes widened. "Oh, yeah, thanks," she added.

Miranda smiled fully now. "I'm just glad Invictus gave me the strength to heal us both."

The three stood in silence until the miasma dispersed. With a sigh, Celyth picked up her torch. "Okay, so now what? Do we put the field trip on hold?" Her normally sarcastic, teasing tone was back.

Miranda grimaced. It could take two days of underground travel to get back down the mountain. "Not yet. Let's give your idea a go."

Arlindra smiled as Celyth celebrated. She exclaimed, "Finally! If there's a monster at the heart of this, we're going to be so famous.

We went to the center of The Unbinding and stopped the Umbrals before they became a serious problem!"

In truth, Arlindra and Celyth had been adventuring for a few years before meeting Miranda. They were from Mystalon, an ancient elven society which broke away from Claston centuries before The Unbinding. Their fathers were brothers serving as Sages there, an elected council that made decisions for their reclusive people. The cousins had no interest in political careers and opted to adventure instead. They both received the finest training and built reputations in Mystalon. When Umbrals began appearing three months ago, however, they were dispatched to investigate possible causes. Their work led them to K'tal H'yuck a month ago where they met Miranda. The priestess was working with the draikin to protect access to the Dundoi Mountains. After the cousins explained what Umbrals were, Miranda was more than excited to help, having dealt with shadow creatures in her previous adventures. Nobody had reached Argentum since The Unbinding, and they navigated the cavernous mountain path to the magical necropolis. It was now abundantly clear that Umbrals were not the same as the shadows created by Indervill's power at the Astral Spire. They were connected to locations of arcane significance.

Arlindra's snark pulled Miranda from her thoughts. "Yeah. If there's a monster, it's going to be that easy to stop."

Miranda giggled. Sometimes the cousins reminded her of Justin and August. Celyth retorted, "You've got me on your side, of course it'll be that easy."

They exited the hallway complex connecting the outer ring of buildings and headed through a large courtyard toward the main palace. Miranda could feel the mana continuing to thicken as they approached. She inhaled, hoping to replenish the magic she used fighting the Umbral. As she concentrated on the metaphysical ambience of the palace, she realized the abundant ether in the air was stale. It was still usable, but it had stopped flowing. She stopped about two hundred feet from the central palace doors. A circular path with a large fountain in the center welcomed them toward the heart of the palace. Miranda paused to marvel at the beautiful building for a moment. It was a white, marble step pyramid sloping up one hundred feet. There were numerous spots for defenders built throughout the architecture, but they were integrated into the design. It looked beautiful instead of secure. "I've never seen anything like this," she whispered, mostly to herself.

Arlindra chuckled. "I don't think any of us have," she commented, also sizing up the strange, central building of the palace. The base floor of the pyramid sprawled two hundred feet on one side. The pyramidal grade was sharp, but there were patios and balconies built throughout the intricate architecture. Faux columns had been carved into the marble at every window and door. It was truly magnificent.

Celyth grunted. "Well, are we going to stare at it, or are we going to conquer it?" she asked, enthusiasm dominating her voice.

Miranda shook her head, "The magic is strange here. The air is full of mana, but it seems to be stagnant. It's not moving like I would expect. I could feel the arcane stream out there," she said, gesturing back to the hallway complex. "It's not moving here."

Arlindra looked around, asking, "Does that pose a danger?"

Miranda shook her head. "It's just different. Let's proceed with extra caution," she recommended. She took a moment to pray for Invictus's standard protections, and they approached the front door to the palace at the end of the path from the outer palace complex. There was no water in the elaborate fountain, also made of marble. A beautiful relief of ivy had been carved into its base. A tower of faeries sat in the middle, and the statues at the top had large pitchers that would have poured water into the base, keeping the water flowing.

Celyth and Arlindra held their torches up. They had no idea what time it was as they traveled mostly underground for two days to get to Argentum. Since they arrived, there had been no light in the sky and no natural sounds. The silence made Arlindra uncomfortable, as even the winter nights in this region should have been full of noises. Quilli birds normally nested this high in the mountains, and they were noisy when hunting insects and larvae in the dark.

Miranda stopped as they stood mere feet away from the door. The mana exuded a pressure on the three of them, but only Miranda understood the sensation. "Can you feel that?" she asked the cousins.

Celyth nodded, a look of concern in her eyes as she peered at the grand palace doors. They were large, ornate double-doors, each ten feet high and eight feet wide. "It's like a hex or a curse is slowing me down. Like my own power working against me," she commented.

Arlindra started to speak, but then she blinked out of existence. A moment later she reappeared mid-sentence, "and it's making me lose control." She gasped before disappearing again, reappearing intermittently.

Miranda closed her eyes and concentrated on the mana within her. It swirled and responded as expected, so she let it rest. "My gift is not unstable, for whatever reason," she shared.

Celyth started to back away from the door. As she did, she felt herself reverting to her normal speed. Arlindra was able to remain firmly in the primary dimension as she also withdrew. Miranda watched them as their uncanny magic settled, then she turned back to the doors. She reached out, still about fifteen feet away, and she activated her draconic powers. This time, she mimicked Naomi, using telekinesis to open the doors.

As she did, the three gasped in horror as a horde of Umbrals spilled out from inside the palace, melting into the courtyard outside. What they had seen of the demonic shadow before paled in comparison to the nightmares before them. Many of them were incomplete and unrecognizable, but some had distinguishable shapes. Some were draconic in nature, but others were covered in tendrils and appendages. Miranda quickly backed up to her new companions, keeping her eyes on the threat emerging from the building in front of them.

Celyth spoke first, "Yeah, I really was going to walk right up to the door and open it. Bad idea."

Arlindra laughed. "We're seriously outnumbered here, and you're still cracking jokes." Her laugh was authentic, though. Celyth's spirit was unbreakable even in the face of mortal danger.

Miranda weighed her options. The mana was thick here, but it didn't flow. She could replenish immediately, but she didn't know how long the ether would stay abundant if she began using stagnant arcane energies. "Wait," she whispered. "This place is like me, the magic pools here." Her eyes lit up with the realization. "This is incredible, a location like me!" She realized the Umbrals were closing in on them. "Hang on, ladies," she warned as she activated the magic stored inside her. A bright, purple circle of light appeared underneath the three of them, and three smaller white circles radiated under them individually.

As the spell pulled them through time and space, Miranda detected something wrong with the teleport, and she could not see their destination. She increased the amount of magic spilling from her essence, and she whispered a prayer to Invictus. "Sword of Justice, protect us from harm and lead us to safety." She sensed friction as the spell transported them, and she continued to boost her magical output. After expending nearly all of her mana, she felt a breakthrough. She glimpsed their desired location in her mind and forced a successful teleport.

They appeared in the town square of K'tal H'yuck. Miranda immediately lost her balance, and her hair had lightened from its normal deep red to a bright pink. Arlindra reached out to help Miranda stabilize, but they were both too disoriented. They tumbled to the ground.

Celyth started laughing, finding her own balance. "We're not even at the tavern yet and yer both too drunk to stand!" she taunted.

Arlindra glared up at her cousin, then looked back to Miranda with concern. "Are you alright? Your hair! It's happened again." she commented, still astonished to see Miranda's hair change as her mana depleted. It sparkled its new, pastel hue in the torchlight of the city square. The clock on the well-lit tavern showed the time as ten minutes after midnight. All of the shops were closed and dark.

Miranda shook her head, trying to find her voice after expending so much magical energy. She struggled to speak. "I-I'm fi-fine," she insisted, sounding as if she were freezing. "The h-hair ch-changes when I'm-m running out of m-m-magic," she explained. "As I said before, it's not lethal. D-directly at least," she shuddered as she spoke. She reached into a pouch on her belt and withdrew a purple leaf. It was a solisberry bloom, a flower from another of Espa's sacred trees. Naomi had the wise idea to snatch a handful of the leaves from the solisberry tree at the Astral Spire. The tree thrived on magic, and its blooms accelerated the flow of magic through a person when consumed. Miranda placed the leaf in her mouth and let it dissolve. As it did, her hair started to darken, though the leaf only replenished enough mana to keep Miranda from passing out. "I'll be fine," she promised, less shaky now.

Celyth and Arlindra sighed. It was hard to argue with her when she was smiling and downplaying her own fatigue. Celyth finally jabbed, "So what would happen if you, like, dyed your hair?"

The three of them laughed, and Miranda answered, "That's a good idea, maybe then I won't scare people so much when it changes colors." Celyth reached down and helped Miranda stand, and Arlindra stood with an athletic maneuver, going from the ground to her feet in an instant.

"You wouldn't dare!" a voice interrupted them. The three turned to see an elf with golden hair and gray eyes. He held the reins of a pegasus in one of his hands, and it seemed he had been watching them since they appeared.

Miranda shrieked with joy. "Evan!" She ran to the elf, nearly tackling him with a hug.

Evan laughed and planted his feet firmly, wrapping his free arm around Miranda's waist and squeezing her in return. "Miranda!" he exclaimed, not at all surprised by her reaction. He let her go as she stood straight. "Besides, your friends need to know if you're napping or if you've overdone it and used up all your magic," he teased.

Miranda smiled broadly, but Celyth interrupted. "Wait, who is this guy?" she asked, looking Evan over. She was a little taller than him, but she thought he was built more like a dwarf than an elf. If it weren't for his ears and his clean-shaven face, she might have thought he was definitely a dwarf. "He certainly lifts," she finally remarked.

Evan's face scrambled with confusion. "Wait, lift? Lift what?"

Arlindra's eyes narrowed. "Apologies, Evanthalus. Miranda has told us a lot about you. I'm Arlindra Fernith," she explained, trying to prevent confusion. "My cousin, Celyth Fernith, here," Arlindra gestured to the elf with purple hair. "She means you train like a warrior and it's evident in your build."

Evan laughed and Celyth made an exasperated face. "Oh yeah! Evanthalus, the cute one, right?" she blurted without warning.

Everyone froze for a moment before a wave of awkward laughter overtook them. Miranda decided to get ahead of the sudden, embarrassing exposure. She now knew better than to disclose such random thoughts to her less-discreet companions like August and Celyth. "Wait, Evan, why are you here?" she asked, a terrifying feeling spreading throughout her body. She was so happy to see him she didn't consider the implications at first.

Evan's face turned grim. "The fight against Farzg is becoming more complicated by the day. In the last couple of months, we've started to come across dragon eggs on his slave ships." He looked at Arlindra. "It is an honor to meet you, Arlindra. And you, Celyth. If you travel with Miranda, that tells me all that I need to know about you, and I already consider you an ally and a friend." He spoke with confidence and poise.

"Damn, you really are cute," Celyth taunted. "I mean, yes it's nice to meet you," she added, trying to sound formal and failing by a large margin.

Miranda's eyes scanned the square. "Evan, why don't we get something to eat and drink, and we can trade information."

The three of them spent the next couple of hours late into the night at the tavern. Evan explained the increasing frequency of dragon eggs in Farzg's henchmen's possession. Miranda deferred to Celyth and Arlindra to explain the Umbrals. About three months ago, strange shadow-like creatures began forming at random in the isolated city of Mystalon. The Sages, the governing body of the independent elven kingdom, dubbed them "Umbrals." Though they were fairly easy to dispatch, they were still concerning as the Sages feared the aggressive shadows may attack children or someone otherwise defenseless.

Then, they described the Umbral they faced in Argentum. Not only was it stronger, but it wielded magic power. Its lingering, magical miasma was also very different.

Evan furrowed his brow and asked, "So you've only fought one with extra powers? And you're sure it's not just some uncanny magic gone wrong?"

Miranda tapped her chin. "Definitely not just uncanny magic gone wrong. The palace at Argentum was brimming with magical energy that didn't flow. It's like the arcane stream is pooling up there, close to where The Unbinding supposedly happened," she explained, describing the large number of creatures spilling from the palace when she opened the door.

Evan's lips were drawn tight in thought. "I don't know if Erk would have any better idea than you do, Miranda," he speculated.

She nodded, her braids bouncing off the breastplate of her battlemail. "I feared that would be the case as well. It's odd that he'd send you all this way alone, though. Wait," she paused and then grinned. "This was dad's idea, wasn't it?" she asked with a giggle.

The elf cousins listened intently. Arlindra was trying to help piece together the puzzle, but Celyth was waiting for any kind of gossip she could draw out of the conversation. Miranda mentioned her dad, which brought Celyth's questioning. "Wait, I thought you were an orphan?" Her eyes narrowed with suspicion.

Miranda laughed. "Oh, my modai-rin. Thomas Selasine. He adopted me, remember?" A gentle patter of late winter rain pelted the roof of the tavern, filling a momentary lull in the conversation.

Celyth's eyes widened in response as she skimmed her memories. "Oh yeah, sorry. You talk about the dragon dad a lot, too. I think there are more orphaned heroes than runaway heroes. How does that happen?" she asked, the joke evident in the tone of her voice.

Evan and Miranda chuckled, but Arlindra rolled her eyes. Evan nodded and responded to the original question, "Well, yes, His Holiness and Commander Burchard made sure I had a pegasus, but Erk was the one that insisted we needed to get your input." Evan gave a small smirk. "He misses you, you know."

Miranda's eyes filled with bittersweet tears. Though the cousins had been with her for a month, this was the first time they saw the depth of emotions Miranda expressed without hesitation. "I miss him too, so much, honestly. Everyone." She breathed deeply, however, and calmed the wells of tears that could have spilled at any moment. "I've learned so much here with the draikin though. I think we should probably escalate both of our problems to a wiser entity." She spoke with confidence now, and her normally sweet smile was a little ambitious.

Evan tilted his head. "But I said Erk probably wouldn't know about the Umbrals," he started but trailed off. His eyes widened, and he protested, "Oh by Lexcord, Miranda, no!"

Celyth and Arlindra traded a confused glance. Miranda nodded vigorously and said, "If Erk didn't know what to do, who would he ask?"

Evan let out a deep sigh. "But it's too dangerous! Plus, how will you reach them?"

Celyth tapped the table. "Uh, 'scuse me. But who? Reach who? Ask who?" she questioned, shaking her head in a way that insisted on a response.

Miranda's lips pursed up into a small smile as she explained. "We should probably seek out the eldritch dragon, Ezelbrecht, and ask them. Besides, they owe me an apology."

Arlindra's eyes narrowed. "I've never heard of such an entity," she warned, politely requesting more details.

Miranda nodded and replied, "They are a child of Gorthran the Dragon King. They are ancient, and they know much about magic and the arcane stream. They helped me learn about myself, and I think Ezelbrecht could help us again." She smiled at Evan. "Besides, there's more than one way to reach Olvidado."

Evan sat back on the bench and took a deep drink from a mug. "Well, I'm not letting you go to Olvidado by yourself. Erk has told the story half as many times as he tells people about you healing me. Which is at least once a day," he partially joked.

Miranda giggled but turned serious as she looked at Celyth and Arlindra. "The first time I went to Olvidado, Ezelbrecht tried to force me to stay with them because of my unique heritage. It was way easier to teleport people back then," she lamented a bit. "Ezelbrecht is an evil being but is most interested in self-preservation and restoring dragons to their original, natural conditions. I believe their advice will be of the utmost help, even though it will be incredibly dangerous to obtain." She let out a swift breath. "You are welcome to accompany us, though."

Celyth pounded a fist on the table and smiled broadly. "If they get uppity, you'll need me. I can shoot this Ezelbrecht right out of their cocky attitude, yeah?"

Arlindra laughed. "Nature is full of many paths. Some are very dangerous, but hiking them can be very rewarding. The most beautiful trees grow in the hardest to reach places. I would not miss such an opportunity."

Evan asked again, "Still, you haven't told me how you plan to reach Ezelbrecht. Olvidado is in The Isles Known for Nothing," he complained.

Miranda's eyes softened and she gave her normal, pretty smile. "Let's discuss the details in the morning. I'm still wiped out from that teleport." She kept the details of her experience during the spell to herself, but she suspected Jacques's disappearance during the Battle of Beriton was not a mishap. Something was wrong with teleportation magic.

The others agreed with her sentiment, and the cousins bid Miranda and Evan goodnight. Evan and Miranda sat talking for another hour. They reminisced about their time on *The Nebula*. They spent a month sailing through the Solar Sea and Ignia Sea after their previous conflict with Gelidor. On the surface, it was a hunt for slavers in the southern waters, but honestly it was a chance to give Miranda some time to breathe. After Selasine cured her from the usurper's curse, she was unwell for almost a week. It was not like the magical induced sickness caused by Vortex the Lich, but instead it was as if Miranda's body and essence were both grieving. She had sacrificed a nearly unlimited gift to save countless lives after being transformed into a dragon. They won the final battle with minimal casualties, and Miranda did not regret her decision at all. It just took the rest of her essence a while to catch up. After she recovered somewhat, she felt very free and excitable, and they visited the islands of Tibot and Tobit with Erk and the others. They also shared time together in Nulodia during an evening Erk arranged for them. She and Evan were both fond of their time together.

Eventually, Miranda went to rest. Evan waited a bit, having one more mug of ale before getting his own room in the sleepy little tavern. A lone draikin was left at the bar and had almost a dozen mugs before him. He wore flowing robes and looked to be deep in concentration, not intoxicated. Evan smiled and remarked, "If you find any solutions in meditation, master monk, please share your enlightenment."

The draikin snapped to attention at once and smiled. His scales were a brilliant silver that glinted in the candlelight. "I only share that kinda thing with my drinking buddies," he replied.

"May Lexcord smile on us, and let us share a drink soon then," Evan said as he headed up the stairs. Miranda insisted the stables would be fine for his pegasus, and she held the proprietor in high regard. There was a lot on Evan's mind, but somehow, he felt at peace. He felt like he found something he had been missing for a while now. Evan knew that following Miranda to Olvidado would cause Selasine and Erk to worry, but he had confidence in Miranda's plan. The others could learn of the journey afterward. He fell asleep with his stomach still in knots and confusion in his mind.

Invictus and Lexcord stood side-by-side in the primordial place, the dimension of the gods of Espa. Here, divinities could see all of mortality and had access to the knowledge of the universe. They could not fight the other gods here, nor could they wield their incredible powers. Instead, they could change reality by sending their divine essences from the primordial place to the primary dimension where mortals lived. If the gods wanted to intervene directly, their avatars would have to descend to the mortal coil where they, too, would be mortal. Though it was unlikely that even the strongest denizens of Espa could kill a deity, it had happened more than once in history. Most of the gods were welcome in the primordial place, including the god of madness and chaos, Indervill. Na'agamlor, the god of greed and corruption, had not learned of a way into the primordial place. Nevertheless, while in the primordial place, the gods mostly kept to themselves.

Today, however, a familiar and intrusive presence roused Lexcord and Invictus from their vigilance over their followers. A booming voice echoed around the primordial place. The gray and golden clouds of this dimension swirled as it spoke. "It's been a while, yeah?"

Invictus slowly opened his eyes and looked around the dimension of the gods. "Tyrdrac. I'm afraid it hasn't been long enough," the god of justice and order rebuked the mortal. The booming voice was the arcane manifestation of Dalyn Tyrdrac, the sorcerer that accidentally broke magic by fusing his own essence into the stream. The gods who revered order and security for their followers were not pleased with the results of Tyrdrac's actions.

The voice decreased in size, and a ball of light appeared before the two deities. It looked like the orb was crackling with pure energy. "I'm starting to worry about the arcane stream. Pieces are going missing in here. Do either of you know what that means?"

Lexcord smirked. "You've learned to control your voice, master Tyrdrac," she said coolly. "And you've come to consult the gods again on something that you broke on your own," she chastised.

The ball of light jittered with excitement. "I know, I learned this from Miranda. Who I'm very worried about, by the way. If pieces of the stream are disappearing, then something dangerous is going on in the mortal realm."

Invictus shook his head. "She is thriving. Her prayers ring through stronger than ever, and her faith in herself has grown many times over."

Dalyn groaned. "That's all what we'd expect from such an exceptional woman, I know. But don't forget that she's a dragon. She's made of magic, just like they are. Actually, so much of the universe relies on the arcane stream. If pieces are going missing, you should probably show a little more concern, mister sword," Dalyn finished, his voice inflecting his sarcasm openly. He used Invictus's title, The Sword of Justice, so rudely and informally.

Invictus scoffed but understood the mortal's insistence. "Very well, Tyrdrac. What do you propose we do?"

Dalyn's light ball shrugged. "Perhaps nothing until we can identify the cause of the arcane stream breaking apart. This time, I promise I didn't do it. And I'm pretty concerned because I'm on the chopping block just like anything else that relies on magic."

Lexcord nodded, her silver hair sparkling in the light generated from the golden clouds and Dalyn. "We will keep our consciousnesses watching for anomalies. Do you have any recommendations for us, sorcerer?" she asked, gentler toward the entity than her more disciplined brother.

"Yeah, try to figure out if the mortals are doing something different with magic. Maybe they're using it in a way that they shouldn't be? Check on Miranda, too, if there's something happening to magic, it's likely going to pull her in somehow. Maybe have a chat with some of the eldritch entities down there in the mortal world." The light ball started to lose brightness. "It's difficult to come talk to you, but it's getting easier. For now, though, there's no way I can do anything except keep you posted on the state of the stream. And I didn't think I should wait with this info even though it's not much," he warned as his orb broke apart.

Lexcord replied as the magical entity dispersed, "Rest assured, Master Tyrdrac. We will take your warning earnestly. Do return if you learn anything before we do."

"Thanks, I will," Dalyn's voice called back, the booms in the primordial place echoing.

Invictus stared across the primordial place when he caught a glimpse of black clouds coalescing. After a moment, he and Lexcord could see the avatar of Aylabrax, an evil goddess who served as a thorn in the side of justice and order. Aylabrax's avatar was dressed in a gray, nondescript robe, and black hair covered her face. She looked very unsettling, even to the other gods. Furthermore, she rarely came to the primordial place, as she preferred to feed on the fear and souls of mortals. For her to return to the primordial place, both Invictus and Lexcord worried a terrible situation was afoot in the primary dimension.

Aylabrax intentionally kept Lexcord and Invictus far away. The gods could not force interaction, but it was apparent Aylabrax wanted to be seen, and Lexcord and Invictus complied with seeing her. She did not allow them to approach. Instead, she raised a finger and pointed into the golden swirls in a cluster of clouds. She created a vision within them. She showed the other gods the horde of Umbrals escaping the palace at Argentum hours before. The shadows crawled all over the central structure and filled the courtyard, but they did not stray far.

Invictus grumbled to himself. "This is some kind of trap that she's set, I just know it."

As Lexcord nodded to agree, Aylabrax appeared between them. "It's not a trap," she said in a deadpan, monotone voice. It was soft and her manner of speaking was abrupt. "I just wanted to show you," she explained, which only created more questions for the deific siblings.

The god of justice, Invictus, and the god of truth and good, Lexcord, watched the vision of the Umbrals with growing concern. While they were distracted, Aylabrax sank into the clouds creating the illusory ground in this dimension. Beneath them was an expanse of green, viscous liquid that served as a representation of all the knowledge in the universe. She swam through the liquid, seeking information outside of her normal channels. She sought information about the arcane stream, but it was too plentiful. She could not articulate specifically what she wanted. Frustrated, she tried to seek out an entity instead. She sought Gorthran the Dragon King. The eldritch god broke himself into shards and poured his entity into the arcane stream eons ago, creating evil dragons. Still, Aylabrax wondered if there was a way to communicate with Gorthran.

The only information left in the universe about Gorthran pointed Aylabrax to Ezelbrecht.

Chapter 3
Pain and Promise

"Pursuit of power is a foolish endeavor. Instead, followers of the light should pursue humility, wisdom, and discernment. Such traits foster conviction, reason, and order. It is no surprise that many abandon the pursuit of power upon mastering these. Together, they provide an overwhelming power against beings with evil thoughts." – Lexcord's Reflections

Yuvina's breath was quick and shallow. She lay on a sophisticated, sinister examination table, waiting for Doctor One to return to the laboratory. Yuvina refused the restraints, and Doctor One did not insist. She could endure the transfusion. She had, after all, suffered much worse at the hands of people who considered her lesser thanks to her lack of uncanny magic. She shuddered with tense anticipation as the prospect of finally being set free of this curse materialized before her. She looked around again, and Doctor One's laboratory was especially well lit. It was brighter than daylight and the walls were made of porcelain tile. They reflected the already brilliant luminance of the room, giving it a stark, white ambiance.

A door opened, and Doctor One entered the laboratory with an excited step. He skipped toward the examination table with his arms full of wooden contraptions and glowing gemstones. He spoke to Yuvina as if they were old friends by this point, but his very presence made her fur stand on end. She felt as if she was compromising something she shouldn't by associating with Doctor One, but if the higher ups of The Forgotten trusted him, then she knew she should too. He gave a warning, "I've prepared some chemicals that should reduce the overall pain you will experience, but you will be barely lucid. Pay attention to the visions, do you understand?" he lectured, his voice patronizing. "You're absolutely certain you don't want the restraints? It's for both your safety and the efficacy of the infusion," he explained.

Yuvina shook her head. "If I can't handle the pain from a device, how am I supposed to handle these powers?" she insisted, feeling like such an alteration to her life should be more painful than anything she had ever experienced. She needed the infusion to hurt so she would remember the pain inflicted on others as a result of her powerlessness. Her whole family suffered because she was weak. She didn't ask to be born without powers, and she'd give anything to get them. She wanted to prove that now.

Doctor One shrugged. "Well suit yourself, but if I were you, I'd go with the restraints." He set the devices on a table pressed against the wall to Yuvina's right. He then spilled the stones out of his arms, and they scattered across the table. "If my theories are correct, we should be able to infuse you with five different powers. One for each of your limbs and one for your torso. We could try one for your tail, but I am afraid for your safety," he grumbled and shook a finger at her. "And we certainly wouldn't want to try one on your head. Every time I've tried that, things have gone badly." His common accent was strange to Yuvina, though she suspected that it was Star Coast, a kingdom in East Espa.

The doctor continued speaking, "So, you say you prefer to wield two weapons. I decided we would attach the lacrima-deum from the shield dragon to your torso. I theorize this will provide you with an incredible fortifying power."

Yuvina growled gently. "What happens when you attach a device to an animal's head?" she asked, trying to extract information. She found herself lusting for as much power as could be managed in this exchange. And if she died trying, she wouldn't care.

Doctor One scoffed. "Well, child. Simply. They go insane. Some eat themselves. Others run in circles until their hearts burst from exertion. Others talk to themselves until they wither away from dehydration. Who would have known that the rodent language contains four thousand unique expressions?" he rambled.

Yuvina's whiskers trembled. "What kind of powers would you

anticipate gaining from attaching a device to the mind of an intelligent creature?" she asked, willing to take such risks.

The elf's face twitched with a little anger. "Nonsense, foxkin. I'll not risk what is guaranteed for what might be. Don't be so rash," he objected adamantly.

The kitsune let out a resigned sigh. "Fine. So, what happens with the shield dragon lacrima-deum in my torso?"

Doctor One's look of frustration jumped from anger to enthusiasm. "Oh, it's marvelous, I think you'll love it. You should be able to transform your skin and your fur to stone. Maybe even steel!" he predicted. He practically sang as he picked up a large, wooden device. It was a two-foot, rectangular piece of eolnut wood. From each of the four corners, two-inch spikes protruded downward. Though they were somewhat long, they were extremely thin. The tips resembled sewing needles. On the top side, a small recess was surrounded by a spiky, wooden ring that would scratch anything placed into it. The gemstones Doctor One brought seemed shaped especially for this infusion.

Yuvina sat up straight. The device was meant to fit in her back. As she did, Doctor One shuffled in his jacket and found a smaller, medicinal needle. Healers had developed such technology through careful research, and they had identified what herbs and chemicals could be distilled into injectable medications. She assumed he was planning to inject her with something to ease the pain of the infusion. "I'm sorry Doctor One, but I am far too eager for speculation. Please, just begin," Yuvina insisted.

He shrugged again. "Have it your way, then," he concluded as he pressed the needle between her shoulders. As he injected the substance within, Yuvina could feel a cold swirl spreading from between her shoulder blades, radiating out like a tree's branches. Doctor One rubbed the spot where he had given her the injection. "Can you feel that?" he asked.

Yuvina shook her head. "Barely. Hurry, then," she pressed.

Doctor One sighed. "Not yet. This is also necessary. The pain will affect your entire body," he warned. As he did, he withdrew a different injector. "This one is fine in your arm," he said as he injected the substance before she could react.

She snarled a bit, her snout curling up. "What does it do?"

The elf waved nonchalantly to the air, "It makes you free, child. Just wait."

After fifteen minutes, Yuvina was very sedated. She didn't feel the prick when Doctor One inserted the device into her back, puncturing her skin and organs in the most miniscule but possibly painful way. She also didn't feel the transfer of energy as the doctor placed the shield dragon egg lacrima-deum in the device. The power from the gemstone began to flow into her body, and the crystalline manifestation of magic began to dissolve into visible particles. The wooden device drew them into a spiral of mana that then fused with Yuvina's body. As it did, her body responded, wracked by pain. Thanks to the medication administered by Doctor One, however, she did not feel it to its full effect. Instead, she began to remember why she was willing to go to such great lengths to find a way to finally be important.

Yuvina smelled smoke. She sat up in her bed and rubbed her eyes, sniffing the air carefully. The offending, acrid odor was close but not immediate. She let out a yawn and stretched, sliding out of bed. As an adolescent kitsune pup, she had as much responsibility for keeping the den safe as anyone else.

That was Yuvina's problem though. At fifteen years old, she was the only one of her siblings that had not manifest an Unbinding power. Her older brother, Aizari, found his uncanny magic at twelve years old. That was six years ago, and Yuvina's twelfth year passed without any changes between her and the mana. Now that she was fifteen, everyone around her was certain she would not find a connection to the arcane. Their little sister, Eileen, had recently turned twelve and manifested her power the year before. Yuvina was afraid she would not be very helpful if there was some kind of danger happening in the den.

It didn't matter, though. The smell of smoke was enough to bring every kitsune out of their homes and to the center of the thicket they called their den. Numerous foxkin lived in their community, existing in harmony with nature. Their enclave was nestled into the root complexes of the massive trees of The Tymbyrwylde, a region beginning one hundred miles southwest of Claston. The dense forest consisted of eldritch trees unlike any others in Espa, and The Tymbyrwylde stretched over one hundred miles east to west. The trees stood at two hundred feet tall and were incredibly resilient. They could not be cut down because they regenerated too quickly. They could, however, be cultivated and reshaped. Their green, spindled leaves were massive and supported ecosystems in the canopy above and on the ground below. Creatures that revered nature, like the kitsune, called the massive, ancient forest their home.

As Yuvina covered herself in a stitched leaf robe, she heard her parents stirring. She opened the door to her room, and the smell of smoke intensified. Her nose twitched with anxiety as her instincts took over. Their house was not very large; it was just five bedrooms and a sitting room. It was a circular home built into a hollowed root of a Tymbyrwylde tree, as were many of the dwellings in this den. The kitsune dined together as a community in the hollow Tymbyrwylde tree root in the center of the den. Yuvina was the first of her family to emerge from their home, noticing a number of her neighbors had already identified the source of the fire.

Yuvina's eyes filled with tears; the community center for her family and neighbors was fully engulfed in flames. She felt a sudden fear course through her. If somebody could set a Tymbyrwylde root ablaze, then they must wield immense power. Yuvina heard shouting from behind her; it was her father. "By Lauerili, how?" he asked, his voice a deep, angry growl. He invoked the name of the kitsune deity, a thirteen tailed foxkin who ascended to godhood through their faithfulness to the earth mother, Gaiater.

Another voice added, "Don't hesitate, father." It was Aizari. "Our powers are ice and water, we can save it." The young kitsune stumbled over Yuvina as he burst through the curtain over the house's entrance. He yelped with shock, causing Yuvina to jump forward. She realized her brother and father must have seen the commotion from the windows of their home. Aizari was springing into action. "Yip! Yuvi, what are you doing?!" he shouted in annoyance.

Yuvina scrambled to turn and face her brother. She bowed and stepped out of his way. "Sorry, brother, I smelled smoke, and I came to investigate," she explained. The entire den glowed with a deep orange hue as the massive Tymbyrwylde tree root burned in the center.

Aizari snarled a bit. "And what did you think you were going to do to it? Spit on it and smother it with shame?"

Yuvina stood straight and began to retort, but she snapped back into a bow, lowering her head in fear and deference. "I'm so sorry, brother, I—" she began, but he interrupted.

"Save your words, Yuvina. The only thing worth anything right now is action. And I'm afraid there's not an action you can take to help. Just stay out of the way, okay?" he chastised and then sprinted toward the community center.

Yuvina stayed bowed to hide her tears. As she expected, her father emerged from the curtain as soon as Aizari left. She may have masked her tears, but she couldn't hide her sobbing.

Her father, Tsuyoi, looked at her with pity. "Come, my daughter," he ordered and extended a paw to her. She stood and approached him. He wrapped his arm around her. "I will scold your brother for his words, but his sentiment is correct. Without a useful power or way to contribute to a crisis, you could make things worse if you end up in danger trying to help." He shook his head as he patronized her. "I just want you safe, and I know it frustrates you. But please, Yuvina. Stay here. Let me and Aizari handle this alone."

She felt her sadness and submission turn to spite and anger. She snapped her head up at her father and the whiskers on her short, light gray snout trembled. "Fine, then," she said and stamped her foot.

Tsuyoi sighed. "I have work to do. Now stay put." He ran toward the community center which could be easily seen from all of the houses built into the root complexes of the Tymbyrwylde trees. The building serving as the community center was the hollowed remnant of the largest root in the nearby den. To further complicate the situation, the roots were still very much alive and thrived with the kitsune dwelling within them. Intense, magical fire was necessary to burn a living Tymbyrwylde tree, and the situation concerned Tsuyoi.

Yuvina watched in petulance until her father arrived at the root in the center of the den about one thousand feet away from their home. She snarled to herself in frustration. "I just want to help!" She had heard that people of all kinds occasionally found their Unbinding powers just when they needed them the most. She theorized that maybe she just needed to be in a little danger for it to unlock. Thanks to her dad and brother, she was never allowed to help. She was coddled like she was sick or in pain constantly. She hated it. She might not have had an Unbinding power, but she could still find a way to help. With all of her defiance showing, she rushed across the den toward Wise Telkut's house.

Wise Telkut was one of the village elders who always encouraged Yuvina to be strong in spite of the fact she was born without any obvious uncanny powers. She desperately needed to seek his counsel as she wanted to prove she could be helpful. Her brother was mean, and her father was wrong. As she arrived at the correct root cluster, she found Wise Telkut's home. It was also a good thousand feet away from the fire, but from an area adjacent to her home. She rang a bell hanging outside.

A voice from within replied, "Come in, Yuvina." He already knew it was her, causing her to blink with determination.

She bared her teeth and pushed through the curtain into Wise Telkut's sitting room. She asked, frustrated, "How did you know it was me?"

Wise Telkut hummed and chuckled. "Because, child, there's a crisis and we're both powerless to do anything about it. Come in, have some tea, yes?"

Yuvina's whiskers trembled. There was no way he could just distract her while the community center burned. "Wise Telkut, please. I know I can help my brother and my father! I want to help put out the fire! Couldn't we band together and carry buckets of water to help? The well is deep and our supply of buckets is plenty!" she shouted with excitement. "Not everyone has an Unbinding that can help, but anybody can carry a bucket!"

Wise Telkut laughed. "Of course, child. But! A blaze of that magnitude is more than the natural waters of Espa can douse. The arcane stream, though fractured, is the only flow that can stop those flames."

Yuvina narrowed her eyes. "How do you know that?" she growled.

Wise Telkut sighed. "Please, understand, Yuvina. Somebody set that fire intentionally. The question is not whether or not they stayed, but rather where they are hiding." The old fox looked as wise as he sounded. His fur was a whitening silver as he was an aged kitsune of seventy years, a comparable lifespan to humans. "If I were still a pup, I'd be out there with your father and brother, ready to extinguish the aggressor that has violated our den." His voice changed to a growling anger Yuvina had never heard before.

Yuvina barked in reply, "Would you stop?! You've never told me to just stand aside! This isn't fair!" she huffed.

The old foxkin sat down on a chair made of gnarled Tymbyrwylde bark. It was upholstered with the thick leaves of the trees that made up their homes. It would take years for the leaves to completely dry and wither. As he sat, Wise Telkut looked up at Yuvina. "You're right, but the fairness of the situation was never the question. You should act in wisdom. Discretion. Realize when something is bigger than your pride, and act accordingly," he lectured.

Yuvina could not believe what she was hearing. Wise Telkut was the last person she expected to tell her to hide from something just because it was dangerous. "You're wrong! And I'm going to prove it!" she spat in reply. Before Wise Telkut could object or try to stop her, she turned and stormed out of his home with a frustrated growl.

In a moment of lucidity, Yuvina looked around. Her mind had come back to the present, and she felt very groggy. Then searing pain coursed through her back. The medication that had allowed Doctor One to put the device into her torso was wearing off. She started to whimper as the pain intensified.

"Now, now, not yet!" Doctor One said, having watched his test subject carefully for the last hour. He took a handful of leaves from a tray set up next to the examination table, and he offered them to Yuvina. "Solisberry leaves. They should put your body in tune with the arcane stream if you eat them. It will ease your suffering."

Yuvina complied, nibbling the leaves from Doctor One's hand. They were bitter and made her mouth tingle. As she chewed, the elf prepared another needle to renew her sedation. After he injected the chemicals, he offered Yuvina some water, and she lapped it with intense thirst. She never fully lost consciousness, but she felt like she could see her memories replaying in real time. She kept reminding herself to pay attention as the doctor had instructed.

Yuvina watched her brother and father using their uncanny magic to fight the blaze engulfing the community center. She was in the middle of a sprint across the den toward a nearby well; each section of the den had plentiful water provided by four wells dug in the areas between the homes of the kitsune and their community center. As she neared the well, her stomach sank to The Rift. The orange glow from the fire revealed armored humans emerging from the darkness beyond the edges of the flame's light. She started to panic as she thought about Wise Telkut's words. This was her chance to help.

Yuvina yapped frantically, a warning sound to nearby kitsune. The armored humans were entering the den from the main path to the west, but Yuvina could not see any townsfolk ready to offer resistance. As she gave the warning, she heard other voices join her. The humans did not change their pace, and they marched in formation toward the burning community center. Aizari and Tsuyoi were still visible outside the burning root, her brother using fantastic waves of water and her father conjuring large pillars of ice that dampened the heat of the fire. Within moments, the entire den was abuzz with yapping kitsune warning the den of the attack.

Before Yuvina could make any decisions, the humans broke formation. At first their movements made no sense, but Yuvina realized they were fanning out toward the outer ring of the den. There were twenty invaders, and they moved outward in a circle. The kitsune were not a warlike people, and they did not keep many crafted weapons ready. Instead, they relied on their fox-like features and natural weapons to defend their home. As the humans neared some of the kitsune, the foxkin sprung into collective action. Groups tried to overwhelm the humans, but they were disciplined fighters, capable of keeping the kitsune at bay. Then, the uncanny magic began to fly.

The attackers wielded a wide range of destructive Unbinding powers, and once a kitsune responded in kind, the humans lost interest and stopped targeting the resisting foxkin. It soon became apparent they were trying to isolate kitsune with uncanny magics that were less destructive in nature. Lightning bolts and fireballs were traded between sides, but the spells did not affect the humans much. Yuvina watched in horror until she recognized she was now under attack.

Her fur stood on end as she felt somebody's eyes on her. Still close to the well, she realized she was a long sprint away from her house. Just as she started to run, a gust of wind blew her down. One of the humans stood fifty feet away from her, dragging a two-handed blade in his right hand with his left extended in her direction. Yuvina yelped with surprise as she hit the ground, scrambling quickly on all fours to make a running recovery. Her athleticism was admirable, and she was one of the fastest adolescents in the den. She kept her momentum and was in a mad dash toward her home, missing only a step when she impacted the ground. Her blood turned cold, however, when she heard the human shout in a language she did not understand. She saw a few of the others were now in pursuit, and they were positioned to cut her off.

With her home no longer an option, Yuvina cut sharply back toward the community center. The invaders continued to shout, but she didn't care. She began to cry as she ran. Everyone was right. She really was useless without some kind of power, and now she was being targeted exactly as Wise Telkut warned her. She shouted to her family near the community center, which was still burning. "Father!

Brother!" she barked in a higher pitch than usual, reflecting her fear.

As she neared, her father was doubled over with exhaustion. Aizari had taken a defensive position, creating blasts of water to serve as a warning to the humans in pursuit of Yuvina. "Hurry, sister," Aizari shouted back to her.

Four humans formed a line and began to approach. "Surrender the helpless one, soldier, and we'll spare you," one of them ordered, the voice deep and terrifying. It spoke the kitsune language fluently. Yuvina ran past her brother, stopping beside her father, panting from the exertion. Her ears were pinned back, and her tail was curled under in fear.

Her brother sneered. "Yeah, forget about it. Leave us alone." He let out a warning yip and another blast of water.

Tsuyoi stood and turned to face the aggressors. One of the humans replied, "Alright, then. You asked for this." They drew swords from their backs and began to charge.

Yuvina watched as her brother and father fought against the humans, but they were too exhausted and outnumbered. It felt like time stood still as Yuvina watched them slay her father and then her brother in a matter of seconds. She stood, petrified with fear as one of the attackers approached her with caution. When it became apparent she was in shock, he moved toward her and threw something in her direction. A ring of light formed around her body and restrained her. She could still walk, but her arms were bound to her sides. All she could think of was Aizari telling her to stay home. If she had just stayed home, she would have been safe. The entire plot now made sense; these evil humans had set the community center on fire because it was the only building in the den visible to outsiders. Then, as the kitsune responded to the crisis, the aggressors found what they wanted: the den's inhabitants. Thanks to her stubbornness, her father and brother were dead. She was being taken, but she didn't know where. Her heart ceased to feel anything except her own weakness. She couldn't even muster a tear over the weeks that she was trafficked.

As Yuvina became cognizant, she felt a dull pain throughout her body. She mumbled with a groggy voice, "Doctor One are you here?" She tried to look around, but she was incredibly disoriented from the medicines.

"Yes child, the procedure was a success!" he cackled. She was still in the bright laboratory and on that same, terrifying examination table. His voice continued to gloat, "Very, very soon you'll have a power unlike anyone else! Power given to you by me! The incredible Doctor One!" His voice was maniacal.

A sharp pain pierced Yuvina's entire existence. She whimpered a bit but tried to maintain her composure. A headache swirled behind her eyes, causing her to close them. There was a new sensation in her, but she didn't understand it. "I think I need to sleep," she murmured.

Doctor One clapped his hands. "Yes, yes. Rest. You will probably be fitful for a while, but you need to hone your focus so you can manifest the gifts I have bestowed upon you!" His enthusiasm was encouraging, but it seemed excessive to Yuvina. He continued, "You need to rest before the next steps, so yes, come with me."

He led her out of the laboratory to the hallway with bedrooms. She picked the first door on her right, a lavish chamber filled with opulent furniture. She still wondered how it was possible to have such a nicely furnished home and operational laboratory in the Ermen Moors dozens of miles north of Nulodia. She pushed the thoughts from her mind and collapsed onto the bed.

She became more aware as she tried to fall asleep. As the medication wore off, the pain returned. She had been stabbed before, and this wound felt similar. Fortunately, these punctures were much smaller. Doctor One put some bandaging on her, though.

Yuvina sat upright with urgency. She murmured to herself, "Aren't most physicians usually clerics?" She wondered why he didn't use a healing prayer instead of all of the herbs and medicine. Yuvina gripped her temples with her paws. "What kind of doctor are you then?" she asked to the empty, dark room around her.

The new sensation she had felt since she became conscious still permeated her. Doctor One mentioned the operation was successful; perhaps this was what the arcane stream felt like? She focused on that unseen pressure, ignoring the pain radiating in her head. Her heart rate accelerated as if she were running. Something was moving through her, and her body experienced intense tingles. The longer she concentrated, the more comfortable she became with the feeling. After what seemed like an eternity, the flow within her surged out of control. In a brilliant flash, a ring of glowing orbs formed around Yuvina's body. There were twelve in total. As they appeared, Yuvina felt the previous pressure diminish. Was this it? Did she finally have a power?

Yuvina's eyes filled with tears of relief. It wasn't what Doctor One theorized, but she was overwhelmed by the fact anything happened in the first place. She was still in an incredible amount of pain, but now it was coupled with an anxiety to understand her new capabilities. As she leapt out of bed, the orbs began to orbit her body. They moved with random trajectories. Each was the size of an apple, and they glowed bright white, illuminating the room. Yuvina bounded toward the door, and the orbs matched her speed with mystifying ellipses. She froze, marveling at the lights following her every move. She really wanted to know what they would do.

She rushed into the hallway of the bedroom wing, and she turned immediately left into the parlor. Doctor One was resting on a lounge, reviewing something on a scroll. His eyes cut toward Yuvina, a swirl of colors reflecting the light of the orbs surrounding the kitsune. His face twisted into an intense smile. "Yuvina, my child! You've already done it!" he shouted, using her name for the first time.

Yuvina blinked. "Doctor One, is this my new power?" she asked with increasing excitement evident in the pitch of her voice.

His smile changed from intense to sadistic. "If I'm correct, it will protect you from this," he said. With no more warning, he withdrew a small device glowing a brilliant blue. It looked like a magic wand, but it was made of metal and gears. As he pointed it at Yuvina, a crackle of lightning buzzed at the tip of the clockwork wand and burst into a stream of electrical power. In the single instant the lightning should have struck Yuvina, one of the orbs floated between her and the attack. It absorbed the entire magical discharge given off by Doctor One's device.

Yuvina flinched and kept her eyes closed until she was sure she had not been struck. She opened them slowly to see the orb that blocked the spell was now glowing blue. "It changed! What does it mean?" she asked, her mind still trying to come to grips with the current situation.

Doctor One grew even more excited as he saw the results. "Just as I suspected! It's the Magic Mirror spell!" He jumped, laughing hysterically. "There are wizards who live one hundred lifetimes and never master that spell! Absolutely incredible!" he shouted. "Yuvina, you'll be invincible with this power!" He used her name again, which she found odd.

Something flashed from underneath Doctor One's tunic. A barrage of knives materialized, aimed at Yuvina. With just a gesture of Doctor One's wrist, they flew at her, powered by an unseen, magical force. The orbs swirled without Yuvina's command, swooping into the path of the blades, deflecting them with ease. Even the blue orb still flew in time with the others, helping protect the one who conjured them. The other eleven turned a dark, steel gray after being hit by the knives. Doctor One then ordered, "Now Yuvina! Will the magic inside you to fight back!"

Yuvina blinked, not understanding his meaning. She focused on the sensation from before, exciting the orbs as they continued their orbits. Somehow, she could communicate with the spell. Her thoughts echoed the doctor's words. "Fight back!" she commanded. Suddenly, all twelve orbs spun in a wild circle and drew close to her. They went around her waist, six inches away from her body, all following the same circular trajectory. As she continued to concentrate, they coalesced into a bright light. They exploded in a shockwave through the parlor. The force blew furniture all over the place, destroyed vases and clay statues, and knocked Doctor One over in spite of the fact that he possessed a magic barrier of some kind. The beautiful chandelier shattered, raining crystal fragments all over the room. Yuvina's eyes widened in horror at the destructive capability of her protective power. Her look changed quickly, though, as she noticed Doctor One stood and began to jump again. The kitsune smiled instead, shouting "It worked!"

The elf gave a pleased but maniacal expression. His experiments were finally paying off. "You are fully bonded with the arcane. You see, this shows great promise. You! You show great promise." He ran to Yuvina, looking up at her. She stood at five feet and six inches, and there was a meekness about her that belied her thirst for power. She now smiled, however, an expression that was rare for her. Her heart soared, and she perceived this change to be the cure to her affliction.

Doctor One tapped his chin. "Now that it's settled, go rest, child. Use your power if you're in danger. The Magic Mirror is an incredible spell."

Yuvina nodded. "Thank you, Doctor One. You've changed my life."

His insane smile emerged. "And you've changed the course of history, child. I will repair that which was destroyed."

Yuvina tried to sleep, but she found her thoughts restless. She wondered if she would have been able to stop the slavers that killed her brother and father and took her far from her home if she had this incredible power from the beginning. She never returned out of shame for what she had done. She knew her mother and Eileen would be better off without the continual reminder of her disgraceful weakness. Even the slavers lost interest in her once it became clear that she had no Unbinding to add to her value. She was sold a few times and placed on a ship, but some pirates liberated her and took her to Nulodia. The pirate captain that had saved her was an incredible giantkin that Yuvina remembered well. Her name was Naomi, and she was kind to Yuvina. Once the kitsune told the captain that she did not want to return home, Naomi took her to Nulodia.

Life in Nulodia was not necessarily terrible, but finding work could be hard. People with the right types of uncanny magic could do specialized work for great pay. People with useless or destructive magics still found themselves employable, usually in a way that was complimentary to their gifts. Yuvina and The Forgotten had been petitioning the government of Nulodia to outlaw discrimination based on people's Unbinding powers, but so far there had been no response from the city council or the Church of Invictus. Even they must discriminate against The Forgotten, she thought.

None of that mattered, now. Yuvina wondered if she could still call herself part of The Forgotten, especially with a gift so noticeable and powerful. She closed her eyes and tried to drown out her thoughts, but she found herself brimming with excitement. Things would finally be different, and she would be important.

Over the course of the next month, Doctor One infused Yuvina with four more lacrima-deum. The ones in her arms allowed her to wield her daggers with blinding speed and overwhelming strength. One in her left leg allowed her to cause the ground around her to become sticky, and the other allowed her to perform even more incredible athletic stunts. While she practiced using her new powers, Doctor One monitored her closely. He also sent word to his allies that he needed to meet with them soon to show them his newest discovery. His research assistants Doctors Two, Three, and Five were glad to hear of the experiment's success, but they could not come to the moors right away. A ripple of events far to the east had caused chaos in the kingdom of Claston in the last few months. According to reports Doctor One heard, the king of Claston was killed by a mighty purple dragon unlike anything recorded in history. He wanted to see and dissect this creature with his own eyes and hands. It sounded fascinating.

Still, someone close to Doctor One did respond. As Yuvina

continued to train and understand her powers, a strange man arrived at the estate. He reminded Yuvina of a small giant. He was a frost giantkin, and he had a long, white beard. His eyes were purple, and the tone of his skin was pale violet. He was two feet taller than Yuvina, towering over her and Doctor One.

The day he arrived, Yuvina was in the laboratory practicing attaching her sticky powers on surfaces other than the ground around her. If she stomped with her left foot, a thick viscous gelatin would pour out from her in a thirty-foot radius. She learned fine control over the adhesiveness of the goo, and as such, Doctor One theorized she could use it to climb vertical surfaces if she could activate the magic with her left foot against a wall. He always lectured her, "Creative thinking is the only thinking. Everything else is worthless."

Yuvina stood motionless, her feet planted against the wall. She was standing horizontally four feet up, the adhesive spell rooting her in place. She and Doctor One heard a bell ringing outside the complex. She dismissed the magic and ran down the wall, her vulpine agility now enhanced by her powers. The two of them went to the front door where Doctor One dismissed the enchantment on the lock with his secret word. When the door opened, there stood the tall stranger, accompanied by a shocking visitor. Yuvina gasped. It was the head of The Forgotten, a human by the name of Seiv Everdusk. He smiled as soon as he saw Yuvina.

Doctor One did not give time for introductions, he simply ushered the two of them into the parlor. Yuvina had continued to use the parlor to work with her incredible defensive gift, and it was in utter shambles. Almost nothing was still intact. The doctor shouted, "Alright Yuvina, let's show them. Do it! The Magic Mirror! Eldon, Seiv, watch yourselves."

Yuvina nodded, having rehearsed demonstrating her power. Seiv watched in awe as the young kitsune who he had known for several years now manifested the Magic Mirror spell. The orbs formed around her, and his jaw dropped. He murmured, "This is greater than I ever anticipated. Doctor One," he said, looking toward the scientist. "You were right. You have the cure. The Forgotten are free of their curses. Not only that, but I want to see this in action. Allow me to prepare."

Seiv had no arcane powers like everyone in his organization. Himself and his lieutenants, however, were experienced priests of Pulhash, and they lived their lives with their deity's chaotic philosophies. They wanted justice for those who were treated as lesser, and they organized The Forgotten as a platform to spread Pulhash's methods and philosophy. Seiv stood tall and prayed with a shout, "Only fools leave the house without a shield. Help me, mighty avenger!" Four disc-shaped shields of light appeared in front of Seiv.

The giantkin rolled his eyes. "I won't need to prepare anything. I will, however, test that this is the Magic Mirror you claim it is."

Doctor One jumped up and down again. "Yes, yes! Farzg! I want to see your *full* power!" he shouted with an enthusiasm Yuvina didn't recognize. It almost sounded fearful to her sensitive ears.

The twelve orbs of light orbited Yuvina again. She stood tall and had a cocky grin on her snout. Her whiskers trembled with eagerness. She yapped, "I'm ready!"

Farzg rolled his eyes again. His voice was languid and condescending. "If you die, child, it's because this fool has lied to me. I do not like to commit violence with my own hands, but it is necessary to verify the doctor's theory. Goodbye."

Farzg held out a single hand in front of him and the temperature in the parlor dropped rapidly. After a moment, he held out his other hand, leaving his arms outstretched. He inhaled and lowered his massive body into a deep fighting stance. The temperature plummeted, and an arctic gale blasted Yuvina. One of the orbs drew near Yuvina and began to absorb the magic in the atmosphere. It neutralized the dangerously low temperature. It filled with a blue color, causing Farzg to smile.

Doctor One was wearing a jacket Yuvina had never seen. It was made of the same clockwork material as everything else the eccentric elf had. It glowed red, presumably keeping him warm as the air became frigid. The shields around Seiv warded the cold somewhat, but he was shivering. The air filled with freezing fog as ice formed all over the room. The sublimating wisps served as reminders of the lives lost to the unrelenting power of the cold.

The orb that had protected Yuvina was almost full of blue. Farzg moved his hands from in front of him to his sides, extending them in a threatening gesture. With his deep fighting stance, he looked like a monk ready to spring into action. Instead, he drew his arms in and then punched toward Yuvina. A massive geyser of ice shot from Farzg's fists, stretching twenty feet in diameter. The orbs around her swirled with incredible speed, nullifying the magic of the attack on contact. Each one of them turned cold blue. In an instant, a return blast knocked Farzg through the stone wall of the estate. Seiv's shields shattered, and Doctor One had run out the front door.

Farzg lay on the hard ground of the Ermen Moors. He was thrown at least one hundred feet outside the complex. He did not feel any pain from the blast, as he was immune to the effects of cold and ice. His dense bone structure made him especially hardy, but his skin was as solid as the densest glacier. Injuring him with fire magic was likely the only way to hurt him. He sat up, looking at the large hole in the wall of Doctor One's estate.

The mad-elf ran toward him. Farzg heard the scientist's voice long before he could see the insanity behind Doctor One's eyes. The elf ranted, "Well, now, Frozen Death? How's that for a demonstration? The girl is my creation! I will become a god!" He did not even acknowledge the hole in the building. He walked up to Farzg with a smug bounce in his step.

The giantkin gave a deep, evil smile. "She's perfect then. I'm encouraged by your success, as I came to talk to you about a problem we're having." Though he remained on the ground, he was still eye level with the standing elf. Farzg sneered as he continued, interrupting Doctor One before he could begin a rant or lecture. "You see, the Church of Invictus cuts me off at every turn." He rolled his eyes as he spoke. "If I am to procure you more eggs, I will need more mercenaries. I will also need someone or something to deal with the church's efforts. I have lost dozens of eggs to them."

Doctor One's eyes narrowed. "Church of Invictus you say?" he clarified in a suspicious tone. "Why is the Church of Invictus concerned with my eggs?"

Farzg sighed. "They're often in transport with the rest of the cargo I traffic. If it weren't for that other cargo, your eggs would cost you a great deal more than they do now, fool." The giantkin only cared for the profit to be shared in his relationship with Doctor One, but as the church tightened their grip on Farzg's operation, he needed to play shrewdly. "I hear they are hoarding your eggs."

Doctor One's smile darkened. His visage was more sinister than Yuvina had ever seen. She and Seiv were now outside, watching the elf approach the much larger giantkin who continued to sit on the ground. Doctor One spoke in a deep, malicious voice, "If it is the church that stands in our way, then we must play as equals. I will seek my deific favor tonight, then. We must act with the same forces as our enemies. And we must overtake them with our superior planning and strategy."

Farzg stood, dusting off his elaborate, royal robes. Yuvina had never seen anyone dressed in such a way, and she could not identify the significance of his attire. The frost giantkin spoke in his slow, condescending voice, "Very well. If we can recover the eggs, I will reduce the price per egg in the future. Dealing such a blow to the fanatics would show the superiority of our alliance." The two of them began to walk back toward the front door of the complex. Yuvina could understand most of their conversation thanks to her naturally keen hearing.

"I am ready for the next phase of my experimentation. I must find a way to fuse the heart of a lacrima-deum into myself. This is the goal we have been working toward. If I am correct, then the lacrima-deum heart is the shard of Gorthran or Saraix that was thrown into the arcane stream." His voice became clearer as they closed the space between them. "If the Magic Mirror is a possibility from just the lacrima-deum formed from a shield dragon egg, then the hearts will yield incredible results." His voice was collected and calmer than Yuvina had ever heard, and his expressions were more unsettling than normal. She felt queasy. Doctor One then looked to Seiv. "And in the process! We can heal those that have been forgotten by the stream. Help us collect eggs, Everdusk, and we will make enough lacrima-deum so The Forgotten can become more powerful than any organization in history!"

Seiv gave a wicked smile. Seeing Yuvina was all the proof that he needed. "Then I will stay to be infused myself with the power that you have promised."

Doctor One tilted his head and looked up at Seiv, who stood around six feet tall. "And what do you offer in return? I need more eggs, or there will be no more lacrima-deum."

Seiv looked at Yuvina. "Would you be willing to work for Doctor One? You are still part of The Forgotten though you now have uncanny power. We need to collaborate with him to carve a new future for children born without magic." His voice was sincere but authoritative.

Yuvina's whiskers trembled a bit. It sounded wrong, and Doctor One was scaring her. Nevertheless, she convinced herself that it was for the greater good. So many people who felt powerless could be given a gift that would add so much to their potential. "Very well. What would you have me do?"

Doctor One scratched his chin again and his insane smile returned. "I need you to infiltrate the Church of Invictus and find out where they are keeping the dragon eggs. Then I will give you a way to bring them to me." His voice was no longer serious, but wild again.

Yuvina nodded in agreement. "How will I infiltrate a church if I am not a member of their folds?"

Farzg interrupted. "They are a trusting lot. Fight on their side for a while. They'll value you without your faith being tested. They are even in league with pirates now. I do love to see the law pick and choose who wins and who gets hunted," he spoke, his voice dripping with disdain. "It's best to do so with complete sincerity, however. Your faith may not meet a test, but your heart will be judged by the Judges of Heart. Any doubt or hesitation would reveal you to a Judge of Hearts."

Yuvina only knew the Church of Invictus served as law enforcement in the city of Nulodia. She always tried to avoid them because she was often trespassing in order to spy on Wielders, the name given to those with uncanny magic by The Forgotten. She replied, "Very well. But I don't think I can just walk in the front door and volunteer."

Doctor One's smile stretched further. "I am owed a favor by The Lady in Mourning. I mourned the loss of my magic, but I did not lose my genius. I will seek her guidance in this matter."

Yuvina gulped. She had no idea who The Lady in Mourning was, but it was concerning to her that Doctor One was a physician who refused to use healing prayers. Though she was not a cleric, The Forgotten tended to follow the tenets of Pulhash, and Yuvina was no exception. Infiltrating a group that was hoarding eggs would not be the worst action she could take. It was worth the dishonesty for the end result: liberation of The Forgotten. She sighed deeply. "Very well. I will trust your guidance, Doctor One. And you, Master Everdusk."

The giantkin gave a haunting smile. "And I am Eldon Farzg. The Frozen Death. The church has done me great harm and has stolen the means to cure those that share your former condition." His lips were purple and dry, and his eyes teemed with malice. Yuvina shuddered as he continued, but the condescension in his voice was gone. "You wield an incredible power now, one that withstood the entirety of my Death Geyser. Only one person has ever been hit by it and lived." His purple eyes narrowed, the glow making him seem like an otherworldly being. "Now there are two of you."

Yuvina's heart swelled. Her power had earned his respect. She didn't know much about this Farzg, but he was incredibly powerful. Now she understood Aizari's cockiness when they were children. If she had this power back then, he'd still be alive. Then she could have rubbed it in his face that she had a much stronger power. Yuvina of the Magic Mirror had a delicious ring to it.

Doctor One pulled Farzg to the side a moment later, speaking quietly. "I am calling in my favor with Aylabrax. We have a trip planned to another plane soon. I am seeking the primordial place. Aylabrax is to take me to Olvidado, and I have lacrima-deum from an astral dragon to help me reach the primordial place from there. I need answers to my problem with the dragon hearts." His voice was hushed and serious again, noticing Yuvina and Everdusk were still engaged in conversation. "Instead of a device, we will have Aylabrax do the dirty work. The fox will be just a pawn, a small sacrifice."

Farzg's eyes narrowed. "I thought she was your pride now? Your successful experiment?"

One rolled his eyes. "She's just as disposable as anyone. Besides, the magic is likely to kill her anyway. We'll have her infiltrate the church in a way that not even she suspects her own motives. And upon her success, we'll recover a bounty of eggs."

Excitement gripped Farzg's face. "Do elaborate, then. Your genius never ceases to entertain me." He meant it literally; Farzg found One entertaining enough to continue working with him, which was rare. Usually, the frost giantkin got bored with even his most lucrative clients, and his ensuing rudeness would lose him contracts. Still, the most connected criminals knew Farzg was more than capable, and they would feign attempts to keep the giantkin invested in their enterprises.

Doctor One's eyes narrowed with malice. "The Dark Command," he explained without another word.

Chapter 4
Return to Olvidado

"Bathe in The Currents, spawn of water. Let Remora's unholy embrace guide you to the corners of the universe where mortals are forbidden." – The Unhallowed Scriptures of Remora

iranda sat in front of a mirror on an antique vanity, trying to gauge how much the arcane stream flowed through her overnight. Her hair looked red in the dim light. She didn't want to braid it yet if she had not recovered enough mana to restore it to its normal, cool crimson hue. She sighed. The last five months taught her to rely less on her draconic gifts, and, as a result, she mastered some incredible prayers and curses. She could call the simplest blessings by name, but she preferred the recitations anyway. Selasine was the only priest she had ever met with such faith in the Sword of Justice who could do so, but now Miranda was also capable, much to her own surprise.

The arrival of the cousins at K'tal H'yuck, however, marked the end of that period of spiritual growth. Navigating the tunnels between the Dundoi Mountains and Selian range forced her to give equal weight to the reserves of power available to her. Fighting the Umbrals in Argentum reminded her of the necessity of honing her draconic gifts. She needed them to protect her friends and family. She ran a brush through her hair, reflecting on everything she learned living among the Draikin.

Miranda had arrived in K'tal H'yuck at the end of her last adventure, which spanned the months of The Flourishing and The Harvesting. It was now early in The Resting, a quiet, winter month in agricultural communities like Devitus far to the east. She had a home there, but she was not content to live the quiet life of a noble in a sleepy farming village. Her adventures with Erk and Selasine awoke a desire to help the world with meaningful action, and she understood the burden of being the deciding factor in a conflict of monumental scale.

Though Miranda did not want to see discord of such magnitude in her personal adventures, she did want to learn how to be a vigilant and faithful warpriest. Upon her arrival five months ago, the draikin were struggling with new bands of egg hunters, adventurers who made the majority of their wealth by stealthily acquiring dragon eggs and selling them on the black market. It made Miranda sick to think about it. Fortunately, when a dragon egg was destroyed, the godshard within would recycle through the stream to be born again. She had learned so much serving as the priestess of Invictus in this community of draconic people, including understanding the lives and customs of the draikin, their creation myths, and their modern relationship to dragons.

Miranda stared into the mirror, lost in her thoughts. The Unbinding was especially cruel to dragons. It took away their innate magical powers, including their ability to wield their incredible breath weapons. They were practically helpless, and that worried Miranda. Fortunately, the Dundoi Mountains had come to be known as a safe place for dragons and their eggs over the last century. It reached south as an extension of the Trollcrag Mountains, which stretched five hundred more miles to the east. Just to the northeast of Dundoi sat the Selian Range, the densest part of the Trollcrags. Nulodia lay one hundred miles to the west, and the fertile Starlock Plains spanned to the south. Dragons could seek refuge in the Dundoi Mountains if they were being threatened or hunted. The draikin of K'tal H'yuck built their settlement inside the only passable access to the peaks above, and it was styled after the fortresses built by the Drakinskäld in the Dracon Wars over three thousand years ago. In many legends, the Drakinskäld were fierce warriors that were dragons who chose to be born as humanoids rather than in the likeness of Saraix. By fighting alongside human, orc, elf, and dwarf, the Drakinskäld turned the tide of the Dracon War in favor of the humanoids. The draikin believed that a single shard of Saraix could have given birth to hundreds of the Drakinskäld, creating the ancestors of the draikin. Miranda wasn't so sure about the validity of that part of the story. Still, the fortress was strong, and it would take an actual army to get through to the dragons who had taken refuge in, on, and around the mountain.

To make the region more interesting, Argentum sat high between the Dundoi Mountains and the Selian Range. Miranda was glad they were able to investigate the ruins, but the Umbrals concerned her. Now that Evan had arrived with news that slavers were trafficking dragon eggs as well, she was more than concerned; she was afraid. Ironically, she was so afraid she reached into the depths of her mother's memories to find a way to Olvidado without traveling to the Isles Known for Nothing, which was over six hundred miles to the southeast. Erk had shown her how to reach Ezelbrecht's home, but the pirate didn't fully understand what made it possible to reach the forgotten island there. With Reshiria's knowledge helping her in unexpected ways, Miranda knew how to reach Olvidado from almost anywhere in Espa.

Miranda smiled at herself and began to braid her hair, satisfied with its color. As an orphan who grew up in a monastery, she never expected she would be important like this. She would have been content to help the townspeople of Devitus in the smallest ways, and she would still help them if she thought that was the best use of her time. Their struggles mattered to her, but she feared for their futures if she shirked her destiny. In truth, she still wasn't sure what her destiny was. Maréli, the Chief Healer for Invictus's church in Nulodia, made Miranda think she should seek a way to heal the arcane stream from The Unbinding. A feat of that magnitude seemed foolish in the current moment. Instead, she saw the intersection of the church's confusion about dragon eggs and the increase in poaching efforts in the Dundoi Mountains. Her efforts with the draikin had made her very protective of dragon eggs. She wondered if the growth in egg trafficking was somehow connected to the Umbrals.

After Miranda finished braiding her hair, she slid a beautiful sapphire comb into the back. It fit snugly in her hair which was pulled forward in the style of Invictus's healers. She was dressed in her battlemail, ready for travel. She prepared to share her plan with the others over breakfast, and they could make decisions together.

As she descended the staircase into the dining room of the inn, she could see Evan, Celyth, and Arlindra gathered at a table on the far side of the long building. The bedrooms sat on the east side, and the dining hall was on the west side. Though the draikin were not very tall, they built their settlement with buildings of various sizes.

Public spaces were usually comfortable for taller people, and this tavern, The Copper Crescendo, was no exception. The dining room stretched out one hundred feet past the end of the bar, which sat just to the left at the bottom of the staircase to the bedrooms. The bar on the north side of the building welcomed patrons entering from the southside entrance. About fifty feet to the right of the entrance sat a magnificent stone fireplace. The building was made of cured oak and cedar, giving the place a pleasant, woody smell. Miranda had enjoyed that scent every morning since arriving in K'tal H'yuck.

She approached the table with bold steps, drawing her companions' eyes to her. As she neared, her musical voice sang out a greeting for all three of the elves, "The Silver Maiden bathes in the dawn, welcoming the warmth of light." Miranda beamed at them.

Evan gave a deep sigh of relief, noticing her hair had darkened to its appropriate shade of red. With a confident smile, he replied, "And may we serve as lights of Lexcord, warming Espa with truth and righteousness."

Celyth and Arlindra looked at Evan. Celyth gave a grin and narrowed her eyes, "I thought you said you weren't a priest like Mir." Arlindra pursed her lips in thought, giving her chin a gentle rub.

Miranda laughed, "No, he's just well versed in the teachings of Lexcord. The goddess of the elves, you know, like all three of you. I mean she's a goddess for everyone, but," she started to stumble over her words. "I mean. Not everybody who knows a catechism is a priest," she finally explained. She forced an awkward smile, the confidence from before wavering.

Arlindra chuckled and Celyth laughed. Arlindra snarked, "After a month with you, it's hard not to pick up on the catechisms."

Evan grinned with nostalgia, explaining, "I spent a month with her on my brother's ship. That's where I learned the sayings myself."

Miranda feigned innocence with a shrug. She took a seat at the round table and looked behind her at the sparsely populated dining room. A few of the regulars were present, including Master Zeak, a silver scaled draikin who practically lived in The Copper Crescendo. He was a strange draikin, but he grew more enlightened as he spent time at the bar. She turned her attention back to the table and asked, "All the way in the back corner? Isn't this a little cliché?"

Evan gave a cheeky smile as he replied, "I'm surprised you haven't found yourself here more than once since you began adventuring!"

Miranda blinked for a moment as she realized she sat at this table dozens of times to gather and share intelligence about egg poachers.

Master Zeak was one of the agents who kept track of outsiders in an effort to identify which ones had hostile intent. They had interrogated people at this very table together. Another time, they had too much to drink and Zeak's companion, Cas, had to help Miranda back to her room. As she broke from her thoughts, she said, "Okay, it's a good spot." She shook her head in disbelief.

Everyone gave a quick laugh, and Miranda sheepishly looked at the table before them. Evan had already secured breakfast, and the plates were still steaming with warmth from the kitchen. The cold winter air creeped through the windows to this back corner, far away from the fireplace in the center of the tavern. An assortment of winter berries, cheeses, eggs, and a bit of ham had been scrambled together and stuffed between toasted bread. Miranda narrowed her eyes at Evan and asked, "You let Celyth order the food, didn't you?"

He tilted his head as he replied, "How did you know?" His voice indicated surprise.

Arlindra laughed. "The hot breakfast options aren't cheap this time of year. I became a ranger because I like food, and I like to find great food. But," she snapped, cutting her eyes at Celyth.

Celyth's eyes widened, the green within flashing with incredulity. "Hey! He offered to pay for it *after* I ordered," she protested.

Evan laughed. "Of course, that's why I offered. Miranda's friends are my friends, although working with the church is about ten percent of a pirate's salary." He then twisted his lips into a sarcastic grin as he bragged, "But per church contracts, we still get to loot the bad guys."

Miranda leaned forward and her voice deepened in disbelief. "Evan, nooo," she whispered, holding out the 'o' sound as she usually did when expressing shock.

He laughed to diffuse his insinuation. "We donate the excess to helping freed peoples find their feet. There's a lot of costs associated with running The Neb and The Blur. His Holiness and moshirote figured it was the best way to keep the pirates operational. And bad guys aren't as rich as Gelidor was. But ten percent of a pirate's salary?" he continued, his face going from playful to serious. "Ten percent is still more than anybody would ever need to survive. So, I'm going to share that with my friends when I can."

Miranda could hear the sincerity behind his words. As a young elf, he was part of a noble family. They moved to Claston before he was born. He knew times of plenty, but after the civil war broke out between Gelidor the Usurper and his subjects, Evan knew more loss than anyone should. He lost both of his sisters and his parents in those conflicts, and Gelidor cursed him as well. Miranda thought it was wonderful he had a giving heart after all he had been through. She finally spoke, "Well, Evanthalus, your kindness is outmatched. I suppose a meal is worth knowing the plan. Right?" she teased.

Evan nodded, his expression now neutral. Celyth and Arlindra began to eat while Miranda explained the plan between bites of the breakfast sandwiches. Her tone was very different than Evan remembered. Even in their philosophical conversations, she maintained a certain whimsy unless she became emotional. She could speak very passionately about topics, but sometimes it caused her words to catch in her throat. Now, she sounded like an experienced leader briefing her team. "The plan is to move south toward the Starlock River. There are plenty of bayous that stretch to the south alongside it. They go for miles."

Arlindra bobbed her head in agreement, adding, "We passed through several villages in those marshlands south of the Starlock. We even had to travel through the swampy region on a raft for a while."

Evan leaned forward. His eyes sparkled with mirth, but they were narrowed in realization. His mouth parted as if his words were stuck on the back of his tongue. Miranda tilted her head in his direction, her braids angling with her gaze. She smiled and asked, "You see where I'm going?"

He nodded and replied, "You mean to tell me we can reach Ezelbrecht from any body of water?" He blinked in disbelief for a moment.

Miranda gave a nervous giggle, her poise deteriorating a bit. "Well, not exactly. But you do need to be on certain bodies of water to reach them. Something my mother calls 'The Currents.' And only certain people can go." She glanced down at the table and rocked back and forth for a moment, indicating she was stressed. She took a deep breath as she continued, "I'm one of the people who can go because I've been there before. The only reason Erk could go is because Vortex told him how to persuade The Currents to obey him." Miranda shuddered at the thought of the ancient lich. "My mother's memories fill my mind sometimes. That's how I know how to reach Olvidado. She used these very same bayous to go there once. And that's why I know it will work."

Evan's face was twisted into a handsome smile different from Erk's. Miranda found herself staring, waiting on him or the cousins to respond. Evan spoke first, and his voice made her heart flutter. "I wondered all night long about what you might know. His Holiness and moshirote would be proud," he commented, the mirth in his gaze growing.

Arlindra gave a nod of approval but had no questions. Celyth shrugged, which Miranda knew was at least her signal of compliance. They finished their lavish breakfast in relative silence, the cousins only breaking it to discuss gossip they heard about Elitirin, a Sage back in Mystalon. Miranda was shocked to learn Elitirin sold tracts of land to outsiders who paid her with foreign currency. Well, she at least feigned a bit of shocked body language. She wasn't sure what Arlindra and Celyth meant while they were discussing the details. Evan didn't seem to be listening as he ate his sandwich.

As they left the tavern, Evan left a generous, extra sum for the proprietor. "Just in case you need something for the pegasus," he explained, though Miranda knew it wouldn't be necessary. Pegasus Knights would collect the animal if the companions did not return in a timely manner.

Before they walked out the door, Master Zeak, still seated at the bar, called out, "Hey, Mir'thax!"

Miranda spun around, her draconic name in common sounding out of place. She returned a loud but floaty, "Yes?"

Zeak laughed. "Leaving without me's a terrible idea, but I'm really not in the mood for an adventure right now. Still, I know you gotta go. I'll hold things down here, got it?"

Miranda's lips broke into her sweet smile, and she lowered her volume. "Of course, Master Zeak." The inn was quiet this early in the morning, anyway. The sun had only been up for an hour, and it was the heart of winter. Short days meant extra sleep for those who relied on the sun for their work.

They departed two hours after sunrise. They could reach the Starlock River near sunset on foot, and they intended to travel hastily. A dense, deciduous forest stretched from the Dundoi Mountains to the Starlock River. This deep in the winter, most of the trees were bare, but some vegetation still thrived in the cold. The leaves that fell in autumn were decaying on the forest floor, covering it with a rich humus. It filled the region with a delightful, natural scent. Frostberry bushes were in full bloom, providing a floral supplement to the earthy smells. Miranda savored the aromas for the entirety of the journey. As they neared the river, the sun had just settled beneath the northwest horizon, its final rays of light filling the evening sky with tones of deep purple and teal.

Miranda was surprised they made it so far without incident. To be fair, though, most of the dangerous wildlife for the Dundoi region was deep in winter hibernation. She had convinced herself the journey south would be a constant battle against stray Umbrals, but she was glad she was wrong. She felt like she had a tendency to make a problem bigger than it needed to be, and such thoughts fueled her anxiety about the situation. She knew going to Ezelbrecht was probably the wisest choice, even if they were not the kindest dragon in existence.

The four found a small settlement close to the river that had no inn. They secured a river raft from a friendly orc who knew the area well, and Evan made sure to spare no expense. The vessel was made of several buoyant logs tied together and pitched on the bottom. A small mast was built into the center, and it had a circular bench built around it. Long oars were fixed and tied to each of the corners. They were long enough to reach while seated at the mast. The raft was ten feet across and fifteen feet long. It could seat all of them easily.

Celyth tied off their transport while Miranda and Arlindra set up camp about a thousand feet to the west of the settlement. They built a fire and had cold rations for their evening meal. Evan put his personality to work, visiting with the people in the settlement. There were no confirmed reports of Umbrals in the last month, a sign the strange shadows were sequestered to regions rich in magic. The journey tired them, though, and eventually they gathered around the campfire to rest. Miranda pitched a small tent that would be somewhat helpful if it rained, but Evan and Celyth merely laid out sleeping mats stuffed with down. Arlindra chose a nearby tree to sleep in, and she prayed to the earth mother to protect their campsite. She climbed up into the tree, finding a branch that supported her easily. She watched over the camp from her perch.

Evan lay on his stomach, the pillow of his bedroll supporting his chest. Celyth wasted no time falling asleep, and only Miranda could see Arlindra resting on the tree's branches in the darkness. Evan noticed Miranda being restless, and his voice was barely louder than the fire, "Trouble sleeping again?"

She rolled over onto her stomach as well, looking across the fire where Evan lay. The opening in her small tent would only cover her head if she withdrew within, but she left it open. "Yeah, just a little. I could feel excitement building as we reached Argentum, but I wasn't expecting to be running to Ezelbrecht barely a day later." She let out a sigh, but then she giggled. "I should have known that I would end up fighting Farzg as well. He doesn't seem to be very good at making friends, but he is very talented at making enemies."

Evan's countenance seethed with anger for a moment as Miranda said the slaver's name. He calmed and replied, "You are correct. An evil of that magnitude will only grow. I think he's feeling the squeeze, though, as he's becoming more and more reliant on Death Pirates instead of his own henchmen. And if you can call Death Pirates friend," he paused and took a deep breath.

Miranda saw the emotion swell within him. "After what he did to Iria and Telisi, and Haelia too." Her voice was somber. "And everybody he's ever hurt. He deserves everything that you and Erk and Naomi and Dad throw at him." She gave a cheeky smile. "Pour out the wrath of justice."

Evan felt the tension in his mood dissolve. Miranda understood and knew just what to say. She had earned the church title "Judge of Hearts," an accolade she shared with Selasine. It indicated they could see people for who they were, and they knew how to reach people in spite of facades or masks. When Erk kidnapped Miranda, she tore down the front he created as a dread pirate. Evan smiled across the fire to her. Miranda probably understood his own heart better than he did, he thought. "We will. But then what?"

Miranda had missed her conversations with the Lancethinas brothers. She giggled, "Then you're free to live without the burden of vengeance. The pain of our losses will never truly heal, but delivering justice to those who caused that pain might help." She gave him a soft smile. "And there's only one way to deal with Farzg, and I'm— I'm not strong enough to do that." She stumbled a bit as she spoke.

Evan blinked, trying to understand her meaning before responding. "You don't think your gift is strong enough? Or you?" he asked. Miranda was not insecure, but at times she could downplay her own value. She would barely let Erk give her credit for her nearly single-handed defeat of the usurper and his Death Pirate allies months ago. Evan thought she was fully strong enough in power and conviction.

She closed her eyes for a moment and her body glowed with a golden aura. "Partially the gift. But mostly, I don't want to be the one who kills in the name of justice. There are those with the right dispositions, and I believe that's the team hunting him now." The golden aura faded. "Even now, I'm fully powered, but the best I could do is maybe an earthquake. Or a teleport for us." She twisted her lips, slightly perplexed. Her recent teleport made her shudder with worry. She pushed those concerns aside as she murmured, "And even then, what good is that against somebody like Farzg?"

Evan nodded in understanding. "There's a strength in you. You share it with His Holiness. It's a strength Farzg fears. Even more when it's connected to allies like moshirote and me." He gave a sly, sinister smile. "Yashirote Iria left Claston because she couldn't bear the pain of the war," he said, using the word for older sister in formal elven. "She was like you in a lot of ways, but the killing she was forced to do broke her spirit. I don't want you to ever feel like that. There is a perfectly capable blade by your side. And I can carry that burden with you."

Miranda's heart fluttered in her chest again. She hated the idea of causing harm to others so much, but she knew violence in the name of justice was sometimes necessary. Evil beings used violence to oppress, and sometimes the only way to stop them was through equal brutality. For some reason, Evan's offer to take that burden with her gave her a light feeling in her stomach. Instead of a lecture on the necessity of violence, he simply accepted how she felt and validated it with his understanding. She could see a different facet of him right now, and she liked it. Her sapphire eyes sparkled in the campfire as she stared at him in disbelief, struggling internally to understand what she felt. "You've left me speechless," she finally replied.

Evan's lips broke into a caring smile. "Then rest, Miranda. We've got a busy day tomorrow."

He was right, she thought. Her battlemail was laid out beside her tent, glinting in the light of the fire. She reached over to a bag on her belt containing useful potions, salves, and medicines. In it, she found a small music box wrapped carefully in cloth. It was adorned with beautiful gemstones and sparkling metals. She wound the gears, and the melody helped her drift off. She was thankful nobody else seemed disturbed by it; the song it played put her at ease and helped her rest.

The next morning, Miranda awoke to a sizzling sound followed by a delicious aroma. She opened her eyes, looking out of her tent to see Arlindra with a camping pan held over the fire. Miranda sat up and pushed her bedroll off. She squirmed out of her tent. Evan and Celyth were about thirty feet away, standing with the raft. They were engaged in conversation and getting along pleasantly. Arlindra greeted the awakening priestess, "Good morning, nen'li." She used the elven word for friend, an indication she had grown to trust Miranda over the last month.

There was already enough sunlight in the sky to see clearly. "It seems as if I've overslept," Miranda apologized.

Arlindra shook her head. "Nonsense. Our natures dictate our body's need for sleep just as it does for food. The acuity of the mind is more important in battle than the swiftness of one's blade."

Miranda blinked with an impressed expression. Arlindra's wise sayings reminded her of some catechisms. "I wouldn't have said it quite like that, but thank you for understanding," she replied with a laugh. She donned her armor and packed up her things. As she finished, she helped Arlindra complete breakfast preparations. The ranger had acquired some fatalfly eggs, a creature akin to a bird-sized wyvern. They were notoriously aggressive creatures, but their eggs and meat were delicacies.

Arlindra wrapped the eggs in some flatbread. After smoldering the fire, the two of them joined Celyth and Evan by the raft. Arlindra gave everyone a serving of the food she had prepared. "We can eat on the way," she commented.

Miranda nodded, "Sorry for waking so late. Are we ready?" she asked.

Evan gave a broad smile and answered, "At your orders." He stepped onto the raft, which seemed sturdy enough. Celyth joined him, bounding to the far side and using an oar to push the raft closer to the shore.

Arlindra gave a lithe step onto the vessel, turning and extending a hand to Miranda. She helped the priestess onto the raft, adding, "Don't make me drop my food. You know that's unforgivable," she warned as she took a bite. She was graceful and eloquent, but her love of food overpowered her manners.

Miranda laughed and took a bite of her own breakfast. "A crime so heinous, it's not listed in the *Vexilatus*." The Church of Invictus had many texts, but the *Vexilatus* outlined acts of chaos and prescribed penance for them.

As they boarded the raft and set down their packs, they took a moment to eat. The vessel drifted into the slow current of the Starlock River. The water was murky and listless here, and trees grew along its banks and even in the water itself. The four took turns rowing, moving across the river into the great bayous of the region. After an hour of aimless floating, a dense, unseasonal fog grew around them. Visibility was very important in the swamps, as they had to navigate around trees and thick vegetation several times within the first hour. Celyth groaned. "It's too cold for fog."

Arlindra agreed but voiced her concern differently. "This could spell trouble for our ability to navigate."

Miranda closed her eyes and inhaled. "The Currents call to us," she explained. "Keep pushing forward."

Evan sat on the bench under the mast. "Aye aye, cap'n," he teased.

Miranda turned to look at him, her eyes wide in disbelief. "I thought that was a title reserved for Erk the Radiant!" she replied in shock.

He laughed, turning the oars again. He thought she was cute when she was in denial. "Brace yourselves, rough patch," he warned.

They felt the bottom of the raft scrape over a submerged tree root. It wasn't as rough as Evan anticipated, but he wanted to be cautious. These waters weren't as deep as the ocean, but they could be equally dangerous. As they continued, the fog thickened until the water beneath the raft was no longer visible. Miranda would have to expend mana to enhance her vision through such a hazard, so she opted for low visibility like everyone else on the raft.

They noticed, however, the water's movement accelerated. At first, Arlindra and Evan voiced concern, but they realized the obstacles in the swamp were no longer a threat. The air smelled salty, and Evan exclaimed, "By the gods, we're on the open water!"

Miranda's smile was small. "Yes. Olvidado," she commented, gesturing in front of the raft. The fog dispersed, revealing a narrow beach surrounded by towering, rocky ridges. The wafting clouds obscured the sky, but the darkness of night loomed just behind the billowing haze.

Evan's heart raced with excitement. He held onto that feeling as long as he could, reaching out to grab Miranda's hand. Her eyes widened with surprise as he squeezed. He said in a mesmerized tone, "You're truly amazing, Miranda. You've brought us to Olvidado!"

Her cheeks flushed a little and she nodded, her braids bobbing enthusiastically. "That's what I set out to do!" she replied, an awkward tenor in her voice.

He realized he grabbed her hand and gently let it go. "Apologies. This is exciting, Erk has told me about this place so many times, and I'm afraid my memories of coming here were mostly lost when you healed me!"

Celyth and Arlindra exchanged glances and narrowed their eyes, but they were entertained by the awkwardness. Miranda watched the beach as they paddled the river raft up to the shallow sands. It was difficult to avoid getting their feet wet, but Evan and Arlindra jumped into the shallows first. They pulled the craft toward the dry beach. Miranda and Celyth followed, the light vessel sliding onto land. They tied it off to a nearby tree just in case Olvidado had a tide. Miranda honestly didn't know, and neither did her mother.

As they tied off the raft, Celyth commented, "Hey, looks like somebody is already here."

Miranda looked in the direction Celyth pointed, and the priestess saw a small skiff she recognized. The first time she came to Olvidado with Erk, Selasine, and August, she rode in that boat. Furthermore, upon their previous arrival, she felt an overwhelming sense of evil and dread, and it made her panic. This time, she welcomed Olvidado with hysterical laughter. "Sword of Justice, that's how I got here the first time!" she said through fits of giggling.

When she explained, her laughter became contagious. Evan added in, "Wait, so if the skiff is still here, does this mean we'd end up in Yendralia if we took it instead of the raft?"

Miranda's eyes widened. She teleported herself and her companions back to Yendralia after her first experience here. She wasn't sure how to leave the island, so she closed her eyes and focused on the mana within her. For her to use Reshiria's memories, she had to scan her own mind and the magic inside for answers. Miranda did not always know which question to ask, but if her mother knew the answer, Miranda also seemed to know. As her mind contacted the ether, she found her mother's voice. Fortunately, this question had an answer in Reshiria's memories, and Miranda found it. "Ezelbrecht will send us back based on our destinies. Mother always ended up back where she started, but that doesn't seem to be the only possibility."

Evan nodded, and Arlindra looked around. The fog had broken up just a few feet away from the beach, but the landscape here was dark and sinister. The ranger commented, "It does look as terrifying as you described."

Celyth started to light a torch, but Miranda gripped her holy symbol and prayed, "Sword of Justice, pour out your light and righteousness. Push back the darkness with your holy daylight." As she did, the miniature scales of justice hanging from her neck began to glow. It illuminated a sphere around them as if it were noon with

Miranda as the source. However, they could still see the dark at the borders, pressing against their bubble of radiance.

Celyth found it unsettling, especially because what she could see was otherworldly and nightmarish. Gnarled, black trees stretched up dozens of feet in the air, and strange, dry vegetation littered the craggy ridge surrounding the beach. As Miranda's prayer lit up the area, the group could see a single path descending into a gorge. It disappeared into the darkness. "Think there's anything to fight down there?" Celyth asked after taking in the surroundings.

Miranda tilted her head, putting her braids at an angle. "Last time I was here, there was a fight in the gorge, but I don't feel Ezelbrecht's immense evil from here. They must be aware of us and are welcoming us."

Evan let out a deep breath. In his mind, that sounded promising. He had heard Miranda was extremely sensitive to Ezelbrecht's presence. If she felt safe at this moment, he hoped they had nothing to fear from the eldritch dragon. "Then let's pray for our safety and stay vigilant," he finally added.

The four spent six hours traversing the gorge, arriving at the massive entrance to Ezelbrecht's lair. As the cave came into view, Celyth began to complain about the lack of monsters to fight. Arlindra rolled her eyes, but Miranda giggled. Evan was concerned Celyth might have a violent streak, but he correctly blamed her background as a trained fighter and master archer. As they neared the opening, Miranda hesitated for a moment. She called out in the draconic language, "Ezelbrecht the Gray. It is I, Mir'thax Toi'landra," she identified, using the form of her name given to her at birth. It was a draconic phrase describing Miranda's heritage perfectly. Her father was an incredible, fire-breathing, red dragon with a good heart. Her mother was a ruthless and cunning blue dragon capable of breathing bolts of extraordinary lightning. Miranda's dragon name meant "of fire and lightning," but she preferred to use the common form of her name. She continued her introduction, "I seek your counsel regarding the safety of dragons and their eggs."

A burst of wind rushed from the cavern, blowing everyone's hair and clothing. Celyth and Arlindra instinctively readied their weapons, interpreting the sudden gust as an attack. Evan stood close to Miranda, who did not react. He asked her, "Was that Ezelbrecht? What did you say in that language?"

Miranda turned to him with a gentle smile and meek nod. "I said hello. They've invited us in. Let's go." She turned to look at the elf cousins. "I don't think the weapons would help much with Ezelbrecht. And make sure to be deferent if they seem cranky." The music in her voice was far too playful to be walking into a deadly situation, the cousins thought.

Arlindra and Celyth nodded and shouldered their bows. As they crossed under the rock into the cavern, Miranda's Daylight prayer ceased. The cave was not dark, however, as a pale, silver light radiated from deeper within. Stalactites and stalagmites of varying sizes made the cavern busy but spacious. Everyone followed a step behind Miranda as she walked toward the center. Evan began to worry, and the light in the cavern allowed him to glimpse the wings of a dragon of incredible size. His heart leapt into his throat.

"Mir'thax. I thought I'd never see you again," an intimidating, powerful voice called out.

"I had only hoped you wouldn't, great Ezelbrecht," she replied, her voice emotionless but bigger than usual. As she responded, the four emerged from the darker part of the cavern into a central area large enough to house a dragon many times larger than average. There was no dragon hoard, and the pale light of this place made colors difficult to distinguish. Ezelbrecht sat in this open space, their long tail curling around a stalagmite and into the darkness. They waited on all four feet until the group emerged. They then stood on their hind legs, their neck towering fifty feet into the air. Miranda continued her response, "But the mortal realm faces a new threat of special interest to those of us with draconic blood."

Ezelbrecht's eyes narrowed, and their maw broke out into a horrifying smile. They lowered their neck, bringing their face so close Miranda could reach out and touch it. Evan felt a fear deep in his stomach that made him feel powerless. Celyth's bloodlust turned to quiet compliance, but Arlindra marveled at the size and uniqueness of the eldritch dragon. She knew it was unlikely she would ever see anything of this magnitude again in her future. Ezelbrecht retorted, "So it is you, the impossible dragon, who wants to be a champion in the struggles of the old ones?" Their voice dripped with condescension so thick it made the cousins feel queasy. Evan's heart raced.

Miranda lowered her head in humility. "I could never make such a claim. I am neither a shard of Gorthran nor Saraix. But I am the child of both. My purpose is to help and to heal, nothing more, nothing less. And those who wish the opposite are seeking dragon eggs with intense fury. I merely wished to beg the counsel of the oldest and wisest of our kind."

Ezelbrecht's smile softened and became neutral. "The daughter of Reshiria nothing more than a healer?" they hissed. "Humans are so commonly arrogant, more so when they possess the power to defend their arrogance. And you," Ezelbrecht's tongue flicked past Miranda, whipping right between Evan and Celyth. "Your humility is sincere. You've embraced part of your destiny, and the fear I tasted in you is now gone."

Miranda cycled her breath, and her companions relaxed as Ezelbrecht seemed amenable to the conversation. Miranda replied, "As always, you are correct in your assessment of my heart. I don't understand my destiny, and I am confident it will materialize in the future. For now, though, I am worried about the destinies of others. The shards of Gorthran and Saraix."

Ezelbrecht gave a gentle nod, staring into Miranda's blue eyes with intent. "I can see you already know what happens to a dragon egg if it is destroyed. So, ask your question, fire and lightning."

She stared back, the pale light giving Ezelbrecht's eyes a silver shimmer. "Besides alchemy and," she shuddered as she spoke. Ezelbrecht simpered, appreciating her genuine disgust. "And eating them, what ridiculous reasons would mortals have to pursue dragon eggs?"

Ezelbrecht's cold, evil heart filled with joy. To them, Mir'thax was superior to all humans. They were glad that their last encounter did not keep this unique dragon-human away. To hear her refer to egg thieves as mortals so casually meant she was coming to grips with the power of her entity. They replied, "Dragon eggs are intense conduits of mana. Their pull is not unlike the solisberry tree, but it is more concentrated." The dragon flicked their tongue again. "They spend half a century gathering the ether from the arcane stream. It shapes them into the dragon they will become. If that dragon is of fire like your father, then the egg stores ether suitable for fire magic." Ezelbrecht's smile widened as they saw the realization in Miranda's eyes. Still, they continued, "Likewise, your mother's egg favored the mana particles that could generate lightning. What do you think all of the eggs have in common, though?" they asked, putting Miranda on the spot.

She stood tall as she replied. "The shards of Saraix and Gorthran," she stated, confidence permeating her. Evan was enthralled with this woman who had healed him, standing face to face with an eldritch dragon so comfortably. Celyth realized Ezelbrecht was not a fight she would want to joke about, even if the ancient dragon lacked their breath weapon. Arlindra listened, observing their surroundings. In some sense, Miranda's companions felt invisible or at least so insignificant Ezelbrecht did not bother to acknowledge their existence.

"Correct," the dragon hissed in return. "There is something you must understand, though. As magical conduits, it is possible a mortal has begun tampering with the eggs in order to take advantage of their affinity with the ether. I welcomed you to Olvidado for two reasons. The first is that my goals and your goals are currently aligned. The second," the beast grew enraged as they spoke. "The second is to tell you how you and I are different. And why that matters."

Miranda's eyes widened. Ezelbrecht had been expecting her, and that gave her conflicted feelings. She replied, "I am honored to receive your wisdom."

The eldritch dragon's eyes narrowed. "You are. You see, you are an impossibility in the sense that two, living, breathing dragons created you. I, too, was created, but I was created by Gorthran himself." The cavern quaked when Ezelbrecht spoke the Dragon King's name. The beast brought their face closer to Miranda, but she did not reach out to touch them in wonder as she did months before. This time she stood, defiant and justified. Impressed with her growth, Ezelbrecht continued, "Legends say Saraix broke herself into many different numbers of shards. I know the exact number."

Miranda's expression went from strength to shock. The beast before her paused, giving her a moment to interrupt, but she said nothing. She knew Ezelbrecht would share what they wanted regardless of her questions or speculations. As she calmed, they added, "Nine thousand, nine hundred and ninety-nine. There were almost ten thousand shards of the Dragon Mother broken and put into the arcane stream. Gorthran's number is different."

The cavern rumbled a bit again, moved by unseen forces. Miranda's sapphire eyes bent into a glare, and she made a scrutinous face reminiscent of a dragon. Reshiria's memories spilled into her consciousness. She recited the number with defiance, "Nine thousand, nine hundred and ninety-four."

Ezelbrecht laughed, raising their head to the top of the cavern. "You truly are a dragon, Mir'thax! Your father was born of my mortal enemy, but your mother."

Miranda's scrutinous face twisted into something sinister, a new expression. "Hello, grandfather."

Ezelbrecht's scales burst with color in the pale light. They cycled through chromatic and metallic hues, even reflecting otherworldly shades that could not be described. Ezelbrecht said in a shout of triumph, "Correct, child. I am the six shards of Gorthran left to preserve himself as an entity." They lowered their head, drawing near Miranda again. "However, I, Ezelbrecht, have always had a mind of my own. I contain what is left of the Dragon Father, but I am my own being. I was the strongest of his chosen children, and so it is my face and my name that manifests in this universe."

Evan's jaw slacked in disbelief. Celyth and Arlindra traded glances. None of the legends ever mentioned this part of the story. As they stood behind Miranda, they could not see the dark expressions now twisting her countenance. Miranda replied, "I have felt the power that courses through me. And I have all of my mother's memories. I'm sure you know of my plight," she continued. She still had a wicked smile on her lips, which Ezelbrecht relished. "We are very different because you are the manifestation of a god. I am but a mortal dragon. An Abyss of power divides us."

Ezelbrecht nodded. "Do not forget I can still see the stream child. This is why you are here, and for no other reason."

Miranda blinked with confusion. She didn't understand their meaning.

The dragon continued, "You see, my children are beginning to disappear. Out of my progeny, at least four hundred shards have gone missing since you came to see me last."

Miranda leaned forward slightly. "Missing? Can you not see them?"

The beast shook their head. "Not in the stream, nor did they hatch. If the egg was destroyed, I would see their shard in the stream. If the dragon was born, I could call their name and find them. They are part of me, and I am part of them. But four hundred, simply gone."

Miranda's dark expression turned into one of horror. "And of the Dragon Mother's?"

Ezelbrecht's maw twisted up into a sickening smile. "Over five hundred. There are almost one thousand dragons missing from the ebb and flow of magic."

Evan gasped, putting the pieces together. He blurted, "By the gods, the stream is bleeding."

Ezelbrecht's eyes snapped to Evan. They continued to smile,

"Welcome, Evanthalus, brother of Erilkaiden, Thief of Light." The smile melted. "In a way, it's fitting you accompany the girl this time. You owe the dragons your life."

Evan nodded in deference. "Of course, great Ezelbrecht. And that I continue living is a testament to your mercy."

Miranda interrupted, "Though my heart is like my father's, my ambitions are like my mother's. Reshiria would not stand by and let the dragons disappear. Though my power pales compared to yours, I bear the strength of my heritage and my chosen god. What is happening to the godshards?" she asked pointedly.

Ezelbrecht let a burst of air out of their nose, causing another gust of wind like the one that greeted them at the entrance to the cavern. "I do not know, child. But I guarantee that it's connected to the increase of trafficking in dragon eggs. If you answer that question, then you'll answer all four questions currently in your heart."

Miranda turned to look at her companions. "Then the Umbrals are connected to this as well?"

The eldritch dragon moved their maw gently before replying. "As I said, find out what is happening to my children, then you will have your answer."

Celyth and Arlindra nodded as Miranda turned back to them, hoping the answer would help them on their quest. Miranda looked up at Ezelbrecht and clarified, "Then we will investigate what is happening to the eggs. Is there any chance that faekin have a role in this?" she asked, sharing the information Naomi had passed to Evan in his last debriefing.

Ezelbrecht nodded. "The faekin are all magical, but magic does not constitute their life force as it does for us, Mir'thax. Instead, it feeds them as a source of sustenance. Follow these leads, and when you find what is happening to the eggs, you may find the godshards as well."

Evan understood Ezelbrecht's motivation then. He couldn't wait to get back to Nulodia and brag about visiting Ezelbrecht without almost dying. Still, the situation was grim, and he was concerned. Miranda's parents would have had shards in the arcane stream; he then thought the worst. "Miranda," he whispered.

She turned to look at him, and Ezelbrecht also turned their attention to Evan again. The dragon replied in a patronizing voice, "I haven't seen them in almost thirty, but their shards disappeared a little less than twenty years ago. They were the first to go missing."

Tears surged to the corners of Miranda's eyes. She spoke with her father and mother in the arcane stream, but their essences seemed separated from the flow of magic. Her heart raced with panic. To find them, she had to touch their crystalized gemstone with her mana body while she was lost in the tides of ether. That glassy substance was very similar to the crystalized magic in Evan's sword. The panic started to eat away at her composure. She looked from Ezelbrecht to Evan, "Evan, will you show me your sword again?" Her melody was timid and fearful.

He nodded and withdrew it, noting Ezelbrecht's size would have made the weapon ineffective anyway. Miranda reached for it, a tremble in her hand. She looked into the pommel of the sword made of strange metals and clockwork pieces. As she took the hilt in her hand, a gear began to turn, causing the gemstone and the blade to begin glowing a faint, pink color. She slowly turned to Ezelbrecht. "My parents were turned into gemstone statues resembling the stone in this blade." She held it out for the dragon in a non-threatening way.

The beast narrowed their eyes and flicked their tongue around Miranda. "Crystalized magic?" they hissed. The cavern fell silent as Ezelbrecht had no immediate answers.

Miranda continued to explain, "These weapons are becoming increasingly common, and they use these gemstones as a source of power. Is this what's taking the shards from the stream?"

Ezelbrecht flexed their maw in genuine thought. "If mortals have learned to crystalize magic, then Espa is doomed. Magic should not manifest this way in the mortal dimension. This is anathema."

Miranda nodded in agreement as she returned the sword to Evan, trying not to break down in front of the eldritch dragon who seemed to respect her at least. Her parents were waiting to be called, but they were trapped. She thought she knew exactly where their godshards were. She had to get back to Devitus.

The dragon smiled. "You know where you're going then, yes. Leave from whence you came. I will send you close to your destination as a show of our mutual struggle. Do not think this makes us permanent allies, Mir'thax. You belong to neither me nor the Dragon Queen. You have proven yourself to be just as human as you are dragon in this moment, and I have grown tired of your presence."

Miranda bowed her head in deference. "I will depart at once, O Great One," she said in a hushed, hurried tone.

As they turned to leave, Ezelbrecht had an afterthought. "Beware, though. Aylabrax the Devourer of Souls came to see me just yesterday. She wanted to know about the godshards, too. I told her nothing. She left. Her power is invalid here, as is that of the one you call Invictus." Ezelbrecht yawned. "Plus, she's still here on the island. Or at least it feels like she's here. You probably won't see her. She's not hunting for you."

The four did not stop, understanding the seriousness of Ezelbrecht's previous rebuke. Miranda called back, "Thank you again, great Ezelbrecht." The companions did not turn around to see the ancient, evil dragon's lingering, sinister smile.

They said nothing until they arrived back at the beach. Arlindra helped them navigate the ascent out of the gorge in the safest way with only hand gestures. As the walls of the gorge began to get low, they could hear the water splashing on the beach. Once Miranda's Daylight prayer poured onto the vessels, they noticed a humanoid of some kind now lay on the raft.

"What the," Evan hissed as he saw the silhouette of the person first.

Miranda looked around, and the cousins drew their weapons. Evan pointed fifty feet down the beach, the water behind the raft starting to billow with fog. As Miranda's eyes found the person, her first instinct was to run and investigate, but this seemed a little too suspicious. She hoped they weren't injured and in need of her assistance.

Celyth prepared three arrows and gave a nod with her chin toward the raft.

Evan held his hand up toward Celyth and broke rank to approach the stranger. Miranda followed close behind, and Arlindra and Celyth split the difference to the sides, weapons at the ready. He looked closely and called back, "It's breathing, but it's unconscious."

Miranda kicked herself mentally and rushed forward. She pulled a cloak from around the creature's head, and she saw the face of a beautiful kitsune, eyes closed in repose. As Miranda touched her to check for vitals, she felt a weird static sensation. "Ouch!" she shouted as she jumped away from the foxkin, sparks sputtering everywhere after they made contact.

The sudden, magical backfire caused the foxkin to awaken, and she scuttled backwards on her paws, pressing up against the mast of the raft. "Who are you? Where am I?" she asked in a panic.

Miranda looked at her hands, dumbfounded. She hadn't

experienced that before, and she wasn't certain what it was. It didn't seem like it drained any mana from her, but it was definitely a surprise manifestation of arcane energy. As she stared at her hands, Evan replied to the kitsune, "We're an adventuring group in a remote location only reachable with very specific knowledge and circumstances. I'd say we're past introductions, wouldn't you?"

The kitsune blinked in disbelief. "I promise, I mean you no harm. I do not know where I am, nor do I know of these circumstances of which you speak." She panted, her eyes darting around the beach in trepidation. Celyth and Arlindra shouldered their bows and approached the raft. Evan stood on the shore, holding the rope to the raft in one hand and his strange blade in the other.

Miranda finally let go of her confusion and looked up at the foxkin with empathy. "I'm sorry I startled you. My name is Miranda, warpriest of Invictus," she said in the sweetest voice she could muster, the feeling of worry regarding her parents still urging her to hurry.

"Yuvina. I'm Yuvina," the kitsune replied. She immediately wanted to stab herself. She gave them her real name! She screamed at herself internally.

Evan smiled. "Well met, then, Yuvina. I am Evanthalus. We really are in a place that's almost impossible to get to by accident. Where are you from? Where were you before you woke up here?"

Yuvina looked nervous and wanted to run away. She shook her head. "I'm from the Tymbyrwylde. And, I..." she looked down as she trailed off. She tried to remember, but she couldn't. She honestly had no idea where she was before she woke up here.

Miranda gave a sincere smile. "Are you injured? Have you lost your memories?"

Yuvina nodded. "It seems to be a small timespan, maybe a week. A month? I don't know what day it is, so I have no frame of reference."

Evan replied, "Does that mean you have no intent to see Ezelbrecht?" His eyes were still narrow with distrust.

The foxkin's nose twitched. "Who?"

Celyth leaned forward. "Well, there's four of us and one of her. I say we drag her back with us and find out what's really going on." She cracked her knuckles and her green eyes burned with curiosity more than malice.

Yuvina's eyes widened, "Oh, gods. Please, don't hurt me, I truly mean you no harm." She trembled with fear, but internally, she seethed with anger. These people were most certainly Wielders, and Yuvina knew she could not trust them.

Miranda and Evan looked at each other. They knew how dangerous this might be, but they silently agreed they couldn't abandon her here on Olvidado. Evan asked pointedly, "Are you armed?"

Yuvina nodded. "Daggers. Four of them."

Miranda whispered a prayer to Invictus. As she did, the dim colors reflected by Olvidado's nightmarish landscape began to distort. She could see Yuvina radiated with an aura of goodness that was sincere but undisciplined. Miranda gave a nod to Evan before saying, "Very well, Yuvina. Please accompany us back to dry land."

The kitsune mumbled, "Okay." The fear in her voice was tangible.

The five began their journey into the fog with more questions than they began.

Aylabrax's mortal avatar was disturbing. The black hair draped in front of her face gave her an unsettling appearance, but it was the overwhelming aura of darkness and evil that spoke to her true nature. She was known as the devourer of children, as her presence caused them to wail with terror. She had only one goal, however: to increase her own power. Her followers did not reach out to her in the primordial place; she preferred to walk among mortals. Instead, those who served her in the pursuit of individual power would often find themselves a personal audience with the dark goddess. The relationship was usually that of parasite to host, Aylabrax using her immense power to siphon what value she could from her followers. They shared willingly, in many cases, but most of her clergy ended up as another soul in her collection.

Doctor One, however, was different from Aylabrax's followers. The eccentric former wizard had an intellect that superseded Aylabrax's immense power. His madness reached into corners of the universe not even Aylabrax considered. His lack of people skills did not hold him back, either, as his discoveries and ideas always drew people to him. The Lady in Mourning stood on the shores of Olvidado with a kitsune in her arms. Doctor One was looking down into the gorge. He whispered, "Hurry, dark one. They are returning."

Aylabrax placed the kitsune on the raft. She had used her primary power, Devour, to eat the foxkin's memories of the last month. After being infused with lacrima-deum, she radiated magical energy, tempting the dark goddess to consume her entire essence. Aylabrax did not, however, as the kitsune's value would prove much greater long term. "Now, for The Dark Command," she murmured, monotone. She whispered in a language that no longer existed in Espa. Vapors of power emerged from her lips, wafting through her hair and into the kitsune through her nose and mouth.

Doctor One turned to watch The Lady in Mourning work the ancient magics. There were dangerous powers residing outside the arcane stream and the gods, but most of them had been purposefully forgotten by history. Some of the gods themselves relied on that bygone arcana, a poorly understood but unimaginable strength.

The dark goddess continued breathing vapor until she finished chanting her words. Her voice was rigid and bored as she explained, "When she sees the eggs, she will use the power. It is beyond her control; I have made it so." Aylabrax stood. Her mortal form only wore a knee length, ragged gown. It was once white, but it had turned a deep, bland gray thanks to the evil energies stirring within her. She looked like a horrible spirit returned to the mortal coil for vengeance, and, in some respects, that was an accurate depiction of her entity. The target of her revenge, however, had been lost by even her own memory.

Doctor One approached her. "Now, it's my turn."

Aylabrax said nothing, walking past Doctor One into the gorge of Olvidado. The darkness did not matter to the evil goddess, and Doctor One's monocle allowed him to see in the dark. They did not descend far before they saw a bubble of daylight deep in the gorge below. Aylabrax hissed, "Invictusssss." The sound of snakes echoed throughout the gorge.

The mad doctor stopped and looked down. "What about him?" he sniffed the air as he spoke.

Aylabrax's body shook. "I want to consssume them. They possess great power. Their sssouls are immenssse." She licked the dead, dry lips beneath her hair. "One of them carriesss three soulsss, even! The dragonsss," she finished, still drawing out the 's' in her words as if she were a serpent.

Doctor One insisted, "You won't be able to consume the dragon down there unless I get the information I need. If you want to use your Devour on Ezelbrecht, you'll have to get them off this island first. Quickly, we haven't much time." He placed a device on the ground. It looked like a person-sized plate with a single lacrima-deum extractor attached to the base on a three-foot-tall stand. The extractor was made of eolnut wood, and it had many sharp points meant to puncture the crystallized magic. Olvidado was a plane between planes, resting just outside the primary mortal coil and the primordial place of the gods. Na'agamlor the corrupt merchant god could not afford a way into the primordial place, but Doctor One found a solution. Using a lacrima-deum formed from the egg of an astral dragon and a teleportation device, a mortal could theoretically enter the primordial place. The trick, however, was to begin in a location that was already halfway there. Intellect was much more valuable than money, and the mad-elf cackled to himself as he placed the entire petrified egg in the extractor. It had been split into two halves so that Doctor One could extract the godshard within, but he used everything else to power the machine.

A faint whirring noise filled the air, but it grew into a low, vibrating hum. The disc of the device lit up, and Doctor One stood on it with Aylabrax beside him. After a few moments, the evil goddess gasped with surprise as she saw the clouds of the primordial place beneath them. She suddenly caught a fearful feeling. Doctor One was already capable of accessing both Olvidado and the primordial place. She wondered if she should expose this insanely intelligent creature to the core knowledge of the universe. She struggled with finding answers in the viscous body of knowledge beneath the clouds simply because she did not know what questions to ask. Doctor One knew the questions and how to understand the answers. Aylabrax decided to carry through with the plan; as of now, Doctor One was no threat to her divinity, and he still had many potential uses to her as a pawn. As he peered into the forbidden corners of the universe, he would endure the madness created by exposure to such knowledge. She could then Devour his mind, and it would exist as a sub-mind within hers. She would have access to that knowledge without risking the miniscule remainder of her own divine sanity.

The two dropped through the plate beneath them as the crystalized egg burned up. The device disintegrated into black miasma behind them as they fell into the clouds of the primordial place. The dispersed magic displaced space-time, and Doctor One knew it would create anomalies connected to his timeline. He did not, however, have the time to spare on an experimental investigation. He was the first mortal to enter the primordial place since its creation over a millennia ago.

Doctor One wanted to gloat about his success, but he was soon overwhelmed by a sensory experience unlike anything in the primary dimension of Espa. Gravity became optional. He felt like he could see anywhere in Espa if he merely thought about that place. Touch, smell, and sight blended together as his mind seemed more responsible for shaping this world than a pre-existing reality.

Aylabrax did not want to risk the other gods detecting the presence of a mortal, so she shielded herself from view. The gods could only perceive each other in the primordial place if their wills were mutual. Most of the time, the gods of good and light left their connections to the evil gods open. Darkness had a tendency to brag, possibly revealing malicious intentions before they unfolded. The evil gods, however, valued their secrecy, and tried to avoid the good gods as they created their sinister machinations. Aylabrax hoped that her will would shield both herself and her guest from the prying eyes of the other divinities.

Doctor One had read numerous texts about the primordial place and knew where the universe's information was stored. He sank below the clouds, splashing into the viscous green liquid. He realized he would drown in this liquid, so he swam back up. As he coughed a breath full of the liquid out, he looked to his dark companion above. "I won't have long. If you want to use this information, you'll get me back to the prime coil as soon as I lose consciousness."

Aylabrax's face twisted into an evil smile, but Doctor One could neither see nor feel it. "Very well," she spoke, her voice deadpan and disagreeable.

Doctor One focused on his own memories as he dove into the green liquid of knowledge. He thought about an inert pocket of energy known as the Eye of the Stream, an anomaly that flowed within the arcane stream. As a young wizard, he isolated that phenomenon during an experiment. His brush with the Eye, however, was only the beginning of this journey. What he witnessed that day inspired every discovery he made after. It seemed fitting, then, that he would seek even more knowledge to assist him in creating a device to siphon divine power from one entity and transfer it to another. The question was so specific that the universal knowledge revealed to him realities beyond his wildest imagination. Not only was it possible to steal the essence of Saraix and Gorthran, but it was also much easier to do than Doctor One hoped. He knew he was right about the godshards months ago, and now he knew how to make them useful. There were ten thousand shards of both gods. Doctor One realized that Saraix had saved only one shard to hide her essence, and that godshard was in the mortal coil.

It was in a vault that Doctor One recognized. The well-protected treasury was encased in a strange, perpetually cold mineral known as snowstone. There were many incredible artifacts and treasures here, but on a pedestal in the center rested a glowing, silver shard. It was encased in a solid manifestation of pressure shedding a subtle radiance. How in Espa had Farzg hidden the godshard of Saraix in his vault this entire time? The frost giantkin would not be inclined to trade such a relic lightly. Doctor One needed to think of a way to remove Farzg from the formula and claim the shard for himself. This would be the breaking point of the frost giantkin's usefulness.

His mind sought a method to use the dragon gods to empower himself, and the answers he found were unexpected. "Sentient arcane underflow?" he mused as a device materialized in his mind. It would convert his body into a lacrima-deum, exhaust it, and preserve his cognizance. With the shard of one of the dragon gods, he could grow in power as an entity of inverted magic. He felt his air running short, but he continued his perusal. He sought the location of Gorthran's shard. That dark godshard was shrouded by the entity of Ezelbrecht, an eldritch dragon of great power. Gorthran, however, rested within the exiled dragon's soul. Doctor One needed to bait Gorthran and Ezelbrecht to escape their exile in Olvidado. Thanks to the unlimited reach of universal memory, Doctor One recognized Gorthran had been plotting his own escape for a decade already. The eldritch dragon had been in contact with a pirate named Erilkaiden, and that elf possessed the power to compress dimensions. If the pirate opened his power anywhere in the central reality, Gorthran could escape. The Dragon Father was angry with One, and the mad-elf predicted immediate confrontation. It was time to escalate his plans. Erilkaiden needed to open his Black Hole somewhere in Espa. He prepared his orders for Sender, his agent in Mystalon. Preferably known as Doctor Five, Sender possessed incredible tenacity and vigor. His Unbinding power was so intense Doctor One wished he could peel back the secrets of such a gift and make it his own. Nevertheless, he trusted Doctor Five and his talents. Before he could finish his plotting, he fell unconscious.

Chapter 5
Law Enforcement

"Blessed are they that carry the blood of the giants." – Gestalt,
King of Earth Giants

homas's back was pressed against the wall in the alleyway. Standing at six and a half feet made it impossible for him to hide, but he needed to try. He lamented that Invictus did not grant invisibility prayers.

From further up the alleyway, he heard a series of clicking sounds. He couldn't see the source, but he knew it was Erk. At five feet tall, the elf had an easier time hiding in the shadows. He also knew a pirate language called Scallywag. After a moment, a series of clicks returned from the entryway of the building across the street from the alley. Thomas figured the source was Naomi, giving an update. Unlike the high priest, she did have an item to turn herself invisible. Since she was nearly as big and tall as Thomas, he thought that it was lucky at least one of them could move through reality without being spotted.

A moment later, Erk's head popped up over a barrel several feet away at the front of the alley. "Nulestotejin, come close. The coast is clear."

Thomas approached the barrel near the corner of the building on his right. There were crates stacked six feet high in front of it, giving Erk a hidden, dark location to observe the street. That same building on the right was the focus of their current investigation. The anti-slaver division of the church had uncovered leads that Farzg had a safehouse inside the city. They were here to serve a search warrant issued by the Council of Four. Thomas asked Erk, "What's she see from the street? Are the kids in position?"

Erk nodded. "Everyone is in position."

Selasine drew his sword and pulled the hood of his cloak off his head. Before beginning this mission, he painted two blue lines down each of his cheeks. The warpriests of Invictus used the makeup to look more intimidating and bolder on the battlefield. He began to do so again because Miranda insisted on wearing the makeup herself. Her love of traditions rekindled his own love for his previous station as a warpriest. Now he was the high priest and commanded the church as a gentle but righteous leader. He was always in the field with his teams. In this raid, he and Erk would take the back of the safehouse, while the Airborne Marines and Naomi stormed the front. The two of them slid further down the alleyway and into an intersecting alley behind the buildings. They turned to the left, noticing there was a makeshift cargo door knocked into the wall about ten feet to the right of the back door of the building. The improvised metal paneling looked heavy, and it was one of the reasons Selasine was able to obtain a search warrant so quickly. Reconnaissance indicated significant activity happening in this place, especially after dark. Reports included both slaver victims and crystallized magic, raising enough suspicion for the warrant.

He and Erk stood close together, looking at the cargo door. Thomas warned him, "I'm going to give Damil the signal."

Erk nodded but remained silent.

A sudden, psychic tingle caught Selasine's attention. A voice radiated through his mind; "Your Holiness?" it inquired.

Thomas gave a half smile. Thanks to the events in Claston, he and Damil were able to rekindle the romance they shared in their youth. Still, if Damil was involved with official church business like this, he maintained the maximum level of formality. Thomas didn't mind, as it was healthy for their personal relationship. "Reporting, High Paladin Starstorm. We are in position to engage. Two entrances, a normal sized door and a heavy cargo door. If you can call it that."

August's thoughts responded. "Airborne Marines in position, one entrance street side. Double-doors. Four windows on each side, six windows above on the second floor."

Selasine's nod rippled through the telepathy. "Understood. Execute the warrant. Go!" he thought, his authority evident in his mental command.

Erk lowered his hands to his sides, and a brilliant flame formed around them. He licked his lips with anticipation and looked up at the high priest. "On your word."

Selasine gripped his holy symbol. "Sword of Justice, I beseech your might. Lend me the strength of your arms, the swiftness of your feet, the sharpness of your mind, and the protection of your shield." As he recited the advanced prayer, his body glowed with a silver and white aura. A lucent suit of armor wrapped around him, and his muscle density intensified. He looked at the door in front of him and backed up to the building behind him. The alley was sixteen feet across, and the makeshift cargo door was made of metal sheets reinforced with wooden bands. He broke into a sudden run, using the strength granted by the prayer to smash the cargo door with his shoulder at full speed. Wood splintered and metal screeched as his enhanced density obliterated the obstacle. In front of them was a small warehouse lined with crates. The sudden commotion at the door exposed six individuals within. It was approximately noon, so even the alleys were well lit.

A person ran into the warehouse from a door on the far side, shouting, "Those church cronies have a warrant! We have to—" they started, then stopped abruptly. "Damn this! It's a trap, at arms!"

Erk called back, "You have to what?" He had joined Selasine, who had also activated his uncanny magic. A dozen Selasines stood between the people in the warehouse and the exit. The images made it impossible to distinguish which one was the real Thomas, and they enhanced his evasion and tactical presence. Erk loosed his own Unbinding power, an intense ray of sunlight that burned anything it touched. He sent a blast just above the head of the person issuing orders, causing him to drop to the ground.

The warehouse was about twenty feet wide but fifty feet deep. A staircase on the far-right side led up to the second floor, and the entrance to the front room was directly underneath a door at the top. Crates were stacked, organized against the walls at varying heights. There was a pile of containers in the middle that the six workers were sorting. They were in various stages of movement at the moment Selasine destroyed the door. The high priest scowled and spoke, his voice terrifying. "Surrender. The church has been granted legal authority to investigate these premises under surprise circumstances. Violence is not necessary."

The person by the door stood after realizing Erk's warning shot was harmless. "You are a fool if you think we'll let you take us alive."

Erk gave a sinister smile. "I'd suggest going with him. He's a lot nicer than I am."

Selasine observed the colorful enemy. His skin had a blue tint to it, and he had long violet hair. "Damn," he hissed. "This is bad," he warned Erk. Though the suspect only stood at around five foot seven and had a slender build, his features indicated he was related to Farzg.

Erk understood the warning. A commotion from the front of the safehouse culminated in a loud crash at the door behind the interloper. The front team must have been moving quickly. The man with violet hair turned and touched the door, using innate magic to encase it in ice. Selasine frowned and uttered a curse. He recited an advanced version of the binding curse, drawing upon Invictus's strength at a deep level. "Reality is composed of beautiful form imposed by creators of order. As we weave this tapestry of life, the threads of disorder threaten to ruin the stitching of the faithful. Bind that which sews chaos!" he commanded, causing a series of red tendrils to burst from his holy symbol. They lashed out and struck the warehouse workers, binding them with intense coils of red light. It caused four of them to fall to the ground, though two managed to stay standing while bound.

"Your curses won't work on me priest," the man close to the door replied as he rushed through the warehouse directly toward Selasine's wall of images.

Erk met him with a blast of sunlight, the fires on his arms now glowing. Just as the ray hit the attacker, he lifted up his hands with a triangle formed between his index fingers and thumbs. A burst of cold radiated out from his hands, creating a thick shield of ice. As the heat from Erk's light connected with the conjured barrier, it sublimated into cold, thick steam.

Within a moment, the room filled with a cloud so dense it completely obscured normal vision, and the warehouse workers screamed in panic. Erk's eyes widened with immediate regret. Selasine gave a mighty swing with his sword, and the steam split, leaving a cone of visibility all the way up to Farzg's henchman.

The strange man looked surprised Selasine foiled his smokescreen. The enemy was mid-sprint toward the cargo door, and only Selasine and Erk stood between him and his escape. "Confound it," the henchman swore as he stopped and stomped his foot. A thin layer of ice spread out from the point of impact, making the warehouse's floor slick. Selasine and Erk did not seem phased until they saw the man's violet hair flip as he turned and ran toward the stairs at the back of the warehouse.

Erk started to chase, but the slippery ice made it impossible to move. Selasine's prayer helped him maintain traction, and he gave pursuit. Still, the ice slowed him down enough for the violet haired man to climb the steps and coat them in ice as well. Erk had to grab some crates to maintain his balance, and Selasine slowed when he realized how dangerous the stairs would be in their new condition. The man taunted as he opened the door, "I'll send me uncle your greetings, Thomas. I'd tell me dad, too, but you murdered 'em. You'll only get what's coming to you if you keep pursuing Uncle E!"

Selasine's eyes widened in shock. "Lenis?!" he shouted.

The man laughed. Though his skin was slightly blue, he had a very pretty face. His cheeks were full, and his eyes shimmered with an otherworldly pink. His long hair was well kept, and his bangs were carefully cut to emphasize his features. "The same Lenis you left fatherless two-and-a-half-decades ago. I'm thirty now, thanks for the birthday letters."

Selasine's cheeks flushed with frustration. "Dammit, Lenis. Don't side with your uncle! I tried to save your father! He turned himself into that glacial bomb, and your uncle didn't care." He pleaded with sincerity, hoping to delay him long enough for backup to arrive. Unless Lenis had access to teleportation, he was trapped even though Selasine was hesitant to follow. Naomi waited out front and invisible for anyone trying to escape that way.

Lenis was the son of Farzg's younger brother, Elnis Farzg. When Selasine and his companions raided Farzg's estate in the north twenty-five years ago, Elnis used his frost giant magic to turn himself into a glacial bomb that would have obliterated everyone and everything for miles. Eldon had been mortally stabbed, so Elnis created a crisis to distract the heroes. They didn't have time to check if Eldon was truly dead, and, as it turned out, he was not. To save the approximately one thousand people rescued from Farzg's compound, Selasine's friend Haelia used her innate powers as a hellspawn to counter the deadly effects of Elnis's bomb. In doing so, she burned up her entire life essence, but her sacrifice that day saved everyone else present. The bomb only destroyed the core of Farzg's estate and Haelia. Her heat kept the blast contained. It seemed Eldon had used Elnis's story to corrupt his nephew who had been living in Nulodia quite peacefully for the last twenty-five years.

The frost giantkin spat back, "You don't know anything about what really happened then or what's happening now. If you're not on uncle's side, you're going to be in a world of pain really soon. The world is changing, Thomas!" he shouted with finality, and turned to run through the door.

As Lenis moved further away, the ice magic dissipated, bringing the floor back to navigable conditions. Erk checked on the warehouse workers that were still bound by Selasine's curse. They looked terrified. "Are you here against your will?" Erk asked quietly to one young human male.

He nodded, the fear in his eyes evident. Erk looked up to see Thomas still staring at the door, the ice on the stairs also disappearing after a few moments. "Do we have captives or operatives here, nulestotejin?"

Selasine looked around, but something in his gut made him suspicious. Before he dismissed the curse, he examined the warehouse workers. His left eye narrowed with mistrust, and he objected, "Something's not right, here. I can't feel their souls." As a Judge of Hearts, he could feel the wills of other people, but the bound individuals reflected nothing metaphysical.

The high priest identified the threat a moment too late, however, as the man Erk was speaking with gave an evil smile. He raved, "You don't have to let us go! We'll get out on our own! Long live His Majesty!" He opened his mouth. A billowing, yellow cloud of thick, acidic fog burst forth, filling the room in seconds. An invisible barrier around Selasine kept the gas from reaching his lungs, but Erk immediately began to cough. The other warehouse workers started to choke too. The putrid attack dispelled Selasine's binding curse.

Selasine started to recite a prayer to help Erk, but the ethereal armor around him shattered. Looking through the translucent smoke, he saw one of the warehouse workers pointing at him. She had trained a bright beam of white light on Selasine. Before he could curse, he started to choke as well.

Erk tried desperately to hold his breath, but the nature of the magical fog already burned the inside of his lungs so badly he had no respiratory control. He attempted to concentrate enough energy into his arms to burn the fumes away, but he felt himself getting dizzy. Then, something hard crashed into his back, knocking him to the ground. Splintered wood rained down around him.

The young man with the Toxic Cloud uncanny magic was standing behind him, the remnants of a crate's lid in his hands. He raised up a sharp, splintered plank and prepared to stab Erk in the throat. Before he could, a massive weight slammed him into a stack of crates, which collapsed on top of him. Selasine's hulking form loomed in the noxious fumes, and Erk felt himself lifted into the air as he started to slip from consciousness.

"Hang in there, brother," Selasine thought, his distress pinging Damil and August.

Damil's voice replied, "Front of the safehouse is clear, Your Holiness."

The returned thoughts felt like choking and suffocation. August's mind returned, "Dammit, I'm on my way, Your Holiness."

A feeling of fear filled Damil's thoughts. "What's going on, Thomas? Thomas, can you think?"

"Acidic fog. Erk in trouble," is all he could reply.

August emerged from the front of the building, activating his uncanny magic. It allowed him to run much swifter than the average warrior of his build. It took him only thirty seconds to run around the large building to the back alley. As he emerged in the intersection, he saw Selasine and Erk laying on the ground. "Teacher! Captain!" he shouted in shock.

A moment later, Naomi appeared beside him. "Oh, no," she whispered, rushing over to her fallen comrades. She fumbled in her pouch and withdrew some healing potions Miranda gave Naomi weeks ago during Miranda's last visit to Nulodia. As her healing skills advanced, some of her potions were potent enough to bring people back from the brink of death. Naomi hoped this batch possessed that incredible potency. She tipped a phial into each of their mouths, causing them to start coughing and sputtering again. Blood trickled down Erk's lip, and Selasine's nose bled profusely. They also dripped blood from their eyes and ears.

A purple light enveloped Erk's and Selasine's bodies, and the burning sensations in their throats and sinuses eased. The taste of blood only lingered for a moment. Naomi's silver eyes lit up as Erk's gray eyes opened and he gasped for air. Selasine sat up, reaching to his temples. "Gods, we've been had!" he shouted as he saw Naomi looming over him.

The high priest stood, still reeling a bit from the effects of the poisonous gas generated by the warehouse worker's uncanny magic. He tried to run, but he was too disoriented.

August caught his meaning, and, in a burst of speed, returned to the front of the building. He saw Lenis running down the street, so he gave chase. August only caught a glimpse of Lenis as they stormed the front, but based on the violet hair, he figured this subject was likely the leader of this operation. In his mind, it made sense for the leader to stand out with something wild like colorful hair. Fortunately for August, he had his incredible speed to distinguish him from others. He caught up to Lenis in a matter of seconds, but a flash of purple in front of him brought him to a stop. Lenis had created a small wall of ice to trip August, but his reaction time was quick enough to slide over it safely, resuming his pursuit.

"Blast!" Lenis cursed, turning to face August a mere one hundred feet from one of the busier streets in Nulodia. During the chase, they managed to get about six hundred feet away from the safehouse.

"Don't do anything stupid, now. You're under arrest. We know that Farzg can be scary. If you cooperate, we can protect you," August promised.

Lenis's eyes filled with an incalculable rage. "That's exactly what uncle said you would say. Why are you lawmen so useless?!" he shouted back and extended his arms to his sides.

Selasine moved as quickly as he could through the empty street, Naomi and Erk right behind him. Valarie and Justin stayed at the safehouse with the rest of the team to begin cataloging evidence and arrest the warehouse worker with the Toxic Cloud magic. As they caught up with the chase, Selasine could see Lenis's arms extend to his sides. He shouted in terror, "August! Get away! RUN!"

August heard Selasine's shouting but didn't grasp what he said. He knew better than to take his eyes off of a suspect, though. He drew a longsword. "That's the definition of something stupid, man. C'mon, your uncle is always one step ahead of us. He threw you under the chariot today."

Lenis's pretty face twisted between anger and fear. He behaved as if he had no options remaining. He started to mutter incoherently, and August felt the air temperature beginning to drop. "I'll be forced to act in violence if you proceed any further," he warned.

Selasine shouted again, "August, don't hesitate! Run! Withdraw!" His desperation was uncharacteristic.

Damil's thoughts ripped through, "August, get away! That's Farzg's Death Geyser!" He had begun reading Selasine's mind, catching on to what was happening. He had to let August know, but the feeling coming from Selasine seemed as if it were too late.

August's eyes widened in horror as he realized his error. The air temperature was getting so low he felt like he could barely move. It dropped much faster than he anticipated.

Lenis's expression calmed. August suddenly thought that the frost giantkin looked beautiful and serene. His long eyelashes fluttered as he drew in a deep breath, and his lips parted in concentration.

"You're an angel of death," August mumbled out loud. The thought echoed between Selasine and Damil.

Selasine began to hope that Lenis's inexperience with the technique might give August a chance. He thought loudly to August. "The Death Geyser causes wounds that can't be healed easily by prayers. It's how I lost my eye, August. Pray for safety if the air is too cold to move. Call out to Invictus, hurry," he encouraged.

August repeated the prayers of protection and elemental resistance. He shouted with a desperate prayer, "Shield me from the cold, Sword of Justice. Stop this angel of death."

Just as August finished his recitation, Lenis drew his arms in and punched to his front. A geyser of ice about a foot wide burst forward, colliding with August's protection prayer, creating a radiant blue and white light coloring the buildings around them. The commotion caught the attention of passersby, and a crowd gathered at the end of the street.

Lenis started to lose his composure, pushing the magic within him harder. The ice chunks pouring from the beam in front of him grew to two feet in diameter. August's protective barrier began to crack, the geyser building up jagged mounds of ice in every direction in front of the paladin. He felt his body's temperature getting dangerously low as the air around him grew impossibly cold. This surge of magic was incredible, and Lenis was relentless with his attack.

August's protection prayer gave the others enough time to catch up, and a beam of intense sunlight raced past August slightly to his right. He followed it to its source; Erk stood by, concentrating his uncanny power directly on Lenis. As the beam contacted the frost giantkin, the air again began to fill with dense steam. The harder Lenis pushed, the colder the air became. It neutralized the most powerful effects of Erk's uncanny magic. The pirate lord cursed to himself and intensified his concentration. It was obvious, however, that Erk hesitated. He was already using more sunlight than he used to bore holes in the hulls of enemy ships. He could not risk his uncanny magic creating a bigger disaster.

Lenis felt the heat from Erk's attack. It was uncomfortably hot, but the further he pushed the temperature around him down, the less it burned. "The colder the air, the stronger the geyser," he mumbled to himself. He inhaled and pushed with his magic.

As he did, the geyser grew in size and speed again. August's heart leapt into his throat as the cracks in his barrier finally gave way. Before the geyser overwhelmed him, he felt himself pushed to the side as Selasine stepped between him and certain death. "Teacher!" he exclaimed, shivering uncontrollably.

Selasine's immense faith was able to conjure a barrier strong enough to stop Lenis's Death Geyser. He was certainly not afraid of this giantkin with a fraction of Farzg's power. His protective barrier pushed the ice debris to the side, and the core of the geyser continued to blast into it. The blue and white lights were visible from all over the city at this point, causing people to marvel as the brilliance danced across walls and rooftops.

Lenis started to scream. Erk stopped attacking with his light ray as the steam became a hazard again. A barrage of daggers rained from behind Lenis as Naomi became visible. She carefully calculated her assault, but Lenis's skin was as hard as the thickest ice while he used the Death Geyser. The daggers couldn't penetrate his skin even with Naomi's telekinetic support behind them. She cursed to herself, and the magic of her throwing daggers returned them to the bandolier wrapped around her thigh. She smirked, however, as she was earth giantkin. She had her own tricks and elemental affinity. She stomped her foot, causing the stone between her and Lenis to fissure, the split running fifteen feet from Naomi to the frost giantkin. As it reached him, the ground ripped open. A crack three feet deep and two feet wide opened up beneath Lenis, dropping him inside. It caused his Death Geyser to stop, and the streets were suddenly quiet.

Selasine walked over to the hole as Lenis collapsed inside. Naomi and Erk approached quickly, and August stood, motionless. Selasine jumped down and lifted Lenis up. He checked for vitals and found nothing. His body was stiff and frigid.

Erk looked around to assess the situation. "We've got a crowd, brother."

Selasine placed Lenis's body onto the surface level of the street. Naomi was already working on closing the fissure and smoothing the stones with precision.

As Selasine climbed out, he rolled onto his back and closed his eyes. Though he was in great shape for his age, that panicked sprint took a lot out of him. He barely got a new protection prayer readied before August's shattered. His heart was racing. He was still very protective of August, Justin, and Miranda. He had grown quite protective over Valarie as well, and he cared deeply for Erk and Naomi. At least today, as far as he knew, everyone was safe.

Erk finally asked, "What happened to the giantkin?"

Selasine opened his eyes. "He froze himself. He wasn't ready to push Farzg's technique like that." He sat up. "And based on his features, I don't think he's got as much giant blood as Farzg, either."

August finally approached, looking down at Lenis. "I could see the fear in his eyes, Your Holiness. And then, it's like," he paused, reaching for the right words. "It's like he knew there was only one option. And he tried to take as many of us with him as he could. And he was so at peace with that." The young paladin swallowed hard.

Erk looked up at him, August's brown eyes shimmering with sorrow. The pirate replied, "When someone has resigned their heart to darkness, they start to misunderstand consequences. Eventually, their minds are so warped that reality no longer makes sense. Farzg had ahold of this one, probably thanks to their similarities." The elf looked at Lenis. "But he chose his own fate. Whether out of fear, hatred, or whatever it might be."

Selasine stood and turned, and a crowd of common people gathered around at a healthy distance. There were around one hundred individuals watching. With his authoritative voice, he called out, "Onlookers! Do not be alarmed. The Church of Invictus is victorious against these lawbreakers, and you are safe. Please be about your day, a full report will be published in the church bulletin at the end of this week."

The crowd murmured for a minute, but then cheers erupted for the high priest. "Long live His Holiness!" they chanted for a moment. Selasine shook his head. He had asked them so many times not to do that. He was simply the representative of his god, nothing more.

"Selasine, the frost giantkin!" Erk shouted.

As the high priest turned, he saw Lenis's body glowing with a bright, blue light with white on the fringes. His eye widened as he recognized this magic too. "No," he whispered. He clutched his holy symbol. Lenis had used the same innate magic as his father. He turned himself into a powerful, glacial bomb more destructive than the Death Geyser. Selasine barely had time to cry out, "Invictus, save us!" as the magical energy within the body exploded into a brilliant wave of massive, sharp ice shards.

Farzg crumpled the note in his hand. "My nephew, you say?"

The messenger nodded. "Witnesses say it was Selasine and his new elite team. The same ones that—" he began to elaborate, but Farzg interrupted him.

"Yes, yes, you don't have to catalog it every time they do something else to hinder me." He was seated behind an enormous desk in the library on his estate. The room was square with an entrance on the south side. Bookshelves lined the walls and had been arranged into stacks on the first floor. Two metal, spiral staircases were in the back corners. The second floor was dedicated to artifacts Farzg had acquired. He had spent much time in this library recently, trying to formulate a plan to combat the impact the church was having on his trafficking business. His sea trade had been nearly destroyed in the last six months. His land routes were starting to feel the pinch, as well. Now, he'd just gotten word his nephew was killed fighting the church earlier that day.

The messenger was a gnoll standing seven feet tall, coming to Farzg's shoulders. His fur was black, and he was dressed in heavy plate armor that shimmered tones of deep green. His name was Echo, and he bowed his head. "My apologies, Majesty." In truth, Lenis was one of Farzg's lieutenants, and so was this messenger. The frost giantkin did not trust many people, and it had taken him a while to think Lenis was ready to coordinate moving goods within the city. "Do we wish to retaliate and inflict fear upon the people?" Echo asked, cautious with his words.

Farzg shrugged. "A terror campaign would be too costly. No, I'm confident the plant we've just dropped into the church is going to do sufficient damage on her own. Patience is the key, Echo."

Echo looked up. "Your confidence in that mad-elf is concerning, Majesty. I do not wish to speak in ignorance, but I fear the power he promises."

The frost giantkin stroked his beard. He respected his lieutenants, and he appreciated their critical feedback. "I've seen it with my own eyes, it has the potential to be very lucrative for us." He licked his frozen lips and wiggled his jaw as he stood. "But you are also correct that the same power could be turned against us at any time. In that sense, you are correct," he repeated, being redundant for emphasis. "There is that potential," he finished, his normally condescending voice now pensive.

Echo sniffed the air and wiggled his snout. It was not getting colder, praise the gods, he thought. His short, bobbed tail wagged a moment. "You are wise, and I am here to serve, Majesty." He growled and gave a swift, confident bark.

Farzg's smile deepened. "I can guarantee Lenis was not killed. He simply did not want to be taken alive. He had great promise, but I would have done the same as he did."

Echo nodded. "The explosion left a crater and cracked a sewage pipe."

The purple in Farzg's eyes shimmered with bloodlust. "Was our dear friend Thomas among the casualties?"

Echo shook his head. "No, Majesty. I'm sad to report there were no casualties beyond Lenis. According to our spies, informants, and faithful."

Farzg slammed his fists against his desk. "Hoxark damn you to the Abyss, Selasine," he shouted. Echo stepped backwards, ready to run out of the library. The hostility in Farzg's voice was graver than Echo had ever heard. "I will gut every one of your precious team like fish. I'll encase you in ice and burn every horrible memory into your lonely, pathetic eye. How dare you? I let you live. We were even." His voice dripped with malice, and it reverberated through the entire mansion.

Echo trembled. He'd never seen Farzg lose his composure like this. He said nothing out of fear.

"I really don't like violence. It's so beneath me." His voice had calmed. "You know, Echo, my friend. In truth, this was meant to happen. I'm going to take my piece for Lenis. But there was nothing but crystalized magic at that warehouse."

Farzg's lieutenant stood at attention. "Majesty?"

The giantkin's lips twisted up into a smile that made his beard curl outward. It was so sadistic and frightening that Echo took off, running out of the library. Farzg calmly sat back down. He sighed and touched a lacrima-deum powered box on his desk. It buzzed with activity, and a moment later, a voice emerged from the device. "Eldon? Eldon, is that you?"

Farzg rolled his eyes. "Of course, elf. Who else would be foolish enough to hope this device would not work?" He sighed.

Doctor One ignored the jab, speaking wildly. "I've just had a wonderful idea. A few months ago, I confirmed something I suspected for a while! It's so fortuitous you've made contact while I was thinking about this very subject!"

Farzg laid his head down on the desk in front of him in defeat. Why in the Abyss did he touch that machine? Why was he so convinced one of this elf's inventions finally wouldn't work as intended? Whatever the elf was doing with these dragon eggs had so much potential, but Echo was right. Farzg thought he might find himself at odds with Doctor One at some point in the future. He didn't say anything. The doctor continued speaking.

"Oh, before I forget. I have some intelligence relevant to the church. I've got eyes and ears all over the kingdoms! One of those church warriors I've been tracking for you, the big elf. Remember that one?" Doctor One rushed through his words.

Farzg nodded and gave a barely audible, affirmative noise.

"Wonderful. I'm glad you remember your own enemies. And you're glad you've got me. Well, the fellow just turned up in Devitus. I've got an underling out there. He's been tracking rumors of a crystallized statue of some dragons or something. It's been about four months, and the leads took my underling to the frontier. But he saw your guy, Eldon! He saw your guy! Well, one of them." The voice was far too excited for Farzg's mood. "He's there with some other church girl with red hair and two other big elves. Sounds like Yuvina, too."

"Okay, and? That means he wasn't present at the fiasco today that got my nephew killed." He lifted his head. "Wait a moment," he murmured, his voice trailing off.

"Yes, yes! Absolutely. Wait, your nephew was killed?" Doctor One finally paused. It wasn't for respect, though. "I was hoping to experiment on him. He would have made an excellent vessel."

Farzg disregarded the comment about Lenis, focusing on the likely location of the pirate's brother, Evanthalus. "You said Devitus?"

The doctor started to rave, "I know, Devitus! So far out—" his voice cut off.

Farzg touched the device again, ceasing contact. "Echo!" he shouted, the sound shaking the entire estate.

A moment later, a small, hyena nose poked into the room and sniffed the air. Echo followed it into the library. "Majesty?"

"Send Elyndandria to Devitus. I have a debt to repay. I'll write the details up for you in a moment." Farzg sounded collected and calm.

"The assassin? You'll pay her fee?" Echo asked, surprised.

With an evil smile, Farzg's voice slowed, returning to its condescending tone. "Double it. It's very likely she'll get killed, but don't tell her that. If she's successful, I'll get my blood price. If she isn't, I'll get the information I need." He slid his chair back and stood. He looked down at a trap door. It led down to his personal chambers and the vault where he kept his most precious artifacts. He said, "The girl with red hair. The dragon girl. Is she a dragon of light? Is she worthy of serving true justice?"

The gnoll chattered his teeth. "What in the Infernia?" he asked, losing his composure at Farzg speaking to the ground.

The frost giantkin stroked his beard in thought. "We should make the contract for the entire group. Evanthalus Lancethinas. Miranda Hyacinth. Yuvina, too. I want to test the girl with red hair. I want to know if she's worthy to face me." He punctuated his order with a harsh, cold voice. "Understood?"

Echo nodded in obedience, but then the contraption on the desk buzzed.

"This scientist is driving me mad!" Farzg shouted and hit the lacrima-deum with his hand. "What do you want, you lunatic?" he shouted.

Doctor One's voice rattled faster than before. He sounded more excited than when he had announced Yuvina's successful operation. "The real, exciting discovery. I was trying to tell you about it, but I was distracted by my update on your enemies. You need to hear this, Eldon. Anyway, so as it turns out, this crystallized magic, or as I call them, the tears of the gods, they are finite! I already knew that. Once it's used up it dissolves, dissipates, turns to dust, boom! But there's something special that happens when those magic particles disappear. Guess what happens!" he rambled.

The question caught Farzg off guard, but he was suddenly very interested in this conversation. "I haven't the slightest, doctor, please continue," his voice was slow and gravelly.

"It has to rip its way back into the arcane stream from the prime dimension! Oh, this is so amazing. It's called arcane underflow! Since I have been isolating the hearts of the lacrima-deum, the magic of the dragon egg is trapped here in our world. The magic is gone, but the hearts are with me, you follow?"

Farzg looked up at Echo then back at the communication device. "Yes, you keep the hearts, but the rest of the magic is spent."

"When the remaining magic is expended completely, it rips back into the arcane stream. And when it does, a creature of shadow is created! Our biggest client in Mystalon described them as 'Umbrals.' It took them less than a month to use all one hundred of those eggs!

Can you believe that?"

"So, when a lacrima-deum is completely expended, these shadow creatures emerge? Why does that matter for us?" the frost giantkin asked.

"When I learned this information, I did some experiments. I put a huge, worthless lacrima-deum into the biggest eolnut conduit I could design. I put the device in a dimensional cage and activated it to drain the magic from the lacrima-deum. Within an hour, the biggest shadow creature I've ever seen appeared! It looked like a dragon without wings. So, onto my idea. You've got people from the church coming after you, right? With the right magic-proofing, you could create a horde of intangible defenders for your little cottage. Are you interested?"

Eldon narrowed his eyes, his suspicions of Doctor One increasing. "Possibly. What must I do?"

"Don't worry about it. I'll send somebody to help you out! Farzg! I'm going to make you invincible!"

Before Farzg could engage further, the lacrima-deum dissolved. The communication stopped. Farzg was finally free of that elf's voice in his office. Still, why did the magic device only work for such a short time? The frost giantkin stood patiently at his desk for an hour. He took that time to pen an assassination order for Evanthalus Lancethinas and his companions. Doctor One had given him plenty of options at this juncture. He planned to see these opportunities to their maximum payoff.

Echo took the order in hand and turned to leave. "So, keep an eye out for one of those Umbrals? Was that what the mad-elf meant when those things are used up?"

Farzg nodded. "Hopefully, the creature will just find its own diversions. Notify me if anyone complains of any shadow creatures. We do want to keep the goods safe, understood?"

Echo nodded and walked away, leaving Farzg to contemplate his complicated relationship with the mad scientist. His thoughts, however, returned to Miranda. He glared with his soul. "I'll test your words, Iria. 'When the champion of the goddess arrives, I will plunge my sword into your unholy heart.' Such bluster." He shuddered and scowled. "I doubt your 'champion' will have the gall to do what must be done to save Espa, foolish elf." He reached into a pouch and withdrew a perfect, beautiful marble. It was white and reflected the faintest hint of baby blue. "I will not lose at the hands of feverish prophecies. But I will not risk my legacy, either." He adored the bauble for another hour in silence and returned it to his pouch, praying to himself for discernment and strength.

Chapter 6
Frontier Wisdom

The Starlock River was an essential body of water in central West Espa. Emerging from a high, mountain cavern one hundred miles to the east of Devitus, the river was over a mile wide at some points. It flowed down the Trollcrag Mountains to the east, and its course positioned it less than a mile to the south of Devitus. As soon as the fog cleared from the waters around Olvidado, Miranda saw the fortified stone walls built to protect the sleepy farming town where she grew up. She felt a bit of nostalgia and apprehension, and she found a touch of homesickness as her emotions swirled. Ezelbrecht sent her here. They were as concerned for Miranda's parents as she was. She never expected to have the same agenda as the eldritch dragon; actually, in her mind, that was no longer a fair assessment. Ezelbrecht was the remnant of Gorthran and should be thought of as a divinity. Miranda struggled with her feelings and her mother's memories.

The group secured the raft and walked toward the city gates on the east side. Miranda paused as they approached, and Evan detected her hesitation. He cast a glance at the cousins and the newcomer, Yuvina. They interrogated the kitsune on their departure from Olvidado, and she seemed to have a genuine heart. She claimed to be a follower of the god Pulhash, a god of liberation. Miranda's broad, religious knowledge provided an opportunity to bond with Yuvina through theological discussion. The foxkin thought the month was still Winter Solstice. She was surprised to learn the month had come and gone. Though Miranda was distracted by her current mission, she promised she would help Yuvina regain her memories as soon as she could. The foxkin was amenable to following these Wielders, as they seemed caught up in something that might be of interest to The Forgotten. Yuvina felt a profound anxiety regarding her missing memories, however, and she wanted answers.

Everyone stood at the city's gate in front of Miranda, waiting as she remained motionless. Evan broke the silence. "Everything alright, Miranda?"

Her gaze glinted crystal blue in the late afternoon sunlight. Her lips broke into an excited smile. "This is the same gate we left Devitus from in The Flourishing." She looked at it again, realizing it was underwhelming. When she departed, the walls were a symbol of strength and protection. Now she knew the extent of the power that existed in the wider world. She fought to stay optimistic, but she wanted to run straight to her estate to check on the statues of her parents. Still, she had a duty to her companions and the people of Devitus. It was time to adopt the persona of public hero she learned from Erk.

The five continued toward the gate. When they were one hundred feet away, the city guard called down, "Identify yourselves, strangers!"

Miranda recognized the voice. The speaker was a guardsman she knew while serving as a peacekeeper. "Lady Hyacinth returns!" she sang back, confident.

"My apologies, Lady Hyacinth. The city stands open for you!" the guard answered. The gate was already open; this town would not likely be the victim of a surprise siege. It sat high in the Devitan River Valley. The rising path to the east was narrow, and the elevation dropped to the west with numerous outposts and villages further down. The Obelisk Tribe of orcs and goblins protected the peaks and ridges from trolls and giants. The Selian Range to the northwest brought early sunsets to this part of the mountains, but it was a secure location thanks to its Obelisk allies and isolation.

Celyth pushed her hands through her purple hair, puffing it out a bit. "So, are you going to go straight there? To your house?"

Arlindra elbowed her cousin and gave a vigorous shake with her head. "Slow down, Cel."

Miranda turned to the cousins and smiled. "I have to let the people know what's going on far outside their city walls. That way, they will be prepared if this brewing storm blows over them." Her voice was relaxed and her composure strong.

Yuvina sniffed the air as they walked under the gate. The smell of the countryside reminded her of home, but the Tymbyrwylde had a richer scent. She followed quietly, Evan walking beside her with the cousins in front of them. Miranda led the way as they followed the streets of the sleepy town. Houses were clustered together with large fields between them. The pastures contained livestock, grazing the winter grasses of the Devitan River Valley. After ten minutes of walking, a small church came into view.

"There it is!" Miranda marveled. That little building is where her adventures began. She increased her pace, causing her companions to shuffle behind her. Even Arlindra struggled to keep up, and she walked notoriously fast. The street traffic was busy further to the north of the church; most of the people were trying to complete errands and return home. As a result, they kept to themselves as Miranda and company passed, sparing only waves and brief pleasantries. Miranda was running by the time she got to the gate leading into the courtyard of the church. A low-sitting stone wall surrounded the church grounds. A barn and a barracks rested in the distance behind the main structure.

Evan called out, "Miranda, wait!" As he did, she came to an abrupt stop about halfway up the path to the building.

A man stood on the steps to the church. Miranda did not recognize him. She called out, "Greetings in the name of the Sword of Justice."

The stranger smiled. He was a human man standing at six feet tall. He had brown hair fully dusted with gray throughout. It was unkempt and wild. His skin was a deep tan and leathery. He was slender, and he walked with a crooked gait. He descended the stairs as he replied, "Yes, faithful one. Greetings. I am Reginald the Scholar."

Miranda smiled in return. As he reached the bottom of the steps, Miranda's companions caught up with her. She replied, "What brings you to the hallowed grounds of Invictus? I trust the bishop has helped you with your needs."

Reginald approached the group. "Indeed, pilgrim. I merely came to discuss a matter of little importance regarding the local school." He was dressed in a white cotton tunic. He also wore a white cloak over his shoulders, perhaps an indication of his academic nature.

Miranda tilted her head, causing her braids to sway for a moment. "Ah! The school. And you are a scholar. I take it you have come to Devitus to serve as a fount of knowledge for the people of the frontier?" She sounded pleasant, but Evan detected her suspicious tone as her voice changed from its airy, melodic resonance. It reminded him of the authoritative way she spoke at breakfast the day before and the confidence she exuded in front of Ezelbrecht. She did not trust this person.

The scholar reached to his face, adjusting his glasses. They caught a slight reflection from the evening sun still peeking from just over the tops of the Selian Range. "Why, yes, in a sense. I am a traveling scholar, though, and I am doing research in the area."

Yuvina's eyes narrowed. The man smelled familiar to her. Evan took a step around the cousins to stand behind Miranda. The priestess continued, "Well met, then. I am but a traveling warpriest myself. I came to seek an audience with the bishop for a blessing."

Evan froze. Miranda never lied, but she understood the value of a lie of omission. She knew their lives were only as safe as their information, another lesson she learned from Erk. In that moment, Evan identified why Miranda dominated his every thought. She took the kindness and gentleness of the monks of Lexcord and wove it into her heart and actions. She added Selasine's conviction and strength. Now, she adapted Erk's shrewdness and Naomi's caution. A warm, adoring feeling surged in Evan's chest. He knew Miranda's estate was the school for the people of Devitus. Its size and practical location on the west side of town made it perfect for such an endeavor. Miranda's distrust reflected her wisdom and discernment. Now was not a good time to be a stranger inquiring about the location where the statues of Miranda's parents were kept.

Reginald cocked his head with intrigue as Evan's body language showed distress. A smile broke out on his lips as he spoke, "Ah, Master Lancethinas. You're quite a distance from the city."

Evan blinked with surprise. "Excuse me?"

Miranda turned to look at Evan then back to Reginald. The scholar continued, "Apologies. As I mentioned, I am a traveling scholar. I am a frequent visitor to the grand cathedral of Invictus in Nulodia. I have heard of your exploits, and we have even met and spoken before."

Evan scanned his memory and replied, "I am afraid I do not recall our meeting."

Miranda interrupted the exchange, "It seems the Devitan region is of great interest as of late. You mentioned research? I grew up nearby, perhaps I can be of assistance. I also may have connections with the school."

Evan could not believe what he was hearing. Her voice found a balance between flirt and command. Plus, all of what she said was technically true but delivered in a way that would have made Erk proud. His own heart swelled, and a profound attraction to her grew within him. She was learning to find the line between her ideals and how to defend them effectively.

The taut skin of Reginald's face twisted up into a broad smile. He took off his glasses for a moment. "How kind of you, faithful one. May I know your name, lady of the Path of the Sword of Justice? You match the description of someone I am looking for."

She licked her lips. "I am Mir'thax Toi'landra. Warpriest of Invictus, Judge of Hearts." Evan continued to squeal with joy internally, watching her continue to guard her hand as well as possible without being directly deceptive.

Reginald looked from side to side. "A draconic name? Fire and lightning?" he asked, puzzled.

Miranda nodded, her braids dipping low. She sensed Reginald's bluff. She suspected he knew exactly who she was. A seething anger formed in the pit of her stomach, and she prepared mentally to confront this "scholar." Feigning ignorance was almost as bad as dodging questions.

Before Miranda's building fury prompted her to action, Evan took another step forward to stand beside her. The scholar stood less than five feet away from them. Evan could not identify this person and regretted not paying closer attention over the recent months. He interjected, trying to extract details from Reginald's story, "Do you work at the university in Nulodia?"

While Evan and Miranda engaged in conversation with the scholar, Celyth and Arlindra examined Yuvina. The kitsune was watching the exchange on high alert. Her fur stood on end, and her whiskers quivered with rage or fear. Maybe both.

Reginald laughed, trying to diffuse the tension. "Oh no, not the ivory towers of wizards longing for times passed. I work for a private foundation." He took his glasses off again and polished them on his tunic as he spoke. "I do not wish to waste more of your time. If you happen to know anything about a crystal dragon statue or Lady Hyacinth, the patron of the school, I would be interested in your time. I can compensate you; I have a generous budget. No expense is too great compared to the value of knowledge. I seek frontier wisdom because the answers are here, not in any tomes or scrolls."

Miranda had a sinking, horrible feeling in her stomach. She was right not to trust this person. Something about him exuded madness and malice. She replied, "I am familiar with her, but I'm afraid I don't know anything about statues shaped like dragons." Evan fought to keep his composure. A subtle twist of words was definitely Erk's mentoring at work.

Reginald replaced the glasses on his face. "Oh? Well, that is at least half fortunate." He paused and gave an evil smile. "I was told Lady Hyacinth fought in the Claston Civil War last year, and she was off adventuring in the Dundoi region. I would need her permission to gain access to the school. I would very much like to tour it and meet the staff." His smile seemed less sinister now, but Miranda was certain of his evil intent. He continued, "I am disposed to give a series of lectures, as well. The future of magical technology, yes? Magic items for every little thing you can imagine. Keeping meat cool and preserved. Running water on the frontier. Better means to defend our settlements. East Espa has undergone significant industrialization since The Unbinding, and such technology could revolutionize life out here in the country if supplemented by a little magic."

As he spoke, Miranda felt the truth behind his words. Based on the weapons she had seen, the crystalized magic gemstones could probably be used to power any number of magical machines. She used her advantage in the conversation to ask, "Magical technology? What do you mean, scholar?"

His face lit up with excitement. "A coalition of researchers in Alabaster and Claston have discovered a source of power better than steam! I would share my recent findings and my agenda with the people of this community in my lectures. If I can find those crystalized dragon statues, I'll be able to prove my theories. The only thing that could petrify an adult dragon like that is an intense concentration of magic!"

Miranda's composure did not falter. She replied, "An interesting theory, but how would you test it? Surely, you would not find a dragon willing to subject themselves to such a scenario."

Reginald laughed. "Oh, but I can simulate it! All in due time, however. I do not wish to share too much. The foundation is very protective of its projects."

Miranda knew of the universities in Nulodia and Alabaster. They were both centers of learning and research, and many former wizards found themselves employed within. She was unfamiliar with private foundations, however, further fueling her suspicions. Since The Unbinding, technology and medicine had made steady advances. As wizards could no longer manipulate the arcane stream, they began to find ways to manipulate the physical world through chemicals, technology, and uncanny magic. Alchemists and artificers became chemists and engineers, using the disjointed condition of magic to their biggest advantage. Miranda contemplated the best way to extract more information. "How long have you been in the Devitan region?" she asked.

The scholar twisted his lips in thought. He replied, "About a week now, yes. I've been checking leads on dragon lairs in the region, but I've come up empty handed."

Miranda decided she had heard enough. "Very well, Reginald. Are you staying locally?"

He nodded. "At The Rusty Fence. I hope you'll make good on your offer to help. You may inquire for me there." He walked forward, and Miranda and Evan stepped aside to let him pass. Celyth and Arlindra stood shoulder to shoulder down the path, taking a moment to look at the scholar. They gave him matching, intimidating glares before moving to let him by. Yuvina was already off the path, her paws clinging to the winter grass with anxiety. She trembled as he walked through the gates of the church grounds on the west side of the complex, turning north to head toward the marketplace.

Miranda watched him until he disappeared behind the buildings and trees beyond the northwestern corner of the church grounds. Evan cleared his throat, causing her to cut her eyes at him. The normally serene pools of blue teemed with electric hostility. Evan's heart skipped a beat. Her stare looked cruel and ruthless. He found the way she had grown in the last five months as interesting as the sweet, beautiful woman she was before fighting against Gelidor. Before he could speak, her gaze softened, and the corners of her mouth turned up into a sly smile.

Evan started to laugh. It was a shock to him, and she knew it. Celyth's brow furrowed. "Uh, what's so funny? That dude was a total creep."

Arlindra chuckled. "I think it has more to do with Mir than anything else, Cel. Just look." She nodded toward Miranda with her chin.

Miranda looked at the cousins in confusion, "What is it?" Then, she spotted Yuvina, still shaking with distress. "Oh no! Yuvina, what's wrong?" she asked, noticing the kitsune's fearful body language. Everyone's attention turned to her.

The foxkin's gaze lingered on the last place Reginald was visible. She shook her head. "I'm sorry, I don't mean to trouble you. I've never met that person, but they scare me. They smelled familiar," she explained.

Miranda grimaced. "I do not believe he is who he says he is. We will keep our eyes on him. He is an outsider in my home. I have the advantage."

Evan nodded in agreement, his mind still swirling with pride for Miranda's deceptive use of the truth. Yuvina relaxed with Miranda's assurance. Celyth gestured toward the church, suggesting, "Well, back to it?"

Arlindra gave an affirming nod. "The quicker you get your contacts made, the quicker you can head to your estate," she commented, running a hand through her wild, blue hair.

Yuvina lowered her head. These people were strange. As a member of The Forgotten, she always focused on the powers possessed by others, but these four acted like uncanny magic was the last thing on their minds. This Miranda woman seemed exceptional, as she was very caring and gentle. The priestess was very distracted, however, and Yuvina's curiosity was starting to build. Though she could not remember her current mission, she had a feeling that Miranda's current path would see them intersect with her objective at some point.

The five entered the church to see Bishop Ekol and four acolytes sitting on the floor beside the wooden avatar of Invictus on a slightly raised dais in the center of the sanctuary. Beautiful stained glass surrounded the circular central room of worship. Benches and chairs were sat neatly in semi-circles around the idol. There was a raised pulpit near the avatar as well, but Selasine never delivered lectures or homilies while Miranda served with him here. The rest of the church could be accessed by two doors on the far side of the chapel.

Bishop Ekol was a paladin who aided in the rescue of hostages in the Battle of Beriton. His bravery caught the attention of Justin, Valarie, and Thomas. Once Selasine had been promoted to high priest, he appointed Ekol as the bishop of the Devitan region. As Miranda and the others entered, the bishop stood, causing the acolytes with him to rise as well. They then saluted, their shield hands on the hilts of their weapons and their sword hands at their chest, palm up to the sky. Miranda smiled, and snapped into a salute in return, stopping halfway down the aisle to the idol. Her companions tripped over each other to avoid running into her. "At ease," the warpriest ordered, ignoring the commotion behind her. With her accolades, she technically held a higher rank in the church than Ekol, even though he was in charge of church operations in the area.

Ekol and his acolytes relaxed. The bishop spoke, "The Sword of Justice smiles on this reunion."

Miranda recited, "May we follow the Path of the Sword of Justice with righteousness and humility."

He nodded in reply. "How may I be of assistance, Lady Hyacinth?" he asked.

Her eyes turned sharp again. "That man who was just here, I need to know what he wanted."

Ekol's lips tightened. "It all makes a lot of sense, now. He was asking about you and the school. He heard a rumor there is a room that is off limits there, and he wanted to know if it was your laboratory. I haven't the slightest idea what he meant." The paladin was a human in his mid-twenties. For him to hold such a high position was impressive, but Selasine knew the appointment would mold Ekol into a strong leader. The high priest even designed a program to send Nulodian acolytes to Devitus for experience following the Path of the Sword of Justice in a rural context. The new bishop continued explaining, "I did not tell him much, only that you had been away for four months. He asked many probing questions, but we truthfully could not answer them. Which is all for the better."

Miranda ran her tongue behind her teeth as she contemplated the implications. "It sounds like he's working with fragmented information and is piecing it together haphazardly. He spoke of magical technology and other promises that may pose a danger to the balance of law and order. Please stay wary." She saluted to indicate it was an order. The clergy replied in kind.

Miranda's melody steadied as she debriefed Ekol and his students. "I bring urgent news and request support from local peacekeepers. I wish to report enemies of the church have become very interested in dragon eggs as of late. Please confiscate and protect any dragon eggs found in the possession of lawbreakers. Though the law does not prohibit the possession of dragon eggs, current circumstances warrant an abundance of caution. Report any eggs you know of or acquire to the high priest of Nulodia.

Understood?" she asked, holding her salute as she spoke.

"Ma'am!" Ekol and the acolytes replied in unison.

With that, Miranda turned to leave the church. Her companions now walked in front of her. As they departed, the sun finally dipped beneath the peaks of the Selian Range. Miranda guided them to an inn in the marketplace area. The sign out front read Mountain Meadows. Inside, she secured lodging for the five of them. She then insisted she and Evan go to her estate alone. The cousins were hungry, and Yuvina was still shaken. They agreed to eat and wait for Evan and Miranda. It took another ten minutes to walk out to the Hyacinth estate.

Back at the tavern as Arlindra, Celyth, and Yuvina were eating, a buzzing sound created a commotion outside the window next to their booth. Arlindra and Celyth sat together with Arlindra on the inside. She reached over and unlatched the window. Her heart skipped with surprise as she recognized the strange creature hovering outside. It looked like a golden lizard with dragonfly wings. It had sharp protruding fangs and two corkscrew horns. Its bulging, insect eyes contained multiple lids, and its blinking was unsettling to people unfamiliar with the creature. It resembled a very small dragonfly-dragon. Arlindra recovered from her surprise. "Nebu!" she exclaimed.

The creature landed on the windowsill. As he did, he voiced a harsh complaint, "I've been flying all over the region looking for you! I went to Dundoi, but they said you went to the bayous. After the bayous, I had to wait until the earth mother told me where you were! Where in the Infernia have you been!?"

Yuvina's eyes widened with wonder. "What manner of beast!?" she yipped.

Nebu turned his head, his wings rumbled and buzzed as he lifted. "I could ask you the same question!" he piped back.

Celyth laughed, and Yuvina blinked in disbelief. Arlindra scolded him, "Nebu you shouldn't speak to someone that way. I'm glad you found me, and I'm sorry I've been moving so quickly. I knew you would find us!" she replied with enthusiasm contrary to her stoic demeanor.

Nebu was a dracofly, a magical animal with a sharp intellect. They often traveled with adventurers bonded with nature. Arlindra was no exception, and Nebu had been her companion for the last five years. Though his attitude was sometimes abrasive, he was eager to be helpful, and he could fly incredibly fast over long distances. He made an excellent messenger. His most recent mission was to return to Mystalon and report the cousins finally found their way to Argentum. Thanks to their recent adventures in the ambiguous space and time of Olvidado, it took him a little longer to return than normal.

Nebu retorted, "There better be a good explanation for this! And you better share that food. It's about time you showed some appreciation. Have I got news for you! You're going to be so shocked that you'll lose your appetite. You might as well give me the whole meal!" He looked at Yuvina. "Hers too." Then he looked at Celyth, whose eyes narrowed before he could speak. "Aw, c'mon, Cel. Just a bite?"

Arlindra interrupted him, "What news do you bring?"

He buzzed his way into the tavern from the windowsill and landed on the table. "Elitirin is at it again! Your dads are starting to get really suspicious of her." Nebu was a foot long, and his wings were pressed to his back. His four lizard-like claws tore greedily at the food in front of Arlindra. In between bites, he explained with his mouth full, "It sheems like she shtill keepsh tryn' shta helf her new freinsh feel at homesh in Myshtalon." Food sputtered as he spoke.

Celyth's still-narrowed eyes grew harsher still. "And nobody with a brain was surprised," she spat with disdain.

Arlindra looked at Celyth then back at Nebu. Yuvina kept her paws close to her food. They had ordered a spread of venison, lamb, and beef with bread, cheese, and a soup made from dehydrated vegetables. The kitsune didn't want to share with the dracofly.

Arlindra asked, "Nebu. Do you know anything about the strangers she's been affiliating with?"

The strange dragon-insect swallowed his food before he continued. "Yeah. Sounds like they're with some people especially interested in the Umbrals. Thinks they know what's causing them. Puts your whole quest in jeopardy, honestly. Your dads aren't happy, not at all." His voice was high pitched and energetic.

Celyth's visage relaxed. "Have the other Sages done anything to sanction her?"

Nebu shook his head, causing the sharp, hairlike spines on his neck to flail. "Your dads tried to get the Sages to investigate her again, but she convinced a bunch of them it wasn't necessary. Said she was transparent. Trying to solve the Umbrals in her own way, since you two kinda suck."

Celyth swiped a fist at the dracofly, causing him to swoop in the air with a couple of loops. "Watch yourself, bug," she growled.

He gave a very humanoid shrug. "Hey, you should've solved the problem by now! Or, at least the other Sages think so."

Arlindra scowled. "These things take time, but leave it to the Sages to grow impatient with the children of their rivals."

Celyth's fist stayed planted on the table. "They'll regret their impatience."

Yuvina stared at the others, scarfing her meal before the dracofly could turn his attention to her. Nebu grunted and replied, "Well. There's probably more going on. I dunno. I just carry your messages, eat your food, and fight with you. Yeah?"

Arlinda cut another slice of meat off the venison on her plate and held it up for Nebu. "Here, after all that running you've done today. Thank you, buggy."

"Don't call me that!" he protested, causing Celyth to laugh again. Still, he took the meat happily, reunited with his master.

Miranda stood in the sitting room of her estate, looking out a bay window on the west side. Night had fallen over Devitus. Though Ezelbrecht rebuked her for being too human, Miranda understood the dragon's true fear. Whatever was happening to the godshards, Ezelbrecht and Miranda hoped it could be reversed.

The bay window was built with a sitting area. It spanned ten feet across and five feet deep. Miranda opened the curtains to let the moonlight in. In the center sat two, intertwined, gemstone statues. They were human in shape. One was red and the other blue. Miranda had been standing here for ten minutes, calming herself. Her parents' crystallized forms were okay. The fireplace sat cold, but Miranda was unconcerned by the elements. This was the only place she could think of coming after leaving Ezelbrecht and discovering her mother and father were missing from the arcane stream. She wished the eldritch dragon had informed her of their disappearances sooner. If Reshiria and Philotrax were the first to go missing, how long had dragons been disappearing? Miranda's concern continued to grow.

The door opened. Evan poked his head in, able to see well in the moonlit room. "Miranda?" he whispered.

She glowed with a golden aura. "Hey, Evan," she murmured. The aureate radiance flashed and dimmed. It was so bright it took Evan's eyes a moment to readjust to the moonlight. "It looks like their statues are fine. But now I'm afraid to leave them here. Should we take them back to Nulodia for safe keeping at the church?"

Evan entered the room, leaving the door ajar behind him. He thought for a moment before speaking, "Maybe we don't need the entire statues? You and Ezelbrecht said something about the godshards, right? Do you think you would be able to figure out what they are?"

Miranda did not respond. She stared at the statues in silence. As it started to become uncomfortable, she shared her thoughts out loud, "When I made contact with them, I was in the arcane stream. They thought they were too. They're not."

Evan nodded, though he didn't estimate Miranda saw his head move. Instead of speaking, he waited, letting her sort out her thoughts.

She continued, "Whatever happened to my parents is likely happening to the dragon eggs." She stepped into the sitting area in the window. She reached out and touched Reshiria's statue. Miranda closed her eyes. She sensed a dense concentration of mana in the crystalline material. She tried to push the flow of the stream into the gemstone, but it was impenetrable. "May I see your sword?" she asked, letting go of her mother's frozen form.

Evan handed it to her, and he also pulled a couple of daggers from other sheaths. "I've got a ton of those weapons. The team has found hundreds over the last couple of months." As Miranda took the sword and a dagger, Evan asked, "What are you thinking?"

Miranda looked at the sword's pommel, a mysterious gemstone encased within a chamber at the base of some gears. She also noted the dagger's stone chamber was in the crossguard instead of the pommel. When she focused on the weapons, they activated, causing the crystals within to glow and the gears to turn. The blades radiated auras matching the color of their respective gemstones. She handed the sword back to Evan, and it deactivated as it left her hand. She then reached into the crossguard of the dagger and felt the sharp bristles of wood locking the gemstone inside. There were four wooden spikes pressed a quarter inch into the stone. "May I?" she asked.

Evan responded, "Whatever you think you need to do."

She wiggled the gemstone inside until she freed it from the spikes. Miranda looked at the crystal in her fingers. It was the size, shape, and texture of a large, unfinished marble. She could see where the wood had punctured it. It was white with bright green marbled throughout. She scanned her mind for information, hoping maybe her mother's memories would help, but they came up empty. She tried to push the flow of mana into the bauble, but it had the same resistance as her parents' statues. "They have to be the same."

Evan watched as she turned toward the statues. "Miranda, what's going on in that mind of yours?" he asked in a pleasant murmur.

She turned to him with a grim face. "What kind of effect does this dagger normally produce with that stone?" she asked.

Evan's eyebrows danced as the question caught him off guard. He replied, "Poison. A sleeping poison, of sorts. It's magical, though, not something that could be treated with regular medicines."

Miranda looked at the stone, then back to the dagger. Without the crystal inside, there was no light. She then stepped toward the statues of her parents. "I'm sorry, Mom," she whispered.

Evan watched with confusion for a moment, but he eventually realized her intent. She pressed the dagger's crossguard onto one of her mother's fingers. The moonlight made it easy to observe as she punctured the finger of the blue statue with the spikes in the chamber. The statues had frozen with such great detail Miranda could see indentions for her mother's fingernails. It broke her heart to do this, but she had to know.

As she forced the dagger enough to embed the wooden spikes completely into the finger, the light returned to the chamber. After a moment the weapon and the statue began to glow. Miranda's eyes widened in shock, and Evan took a step closer. "By the gods," he mumbled, marveling at the streaks of electricity reflecting deep within Reshiria's statue. The blade of the dagger began to hum, and the aura of energy intensified.

Miranda looked at Evan and thought about their last night together on *The Nebula*. Her stomach dropped to the bottom of The Rift. If the weapons were appearing months ago, dragons should have been disappearing before Miranda met Ezelbrecht. Her trust for the eldritch dragon was as dangerous to her as it was to Erk. Why didn't they mention it on their first meeting? She felt a panic swelling in her chest. She started to hyperventilate.

Evan reached out and took her hand in his. His worry rushed his words. "By Lexcord, what's wrong, Miranda?"

A whisper in her mind put her at ease. "Wake up, Mir'thax." Her breathing calmed, though she still panted from surging adrenaline.

Miranda glared at the dagger as streaks of blue and white escaped the aura. She didn't have time to contemplate Gorthran's sinister plans. Perhaps the Dragon Father really did care for Reshiria and only now had the opportunity to send someone to investigate. Her mother's memories muddled with her own, and the confusion fueled her underlying anxiety. She squeezed Evan's hand with strength. "I'm okay. I keep losing focus. What if Ezelbrecht is manipulating us like Erk?" The music in her voice was fearful.

Evan's handsome smile brought her concentration out of Reshiria's memories. He replied with cool confidence, "My brother's desperation came from guilt. Yours comes from love. There's a big difference there."

Miranda pursed her lips with shock. "Evan! Your brother loves you!"

He grinned. "I know, but that's not why he started sinking ships and killing folks. Savvy?"

Miranda's heart skipped a beat. She squeezed his hand harder, causing him to yelp with surprise. Her eyes widened and she shrieked, "By the Sword, I'm sorry!"

Evan laughed and wiggled his hand, still latched to hers. "You're stronger than I look," he joked.

His humor made Miranda blush a bit. The shift in emotion brought her back to the dagger, still pulsating with power from her mother's statue. This experiment confirmed her fears, which had been steadily growing since she departed Ezelbrecht's cave. She spoke with a somber melody. "So, they've been turned into the same thing as the crystals that power the weapons. It's not surprising that Mom made your dagger light up like this."

They watched in contemplation for three more minutes. The hum from the dagger turned into a loud whir, prompting Miranda and Evan to trade concerned glances. The gears accelerated, and the field of electricity destabilized. A loud, popping sound followed by grinding metal indicated that the dagger broke. The sound sent Miranda into a new panic, and she removed the smoking, darkened dagger from the statue of her mother.

Evan speculated, "Do you think it's possible that the dragon eggs are being turned into these stones somehow?"

Miranda's eyes stayed fixed on the dagger. Her lips barely moved as she muttered, "My parents were fully matured dragons trapped as humans. Their bodies became crystalized magic. There's so much there, it blew up your dagger." Her eyes moved from the dagger to Evan. "I'm sorry about that, I didn't know it would go so far."

Evan chuckled and gave a humorous wave. "The dagger is worth far less than the information, right? It seems your parents are too powerful for the weapons, but think of that as a good thing. At least we know dragons, eggs, and the crystals are all connected. Ezelbrecht helped us get this information. Find out what's going on with the eggs, right? And your parents were the key to that puzzle." He looked at the dagger as smoke wafted throughout the moonlit room. He continued, "I'm afraid of the fire that might ignite if you attach one to your father," he warned. Miranda nodded in agreement, handing the broken dagger back to Evan. Four almost undetectable holes were left behind in Reshiria's fingertip. He remarked, "I wager the statues contain too much energy."

Miranda looked at Evan and the busted weapon in his hand. "Can I see the other dagger?" she asked, and he complied. She removed the gemstone that powered this one as well, but she didn't look back to the statues. Instead, she stuck her tongue in between her lips and then pushed her finger into the crystal chamber of the device. She pricked her finger with the four spikes. As she did, the blade lit up. Blood poured out from her finger, causing Evan to respond, "Woah, Miranda! No!"

The light on the blade swirled and lit up the entire room. It resembled a golden sunrise, but a haze of purple permeated the warm light. It caused a low, electrical buzzing sound throughout the room. A dull odor of brimstone and sulfur filled the air. Evan felt a calming sensation wash over him. He could feel the light swirling around and within him, and it seemed to be searching. Any aches, pains, or discomfort he had from travel were washed away. Before he could evaluate this burst of comfort, he saw Miranda's hair rapidly turning pink. "Stop! Your hair!" he shouted, somewhat drowned out by the sound of the light.

She winced, leaving her finger fixed into the device for a moment longer before withdrawing it. The wounds in her fingertip radiated with pain. "Restore to order what was damaged by chaos," she whispered, a purple light enveloping her finger and repairing the damage. The blood on her finger was still fresh, glistening in the moonlight. A wave of nausea overtook her, and she struggled to stand straight.

Evan was at her side in an instant, offering his hand and shoulder to help her steady herself. "These are the stunts my brother would pull. Slow down, talk to me. We can try some of your theories, but with safety measures in place. Just look at you," he lamented, helping her to a nearby chair and guiding her to sit.

Miranda struggled to breathe as she sat, the queasiness shaking her. Evan knelt beside her, the concern in his gaze intense. She spoke with a slow tempo, the music in her voice still present despite being drained. "At least we confirmed one thing." She leaned back in the chair which was covered by a sheet. It was somewhat dusty, but Miranda only needed to rest for a few minutes.

Evan reached into Miranda's healing pouch while she relaxed with closed eyes. Inside, he found a smaller bag which contained blossoms from a solisberry tree. He took one in his fingers and stood. "Hey, try one of these?" he placed his hand close to her mouth as he spoke.

She was disoriented but leaned forward to nibble the bloom in his hand. She felt the magic coursing through it. That accelerated flow restored the mana within her. The blossom was bitter, but she had eaten several of them as needed over the last few months. With her reduced capacity to store mana, she needed to replenish more frequently. After a moment, her nausea subsided. She sat up with a determined look in her eyes. "Don't you want to know what it is?" she asked, frustrated that Evan didn't ask.

Evan laughed, her spirit never wavering. "Of course, Miranda. Please, what did we confirm?"

She gave a serene smile. "Those weapons. They cause the arcane stream to bleed into our plane of existence. That's why the mana poured out of me. What's in those crystal chambers?"

Evan reached back to the blade on his belt. He partially withdrew it, looking into the pommel. "I honestly don't know. But you're right. It draws magic out of the stones, it draws magic out of your mother's statue, and it draws magic out of you."

Miranda's lips pursed up into a cocky grin. "I know I'm reckless sometimes, but I know that your life is only as safe as your information. Sometimes, you have to take risks to gain information. And even then, it's up to us to put together the pieces we understand and safeguard the information that doesn't make sense yet."

Evan knelt again, bringing their gazes to the same height. "You sound just like brother."

Her cocky grin widened. "That's a compliment, you know."

He felt his heart racing. "I know. That's why I said it. What's different about you now, Miranda? Why are you the only person I can think about lately?"

Her grin melted, and her eyes widened. Her lips formed a circle, a face she made while shocked or awed by anything from a surprise gift to an incomparable landscape. "Evan?" she asked. He seemed mesmerized.

He shook his head. "Sorry, sorry."

Miranda giggled. Her hair was still a deep pink, but the solisberry blossom mitigated the worst of the pain. "Don't be sorry. I'm thinking about you, too. But I don't know what that means yet. I'm glad you're here, and maybe the meaning will become apparent as we make memories together, yeah?" She looked at him with adoration.

Evan understood and his cheeks flushed. "Godshards, then, right?"

In truth, Miranda's sudden depletion terrified Evan and connected him with his tumultuous emotions. He now knew his feelings for her stemmed beyond his gratefulness. She saved his life, but that was only the beginning. The way she had grown in these last months proved she was true to her faith but understood life with a wisdom beyond her personal experience. She had the will and strength of a dragon beneath her beautiful exterior. She had the compassion of Lexcord and the conviction of Invictus. No wonder he found her captivating. Still, she was right. Those thoughts needed time to make sense.

Miranda stood and walked to the statue of her parents. "Godshards. You know, I don't even know what that means, in truth."

Evan followed her. "I feel like we have to say that way too often."

They stood in silence for another hour before Evan laid down on a sofa in the center of the sitting room. Miranda returned to the chair she was in before. The two of them slept lightly, guarding the statues of Reshiria and Philotrax. This is what Reginald was looking for. Miranda thought it was time to find out what this outsider knew. She considered using the statues as a type of bait to learn about the godshards, but putting her parents at risk worried her.

Evan snored lightly and interrupted her plotting. A pretty smile graced her lips as she lay as comfortably as her battlemail would allow. Why in the world was Evan thinking about her? She liked the thought of it, but it scared her. Fortunately, there were plenty of other concerns bouncing around in her mind, and she fell asleep trying to be anxious about all of them.

Elitirin examined the lacrima-deum delivered by Sender. Her green eyes flitted with excitement. They were larger than the one hundred he brought three months ago. She brushed strands of her black hair out of her face. She was confident these would be a more suitable power source for the project she and Sender were working on. Together, they collaborated with her knowledge of the three sacred trees of Espa and Sender's knowledge of engineering and magical technology. They were building a time gate, an apparatus she hoped would allow them to travel through space and time to the beginning of The Unbinding.

The aging elf sighed. This was her one hundred and seventy fifth year in the mortal coil. One hundred years ago, The Unbinding ripped her world apart as it had done so many others. Though Mystalon was largely insulated from the chaos following magic's unraveling, her husband was in Argentum when the fabric of the stream ripped open. He vanished without a trace like everyone else in that tragic city. Elitirin wanted to use Sender's technology to travel back in time and prevent The Unbinding from happening. Sender encouraged her by providing her with discounted lacrima-deum.

Elitirin's expertise had always been in magical plant life. She was a renowned manabotanist, and she was one of the Sages of Mystalon. She campaigned on her knowledge of the solisberry, eolnut, and yindai trees growing in the center of the elven city. Since The Unbinding, the pseudomagical society had found new ways to manipulate the mana stored in the blooms of the solisberry tree. Using stills constructed of cured eolnut, the Mystalonians boiled and processed the magical tree's blossoms. When steeped in yinfruit paste, the mana settled in predictable ways. The resulting products duplicated the effects of hundreds of useful spells. They could be distilled into vials or solid discs depending on the consistency of the completed spell. They could be deployed in various ways, including shattering the discs or vials, or consuming them orally depending on the intended effects. Elitirin dedicated her post-Unbinding years to further understanding the sacred trees under her care, and the people of the Namidan District supported her by electing her.

She met Sender on a rare trip to Alabaster. She needed to gather unusual reagents to conduct some experiments, but she had to go through strange channels to acquire them. While seeking the egg of a moon dragon, she met Sender. He showed her technology beyond her wildest dreams. There was a way to crystalize magic into a physical form he called lacrima-deum, magic words meaning tears of the gods. She understood why they would be called such; after all, the easiest way to create the magical gemstones was converting dragon eggs into lacrima-deum through a complex, natural process.

The dragon gods surely cried for the sacrifice of their children's eggs. Thanks to their affinity with the arcane stream and their tendency to isolate mana particles of particular kinds, however, they could be used by mortals with some predictability. Furthermore, they yielded higher mana outputs than magitabs and magisalves, granting access to powerful spells and effects. Sender never shared the full process of transforming eggs to lacrima-deum, but he assured her it was just as harmless as sacrificing the eggs for alchemy or manabotany. Eolnut piercings harnessed the magical energy within the gemstones to power Sender's weapons and simple machinery. Working with Sender's resources, Elitirin discovered how to use eolnut vines as wiring capable of channeling crystallized magic into more complex devices. Sender was so excited about the discovery that he offered to introduce her to his boss and mentor, Doctor One. She declined, however, reminding him that the nature of their partnership needed to remain secret.

That discovery happened a year ago. They began working on their time gate nine months later, using large quantities of lacrima-deum designated as inferior or insufficiently petrified. The process wasn't fully perfected, but the price was more agreeable than whole, crystalized dragon eggs. As they burned through those lacrima-deum, Elitirin was able to coordinate the flow of mana from eolnut extractors so she could fixate the time gate on points in the past. Every moment of history was imprinted upon the arcane stream. Sender told Elitirin of The Eye of the Arcane, an inert pocket of mana which recorded the whole of reality. Elitirin recognized some of the terminology from her training as a wizard, but she shifted to manabotany early in her studies. She trusted Sender's explanation. With precise focus and intense magical output, a person could open the stream to view those moments through the incredible apparatus Sender named a time gate. Elitirin finally found the correct configuration of eolnut wiring and yinfruit paste to look back one hundred years, but she was still unable to change the geographic focus of the device.

Due to her lack of experience with magical technology, she sold a tract of land her family had owned for centuries to Sender and his associates. Over the last six months, he had built a laboratory there that would be able to process dragon eggs. Not only did the organization pay her a substantial amount of money that she could reinvest in the lacrima-deum, but Sender promised to lend her his expertise to its fullest extent. Together, they would find a way to tear open the fabric of space and time rather than magic itself. Sender was confident they could right the wrong wrought upon Espa a century ago.

Elitirin used the entirety of the first batch to configure the day and time visible in the time gate. That was also the first batch of lacrima-deum produced in Sender's local laboratory. They were building the time gate in the greenhouse at Elitirin's mansion on the outskirts of Mystalon. She could receive deliveries with little scrutiny. That was especially fortunate, considering the outbreak of Umbrals that nearly destroyed her carefully laid plans. Though Sages were considered allies in Mystalon, the Fernith brothers recently began to suspect her of dealing too frequently with outsiders. She understood their caution; the Sages had maintained relative peace within the forest of Mystalon for the last one hundred years in spite of the loss of magic. Outsiders could threaten the balance they created in their insulated city, and Elitirin agreed they posed a risk.

Nevertheless, she had seen the capability of the technology developed by Sender and his associates. She made some of that technology viable with her own knowledge of the sacred trees. The Fernith brothers wouldn't understand the scope of her current project and would likely paint her as deranged or worse. The arrival of Umbrals caused them to insist Elitirin's recent activities be investigated, but she managed to persuade the other Sages to respect her privacy. Elitirin assured the others that she was merely seeking a way to deal with the Umbrals. The Fernith brothers only sent out their rebellious daughters to investigate the source of The Unbinding. Her efforts were more tangible. She would go back and make sure the Umbrals were never a problem at all.

The lacrima-deum in her hand was a whole dragon egg split into two. A whole shipment of them arrived the day before, a gift from Sender's superiors. They wanted to see the time gate completed within the week, if possible. It would be a challenge, but Elitirin knew it was for the greater good. In the center of the lacrima-deum, a sliver was missing. She wrinkled her nose in thought. She was anticipating whole, crystalized eggs, but they arrived in halves. A part of each lacrima-deum needed to be removed to "activate the flow of mana." She didn't understand what that part was, but she was a manabotanist, not an expert in crystalized magic. Sender insisted she run as many of these as she could through the time gate in as little time as possible. If his theory was correct, she should be able to make a clear projection of the past and tweak the eolnut wiring to change the geographic focus of the portal.

She wrecked her greenhouse to make space for the gate. Her heart clenched onto the hope of saving her husband, so the sacrifices would be worth it. She cleared out all of the torkoberry plants, the yindai and eolnut saplings, the fungal colonies, and the sulfurblooms. They crammed all of the technology required to build the time gate out here, and Sender's workers placed the large components all over the delicate infrastructure of the herb bins. The metal pieces crushed the delicate plants, destroying decades of careful cultivation.

Sender's builders brought in a marble foundation. They built a copper harness upon it in overlapping, concentric circles. It stood seven feet in height. A pivot device adjoined the harness to the base, and it was thoroughly greased with eolnut oil. The circles were harnessed together, creating a sphere-like structure that would spin when charged with mana. While spinning, they could see the past through a hazy glow. They viewed Elitirin's greenhouse as it was on the day of The Unbinding. The memory haunted her dreams, confirming what day she located with the time gate.

A control mechanism was built ten feet in front of the device. Long eolnut vines connected the control and the time gate. They conducted the flow of mana from the lacrima-deum positioned in an eolnut extractor beside the controls. The rest of the panel was constructed from steel sheet metal, a rare commodity produced by the dwarves of Thaliston far to the north. Sender was well connected. The eolnut circuitry was complex, but it fit snugly inside metal boxes housing a series of levers. With those, she could manipulate the flow of mana through the eolnut vines. Eolnut trees resembled willow trees in some ways, but they thrived by siphoning magic from the arcane stream around them. They were easy to grow near solisberry trees, and there were dozens of them surrounding the solisberry in the center of Mystalon. Their large, viny branches made great conductors for magic energy, and the wood extracted the large volumes of power by piercing a lacrima-deum.

She placed half of the egg in the extractor. The device was a four-foot column shaped like a funnel. The top contained a chamber with various ways to unleash the power within the gemstones. The larger egg lacrima fit on the eolnut spikes, and she impaled the soft crystal on them. It illuminated, filling her greenhouse with an eerie, red light. Elitirin exhaled with anticipation. "Alright. Let's see what happens if we open all the channels with a lacrima-deum this large."

She whispered to herself as she pulled one of the levers on the control mechanism. She pressed a few buttons meant to open more eolnut circuits, allowing for a broader flow of mana from the extractor to the time gate. After a moment, the copper circles began to move, spinning around and within each other. They built speed until they were only blurs of movement. Elitirin pressed another button on the control panel. The lacrima-deum crackled and caught fire. The blaze generated no heat, however, and did not affect the extractor.

She waited for one minute then pressed another button. The machine radiated a deep buzzing sound. She put her fingers around a lever on the far-left side of the control mechanism. It was at its lowest setting at the bottom of the panel, and she pushed it up. As she did, the hum of the spinning circles increased in pitch. They glowed vivid red from the energy contained in the lacrima-deum.

The glow intensified, and the image projected within the spheres began to move. Elitirin saw the day The Unbinding unfolded. She was in the greenhouse when news of Argentum's disappearance reached her. When magic unraveled, all contact with the city ceased. His last communication suggested he was on the verge of discovering Argentum's secret to maintaining a magical monarchy. Elitirin suspected he was close to the epicenter of The Unbinding as a result of his investigations.

She watched herself drop to her knees in the projection. One of her guardsmen brought her the news that all contact with Argentum was lost. She was cultivating a new strain of sweetleaf, a magical plant native to swamps where mana flowed with abundance. She recognized her grief, a confirmation of the machine's accuracy. She found a time close to The Unbinding, a significant achievement.

Thirty seconds of events repeated within the projection. She pressed long slivers of solisberry bark into the eolnut wiring. As she did, the image displayed changed. Sender was correct. By blocking the stream at certain intervals, the locational focus of the time gate would change. It could require hours of experimentation to find Argentum this way, but Sender gave her enough lacrima-deum to power the machine for a week straight. There were one hundred whole, petrified eggs, meaning she had two hundred halves to burn. She'd use them quickly, but she intended to find Argentum with the time gate. She would save her husband. She would find the cause of The Unbinding and possibly prevent it.

After an hour of work, the lacrima-deum was consumed. She replaced it and continued using solisberry bark to block the flow of the stream through the eolnut wires. She put another egg into the extractor after the second half of the fire lacrima-deum was expended. This one released an acidic cloud of gas. She used both halves of it as well, burning them at the same time for maximum power. More energy yielded a clearer projection. She worked late into the night, and after several hours, she located a dwarven and human settlement at the base of a mountain nearby. She estimated it was Glern, the only constructed city in The Tymbyrwylde. She would have to continue her efforts tomorrow. She already used ten of the crystalized eggs. She only had ninety more tries to find Argentum before the next phase of their experiment.

Chapter 7
A Peculiar Petition

"And, in this, we beg your aid. Gelidor, aligned with Na'agamlor, has brought ruin to Claston. Petition the royals of Alabaster and raise an army. The cause of justice has suffered greatly." – Wailindis Lancethinas, Petition to the Church of Invictus in Alabaster

*J*ustin wiped his brow. He was sweating in the cold of winter. Moving all of these crates from Lenis's warehouse to the Peacekeeper Precinct was a taxing task. City law enforcement functioned under a different hierarchy than the cathedral. The Peacekeeper Precinct oversaw and dealt with law enforcement within the city, and they assisted Selasine's teams by processing evidence confiscated in Nulodia. Their headquarters was located across from the grand cathedral of Invictus in the center of town. There was a grand plaza with a magnificent gazebo and well-manicured park between the two buildings. They used three carts to transport the evidence across town to bring it to the Peacekeeper Precinct. Justin looked over to Valarie, who was helping him unload the crates.

She glared at him. "Stop thinking, get back to work, paladin!" she taunted.

He gave her a soft smile. They had been together for seven months now. She appreciated his intellect, discipline, and humility, and he admired her strength, determination, and persistence. Her formal title was Valarie the Persistent, Judge of Retribution, after all. Justin replied, "Trying to stop me from thinking is like trying to stop that guy from eating," he joked with a nod toward the precinct building.

Commander August Burchard stood with his back to the wall, the front entrance of the building about ten feet to his left. He had one leg propped against the wall, and he was currently stuffing a fried quilli bird wing into his mouth. Justin and Valarie both picked up a crate from the cart and walked toward the door. This building was only two stories tall, but it was quite expansive. It stretched over three hundred feet to both the left and right of the front door, and the central building connected to a jail used to temporarily house detained lawbreakers. It sat beyond the two wings of the building, forming an "H" shape connected loosely by the central building.

As Justin approached, he gave a devious grin to his friend. He teased, "Looks like Commander Burchard the Hungry has been digging in the wrong evidence crate. Now the cooking criminals will never see trial."

August held the half-devoured wing inches from his mouth, which sat agape. His eyes shifted between his snack and his friends. His eyes lingered on Justin and Valarie, neither his mouth nor the food moving. After an awkward enough moment passed, August returned his eyes to his food. He stuck it in his mouth, bones and all, tearing the rest of the meat off of the wing. His fingers stayed in his mouth until he pulled the remnants of sinew and bone out, tossing it into a bin nearby. "You really should try out the mess hall here, the peacekeepers eat like royalty," he added, using his propped leg to push himself off the wall. He dusted his hands together, but it did nothing to remove the greasy residue.

Valarie and Justin both laughed. She added, "The quilli bird is hardly the best thing on the menu. You should try the breakfast stuff." When she began her service on the Path of the Sword of Justice, she was a peacekeeper at this very precinct. She arrested over one hundred lawbreakers in her first year, and most of them were connected with services to help them avoid returning to a life of crime. Doing so earned her the title Judge of Retribution, and she was popular with the clergy serving here. She pursed her lips in scrutiny, chastising, "Besides, peacekeepers shouldn't be at the mess hall while they're working."

August feigned an exasperated expression. "Well, good thing I'm a commander then!" he retorted, opening the door for the two carrying crates. Valarie and Justin traded sarcastic glares as they walked past August and into the lobby of the precinct. It was a spacious room that opened out in front of them and to the right.

There were various clergy positioned at desks throughout. Anyone wishing to report a crime or civil dispute could come here and voice their grievances to the church. August slipped between Valarie and Justin. He opened a door immediately to the left of the entrance, however, avoiding the lobby altogether. They went down a long hallway with several doors on the right and barred windows to the left. One of these rooms had been set aside to deal with evidence related to Farzg's operations in Nulodia. It was the next to last door of the hallway. The corridor stretched eight feet across. The windows and doors were positioned twenty feet apart, leaving large rooms to store and organize evidence.

In truth, August wasn't slacking. He was waiting on Justin and Valarie to bring the most critical pieces of evidence into the precinct. Some of it included correspondence between Lenis and Farzg, paper records, ciphered messages, and some of the strange crystals that powered the clockwork equipment. Farzg's men inflicted greater casualties on the church with the enhanced weapons, and the larger crystals resembled fragments of dragon eggs. At least three representatives of the church needed to be present in order to access the evidence room dedicated to Farzg. High Priest Selasine and High Paladin Erista utilized a combined prayer and ritual to safeguard the doors. Invictus's blessing ensured the doors would only open if the right conditions were met. High Paladin Erista was in charge of the day-to-day operations of peacekeepers and acolytes working for the Peacekeeper Precinct. She was efficient and very much appreciated Selasine's willingness to collaborate. Carulus tended to be secretive with knowledge and plans, which lawbreakers might have feared, but it also caused a disconnect between Erista and operations coming out of the cathedral.

After they stored the evidence, Justin and Valarie double checked the paperwork was in order and headed for the front entrance of the building. The door of the evidence room clicked behind them, the prayer enhanced lock making no additional sound to indicate it would also keep the contents of the room safe. The building was made of sandy colored stone, and the doors were crafted of dense iron. Even without the protective prayers, it would be difficult to break into the evidence rooms. As the three emerged in the lobby, Erista was standing in front of the exit with her arms crossed. She was an orc standing at seven feet tall. She had a beautiful black braid hanging down from the top of her head to her shoulders. Her eyes were a glittery pink, and her skin was dusty gray. Her age, however, was harder to guess, as she looked young for seventy-three. Orcs could live to be one hundred and forty, so she was middle aged, technically. Though she looked young, she had a powerful aura about her. A broad array of scabbards adorned her belt, and her presence alone would be enough to keep petty thieves and pickpockets out of the marketplace. She smiled, her tusks tilting up. Her face was generally stern, but her smile was pleasant and contagious. "Everything in order, paladins?"

The paladins stood at attention with impeccable form. "Ma'am!" they shouted in unison, shifting into a salute, each movement crisp, rehearsed, and disciplined. The peacekeepers and acolytes working in the precinct snapped their attention to the front door, surprised at the sudden commotion.

The high paladin entered the salute herself. "At ease, paladins," she ordered, relaxing. Even their hold time for relaxing seemed rehearsed, as they stopped the salute at the same time. Erista thought it was remarkable. "What is His Holiness feeding you over there?" she teased. Her voice was lighter than her intimidating height would suggest, but as a high paladin, it was the aura of her overwhelming conviction that would break the spirit of lawbreakers.

Justin suppressed a laugh, and since the high paladin had put him at ease, he decided to be sarcastic. "Definitely not fried quilli wings," he jabbed.

August's face did not change, but Valarie's gaze snapped to Justin in surprise. He was usually so disciplined that when he broke protocol, it always shocked her. He did it more frequently than one would expect, as well. She gave a tiny smirk, waiting on High Paladin Erista to respond. The orc let out an amused laugh, catching the reference to the snacks in the mess hall. "We'll strike them from the menu immediately, Justin the Watchful," she replied with a humorous tone.

Finally, August reacted. "No, wait, ma'am!" he blurted. Another round of laughter ensued. August turned to look at Justin with an amused grin. "We'll revisit this moment in training," he said with a chuckle.

The high paladin uncrossed her arms. "Glad all is well. We will have the peacekeepers unload the rest of the crystals in the bulk warehouse for evidence. What would somebody be doing with these strange stones?" she asked, hoping the paladins had some kind of news.

Valarie shook her head, her blond braid waving behind her.

"Unfortunately, we don't know much more than they can power the advanced weapons we have been finding lately. It looks like they had enough of these stones in that warehouse to power a small army. Sizes range from pebbles to bricks." She wanted to salute. When Valarie began at the precinct she knew High Paladin Erista as Chief Enforcer Erista. She was proud of her former mentor for attaining the rank of high paladin. Under Erista's guidance, the peacekeepers and acolytes working with The Enforcers kept person-to-person crime at an all-time low in the city. Furthermore, when arrests did need to be made, her policy of de-escalation saved many lives. The rehabilitation programs for lawbreakers were extensive, and she also oversaw those helping people trapped in unfortunate circumstances that encouraged criminal activity.

Still, though the streets were generally safe, not all criminals were merely people down on their luck in need of social programs. Farzg was not the only notorious criminal with a presence in the city, but Selasine was able to use Farzg's wide reaching influence to justify a kingdom-wide church investigation. The Alabaster royals approved a modest budget for the manhunt, but the Peacekeeper Precinct limited their scope to activities happening in the city and the city alone. Erista nodded to Valarie. "Thank you, Valarie the Persistent. And thank you for keeping your collateral damage low." She stared directly at August, her pink eyes scolding him.

His expression of surprise and guilt resulted in a forced smile through gritted teeth. "You've read the report already then?" he asked sheepishly.

Erista laughed. "It's not my place in the hierarchy to discipline you, though I would if I were your commanding officer." She smiled as she spoke. "His Holiness counts your lesson as learned, and I trust his judgment." Then her face turned serious, and she reached out and placed a hand on Commander Burchard's shoulder. "But I don't want to have to read the next report where I find out a brave young paladin with a lot of promise did something ridiculous and ended up unrecoverable as a result."

Justin gulped. Unrecoverable was a special word the church used to designate individuals whose injuries were too grievous to return them to the mortal coil. Fortunately, he had been one of the lucky ones in the past. Moreover, that was one thing that Justin could say he did that August had not done yet, and it would spoil the joke. He hoped no harm so great would befall his friend for more reasons than just his own monopoly on battlefield deaths. Still, Justin couldn't resist the opportunity to share humor with his true sentiments. "Don't worry ma'am. He's more likely to choke on a quilli bird bone than to face harm in battle. I won't allow it."

High Paladin Erista smiled again and withdrew her hand from August's shoulder. "Look over them, Judge of Retribution. That's an order," she said, cutting her eyes to Valarie with a smile.

"Ma'am," she replied with a casual salute.

The paladins departed for the cathedral and the high paladin mobilized her acolytes and peacekeepers to put the rest of the confiscated gemstones in bulk storage. As the paladins walked through the park in the plaza, August walked in front with Valarie and Justin behind him. The tower shields on their backs made them look comparable in height with August, and they were an intimidating presence in motion. The people of the city enjoying the park usually waved to the paladins, and sometimes children would rush them to ask about different kinds of monsters. Kids tended to ask about dragons, vampires, and werewolves, but August and Valarie were shocked when one child asked about wendigos. Justin figured the child was well-read, as he knew about many strange beasts before his tenth birthday. Today, people waved, but nobody approached. The clergy of Invictus were heroes of the city in a lot of ways, though other avenues existed to serve the people.

As they approached the cathedral sprawling on the north side of the plaza, August turned his head to Justin and Valarie, speaking over his shoulder. "Thanks again for handling the evidence, friends. We make a pretty balanced team, yeah?" he remarked, his voice genuine.

Justin nodded in return, a simple smile on his lips. "Any time, elf word for family member." The three of them laughed, imitating the way Erk, Evan, and Selasine talked to each other.

They kept walking and the jokes escalated. In a boisterous voice, August mimicked Erk's introductions, "I am Erilkaiden the Radiant, title upon title, fear me across the seas!"

Justin nearly doubled over with laughter, struggling to walk. Valarie's normally severe gaze was lighter as she, too, found it hilarious. Justin added, "Bad guy, good guy, which guy, I'm the guy!" He pushed his hands in front of him as if he were shooting a beam of light.

A voice piped from behind them. "The likeness is uncanny, Justin. You should do Evan next! Or Naomi!"

The three of them froze. They turned slowly to see Erk dressed in his full captain's garb. His smile was as radiant as his name. Justin raised a hand in greeting, but their expressions all looked anguished. August pursed his lips. He lowered his voice and tried to sound feminine, an odd contradiction in his mind. "I'm Naomi and I'm going to stab you if you're lucky." He tried to sound smooth, and the joke worked.

Erk burst into laughter, adding, "Come now, kids. We have a tendency to mimic our mentors, your imitations are flattery. Caricatured a bit, but at least we know you're paying attention." His humor settled and he smiled. "I've been hanging out in the plaza, waiting for your return. August." He looked directly at the young man.

August stood at attention, Valarie and Justin joining him instinctively. Erk continued, "Thank you for your quick thinking. I owe you a great debt."

August shook his head. "We are allies and friends, captain. I know without a doubt you would have done the same."

Erk gave a vigorous nod, replying, "Indeed, commander. Without a moment's hesitation."

Justin reached up to scratch his head and pushed his shoulders up into a shrug. "Part of the thanks should go to Miranda. Those potions she shared with us were incredible. The fact you and His Holiness survived and were back in action within minutes is almost as miraculous as her healing hundreds of people at once."

Erk and August looked at Justin with a puzzled glance. Erk continued, "Oh, of course. There is no doubt that I will always be extra thankful for her in so many ways."

Justin shook his head, "No, I mean. I didn't mean to cast doubt on your gratitude, sorry captain." He took a breath. "It's just . . . the warehouse people. None of them survived. In fact, the gas was so deadly it eventually corroded the lungs of its own caster. These were low level people, and that power could have taken out two of our most incredible leaders." He seemed to be thinking, caution in his eyes. "Whatever we're getting into is escalating."

Erk's countenance softened. "It is escalating. You are correct in that conclusion, Justin. Unfortunately, the near catastrophe was my doing. I became too quick to trust and caused a moment of hesitation. I wrongly assumed anyone working at the lowest levels of Farzg's criminal empire would be forced there against their will. The incident at the warehouse proves us both incorrect. These were not low-level thugs but trained and thriving criminals in the middle echelons of working with Farzg." His face fell into a grave expression. "That we destroyed their operation with only three near-misses and no casualties is a testament to your bravery and quick thinking. Thank you again, August."

The four stood for a moment in silence. Valarie cleared her throat. "Shall we report to His Holiness?" she asked.

The others nodded in agreement, and they entered the cathedral through the front doors. The magnificent building was a sprawling complex, and the primary entrance led into a large nave. The corridor led straight into a massive sanctuary, and staircases on the sides led up to balconies fifteen feet above the central room. The total space could seat ten thousand people safely. Twelve doors on the north side led deeper into the cathedral. They needed the cathedral's library, so they entered the northwesternmost wing. Selasine's office was on the second floor of the library.

As they approached the high priest's study, Carulus greeted them from behind a desk outside the door. "Faithful ones. Remarkable work on the evidence paperwork, Justin the Watchful!" he complimented.

Justin gave a hesitant smile to the half-elf. "In matters of bureaucracy, your compliments are the highest standard, Carulus the Penitent."

Carulus was short for a half-elf, standing at five feet. He was advancing in years, and becoming a shadow creature formed by the god of madness had not helped his physical appearance. He looked ragged and weak. The bureaucrat continued, "In the future, Commander Burchard, would you make sure to sign all of your reports?" he asked, trying to sound polite.

August blinked in surprise, "Oh, did I miss something?"

Carulus nodded. "Indeed, commander." He stood, finding a stack of parchment leaves. He isolated a few documents that had not been marked or distinguished in any way from the others. Sure enough, August's signature was absent on all four of the pages.

The towering paladin huffed at himself. "Well, how about that. Sorry there, Carulus. Have you—"

Carulus cut him off by placing an ever-flowing quill in his hand. "Of course, commander. It happens, and to err is to be mortal." He gave a sympathetic smile. Before, he likely would have berated the young man for his errors. After his entire world crumbled beneath the weight of his bad decisions, he had learned to be patient and forgiving. August was a fighter, not a bureaucrat. Carulus was learning how his strengths could compliment the strengths of others.

August signed the paperwork as needed. Carulus returned to the desk and put the pages in their correct locations in the stack without bothering to check page numbers. His confidence in his organizational skills was clear. August mused, "You're so much more awesome as a bureaucrat than a general."

Carulus laughed at the paladin's bluntness. "Of course, August, that's how I ended up here. The Sword of Justice has taught me humility in the most painful of ways. It was my own pride that caused the pain. His Holiness has shown me what it means to apply your gifts regardless of the value others place upon them." He paused and gave a gentle bow. "I have been blessed by Invictus and the arcane stream. I will continue to use those blessings to help people in need. After all," he started but paused. He glanced at the door to Selasine's study before continuing. "After all, a person I once looked down on has treated me with nothing but grace and mercy."

Valarie had volunteered to accompany a group of Shield Knights on Carulus's expedition against Erk. She traveled with eight others to Devitus and to the Undine Coast from there. She did not realize their short pitstop in that sleepy frontier town would ultimately connect her to the man she would fall in love with. Furthermore, she didn't realize that those events would firmly shape her direction in service to the church. She saw Carulus in a tragic way, as she once revered him as the high priest. His homilies were invigorating. He had a theatrical way of speaking that really highlighted the spirit of the law. Plus, he knew every single catechism by heart. His descent into depravity made her sad, but she was proud of the way he handled his divine punishment. Everyone knew the moment Carulus stepped out of line his heart would stop beating. It was a condition placed upon him by Invictus personally. Carulus accepted the terms. He truly wanted his heart to beat for those on the Path of the Sword of Justice and the people of the Alabaster Kingdom. Valarie was not a Judge of Hearts, but she knew this was the Carulus she looked up to in her younger days. She expected no less from him. She finally added, "Your wisdom continues to grow, Lord Gaius," she said, using his common name purposefully.

His eyes drew up in emotion. "Yes, yes, Valarie. Your easy forgiveness is unwarranted."

Erk interrupted. "Not at all, Carulus." The elf stepped forward, standing between August and the priest who once hunted him. "Your misguided actions have fortunately fallen on the side of the greater good." Erk smiled cordially, and Carulus lowered his head with guilt. Erk's people had been the victims of unjustified, monarchal violence, and the Church of Invictus should have been there to support them in overthrowing an unjust and unfit ruler. Unfortunately, the church did not have a formal foothold in the kingdom, and Gelidor aligned himself with Na'agamlor, the god of corruption. Erk encouraged the former high priest, "Do not bow your head in shame, priest. You have acknowledged your shortcomings and have staked your very life on making up for your mistakes." He reached out, touching the bureaucrat on the shoulder. "I, too, have much to atone for. I understand the grief you feel."

Carulus's eyes watered. "Oh stop, the lot of you. You'll make me lose my composure. If I cry on duty, I'm afraid the Sword of Justice himself will show up to scold me."

Everyone gave a slight chuckle at his theoretical situation, but they understood. Carulus's route to forgiveness now resided in his actions. He even worked research jobs outside the church part time to raise funds to assist the families that lost loved ones in the tragedy he caused. Thanks to his uncanny gift, that was a very profitable endeavor. Erk finally asked, "Is His Holiness available?"

Carulus nodded and gestured to the door. "Available and expecting you. We've received a most troubling petition."

Erk was in motion immediately. "Be well, Carulus."

Valarie gave Carulus a brief salute and smile, and she joined everyone as they opened the door to Selasine's study without announcement.

The high priest stood at his long table. There were mountains of paperwork everywhere. He stood on the far side with a parchment in his hand. Thomas gestured for everyone to join him without looking up.

Erk spoke first as they entered the room. "Is there news, brother?"

Selasine's eye glanced up from the parchment. "Indeed. A strange petition."

The four rushed to the table. The paladins all saluted, and Selasine stopped what he was doing and set the parchment down. He returned the salute with a crisp snap of his wrists and a stomp of his right foot. It sent shivers down Justin's spine; Selasine had impeccable form, which is one reason he admired his mentor. The high priest picked the parchment back up. "It's from Mystalon."

Erk's eyes widened, "Maldith." He cursed in the language of

giants, something he picked up from Naomi. "Are you serious? Mystalon has been independent for the better part of four hundred years!"

Selasine nodded. "It's a grave situation. Shadow creatures have been appearing. Their description is similar to the shadow beasts Carulus introduced us to." He paused as he looked over the scroll. "But they're not as simple to kill. The weak ones are easy to dispatch, but there seems to be a hierarchy. There were no shadow beasts of this magnitude in the Astral Spire."

Erk listened. The paladins stood at attention, motionless. Selasine continued. "And to further complicate the matter, the petitioners are, wouldn't you know, the brothers who are the fathers of the cousins Miranda has been traveling with."

August blinked in obvious confusion. "Say that again, sir?" he asked.

Justin's eyes cut toward Valarie, but she ignored him. She also didn't understand what Selasine said, but she didn't want anyone to know that. Selasine amended his explanation. "Miranda has been traveling with two elves from Mystalon. They were seeking answers to the source of the shadow creatures there. They thought solutions may reside in Argentum, and they finally found a route to the city. That was all briefly before I dispatched Evan to find Miranda."

Erk's lips twisted up in thought. "And those elves, they are the daughters of the petitioners."

Selasine confirmed with a swift nod. August and Valarie understood now. Justin stayed glued at attention. The high priest continued, "If her timeline has not been interrupted by current events, then I would expect a letter from her soon. I'm going to ask Damil to reach out to Evan in the morning, however. I do not want to take this petition lightly." The wisdom in Selasine's words resonated throughout the room.

Erk agreed. "Mystalon has been insulated for centuries. For them to ask for help from outsiders is a grand display of humility and fear. Whatever is happening, it's happening fast and it's cataclysmic."

The paladins listened in bewilderment. As all three of them were humans, they had heard fairy tales related to Mystalon, the elven paradise of magic. Such a kingdom was a great imaginative story for human children growing up in the era of The Unbinding. The rumors of the kingdom's power had been greatly exaggerated, however, and they were increasingly isolated after magic unraveled. August asked, "Is this something we should get mixed up in?"

Selasine sighed. "I'm not sure, commander. I just find it a little coincidental that Miranda's traveling companions are from the same isolated kingdom that just petitioned the church formally for help." He took a deep breath. "Reason dictates we wait until Damil can make contact with Evan. The slaver caravan raids were a success. Farzg has his fingers as far as the Ezdell Hillcountry, and I'm glad we've dealt them a serious blow that far east."

Erk's expression shifted to a cheeky grin. "What if we set sail immediately? We can get to Mystalon in just five days' time on *The Nebula*." He looked at the paladins. "Besides, if it isn't something you should worry about, we can follow up on the leads of Death Pirates near Tanlin Falls."

Selasine lifted his right index finger in agreement. "Actually, yes. I like that plan." He stood in contemplation for a moment. "There would be no wasted time."

The paladins exchanged excited glances. Sailing with Erk always proved fun. Though they were passionate about their work with The Airborne Marines, their true sailing spirits were awakened on *The Nebula*. Each of them had their own fond memories of the ship and their time with the pirate lord in atonement. Plus, *The Violet Blur* was out on a smaller mission right now. Naomi had probably relegated the responsibilities to the captain of the ship, Annaia. The human had known Naomi for more than thirty years, and Naomi was like a mother and best friend to her. She was quite capable as captain of *The Violet Blur*, a title that Naomi gave her after the Battle of Beriton. August interrupted the planning, "Is *The Nebula* stocked enough to bring five birds?"

Erk's smile widened. "Now that you, His Holiness, and Evan have proven the value, I have gone to my own lengths to, uh, keep a few of the winged beauties handy on the ship." His expression became prideful. "I've had the stable deck refitted. I've purchased six pegasus. These assets are at the church's disposal."

Justin and Valarie grinned. Justin asked, "And our cabins on the officers' deck?"

Erk smirked in return. "Just as you left them, Justin the Watchful."

Selasine's face balanced his own excitement with his concern for Mystalon. "Give me a moment then." He picked up a parchment nearby and began writing. Everyone stood in silence, the ever-flowing quill scratching as the high priest wrote. After he finished, he looked around. "Now it's official. We sail immediately."

As the five of them emerged from Selasine's office, Carulus stood. "The petition, Your Holiness?"

Selasine held it in his hand along with the decree he just wrote. "We set out for The Sea of Undine. I will send official word on the church's stance on the matter after first light tomorrow. We have multiple leads in that region. *The Nebula* is our best bet on reaching them in a timely manner." He handed the parchment he had penned to Carulus.

Carulus bowed and skimmed the new document. "I will gladly complete the paperwork for the incident at the warehouse. As of now, Your Holiness is on a journey of prime importance to the balance of order and justice in the far reaches of Alabaster." He gave a weak smile as he faced the five. "May the Sword of Justice guide your path. Set out with order in your steps and righteousness in your hearts. May Invictus shine his holy light upon you and pour out his judgement in abundance."

August, Justin, and Valarie saluted, and they completed the catechism in unison. "Our steps forward bring the future, but our footprints are the evidence of our deeds. Silver Maiden, guide our hearts; Sword of Justice, guide our hands. Together we depart, and together we shall return." They relaxed their salute. Selasine beamed with pride. Erk watched with sympathy as he saw the mixture of Carulus's joy and sorrow. At least the bureaucrat's heart was in the correct place now. Erk understood that feeling.

The five practically ran to the port district. Of course, this was a serious matter. In the most recent months, the three young paladins had been with the Airborne Marines and their flagship, *The Starstorm*. It was named in Damil's honor after his retirement as High Paladin of The Pegasus Knights. Still, *The Nebula* was a much more luxurious craft, and Erk's reformed pirate crew made for an entertaining voyage. Many were great musicians, and they were all fiercely loyal to Erk and his friends.

Erk allowed the clergy to board first. As the captain came aboard, the crew began to cheer. He smiled with a devious look. He ran to the captain's quarters, and inside he found the cord to ring *The Nebula*'s bell to announce the ship's departure. As he returned to the deck, he looked to his right. Naomi emerged from her dressing room fifteen feet away. It served as storage for the things she liked to keep on her beloved's ship. She looked at Erk, dressed in her full combat attire. She asked, "Where are we off to, honeycomb?"

Erk's face radiated tense excitement. "His Holiness received a petition. We might be going to Mystalon."

Naomi's eyes narrowed. "No way," she hissed in disbelief.

The captain nodded. "Five-day journey to the Undine Coast. The bays are numerous there, so we should be able to find a suitable place to drop anchor. Then we can take the pegasus from there."

The earth giantkin's lips broke into her beautiful smile. "Aww, Erilkaiden! Taking me to kingdoms spoken of only in fairy tales. Who would have known you were so romantic?" she teased, her deep, rich voice capturing her adoration.

The clergy went below deck to assess their cabins. Erk left them unchanged, hoping this day would come sooner rather than later. He let out a big sigh. "We're going to be missing two crewmembers, though." He walked up to the upper deck and stood at the helm of his ship. Naomi followed him, speaking as they walked.

"Miranda and Evan will be fine. I wonder if he's confessed his feelings yet," Naomi commented.

Erk smirked. "Probably. Ever since he's come back from the brink of death, he's been bolder than I've ever seen him. And it's pretty clear that he likes brave, strong, beautiful women," the elf said looking up at his own love. "It must run in the family." His smile was sweet and sincere, and it still made Naomi's stomach flip with butterflies.

She placed a hand on his shoulder as they stood at the helm. Erk calculated the ways the Fernith brothers and their daughters could be connected with current events. Additionally, even if the events in Mystalon were unconnected to Farzg and the dragon eggs, perhaps the magical society there would have more information about their potential uses. He needed answers. "Raise the colors, crew," he ordered.

They raised a deep, purple flag with stars stitched into it. They were shaped in the pattern of the constellation of Saraix. *The Nebula*'s flag was designed in honor of Mir'thax Toi'landra, the dragon who saved so many lives at The Battle of Beriton. Miranda had not seen it yet. Hopefully, Evan wouldn't spoil the surprise. Erk smiled deep in his heart. Mystalon would have been a great place to visit as a wizard. He had not been a wizard in one hundred years. To go now as a pirate indentured to the church was an acceptable consolation prize. Though Gelidor robbed him of most of his family, he had a new family that kept his heart safe from the darkness that nearly consumed him. "Raise the anchor in one hour. Anybody caught deserting will answer to Annaia when she's back in port."

His voice rang across the deck. The crew that could hear him gave an "Aye, cap'n!" shout in return. Erk was home, and his new family was sailing with him once again.

Chapter 8
Power Within

"Born under the auspices of calamity, elves with hair black as night are doomed to a tragic fate. Then again, the fate of all mortals ends with death, an immutable byproduct of life. 'Ware the elf with black hair both as friend and foe." – Elvenscrit,
Chapter Three

The sound of a door closing tore Miranda out of her sleep. Her hand went to the hilt of her sword out of instinct, and she scanned the sitting room as it glowed in the early morning light. The gemstone statues of Reshiria and Philotrax sparkled as radiance from the sun reflected off the dormant citrus orchard on the west side of the estate. Evan was standing with his back to the statues, watching the sitting room door.

"Trouble?" Miranda whispered.

Evan shook his head but kept his eyes fixed on the door. "I think school is starting."

Miranda blinked and stood up, the long skirt of her battlemail rattling. The golden mesh was made of fine adamant rings so small they were almost imperceptible, but the dense metal was quite loud. A voice called from the hallway, "Miranda?"

She recognized it immediately. "Headmistress!" she exclaimed and bolted toward the door. Evan looked around in shock, his eyes darting from the door to Miranda, then following her as she ran across the room. The door was still slightly ajar, but Miranda threw it open.

In the hallway stood an elf with warm, orange hair. She stood at five foot three, and she carried a large, wooden staff. She was the headmistress of the monastery of Lexcord a little way outside of Devitus to the north. Miranda grew up there, and the headmistress was her first true mentor. "It's so good to see you! Welcome home!" the monk greeted.

Miranda smiled with confidence. When she left Devitus the first time, she tried to say goodbye to the headmistress, but she departed a babbling mess. The headmistress taught her to say "see you soon" instead of more permanent farewells. So far, Miranda continued to make good on her promises to see people again. "Thank you, headmistress, and you as well!" she replied to her former mentor, stepping forward to hug the monk.

The headmistress returned Miranda's hug and looked around her inside the sitting room. "I hope everything was just as you left it. This room has remained locked and secure since you departed." She noticed Evan standing near the statues in the bay window. "Oh, I see you've brought someone with you," she continued as she made eye contact with Evan.

Evan gave a kind smile, recognizing her title from Miranda's stories. He addressed her directly, "It is a pleasure to meet the person who showed Miranda so much kindness in her youth. I am Evanthalus Lancethinas."

Miranda took a step backward and invited the headmistress into the sitting room. The monk's movement was graceful, swift, and undetectable. Evan's eyes widened with interest; the headmistress's agility reminded him of The Harbinger training he had been working on with Erk. The headmistress replied to Evan, "Well met, then, Evanthalus. I've heard more stories about you than I can explain." Her comment prompted confusion from Evan, but she deflected by continuing her greeting. "Welcome to Devitus." She glanced at the statues behind him. "I feel like you have a decision to make, Miranda."

The warpriest brushed some loose hair out of her face. Her braids were unraveling, but at least her hair color had returned to normal. The ether purged from her by the dagger did not go far, nor did it disperse back into the stream. It had simply been thrown out and became stagnant, much like the magic deep within Argentum. She reabsorbed most of it overnight, and she had a solisberry bloom. She was brimming with mana. "I do, headmistress. But I don't want to scare dad by just dropping the statues on him."

Evan interjected, "Actually, Miranda. I have news regarding His

Holiness and brother. I wanted to get your input before we present this information to the cousins. It involves their fathers."

Miranda looked at Evan with shock. "What? When did you receive news?" she asked. The headmistress looked up at her former pupil, evaluating her composure. Before Evan could reply, Miranda added, "Oh. Damil. Right?" She was sad Damil had been unable to reach her, and the music in her voice reflected her sentiments.

Evan confirmed with a nod. He looked at the monk, saying, "Headmistress, this information may soon be relevant to your community." He turned his attention back to Miranda. "The Fernith brothers made a formal petition to the Church of Invictus. The shadow creatures continue to wreak havoc upon Mystalon, and they fear it may be a punishment from the gods." He licked his lips, choosing his words carefully. "His Holiness, brother, Naomi, and the Airborne Marines are currently aboard *The Nebula*, and they are sailing toward Mystalon. The shadow creatures are still poorly understood. I relayed what I knew of them to Damil with His Holiness and Commander Burchard present."

The headmistress smiled as Miranda's body language showed her comfort with the difficult decisions in front of her. The warpriest spoke to Evanthalus with directness and confidence. "There is no question or need to consult the cousins. If His Holiness and Erk are in route, then we must also set our course for Mystalon."

Evan's lips broke into a smile. The headmistress beamed up at her former pupil, asking, "And what of the statues, Miranda? I can see that's why you are here. You fear for them. What do I not know?"

Miranda swallowed hard. "Well, ma'am," she started, but hesitated, unsure of what to say. She calmed herself, collecting her thoughts. She restarted with more poise. "I'm afraid my parents' souls are trapped within these statues. They are made of crystalized mana, much like the stones powering strange, new weapons wielded by slavers working for The Frozen Death." She shook her head. "I'm functioning under the assumption whatever happened to my parents is happening to dragon eggs around the kingdom. The shards of the Dragon Father and Dragon Mother are beginning to disappear from the arcane stream. My parents were the first to vanish, and this is what's become of them."

The headmistress made another imperceptible dash from the door to the statues. Evan's eyes jittered with disbelief as he tried to keep sight of the headmistress, but he was certain he could only see her after-images. She reached out and touched the petrified forms and hummed some words. She cycled her breath. Her eyes closed, and she radiated energy. Miranda walked across the room, moving around the sofa Evan had slept on. She watched as the headmistress did something to her parents. She trusted the monk deeply, but she still felt uncomfortable.

The statues glowed with a bright, pink aura. The light flickered off the walls in the sitting room, and Evan and Miranda had to cover their eyes. A buzzing sound radiated from the headmistress and the statues, the pink light enveloping the monk as well. After a few minutes, the sound and the light faded. Evan stood within arm's length of the headmistress, reaching out to keep her from stumbling backwards out of the bay window.

The headmistress's eyes shot open, her body wobbling from the exertion. "Miranda, there are no souls in these statues. There is a dense concentration of power within them, but that is outside of my understanding. I am very well trained in finding the soul of an entity, however, and I can confidently say that there are no souls within." The headmistress turned to face Miranda, standing a foot above her normal height in the bay window. "I never thought to look before. Had I looked sooner, I don't know what I would have found. It has also been nearly twenty years since then," she said.

Miranda clarified in a small voice, "Seventeen years ago." Evan felt his heart break hearing the tone of her voice. The melody was gone. "Just after this last Solstice."

The headmistress realized she sounded too callous in her generalization. "I know, Miranda. Apologies." She appeared by Miranda's side within the same instant. She took the young woman's hands in hers. "The flow of time changes as you age, and as an elf, I forget how long the years feel to a human. So much of your life spent without your parents is worth counting. Because you count the days you've been strong." She squeezed Miranda's hands, covered by her armored gauntlets. Sharp, sapphire gemstone blades jutted out from under the forearms of the mithril gloves, and they looked deadly. The headmistress held her hands tenderly. "And seventeen years ago, your parents were stolen from us in a cruel way we do not understand. But if the same thing is happening to other dragons, you have a responsibility to uncover the truth."

Miranda nodded in agreement. "That's why the situation in Mystalon needs to be investigated. Ezelbrecht said the Umbrals would be connected to this, too." Her face twitched with intensity. "Argentum wasn't the source of the Umbrals. It has something to do with magic, but I don't know what yet. I just want to make sure my parents' godshards are safe before we depart."

Evan turned toward the statues, then to Miranda. "You made contact with them while you were in the arcane stream, you said?"

The headmistress's expression was contemplative. Miranda looked at her with a small smile, then back to Evan. "When I was trapped in the stream, I came to Devitus. Before we came here to my parents, Dalyn Tyrdrac and I even visited the monastery. I gave Emi quite a shock, and she was the only person who detected me."

The headmistress's eyes widened. "She remembers that day well. She even knew it was you, but she wasn't sure what kind of trick you were playing." The headmistress patted her hands around Miranda's gauntlet-covered fingers. "The monks of Lexcord possess a high degree of spiritual wisdom. The Harbingers train their bodies, but The Hammerfist train our spirits in equal measure." She glanced at the statues. "After you spooked Emi, you came here?"

Miranda tried to hide her emotion. "Yes, and I touched the statues with a body I formed from the ether. I could hear my parents' voices and I felt their presence. I stayed there with them until I awoke on top of the Astral Spire."

Evan inhaled, his mind working quickly. Miranda imagined Erk was similarly imaginative and thoughtful at Evan's age, but Evan had a thirty-year experience deficit compared to his brother. Still, he was as smart as he was strong. He started to think out loud. "When you woke up in the Astral Spire, you went straight into action. You did things with the mana pooled within you nobody would have thought possible."

The headmistress cut her eyes directly to Miranda's. The warpriest frowned as she replied, "Carulus had been transformed into a shadow and Indervill came. I remember. I am just grateful the mana flowed so freely there."

Evan tapped his chin and shook his head. "When you spoke to Indervill, you had three voices. Your own, and two others."

The room sat silent for a moment. Miranda looked at the statues, then to the headmistress, then to Evan. She finally spoke, "I remember that, but it's almost like the whispers I could hear before I understood my power. Like the voices were truly not mine. That was not the mana working within me."

The headmistress smiled as well. Evan added, "So something within you spoke with those voices. Has anything else been different since you made contact with your parents in the stream?" he asked, hoping his hypothesis was correct.

Miranda nodded again. "Ever since then, I've been able to access my mother's memories." A sudden feeling of hope flowed through her. She sensed her father's hand on her cheek like she did months ago in the arcane stream. She felt her mother's will swelling inside her. "Oh, Evan! What did I do?" she asked, fear choking her hope and her voice.

The headmistress hummed again, holding on to Miranda's hands. The pink light filled the room again, and the monk finished her search after only a moment. "You didn't do anything Miranda. Philotrax and Reshiria, did." The headmistress reached up, touching Miranda's breastplate near her heart. "They've hidden themselves here. Dormant and waiting."

Evan's eyes lit up. "That's why you have your mother's memories then!" he exclaimed. "You carry their godshards with you!"

Miranda blinked dubiously. "It would make sense if I also had my father's memories," she looked back at the statue. "But I only have my mother's."

The headmistress's lips softened into a caring smile. "I knew your father very well, child. You've become more like him than you realize. People were drawn to him for many reasons."

Miranda swallowed hard. She had felt more confident in recent months. She thought it was because her faith in Invictus had shaped her into someone fighting to make the world a better, safer place. Channeling the divine essence of the gods could be taxing on one's body and life essence. Since emerging from the arcane stream, she found she could easily wield stronger prayers. If she had three spirits within her, it's no wonder that her individual power had increased so rapidly over the last year. "They promised they would stay with me. Is this what they meant?"

Evan felt caught up in Miranda's emotions. His own father was murdered by the usurper, and his mother died protecting him from Gelidor's curse. He would protect his own parents' spirits with all his might if he found he held them within his own essence. He was happy for her, giving comforting words, "I think that's a beautiful way to see it, Miranda. And for you to learn their godshards are within you means you can treat their statues as a treasure to keep safe. But it's a large treasure, and quite heavy."

The headmistress remained stoic, and Miranda chewed her lip nervously. She then composed herself and withdrew her hands from the headmistress. "Evan?" she asked.

He did not speak but replied with an affirming nod.

She continued, "Can you warn dad and Erk that I'm sending them something?" She felt intense relief filling her essence. Her parents' souls were safe. She didn't understand how she took their godshards, but she thanked Invictus they were tucked away with her own soul. She treasured the statues, as well, since they were the most concrete representation she had of them. If they could be used to power the clockwork weapons, she didn't want people pursuing the mana contained within them.

Evan replied, "Of course. Where are you planning on sending the statues?"

Miranda's smile turned playful. "A pirate should keep their best treasures on their ship. I'll send them to the dressing room on The Neb."

Her smile was contagious, spreading to Evan. He answered, "Brilliant idea. I'll get the coordinates from brother." He winked and then pressed both of his hands to his temples. Talking to Damil and the others like this felt strange, but it was better than waiting on messenger birds.

Damil's voice pushed back in response to Evan's call. "That was a quick decision!"

Evan felt Selasine and Naomi's minds present after a moment. The high priest thought out, "Nulestotejin. Do you have news?"

Evan thought back, "Miranda wishes to send the statues of her parents to you on *The Nebula*. I think she's going to use her gift. What is the location of the ship?"

There was a brief silence, but Selasine's consciousness returned a moment later. "We've rounded Cape Ember. The volcano can be seen from here." Worry emanated from all minds present.

Naomi's voice added, "Tell her to put them in the dressing room. And, please, be careful with her gift."

Evan replied, "If all goes well, it should be on board within a few minutes. She's decided we will head for Mystalon in response to the Fernith brother's petition." Though it was not customary, any priest, cleric, or paladin of Invictus could respond to petitions for the church's aid. This policy allowed individuals within the church to vet petitions for their seriousness if higher officers did not want to mobilize a formal investigation.

Evan felt three sighs of relief. Selasine thought, "Tell her we'll be there in four days' time. If she sends the statues, do not let her try to teleport you to Mystalon." There was a pause. "Erk insists that is an order."

Evan laughed. "You come tell her what to do, that's not in my bag of tricks. I will keep her safe, however. That's a promise. We'll be in contact as we travel." His thoughts felt playful but sincere.

Damil's nod was apparent in their minds. He could maintain telepathic communication for a while, but it was exhausting. With the volume of messages he expected daily, he preferred to keep group contact short. "Give her all our regards," he thought, closing the telepathy.

Evan opened his eyes and shared the conversation with Miranda and the headmistress. The warpriest stepped up into the bay window, looking at the statues. She closed her eyes and felt the overabundance of mana in the room. The lingering magic from last night was enough to teleport the statues a dozen times. She hoped this wouldn't even change her hair color. She visualized the dressing room on *The Nebula*. She tried to see the world through Erk's eyes, the ether spilling from her. She couldn't hear his thoughts, but she could see a volcano off the port side and open sea to the starboard. They were making excellent time if they had only been traveling for a night. The mana poured faster as she concentrated on the statues of her parents. At one point, she teleported an entire fleet of ships from the Sea of Undine to their home port of Beriton. Two statues would hardly require as much mana, but she had a diminished capacity now. She had faith in her god, the power within her, and her friends. She inhaled, making the final push to shape the universe to her will. A bright purple light burst from her, the aura spilling down the hallways of the estate, out of the windows, and it was visible from all over Devitus.

As the light cleared, the statues were gone. Evan and the headmistress stood motionless, watching Miranda carefully. She stretched out her arms. Her hair remained its normal shade of red. She turned around, smiling. She took her time, calculated the mana requirements precisely, and she was alright. The extra mana left in the air replenished the pools within her.

After a moment, Damil sent Evan a thought confirming the statues were on board *The Nebula* safely. Miranda beamed, but then her eyes narrowed. "We have a mission now, headmistress. I am sorry I could not stay longer to visit, but we must depart for Mystalon with haste."

The headmistress gave her a sweet smile. "I knew it would be a short visit, Miranda. May the Silver Maiden protect you on your way."

Miranda looked at Evan. "We should alert the cousins of the situation right away."

He agreed and reached out to the headmistress. She gave him a firm handshake, grabbing his forearm just short of his elbow. He smiled, saying, "Again, it's been a pleasure. I hope this morning's events won't interfere with the students' learning today. Be wary of Umbrals and dragon eggs."

The headmistress returned his pleasant tone. "I shall, Evanthalus." She looked at her former pupil. "And you." She hugged the warpriest, squeezing her. "Keep using that sharp mind and that unbridled spirit together. I'm proud of you."

Miranda's eyes shimmered as she felt tears welling. "Thank you, headmistress." She started to walk toward the door, adding, "We can lock this room back up, right?"

"I will," the monk replied.

Evan joined Miranda in the hallway, the headmistress still waiting within the room. Miranda waved gently, "See you soon, headmistress!"

The orange ponytail bobbed up and down, "Of course. See you soon, Miranda." After the priestess was out of earshot, the headmistress looked at the floor. "I just hope you will forgive me."

As they walked down the dirt road from Miranda's estate toward town, they met Celyth, Arlindra, and Yuvina on their way toward the mansion. The purple light all over town got their attention, and they feared there might have been danger. Evan and Miranda ran toward them, and the cousins and the foxkin stopped walking. Miranda waved as she approached, and Evan stayed a step behind her. They met on the path about three hundred feet away from Miranda's estate, close to the roads leading back into town. Most of the trees were barren in the deep of winter, and the bustling marketplace was barely visible on the other side of a dense thicket another thousand feet away.

Celyth spoke as they approached, "Was it a good fight at least? I'm going to be really mad if I wasn't invited to a good fight."

Miranda laughed. "No, nothing of the sort. I sent the statues of my parents to Evan's brother, Erk. They should be safe on his ship. And their godshards," she said with a pause. "As far as I understand, I think I have their godshards within my own essence now. It's why I have my mother's memories and my father's confidence. If that was the case, why didn't Ezelbrecht just tell me that? They can see the shards!"

Arlindra's eyes narrowed as she replied. "Perhaps they wanted to be coy and guide you to the answer in the most inconvenient way." Nebu was perched on her right shoulder, his dragonfly-like wings buzzing and twitching.

Yuvina felt out of place, but Miranda's promise to help restore her memories kept the foxkin close to the cousins. Last night over dinner, they connected on a personal level, but she ultimately knew she had no place among these people with incredible powers. Her tasks lay in the shadows, surveying and understanding people like these adventurers. The more information she could gather, the more she could report to The Forgotten. For now, she remained silent, watching.

Miranda speculated, "I think Ezelbrecht wanted me to test the statues of my parents. Crystalized magic powers the weapons, and my mother's statue overcharged and destroyed one of Evan's daggers. It's a fair conclusion that whatever is happening to the eggs is what happened to my parents." She stood at attention after she finished speaking.

Celyth lost interest and began daydreaming. Evan said, "And the Church of Invictus made contact with me this morning."

Arlindra asked, "Is there news, then?"

Miranda looked between her friends. "Your fathers have petitioned the church for help with the Umbrals."

Nebu stood, his tiny dragon legs stretching. "I had a feeling they were gonna do that!"

Celyth's attention snapped back to the conversation. "You said Dad did what? Asked for help?"

Miranda nodded. "They filed a formal petition to my dad in Nulodia. The high priest. And he's on his way to Mystalon right now!" she said, excitement building in her voice.

Nebu's wings started to buzz, and he hovered close to Arlindra's face. Celyth frowned in thought, and Yuvina listened with anxiety. Arlindra broke the hesitation in conversation. "We should return, too, then. Finding Argentum has been a fruitless endeavor, after all." She sighed, feeling helpless.

Miranda noticed the elf's discouragement, reaching out to touch her left shoulder. "I didn't realize it, but last year I left from Devitus toward the east. I was with an army. We rode right by Mystalon! I bet with your guidance, we could reach your home in just a few days' time." She smiled, casting a glance to Celyth. "I would gladly accompany you to your homeland and give my best effort to solve the Umbral crisis."

Arlindra looked at her new friend. They had known her for such a short time, but she enthusiastically volunteered to help at every turn. The ranger's disheartened face shifted, a rare smile gracing her lips. Evan interrupted to add, "And where she goes, I go. My brother and his betrothed are also on their way to Mystalon. They fear Farzg may somehow be involved."

Celyth replied, "If you can keep up, cousin can get us there in five days."

Arlindra glared at Celyth, "Three days if you can keep up, four if you can't. Five if you're really lazy and make me take care of camp duties." She turned back to Miranda. "I am worried about my father and uncle. They have risked their lives by petitioning the church. The Sages will not take kindly to outsiders being invited to solve Mystalonian problems."

Yuvina yipped, more out of impulse than anything else. "Tradition and authority create prideful leaders that would sooner see their kingdoms burn than to admit weakness. Your fathers are truly wise to seek outside help, even though that puts them in danger."

Arlindra inhaled with concern, looking at Yuvina. "I am proud of him. And I'm not going to continue with a fool's errand while the other Sages plot against him. We should leave right away."

Miranda also looked at Yuvina. "If you wish to return to Nulodia, I would gladly pay to have you escorted—"

Yuvina stopped her with a playful growl. "But my memories? I need to know where I have been this last month. That you found me on Olvidado only fuels my suspicions I was meant to travel with you for a time. If you'll allow it, I would like to journey to Mystalon with you."

Celyth put a hand on the foxkin's shoulder. "Of course, foxy. I want to hear more stories like last night. The Tymbyrwylde sounds like a place I'd like to visit."

Yuvina giggled and knocked Celyth's hand off her shoulder. "I told you not to call me that," she protested, but did not seem angry. In truth, Yuvina was also shocked. In her experience, people with powers of this magnitude were usually arrogant and self-serving. She had documented thousands of them and their misdeeds for The Forgotten. These adventurers were unconcerned with her powers, and they granted her trust with little hesitation. Learning of Miranda's heritage intrigued Yuvina, and she planned to keep her lack of powers secret as long as possible. Miranda's determination to help her regain her memories earned the priestess Yuvina's skeptical trust. The kitsune needed to understand why they would even want to help her.

Arlindra punched her fists together, and Nebu blurted out, "You can ask them not to call you something, but that's only going to make it worse!" He zoomed a circle around Arlindra's head and landed in her hair.

Miranda brought everyone back to the matter, saying, "Then it's decided, we'll travel together. We have no time to waste then. On to Mystalon."

Miranda and Evan quickly understood what Celyth and Arlindra meant by "keeping up." Arlindra was capable of finding routes through the densest parts of forests and up and down impossible ridges. Yuvina was at home moving through the wilderness southeast of Devitus. Evan and Miranda struggled, but they were persistent. Miranda even used a prayer to boost their endurance for the journey. After traveling all day without rest, they stopped shortly after the sun had set.

They made camp under a rock formation with a shallow cave. It was ten feet deep, but the ceiling sloped up and out like a cone. The area was an outcropping on a ridge above a forested area to the southeast. Another ridge stood above this one, making the area easy to protect from magical beasts and other threats.

Celyth felt uneasy as she built a small fire just outside the shelter of the cave. "Cousin," she said.

Arlindra nodded but said nothing more. Evan and Miranda traded glances. They were rolling out their sleeping mats in the cave. Yuvina sniffed, sitting nearby the kindling fire. The foxkin added, "She's right."

Evan tilted his head. "Right about what?"

Yuvina growled a bit. "We're being followed. I can smell them. Elf. Female."

Miranda beamed. "Your senses are incredible, Yuvina!" She closed her eyes and spun the mana within her. She shaped it to enhance her own sense of smell. As she opened her eyes, she also sniffed the air, but it was an immediate overload, causing her to scream in surprise.

Celyth and Arlindra both drew their weapons. Evan's eyes cut to Miranda, but he saw nothing apparent. Miranda pinched her nose and moved quickly toward the fire. She dismissed the spell right away. "By Invictus, that hurt! How do you handle so many scents all at once?" she asked, the music in her voice curious and excited. The cousins rolled their eyes and shouldered their bows.

Yuvina looked up at Miranda with a puzzled expression. "What do you mean?"

Miranda sat beside her. "I know I was really vague explaining things earlier, but my parents were dragons trapped in human form after The Unbinding. They were somehow turned into statues of crystalized magic, which is what I sent to *The Nebula* earlier today."

Yuvina's nose twitched. "And what does that have to do with scents?"

Celyth and Arlindra rummaged through their supplies for food. Evan had taken out a small prayer book and was reading comfortably in the dim light bouncing off the back of the cave. Miranda looked at Yuvina, still pinching her nose. It made her voice nasally. "I don't have an Unbinding power like most other people. The arcane stream flows and pools within my essence. I can shape the power to do almost anything." She let go of her nose and giggled. "I tried to use my power to enhance my sense of smell like I do my eyes. I can see in the dark like a dragon. But I tried to smell the world as you do, and it hurt."

Yuvina's maw opened in disbelief. "Why would you want to smell the world like I do?"

Miranda smiled at her as she had so many others, but for some reason her innocence and wonder did nothing to garner Yuvina's openness. The kitsune was reserved, and Miranda could sense deep sadness in her tale. Miranda thought back to the moment on Olvidado the day before, when she touched Yuvina and it created magical sparks. She finally replied, "Because I want to understand you better." Her own voice was firmer than she expected, realizing a soft approach would not work.

Yuvina closed her mouth after a moment. She sniffed again and turned her eyes to the fire. "You learn how to make sense out of what you smell over time. It's like learning to see with your nose, that's all."

Miranda inhaled. She stirred the magic in her again, recreating a simple spell wizards once used to see the arcane stream. Erk described the spell as a necessary tool for all magic users, but since

The Unbinding, the stream's flow had been hidden from the view of most mortals. Miranda, however, could use the idea of the spell to shape the mana. As she peered into the ebb and flow of magic, she saw five distinct strands of mana flowing through Yuvina. She looked at Evan, seeing only a faint stream flowing through him in the cave. That was the connection all living creatures had with the arcane stream, and it was particularly strong for elves. The cousins each had a single, bright strand flowing through them as they sat in the cave now, snacking on some pecans Arlindra gathered as they traveled that day. The strength of that flow indicated the two possessed powerful arcane gifts. The warpriest looked at Yuvina, "The mana flows through you differently than everyone else."

Yuvina's eyes tore from the fire to Miranda. "What do you mean?"

Miranda's lips tightened. "You said you've lost your memory of the last month, but what do you remember before that?"

Yuvina fixated on the fire again as fear swelled in her stomach. How could the stream flow through her? What happened in this last month? She worried for her own safety, and she decided to be forthcoming. "I don't understand what you mean about the stream. I was born without an Unbinding power. I belong to an organization of people who are unable to reach the arcane."

Miranda felt the honesty in Yuvina's tone. "What is your organization's mission?"

Yuvina's eyes returned to Miranda with a bit of disdain. "To cure our affliction, of course."

Miranda remembered a time when she thought she had no uncanny magic. She looked at the fire for a moment, then back to the foxkin. "Affliction? You see your lack of magic as an illness?" She instinctively turned to look at Evan.

Yuvina gave a swift, single nod. "Why else would people treat us as if we are sick? Or look down on us for our lack of Unbinding." She felt herself getting emotional, but she continued speaking, "Or you're so powerless that you can do nothing but stand and watch as your family is murdered before you." Her words started to waver as tears filled her eyes.

The warpriest's expression melted into sympathetic concern. "Oh, Yuvina. I'm so sorry." This was the sorrow Miranda, Judge of Hearts felt as she spoke to the foxkin. She estimated Yuvina had already heard that people with gifts are often powerless, and she knew that conversation would yield nothing but frustration. Instead, she focused on an uplifting way to approach the subject. "You may not think so, but I can see you have a power within you. Something that can only come from who you are and what you've been through."

Yuvina already knew where this lecture would go, however. For a moment, she thought Miranda might be different. If the warpriest had a power as incredible as she described, she could never understand what it meant to be completely powerless. Instead, Yuvina found herself shocked as Miranda continued. "You've learned how to survive when the rest of the world is against you. People with wicked hearts are even crueler to those who they perceive as weak or lesser. The fact that Invictus has not addressed discrimination faced by people born without uncanny magic is an oversight."

The foxkin blinked in disbelief. "Wait, what?" Nobody had ever acknowledged her weakness, nor had they acknowledged the failures of institutions to help The Forgotten in their social struggles.

Miranda nodded, her braids now in terrible condition. She sighed and pulled the sapphire comb from the back of her hair. She began to undo her braids as she continued speaking. "I mean it! You've got a survival strength not many people would find going through what you've been through. You're still fighting."

Yuvina's jaw slacked, and the foxkin watched as Miranda combed out the tangles from her unraveling braids. "If everyone thought like you, we might not need secret organizations to protect ourselves."

Miranda tilted her head a bit as she combed, dried leaves having somehow matted between twists of hair. She really should have covered it or tied it back like Celyth. She responded, "I know I don't speak for everyone, but I try to weigh the truths of people's hearts. I can see that yours is broken, and I understand why. If society has failed you, it's because Invictus has failed you. After we solve this problem with the Umbrals in Mystalon, would you like to meet with my dad?" She managed to get the leaves out of her hair by the time she made the offer.

Yuvina sat speechless. Who was this woman boasting such great power and yet immense gentleness? How could she be the first Wielder Yuvina ever met who acknowledged the struggles of the weak and the failures of the strong? Her whiskers twitched, and tears soaked into the fur on her cheeks. On top of careening into danger for the cousins, she was already planning a way to bring Yuvina's complaints before a high-ranking member of an organization that had largely ignored the pleas of The Forgotten. "What do you stand to gain from such charity?" she asked.

Miranda blinked and made eye contact with Yuvina. "I get to live in a better world where all people are treated with dignity and respect. I get to be surrounded by happy people who feel safe, and I get the honor of being one of the peacekeepers that keeps them safe." She resumed combing the tangles out of the other braid.

Yuvina wasn't sure what to say. Her answer was so candid, the foxkin decided she trusted Miranda. "Thank you."

Miranda smiled, but then she poked her tongue out of her mouth up toward her nose. She found a particularly tangled clump in her hair. Her eyes crossed as she pulled the hair in front of her, trying to focus her strength on her grooming. After a few brutal pulls, the tangle let free. Miranda then smiled again. "There's no need to thank me. I know that it's naïve, but I would hope somebody would fight for me if I felt powerless. Actually," she paused. "I didn't know I had any kind of power until just last year. I found joy in just helping in any way that I could, but I lived in Devitus. As you saw, it's not really a dangerous environment. A little hard work is a power of its own on the frontier," she explained.

Yuvina's whiskers trembled. She sniffed the air again. Something had changed. "Miranda," the kitsune interrupted.

"Yes?" the warpriest replied, blinking.

"Move!" Yuvina shouted and jumped so her legs were perched beneath her. In an agile, standing motion, she scooped Miranda off the ground and dove forward. As their bodies connected, magical sparks sprayed in all directions. Not even a full second after Yuvina moved Miranda, a blast of fire exploded where the warpriest had been sitting. It washed out in a sphere, filling the air with magical flames.

Evan, Celyth, and Arlindra jumped to attention. They had not settled in for sleep yet, thankfully. This time, the cousins drew their bows with purpose. Evan drew his clockwork sword and dagger, the lights in them whirring with energy. As the Fireball cleared, they saw Miranda and Yuvina on the fringes of the blast zone. Fortunately, the magical fire did not spread. The targets evaded the majority of the heat, and Miranda's armor shielded her as well. Yuvina stayed in motion, doing a somersault to return upright. The sparks ceased after she broke contact with Miranda.

Evan ran forward, scanning the darkness for signs of movement. The winter moons were still bright even though they were waning. He couldn't see anything, though. There was a ridge opposite the cave, and an attacker would have any number of vantage points if they were skilled enough to navigate the terrain.

Celyth and Arlindra prepared to fire magitab flare arrows. The light would disorient an attacker relying on sight, they hoped. They shot toward the ridge at different angles, causing magical, bright light to illuminate the campsite and surrounding area. A rocky path descended into a heavily wooded area to the left of the cave. Arlindra chose this space due to its defensibility, especially with somebody trailing them all day. The interloper would have to confront the group at their own peril.

Miranda stood, giving Yuvina a bewildered look. Instead of fear or surprise, Miranda only marveled. "Yuvina! You're incredible! Did you see!" she continued, losing her composure in excitement. "You saved both of us!"

For some reason, Yuvina couldn't help but smile. Nobody had ever reacted that way to her saving them, either. "Be wary!" she yipped.

Miranda nodded. She had left her tower shield in the cave. They were exposed to another assault, but even with the flare arrows lighting the ridge, she could make out no attacker. She gripped her holy symbol and prayed, "Sword of Justice, hear my voice. Your faithful are at the mercy of the unjust. Surround the enemy with your holy fire. Rain down your judgment!"

After she recited the curse, a pillar of purple fire ignited around a tree on the ridge. It spiraled fifty feet into the air, as if the essence of Invictus manifested a finger of flame, both burning and giving away the location of a presumed assailant. The purple flames enhanced the eerie glow shed by the flares. The entire crevice was lit brighter than day.

Evan sprang into action, but he sheathed his weapons. He coordinated his sprint by bounding almost side-to-side, running sixty feet from the cave to the ridge, and then he jumped. He leapt onto a low hanging branch of a large evergreen tree, but during his next bound, he turned his body sideways with his left side parallel to the ground. His feet planted firmly onto the trunk of the next tree in his path. He converted his momentum into an upward leap that allowed him to grab a branch hanging ten feet higher in the air. With a swift kick, he propelled himself back and then forward, launching himself onto the ridge in a salto. By the time he landed, the purple flames had burned out. The tree was unscathed, but a figure stepped out from behind it. They were covered in a distinguishing aura of purple, which Evan assumed was a result of the curse. They matched Yuvina's estimate of the stalker from today; it looked to be a feminine elf slightly shorter than Evan. She wore a bodysuit which covered her from neck to toe. A dark cloak draped over her shoulders, giving her a menacing silhouette.

The cloak billowed with sudden movement as she sprinted toward Evan, prompting him to draw his weapons. She hissed, "Target confirmed." Then, a flash of light beamed from the cloaked figure's hand. Evan struck the light with his dagger by swiping it in front of him. The magical enhancement of the blade deflected the magic force following the light. A surge of excitement filled him with boldness, and he returned the assailant's charge. As they neared striking distance, the mysterious figure leapt through the air with an acrobatic maneuver, spinning her body horizontally with unbelievable agility. As she did, Evan saw the rain of daggers only a moment before they reached him. He parried furiously, his muscle memory and coordination connected from recent training with Naomi. The attacker hit the ground with poor form, rolling toward the edge of the ridge. Evan redirected his momentum with a tumble of his own, jumping back toward the attacker.

He heard a shriek as he closed in on her location. He hesitated enough that he caught a glimpse of her teal eyes shimmering with intrigue in the flare light. A flash of lightning discharged from the assailant catching Evan off guard. He took the bolt straight to his body, blasting him backwards twenty feet into a rock wall.

As the cloaked attacker stood, seven loud plinks knocked her forward, causing her to fall from the force. Her magical armor shielded her from the razor-sharp arrows' most lethal effects. Arlindra and Celyth looked at each other with cocky smiles. Arlindra said, "I hit her four times."

Celyth's lip twitched. "Quality is better than quantity anyway. Mine hit center mass."

Yuvina scrambled up the side of the ridge, using her agility and paws to balance precariously in places as needed.

Miranda started running toward the ridge when Evan did, but he was so swift that by the time she arrived at the base, she heard the lightning crackle above. She snarled with protective instinct, and the mana within her propelled her into flight right up the side of the ridge. She took off just after the volley of arrows shattered into the attacker's armor. As Miranda arrived at the top, she drew her sword and swiftly overtook the cloaked figure on the ground.

The assailant turned toward Miranda, surprised at the arrival of a new enemy. Miranda's blade was in her face before she could manage a counterattack. The assassin shouted, "Stop, priest!"

Miranda's face quivered with rage. She recited an advanced version of the binding curse, hoping it would immobilize an enemy with a powerful will. "Reality is composed of beautiful form imposed by creators of order. As we weave this tapestry of life, the threads of disorder threaten to ruin the stitching of the faithful. Bind that which sews chaos!" she yelled.

Red tendrils flashed into existence around the cloaked figure. She squirmed against them, but as she struggled, pain surged through her body. She had faced priests capable of such curses before, but usually the tendrils broke due to her extraordinary presence. Faith was a weak weapon, she thought. The flashes of pain, however, caused her to stop struggling for a moment. Whoever this priestess was, Elyndandria had underestimated her greatly. The advanced curse was unexpected. Still, the assassin could endure pain if needed. She could not afford to be bound and questioned. Her struggle resumed with intensity.

Miranda rushed to Evan's side, finding him gasping for air. His magical armor absorbed some of the blast, but the electricity still gave him a grievous injury. With indignation, she prayed, "Restore to order what was damaged by chaos." A swirl of light surrounded his entire body, comforting his pain. The injuries mended with a cold, tingling sensation. Miranda stood, satisfied Evan would be okay, and she returned her gaze to the attacker. The flare arrows began to die down as Yuvina bounded onto the top of the ridge.

In the time it took Miranda to heal Evan, the assailant had broken free of the divine curse. Yuvina drew her daggers, and her tail twitched with anticipation. Miranda held her sword in front of her, approaching cautiously.

The attacker glared, her eyes barely visible now as the darkness covered them. Miranda's enhanced vision resisted the environmental hazards, but the attacker and Yuvina struggled as the flickers in the darkness assaulted their vision. Miranda took that moment to try another divine curse, "Invictus, hide us from the eyes of our enemy. Hamper the vision of chaos; rend them lost in their own darkness."

The world darkened more in Elyndandria's perception, but her mind fought ruthlessly to resist the divine powers surging over her. With a frustrated growl, she activated her uncanny magic. A sonic pulse burst from her as the epicenter, blasting Miranda away from her. As the shockwave hit Yuvina, a ring of glowing orbs formed around the foxkin's waist, spinning with incredible speed. The orbs absorbed the force. Yuvina's eyes widened with disbelief, the magic manifesting around her in a way she did not understand. The orbs whirred, turning bright red. They coalesced into a single beam of white light reflecting onto the attacker, flinging her into the same rock wall as Evan. She crashed with enough force to shatter the entire ridge above, causing chunks to cave in on her.

Yuvina stood in awe, looking at her paws. She felt an energy leave her body, but she was not sure what caused it to happen. She thought about what Miranda said about the stream flowing through her differently. Was she correct all those years ago about the stress of combat bringing out her Unbinding? Who was this Miranda, and how did she understand her so easily? It made no sense for a power to manifest now, not when she had been in mortal danger so many times. Something had to have happened in the last month, but she couldn't remember.

The pile of rocks over the assassin shattered with another concussive blast showering debris over Miranda as she lay prone and Yuvina as she stood near the edge of the ridge. Evan was safely tucked beside a rock that shielded him from the attacker's blast. Dust wafted into his face as he sat up, his body quickly recovering thanks to Miranda's prayer. He coughed but gripped his weapons tightly in his hands.

As stones pelted Miranda, she covered her head with her armored hands. Justin had insisted she start wearing a helmet, but she didn't like how it felt. She wore the braids of a healer for a reason, but in this moment, she felt tension in her core. She had been averse to violence in the past, and she even hesitated to kill the usurper of Claston. But now she understood violence would be necessary to protect herself and her friends. She let a cruel thought rise in her mind. She could not be a healer when working against forces so vile. She needed to know what this attacker's intentions were, who sent them, and why. She struggled to shape the mana into a psychic attack targeting this assailant's memories. She wanted to see them as clearly as she could her mother's when they surfaced.

A beam of purple light surged from Miranda, still shielding herself from rocks. It enveloped the attacker, still buried underneath some rubble. As it connected, it glowed brighter. This individual's willpower was incredible by all accounts. Miranda felt the enemy's mind push back, and she reflected on the previous struggles she had with mind-affecting magic. Her own presence was previously meek, but over recent months, her confidence grew. Her will surged harder, using the sheer psychic weight of the mana to obliterate the attacker's willpower. The pushback demanded greater quantities of ether to overcome, and Miranda's hair began to turn pink. She kept forcing her will, however, and her hair lightened at an alarming rate. The mental block she felt crumbled, and she invaded the attacker's mind with righteous fury.

Echo handed Elyndandria the official contract of extermination. Evanthalus Lancethinas and companions. Identified recently by Reginald the Scholar, Doctor Thirteen. They were in Devitus, and by the time Elyndandria's teleportation device arrived, the quarry had already moved southeast. She had several wands and tricks at her disposal, but the tools the doctors gave her were incredible. She had made over one hundred marks in the last season and had accumulated so much wealth, but she could not stop killing. Not until she found Veronica.

Miranda kept trying to sift through the attacker's memories while she was inside her mind. Elyndandria was her name? She was chasing them on behalf of this Echo? No, Echo had to be some kind of intermediary. Who was Veronica? Furthermore, who would want to take out an assassination contract on Evan? Farzg? Eldon Farzg? Why?! Elyndandria's mind did not have all of the answers Miranda wanted, but she found enough information to understand the nature of this assassin's mission.

While Miranda was bound to Elyndandria's mind, the warpriest realized she was losing consciousness. She pushed the mana too far, and she was about to pay the price. The elf's thoughts became mentally audible. "You're lucky you're more gifted than Farzg estimated. I can see you looking where you shouldn't be looking, priest. Your own god should curse you for such vileness."

Miranda's returned thoughts were scattered, but they teemed with uncharacteristic hostility. "Let's pay for our crimes together, then. Who are you? Why are you—are you here? When did you meet Reginald?" She lost consciousness before she could listen for answers.

Evan and Yuvina pulled the assassin's body out of the rocks. She seemed lifeless, but so did Miranda. Evan set a solisberry bloom under her tongue, then he put another in her mouth after it dissolved. The cousins joined them on the ridge, waiting patiently as Miranda recovered from her incredible exertion.

As everyone's focus was on Miranda, the cloaked assassin regained consciousness. She was thankful Farzg paid her for a previous mark with a ring granting her rapid regeneration. When she was sure she had the strength to retreat, she did so with surety and swiftness. By the time Miranda's companions reacted, Elyndandria was gone.

This mark was worth ten times the bounty she was offered. Farzg had nearly gotten her killed by sending her after a misleading quarry, and he had much to answer for.

Lexcord and Invictus were in the primordial place, listening to the prayers and supplications of their followers. A premonition rippled throughout the golden and gray clouds before them, and in it, they could see Aylabrax walking alongside an elven mortal. They radiated dark energy, the volume of which pushed into the primordial place and disrupted the vision.

Though the dimension of the gods was a metaphysical space with flexibility in manifestation, the Siblings of Order preferred the shapes of their mortal avatars.

Invictus drew his sword. "Sister," he said in a deep, foreboding voice. His dark skin glimmered in the light reflected from the golden and gray clouds surrounding them. The numerous braids in his hair shook with dissatisfaction. "The Lady in Mourning is complicating this conflict. Her presence should be mitigated."

"I see it too, brother," Lexcord replied. "Aylabrax has gone too long unchecked in the mortal coil." She pulled a hammer off a clip on her belt. "I should go. Your church is at war," she reasoned.

He shook his head. "Your followers are more numerous. My faithful should be safe with you, sister, if you would be so kind to grant their prayers in my stead." He smiled with confidence.

Lexcord's silver hair whipped around her face as she concentrated on her brother's followers, creating a gust in the primordial clouds. Though her own faithful numbered in the millions, Invictus's purview of law and order gained him significantly fewer followers. Those who walked the Path of the Sword of Justice were focused on acting in the name and spirit of their deity. She nodded and replied, "Of course, Invictus. Though, if you cannot find success quickly, you should return, and we should trade places."

Invictus agreed, "Your holy light would certainly extinguish her darkness, but I would not risk harm befalling the Silver Maiden. Let me intervene for now. I fear her plans are escalating."

Lexcord's lips drew up into a grim expression. "And none of our followers near the conflict are even aware of her proximity."

As she spoke, they felt the pressure of the arcane stream weighing on the primordial dimension. Invictus looked around, his long, black braids following the tilt of his head. "Tyrdrac?" he asked.

The sorcerer replied, "It's me, and I bring horrible news. Within the last couple of days, the stream has thinned noticeably." His voice permeated the primordial place. "I still have no idea what's causing the stream to bleed, though."

Lexcord's grimace grew darker as she replied, "The dragons. Can you see the dragons in the stream?"

Tyrdrac paused before replying, "Not really. That's more likely something you could expect from Miranda," he explained. "My grandfather was a dragon, but I don't have the same kind of connection as she does."

Invictus frowned. Miranda was well-known by the Siblings of Order. Her name, however, continued to grow in importance as the current conflict unfolded. "Miranda," he whispered, and the clouds swirled before him. He saw her and her companions as they approached the borders of Mystalon. "She is far from Aylabrax, at least. The Lady in Mourning is in the Dundoi region."

Lexcord protested, however, "Was Miranda not just in the Dundoi region herself?"

Tyrdrac interrupted, "She's not hard to keep up with from the arcane stream, the whole thing flows through her." He provided no physical avatar to interact with the deities, but his presence was clear and known. "You might not have noticed, but she went to Olvidado. I've been following her since we met and she's easy for me to find." There was a pause. "Well, it's the most entertainment I've had in a century. You can't blame me. I'm not being creepy, I swear."

The deities remained silent, returning their focus to the clouds showing them the past as easily as the present. As they began to look through Evan and Miranda's memories, the green, viscous liquid beneath them bubbled up into the clouds. They witnessed everything from Miranda's departure from Olvidado through the present in only a matter of moments. Invictus and Lexcord traded glances. The Sword of Justice spoke, "Aylabrax used Devour on the kitsune and left a portion of her unholy power inside the foxkin's mind. I insist that I go now, as justice must be dealt."

Lexcord's face became fearful. "Brother, let me go first. I will see to the kitsune immediately, and then I will hunt for Aylabrax in the Dundoi region. The fox must be healed before something tragic happens."

Tyrdrac reinserted himself, "Um, but something tragic is happening and it's happening fast. The stream, right?"

Invictus closed his brown eyes. "Then my mission is all the more required. Sister?" he said with an interrogative tone that sounded bittersweet.

Lexcord tilted her head to the side. "What of the foxkin?"

Invictus gave her a pointed, assured look as he spoke. "I have faith in my followers, just as they have faith in me. Miranda is miraculous; I know that she can defeat what is left of Aylabrax, as I can pour more of my own divinity through her essence than was left behind by the Lady in Mourning."

Lexcord understood. "Very well," she replied, giving a single nod. "I will answer her prayers in your stead, as well as every other. The Sword of Justice will walk among mortals for a time, a dangerous sign."

Tyrdrac repeated, "Still, if you don't stop the stream from bleeding, magic could see serious consequences." Both of the deities snapped their attention to the arcane presence around them, incredulous. The sorcerer continued, "I know I'm not one to talk, but I just don't want to see it get worse. I feel responsible," he lamented.

Lexcord gave a harsh glare. "And you are, Tyrdrac. Hopefully we find answers in pursuit of Aylabrax."

Invictus donned a golden, radiant helmet. It glinted in the light of the primordial place, contrasting with his dark skin and hair. His broad features scrunched into a judgmental look of concern. "Keep your eyes on the girl, Tyrdrac. I have a feeling the answers we all seek are centered around Miranda. I just hope my intervention will even the odds in favor of our faithful." As he finished speaking, a glowing, golden circle opened beneath the Sword of Justice. Sparkles of white light sublimated into the air as wisps, flickering up ten feet before dissipating into nothingness. "I will be in the prime dimension within a day."

Invictus fell into the circle of light, prompting Lexcord to close her eyes. "Farewell for now, brother. I, too, will pray for your safety."

Tyrdrac gave an exasperated sigh. "My entire life, I struggled to understand how mortals have faith in you gods. But I see why it works now."

Lexcord's attention returned primarily to the voices of her and her brother's followers. "Why is that, sorcerer?" she murmured in reply.

He answered, "Your faith in them is just as strong. And that is what separates deities of good from those with dark hearts. I'm touched, honestly."

Lexcord simply smiled. Tyrdrac's gradual changes of heart were encouraging to the goddess of truth and beauty. "Keep an eye on them, please?" she repeated. Tyrdrac departed in silence.

Chapter 9
Infernia Unleashed

"Arcane underflow is the byproduct of abusing the blood of Genesis, the arcane stream. By holding magic outside of the flow, a hole is carved into the primary dimension. What would happen if a magical creature's body was used to carve such a hole?" –
Santiago Eb'lin, *The Tears of God*

laric Fernith rolled up a scroll in his hand. The messenger waited patiently until Alaric dismissed him. "Fetch my brother on your way out," he ordered as an afterthought.

The messenger departed in silence, and Alaric's brother, Evander, arrived a few moments later. Alaric was in his study, a modestly sized library full of magical tomes and scholarly texts. The dense forest of Mystalon created a heavily shaded ambiance, and the back of the study had a glass paned window that let in the specks of light finding their way to the surface. Alaric spoke before Evander could close the door, "Three days."

Evander turned to his brother. "You mean to tell me the church made a decision so quickly? They let Claston burn for a century!"

Alaric nodded. "I'm shocked as well. I didn't anticipate such a swift response. We will face backlash for this much sooner than we anticipated."

Evander's face was grim. "The solisberry is lit with energy. Wikton thinks a huge concentration of mana has been dispersed nearby, and the solisberry is drawing it in like a conductor."

Alaric stood. "A discharge of mana? It's been a century since we could do anything more than whatever the universe decides to bless us with. The incantations are ineffective, and magic is difficult to seal within objects. Unless somebody is dispelling an armory of magical weapons, there should be nothing of the sort possible." His face was drawn up with worry as he spoke.

Evander replied, "Any word from the girls?"

Alaric shook his head. "Nebu's last report indicated they found more Umbrals. The warpriest they are traveling with, however, has come into information that dragon eggs are being targeted by smugglers and slavers. An additional elf of Clastonian nobility now travels with them."

Evander nodded. His hair was a soft green, and his purple eyes reflected his growing concern for his daughter and his niece. "Should we warn them the church is going to intervene?"

Alaric looked to his desk for a moment but then stepped around it. "If we tell them, they will be here before the end of the week." He stood face to face with his brother, as they were both just shy of five and a half feet. Alaric's hair and eyes were both a royal blue that looked especially dark in the shadowy lighting. "Besides, the warpriest is the daughter of the high priest who responded to our petition. I don't think that's coincidental, especially considering the prompt answer from Nulodia."

Evander smiled. "So, Celyth really isn't too abrasive to get along with others."

Alaric laughed. "She's a perfect compliment to Arli. If it wasn't for Cel, I don't think my daughter would speak to a soul other than me. Not even her siblings."

Evander was the younger brother at one hundred and twenty-five years. His brother was fifteen years older and had always been a great mentor and friend. The Unbinding happened a decade before Evander reached elven adulthood, and he was proud to be by his brother's side as they rebuilt their reclusive society. Their continued access to magic was thanks to the sacred trees of Espa. The yindai trees were the most numerous, and ether concentrated within the pulp of their fruits. They could be used to make anti-aging creams around most of the world, but in Mystalon, the Sages had discovered how to use them as the base in a magisalve or magitab, the respective names for the liquid and solid manifestations of Mystalonian magic. Furthermore, the oil of the eolnuts was an excellent lubricant for the machinery built by the dwarves of Acero. The Fernith brothers were proud of the discoveries made by entertaining outsiders to their society.

Alaric was one of the former wizards who perfected the process of steeping yinfruit pulp in a solisberry broth. The magic substance was exposed to eolnut several times throughout the process, depending on the spell to be duplicated. Though they could not recreate all magic with their methods, they could at least use it as a tool as they had for centuries before. Alaric was well respected, but he was young compared to the other Sages. They accused him of being too open to foreign ideas, and they were correct. One reason he sent Arlindra and Celyth to the outside for solutions was to expose them to the greater world. Mystalon's future would be bleak if they remained isolated in a time when the world could use their magical technology. By using all natural elements, the Sages were confident that their tinkering with the arcane was just as safe as casting spells as a wizard.

Evander's response broke Alaric out of his thoughts. "You'd think Cel and Arli were siblings if we didn't know better." He laughed. "They're practically twins born a year apart."

Alaric gave his brother a sorrowful smile. "Their bonds are forged in tragedy, much like our own," he replied. He spoke of the loss of Evander's wife and Celyth's mother, Kiriana. She passed from a mysterious illness a couple of years ago, and Celyth struggled to cope with the loss. Alaric placed a hand on his brother's shoulder.

Evander nodded in reply but spoke no more. Sadness swelled within him.

Alaric gestured to the door behind his brother, "Come, let us walk to the arboretum."

They left Alaric's home, continuing their conversation as they walked through the streets of Mystalon. The paths were paved with a smooth stone that glowed in the forest ambiance created by massive trees spanning above them. Before The Unbinding, the founders of Mystalon used magic to build a city deep within the Mystalonian Forest. Like the Tymbyrwylde, the trees here were enormous and ancient, but they were also remarkably different. They did not provide harmonious living spaces, and their teardrop-shaped leaves were not precious. Their trunks towered high into the sky, stretching up at least one hundred feet before the branches even began to form the canopy above. Furthermore, each tree could easily reach fifty feet in diameter, making them both vertically and horizontally imposing. They stayed green year-round thanks to the coastal climate of the region.

The size and majesty of the trees, however, created a unique ecosystem under their branches. The Mystalonian trees grew at least two hundred and fifty feet apart, and many, smaller plants and fungi thrived in the loam created by the never-ending shower of leaves from the canopy above. The forest stretched almost one hundred miles from east to west, and the city of Mystalon was built in the central region. A group of elves departing from Claston far to the east chose this location nearly four hundred years ago based on the concentration of mana in the depths of the forest.

The people of Mystalon organized their city around sixteen Mystalonian trees that grew at the edge of a clearing. An incredible solisberry tree dominated the center of the central glade. Though it was the same size as the Mystalonian trees, the solisberry tree prevented the other, towering vegetation from encroaching upon it. Nevertheless, smaller yindai and eolnut trees grew in abundance among the roots of the solisberry, and they thrived thanks to the ever-flowing, plentiful mana there. To aid their growth, the Mystalonians constructed a massive glass and mithril frame to create an arboretum around the solisberry tree. Within, an incomparable botanical garden blossomed under the purple blooms of the sacred tree. In this somewhat artificial environment, the elves managed to cultivate massive groves of Espa's sacred trees and other plants, and this area received the most sunlight in the entire Mystalonian Forest. Alaric and Evander walked toward that dome from the center from Alaric's home district, Haerulf.

The sixteen Mystalonian trees closest to the solisberry formed a circle around the arboretum. Each tree represented one district, and each district was home to approximately one thousand elves. Every district elected a Sage to represent them, and both Alaric and Evander served their districts as representatives. The buildings in Mystalon were made of stone and wood. Their architecture was magnificent, with ivy and wooden textures dominating the facia and columns of the post-and-lintel entryways. Incredible glass rotundas graced many of the homes, creating an inviting and open feel to the forest city.

Alaric did not look at his brother as they meandered through the city, but he continued the conversation in a hushed tone. "As far as it goes, our daughters are likely to return. They will also be in danger. I estimate we'll hear from Nebu again soon," Alaric said, the street glowing beneath him. "If we are convicted of consorting with outsiders, they will likely pursue Arli and Cel in the same way."

Evander nodded in agreement, walking in pace with his brother. Although they spoke in quiet voices, they still waved cordially to passersby. The Mystalonian social hierarchy required them to be friendly to everyone in public. Public servants were held to an especially high standard, and the Sages were required to be the most economically productive members. Mystalon was a society that functioned without money. Most of the produce and sundries in the marketplace were magically fabricated or enhanced. Citizens took their share as needed, and many of them worked to produce the goods in the first place. Land ownership was granted to families, and strict social rules maintained a balance of privacy and independence. As they approached the arboretum, Evander replied, "Either way, I hope the church can help provide answers. Otherwise, we're putting our necks on the line for no other reason than to shake up Elitirin's coalition. The people in the middle ground will be really pissed off at us. We might even lose Wikton's support." He sighed.

Alaric gulped. Wikton was the only reason that Elitirin's coalition had not managed to oust them from the Congress of Sages. They were chosen by the people in their own districts, but a supermajority of twelve Sages could remove another if they were accused of certain misbehaviors. As the governing body of Mystalon, they often had to interact with outsiders, but it was meant to be done in transparent ways. Elitirin accused the Fernith brothers of consorting with outsiders while she sold some of her family land in exchange for foreign currency. Even with such hypocrisy, Alaric could not unify the Sages against her, nor could she against the Fernith brothers. Wikton, the eldest of the sixteen Sages, had long sensed calamity would befall Mystalon. To exacerbate his fears, when the Umbrals began appearing a couple of months ago, Elitirin began behaving suspiciously. Land on the outer reaches of the forest had little value beyond grazing pasture for the zaligoats, an herbivore that fed on the leaves and bark of the Mystalonian trees. A party of Mystalonian hunters returning from a hunt in the grasslands to the southwest of the forest claimed they had witnessed a massive construction project on outer lands belonging to Elitirin. A return trip to that part of the forest, however, showed no evidence of development. The Fernith brothers thought she was hiding something. So did Wikton. With no visible evidence, the rest of the Sages agreed there was no need to investigate Elitirin's activity on her property. If outsiders had purchased it to graze zaligoats, then the other Sages were surprised that Alaric was not onboard; after all, he seemed to be the most open to outside ideas and communication.

Neither of them said another word as they crossed over a small bridge made of the same glowing stone that paved the streets. An artificial stream had been dug around the perimeter of the arboretum. The dome curved up rapidly more than two hundred feet in front of them. Inside, they could see the dense canopy of various vegetation that blossomed alongside the eolnut and yindai trees. The afternoon light was bright here in the solisberry garden, but it was supplemented by the purple glow of the solisberry blooms. Towering above everything else in the center of the dome sat the magical, sacred tree. Its branches climbed up and outward, rising nearly to the top of the massive structure. Its roots stretched in all directions from the gargantuan trunk, towering higher than even some of the other trees. This was the most important plant in the arboretum: the solisberry tree, the key to Mystalon's way of life.

As they entered the arboretum, the air was warm and humid. The sound of agitated jungle birds filled the air. The solisberry tree's immense flow of mana created a gentle breeze throughout the environment. The glass surrounding this structure was tempered in such a way it trapped heat inside the dome, and the windows could be opened to let heat escape with hinges built into the mithril frame. Alaric finally spoke in the cover of the noisy environment, "Wikton was correct. Just look at the way the blossoms are shimmering. The birds are bothered, and the butterflies are hiding."

Evander looked up at the tree. The flowery blossoms would occasionally produce a purple light as they were filled with ether from the arcane stream. According to most theories, solisberry trees were anchor points for the flow of magic. The entirety of the stream could flow through the magnificent trees in only a day. A single blossom would normally shimmer once a minute or so, but Alaric and Evander understood Wikton's concern.

Some of the blooms on the tree stayed perpetually lit. Others rapidly flickered with energy, and the spear tipped dark green leaves around them shimmered as they reflected the purple light. Evander let out a sigh. "This is foreboding. Why won't the other Sages pay attention to the warning signs?"

Alaric shook his head. "Denial. Cowardice. This is clearly connected to the Umbrals. The tree hasn't looked like this, never in my hundred and forty years." He was further disturbed by the lack of people in the gardens. In the daylight hours, many came to enjoy the sunshine or the beauty of the gardens. There was not another soul around right now, which put him on edge. "Where is everyone?" he asked, the tension in his voice rising.

Evander walked toward the tree. "Brother, do you see that?"

Alaric was only a step behind him, "See what?" He peered up into the solisberry tree's branches. In his frenzied search, he caught a glimpse of movement on a branch close to the trunk of the resplendent tree. His brother began running, and Alaric kept pace with him.

Evander grumbled, "C'mon, I know I wasn't imagining it." He growled and reached into a pouch, withdrawing a small, chalk tablet. He placed it in his mouth, and after a moment his eyes began to glow. His enhanced senses confirmed what his elven eyesight had only barely recognized. "By the gods, brother."

Alaric's expression was alarmed. He could still only see glimpses of movement, but never a source. Though it was more prominent near the trunk, he could occasionally see something in a branch. "What do you see, Evander?"

"Umbrals. But they seem different. They don't want to be seen. They are hiding." Evander continued walking toward the solisberry tree. He was among the towering roots now, some of them jutting up to fifteen feet high in places. "But they're huge!" he exclaimed, drawing a sword. "The ones from the forest and in the streets were elf sized, but these are huge."

Alaric rubbed his eyes and started to squint. Then he understood. In between the shadows of branches and crevices in the tree, massive, shadowy blobs were immersed in darkness. The movement came from the flickering in the brilliant purple light that cast the ominous shadows in the first place. As Alaric identified what he was looking for, he felt his heart sinking. "Have I gone mad, or do they look to be made of flesh and bone?"

Evander shook his head. "I only count seven. We should dispatch them as we have the others, with a jolt of sacred light."

Alaric's instincts told him not to approach the tree. "You've magically enhanced your vision, brother, I don't think you can see what I can. Dismiss the spell! These are not Umbrals as we know them," he pleaded, terror coursing through him. The shadows reminded him of his only encounter with a dragon, gripping him with an unnatural fear caused by their intense, magical presence.

Evander stopped fifty feet from the trunk of the solisberry tree. The diameter of the trunk was two hundred and fifty feet, taking up a significant portion of the center of the dome which stretched one thousand feet across. He willed the magical outlines in his vision to stop and gave his eyes a moment to adjust. There in the shadows, he could see creatures with textured skin. They resembled shadows to an extent, but they were clearly corporeal. They were nestled into the shadiest parts of the tree, but occasionally light would reflect off a set of black, watching eyes. They were twice the size of an average elf. As the brothers observed, the shapes became clearer. They looked like gigantic lizards clinging to the protection of the massive tree.

Alaric whispered, "I knew it. The previous Umbrals were just a reflection of something else. Fragments."

Evander started to take steps backwards. "And these appear to be whole. Complete. Are they doing something to the tree?"

The older brother stepped in front. "I have no way of knowing that. I can no longer see the stream, and there is no magitab to help." He craned forward, his eyes sparkling in the flickers from the solisberry blossoms. "Careful, they're moving," he hissed, pausing his movement.

"We should alert the Sages," Evander recommended.

Alaric nodded. "Just back up slowly; something about the tree has them mostly dormant for now. Perhaps the flow of mana eases their aggression," he commented as he walked backwards. His eyes never left the Umbrals that noticed his presence. As the brothers backed away, the creatures settled back into the shadows under the branches of the solisberry tree. "Your idea is wise. I will head to Wikton personally."

Evander started to turn toward a different exit. There were numerous doors along the perimeter of the arboretum, and the gardens within were carefully cultivated by members of all districts. He added, "I'll go to Shaelides, then. They can send word to Diamandra and Yalista. Umbrals on the tree is a potential crisis."

The brothers split up, Alaric running for the Garand district in the northwest of Mystalon while Evander made for the northeast section, the district of Galathan. Wikton and Shaelides were their closest allies among the Sages, but now was not a time to be political. Whatever was happening needed an explanation and a solution immediately. Sages outside of their coalition like Diamandra and Yalista would be more likely to heed a warning from Wikton and Shaelides.

Alaric arrived at Wikton's home near the base of the tree known as Garand. He yanked the cord of a bell hanging outside, ringing it with urgency. He looked inside the well-lit rotunda to the right of the front door, and he saw movement within. A moment later, the door opened, and an aged elf stood before him. He was hunched to a little under five feet, and he carried a metal cane in his left hand. His white hair spilled in waves down his back. "What is it so close to lunch time, Alaric? I'm a geezer, boy, I need my sustenance!"

Alaric's expression remained grim, causing Wikton's teasing demeanor to shift. Alaric explained, "Evander and I just went to visit the tree, and we both witnessed Umbrals clinging in its shadows. We agree there is something abnormal happening. Please spread the word to the other Sages. We'll be waiting on the north side of the arboretum." He spoke quickly but clearly.

Wikton looked down for a moment before peering up at Alaric. "Are you sure they were Umbrals, boy? It sounds like you've got doubts weighing you down."

Alaric turned for a moment, looking at the Garand district around him. He turned his attention back to Wikton. "They seemed to be flesh and bone, somehow. Not their normal, incomplete nature. Their shapes vary some, but they are like large lizards. Draconic, even." He took a deep breath, continuing, "Please. Alert someone who will listen to you like Diamandra. We need the Sages to respond, the solisberry may be in danger."

Wikton nodded and drew his head up. "Get back to the tree, then. I'll spread word." He groaned. "I knew it was only a matter of time before it all got ugly. Well, I can't say I'm surprised." He stepped out of his house.

Alaric began to return to the arboretum. "Please hurry, Wikton," he pleaded. As he scurried back through the streets of Garand and toward the dome in the center, he could detect an anxious increase in activity between the districts. As he entered the less-populated space between the district trees and the dome in the center, he saw Elitirin facing the glass structure from the east side. He approached the other Sage cautiously, covering significant ground to reach her. She stared in shock at the solisberry tree.

"Alaric?" she asked, her eyes never leaving the dome.

"Yes?" he replied gently, his voice softer than usual.

"Is it true? Are there creatures consuming the tree?" she asked, a fearful tenor in her voice.

He shook his head. "We can't know that for certain; the solisberry is an incredible tree. The creatures may merely be drawn to it. Who brought you word?"

Her eyes finally broke away from the dome. "Deritax. Someone went to the tree earlier and there were strange creatures. They ordered the evacuation an hour ago." She looked at him in disbelief, "Do you mean, you didn't get the warning?"

Alaric narrowed his eyes. Nobody had informed his coalition of creatures on the tree, and now the secret was in the open. It became apparent that Alaric and Evander were purposefully not informed. He glared as he spoke, "Dammit. This was not something that should have been political! What if the tree is in danger?"

Elitirin returned her gaze to the dome in the center. "Do you have any faith that your daughters will learn what is causing these creatures to appear? I do not mean to sound cynical," she backpedaled. The tone of her voice, however, was despondent. She sounded heartbroken.

Alaric's glare softened. "I'm afraid that they are likely on their way back to Mystalon as we speak. As I reported before, Argentum was a dead end, plagued by Umbrals of its own."

She sighed. "What do we do?"

He smiled and replied, "We just take them out like we've done all the others." He walked toward the arboretum.

Elitirin stood, motionless and fearful. She knew in her heart what was causing the Umbrals now, but she was so close to unlocking the time and space she needed. If she could go to the past and prevent The Unbinding, then all of the suffering in the present would go away. Still, she needed time that had run out. She already exhausted the one hundred complete, crystalized dragon eggs Sender had given her. He promised her another one hundred if that "Didn't do the trick," as he put it. A horrible feeling took over Elitirin's core, making her worry for her people and her actions. What if she had been duped by Sender? It didn't make sense to build a laboratory so close to Mystalon if he was going to betray her. The eggs needed to be processed quickly to power the device, and their sources were plentiful in this region of the world.

Alaric entered the arboretum again, directly approaching the solisberry tree in the center. As he did, he could see the lizard-like creatures as they scurried in the shadows. He drew a rapier from a thin, obsidian scabbard on his belt. He was swift on his feet, and he thought he would start the process of eliminating the Umbrals on the tree. If the others were on their way, he wanted to show his proactiveness in destroying this threat to their way of life. As he approached within fifty feet of the trunk, however, the creatures grew agitated and congregated together. Evander was not exaggerating when he said they were huge; all of the previous Umbrals combined would not be enough mass to equal one of these. The closer Alaric walked to the tree, the more clearly the large shadows showed interest in him.

He came within ten feet of a cluster of four Umbrals. Their forms were distinct at this distance. The shadows were dragons without wings. Though these manifestations initially looked to be ghostly, the afternoon sunlight gave form to their dark bodies. He swore they were tangible, physical creatures. Alaric froze, thinking about the implications of the shadows' forms. "Dragon eggs?" he asked. "Smugglers, dragon eggs. Now the Umbrals are clearly dragons." He started to walk backwards, the shadows stalking him slowly. Their interest really was the tree, as their hostility ceased after Alaric was about fifty feet away. "Something isn't right," he grumbled.

At that time, he heard a shout from the other side of the massive solisberry trunk. "Alaric! We are here!" It was his brother's voice, but Alaric wondered who 'we' might include.

"I'm here, brother," he replied, his voice gruff. "The Umbrals are territorial over the tree, and they lack the mindless hostility of previous manifestations. Can anyone explain what is happening?" he shouted back.

There was no immediate response, but as Alaric withdrew, the Umbrals ignored him again. As time passed, more Sages arrived, all of them confirming the existence of the Umbrals on the tree. They stood helpless for hours, nobody brave enough to provoke the creatures for fear they might retaliate as a complete group. Due to their size and numbers, the elves of Mystalon dared not initiate hostility. They spent the next day observing as shadows crawled all over the tree. The consensus was they seemed to be shadow dragons without wings, though a few insisted that they were a type of lizard common in the eastern reaches of the world. There were one hundred in total, a damning number for Elitirin. Whatever followed, she knew that she was to blame.

The shadows remained dormant on the tree for another day. Afterward, horrors unimaginable befell Mystalon. The draconic shape of the creatures held true in their manifestation of power. They began to leave the comfort of the tree, boldly dispersing groups of elves with breath weapons of many varieties. Some breathed fire and lightning, and others clouds of corrosive gas and geysers of acid. The intensity of their attacks could not be blocked with protective magisalves, nor could the creatures be extinguished with simple magical attacks. They wreaked havoc on the city for twelve hours before withdrawing to the tree. The Umbrals waited there for another twelve hours before attacking the city again. The citizens of each district barricaded themselves into easily defensible areas, but the Umbrals were drawn to magic. Anywhere magisalves or magitabs were stored, the dark creatures would arrive to consume them.

To make matters worse, the Sages had to face questions from the people. These were the very beasts Celyth and Arlindra left to investigate, but they had not returned any answers yet. The elves of Mystalon began to grow fearful and weary, and after just two days of standing off against the creatures, the magical society lay in embers. Most everyone had disposed of their magical items and tools. Water producing magisalves were all used to make water for prolonged barricades. In more than one instance, a citizen tried to smuggle a magical heirloom into a secured position, only for the entire group to be slaughtered by an Umbral.

Late on the second day of fighting, the third wave of attacks began to subside, and the creatures returned to the tree. Alaric, Evander, Wikton, and Shaelides coordinated a multi-group effort for mutual defense against the creatures. There was a structure reminiscent of an elven castle in the Galathan district, and the Fernith brothers had organized a position within to keep the beasts at bay. It became apparent that great effort would be required to destroy the Umbrals now, as it took nearly one hundred casualties to kill a single beast that broke past the posted guards. Mystalon had no military, only militias that could be organized to use magical tools in creative ways to ward off outsiders. Their tactics were so effective that their small, reclusive country had staved off invasion dozens of times, even against invaders with armies many times the size of their humble population. Now that the threat came from within, Mystalon was on the brink of collapse, and the beasts that brought such destruction were unyielding.

On that second day, Alaric stood on the fortifications of the miniature citadel. He watched as the Umbrals withdrew to the arboretum as they did every twelve or so hours. Night had begun to drench the forest in darkness, but the winter moonlight bathed the center of Mystalon in eerie, silver dread. The people could barely fend off individual creatures in large groups, and across the city in three waves of attacks, only three of the creatures had been destroyed. When they died, their bodies exploded in a cloud of black miasma unlike the weaker Umbrals. The destructive outcome was almost as deadly as their living presence. He sighed deeply, and his ears twitched with anticipation. He could hear a low rumbling sound.

"Nebu," he whispered. The exhaustion of continual conflict caught up to him, and he sat down. Within a minute, the energetic dracofly popped up over the wall of the citadel. "Please tell me my daughter and niece are in Alabaster and safe," Alaric pleaded.

Nebu shook his draconic head vigorously. "They'll be here tomorrow. They're traversing the wilderness between here and Devitus. That's where they ended up when I finally found them. But I've got news! The warpriest and the newcomer are pretty sure that the dragon eggs are being turned into crystallized magic. Dragons are pretty weird, apparently." He landed on his back legs, crossing his arms as he complained. "But those crystals power all kinds of cool weapons. Like an energy source."

Alaric stood, his expression grave. "A power source," he mumbled. Then his jaw slacked, "By Lexcord, no." He held up a spyglass, a piece of non-magical technology rounded up from somebody's grandmother's box of antiques. He kept watching the tree for signs of deterioration, but nothing alarmed him at this point.

Nebu flew up to hover at face level with Alaric. "So, what have you got? City looks pretty rough," the dracofly remarked sarcastically.

Alaric rolled his eyes. "Yes, Nebu. There are nearly one hundred incredibly powerful Umbrals wreaking havoc on us in twelve-hour waves. Can you get a message to the other Sages for me? Tell them that tomorrow my daughters will be returning with reinforcements."

Nebu snorted. "Oh gods, you want me to talk to the snobby one?"

Alaric nodded. "If my estimates are correct, Elitirin will likely be with her allies. It's impossible to fight these beasts in small numbers, and getting caught by them is a death sentence. Please, tell me, are the warpriest and the newcomer strong?"

Nebu gave Alaric a cheeky grin. "Oh buddy, you don't even know what's happened! They've picked up a kitsune friend too. This fox can use the Magic Mirror, it's incredible!"

Alaric looked to Nebu with immediate hope. "The Magic Mirror you say?" His eyes widened with excitement. "If she has the Magic Mirror, then maybe we can save what's left of our city!" He started to fidget nervously. "Wait, where did this foxkin come from?"

Nebu shrugged. "I dunno, she's lost about a month's worth of memories. Really cool, though. Seems to be good at heart and all that. Miranda has really taken to her."

Alaric tapped his chin. That was the warpriest's name. "And the warpriest, what of her power?"

Nebu flailed. "Like I told you before, it's kinda wild. She can do almost anything, but if she pushes it too hard, boom. Out like a candle in the rain. She tried to explain it to me, but I didn't listen. She was eating something Arli made, and it just looked so good. Like, I'm still having dreams about that lambchop." The dracofly flew a circle around Alaric's head. "Hey, trust me, when they get back, they're going to solve your Umbral problems in no time!"

Alaric frowned. "I hope you're right, Nebu. And please. Tell Arli and Cel to be safe. These creatures are as strong as the dragons of yore."

Nebu gave a nod. "Well, I'm going to fly while it's safe pops. Be back tomorrow with Arli!" he whizzed around one more time before making his typical messenger circuit through the city. When he announced the Fernith daughters were returning, he was met with cries to tell them to run. When he followed that announcement with news of them bringing outside help, he was met with silence and confusion. He didn't stay long enough for questions and departed Mystalon within the hour. Funny, he didn't see the snobby one at all. Maybe she finally got eaten. Nebu knew Arli would scold him for such thoughts. Which is exactly why he wouldn't mention it to her.

Alaric stared at the arboretum until he became delirious with exhaustion, dozing off with the spyglass in his hand.

Elitirin descended the stairs into the underground laboratory. Sender had been here continually for the last two months, tinkering with the power crystals that allowed her to operate the time gate. She called out gently, "Sender, hello? Are you here?" She was met by silence, which was unusual for the laboratory.

As she reached the bottom, she was in an equipment room. The walls of this place were made of porcelain tile, and they reflected the light from several crystals fixed into extractors on the wall. She felt a nervous sensation as she walked toward the door that led into a more controlled part of the laboratory. It had a lacrima-deum affixed beside it, functioning like a heavy-duty lock. She touched the power crystal, its jagged edges once the promise of hope for her people. To her surprise, the door opened as she touched it. She walked through, the clockwork mechanisms hissing loudly as the door slid shut behind her.

In this new room, she could see Sender at the far end. "Sender! Something is wrong!" she voiced. As she approached, he looked incredibly focused. He was leaning over some sort of device, looking down into it, his eyes pressed against it.

He stood, his gaze lingering on the contraption. His red eyes sparkled with excitement, and he brushed his wiry, black hair out of his face. It was thinning, but he maintained it long. He looked to be a human around forty years. He replied to Elitirin, "Oh, nothing at all is wrong! In fact, everything is going according to plan!"

Elitirin froze. "Excuse me?" she asked, her voice incredulous.

Sender smiled broadly. "Exactly to plan! You see, Doctor One had a theory."

The elf stroked her black hair nervously. "Who is Doctor One? What theory? Sender, the gate is almost finished. What do you mean?"

The human laughed hysterically. "Time gate? Did you really think such a thing possible? No, you were merely a willing participant in an experiment you did not understand. You don't think that one hundred full, egg-sized lacrima-deum would be so inexpensive, did you?"

She blinked, the fear in her body growing. "I don't understand what you mean, Sender. Quite frankly, you're starting to terrify me."

Sender made a broad gesture to the room around them. "This laboratory was a temporary setup. I was only here to get what I needed from the plentiful dragon eggs in the region. The Tanlin Falls proved to be a most fruitful endeavor. I didn't have machinery to exhaust the lacrima-deum made from those eggs gathered near the falls, but I did have you! So eager to burn up a power source you didn't understand!" He laughed again, pointing at a long trough full of viscous, deep-red liquid. "Place a dragon egg in here, apply one pound of ethereal pressure, the faeblood will trap the magic inside. Let it sit for one week under those conditions, and you'll have a fresh lacrima-deum. The tears of the gods weep for your mistake, Elitirin."

"Explain yourself!" she demanded. She withdrew a dagger from under her cloak.

A sadistic smile crossed his lips. "You see, the eggs become crystallized magic that power our devices. I do not need that stored energy, I only need a sliver of the egg. I gave the rest to you. If magic crystallizes here in the prime plane, what do you think happens in the arcane stream?"

She furrowed her brow. As a manabotanist, she contemplated the implications. Her eyes widened in terror. "An imbalance in the stream?" she asked.

Sender nodded enthusiastically. "Yes, and the universe corrects such an imbalance by creating a negative equivalent on this side of reality! That's how your precious Umbrals come into being. When the magic of a lacrima-deum is burned up, an Umbral forms to correct the balance of magic between the planes. Doctor One confirmed this to me only the day before I delivered one hundred complete eggs to you!" He laughed and pointed at her. "Your narrow focus has destroyed your entire civilization. I love to teach science and morality! The future is for those of us who can see through foolish moral codes of mortals and reject them. Doctor One will usher in a new era." Sender licked his lips eagerly. "And I, his assistant, Doctor Five, will be there at his side when he ascends to godhood."

Elitirin felt a new type of anger, fueled by her own naivete and Sender's wicked intent. "You'll pay for your callousness!" she shouted and lunged at him with the dagger in her hand.

He smiled, brandishing a small coin. It glowed in his hand, covering him in a protective aura. As Elitirin's blade should have connected with Sender, he disappeared and appeared behind her in less than a second. A low hum echoed throughout the laboratory. He hissed, "Oops."

The room started to shake. Elitirin turned to glare at him, full of helplessness. "What have you done, Sender? Answer me!"

He cackled and started to walk to the door. "I'm just tying up some loose ends. Doctor One is finished with this region, and this laboratory no longer needs to exist."

The shaking intensified. The porcelain tile walls began to crack. Elitirin then closed her eyes and focused on her own uncanny magic. She focused on the plant life all around them in the underground laboratory. Sender closed the top of the laboratory as he exited, the shaking around Elitirin growing stronger still. She made the mistake of trusting an outsider, but she would not let him destroy the evidence. Acting on the promises he made was the most logical decision for her, but discovering his true intentions made this a vile act the whole of Mystalon needed to see. She used her uncanny magic enhanced by her own life essence. Her desperate push strengthened the roots and branches of nearby plants, holding the laboratory together. In spite of her effort, the shaking caused the building to rupture. She kept pushing her gift until she lost consciousness. The ceiling collapsed around her as the world went dark.

Chapter 10
Crisis and Hope

"When 'justice' is burdened by bureaucracy, only the bureaucrats win." – Eldon Farzg

elasine dismounted his pegasus. The Mystalonian Forest glowed orange from the flames bellowing deep within the city center. He stood about half a mile from the edge of the treeline, looking into the night sky with worry. A clamor behind him indicated Erk was landing, and he handled his pegasus surprisingly well for a sailor. "Woah, easy," the elf said as his mount's hooves contacted the ground at an alarming speed. Selasine's gaze did not break away from the top of the forest.

Naomi landed behind Erk with much less commotion. August, Justin, and Valarie landed with her, everyone struggling to catch up with Selasine. He had the most experience with the beasts, and it showed. Still, flying proficiency would not be enough to right the horror Selasine saw before him. Mystalon was already burning, and the Church of Invictus arrived too late again. Selasine was worried he would have to muster an army, which was a paperwork nightmare.

Erk stood at his side a moment later. He said nothing, staring at the glow in the night sky. The others joined a step behind, looking up in silence. Selasine finally spoke, "The Umbrals should have been a higher priority since Miranda informed us of their existence. This is a disaster that I'm partly responsible for." He sighed.

August gave him a forceful pat on his back. "Don't go making yourself out to be bigger than you need to be. One crisis at a time is all anyone can ask, and priorities change when information changes."

Erk nodded in agreement. The high priest would have said the same to the paladin had he tried to blame himself. The pirate lord added, "Besides, now that we are here, we can render aid as intended. Come, we must not dally." He mounted his pegasus again. "To the heart of the city."

Everyone followed Erk's lead. It took another hour to reach the sixteen trees sitting over the top of Mystalon. As they sailed over the boughs, they saw smoke pouring from ruined buildings. The flames lingered, embering in the stone. The haze was black and dense, smothering the air with the smell of char and soot. The core Mystalonian trees at the district centers were half a mile apart on average. The solisberry tree flashed in the clearing at the center of the city, the dome around it wrecked.

The sounds of conflict echoed from numerous points throughout the city. The sprawling neighborhoods beneath them smoldered in ruins. The blocks spiraled out from the sixteen trees at the district centers. The glowing stones of the streets created enough light to see well in the deep shadows of a forest night. They were, however, fractured in many places, and the stones lost their luminance after being shattered. A terrified scream attracted Naomi's attention to the street one hundred feet below. She shouted, "Look out!" and spiraled her pegasus downward onto the street.

Erk used the aerial position to evaluate the situation, and the paladins descended behind Naomi. The pirate lord looked at Selasine, and they maneuvered their mounts in a turnaround. The high priest asked, "Problem?"

Erk peered at the scene unfolding. He spotted a group of elves running, and his keen eyesight noticed the danger up the street. He gestured with his left hand and drew a short sword with his right. "There!" he shouted, spurring his pegasus into motion. Selasine followed him without question.

A huge, lizard-shaped shadow pursued a group of Mystalonians through the main street of the district. The elves were heading toward the Mystalonian tree in the center, and the creature sprayed jets of prismatic energy from its maw. The breath weapon exploded against stone and ignited any exposed wood.

Selasine cursed to himself. "Talirix Volïs." He used his legs to drive his pegasus into a direct assault.

August landed in position to intercept the shadow creature with a maneuver known as a dive dismount, and his pegasus ran a safe distance away. The others lacked the commander's aerial combat training, and they had to make the spiraling descent for beginners. Their landing took a minute longer than August's, and they headed toward a smaller tree to tie off their pegasus. Valarie, Justin, Erk and Naomi ran to support August against the shadow monster now charging toward him.

Selasine's diving strike from the air slowed the creature's attack. The high priest recognized the creature as an Umbral, but it looked tangible instead of shadow as he expected. The surprise didn't change his course of action. His sword connected with the monster's face as the pegasus galloped through the air with fierce stomps. The beast's hooves crunched into the side of the eight-foot-tall creature, and Selasine saw its draconic features. His blade tore in a downward angle from the Umbral's eye toward its neck. The pegasus trampled on the dark dragon's shoulder, allowing Selasine to guide his mount upward. "It's a dragon with no wings," he grumbled to himself while taking scope of the damage he did to the beast. He prepared for another assault. Before he could engage again, however, the beast retaliated with its prismatic breath weapon.

A light filled the creature's maw, and a moment later, a rainbow-colored beam blasted toward Selasine. The high priest thanked Invictus for the distance between himself and his target. He prayed, "Sword of Justice, we seek refuge behind your shield! A great calamity befalls the faithful. Disinherit the legacy of the wicked!" As the prismatic attack connected with Selasine and his pegasus, lightning crackled out in a sphere. The advanced protection prayer converted the mysterious energy into harmless electricity, and it discharged with a heavy thunderclap. Selasine shouted and activated his uncanny magic. His innate ability duplicated the image of his pegasus mount in addition to his own. Now the massive beast had to contend with a dozen riders descending to engage it.

To exacerbate its vulnerability, the pirates and paladins arrived within engaging distance. Justin and Valarie firmly planted their mithril tower shields in front of them, charging toward the dark dragon with confidence. August used his uncanny magic to increase his movement, rushing to the beast's left side. Naomi charged toward the draconic creature's right flank. Erk stood behind the Shield Knights, activating his uncanny magic. Flames swirled around his arms. The people of Mystalon stopped to watch, surprised by the sudden interlopers on the streets.

Selasine's mind raced in the midst of combat. The slavers had been trafficking dragon eggs, and these creatures resembled dragons without wings. Furthermore, this beast did not match the description of "Umbral" as provided by the Fernith brothers. Though he had never faced one, the high priest realized he and his allies were engaging with a creature almost as formidable as a fully grown dragon. He began to suspect the dragon eggs were connected to these otherworldly beasts with scales as dark as shadows. Selasine's dive exposed the Umbral's left side, allowing August to score a stab in the monster's left abdominal muscles. A spray of daggers pierced the beast from its right, an unseen force propelling them with deadly weight. Naomi crouched as she threw the knives with a steady rhythm, their enchantment returning them to the bandolier strapped to her right thigh. Though each individual knife was insignificant alone, the barrage was savage enough that the wounds she caused were graver than those inflicted by Selasine and August.

The hulking, dark form snapped its attention in Naomi's direction, turning hard to its right side, putting August and Selasine directly behind it. The beast sprayed a sudden rainbow jet, striking Naomi. It enveloped her with a prismatic halo. Her eyes rolled back into her head, and her silver ponytail bobbed. Erk shouted and unleashed a torrent of sunlight into the beast's left side. Selasine and August tore into the Umbral's haunches from behind while Valarie and Justin unleashed a series of attacks that would have disemboweled a biological creature. Instead of innards, however, a spray of black particles spilled from the Umbral's wounds.

Naomi looked at herself coated in the prismatic aura, and the full force of the dragon's strange beam unleashed. Her magical armor provided little protection against the mystifying attack. She felt herself losing control of her senses. Her body numbed, and she stumbled to the ground. A burning sensation filled her essence, and breathing hurt. A concussive implosion centered on Naomi followed a moment later. The beast's rainbow-colored breath was an aberration of the arcane stream. The effects were devastating and random. The earth giantkin shrieked as the implosion sucked the air from her lungs. She had felt pain before, but this combination was something new. The breath weapon targeted not only her body but her very soul.

Selasine shouted, and a blur of the high priest bounded through the air toward Naomi. August tested the tangibility of the creature, making an agile, running leap onto the beast's back. He landed comfortably on solid scales, but then he realized he was in hostile territory. The spines on the Umbral's back lashed out at him; though they were flexible, they were sharp. August almost lost his balance as another wave of force hit the dragon from the side as Erk intensified his solar beam. Valarie and Justin wailed against it with such ferocity they could have broken the ranks of an entire battalion of common soldiers.

August ran along the spine toward the head, swiping the Umbral's spines away with his longsword. As he passed the draconic creature's shoulders, he noticed shredded stubs where wings should have been. They looked torn as if they had been amputated with a serrated blade. A dark miasma seeped out of them, an unclosing, magical wound. August knew this tiny detail was significant, and he tucked it away in his mind. Still, whether this beast was suffering or enraged did not matter. It was threatening lives, and he had to put an end to it. He charged up the neck of the Umbral and leapt into the air. With great precision in his footwork, he timed and angled his jump so his sword would pierce the base of the creature's skull.

As August delivered the hopeful attack, Selasine dismounted his pegasus and examined Naomi's injuries. The rainbow breath was a mystery, and Selasine did not have time to make speculations. He prayed a requimist, a sorrowful sacrificial prayer that exchanged life force for intense healing energy. Naomi started to scream as her senses returned, but the prayer filled her with a soothing coolness. It replaced the pain with comfort. She felt her flesh mending, her entire body moments away from dissolving as the result of an unseen, corrosive energy which seeped into every part of her being. As she recovered her faculties, she stood up. She saw the dark beast diving headlong into a lunge aimed at her. She dodged with an acrobatic roll, the beast's strength waning. August's sword did not disable the creature as he had anticipated, but it did cause another intense spray of bleeding magic particles.

Selasine backed away from the dragon, but the requimist took its toll. He collapsed, the prayer exhausting him. The Umbral closed in on Selasine, pulling its head back. August, however, was still on top of the terrifying beast. He pulled his sword from the monster's skull and stabbed again, accelerating the rate of arcane bleeding. The particles dissipated with a crackling noise, and a light began to glow inside the creature's translucent body.

Valarie shouldered her shield so she could strike faster. Justin activated his uncanny magic, turning his skin to stone to protect against the Umbral's physical attacks. The draconic shaped form could not retaliate against so many assailants hitting all of its weak points. Still, the paladin's hardened skin kept the beast's back claw from impaling him as he and Valarie assailed its side. Valarie's uncanny magic enhanced her unrelenting stabs, granting her additional swiftness and accuracy. She wreaked havoc on the magical creature, and between August and Valarie, it was losing magical essence at an incredible rate.

Just as the Umbral collapsed, the glow within created an audible, pulsing sound. It brightened, and an intense pressure filled the air. It reminded August of Lenis, and he looked toward Selasine, "Your Holiness! It's happening again! Just like Lenis!"

Selasine gripped his holy symbol with a grimace. Another prayer was going to hurt, but he had no choice. "Sword of Justice, contain the wrath of our enemies!" As he did, a bubble formed around the Umbral, and the creature's magical body detonated with rainbow colored energy. Thanks to the prayer, the bubble contained the blast, but the dispersing energies caused it to burst. Water erupted into the air, creating a prismatic shower of neutralized magic rain. The companions exchanged looks of disbelief as cheers erupted from the onlookers.

Naomi felt alright, everything considered. That rainbow breath assaulted her with many forms of magic, and she only resisted a couple of effects. Selasine's sacrificial prayer spared her incalculable pain and certain death. She understood the kindness that her old friend Iria saw in him, and she let that gratitude swell. "Thanks, Thomas," she said with a smile, looking into the heart of the watery aftermath of the Umbral's self-destruction. The raindrops fizzled into black sparks of magic, sublimating into the atmosphere around them.

The high priest smiled through physical pain and spiritual strain. "Of course, Naomi." The Catechism of Containment was exhausting. It was a niche prayer reserved for demons of the highest order, many of them dying in glorious, destructive infernos. He had employed the prayer twice now in less than a week. He used it to minimize collateral damage after defeating Lenis, and now against the Umbral. He was glad that it worked against more than demons, but he felt the fatigue in his soul.

Erk called out through the pouring water and wisping particles. "What in the Infernia was that?"

Justin described its elements rationally, shouting louder than necessary. However, his voice drew more cheers from the crowd, as his diagnostic vocabulary inspired confidence. "Sir! Confirmed draconic form, minus wingspan. Confirmed breath weapon. Enemy does not contain simple draconic biology. Commander Burchard's assault is evidence." He started to salute. "We face tangible but simultaneously illusory dragons."

The pseudo-shower subsided, and the air cleared of black sparks. Selasine's former students marveled at the range of prayers he had mastered. They also knew the level of strength and faith it required to draw out such specific manifestations of their god. As clerics relied on prayers, paladins depended on a continual infusion of their divinity's essence. Though their prayers were limited in scope, they bore the very power of their god in their presence and actions. While that had its advantages, Selasine's experience as a warpriest was evident in every new situation the young paladins encountered. A year ago, Justin and August were constantly impressed by their mentor on the frontier. Their awe of Selasine continued to grow. His experience empowered his faith and made him an indispensable ally. They were now grateful to call him teacher and friend.

Selasine's body ached from the prayers and sudden exertion of fighting the Umbral. He sat down, his breathing ragged. The sacrificial healing prayer brought him to the brink of exhaustion. He looked up at his team. "Answers. We need answers. Talk to the people."

The paladins saluted and turned to face the people watching closer to the Mystalonian tree at the center of the wide street. As they moved away, Naomi and Erk slid onto the ground close to Thomas. The pirate lord's gray eyes reflected genuine concern as he asked, "Nulestotejin, are you alright?" His voice was a bit shaken.

Naomi, too, felt worry stir within her. She cursed at her slow response, blaming herself for getting caught in the way of the shadow dragon's breath. She was relieved when the high priest laughed.

Selasine responded, "I'm fine, Erk." His voice was relieved but fatigued. "I'm just getting too old for adventuring, that's all. I've sustained significant injury in the last two brawls." He stood, taking a moment to do so with grace and dignity. Erk and Naomi rose as well, Selasine and the giantkin towering over Erk. "Let's help the kids with the questioning," he ordered.

Erk replied, "We just defeated a dragon without wings. I pray to Lexcord that Miranda is getting close."

Selasine's face was grim. "Damil said they could see the forest as of this afternoon."

The three of them turned to join the paladins in speaking with the elves fleeing from the Umbral.

Celyth groaned as they descended the last ridge overlooking the Mystalonian Forest. As the sun set, they could see the fires burning in the heart of the city. The elven warrior hit the ground running. Arlindra was right behind her but using more caution. She shouted, "Wait, cousin, no amount of rushing will change the situation!"

Nebu called out from Arlindra's shoulder, clinging to his master's armor. "Seriously, the city is in really rough shape. It's ugly in there, Cel. I'm not ready to see it again! It's the stuff of nightmares!" He started to rave, his voice emotional and overdramatic.

Celyth shouted back, "Tell that infernal bug to shut up!" Then she turned, jogging to cover the half mile between them and the forest. Evan, Miranda, and Yuvina descended the ridge much slower, the kitsune serving as the rear watch for their group. Her sense of smell could detect people up to half a mile away, and they did not want to be caught by surprise again. Ever since their fight against the mysterious assassin, Yuvina had grown very fond of these people. They acted with selflessness and concern, and they intended to use their powers to save others rather than enrich themselves. Yuvina felt like that was the lesson she needed to unlearn in order to unlock the power within her, and she was grateful to Miranda for having shown her that. Now that she had access to an Unbinding, she still wanted to fight for the people who had not found their own uncanny magic. She hoped her assistance in this mission would earn Miranda's continued favor and enthusiasm.

Arlindra waited at the base of the ridge for everyone to catch up. Nebu huffed, "I only have four legs. Why does she keep calling me an insect? A crisis is no reason to forget fundamental biology." The dracofly sat on Arlindra's shoulder in protest.

Miranda looked toward Celyth, asking, "Is she going to be alright? Her haste is concerning."

Arlindra's lips tightened with anxiety. "Cousin is worried about our fathers, that's all. She's not necessarily worried about the rest of Mystalon." She cleared her throat as she spoke. "I'm only concerned about the needless destruction of life. Especially the trees," she said, trailing off in a sad voice.

Evan patted her on the shoulder in encouragement. He walked

from behind her toward the edge of the forest where Celyth waited impatiently. He gave her and Miranda both a nod as he moved, saying, "Let us hope our arrival minimizes casualties, then." Yuvina bounded behind him, giving Arlindra and Miranda an insistent glance.

Miranda tried to give a comforting smile, but she felt awkward. She couldn't imagine how anxious she would be if she returned to Devitus and found it in ruins. The warpriest finally added, "We'll save everyone we can, okay? If these are super Umbrals like the one in Argentum, we'll just have to take them out. I'm here to help," she reassured. She then hustled toward the treeline.

Arlindra let out a deep sigh, following Miranda toward the others. Her new friend was right; one crisis at a time.

It took two hours for Arlindra to guide them through the forest, approaching the city from the northwest. As the city came into view, the devastation was absolute. The conflict had been raging from the furthest reaches of the city to the dome in the center. Celyth pointed to one of the central Mystalonian trees, commenting, "That's Garand. Wikton's district. We might be able to find a source of information there." She looked to her companions. "Thanks for coming with us. You're some of the first outsiders to reach the city in centuries, and in my eyes, you're more than welcome."

Miranda smiled. "It's an honor, Celyth. Let's go," she ordered, marching toward the tree Celyth had indicated.

A few outlying buildings survived the carnage, mostly storage barns and grain silos. Arlindra spotted an anomaly on the roof of a barn. She hissed, "Stop! Nobody move." She froze in place. Her eyes locked onto the building off to the right of the dirt path leading into the Garand district.

Evan squinted and cursed. "By the gods, I see it." He drew his clockwork sword and stopped beside Arlindra.

Miranda and Yuvina responded with clumsy attempts to stop in place, and they stumbled into each other. The spray of magic sparks did not surprise them this time, but they broke apart quickly. Miranda followed the ranger's stare, observing the storage barn carefully. Her enhanced vision perceived the Umbral on the roof with great detail. It was eight feet tall at its shoulders, and it was definitely draconic. "Invictus, spare us a tragedy," the warpriest mourned. "What manner of beast do you see?" she asked the others, watching as the shadowy dragon paced from the front to the back of the barn.

Celyth peered at the building. The barn was at least two hundred feet away, and the orange haze coming from deeper within the city lit the outskirts with an eerie radiance. "It just looks like a big Umbral."

Yuvina shook her head. "I detect no scent. My eyes see only a lizard." Her whiskers shook.

Evan understood Miranda's concern. He could distinguish the monster's draconic features. "Have any of the other Umbrals manifest as a dragon without wings?" he asked.

Arlindra and Celyth shook their heads. Arlindra replied with more questions. "You think these are dragons then? Does that mean it's likely that dragon eggs are involved in their creation?"

Evan nodded. "Ezelbrecht indicated all of this was connected, and I can't deny what I'm seeing. Based on all of your stories, this looks different from the average Umbral." He spoke with confidence in his deductions.

Celyth interrupted him, "To be honest, I wouldn't even call that an Umbral. It's too real. It looks like it belongs here. The other Umbrals never seemed like they belonged. They had no form, but this is obviously a dragon." Her nonchalant shrug belied her frustration.

The five approached the barn, watching the dark, draconic beast stalking the length of the roof of the storage barn. The building stretched twenty-five feet into the air at its apex, and it had large cargo doors on each side. The creature on the roof seemed determined to keep its eyes on all of the exits, but it was proving impossible. Its movements were frantic, behaving like a predator losing its prey. Evan asked, "Does it see us?"

Miranda inhaled. The arcane stream flowed so thickly here that she would have a nearly unlimited supply of magic. She prayed the advantage would not be necessary. As they came within twenty feet of the storage barn, the stalking shadow on the top of the building stopped and turned its attention to Miranda and her companions. It hissed, a feature that surprised the cousins. "It's alive," Arlindra said in bewilderment.

The creature was more interested in the interlopers now, and Miranda caught a glimpse of several elves looking out of the windows and doors on the north side of the barn. She wondered what they were doing previously to keep the beast at bay. She drew her sword and readied her shield. "Umbral or not, these beasts are the source of grief in Mystalon. We must extinguish the chaos," she ordered. Evan's heart stirred with inspiration. Miranda spoke with such confidence that he understood what the headmistress implied. This was the bravery and resolve of her father. She pointed at the dark dragon with her sword and shouted, "May Invictus pour his wrath upon you, agent of chaos!"

Evan rushed forward and the cousins took up positions on each side of Miranda, preparing their bows for an initial volley. Yuvina focused on the feeling of the magic inside her. She learned how to call her uncanny magic at will thanks to some guidance from Miranda. Somehow, she felt like there was more power within her essence, but for now, she had a last line of defense. She ran toward the storage barn as well, her steps light and agile.

As Evan and Yuvina drew near the building, the creature on top inhaled and discharged a yellow ray of light from its maw. Instinctively, Evan and Yuvina leapt upward, their training and reflexes allowing them to dodge the beam and convert their momentum into powerful jumps. The beam's effects were not readily apparent, but both the elf and foxkin knew it would be unwise to test the strange creature's powers. A barrage of arrows rained down on the shadow dragon's center mass as Celyth and Arlindra unleashed a series of focused shots. The arrows burst into fire as they pierced the Umbral. It let out an audible roar in response, charging up its breath weapon again.

Yuvina and Evan closed in on the beast's sides, Yuvina pouncing onto its front left shoulder and Evan trying to assault the Umbral's draconic chest from its right. As they attacked, it sent another blast of light from its mouth toward Miranda and the cousins. They all ducked behind Miranda's shield, a tactic they had used a dozen times fighting monsters in the caverns near Argentum. When the light contacted the shield, however, the tower of mithril disintegrated after four seconds of exposure. Miranda's eyes widened with shock; she had never considered such an attack possible. Her shield simply turned to dust, leaving herself and her companions exposed. Fortunately, the light ceased as the shield was destroyed. Her brow twitched with frustration at the sudden development, but she understood how unpredictable magic could be. She walked forward, holding her sword at a downward angle.

Meanwhile, Evan had punctured the beast several times with his sword. The draconic forelegs raked and swiped, but Evan was too nimble. Yuvina also discovered additional threats on the shadowy beast. Its spines swiped at her as she stood on the Umbral's shoulder. She took a dagger in each hand and jumped, tearing her way from the top of the shoulder to the elbow of the beast's left forward arm. As she landed on the roof of the barn, she felt a sensation similar to the first time her power activated in the fight against the assassin. This time, the urge came from within her arms; as she focused on the feeling, her muscles brimmed with strength. She unleashed a flurry of slashes that were faster and more vicious than any assault she had ever given. The beast made a swipe at her with its injured foreleg, but she backflipped out of the way with ease. As she landed, she felt the mana flowing through her; her combat abilities had been enhanced. She looked toward Miranda out of instinct, hoping the young priestess would also have answers about her improved fighting prowess.

Miranda's red hair shimmered in the flickering orange light of a city on fire. She looked up at the Umbral, pity filling her heart. Arlindra stood close to her, and Celyth stayed back to cover them if the beast began to use its disintegrating breath weapon again. Miranda was about ten feet away from the creature, watching its essence spewing from its injuries in black sparks. "I feel like I know you," she whispered.

The shadowy figure stomped and planted its front legs, unable to stop the unrelenting assault from Evan and Yuvina. It stretched its draconic neck down, giving an agonizing roar. The beast was close to giving up. Miranda held her sword firmly in her right hand, but she lifted her left toward the Umbral. She stretched out her fingers and focused on the ether collected inside her. Arlindra looked at her with curiosity. A moment later, purple lights emerged from Miranda's fingertips and wrapped themselves around the shadowy dragon. The warpriest closed her eyes as the magic connected her to the monster. The air around Miranda became agitated, and a swirl of energy surrounded her, causing her braids to whip. She opened her mouth and inhaled. The mana in the air replenished the energy she was using to analyze the Umbral. She wasn't sure how to shape the magic exactly like she wanted, so she discharged enough mana to copy the shadow dragon's features. Erk described summoning spells to her on their return voyage to Nulodia during The Harvesting; she was certain she could use such magic to evaluate this strange creature. It was formed of decayed arcane energy, and the sensations returning from her spell made little sense.

Miranda opened her eyes and looked at the dark dragon on top of the storage barn. She could see the elves inside looking at her with fear. The only emotion she could read from the beast was a terror greater than any known to mortals. She spoke in the draconic language, "You wretched beast. What has befallen you?"

It replied in draconic, "Missing. My soul is missing!" Everyone around them heard the guttural expressions of the language of dragons, but only Miranda and the beast understood.

Evan and Yuvina stopped their attack, jumping several feet away from the dark-scaled monster. Its injuries continued to spray black sparks. Miranda continued speaking, relying on her mother's memories to communicate in draconic, "Where is your soul?"

The creature left its neck stretched down. In this posture, it stretched fifteen feet from head to tail. It hissed back, "Separated! In the magic!" It reared its head back to strike, but Miranda pulled hard on the purple energy connecting her to the beast. As she did, the essence of the shadow dragon unraveled into a cloud of lingering, black particles. The warpriest let out a deep sigh. She would not be able to replicate this creature by shaping the mana; its very nature seemed to be antithetical to the flow of the arcane.

Arlindra watched Miranda as the priestess contemplated the information she uncovered with her summoning spell. Celyth approached from behind as the threat disappeared. Evan and Yuvina jumped down from the low point of the roof of the barn, the ten-foot leap nothing for their agility. Miranda looked around, noticing everyone's expectant gaze. The elves inside the barn celebrated with each other, recognizing that they had been rescued. Evan spoke first, "Miranda, did you overuse the mana?" he asked.

She shook her head. "I tried to use the logic of summoning magic to understand the creature, but I have more questions now than before," she explained. Her eyes stared off into the distance. "My mother and father are agitated." Her hand instinctively clutched her chest, and she sat down on the ground.

Evan was at her side in an instant, and the others gathered around her a short distance away. Miranda shook her head again, her braids swinging back and forth with the motion. "This doesn't really make any sense. The Umbral was clearly using magic to power its breath weapon, but its body was made of stagnant magic particles." She held her left hand up, looking at it. "It's like a pocket of magic that shouldn't exist."

Evan gazed at her, concern and admiration in his eyes. He had only practiced one summoning spell before The Unbinding, but

Miranda's choice to use that type of magic to investigate the creature was genius. She would have made a great wizard in her own right before magic unraveled, and her mind had magical intuition most aspiring wizards lacked for decades. He replied, "What do you mean by stagnant magic?"

Miranda squinted in thought. "Dragons rely on magic as much as biology for survival. It concentrates in their bodies while their bodies are formed in an egg. The godshard then draws the arcane in a continual flow during a dragon's life," she whispered, thinking intently. Her eyes widened and she looked directly into Evan's beautiful gray gaze. "The godshard was missing! When I spoke to the creature, it said its soul was missing. Maybe that explains the lack of wings?" she asked, her mind moving quickly. "These Umbrals are just fragments of stale magic left behind when the godshard is taken from the egg. They can sense their own incompleteness and are lashing out."

Celyth sat down as well, looking around. "Looks like the Sanlin property." She licked her lips, also deep in thought. "That's all fair, but the Umbral near Argentum looked like some kind of demon. Why are these specifically shaped like dragons?"

Evan looked to the ground, scanning his knowledge of magic. Yuvina, however, answered the question. "You must understand, though wielding magic is new to me, I am well versed on its function and theory." She stepped forward. "When mortals wield the arcane stream, it merely shapes it into something temporary in most cases. Sometimes magic can be trapped here, though."

Arlindra and Celyth looked to the foxkin with interest. Her words made sense to Evan and Miranda as well, but they weren't sure what direction she intended to take in her thinking. The kitsune continued explaining, "Intense concentrations of discharged magic often leave an imbalance on this side of the arcane stream. Those magical anomalies can vary, however; it seems that taking the godshard from a dragon's egg leaves a similar imbalance. That's my guess, at least."

Miranda stood up, her heart racing. She felt like Yuvina was onto something. She replied, "Then let's operate under the assumption that the Umbrals are manifestations of a magical imbalance." She glanced inside the storage barn, noticing there were six elves inside. She spoke in Alabaster Common to them, "Greetings, Mystalonians. The Umbral pursuing you has been slain."

A voice from inside replied, "Are those the Fernith kids?"

Arlindra and Celyth both faced the storage barn. "Celyth?" the voice added.

"We are here," Celyth responded. "Are there more beasts like the one pursuing you?"

An elf emerged from the barn. "Thank the gods you've returned. There are one hundred of these dragons destroying everything in Mystalon. In just three days' time, they've consumed as many of our magisalves and magitabs as they can get their talons on." He seemed frantic. "They are drawn to any source of magic. They cling to the solisberry tree for hours on end."

Arlindra recognized the elf as a skilled artisan from Wikton's district. She asked, "I don't suppose anyone figured out what caused them to appear, did they?"

The elf was still terrified. "Not at all, Lady Fernith. Although Sage Elitirin has been missing since last night."

Nebu stood up on Arlindra's shoulder and confirmed with a nod. "Yep, I didn't see the snobby one when I made my rounds yesterday. All the other Sages are accounted for."

A different voice called out from the barn, "Arli! Cel! You've gotta save us!" It was Wikton's great grandson, an adolescent elf with rebellious tendencies like the Fernith cousins.

Celyth gave a reassuring smile, "Count on it, kid."

Arlindra turned to her companions. "Look, if Elitirin is missing, we should forget about the city for now. If there were answers here, dad or uncle would have already uncovered them. It's against the rules, but I say we need to investigate Elitirin's land. Remember the rumors?" she asked, looking directly at Celyth for confirmation. "I saw it with my own eyes," she insisted. Celyth gave a slow nod of agreement.

Nebu shook, buzzing his wings loudly. "I told you! That elf is bad news. Has been since the Umbrals started appearing."

Miranda twisted her lips in thought. "The solisberry at the center of your city causes the mana to flow as thick here as it did at the top of the Astral Spire. I can help in any way you need." She offered her help genuinely, reaffirming Miranda's selflessness to Yuvina. Evan looked concerned, however. Before he could speak, Miranda continued, "Don't worry, Evan. I know my maximum is a lot smaller than it was, but I know I'm not going to run out here in Mystalon."

He laughed, "You're not supposed to read my mind. Speaking of, let me report our discovery and plan to Damil and His Holiness." He looked around again, sheathing his weapons. He gave a final smile to

Miranda before raising his fingertips to his temples, connecting his mind with Damil's. As he began to make his report, those around him continued talking.

Celyth added, "Her family's land is all the way on the edge of the forest. Southwest side. If there's nothing there, we'll be wasting a lot of time," she warned.

Arlindra nodded, "Be that as it may, we stand a better chance at finding answers there. Which we need if we're going to fight effectively. I really hope we're not too late to save Dad and Uncle," she finished, looking to the ground with sadness. "But it won't do any good to save them without answers. They'll stay here and fight to the death if we can't answer all of their questions."

Miranda understood, her lips curling up into an excited smile. "Then let's look for answers. Did you say it was in the southwest corner of the forest, Cel?" she clarified.

Yuvina and Evan traded troubled glances. Celyth confirmed with a nod, grinning because Miranda used her nickname. Arlindra caught the exchange, smiling internally. Miranda cycled her breath and put her fingers together, forming a triangle with her index fingers and thumbs. She focused on the mana flowing through the Mystalonian Forest to locate the southwestern corner. A bright, white circle formed underneath them. As they stood in the center of the spell, they felt like they could see the whole of space and time for just an instant. In the very next, they were standing in a poorly lit corner of the forest.

Miranda shuddered. She met the same resistance during the teleport as the egress from Argentum, but the abundant mana nearby made the arcane pollution easier to clear.

Mystalonian trees towered overhead in this part of the forest, but smaller shrubbery had been uprooted and discarded. A large section of earth had been disturbed, and a sinkhole had formed. The crevice was one hundred feet in diameter, but on the west side of the crater was a bundle of tree and plant roots firmly wrapped around something. It rested on the surface on the edge of the sinkhole.

Miranda whispered the Daylight prayer, causing her holy symbol to light up the area. Arlindra gasped and hissed, "Look, there!" She pointed to a ten-foot-wide pipe sticking out of the dense wood and vines wrapped around the ambiguous structure across from them. The vegetation held the structure to the edge of the wall, but the ground seemed loose. The five walked around the larger area of ruptured surface. The sides looked so tenuous that even a slight disturbance could cause the edges to sink into the terrifying darkness below. It went further down than Miranda's prayer, implying a significant drop.

When they reached the pipe in the roots, Arlindra gave it a cursory inspection for boobytraps. The mass of vines clinging onto this pipe looked unnatural, but Elitirin was a manabotanist. Her connection to plants transcended magic. With a grimace, Arlindra turned the wheel on the pipe's covering, loosening it enough to open. When she let go of the dome-shaped lid, it clanged, causing the half-suspended structure to shake precariously. She gave a frightened look to her companions, who all gave her stares of disbelief.

She mumbled, "Yikes. Sorry." She rejoined Miranda and the others on firm earth.

Miranda looked down into the sinkhole. "You know, why don't we do this the safe way." She took a step back and let the mana swell within her. The arcane flow was slower here at the edge of the forest, but it was still many times stronger than the average location. She used the magic within her to lift the bundle away from the wall, placing it firmly on the solid ground beneath the Mystalonian trees. The vines and roots enveloped a structure thirty fifty feet long and thirty feet wide. Arlindra scrambled on top of it, climbing back up to the upright pipe on one end of the structure.

Miranda grabbed a handful of roots, but she felt Evan's eyes on her. His concern was flattering, and he had seen her pour out way too much magic just a few nights before. He would just have to learn her new limits, she thought to herself. She looked at him with a coy expression. "You're just going to let me climb this thing in all this heavy armor?"

Evan snapped to attention, realizing that he was dawdling. "Oh, right!" he replied, looking at the twelve vertical feet of roots and vines before him. With a couple of carefully placed jumps and kicks, he was at the top in just a moment. He laid down flat and extended an arm to Miranda, who then jumped with much less grace than Evan. She managed to get ahold of his hand, however, and he pulled her up with ease. She giggled on the way up, the sapphire blades in her gauntlets shredding through the vines wrapped around this mysterious structure. Evan practically caught her, yanking upward and trying to stand as Miranda's weight reached the top. She fell into him clumsily, and he broke their fall.

Miranda gave him a puzzled look. "Were you trying to throw me?" she asked, her lips forming a small, bewildered circle.

Evan shook his head, feeling her weight pressing him into the sharp wood beneath them. He managed to land prone, and Miranda was sitting on his chest. She stood up, the skirt of her battlemail clanking against the metals in Evan's armor. She extended an arm to him and helped him stand. Yuvina hopped up the side, climbing the wooden bundle with as much ease as Evan. Celyth also climbed up. Evan answered, "No, just being a little overly ambitious with my maneuvers. Sorry, I hope I didn't hurt you."

Miranda laughed. "Even if you did, I'm a priestess, remember? Invictus can heal most injuries through me, even broken bones!" she explained with excitement. Evan knew she focused on the path of the healer before facing Gelidor; now, she was an experienced warpriest with extra potent healing capabilities. It was a combination that made anyone fortunate to have Miranda on their side, even before taking her other gifts into consideration. Evan gave her a confident grin.

Arlindra interrupted, "It smells dangerous." She peered down into the pipe. "Miranda, you first? You have the light."

Miranda looked at the pipe, then to Arlindra. "But I'm claustrophobic!" she said with an exaggerated whine.

Celyth blinked incredulously. "You what?"

Arlindra rolled her eyes. "You always say that."

Miranda giggled. "Yeah, okay. I'll go first," she replied. She would have continued teasing her new friends if the circumstances were not so immediately dire. Now was not the time for jokes. She climbed up the pipe which protruded six feet out of the top of the mass of vines and roots. Looking down, she saw a ladder leading into a white room with long shadows thanks to her Daylight prayer.

She climbed down, listening for threats. As she reached the bottom, she felt magical pressure coming from behind a door opposite the entrance at the ladder. A glass panel separated this entryway from some kind of laboratory. It let enough light through that Miranda could see more of the white, porcelain tile making this place very bright. Arlindra was right behind her with Celyth nearly stepping on her cousin's head to get down the ladder.

Miranda stood at the glass for a moment, staring into the other room. She noticed a person inside, causing her to shout, "Someone's in here, and they look injured!" The room was partially collapsed with chunks of the ceiling scattered about.

Arlindra rushed to the door, inspecting it. It was made of metal and had a clockwork locking mechanism with a power crystal affixed to it. It resembled the ones in Evan's weapons. She touched it, but it did not respond. "Does this open the door?" she asked.

Miranda touched it as well, but it remained inert. She furrowed her brow and pushed mana into the crystal. It glowed for a moment then disintegrated, flaking into a white cloud. As it did, the door clicked and relaxed. The gears released, allowing Arlindra to push it open.

She and Celyth rushed to the figure laying on the floor in the laboratory. Evan and Yuvina were now in the entryway, assessing the situation. Miranda joined the cousins, finding Elitirin lying in a pool of her own blood.

As Arlindra touched her, checking for vitals, the Sage's hand reached out and took Arlindra's. "Is that you, Arlindra?" she asked, her voice weak.

"Yes, Lady Elitirin. We're here to help. What has happened?"

Miranda clutched her holy symbol in her hand. She knelt beside Elitirin and prayed, "Restore to order what was damaged by chaos!" A glowing light covered Elitirin, causing her physical wounds to close. Something else, however, kept her on death's door.

"Your prayers are appreciated, foreign healer," she said with sadness in her voice. "Honesty. Honesty," she murmured, delirious. She continued, "Please, Arlindra, Celyth, listen to me. I prayed that somebody would find me before my time ran out. How fitting that it is both of you with outsiders in your company." She struggled to breathe.

Arlindra tried not to look callous as she held her father's greatest political opponent in her arms. Celyth crossed her own arms, wondering why Miranda's prayer would not be enough. Evan and Yuvina watched from the doorway in silence. Elitirin continued speaking, "I expended the entirety of my life essence to preserve this place. I die in shame, but I have knowledge that must be passed on. Please, save our homeland."

Miranda gave a concerned look to Arlindra. The ranger seemed uncertain, but Miranda gave her a confident nod and a smile of determination. Tears filled Arlindra's eyes. She looked down at Elitirin. "Tell me your story, then. May the truth save Mystalon."

Her next words, however, made Celyth's and Arlindra's blood turn cold. "Mystalon, and your mother, Arlindra. I know where Vanesa might be."

Chapter 11
A New Enemy

"The solisberry tree is possibly not a plant at all. The blooms do not grow new trees, nor do they produce pollen and sap. They are more resilient than Tymbyrwylde trees and sturdier than Mystalonian trees." – Marin Elitirin, *The Sacred Trees of Espa*

uvina sat on the ground outside, looking up at the laboratory covered in roots. Something about the interior of that place made her uneasy. It felt familiar, but she'd never been there. It filled her with a sense of dread. The longer she traveled with Miranda, the more she was certain something horrible happened to her in the last month. This new power within her was incredible, but she wondered what kind of price she paid for it. Miranda said that to her on their second night of travel across the low mountains in the southern Trollcrags. Yuvina could still hear her words, "It seems like everyone wants power, but power has a price. My gift came at the price of my parents and made me the center of an international conflict." The kitsune had never considered the nuance in the lives of people who were born with powers, regardless of their source. Accepting that, however, meant accepting she began paying the price for her current situation fifteen years ago when her brother and father were cut down before her. She trembled with anxiety as her companions emerged from the laboratory.

Evan hopped down first, prompting Yuvina to stand. He helped Miranda navigate down the branches wrapped around the cylindrical structure. Arlindra and Celyth competed for the quietest landing, and Celyth frowned when the buckles on her equipment rattled. Her cousin, however, clenched her fist and made a celebratory gesture in complete silence. Yuvina licked her maw with anticipation as everyone reached the ground.

Miranda noticed the kitsune's agitation and asked, "Yuvina, are you alright?"

She fluffed up her fur and shook her body. "I'm sorry. That place spooked me. As I said, I felt like I have been there before, but I have no memory of it."

Miranda looked at Evan, twisting her lips in thought. She explained the situation to the kitsune. "Sadly, we were unable to save Lady Elitirin. Even my gift was unable to restore enough of her life essence to give her a chance to continue. If only we had arrived sooner," she lamented.

Arlindra reached over and placed a hand on Miranda's shoulder. "Don't blame yourself, nen'li. Elitirin's fate was wrought by her own hands; I am just glad to see that, in the end, she was willing to sacrifice herself to save others."

Yuvina's ears twitched. "Does this mean you've uncovered information?"

Miranda nodded and replied, "Elitirin has been burning power crystals non-stop for weeks now. The smaller crystals created the incomplete, weak Umbrals without form. She was betrayed by a man called Sender who knew that burning the crystals would create Umbrals. The more complete the crystal, the more complete the Umbral," she continued, looking to the ground.

Miranda detected Celyth's increasing anxiety as the warrior added, "To make the crystals, they have to soak dragon eggs in leprechaun's blood, or something like that." She shrugged. "Did you all really understand the nonsense Elitirin was talking about? Negative arcane underflow? Positive stream conductors? Inhibitors? Is that really all related to the eggs?" she asked, uncertainty in her voice.

Arlindra glanced at Evan and Miranda. Evan's magical knowledge was elementary, and Miranda's was skewed by her relationship to the arcane. Miranda gritted her teeth, unable to respond to Celyth's confusion. The warpriest elaborated, "The best I can tell, Sender and his ilk have a gruesome process to turn dragon eggs into crystalized magic that they are calling lacrima-deum. Those are magic words that mean tears of the gods." She spoke with a questioning melody, however, realizing she had borrowed her mother's memories to translate the words. She shuddered and continued, "When a lacrima-deum is exhausted, it creates an Umbral thanks to the imbalance of magic trapped on this side of the arcane stream. It stales and leaves behind magical footprints."

Yuvina's whiskers shook with excitement. Her maw curled up in a smile. Ironically, she understood the conversation. "The Umbrals must be a negative arcane underflow reaction. Since the stream has been choked of mana for a time, once the energies are burned and returned to the stream, it could theoretically manifest as sentient arcane energy. Such an entity would be drawn to magic." She looked to the northeast, the direction of the city from Elitirin's property. "And in a kingdom like Mystalon, there's no shortage of magic for them to find."

Celyth blinked again. "You mean you understood all of that magic gibberish?"

Yuvina smiled. "Remember, I've been trying to cure a lack of magic for the last ten years. If eggs are positive stream conductors, it means the stream passes through them and settles. Much like it does for Miranda and a solisberry tree. Their essences contain the fabric of magic." She thought long about her knowledge. "You know, I feel like I know more, it's just out of reach." She scratched her chin.

Miranda looked at Evan. "That means when the gemstones on your blades are exhausted, more Umbrals will be created."

Evan looked at his belt. "I'll be rid of these cursed abominations the next time I have access to Erk's armory."

Miranda's eyes lit up. "Oh! Evan! You have to tell dad and Damil! The source of the Umbrals!"

Evan's gaze snapped to meet Miranda's excited expression. Her cheeks flushed and her eyes glanced away. He responded, "Oh yeah! We should be able to meet them. They were arriving as we did earlier in the evening." He raised his hands to his temples with urgency, happy to make a productive report.

Damil's thoughts pushed through, "Hey, Evan. Do you have news?"

Evan's nod manifested through the telepathy. "We've discovered the source of the Umbrals. We've confirmed the creatures we now face are also Umbrals, and they are created by burning through the power stones we have been finding."

As Evan pressed his thoughts toward Damil, he felt Selasine and Naomi present. Selasine's mind returned, "Is that so? Is it connected to the eggs somehow?"

Evan's thoughts reverberated with confidence and a touch of anger. "The power crystals are created using dragon eggs. That's why Farzg has been trafficking them so prevalently. The process is horrific. If we don't stop Farzg, then there could be Umbral outbreaks like this all over the world, savvy?"

Selasine thought back, "Is there any reason they would be drawn to the solisberry tree? Even now, the beasts are withdrawing there."

Evan's eyes opened and he gazed at Miranda for a moment, remembering her theory. He then closed them and returned his thoughts to his allies, "Based on what we learned from Elitirin, the lacrima-deum were still somewhat incomplete. They had something removed from them before Sender gave them to Elitirin. Miranda believes that missing piece to be the godshard." There was a pause in his thoughts. "The Umbrals are incomplete dragons; they are missing their souls. They are looking for them in the stream as it flows through the solisberry tree."

Miranda watched as Evan communicated. She felt anxiety building within her. She had not seen her adoptive father in three months. Now that they understood the source of the problem, they had nearly one hundred Umbrals to destroy. She was excited to fight by Selasine's and Erk's sides again. Still, she had to be patient while Evan made his report and organized a rendezvous. Celyth, Arlindra, and Yuvina also watched in silence. If the cousins could be patient at a time like this, then so could she. Miranda smiled, returning her gaze to Evan.

After a few more moments, his eyes opened. "A message from Alaric Fernith," he said suddenly.

Arlindra's expression brightened. "Father! What are his orders?" she asked.

Evan nodded. "We are to meet at the old citadel in the Galathan district. The whole of Mystalon is in shambles, but the survivors from Haerulf, Pleidis, and Garand have been putting up a defensive fight there for the last couple of days. Their resources are running thin, and they could really use some reinforcements." He started to smile, his eyes lingering on Arlindra and Celyth. "His Holiness is currently leading survivors from all districts toward the old citadel. Everyone is waiting on your return, Ladies Fernith. We should move now, the Umbrals are withdrawing to the tree."

Celyth's eyes remained cold, her green gaze flickering in the Daylight prayer emanating from Miranda's holy symbol. "They want us back now when our skills will save their asses."

Arlindra put a hand on Celyth's shoulder. "I know you are angry, cousin. Bitter. Even Hai-Yashir would have—" she started.

Celyth interrupted her abruptly, "Why are you so forgiving, cousin? Hai-rin died because of their backwards ideas! We needed a healer, not more yinfruit garbage! But now that *they* need help from the outside, they're more than willing to take it." She looked incensed, her eyes flashing with fury. Nebu tried to look as small as possible on Arlindra's shoulder as Celyth shouted, "As far as I'm concerned, the rest of them sealed their fates when they killed my mother!"

Miranda, Evan, and Yuvina exchanged glances. This was part of a tale they had never heard. Miranda wanted to offer comfort and condolences to Celyth, but she could tell that the elf was especially agitated. Over the last year, Miranda learned to read people's emotions much the way Erk did. Now was the time for action, not tragic tales and justifying divisions. Before Arlindra could respond, Miranda insisted, "That's not fair, Celyth!"

Celyth's eyes cut to Miranda with hostility, but the warpriest looked overcome with emotion. The elven warrior wanted to lash out, but Miranda's sapphire eyes were full of truth and righteous indignation. Miranda continued speaking, her voice commanding and authoritative. "You left your home to find a solution to the Umbrals, and now you're back with answers. You've proven that reaching for outside help is the right thing to do sometimes. You and your family have suffered enough, and your efforts can prevent more tragedies in the future." She stood at attention. The conviction in her voice was not from Philotrax nor Reshiria; this was who she was in her heart. Her musical voice choked with pain and empathy, "You have the chance to prevent more tragedies, the same kind that have broken your heart. You have suffered plenty, do you really think you need to pass that pain onto others?"

The anger in Celyth's eyes turned to sorrow. Arlindra hugged her cousin. They truly were sisters at heart. The ranger spoke, "Come, now. What's better, poisoning yourself with bitterness, or proving to them that you were right? Now's our chance. Espa is so much bigger than Mystalon, and I'm ready for this nightmare to be over so that we can go back out there. Father and uncle can clean up the mess." Arlindra released her cousin and looked into her eyes. "We've got new enemies now. Farzg is moving the eggs that destroyed our home, right? I don't think the Sages would debate for one second now that Elitirin is gone. You know what we need to do."

Yuvina's eyes filled with tears. Even with immense powers at their disposal, the cousins still faced a tragedy similar to hers. The kitsune started to wonder if she would even be alive now had she been born with some kind of magical ability. Watching from the shadows for so long had skewed her view of those with uncanny magic. She felt like she needed to see Seiv Everdusk soon to discuss her future in The Forgotten, especially now that she had discovered a gift of her own. For the moment, however, she wanted to help resolve this conflict. Her uncanny magic would be useful against incredible beasts like the Umbrals. She had a duty to stay; Miranda helped her uncover her uncanny magic, and Yuvina wanted to start doing the things she promised she would do if she had magic of her own.

Celyth took a deep breath, looking at Miranda. "I guess you're right. And to help father and uncle, we'll have to help those other morons." She shrugged, wiping a tear from her eye. "It's like collateral damage, but the opposite."

Her phrasing elicited a laugh from everyone except Nebu, who was still trying to go unnoticed. Evan asked, "Does that mean we can rely on you to guide us to the citadel in Galathan?"

Arlindra and Celyth both nodded in agreement. The ranger added, "It's not much of a citadel, though. Mostly a replica, a historical building of sorts. Reminiscent of the wars that pushed the original Mystalonians away from Claston."

Miranda turned toward the center of the forest, the fires glowing brightly. The warpriest speculated, "If the Umbrals are withdrawing to the solisberry tree, then now is our best chance to unite with our allies. We need to rest soon, as well."

Arlindra and Celyth began walking toward the city. Celyth commented, "It's only a few hours on foot to the heart of the city from here."

Miranda gave a cheeky smile. "I'll be able to recharge closer to the solisberry tree, too. Let's save our energy," she said, pressing her fingers together in a triangle again. Miranda was shocked when they met no resistance in their magical journey, further confounding her expectations about teleportation magic.

In another instant, the six of them stood five hundred feet to the north of the dome over the solisberry tree in the center of Mystalon. As they gained their bearings, they saw numerous, hulking Umbrals making their way back into the dome. Many of the panes of glass surrounding the structure had been shattered, allowing the beasts easy passage under the mithril frame. They saw dozens more shadowy dragon figures swarming toward the tree in the distance.

Arlindra was the first in motion, "Come. Galathan is northwest of the arboretum."

The others joined her, moving across Mystalon while the Umbrals withdrew. Within the hour, they were near the base of a Mystalonian tree surrounded by ruined houses and other buildings. The Umbrals had wreaked wanton destruction on the city. The glowing, paved streets were completely shattered, only shining their light in a few places that miraculously escaped the devastation. The beautiful architecture of the stone buildings now rested in piles of rubble, and wooden buildings were obliterated by fire and lightning. Many of them were still ablaze, ignited in this last assault from the Umbrals. Celyth looked at the scene with disdain. Arlindra tried to ignore the details, focusing on their destination.

The only sound in the streets was fire. Yuvina shuddered, the spectacle reminding her of when she was taken from The Tymbyrwylde. Evan thought back to the way Gelidor's men destroyed his family's estate in an attempt to consolidate power. As they came to a neighborhood with numerous structures ablaze, Miranda sighed. She focused on the mana in the air, drawing as much of it to her as possible. She then created several small storm clouds that began raining over the fires. Nebu stirred for the first time since Celyth's outburst. "I mean, the gesture is nice and all, but I don't think putting out the fire is going to help!" he taunted.

Miranda simply smiled. "The sooner the fires are out, the sooner the Mystalonians can rebuild." The music in her voice was sincere and heartfelt. As she spoke, Evan's heart surged into his throat. It was Miranda's infinite optimism which saved his home kingdom. He felt honored that he was entering into battle by her side this time. The warpriest looked around. "Where is the citadel?"

Arlindra gestured to what was once a wide, glowing street. "This way," she ordered, navigating the rubble left behind by the fighting. After another ten minutes of walking, they saw the building in question. It stood forty feet high, and the remnants of a ten-foot wall surrounded it. It was a three-tiered defensive structure with numerous turrets and crenelations making it practically impregnable. Miranda realized what Arlindra meant; the building was imposing, but it was smaller than what she expected of a fortress. The front gate of the citadel was utterly destroyed, but a battalion of armed Mystalonians stood out front. Arlindra raised an eyebrow with concern. She recognized several of them as citizens of the other northern districts of Slanodon and Uyin. Part of her was glad to see the unity, but it came at such a steep price.

A voice bellowed from behind the companions, "You're late!" It was a gruff with a common accent similar to Miranda's.

Evan turned with a smile on his lips. Celyth and Arlindra presented weapons, and Yuvina crouched low, scanning for threats. The overwhelming smells of the burning city masked the interloper's scent. Miranda, too, turned with eager surprise, her blue eyes wide with joy. "August!" she called back and broke into a run toward the source.

On the broken path behind them stood three paladins and about two dozen Mystalonians. Miranda closed the hundred feet between them in seconds. August laughed and hugged Miranda as she launched herself into him. Justin and Valarie looked at each other with small, adoring smiles, but then Justin gasped.

"Miranda, where is your shield?" Justin demanded without so much as a greeting.

As the warpriest broke away from August, she turned to Justin and Valarie who were standing to August's right. They were not in their usual formation as they guided the Mystalonians to the citadel. Miranda's cheeks flushed with embarrassment, "One of the Umbrals turned it into dust with a yellow breath weapon made of light," she explained.

Justin blinked, then Valarie elbowed her boyfriend. She stepped forward and hugged Miranda, saying, "It's good to see you! Don't mind him, we'll put in a requisition to get you a new one as soon as we're back in Nulodia," she said, winking.

August laughed, and Justin sputtered, "Hey, I was just worried! Sounds like the shield saved her from Yellowbreath."

Miranda blinked. "You mean it had a name?"

Justin grinned. "Well, a nickname. I suppose if you encountered it, then you ended it?" he asked confidently.

Miranda confirmed with only a nod as her new companions and Evan joined her next to the paladins. Miranda looked around, "There are probably a lot of introductions to be made, but now is not the time. Shall we accompany you to the citadel?"

The paladins saluted in unison, prompting Miranda to do the same. As the group approached, now thirty strong, the paladins took the lead. They stepped forward to speak with the city militia. After a few moments, an elf with royal blue hair emerged from the hallway exposed by the destroyed gate to the building.

Arlindra rushed forward, shouting, "Modai-rin!"

Celyth was right behind her, "Modai-moshir!" she shouted.

Alaric's relief was visible in his eyes. "Yolasha! Yolen!" he called back. There were at least fifty people present now including the militia members outside the small citadel. The crowds melted away as Arlindra and Celyth overwhelmed Alaric with a forceful hug. Miranda's eyes lit up with excitement and her lips pursed up into a happy smile. Yuvina watched in heartbroken silence. Evan's eyes lingered on the citadel, giving an excited smile of his own.

"Your daughter and niece, I presume?" a warm, methodical voice asked in the awkward quietness that fell during the reunion. The reason for Evan's smile became apparent as Erk, Selasine, and Naomi also emerged from the ruined entryway.

The paladins and Miranda all stood at attention; the high priests of the Church of Invictus outranked all other clergy but the Council of Four. Celyth and Arlindra took a moment to observe the newcomers, and Celyth blurted out, "Erilkaiden, Dad, and Naomi." She pointed at each one of them as she spoke.

Erk and Naomi burst into laughter. Selasine smiled, tenderness in his eye, "Well met Celyth. Your father is waiting for you in the citadel," he explained.

The sarcasm in her expression evaporated. "Modai-rin!" she called, rushing past Alaric and the others to enter the citadel.

Alaric gave a saddened look to his daughter. "You were wise to go directly to Elitirin's property. I am proud of you," he began, his voice filled with emotion.

Arlindra embraced her father again, but her eyes were locked onto Selasine. The hallway behind the wrecked entrance was ten-feet wide and ten feet tall, and he seemed to occupy most of that space on his own. Naomi was almost as physically overwhelming, and the Erk character looked equal parts deadly and handsome. She smiled at the people she would have called Miranda's family but said nothing.

Erk's face was drawn tight with worry. Selasine patted the elf on his shoulder as he stepped forward to address the faithful. The militia was organizing the citizens escorted by the paladins. The high priest looked at his pupils, giving them a stern examination. The world seemed to stop as he stood tall then saluted. His form was impeccable. His left hand gripped the hilt of his sword in the same instant that his right palm turned up to face the sky. He then began a catechism none of his former students had ever said with him. "On this day, we face great calamity. Justice has been wounded and order bleeds at the hands of chaos."

Valarie's eyes cut to Justin. August stared back in disbelief. Justin shook his head, not expecting the catechism. Miranda's musical voice replied, "In these days, may the hands of Invictus heal the wounds. Now is not the time for more bloodshed, but for mending." It was one of the healer's catechisms. She stepped forward, walking up to the high priest still holding his salute. Right now, she was in direct violation of so many protocols she could have been reprimanded. She then snapped into her own salute, her eyes filling with tears and a smile on her lips. She thought of him as a father, and rightly so. After she had been overcome with violent thoughts while facing the assassin, she felt a turmoil stirring within her heart. He had chosen the perfect catechism to greet his daughter whose mind was struggling with the impulse to use violence to solve conflict more efficiently.

Selasine maintained a stern look on his face for a moment after Miranda saluted. His posture then relaxed, and a smile broke out on his lips. "At ease, yolasha," he said, her embrace clanking their armor together before he could even finish his command. Justin, Valarie, and August eased their postures. They all smiled as their little adoptive family reunited.

Arlindra interrupted their reunion. "Miranda! Where is Yuvina?" Her voice was panicked.

Miranda released Selasine from her embrace but stood close by him as she turned to look at the crowds. She shook her head as she searched.

Evan, Erk, and Naomi had gathered a short distance away. Evan cursed as he overheard. "By the gods. Yuvina?" he called, also scanning the crowds.

Selasine heard about the foxkin from Evan's reports. Her missing memory concerned him, as he only knew of two forces in Espa that could tamper with a person's mind with such precision. "Should we organize a search?" he asked, not seeing any kitsune in the crowds of displaced elves.

Miranda giggled. She responded, "I can still feel her close. I think the crowds spooked her." She looked at Arlindra. "Don't worry. She'll be back with us when it matters."

Arlindra gave a nod. "I suppose you're right." She had grown fond of the kitsune over the last few days; they were both perfectly content keeping to themselves, but Yuvina's talents and intellect impressed Arlindra. Yuvina was not overbearing and did not pry too much. In Arlindra's mind, those traits made Yuvina a perfect friend. She sincerely hoped the foxkin was okay wherever she had gone.

Selasine put a hand on Miranda's shoulder and looked down at her. "You've gone and gotten yourself mixed up in another crisis, kid."

She sheepishly looked up at him with a grin that only happened when she forgot an important catechism. "I can't really stop destiny, can I?" she asked and shrugged.

Selasine gave a content sigh. "Speaking of destiny, we have a plan to discuss. For now, however, everyone needs to rest. I will collaborate with Alaric and the other Sages. We will brief everyone in the morning before the Umbrals begin their next rampage."

Miranda couldn't argue with his logic and was content to follow her dad to a dining room converted into indoor campsites. Naomi had prepared a space for her companions complete with plush bedrolls and pillows. She had even placed a few pieces of luxury furniture around their claimed space. Everyone except Selasine and Erk found a spot. Celyth arrived after visiting with her father for a while. As Arlindra chose the space furthest from the group, Nebu buzzed his wings. He asked, "So, you're telling me this Naomi character was prepared for this? Look at this stuff! It screams luxury! Is Naomi a queen or something?"

The giantkin laughed, lounging on a luxurious chaise and covered in a billowing silk gown. "Yes, dracofly. I demand luxury for my crew and my friends. I keep enough on hand to make sure all of my girls have a comfortable place to sleep if we have to rough it inland." She sat up, causing Nebu to take flight and hover near Arlindra's face.

Miranda yawned and laid down on a plush blanket that felt like a mattress. She had taken off her armor for the first time in three days and felt intense relief. She wanted a bath, but Naomi did not bring the magical tub from the dressing room on *The Nebula*. The dining room was large, stretching out one hundred feet by forty feet. Other groups formed camps of their own, and everyone seemed on edge. Miranda would have to wait for that bath. She had changed into an oversized cotton shirt that might have belonged to Selasine at one point, but it made a perfect evening robe for her. The chatter of everyone around her faded, and it sounded like Nebu and Naomi were still discussing the lavish furnishings she kept in a pocket dimension.

As everyone began to settle into their places, the paladins were laid out in the center area of the makeshift camp. They had placed their bedrolls and tucked them under a few luxurious blankets Naomi had lent them. Evan saw Miranda settling in for sleep across the campsite and maneuvered his way across the bedrolls, attempting to move with such swiftness that nobody would notice his passing. August, however, decided to make the obstacle course semi-lethal by grabbing Evan's ankle as he tried to glide over them without touching the ground.

As Miranda's mind started to contemplate the events of the day, a flash of blond caught her attention. Evan was mid-air, about to faceplant directly into Miranda. The sudden movement caused Miranda to shriek with surprise, and she activated the mana within her on instinct. It suspended Evan in the air, about a foot away from Miranda's face. Her eyes were wide, and her mouth took its distinct, round shape of shock. She sat up on her elbows.

Evan grunted, the momentum of his fall cushioned by an unseen force. Behind him, August and the others laughed, the childish prank going perfectly. Evan looked up, his blond waves falling haphazardly into his face. Miranda's stomach jumped up into her throat. She could barely see his gray eyes through his scattered hair, but they were so beautiful she lost her breath. He looked right back into her pools of blue, her surprise endearing and cute. He laughed awkwardly, "Oh, thanks."

Miranda twisted the mana a bit so she could guide Evan's hovering form to another soft blanket beside her. She dropped him from about six inches in the air, causing him to land with a soft thud. "Time-out," Miranda said, her voice teasing and pouty.

Naomi watched the two of them intently while almost everyone else began trying to sleep.

Evan rolled onto his back. "Ouch," he prodded.

Miranda giggled. "You know better than to pull stunts around August."

He laughed. "Just goes to show I still have a lot of improvement to make." He had changed into green, silk pajamas that looked a little small for him. He must have appropriated them from Erk after his curse was lifted, Miranda thought. He propped himself up on an elbow and rolled onto his side to face Miranda. He pulled a pillow from nearby under his chest. "I want to be like the headmistress. Her movement was incredible."

Miranda tilted her head, her hair unbraided. Because she wore the unique, front-hanging braids so often, her hair seemed most normal when it was pulled forward. She brushed some out of her face, replying, "You're on the wrong path, then. The Harbingers and The Hammerfist are very different."

Evan cocked his head down, "Oh, is that so?" His voice indicated curiosity.

She nodded in reply. "Remember how the headmistress could also look for my parents' godshards?" She placed her hand close to her heart.

He nodded. "She mentioned The Hammerfist. I only know that The Harbingers are an elite fighting force. Hammerfist training doesn't focus on weapons at all."

Miranda's lips twisted into a coy smile. "And that's why the headmistress can move faster than light, and August can trip you."

He grinned in return. "Fair enough. What about The Hammerfist is so different?"

She laid down on her back, her hair cascading over her shoulders and onto the blanket. "They don't study weapons because they don't like violence. They rely on Lexcord's spiritual guidance to train their bodies, minds, and souls to perfect harmony. And then they can do really crazy flips," she started to ramble. Evan had given her the perfect topic, as he wanted to know more about the reclusive monks. "It's like their bodies break away from the physical. The masters look incredible when they train together. I think you'd make a terrible monk, though."

Evan's lips parted in surprise, "Why so?" His voice was slightly defensive.

Her shy smile seemed small, and her stomach was still caught in her throat. The feeling intensified when she started to speak, "Well. For starters, I think your hair is pretty, and you'd have to shave it. Second, the masters are patient, contemplative, and reserved. You're contemplative, at least."

He laughed out loud, provoking August to snore deeply for a moment. The paladin had somehow already fallen asleep. Evan liked her reasoning, and it filled his stomach with butterflies. "Please, tell me why else I'd be a terrible monk." His voice was suave now, indicating his feeling in the conversation had changed.

Miranda raised an eyebrow and her jaw slacked with incredulity. "Evanthalus! Fishing for more compliments. You're reaching a new low."

She caught him so off guard his eyes bulged, and his mouth elongated in an ashamed expression. Then, hesitating for only a moment, his smile returned. "And every time I hit a new low, there you are to pull me right back from the depths." He fluffed the pillow. She rolled on her side facing Evan now, but her normally sparkling eyes were closed. The torches lighting the room were somewhat dim since they were likely mundane. The Umbrals would have come looking for the everburning variety. Still, in this light she looked beautiful and serene.

She replied, her voice lowered to a murmur, "Then stop trying to live like you're trying to recover thirty years and start living like you have three hundred more to look forward to."

Evan smiled. Her words were harsh and straightforward, but she was right. He spent every moment focused on honing his skills because he felt like he was working from a deficit. In a way, he had been compensating for his loss of Unbinding power. Miranda could see right through that insecurity, which is what prompted him to glide over the resting paladins in the first place.

A voice hissed from a window on the second floor above. "I heard a scream. It was Miranda. Is she alright?"

Evan looked up, spotting Yuvina perched in a second story window. He raised his finger to his lips, hoping she would see that everything was in order. After a moment the kitsune relaxed, laying back in the window's opening. The citadel's walls were thick, though they had taken substantial damage in some places. Evan's smile persisted. He felt like something big was going to happen tomorrow, but he wasn't sure what that might be. Still, he had an excitement lingering in his spirit. "Goodnight, Miranda, Judge of Hearts," he whispered.

Miranda's soft breathing helped him ease into a gentle rest of his own.

Naomi's silver eyes glittered. She was right, as per usual. They were cute together and complemented each other's strengths. She relaxed in the chair, Arlindra having dozed moments ago. Nebu had tucked into his master's hair. Celyth seemed strangely delicate in her sleep. Justin and Valarie embraced while they rested, and August's snores were sporadic. Miranda and Evan were close together, and their mysterious fox friend slept a story up in the windowsill. Naomi looked over them all protectively. She already knew what the Sages had decided and why that heartbreak needed to wait for tomorrow's light.

Eldon Farzg stroked his beard methodically while he gazed out the window in his study. He admired the grounds of his marvelous estate. The complex consisted of a main villa with a welcoming courtyard out front. The architecture was reminiscent of the castles built by frost giants throughout history. The material was ivory, marble, and a beautiful, white stone known as snowstone. It was a magnificent rock that was perpetually and magically cold. Pillars were built with a deep blue granite with no magical properties in spite of its mystic shimmer. Large windows revealed opulent rooms within, and the villa included numerous wings and icicle-shaped spires. Enormous statues and fountains decorated the path leading from the courtyard to the gates of the estate. A large, fifteen-foot wall had been erected around the villa, and the complex sprawled for miles outside the central area. Six small fortresses were strategically positioned beyond the wall. They housed Farzg's highest ranking servants when they were not deployed. They also served as an additional guard against anyone foolish enough to approach Farzg's estate on foot. The dirt road departing his property disappeared into The Lichwood ten miles away.

Farzg sighed with boredom. Not even his magnificent kingdom could distract him from his current predicament. There were very few things in the universe he feared, and the meddling of dark gods was one of them. Doctor One's technology offered Farzg the keys to command an unparalleled criminal empire which undermined the despotic theocracies of Alabaster. At this point, however, it was becoming clear to Farzg that Doctor One's ambitions went beyond the scope of correcting the balance of order and chaos. His plans seemed impetuous, and Farzg preferred to operate with calculated moves.

A knock rattled the door, pulling Farzg out of his thoughts. "It's open," he replied, continuing to stare out the window.

Echo's voice sounded panicked, "Majesty!"

The frost giantkin turned around to see Echo mere steps behind an athletic elf in a bodysuit and cloak. Her teal eyes flashed with anger under the hood of her draping as she approached Farzg, who stood motionless. He stared in disbelief as Elyndandria stopped inches away from him, the frost giantkin towering over her. She pulled the cloak off her head, revealing short, black hair. Her face was somewhat long and pretty, and a scar descended from above her right eye, across her nose, and down her left cheek. Though her eyes were such a light color, they reflected pure malice in this moment. "Eldon, are you trying to get me killed?"

Farzg cycled his breath. He chose Elyndandria thanks to her reputation for efficiency, but he was not surprised this mark proved too much for her. "You are the professional, Elyndandria. Did you make the mistake of attacking them all at once?"

Elyndandria's nostrils flared with anger. "You know that's how I operate. The woman with red hair invaded my mind, Farzg. They had resources you didn't warn me about." She paused to maintain her composure, but her face contorted from the strain. "Furthermore, they weren't where you said they would be. I had to do recon. That Reginald guy is a creep." She sighed. "I don't know what you're getting into, Farzg. But you should get out while you're ahead. That group with the Evanthalus guy is incredible. You should have warned me."

Though Farzg was physically more intimidating, Elyndandria's presence rivaled The Frozen Death. He had full faith in her ability to survive; he had, after all, given her an incredible ring of regeneration. He realized she was probably angrier about missing a mark than the details missing from the contract. "How about this, then. I will pay you the full bounty for a full report on the activities and capabilities of the enemies you faced on this mission." His voice lacked its usual air of condescension. He respected Elyndandria, and he had deceived her intentionally. The notorious assassin would either succeed in her mission, or she would acquire important knowledge through failure. He was willing to pay her substantial fees for even a failed mission. "Does that sound fair?" he asked, a rare sincerity in his voice.

Her lips quivered in rage as she responded, "Not until you tell me every disgusting detail of what you're mixed up in and why you would send me halfway across Alabaster to eliminate a pointless target."

Farzg gave a nod and gestured toward the desk in his study. Elyndandria didn't move, staring up at the frost giantkin with persistent rage. He heard the door to his study click shut as Echo departed. Resuming his usual, haughty tone, he explained, "I am currently being targeted by the Church of Invictus. It seems a coalition of fools has formed to stand against me."

Elyndandria interjected, "You can't feign surprise, Eldon. They ruined you once already." Her voice dripped with sadism.

Farzg's eyes narrowed, and he continued speaking. "The priestess Iriliandria was the one responsible for my first loss, and I paid her what she was owed. I paid it double to Thomas, the new high priest. It's his vendetta against me that fuels the church's movements."

The assassin sneered. "As always, your ego will be your downfall. It might even get you killed this time. The only fool I see here is you, Eldon." The hostility in her tone would have normally been a death sentence while speaking with Farzg, but the frost giantkin was neither offended nor surprised.

He replied, "You are correct based on the facts as you know them. I should have killed Thomas when I had the chance. There are only two of them left. In all honesty, Elyndandria, it's not the church that concerns me now," he continued, walking to the far side of the desk in his study. He sat in a chair placed for visitors.

Elyndandria stood in silence for a moment, watching him walk around the desk and sit. She understood the gesture; in his own way, Farzg was admitting his mistake. He thought of himself as some kind of king, but Elyndandria did not entertain his fantasies. She simply carried out his dirty work when he was willing to pay her price. She walked over to the elaborate throne-like chair now sitting opposite the frost giantkin, and she eased herself into it. Her senses stayed on edge, expecting a trap or worse.

Farzg continued speaking, "I have recently taken numerous contracts from a former wizard that calls himself Doctor One. He is, however, no physician."

Elyndandria scowled. She was familiar with this group, their technology, and their operations. "Reginald. He said he was Doctor Thirteen?"

Farzg nodded. "Doctor One calls his closest associates by the same title and a number. I have met Two, Three, Five, and Thirteen. They are all eccentric, but their value is evidenced by their inventions."

Elyndandria had met some of these "Doctors," and she was using their technology to eliminate targets more efficiently. They were, however, very strange, and the assassin tried to minimize contact with them by procuring their devices through Farzg or other sources. "Agreed, but what does any of this have to do with the fool's errand you sent me on?" she retorted, impatience in her voice.

The frost giantkin closed his eyes, taking time to weave his words. "In short, I learned Doctor One is in league with Aylabrax the Devourer. Her arrival in our current scenario perplexes me and fulfills a prophecy."

The assassin leaned forward and placed her hands on Farzg's desk. The oversized furniture made patronizing body language difficult. Disdain resonated in every word as she replied, "Have you gone and joined a cult? What prophecy are you talking about? I thought this was just a revenge kill, and now you're rambling inanities!"

The air temperature dropped, coating Farzg's stone desk in frosty condensation. His violet eyes opened with a flash of anger. He frowned and glared at Elyndandria, causing the assassin's expression to shift from condescending to on guard. She tilted her head up a bit and scowled in return. She removed her hands from the desk and crossed her arms. She amended, "Sorry. You're scaring me, that's all."

His frown melted into a pained expression. "A decade ago, I cornered a pacifist. I knocked on her door, and she recognized me on sight. She looked heartbroken to see me as one does when they know their life is over." He shuddered as the air returned to a comfortable temperature. "Her words spared her life another hour. I knew she had the gift of Foresight right away."

Elyndandria leaned forward with genuine interest. "She was an elf, then. What color was her hair?" she asked, reaching up to touch her own black locks.

Her casual mannerism surprised Farzg and brought a smile to his lips. "Darker than the raven, Elyndandria."

She replied, "It fits *Elvenscrit*, though the gift is rare."

Farzg raised his hand to his beard, running his fingers through the coarse, white hair. He furrowed his brow and said, "Yes, and we both know the golden-haired prophet." His smile turned sinister. "Nevertheless, this pacifist. When she opened the door, she said 'You're early.' Not hello, not a cry to the gods, not a plea for mercy as so many do. Simply, 'You're early,' and I paused. She was absolutely correct. I arrived two days earlier than I intended."

Elyndandria's teal eyes sparkled with intensity as she listened. Her normal, intimidating expression softened. Farzg continued his story. "Before I could respond, she invited me into her home for tea. I thought it was a ploy at first, but she had the table set for two."

The assassin glared, but the frost giantkin interrupted her before she could object. "It was set for an elf and a person of my stature. An extra-large kettle and teacup. She was waiting for me, Ely. I was intrigued. I suspected poison, but she prepared everything in my presence. By the time the kettle screamed, I was dying to hear her final plea."

Elyndandria's glare shifted to shock, and her lips parted in awe. Farzg closed his eyes again. "I learned that Thomas was not home. He would not be returning for a day, either. In the meantime, she did not beg nor did she intend to beg. She explained her gift. Then, she made a prophecy that has lingered on my periphery for the last decade."

Winter wind howled outside, filling a minute of silence. Elyndandria finally murmured, "Eldon, what did she say?"

He cleared his throat. "The darkness will devour after you've touched the silver light. Your crusade will end in ruin if you betray the radiance. The Judge is the only piece that can stop The Executioner for a reason."

Elyndandria crossed her eyes in confusion. "What in the Infernia does that mean?"

Farzg tugged on his beard as he replied, "I would like to show you something. Please, Elyndandria, open the trap door beneath you."

She raised an eyebrow. "To the vault?" she asked, feeling her avarice surge.

He replied, "Yes. That's where we'll find the silver light."

Farzg took Elyndandria to his vault. The trap door under the desk descended to a royal court, and Farzg's bedroom was behind the dais leading to the throne. In his quarters, another trap door opened to a metal shaft. It descended twenty feet, and a steel door with a valve wheel was shut tight at the bottom. The frost giantkin reached out and cooled the door, causing the wheel to turn as the drop in temperature operated the mechanism. It opened to a large, circular room with a diameter of one hundred and fifty feet. The roof was concave, and the walls were made of snowstone. Strange, trumpet-like bells were positioned haphazardly throughout the walls and ceiling. They resembled pipes running out of sight behind the snowstone. The room was overflowing with treasure and coin, but none of that interested Elyndandria. She only took her payment in magic items left as relics from before The Unbinding.

On the far side of this room was another valved door. Farzg used the same method to open it, but the cold was more intense. Elyndandria lost the feeling in her extremities due to the sudden freeze. "Gods, you're terrifying Eldon," she commented.

He rolled his eyes as the door opened. "I know," was all he said, gesturing inside. The treasure room was a twenty-foot square room encased in snowstone. Chests lined the walls, and a stone display pillar sat in the center. Upon it rested a sliver of silver metal about a foot long. It tapered to a fine point, and the thick end was shaped like a clover with a golden heart etched into the center. An intense halo of white light surrounded the sliver, creating a globe of pressure functioning as a physical barrier. It hovered six inches above the pedestal. Elyndandria wasn't sure what it was, but she found it captivating.

Farzg reached out to the piece of metal and nudged the aura with his fingertips. The whole sphere rolled. He explained, "This is the soul of Saraix, the Dragon Queen."

Elyndandria's eyes widened. She protested, "How in Espa did you come across the soul of a god, Eldon? Are you sure it is what you think it is?" She squinted, examining the beautiful artifact. It glimmered, the silver pure and reflective. "Though The Unbinding has severed me from magic, I can feel its overwhelming power," she murmured, hypnotized by the radiance.

The frost giantkin laughed. "You are wiser than me, Elyndandria. I provoked her. And in her soul, there I found the silver light Iriliandria warned me about." He placed his fingertips on top of the aura, grinding it against the pedestal. It generated no sound. "I received this beauty as payment for a contract with The Merchant."

The assassin sneered. "Ew. That guy is the worst. Why would you deal with him? He's more arrogant than you."

Farzg chuckled and picked up the shard of Saraix with both hands. "He found a way to purchase immortality. I might not like him, but I have a tendency to play nice with entities unaffected by my Death Geyser."

She spat. "You're such a pushover."

He smirked. "And here you are, doing my bidding."

The malice in her eyes lightened. "Loyal patrons earn loyalty. Na'agamlor is far from loyal. His gifts profit nobody but him."

Farzg frowned with agreement. "While that's true, I found enough mutual benefit to accept the contract. The Merchant wanted a particular type of dragon egg in exchange for this precious relic." He held the shard of Saraix toward Elyndandria. "I sealed my fate when I murdered the priestess. I know the prophesied future." His eyes lingered on the shard. "I plan to change that future, but I know what will happen if I cannot."

Elyndandria's mouth hung open. She asked with unusual hesitation, "What happens, Eldon?"

"Regardless of the outcome of the pending conflict, my

possession of this item must end. I have seen fools try to fight prophecies with such ferocity that they weave the destiny themselves." He shook his head. "Now that darkness devours, Iriliandria's Foresight advances. Seven eyes fixed to the silver light, but only the teal raven can fly her to safety."

Elyndandria sputtered, "I-is that supposed to mean me?!" Her eyes bounced between Farzg and the shard. She took a step back, feeling the divine power of the Dragon Mother weighing against her.

"Aye," he replied, his gravelly voice deeper than normal. "I sent you after Evanthalus, but my objectives were two-fold." His gaze dropped to the artifact in his hands. "The Dragon Queen instructed me to give her soul to a dragon of light. I believe that dragon is the girl with red hair."

The assassin perched her hands on her hips. She replied, "Why would you side with your enemies, Eldon?"

He returned his gaze to Elyndandria. "I'm not. You saw her fighting firsthand. You said she invaded your mind. Is she not a worthy opponent?"

Elyndandria paused. She combed her memories for information before she responded, "The same girl who killed Na'agamlor's agent in Claston. This Mir'thax as she is called. If she's already so powerful, why would you willingly offer her the shard of a god?"

Farzg's sadistic smile returned. "She won't get the shard unless she can kill me, Ely. The second purpose for that contract was to test her resolve. She broke a sacred tenet of Invictus when she invaded your mind against your will." His smile broadened. "I believe she is the only living soul in Espa who stands a chance against me in combat. She is convicted, but she is bendable. Unlike her fellow clergy, she is willing to go any distance to defend her ideals."

The assassin's jaw slacked with frustration and disbelief. "Y-you used me as a test?!" she shrieked.

The sadism in the frost giant's smile shifted into utter cheek. "Come now, Ely. I'd never do something so treacherous to my favorite assassin." He stood tall, shifting the soul of Saraix into his right hand and holding it out to her. "When Miranda heads north to face me, I need you to take this to the Eastpoint Lighthouse. I will send you further instructions through the portal chest I have hidden there."

Elyndandria's head jerked with intrigue. "You have a portal chest hidden off the coast of Claston? How predictable." Anger seeped into her expression. "You really believe these prophecies, then. You're taking steps as if they're going to come true."

The violet in his eyes flashed. "Every prediction made by Iriliandria has come true. I have every reason to believe her, and I will not have that aspect questioned." He let silence hang between them for a minute before continuing. "I also believe the future can be bent by powerful wills. Elyndandria, please understand I'm not doing this because I am afraid." His evil, maniacal smile sent physical and emotional chills through the assassin as he finished his rant. "I am doing this because, if I am successful, I will have defied the will of a god. I will have defied the will of the universe, and I will soon ascend to godhood."

Elyndandria took the shard in her hand with a look of disgust. "I thought you were different, but you're worse." She shrugged, feeling the intense magic radiating within Saraix's soul. She felt an entity watching her, and she smiled. "It's comforting to hold."

Farzg turned to walk out of the vault. "Doctor One's end goal is more sinister than I realized when I met him." He reached inside his robe and withdrew a device. "When shadows cast their terror, justice will be nigh. Revenge hides in trust while the avenger fulfills his destiny."

She put the shard of Saraix in an extradimensional pouch. She followed Farzg, asking, "Another prophecy? What is that thing you hold?"

He showed her the contraption in his hand. It was a wand of eolnut wood just short of a foot in length. It ended with a large chamber designed to house a lacrima-deum. "This 'thing' reveals Doctor One's hand. It's called a diffuser. It differs from the extraction chambers in the weapons. Those are engineered to make the most out of the stones, but the diffuser wastes the magic within them in seconds."

The assassin contemplated the crystals powering her own Doctor-created weapons and accessories. When the power was exhausted, the items became inert. She wanted to express anger, but she felt lingering warmth in her soul as if the Dragon Mother had reached out to encourage her. Elyndandria's reply was gentle. "Why would you waste the stones? They're quite useful and expensive to replace."

The frost giantkin smiled. "Therein lies the true objective. When these stones exhaust their power, they create creatures made of arcane underflow. My intelligence suggests they are called Umbrals. The bigger the power crystal, the bigger the beast."

Elyndandria's expression remained neutral. "In other words, these are the shadows in your prophecy. The diffuser can create them in great quantities." She felt uncertainty and anger, and her emotions finally pushed through that wall of peace. Her lips twisted with frustration, and she said, "Another weapon in the arsenal of the mad scientist."

Farzg replaced the diffuser in his robe. "There's no hope of making a coordinated attack with the shadows, but they could serve as agents in a terror campaign." He gestured back toward the contents of his vault. "Dearest Elyndandria, I wish to employ your services again. Take your payment for the contract against Evanthalus. I consider it complete." He paused, raising his voice to a feigned pleasant tone. "I would also like to pay you for this next task up front. Select a dozen items from my personal treasury. There will also be additional payment when you reach the Eastpoint Lighthouse."

The assassin detected no treachery in Farzg's tone. He was serious, causing her to narrow her eyes with suspicion. "This is unusual. What do you know that I don't? Spit it out Farzg. I've played your game for a decade for one reason. You've yet to keep your promise."

The frost giantkin's sadistic expression returned. "Then let me rectify that. The first part of this job will be in Nulodia. We will use diffusers to strike the city with terror, but only to cover a greater operation. Doctor One and my own sources suggest the high priest and his entourage will be absent for a few days pending some disaster in Mystalon." He stroked his beard again, his gaze softening from evil to ambitious. "The church has confiscated so much lacrima-deum, we need only get operatives inside their warehouses. While the church is distracted by the fallout, I will reach for the real prize."

Elyndandria raised an eyebrow. "Which is?" she interrogated.

The giantkin's eyes now shimmered with greed. "An evidence locker with a certain soul prism you wish to retrieve. I had given it to my nephew for safekeeping, but the church managed to take it after raiding his warehouse." Farzg watched Elyndandria squirm in anger. His condescending tone returned as he discussed business. "It will also be a chance for me to remind Thomas that my reach is infinite. He failed to heed my warning. But none of that fiasco should worry or concern you. I need you to dig into the truth about this Doctor One."

The assassin tilted her head with confusion. "Recon? You want me to investigate somebody? Fine. I have no problem taking your treasure now, but if I don't get the soul prism, I walk."

Farzg's lip curled with annoyance. "Fine, assassin. Consider my generous offer as insurance you will get your wish."

She had not carried out a reconnaissance mission in years. Getting this close to reclaiming her husband's soul prism required her to exercise the most vicious of her skills. Investigating a mad wizard, however, sounded like a promising change of pace. "You've got a deal." She collected twelve items including wands, weapons, and enchanted jewelry.

As Elyndandria took her due, Farzg explained. "Doctor One claims he was once a professor at Breckinshore Ridge Magic Academy. I would recommend beginning your investigations there." His voice grew bored. "His genius is evident, but his stories are convoluted. I trust you'll find answers at the academy." The frost giantkin shuddered. "Aylabrax took One to the primordial place. Since his return, his demeanor has been even more unstable. We need to understand his motives and to keep Saraix's soul out of his grasp. Regardless of outcomes."

The assassin narrowed her eyes again. "Fine," she spat.

"We'll fly to the Ermen Moors immediately then. Are you afraid to ride on a dragon?" he asked.

Elyndandria shook her head in disbelief. "Excuse me?" she replied.

Farzg's smile and tone were both boastful. "My pet and friend, Glacirix. A swift and fierce white dragon loyal to me and me alone."

She replied, "I'm not really afraid of giant lizards."

Farzg tilted his head down with a dark smile. "Though The Unbinding has slowed him somewhat, Glacirix can still fly. We can be at the moors in a few hours. From there we can infiltrate the city through One's network." His voice rumbled with excitement. "We'll meet with my lieutenants remaining inside the city. We will unleash a plague of weak Umbrals. You and I will go to the headquarters where they keep their most precious evidence. There, we'll find what you seek and what you need to see my will complete."

Elyndandria joined Farzg at the door of the vault. "You're being too vague, Eldon."

Farzg turned his palms up with dismissal of Elyndandria's complaint. "I'll spell it out then. We are going to reclaim the soul prism and the key to the portal chest. After you depart for the Eastpoint Lighthouse, you will wait to learn the outcome of my conflict against Miranda. If the dragon girl is victorious, you must make sure One meets his ultimate end as a result of giving Saraix's soul to Miranda."

The assassin sighed. "Are you giving up Farzg?"

He shook his head. "Not in the least. There's less than a percentage point of likelihood the girl can destroy me. But it's within the realm of possibility. So, if you wish to ply your trade beyond the next equinox, you'll make sure Doctor One does not upset the balance of this dimension. I have overplayed my alliance with the scientist, and as a result, I've created two sets of powerful enemies." His cracked lips opened with a sinister smile. "Make no mistake, I do not intend to die. But if I die at the hands of a worthy opponent, then at least I will leave my imprint on this universe." He allowed a moment to pass, watching Elyndandria shift uncomfortably. He blinked before continuing, "I do not consider One the worthy opponent. I will face this Miranda, however, and the conflict will test my strength against Thomas's legacy. It is time for the hypocrisy of the Sword of Justice to be exposed, or for the church to do away with me as they've wished for thirty years."

She glared at him. "You're asking me to cooperate with your murderer."

Farzg's eyes narrowed. "It's not murder if it's revenge."

Elyndandria's expression was equally malicious. "It is if the law says so, and the keepers of the law do hate to have that thrown in their face."

Farzg shook his head in adamant disagreement. "Let's not kid ourselves. They've issued a kill-on-sight warrant for me, and I find it hideously distasteful. This conflict will end in violence, and I do hate getting my hands dirty." His smile became more peaceful than the assassin expected. "Besides, we deserve to die, by all standards, even our own. I would kill myself and take my own place if that were possible or necessary. And you'd do the same." His smile shifted, however, causing Elyndandria's soul to fill with disgust. "Would you not? You thirst for the same power I do. I am just blessed enough to take my rightful place as a god."

Elyndandria spat, looking at the masses of wealth stacked around them in the vault outside of the true vault. "Whatever, Eldon. Spare me your philosophical posturing. My husband deserves to have his slumber interrupted, but you stole his prism just when it was within reach. I intend to right that wrong and to harvest the blood that's mine."

Farzg sighed. "You sound just like the church."

Elyndandria's eyes filled with angry tears. "And you're a coward, embracing death."

The frost giantkin gave her a hideous, frustrated grin. "Just wait until you see the Infernia I unleash on the girl. If you are giving her the shard, then I could not bend the universe to my will. She will not acquire so much power without proving herself first. Miranda is different from Thomas, and I am eager to face her."

Elyndandria frowned. "This is becoming pedantic. I'm not interested in your rivalries, Eldon. Let's quit wasting time." She spoke no more, disturbed by Farzg's behavior. His current death wish was uncharacteristic. Miranda stole Elyndandria's secret, and the assassin knew the girl's strength of will. Farzg had bitten off far more than he could chew, and the assassin's emotions tugged between fear and smugness. She shrugged, walking past the frost giantkin toward the exit of the frozen vault in seething silence.

Chapter 12
Erilkaiden Thief of Light

"There are four spells forbidden by the universe: Black Hole, that which destroys reality itself. End, which destroys life and soul together. Meteor, a destructive barrage of planetary scale. And Thaumaturge, a combination of the arcane and the divine." –
Kzar's *Forbidden Spells and Rituals*

Miranda opened her eyes to daylight mixed with the glow of a city burning. Ash and smoke wafted through the air even within the miniature citadel, but she knew how bad the reality looked outside. As she sat up, she realized all of the elves and Naomi were gone. Most of Naomi's furniture and bedding was also gone, indicating she did not anticipate needing to camp in Mystalon again. A sudden, uneasy feeling clutched Miranda's chest.

She stood up, finding Justin and Valarie sitting on their bedrolls nearby, braiding their hair. They already had on most of their armor. August was still asleep. Valarie smiled, noticing Miranda first. She called out, "Good morning, miracle dragon!"

Miranda blinked slowly, raising her knuckles to her eyes and rubbing them. "Good morning, sword queen," she replied, relentless exhaustion evidenced in her voice. The music was weak this morning.

Justin also looked up from his task, "Oh hey, Miranda!" He beamed for a moment, "I'm glad to see you're not as given to sloth as the commander," he teased. Ironically, though Justin and Valarie performed commendably in the final battle against Gelidor, August ended up with a higher rank by joining the Pegasus Knights. Due to their flexible nature, Pegasus Knights needed to command ground battalions while reporting appropriately in their own hierarchy. Commander was a varied position within the church, and August's command really only mattered in battle.

Miranda woke up quick enough to smirk at the huge paladin as he snored lightly at the mention of his title. "You've always been the first one to wake up, Justin," she replied, the melody in her voice waking up with her.

Valarie's smile became sinister. "Not anymore. Now he's the lazy one," she joked.

Justin's eyes dropped to his dark blond hair as he corded the braids tightly. He only had shoulder length hair, so his braids were short, but he still insisted on participating in the tradition. "I mean, it takes me a little less time to get ready," he commented.

Miranda sighed, the current situation weighing on her. "Not faster than the elves, though," she remarked, noting they were the only four left in the camp. Even Yuvina had disappeared from the window. "Or Yuvina," she added, her eyes lingering where she had heard the foxkin the night before.

August's voice entered the conversation. "I think they're carrying out the plan."

Everyone's eyes snapped to August, and Miranda responded, "Plan? There is a plan already?" Her heart started to race with panic.

August sat up, giving a theatrical yawn. His brown hair was not long enough to braid, but the Pegasus Knights tended to keep short hair. Though he used to have a small, brown beard, August now kept his face clean shaven. "I don't know what the plan is, but I've seen this kind of thing before."

Before August finished his sentence, Miranda was up and moving. Her body language was somewhat flustered as she nearly dove into the golden-colored, long skirt of her battlemail. Her hair fell into her face, causing her to flail a bit in frustration. August continued, "Aw, Miranda. Don't freak out. If they didn't share the plan with us, it's 'coz we probably have a different role to play."

A stern, deep voice interrupted them, causing one second of abrupt chaos. "Correct, Commander Burchard." It was High Priest Selasine. His massive silhouette emerged from the door entering the mess hall. He was neither armed nor armored, wearing the ceremonial robes of the High Priest of Invictus.

In that second of chaos, Miranda tripped trying to get her

armored boots on, falling onto a bedroll nearby. Justin leapt to attention, causing Valarie to fall backwards to avoid her boyfriend's elbow. A moment of awkward silence passed before August chuckled. Miranda tried to regain her composure as she stood up, "Modai-rin!" She had a habit of calling him the elven word for father, likely a result of spending so much time with Erk. The pirate loved titles and accolades, and he thought that modai-rin was the perfect word for Miranda to call the man who adopted her.

"Yolasha," he replied, smiling broadly. His expression was short lived, however, as his face looked pained with worry and sadness.

Miranda walked toward Thomas as she situated her breastplate and shoulder pads over her torso. "Can you help me with my armor?" she asked in a rushed voice.

The sadness in his eye made Miranda's heart leap into her throat. He gestured for her to come closer, and she approached him with her back turned toward him. He tightened the straps and belts on the back of her breastplate. "Did you bring your vestments, yolasha?" he asked.

She held her arms out to her sides parallel to the ground while Thomas continued to fasten her armor. "Of course," she replied, glancing back at her bedroll.

"August is right. You all have different assignments today. These assignments will be out of the ordinary. Remember, we are outsiders here. We could not have prevented the events that will transpire here today; the Umbrals will be on the move again within a few hours. Erk has gone with Alaric and Evander to the tree."

Miranda felt the last buckle click and turned to face Thomas. She tried to stay calm, but she was worried for Erk's safety. "What will they do?"

Selasine stared at her for a moment. He could feel her concern, and with her emotional sensitivity, he was certain she could feel his. "Oh, yolasha. Erk's Unbinding power is not what most people think it is."

Everyone in the indoor campsite froze in place, even August who was standing up. He had slept in his armor for some reason, it seemed. Miranda tilted her head in confusion as she protested, "Wait, what? I've seen it dozens of times!"

Selasine looked at the ground. Justin interrupted, "One person with two uncanny magics has never been recorded, though I guess it's theoretically possible." He looked at Miranda, her blue eyes darting between Justin and Selasine as they spoke.

The high priest breathed deeply. "Commander Burchard, you have your orders. Valarie the Persistent, Justin the Watchful, report to Naomi in front of the citadel. She will brief you there."

The paladins stood and saluted. "Sir!" they replied in unison. Selasine gave an unusually lax salute in return.

Miranda felt like she had been here before. Her stomach was in knots, and she assumed everyone knew something she did not. "Dad, please," she whispered, her eyes filling with tears as her friends finished packing their camp area.

Thomas took her by the hand and pulled her in for an embrace. She leaned into him, the normal safety of his hug not providing the right kind of reassurance this time. As the paladins finished packing, they gave another salute to Selasine.

Valarie also hugged Miranda as they walked by. She whispered, "I don't know what's going on either, but just so you know, I'm here, okay?"

Miranda nodded, closing her eyes to try and maintain her composure. Her instincts were screaming with suspicion, and she knew she was not going to enjoy the following conversation. August patted her on the back as he walked by, but Justin also stopped. He raised his right fist to the center of his chest, banging it a couple of times on his armor. "Judge of Hearts," he said, reminding her of their duty here as followers of Invictus.

She pushed away from Thomas a bit, a small smile returning to the corners of her lips. "Judge of Action," she replied. She nodded to say goodbye as he smiled and departed.

Thomas looked at Miranda with tenderness. "Erk's uncanny magic will be able to eliminate the Umbrals before they begin rampaging again."

Miranda started to shake her head. She replied, "There's no way he can defeat all of them on his own, we should be there to help him!" She rushed back to her camp space and began collecting the rest of her things. She fastened the belts to her waist which held her scabbards and healer bag. She reached into her adventuring pack digging through her supplies to find her ceremonial vestments folded neatly in the bottom. She looked at Thomas, "And why did you ask about these?"

The high priest took a deep breath. "Put them on, Miranda. Today, your duties will hopefully include more priestess things and fewer war things."

She stared blankly until she lowered her eyes to her robes. "I can't fight in these, and Erk is going to need me," she started.

Thomas walked to her from the doorway as she spoke. He gestured to a table and a chair nearby. Miranda stood incredulous for a moment, but in a huff, she took a seat. He knelt beside her and took her hands in his. The mithril of her gauntlets was cold to the touch. "Nobody can be near Erk when he unleashes the full power of his Unbinding. It's too dangerous."

The tears threatening her eyes finally became heavy enough, and one spilled down her cheek. "He'll exhaust himself trying to fight them all alone." She felt desperation starting to clutch at her. The same elf who kidnapped her months ago had become so dear to her that the thought of him in danger sent her into a panic. "Please, Dad, I can do anything with my draconic power."

Selasine nodded in agreement. "Of course you can, yolasha. You are incredible, and you are full of courage. But Erk has to do this alone. Naomi will be the closest to him; he will be fine. The solisberry tree and the arboretum, however, will not."

Miranda's eyes widened and her mouth opened. Another surge of fear coursed through her body. "The tree?!" she replied, the music in her voice full of despair. "What is he going to do to the tree?"

He looked into his daughter's eyes. Miranda noticed he looked especially wise in the robes of the high priest. Then, she began to understand. If Selasine was resigned to let Erk do this alone, then he truly thought this was the best course of action. Hearing the tree was in danger, however, made Miranda worry for the Mystalonians. Selasine interrupted her thoughts with his explanation. "Erk's solar beam is only a byproduct of his true uncanny magic." She stared at him in silence as he continued, "If he does not discharge the light but continues to draw the mana in, he can unleash an attack so devastating that nothing will be left, not even the ground beneath his feet."

Miranda's tears were flowing freely now, "He can't do that! If he destroys the tree, then Mystalon will be lost! We have to take the Umbrals down one at a time, as a team. We can save the tree and what's left of the city!" Her voice was shaky but determined. She felt the mana swelling within her and she closed her eyes. With focus, she could feel the entirety of the arcane stream as it flowed toward and away from the solisberry tree in the center of the forest. She took in so much of it that she radiated a golden aura.

Thomas squeezed her hands in his. "Please, Miranda, listen. There were twenty thousand elves in this city three days ago. It's hard to say now, but there may be fewer than five thousand remaining. Umbrals pursue magic to consume it, and now that the Mystalonians have run out of magical items to distract them, the Umbrals—"

She interrupted him, "Oh, no." Her breathing accelerated, "The magic inherent to the elves." She started to cry again, eliciting an embrace from Thomas.

He nodded as he held her. "These beasts are like you Miranda. They have the power of the universe at their disposal, and when they break from the tree, they are nearly invincible until their strength fades. As long as they have the tree, they will be unstoppable." He broke away from the hug, "I'm afraid Mystalon is already lost."

She had not cried this profusely since Carulus provoked her into using the mana within her to heal troops he callously sent to slaughter. "Then I can just use my power to rebuild the city," she said, sniffling. "If the tree is still here, I can work! Day and night. I can use my powers to kill the beasts too, let me go to the tree with Erk! Tell Damil to tell him to stop!" She started to hyperventilate, realizing that the situation was graver than she had imagined. Her empathy for the Mystalonians and her love of the solisberry tree drove her to profound sadness. It was similar to how she felt for Erk, Evan, and the people of Claston when she learned of their struggles as a result of Gelidor's depravity.

Thomas felt his heart break for her. Even Invictus's mortal avatar would struggle to fight the Umbrals in such a quantity. "You might have unlimited mana here, yolasha, but neither your body nor your essence are infinite. If you burn so much mana through you for hours on end, what will happen to your body? What if you burn away more of your draconic essence in the process?"

Miranda started to sob uncontrollably. Her reasoning could not catch up to how she felt. She realized that the situation in Mystalon was so dire that the Sages were willing to sacrifice their way of life in order to protect their homeland. If they went that far, why shouldn't she? These people deserved a chance to rebuild, and she could help. Furthermore, she cared so much for Arlindra and Celyth, and even Nebu. This was their home; she couldn't imagine Arlindra would agree with destroying the tree. "Please, dad, I have to do something. What can I do? I have the arcane stream and all of this power, but why do I feel so weak right now?" Strands of crimson hair frayed everywhere, sticking to her face where her tears had soaked her cheeks. Her face was red from the buildup of emotion.

He pulled her back into his arms. "Because even though your

body and your essence might be limited, your capacity to care for the struggles of other people is infinite." He closed his eye as he held her, remembering how she insisted on helping Erk once she learned of the elf's plight. In the end, she was the deciding factor in that conflict. "That heart. These people are going to need just Miranda. Not a miracle worker, not a dragon, maybe not even a priest." He broke away from the embrace again. "You'll know what your mission is when the time is right."

She tried to catch her breath, sniffling loudly in the process. As her mind caught up to her feelings, she began to process Selasine's words as both father and high priest. She was perplexed Erk had never shared the true nature of his Unbinding power with her, but she knew she never actually asked. "Look at me, breaking protocol, being a crybaby," she jeered at herself as she wiped her tears.

Thomas squeezed her hands again. "The law permits you to have feelings, and Lexcord demands that you embrace them." His voice was comforting but light. "And what kind of high priest would I be if I valued protocol over my daughter's feelings?"

Her nose and mouth trembled a bit together. "Are you sure Erk is going to be okay?"

Selasine gave a silent nod.

She stood, unfurling the vestments she had been holding. A corner was dampened by her tears. She took off her mithril gauntlets, as the spikes would have made it impossible to put on her robes. She pinned them around her neck and slid her arms into the sleeves. They were deep purple and flowing, but very light. The words "The Sword shall never surrender to the forces of chaos and evil" were embroidered around the collar. A golden border had been stitched into the hems. Part of the vestments included a stole that was blue, designating her as a warpriest. The scales of justice adorned the back of the robes. Miranda found a brush in her pack and started to braid her hair. She looked at Thomas with tears still lingering in her eyes. "They'll need Miranda, healer of Invictus," she said, her voice ready to break.

He sat with her as she braided her hair, taking her time. Thomas tried to distract Miranda with a bit of small talk, asking about the cousins and Yuvina. She recounted their journeys from K'tal H'yuck, Olvidado, and Devitus. About half an hour passed as she finished readying herself and followed Thomas to the front of the citadel. They could see some Mystalonians in the courtyard as the two of them approached the shattered entrance to the fort.

They stopped shortly outside the broken gates. The glass dome that could once be seen from almost anywhere in the city was now in shambles. As they walked through the broken streets, the Mystalonians followed them. Whispers and speculations circulated among the crowd. Some of them began to cry, which is when Miranda's work began. A human in ceremonial robes with bright blue eyes and rich red hair made her an interesting distraction to the people of Mystalon. As they walked through the streets, she talked with the elves who were fearful and weeping. She offered to walk with them, giving them the blessings and strength of her chosen god.

She shared with them the Catechism of Grief, reciting, "We are bereft, Sword of Justice. Though Invictus is mighty, the destiny of mortals reaches beyond the sands of time. From creation to end, comfort our hearts, rest our minds. May we walk the Path of the Sword of Justice with solemnity and humility." Her voice was musical and powerful, comforting their hearts.

As Lexcord heard Miranda's prayers, she poured light through Miranda's body. As the priestess started to shine, people nearby felt the sympathy and regret of the gods whose presence had been banished from Mystalon until this very moment. Though the light did not remove the grief, it added the hearts and minds of the gods of good to their cause. Some of the people felt this tragedy was unfolding because they turned their backs on the gods hundreds of years ago. Others blamed it on outsiders, and others still on insiders. Their need for blame, however, washed away when it became clear that Lexcord was still with them. They needed only seek the gods of their own accord, and many of them immediately offered unscripted prayers to Lexcord, pouring her light and comfort through Miranda.

Selasine managed to smile as they continued to walk through the broken city, Miranda glowing like a beacon of divine hope instead of unlimited power. She found her mission.

As she walked, surrounded by hundreds of people now, a soft, fuzzy sensation filled her hand. She looked to her right in surprise, finding Yuvina there, holding her hand and walking in stride with her. Before Miranda could speak, Yuvina said, "If I stay with you, I'll be okay in the crowds." As their hands connected, instead of a sudden, electrical backfire, the two of them produced a stream of bright, ethereal particles. It flowed from their palms to the ground below like a steady, winter snowfall. As those lights faded, they moved in the direction of the solisberry tree.

Miranda's lips turned up into a soft smile, "Of course, Yuvina."

She squeezed the kitsune's paw reassuringly, and the crowds began to arrive at the edge of the Galathan district.

Selasine frowned with sorrow. The crowds then truly began to weep. The light shining from Miranda intensified as it seemed Lexcord wanted to embrace the entire crowd. Yuvina's nose and whiskers quivered.

Where there was once a beautiful arboretum, a massive flame had engulfed the entirety of the gardens and the solisberry tree within. Then, Miranda and Yuvina saw something unfolding nearby that caused their hearts to drop to The Rift.

✻✿✻

Earlier that morning, Arlindra woke to her father's voice. "Arli. Arli, it is time," he whispered. She felt his hand on her shoulder. She roused quickly, her instincts taking over. She stood straight in a single motion. She cast a quick glance around the room, noticing Evan and Yuvina were gone. Naomi had put a metal rod on the ground that opened a pocket dimension. She was putting her nice furniture and sleeping bags away. She still had an abundance, even after giving so many to the Mystalonians. Evander was having a bit of difficulty waking Celyth. Arlindra's cousin had one of Naomi's pillows pressed over her head, refusing to respond to her father. He gave an exasperated shrug after a moment.

"Good morning, Modai-rin," she said, looking at her father. Nebu stirred at her sudden movement, but he flitted his wings and remained curled up in her hair.

"Come, there is much to discuss. I will elaborate on the way. Ready your things, I do not think there will be time to return."

Arlindra did not have anything to pack. She slept in her leather armor and tunic, which were both protective and incredibly comfortable. The bedroll was Naomi's, and the ranger didn't unpack any of her camping gear. She grabbed her bow and quiver, giving a nod to her father. She brushed her hair out of her eyes but left the rest as a wild nest for Nebu in the meantime. He could groom it for her later. "Ready," she said, her light blue eyes awake and alert.

"So quickly?" Alaric replied.

"Wasting time isn't really one of my strengths," she returned with pointed sarcasm.

He gave a half smile. "In most circumstances, I'd say I was proud of your preparedness. Today, I am just sad that such a heavy burden sits on our shoulders." They began to walk from the converted mess hall to the front gate of the citadel.

"Where has Evanthalus gone?" Arlindra asked as they walked.

Alaric looked forward as he talked. "He is out front with his brother, Noble Pirate Lord Erilkaiden."

"Erk," Arlindra amended, recognizing the pirate's name from Miranda's stories.

Her father cleared his throat. "Ah, yes. His common name. He seems more like nobility than a pirate, though," he continued.

Arlindra's pace was brisk, forcing her father to hustle to keep up with her. Thanks to her haste, they emerged from the broken doors of the citadel in less than a minute, finding Erk and Evan waiting in the courtyard. The morning sun had started to peek through the dense canopy of the Mystalonian Forest. Arlindra was glad to note the Umbrals did not bother the grand trees of the districts. Her father was about to begin introductions, but Arlindra spoke first, approaching the brothers with confidence. "Evanthalus," she acknowledged with a nod. Her eyes turned to the pirate. He was dressed in a red captain's jacket with accents of black fabric and golden metals. He had no hat or eyepatch, and his flowing blond hair spilled down to his shoulders. His face was handsome, and he looked to be approximately her father's age. "And Erilkaiden, I presume?" she asked.

Erk smiled. "Alaric's daughter. Arlindra, was it?" he replied.

Alaric was stunned. His daughter was not known for bold introductions, and she preferred working alone. Perhaps her short time outside of Mystalon had sharpened her confidence in others. She replied, "Indeed, master pirate. I've been shuffled through plenty of reunions and debriefings over the last ten hours, please be straightforward about the plan."

When Arlindra spoke in the converted mess hall, Alaric had not expected this level of readiness. He started to suggest a longer introduction, saying, "Yolasha, do you not find it wise to—"

Arlindra interrupted him in response, saying, "Of course, Modai-rin. But I know Evan to be quite a capable warrior, and I trust Miranda with my life. She has spoken very highly of Erk, and I trust him with the same weight Miranda does." She offered her rare smile. "It is an honor to meet you, but I fear we have no time to dawdle."

Erk looked at Alaric and Evan for a moment before looking back to Arlindra. He added, "Likewise, and I share your sentiment. I can tell we are cut from similar cloth, Arlindra."

Alaric smiled in spite of his daughter's impatience. He started to share the plan. "Very well. Arlindra, we need you to collect eolnut, yinfruit, and some blooms and seeds of the other trees we have cultivated in the arboretum. Normally, we would have relied on Elitirin for such a task." He paused and looked at the ground as his voice trailed off.

Arlindra replied, "Understood. And what of the solisberry? Though the Umbrals are scattered through its boughs, I could still acquire some blossoms."

Alaric blew his breath out, causing his cheeks to puff. He responded, "It would be beneficial to your friend to replenish her supply of blooms. Since the boughs are so high, Naomi has been dispatched to acquire them using her telekinetic powers. If you have a method of collecting more, by all means, do so." He grimaced before he continued, "There is another, riskier plan in place to save the solisberry tree. Mere blooms would not be enough to regrow the tree."

The ranger narrowed her eyes. "That confirms it, then. The plan truly is total destruction. By what means will it be wrought? The divine?"

Erk looked at the ground. Alaric explained, "Erk possesses an incredible uncanny magic. The force of an imploding sun."

The pirate lord nodded, interjecting, "Though people know me as Erk the Radiant in the Solar Sea, I am known to the universe as Erilkaiden, Thief of Light." He straightened his jacket as he spoke, now looking at Arlindra. "I'm afraid that the true nature of my uncanny magic is far too dangerous to employ under normal circumstances. However, based on the dire nature of the situation, it is the only swift option that will eliminate a threat as grave as the Umbrals without significant casualties."

Arlindra tilted her head forward a bit, giving Erk a judgmental look. She retorted, "The trees are casualties." Her voice was stern.

Evan nodded in agreement. "Though I am no longer bonded to the arcane, even I can feel the immense mana flowing here. This will be a historical loss. Do you still have the potion Elitirin gave you?" he asked, looking at Arlindra.

Arlindra reached inside her armor, withdrawing a small, crystal vial. It hung around her neck on a mithril chain. "She said I would know when the time was right to use it." She tucked it back into her tunic. "It will accelerate plant growth by decades over the course of a few minutes," she explained, but then realized how her task would be connected to saving Mystalon's way of life. "Oh, I suppose that also includes trees," she added as her thoughts caught up.

Alaric smiled, and Evan nodded again, replying, "I'll be with you in the arboretum to watch for Umbrals and aid with the evacuation effort."

The ranger started to walk toward the arboretum without additional questions. Evan, Erk, and Alaric fell in behind her, continuing their conversation in motion. Erk spoke first as they navigated the Galathan district, asking, "How much of the solisberry tree will you need to try to replant it as a shoot?" The question was ambiguously directed, hoping that either of the Mystalonians may have an answer.

Alaric responded, "I have no idea. I'm assuming more is better."

Arlindra added, "You'll want to get at least a full branch." She stopped suddenly and crouched to the ground, observing the shattered path beneath her. The mid-morning light reflected gray from the destroyed pavement. "What do you think will happen to the mana stream if you destroy a solisberry tree? The earth mother is crying." She touched the stone beneath her, closed her eyes, and whispered a prayer.

While Evan was cursed, he could see the flow of the arcane stream. In that state, he had slain many of Gelidor the Usurper's henchmen with his enhanced uncanny magic. Due to his experience with the stream, he replied, "The mana concentrates in the solisberry tree like it does Miranda. Its essence will be dispelled back into the stream when it is destroyed by Erk's Unbinding power. The fires will not harm it. It's what follows that will destroy the tree and the Umbrals."

Arlindra stood and continued walking toward the arboretum, not even glancing back. "If you can get a six-foot branch or bigger somehow, the solisberry might have a chance. Still, the earth mother will weep." A tear trickled down her cheek as she led the older elves through the streets of Mystalon at a pace Erk and Alaric had difficulty keeping. Evan's recent travels with the ranger prepared him for her quick step.

Alaric, jogging, asked, "How are you so sure, yolasha?"

She breathed deeply, slowing her pace. "Elitirin." She moved slower than a walk now. "Before she died, she told me everything. As I explained last night, she also feared for the solisberry tree. She told me if the tree dies as a result of the Umbrals, we could rescue it with as little as a six-foot branch." She stopped and turned around, anger in her eyes. Before she revealed what Elitirin told her about her mother, she let out a deep sigh. She changed the direction of her next rebuke, "If you had just told us the plan last night, this could have all been resolved already. Why did we wait until the eleventh hour to try and rescue the sacred trees?"

Alaric approached his daughter and took her hands in his. "You were all exhausted. The Umbrals sleep longer than we do. Though they will begin stirring within the next few hours, they will defend the tree even while hibernating." He then noticed Naomi walking on the path behind Arlindra, having rounded the next corner marked by an utterly destroyed apothecary. "Besides, there was still much reconnaissance to do while you rested. The plan still isn't set in stone. We are having to adapt quickly whenever we learn of new information."

Arlindra did not like her father's reasoning, but she was refreshed and alert. The rest helped more than she wanted to admit. "Very well," she said, turning around to see Naomi.

The giantkin had a grave look on her face as she approached. "They can see me when I'm invisible, and they will attack if you even so much as pluck a bloom." She spared no time for greetings. "Fortunately, there are plenty of blooms in the upper boughs that I could pluck from far enough away that the Umbrals dared not approach."

Erk gave a triumphant look, "Then make sure you cut a six-foot branch. The manabotanist disclosed that information to Arlindra last night, but we didn't ask the right questions until this morning."

Naomi's eyes narrowed, stopping only after she had passed the four of them on the path. She turned to face them. "Six feet? Can do, honeycomb. I'm going to fetch the paladins. Their tower shields will give me some cover, and the pegasus maverick is one hell of a bodyguard." She winked at Erk. "You better hurry, I think I agitated the beasts stealing the blooms. Don't you dare start until I have that branch somewhat secure. My telekinesis has a good reach, but my control over the earth requires more focus these days." She gave a loving look at her betrothed. "Promise you'll wait for my signal for phase two, darling?

Erk nodded solemnly. "You have my word. My life and my heart are in your hands." He bowed.

Naomi rolled her eyes. "So theatrical. Maldith. I love you too, honeycomb." She looked at the others. "Hurry now, there's not much time." She made a hasty turn. "One six-foot solisberry branch coming right up. Give me an hour, yeah?" She started to run, turning another corner out of sight.

Arlindra peered at the spot where Naomi left her vision. "Your wife has the right idea," she said and turned around. "Better keep up," she added with a shout. The ranger took off running in the direction of the arboretum.

Evan chuckled as he broke into a swift sprint to catch up to Arlindra. "Your yulesta brother, you hear that?" he teased, his voice excited.

Erk's cheeks turned red as he dashed behind them. "We haven't even set a date!" he objected. His recent months of training made it easier for him to protest as he ran.

Alaric shook his head, a small smile on his lips. The pride he felt for his daughter swelled, and he was thankful he sent her away when he did. She was still standoffish and awkward, but she seemed to be learning to embrace those parts of her personality. Of course, it was convenient that she met the daughter of the Nulodian High Priest of Invictus on her journey. Surely the gods were weaving a great destiny for his own daughter and niece.

As the four arrived at the arboretum, Arlindra spent about an hour gathering eolnuts and ripe yinfruit. She also collected several types of flowers that thrived in gardens with eolnut trees. She harvested the pits of pinplums and ebbilberries which flourished with the yinfruit. A rare species of melon, the Eviscervine, was just ripe enough to pluck. Though picking it interrupted it from growing into a sentient, thorn wielding plant, she could use the seeds within to regrow it. It seemed the other Eviscervines had been devoured by the Umbrals, or they managed to escape the arboretum shortly after the creatures arrived. Some were quite mobile and capable of rerooting themselves if necessary.

Arlindra secured as much plant life as she could safely carry in her pack. She then crouched to the ground, gently pressing the earth with her fingertips. She could feel the earth mother's sorrow as well. Though the earth father would have surely wept too, his presence slept on the tomb of an ancient evil. There were not many solisberry trees in the world. Arlindra was scared of the long-term consequences of losing such a wonder.

Meanwhile, Nebu was awake and aware. He groomed the ranger's hair as she worked diligently to preserve the progeny of the magnificent gardens around them. He kept his usual snark quiet, as he understood his master's sorrow. Erk, Evan, and Alaric kept their eyes on the Umbrals in the branches of the solisberry tree. They did not respond to Arlindra's foraging, but when Nebu flew up to pluck extra solisberry blooms, the Umbrals reacted quickly by scrambling up the massive branches and attacking the dracofly with their breath weapons. After collecting a dozen blossoms, Nebu protested, "I'm too tired now. I really don't feel like becoming Umbral food. I'm going to nap." He then hid in Arlindra's hair.

Erk stopped short as they reached the northern exit of the arboretum. The others turned to face him, but he was looking to the west. The pirate lord spoke quietly, "Naomi is in place and hard at work. Get out of range. Be careful. The Umbrals are stirring." He turned his back on his companions.

"Brother!" Evan scoffed. His tone shifted, however, as he continued, "Keep your promise. Naomi will protect you."

Erk smiled to himself. "I know, moshirin. So, stay back and don't get in the way."

Arlindra looked from brother to brother with anxiety. "What exactly is about to happen?"

Erk swallowed hard. "I am about to manifest the death of a star at the base of the solisberry. The last time I was in such a magnificent place, my world was made whole again." He started to walk toward the trunk of the tree, never turning around. "And now I must destroy such a place for the sake of the future. Please. Stay far away."

Evan nodded to Alaric and Arlindra. "I'm off to help Naomi. Keep the future safe."

Arlindra turned toward the solisberry tree, walking backwards until Erk was out of her sight. She continued backwards until they reached the borders of the Galathan district, watching the calamity unfold before her.

✳☾☽✳

As Erk reached the trunk of the solisberry tree, he was met by a cluster of Umbrals, their size alone able to overwhelm him easily. He noted there were nine approaching, and they crawled down the trunk, stomping toward him. He inhaled. The mana flowed so thickly near these trees, and in this moment, he was never more thankful he had met Miranda. Their trip to the Astral Spire let him experience the magic as it flowed so powerfully. This would be the most devastating, and, hopefully, last time he would ever need to manifest his uncanny magic to its fullest potential. "'Ware, beasts. I am Erilkaiden, Thief of Light. I am here to end your sad existence. May you recover your souls." As he spoke a swirl of light began to envelope his entire body. Normally, it only manifested on his arms, but he drew on the abundance of ether in the environment to accelerate the first phase of his Unbinding power to its fullest potential.

As the Umbrals closed in on the pirate lord, snapping with shadowy jaws and breathing jets of magical destruction at him, the mana burst with incredible force. The plasmatic density of a star surrounded Erk, pushing the Umbrals away from him and dispelling their magical attacks. As the supernova exploded, the mithril frame of the arboretum liquified, and the heat was so intense that all non-magical plant life was vaporized. The Umbrals in Erk's vicinity were pushed back by the force of the expanding, miniature sun, but they were not destroyed.

"Just as I suspected," he said to himself as he continued to focus on the energy flowing through him. His experience as a wizard had afforded him the magical intuition to keep his gift from overflowing by accident. Evan was not so lucky, his desiccating attack overcoming him on the day of The Unbinding. When Erk met Ezelbrecht barely a decade ago, the eldritch dragon helped Erk, but only on the condition the pirate reveal his ultimate manifestation of power to them. Thus, the remnant of Gorthran dubbed him Erilkaiden, Thief of Light, and they named his Unbinding 'Black Hole,' the death of a star deep within the cosmos. Ezelbrecht referenced galaxies, but Erk did not fully understand what the ancient beast intended to say. He could still hear their words.

"You hold the end of everything within you. You are Erilkaiden, Thief of Light. Not even the essence of the universe itself can withstand the destructive capabilities of your gift. Even I fear you, Erilkaiden, and I suspect that you will be the one who sends me back into the stream to become one with my father again. Though I resent you and wish to kill you for that, I welcome such a fate. I have been bored with this universe since the Dracon Wars ended centuries ago. Prove your argument. Use this power for good even once, and I will admit that even I, an all-knowing being, can be wrong."

Erk breathed. "I wish I didn't need to do this in the first place." As he spoke, he locked more of the mana within him. The supernova intensified, and it further pushed the Umbrals back. When fully charged by the mana, they were powerful. "Forgive me, yoshirote'thi. Hai'rin. Modai'rin. Earth mother. Lexcord." The increasing density began to cave in on him, indicating that only a fragment of mana more would initiate the second and final phase of Black Hole.

He held the solar power around him in stasis, the weight of a sun making it impossible for the Umbrals to approach without being destroyed. Almost all of them had gathered around his radiance. The horde of shadows loomed outside the reaches of the impossible light that now surrounded him. He thought back to their experience at the Astral Spire and noted the similarities. A smile crossed his lips. "It's my turn to do the right thing, Miranda. Please, forgive me, as well."

As those words escaped, he felt his heart flutter. "Now! There's three after us!" a thought pushed through. Damil sent the message from Naomi's thoughts.

Erilkaiden looked up to the sky and then closed his eyes. "Run, my love. Get the branch to safety!" he replied. He concentrated on the mana within him, trying to pull as much of it as he could into his essence. As a wizard, it was essential to say the right words to command the magic, and the gestures had equal weight to the success of a spell. Now, it felt intuitive.

Selasine's mind also spoke, "Now, nulestotejin. Do not hesitate!"

Evan's mind also pushed through, "Moshirote! Now!"

At that moment the entirety of the miniature sun collapsed upon Erk, causing the matter around him to begin breaking apart. Time and space slowly began to swirl counterclockwise around the pirate lord. His power compressed the solar magic into a space smaller than the point of a sewing needle. The gravity created by that single, dense point caused the reality to crumble in a radius around it. Not even the solisberry tree could resist the force generated by the center of Erk's Black Hole. Its bark and interior unraveled into fragments of ether, dissipating and flowing back into the arcane stream. As the volume of magic in the environment surged, Erk's power intensified. The Umbrals distorted and joined the light and matter now being infinitely compressed into the center point of the uncanny apocalypse.

Erk heard more voices in his mind as he continued to press time and space into the massive concentration of arcane power. They did not make much sense, however, as he felt himself at one with the arcane stream. He had allowed the ether to fuel his gift to the maximum and unleashed the full fury of his Unbinding for the second time in his life. He always knew what the end result would be, and the night his brother was cursed, he almost unleashed Black Hole to destroy Gelidor and his personal guard. Once his mother sacrificed herself to save Evan and destroy the clerics of Na'agamlor, however, he waited. He knew that in most circumstances, not even he would survive the consequences of this power. Ezelbrecht saved him from falling into the deep pit created beneath him; Ezelbrecht had a long, strong tail and fast reflexes. This time, it would be Naomi's responsibility to save him from falling into the thousand-foot crater created by the aftermath of his magic.

The Black Hole dispelled the hordes of Umbrals around him, compressing their physical manifestations in its gravity. The matter around him was crushed into that tiny space in front of him. Because his uncanny magic also destroyed light, he could not see anything more than flickering tendrils, swirling toward him like the galaxies Ezelbrecht described. His thoughts pushed into Damil's telepathy, "It's done."

To Erk it felt like hours. The entire planet of Espa, however, shook with an earthquake that lasted less than a second.

Chapter 13
Persistent Peril

"The dispelling light is a staple of all magic users, including those that pray for their magic. To cancel truly powerful magic, however, a wizard must exert magical output equal to that discharged by their opponent." – Kzar's Foundational Magic for Apprentices and Sorcerers.

Naomi backpedaled as she dragged a huge solisberry branch away from the arboretum with her telekinetic grab. There were three Umbrals in pursuit, and she had more than one task in the current mission. As she tried to pull the branch faster, the Umbrals began to close the distance. A blur of motion to her right slowed her building anxiety; Valarie the Persistent rushed forward with her uncanny magic to interrupt the Umbrals' pursuit. To her left, Justin the Watchful followed, although his charge was much slower. His uncanny magic only turned his skin to stone, a useful transmutation against physical enemies. The Umbrals, however, could overcome such protections easily, especially when they were fully fed by the mana flowing through the solisberry tree.

The giantkin dropped the branch about one hundred feet in front of her, shifting her focus from the solisberry to the earth. An Umbral leapt into the air, its size and momentum propelling it toward Naomi at unbelievable speed. As she concentrated on the ground beneath her, the dirt and rock surged like a wave, and she rode it out of the way of the pouncing, dark dragon. The shadow of a pegasus and rider appeared overhead. August descended on the attacking creature, landing several substantial blows as he passed underneath its draconic neck with a bold maneuver. The shadowy beast tried to retaliate with its talons, but it was too slow and clumsy.

Naomi heard Justin's voice call out, "Val, August, watch out!" as one of the beasts further away sprayed caustic liquid from its maw. August barely managed to evade with a mid-flight maneuver, and Valarie threw her shield up toward the oncoming splash. The acidic breath corroded her mithril tower shield, weakening its rigid protection. The earth giantkin felt her anger swelling. The magic saw blade she had acquired was supposed to work with very little magical discharge, but the Umbrals were sensitive to magical output. They detected and destroyed it when Naomi was only halfway finished with cutting the branch. She had to use an intense burst of telekinesis to break it away, but in doing so, she unintentionally attracted the attention of the Umbrals to her and the paladins. The fact that Naomi damaged the tree incensed the Umbrals enough that they pursued, putting them out of the range of Erk's supernova filling the arboretum behind them.

"Yoshitoterin!" a familiar voice called out, using the elven word for sister-in-law.

Naomi recognized it immediately. "Evanthalus!" she shouted back, looking around and trying to get her bearings. The Umbral pursuing her stopped to fight with August, so she used her uncanny magic to throw the solisberry branch to the north; it looked much larger than necessary, but Naomi did not want to take any chances. It crashed, causing the Umbrals to chase it, giving Valarie, Justin, and August a fighting chance against the beasts. The branch distracted the shadowy dragons, and they pursued it with abandon.

She saw Evan charging toward them. He had drawn the clockwork weapons she acquired while raiding Farzg's ships in the Solar Sea. She gave them to him not understanding the implications of using them, but their power was truly immense. In their current fight Naomi felt like they needed the unorthodox advantage. They were one thousand feet outside the arboretum on the west side, and Erk's supernova had engulfed the whole of the previous interior. Only three Umbrals pursued the magical saw to its source, but they were fully powered. To make matters worse, Evan pointed to the north and shouted, "We're not the only outsiders here!"

Naomi spared a glance, noticing somebody approaching from that direction. She knew the Sanguile district was that way, but it had been nearly obliterated by Umbrals in the recent attacks. "Can you handle it? I've gotta save Erk!" she insisted, sprinting toward the sun churning where the arboretum once stood.

Evan shrugged. "I'll do what I can," he said to himself. He was reminded of his traumatic silence while his essence was trapped in the arcane stream. He buried his discomfort, focusing on the immediate threat. He dashed toward the interloper approaching from the north, and the paladins continued to engage the Umbrals. Naomi was right in her estimation of Justin and Valarie's efficacy with tower shields, as they were each fighting an Umbral with grand bravado. August had the third distracted as it tried to catch him and his winged mount. Evan's instincts told him to confront the stranger.

As he approached, he noticed that the individual was dressed similarly to Reginald the Scholar in Devitus. Evan's lips curled into a sneer as he drew within one hundred feet of the human. Evan saw his glowing red eyes and black hair, and he felt evil radiating from the smiling scientist. Evan called out, "Identify yourself."

His voice was haughty. "I am Sender, the architect uprooting the solisberry. You are treading on dangerous ground, Master Lancethinas," he replied, fury burning in his eyes as he stormed toward Evan.

Hearing his family name brought Evan to a stop. "Who are you that knows me and refuses to properly introduce himself? That's a violation of hospitality protocol across many faiths and customs!" he replied, unsure as to why he was appealing to somebody he was nearing with weapons brazenly brandished. He resumed his approach, breaking into a sprint. "Who are you really?"

"I'll teach you something of hospitality," Sender replied, reaching into his tunic. He withdrew a small gemstone fixed to a chain, and it created a sphere of energy. Evan saw the magic clearly as he came within fifteen feet. It radiated blue light, covering Sender with an electric, wispy aura. Evan stopped again, evaluating the visible force. Sender smiled, "Ah, fearful of magic now that it has left your body, are you?"

Evan's lips turned up into a sadistic grin, and he leapt into action without a word.

Sender laughed as Evan's blades connected with his body, causing him to disappear. He reappeared about four feet to Evan's left, but he had a long cudgel in his hand. Before Evan could respond, the attacker had secured an uncontested blow to the side of the elf's head. Even if an illusion had caused Sender to move, Evan realized he should have had a moment to react. Instead, it seemed like he was trapped just a second behind Sender. Searing pain radiated from the left side of his head through his entire body. The cudgel shot a jolt of electricity through him once it made contact. It reminded him of the time his sister Iria's Unbinding power accidentally shocked him on a mission, but this was even more painful. The blow knocked Evan airborne, causing him to roll about twelve feet away. Blood poured from the gash ripped into the side of his head, quickly soaking his beautiful, blond hair with a growing crimson stain. Sender continued laughing. He taunted, "You really don't understand, do you?"

Evan tried to convert his momentum into a defensive maneuver. "Damn!" he cursed in common as he rolled into a crouched, upright position. "I understand perfectly fine. You are the 'architect' of the horrors that befell the Mystalonians. And for that, you'll pay!" he shouted as he sprung into another assault. The world was still spinning from the blow he had taken, but he felt oriented enough to attack again.

Still, as his weapons connected, Sender's location changed again. There was another, immediate blow to the head, rendering Evan nearly incapacitated. He could not regain his faculties quickly enough to muster another attack, and he wobbled hopelessly as he tried. Sender's voice changed as he approached Evan, "I am also known as Doctor Five to his unholiness. I am fourth in charge of this operation, and I will show you that you are up against forces not even the gods are prepared for."

The world around Evan swirled harder, and he winced with pain as he tried to orient himself for a brutal onslaught. Before he could muster his strength, however, horse hooves came into his peripheral vision. August descended upon the attacker. The beast would have trampled Sender, but he disappeared and reappeared mid-leap. The four-foot cudgel connected with August's breastplate, knocking him off his mount. The pegasus galloped up into the air but shied away as his rider had fallen off. The gentle beasts lacked the will to fight without riders.

Another cackle of laughter radiated from Doctor Five. Sender looked down at August, then over to Evan. "You think you can save the tree? The tree is the only thing I was sent here to destroy. Stop scrambling for that branch, and maybe you can witness the apocalypse."

Evan stood up, but he stumbled around as if he had too much to drink. His head injuries made him slow and weak. August rolled away from Sender's attack, trying to gather himself as well. Falling off the pegasus had knocked the wind out of him, and he was slow to rise to his feet. As he did, a blunt force smashed him between the eyes, his consciousness evaporating.

Evan growled angrily, "August! No!" and he leapt toward Sender, but a force clubbed him from behind the instant his weapons connected with Sender's body. He too felt his awareness dissipating as the world around him fell black. The last thing he felt was the earthquake indicating that Erk's Black Hole had condensed and imploded.

Naomi ran quickly behind the fires of Erk's supernova as they collapsed. The speed was unlike anything she had predicted, but she had only one thought in her mind: Erilkaiden. She screamed as she closed her eyes, using her connection to the earth to guide her. She could feel the earth being compressed in Black Hole, and the gravity of the spell had ripped the very ground from beneath Erk. As long as he fueled the spell with mana, it would persist and destroy, growing larger and denser with every moment. Erk planned to generate the gravity just long enough to destroy the Umbrals. As the flames from the supernova collapsed around Erk, Naomi felt the earth mother cry. A brief earthquake shook the ground beneath her, but the giantkin was unphased. She felt it coming.

Looking down into the center of the old arboretum, Naomi could see lights swirling in myriad, stretched arms glowing like stars in the night sky. They all churned inward toward a single point, which she thought was probably Erk's uncanny power increased to the maximum. She felt her connection to the earth mother stronger than she had in decades; the last time she felt this close to the earth, she was under attack from an eldritch demon known as The Emissary. She reached down into the ground, pleading for it to respond to her will. "Please, rise. Chase the gravity." She was as close as anyone dared approach, as the solisberry tree was spiraling into the heart of Erk's Black Hole.

A localized, smaller earthquake rumbled beneath her. The earth mother felt the power given Naomi through her heritage, and the goddess responded with enthusiasm. The ground surged below her, mountains rising up underneath Erk as the Black Hole compressed everything within its range into that single, intense gravity point. By this time, however, the gravity was so strong that light was also being pulled into that same point. She could no longer clearly see what was happening beyond the glowing swirls spinning into the middle.

As the force behind Erk's spell subsided, the range of Black Hole's gravity decreased; however, because Erk was the center of this magical gravity, he was no longer affected by Espa's natural gravity. He levitated five hundred feet above the deepest reaches of his attack. As he allowed the mana to dissipate, Black Hole's range deteriorated. Naomi used that decreasing radius to pull the earth beneath them up, calling on the deepest reaches of stone, sand, and dirt to fill in the massive crater that would result from Erk's unadulterated power.

As the earth swelled upward toward Erk, the ground beneath Naomi, Sender, Evan, and the paladins spilled into the five-hundred-foot-deep crater created by Black Hole. The sudden pouring of the earth into its own wound disrupted Sender and the Umbrals fighting Justin and Valarie. Unconscious Evan and August were rattled around in the area outside of Erk's magic. In a fortunate sense, the seismic chaos halted Sender's assault against August and Evan, prompting him to rush toward the solisberry branch Naomi secured earlier. His mission truly was to destroy the tree, and nothing more.

The radius of the gravity became small, allowing Naomi to approach closer as she continued to call for the ground beneath her. "Please," she whispered. For a moment she caught a glimpse of a handsome, dirty elf with green hair. She could feel herself losing consciousness. "Don't fail me again," she threatened the earth mother.

The goddess felt moved by Naomi, softening the rising earth to a fine consistency more like cloth than sand. Naomi pleaded, "Elrune. Erilkaiden. Annaia. Iria," and she saw their faces flash in her mind. She was expending life essence to control the earth to such a great degree, and she felt her vitality escaping. She only pushed her will harder, and Gaiater responded in kind. Though the earth mother was silent, she had a love for all of creation. Naomi's closeness to her heart encouraged the goddess to intervene, minimizing Naomi's loss of life with her selfless press. Many years ago, Naomi endured a decade of slavery before winning her freedom in a fluke accident involving The Emissary. Through those ordeals, Gaiater found Naomi's presence, as the giantkin was able to manipulate earth at will. On this day, however, the earth mother went above and beyond to answer the pleas of the little giant girl who had been calling to her for the last forty years.

As Black Hole dissipated, a fine layer of silt, sand, and soft earth had risen as close as fifty feet beneath Erk. Naomi pushed it up as much as she could manage, and Gaiater filled in the gaps where she was able. As Erk's unconscious body hit that cushioned layer of ground, he didn't feel the pain of his ribs breaking. The softening spill into the middle of the crater, however, caused Naomi to roll down into the sandy center where the solisberry tree once stood. Though they were both still alive, their physical pain was great. They shared their willingness to fight to the end as much as their bonds of love and struggle.

Naomi landed on her back, and she felt her strength waning. The sun shone directly above, but a shadow emerged from the position of Erk's attack. A massive, draconic figure loomed above her as she lost consciousness; she didn't have a chance to contemplate what it might mean.

Valarie and Justin felt the ground shake, but they managed to stay upright by using their tower shields as counterbalances. The cracks in Valarie's shield were spreading. She had been using her increased attack and movement speed to fight circles around one of the Umbrals that was pursuing the solisberry branch. Justin, however, would only strike at the other shadow dragon when it turned away from him. The intense flow of mana through the branch was too much for the mindless creatures to resist. Then, the paladins noticed something that made their stomachs turn.

While they had been focused on assaulting the Umbrals, another outsider had approached and attacked Evan and August. Justin cursed to himself, dividing his focus just long enough that the Umbral was able to smack his tower shield with a shadowy tail at full strength. He flew thirty feet through the air, but as he landed, he realized the earth had softened. It knocked the breath out of him, forcing him to lay back, gasping. After a moment, the ground rumbled as another earthquake shook the area for a moment, causing the earth to shift into the center of the crater. Valarie tried to disengage from the Umbral she was facing, but her increased speed worked against her as the ground beneath her could no longer hold her weight. She sank into the softened dirt, watching helplessly as a strangely dressed interloper began to carry away the last beacon of hope for the Mystalonians.

Sender had the solisberry branch in his hands, and he dragged it away from the caving ground. It was ten feet long and incredibly heavy. Fortunately, Doctor One had given him some lacrima-deum powered gauntlets that enhanced his physical strength enough to make it only a small chore to carry the branch. "Damnable pests. The Umbrals would have drained the tree within the week. It's no wonder they cut a branch so easily. Foolish One. You discounted the interlopers of the Sword." He grunted as he threw the branch furiously away from the softening earth, activating another lacrima-deum powered device in his boots. It allowed him to accelerate fast enough to escape the quicksand-like conditions forming beneath him. "Desperate morons, the lot of them. Clinging to hope." The branch landed on solid ground, and his accelerative boost prevented him from becoming rooted in the quagmire.

Just then, he noticed the Umbral that had been fighting with August was closing in on his location; he knew, however, that the Umbral would be satisfied momentarily snacking on the last remaining branch of the solisberry tree. Furthermore, since Black Hole had destroyed the rest of the tree, this tiny sliver now served as the only anchor for the arcane stream. The entirety of it flowed through such a small portion, and the branch had grown an entire foot in the minute it took Sender to escape Naomi's massive shifting of earth. The Umbral would certainly destroy the church and the rest of Mystalon if it consumed the branch.

A voice from behind him yipped, "I've got the Umbral, Mir!" A kitsune flashed into Sender's vision, leaping toward the Umbral with incredible speed. This was Doctor One's experiment! He was thrilled to see her in action, but he did not anticipate her fighting for the enemy. He wondered what sort of twisted plan Doctor One had concocted by pitting the church, Farzg, the Death Pirates, and The Forgotten against each other. This was an intriguing moment.

A different voice spoke now, singing a threatening melody, "You must be Sender."

He turned around to see a beautiful woman with red hair braided to the front of her face. A purple, ceremonial robe rested over her armor. It looked a little absurd, and it furthered his thought that church customs were ridiculous. "Are you the healer girl?" he asked, emphasizing his condescension.

Miranda's right eye twitched with her building anger. August and Evan lay about one hundred feet to her left, and she pointed at them. "May the healing hand of the Sword of Justice bind the wounds caused by the hands of evil. We face a great peril this day, and we beg the Sword of Justice to pour out his mercy with abundance." A stream of light trailed from her fingertips to her allies, coating them with a white, purifying light. The hemorrhaging in their skulls rapidly reversed, causing them to stir with disoriented groans.

Sender's face twisted up into a horrifying scowl. "You! You're the one who brought down Gelidor!" he shouted. Healers were normally only able to restore life to their allies if they could touch them. This woman was able to heal from a great distance, something that Sender did not think possible. He felt a knot turning in his stomach, but his resolve increased his fury. He continued shouting, "The healer with incredible power who fancies herself a dragon."

Miranda's lips twisted up into a smirk. "I am. And you have found yourself at the end of my blade, lawbreaker. What you've wrought upon Mystalon is immediately worthy of death."

Sender's scowl melted into a sadistic grin.

A few moments ago, Yuvina felt energy surging through her legs and arms as an Umbral pounced on the solisberry branch. Though she was new to heroics using uncanny magic, she began to realize that the stakes of every conflict were now much higher than they had been when she was just a powerless kitsune. She felt the burden of wielding incredible strength, knowing that one wrong move now would undo all the years she had spent trying to cure her affliction. Honestly, she wasn't sure she could call it an affliction anymore. As the energy rushed through her body, she felt her physical abilities enhanced so she could make a running leap at the Umbral and collide with it mid-air.

As she expected, the creature unleashed its overcharged breath weapon. Yuvina sought that new, empowering feeling of her signature attack. The blast of light coming from the Umbral's mouth hit Yuvina, causing Magic Mirror to activate. The orbs swirled around Yuvina with more intensity than usual, alarming the kitsune. She was soon comforted, however, as they flashed a rainbow of colors.

The reflected attack's power intensified ten-fold. The orbs shattered from the sheer volume of arcane energy held within the Umbral's breath weapon, and a rainbow-colored beam of unbelievable power refracted from a point six inches directly in front of Yuvina's eyes. Though both she and the Umbral were airborne, the point for the counterattack moved with the foxkin. The return beam blasted into the Umbral, obliterating its shadowy form in a glorious display of light and a loud, explosive burst. The force knocked Yuvina to the side, landing her close to August and Evan, who were stirring with great anxiety. She did an acrobatic maneuver to break her fall, landing in a rolling tumble with her tail tucked under her and up around her head. As she gained her bearings, she realized that a massive draconic form had appeared in the center of the crater. She growled with uncertainty as the creature's gray scales glittered in the light filtered through the Mystalonian Forest.

As the Magic Mirror shattered behind them, Sender turned his evil smile back to Miranda. "I can see the experiment is going to plan. Now, I will deal with you personally and return your weak friends to their former, moribund state."

Miranda frowned. "The Infernia you will. You're one wrong move away from death, Sender. Do not doubt the fury of the Sword of Justice." The golden aura still radiated from her, causing Sender's mind to race. "Surrender yourself to the mercy of the court and you might find yourself alive tomorrow."

Sender's lips quivered with anger. Everything he knew about this girl suggested that she was weak and lacked the power to make decisions, especially if they involved killing another. She hesitated to kill Gelidor, allowing him to become an incredible juggernaut that nearly destroyed her. There was no way that she would end this confrontation with violence. His anger melted into hysteria as he started laughing. "You! You would lecture me? I'll find no mercy at the hands of your hypocritical deity. You are a fool, warpriest. Immature. Still a child. And you will die with your arrogance."

Miranda cast a glance at Evan and August as they stirred. She breathed a sigh of relief internally, but her resolve was growing darker against Sender. She returned her electric-blue gaze to the mad scientist. "You are older than I, but you are the true fool. You have destroyed an entire society, and you act as if you have some kind of moral high ground. The only thing you have in front of you is imprisonment or death. The choice is yours."

Sender's maniacal laughter intensified. "You still stand before an enemy that you know to be guilty of the crimes you accuse them of, and you demand their surrender? If you were any agent of the law, you would do what your convictions tell you and end my life! But you hide behind a code, and you pretend that you police what is moral and what is right!" His face had turned red as he ranted, and he looked up to the sky theatrically. "You know that I have destroyed Mystalon and nearly killed your friends. If it weren't for you, they'd have surely bled out within a matter of minutes. But, as you always do, you only delay the tragedy." He held his cudgel out in his left hand. "Ironically, you healed your friends only to die."

Miranda felt anxious and afraid, but she held her external composure. "You approach in hostility, further increasing the risk to your life. Drop your weapon and surrender, and you will stand for a fair trial. It is possible that you are being manipulated, and we will be able to stop further tragedies if you share your knowledge with us. Your crimes are unforgivable, but the information you hold is worth sparing you."

A harsh glare filled Doctor Five's eyes. "When One is the center of the universe, then you will know what your true crimes are, priestess. He has been chosen to shape the universe in his image. And he will do so by taking advantage of the weakness of Gorthran and Saraix." He started to walk toward her gingerly, making sure to touch the pendant on his neck. This time, it covered him in a green aura, and he gave Miranda another sadistic smile. "Your friend Evanthalus could not understand how I bewitched him. Neither shall you."

Miranda did not reach for her sword. She stared at Sender with mounting anger. "This is your last chance, Sender. Surrender or face the immediate penalty for your crimes without trial."

"Die, Mir'thax Toi'landra." Sender went from a ginger walk to a sudden charge. He knew that his time-displacement magic would give him one full second of advantage over the warpriest. As soon as she acted, he would activate his uncanny magic, and her weapons or magic would harmlessly hit the afterimage he left behind as he moved into place to crush her skull. The green aura imbued his attacks with the power of poison; he dared not risk allowing her to survive.

Miranda sucked in a deep breath. After she, Selasine, and Erk had destroyed the ancient lich Vortex, the pirate had discussed the existence of powerful, deadly spells with her. He was celebrating the fact that the undead wizard did not unleash any life-ending magic against them, and such circumstances allowed Selasine to destroy the entity with the divine might of Invictus. Miranda remembered the names of some of those spells, and out of simple curiosity had researched them in Erk's library on *The Nebula*. One spell stood out to her: End. It was a simple spell, but the presence necessary to control the arcane stream was immense. In theory, the spell would cause particles of ether to suffocate the life essence of another being. It was the opposite of Gelidor's curse; instead of expelling a person's life essence into the arcane stream, End would use the arcane stream to snuff out the life of an entity. She knew the incantation, but she also knew she did not need it. "Sender, stop! This is your last warning. In the name of the Sword of Justice, I place you under arrest, and you will be tried for your crimes!" The melody in her voice was frantic.

Sender laughed again. "You lack what it takes, warpriest. Now, die!"

With a shift in her resolve, she drew Iria's sword from the ivory scabbard on her belt. Now was not the right time to use such a powerful, mana-intensive spell like End. Plus, she had spent almost two years training to fight with a sword. In her last year of adventuring, she had barely employed the symbol of her god. She was ready to put her skills to the test, but she planned her moves cautiously. As Sender charged at her, she realized that he was overconfident in his own uncanny magic. Whatever he had done to Evan and August, he planned to do to her. Evan was not the type of swordsman to be caught off-guard, and Doctor Five could have broken a barstool over August's head to no effect. As he neared striking distance, Miranda shifted the flow of the mana from lethal intent to a dispelling light. "Sword of Justice, guide my hand!" she shouted, imbuing her with additional, righteous strength.

Sender's smile melted into panic immediately as Miranda's magical sword pierced the chainmail under his tunic, shearing his bottom right rib completely out of his torso. His eyes widened with horror as he realized she had somehow nullified his uncanny magic. He had to activate it within less than a second of his enemy's attack, and his continual reliance on split-second decisions had allowed her to strike an uncontested blow empowered by the magic in her sword and body. "Curse you!" he shouted, the searing pain nearly sending his body into shock. He recoiled from Miranda's lethal strike, reaching into his pouch and withdrawing a healing draught. He chugged it, his body desperate and dying.

Miranda glared as she watched the gaping wound mend rapidly. She bit her lip with anticipation. She felt like she was about to face a worthy opponent in a duel-like situation, something she had only done in training. She felt her heart race, and something else deep within her pulsed. "Let me guide your hand, too, Mir'thax," she heard in her heart rather than her mind. It was her father. She inhaled and exhaled as Sender stood.

The scientist shook the cudgel in his hand furiously. "To the

Infernia with you, priestess. You'll suffer greatly, now. You won't get another free attack." He charged at her again, this time with caution.

As he came within striking distance, Miranda continued to focus her dispelling magic on Sender, preventing him from stepping into the future to attack her with significant advantage. She also let herself act on instinct, her usual over-thinking buried under the encouragement of her father. As Sender's cudgel should have connected with her head, she returned the strike with overwhelming strength. A burst of magic ignited between their weapons, Miranda's dispelling focus neutralizing the magical venom within Sender's weapon but not Iria's sword. The holy energy contained within blasted Sender backwards, and he landed fifteen feet to the left of Miranda.

The warpriest looked around, and Yuvina was now beside Evan and August, helping them gain their bearings. Miranda realized that they were moments from death when she intervened, but she did not realize how much such an injury would disorient them. The kitsune looked back at the warpriest with a pleading look. Justin and Valarie were falling behind distracting the other two Umbrals. The earth had softened significantly, causing the heavily armored paladins to sink. The Umbrals did not stop to attack them, however, as the arcane energy in the solisberry branch drove them wild.

Miranda's eyes cut back to Sender, who had closed the distance between them again. She parried his blows with ease, realizing she could easily maintain her draconic magic while fighting. As she grew more confident with her attacks, she began improvising more. She started to listen to her father's voice, and her sword work went from magnificent to fascinating. Sender went from the offensive to the defensive in only a second. After exchanging several blows with the enemy, Miranda feinted a stab at his chest. As the scientist tried to block, her blow redirected to his arm. Even with his enchanted armor, lacrima-deum-enhanced gear, and incredible reflexes, Miranda still managed to shatter his left forearm with a carefully calculated strike.

"Ak'hnashin!" Sender shouted in a guttural, evil language. Miranda's skin crawled at the sounds, causing her follow up blow to draw up short. Sender tried to activate his uncanny magic again, but found it still repressed by Miranda's dispelling force. "You still hesitate to kill me! You're pathetic!" he hissed as he punched in her direction.

A magical force tried to form, but Miranda's eyes narrowed as she matched the flow of mana. She dispelled a sonic wave generated from a lacrima-deum in a ring on Doctor Five's right hand. She growled at him, the music in her voice lethal. "You stand no chance. I fear no man, no moment, no magic. You are without recourse."

He glared, the pain from his left arm blurring his focus. He had so many magical devices, but under the weight of her dispel, he couldn't use any of them. He watched her closely, hoping she would show signs of weakening.

Miranda smiled internally. She had tucked a solisberry bloom beneath her tongue before the fight began. It helped her maintain a steady flow of mana, and the nearby solisberry branch helped keep the stream abundant. It looked like it had grown to over fifteen feet long already. She could maintain her dispel attack indefinitely at this rate. The music in her voice changed to a somewhat-cocky taunt, "Give up, Sender! You're outmatched."

His expression went from disdain to resolve. "Well then. Allow me to even the odds," he said in a horrifying tone.

Just then Yuvina slid within a foot of Miranda, causing the warpriest to jump to the side. "Watch out!" the foxkin yipped, activating the Magic Mirror again as Sender's body suddenly burst. The flames emanating from him were reflected harmlessly, but they merely masked an abrupt, explosive transformation.

Yuvina felt her heart hiccup. Something about the last activation of her newfound power seemed to draw her very life essence from her.

Sender changed from a severely wounded madman into a beast of tendrils and entrails. Miranda felt queasy at the sight of the hideous demon, recognizing the bane of justice. Furthermore, her dispel no longer worked. This mortal served Hoxark and had traded his soul for the power and body of a demon, a denizen of the Abyss. Miranda was not sure how such a feat was possible, however. No wonder he was so intent on total destruction, she realized. This entity needed to be sent back to the dark corners of the universe. A great maw formed in the center of the amorphous demon as it increased rapidly in size. A fleshy, center mass was supported by tentacles that formed out of visceral, sticky appendages. Fluid gushed from the creature, and Miranda's dispelling magic did not affect that either. Yuvina cartwheeled away from the secretions as they coated the ground in a thick, viscous substance.

Miranda swung her magical sword in an arc in front of her, causing a wave of holy light to disperse. She enhanced it with her draconic gift, imbuing it with a spell that would neutralize biological attacks. She muttered, "Misguided soul, you don't grasp the weight of your actions. Nor do you grasp your own demise." She sighed as she started to concentrate on the mana within her. As she did, a sudden darkness drenched the late morning light with shadow. The unexpected distraction was Ezelbrecht emerging from the crater. Their massive wingspan obscured the sun, stretching at least three hundred feet across. Each flap ushered a blast of wind through the area, tossing Miranda's hair wildly. Ezelbrecht approached the conflict, focusing on Sender's new form with bloodlust in their eyes. They sprayed a geyser of slow-moving cinders, melting the demon's fleshy tentacles. More took their places, however, as they regenerated quickly. Furthermore, Sender continued to grow, reaching a size too large for Miranda to fight effectively with her sword. She felt a surge of anger grow within her.

Justin and Valarie withdrew hastily; the Umbrals they were facing a moment ago had latched onto the increasingly massive demon as if they were parasites. Though demons were not arcane creatures by nature, they did contain an inherently dark power fueled by Hoxark himself. Though demonic energy was poorly understood by mortals, many stories hinted that it was made of the essence of souls, a power irresistible to the shadowy creatures seeking their own. Sender had gone from a small, humanoid presence to a ball of tentacles and a central mass about fifty feet in diameter.

Miranda's frustration peaked as the demon completed its transformation. As the demon grew, she needed to match its now-gargantuan form. Erk had told her about spells that could be used to change a wizard's size, and he explained how Dread Pirate Lord Oorzgo's uncanny magic could change the size of objects. She harnessed the power of the arcane stream to increase her height and density. She started to grow, but the demon before her was more concerned with the shadow now spread over Mystalon.

"By the gods!" Yuvina shouted, stumbling and falling backwards.

Sender's now-demonic voice hissed, "No! Not the Dragon Father!" His massive tentacles flailed wildly as the eldritch dragon sprayed another geyser of extremely hot, ashy magma.

Miranda resumed her assault, "Wrong, that is Ezelbrecht the Gray. They are their own dragon, and they spell all of our dooms." Her focus on size-enhancement magic allowed her to grow from just shy of six feet to over twenty feet, and her sword stayed proportionately long and heavy. Just then, however, she realized Ezelbrecht was using their breath weapon. She snapped her attention from the fleshy mass in front of her to the eldritch dragon. "Ezelbrecht! Have you regained your breath? How have you left Olvidado?!" she shouted. Her voice sounded deep and powerful, a caricature of her usual melody. The change in her voice startled her so much that she chose not to speak any further.

Sender hurled his tentacles at her, but she parried his blows with ease. She realized her own training had equipped her with the skills to fight effectively, but her father's confidence helped prevent her from hesitating. She had little time to reflect, however, as Ezelbrecht's sudden emergence concerned her more than the demon.

"Mir'thax, you fool. I'm a god. I never lost my breath weapon," Ezelbrecht retorted as they tore through one of Sender's flanks, destroying an Umbral in the process.

Miranda glared as she started to wail on the core of Sender's demonic form with Holyfang. Though her density deepened her voice and she did not like it, she had to ask, "Then you are a liar, are you not?" The mass of flesh had been rendered so badly by Ezelbrecht's sudden onslaught the battle now seemed inconsequential.

The eldritch dragon rolled their eyes as they discharged another breath of magma, igniting the fleshy demon in a slow, incendiary burn. They flew directly back up, their wingspan covering the whole of the ruined clearing in shadow. Ezelbrecht's voice changed as they ascended. "I've lied to you as many times as I needed, Mir'thax. You're lucky that you now serve as a pawn in my plot for revenge." A laugh boomed across the clearing as he continued, "Mortals rejoice, Gorthran the Dragon Father has returned to the mortal coil. I have come back to serve as your master, and you are to serve me. Slaves. If you wish to live, you will obey my will!" he shouted.

Miranda felt her heart break, but she could not abandon her focus. She shredded the core of Sender's demonic form with relative ease with Gorthran's help. The Umbrals and the solisberry tree were utterly destroyed, and Sender had sent himself into oblivion. But the Dragon Father now stood before Miranda for a third time.

Around eleven years before the events in Mystalon, Erk found himself staring up at the entrance to a massive cavern. His brother, Drymouth, and his first officer, Jax Slicer, stood beside him.

Drymouth could express no words, and his body language was much less animated these days. Erk worried for his brother, and that concern led him to this cavern. Erk looked to Drymouth with pity and determination, saying, "We should find answers in here, brother. Please hold on a little bit longer." He stepped forward under the mountainside leading into the cave. Olvidado was much more unsettling than The Master had described, but Erk's fear for his brother made him unstoppable in his current quest. He would find a cure for his brother, no matter the cost.

Ezelbrecht's cavern was well-lit in the center. An otherworldly, pale glow reflected off the stalagmites and rock formations in the wider part of the circular, subterranean expanse. In the middle, the three found an eldritch dragon resting deep within.

"You're a long way from home, elf," a voice boomed throughout. Jax reached for a cutlass on his belt. The voice laughed and continued, "Don't bother, pirate. You're just as far from home as the elf."

Erk blinked obstinately and approached the dragon in the middle. They raised their head nonchalantly and looked at the pirate lord with an unamused stare. "How in the Abyss did you reach me? You do not carry the stench of the gods on you, and your Unbinding power is—" they began but stopped suddenly. Ezelbrecht's eyes widened, and they began to smile. A long, growling hiss emerged from the dragon's maw.

Erk did not hesitate as he began to make his request. "Great Ezelbrecht, I have been sent by The Master, Un'harzin. He spoke with me in a strange dimension and told me how to reach Olvidado using 'The Currents.' His wisdom and knowledge are unparalleled among mortals, but not even he could help me with my plight."

The eldritch dragon continued to stare, expressing no emotion beyond their smile. Jax and Drymouth stood a step behind Erk, fascinated by the gargantuan beast in front of them. Ezelbrecht replied after a long, uncomfortable silence. "Un'harzin? This name is familiar to me, but I have not heard it spoken in nearly a century. Nevertheless, anyone with the ability to reach me here has an incredible destiny." They looked at the three humanoids standing before them. "Well not all of you, perhaps. You waste my time and interrupt my slumber. I should slay you where you stand."

Erk swallowed before speaking, his tone apologetic. "We did not mean to disturb you, great one. I merely came to plead a question to an entity wiser than all mortals in existence." His heart raced with anticipation, knowing that the outcome of meeting Ezelbrecht could be dire or incredible.

The eldritch dragon licked their lips. "Then plead, mortal. For I am already bored. And when I am bored, I grow hungry."

Jax felt a drop of sweat run down his forehead even though the cave was relatively cool. His heart also raced; he had been with Erk for ten years at this point and had never encountered anything like this. He steeled himself against the fear coursing through him and spoke, "Pleadin' be pointless in the face of a god. Yer mind already be made, and we's good as dead if you will it. I dun mean to be imp-you-dent, but if I'm still standin' here, then you gots a good reason for it."

Erk's eyes narrowed with delight. Jax had as much intuition as strength, possessing both in abundance. Standing at seven feet tall, the human was impressive by all physical accounts. His record as a pirate, however, was a bit more sullied than Erk would have liked. Still, as his desperation to help Drymouth increased, his requirements for alliances had begun to deteriorate. He was considering taking a young pirate by the name of Zanfur under his wing even though the nuisance tried to challenge Erk at every turn. Zanfur was a dread pirate, known for his willingness to shed blood on the open seas. Such an ally would possibly strike fear into the heart of Gelidor, even. Still, the words his first mate spoke to an eldritch dragon could have been enough to bring their early ends. What he said, however, was true, and Erk recognized the wisdom of such an acknowledgement.

Ezelbrecht's smile widened. "You choose allies well, Erilkaiden, Thief of Light."

Erk blinked for a moment. Jax tilted his head, and Drymouth leaned backward, a rare expression of surprise from the desiccated elf. His skin was taut and dry, and his eyes had all but sunk into his head. Under his horrifying exterior, however, his mind continued to work with full function. His entire mental and magical essence was somehow being pulled into the arcane stream, but the erosion was so slow he figured another ten years would pass before he met his final end. Still, he had to rely on his brother, as his faculties were severely limited in the primary dimension. The pirate lord replied, "I'm sorry, great one, but I am unfamiliar with the title you've bestowed upon me." His hands trembled slightly, anxiety running its course through his body.

Ezelbrecht nodded. "Your ally is correct. The fact that you even found Olvidado means I wanted you to arrive. Please, mortals, have a seat. Allow me to prepare a feast."

Erk scrunched his nose and looked over to Jax, who shook his head. The pirate lord turned back to the eldritch dragon, "There's no need to patronize, either, great one. We are truly humbled to be in your presence. We merely seek your counsel, and I am willing to pay any price. And, yes, before you ask, my own life is a bargaining chip in this. It was forfeit the moment I came into your presence."

The dragon's smile faded. "Very well, mortals. You are both wise enough and brave enough to stand before me. It is fitting that you could see through my condescension. The truth is, I wish to see Erilkaiden's Unbinding power fully unleashed."

Erk's head drew back and up. "Excuse me?" he replied, shocked. "You mean, if I choke the flow of mana and allow it to accumulate to its maximum potential?"

Ezelbrecht merely nodded.

Erk nodded in return. "I cannot say with certainty what will happen, but I know it will be incredibly destructive."

The dragon laughed, the sound hissing off the walls of the cavern with repeated echoes. "There is little that can be done to destroy me, fool. Your allies will wait outside, anyway."

Erk's eyes narrowed. "How do you know? What is it that gives you the gift to see my Unbinding?"

Ezelbrecht reared up, their head in a striking position. "My existence and powers are not yours to question, fool!"

Erk sneered. "Then neither are mine, all wise Ezelbrecht. If mortals are so predictable, so are immortals." He reached up to his head and pulled off his tricorn hat. The skull and constellation stitched into it shimmered in the moon-like light of the cavern. "Kill us all if you like, but Jax was right. We have something you want, or we would not still be standing before you. I only wish to cure my brother of his curse."

Ezelbrecht paused. The hostility surging within them came from a shard buried deep in their consciousness. Though Ezelbrecht was dark and evil, even they understood when mortals had the advantage. "Gorthran, now is not the time!" they shouted.

Erk blinked, his head still perched with antagonism. Drymouth stood motionless, and Jax stepped forward to stand beside Erk. He would face this eldritch dragon alongside his captain, even though it meant certain doom. In his mind, there was no honor in fleeing. Discretion and valor had no home together.

The dragon regained their composure. "You are correct, Thief of Light. It is imperative that I witness the full power of your Unbinding. I will protect you, and only you, from its most destructive capabilities." They relaxed their head from striking position. "Besides, I know you've been dying to unleash it. Maybe if you had," the dragon flicked its tongue as it spoke. "Your brother wouldn't be a dried-up husk. Would he?" They could taste Erk's anger.

"How do you know all of these things?" Erk said, a tremble in his voice.

"I am Ezelbrecht, and I watch all things through the arcane stream. Dragons are creatures of the stream." They gave another menacing smile. "I felt the pulse you gave when you tugged on it that frightful day, Erk. Your intent was made clear, but your reasoning has been lost to me for two decades. I have awaited this story patiently."

Erk's eyes were filled with tears. "Jax," he spoke in a whisper.

"Yes, Cap'n?" he said, standing at attention.

"Take Evan out of here, okay?" he asked more than ordered.

Jax nodded, turning to see Drymouth already heading for the exit of the cavern. "That's damn creepy, but I bloody love 'em," the pirate commented.

Erk's lips broke into a smile though tears strolled down his cheeks. He waited for a few moments after his brother and first officer left the cavern. "If I had unleashed the full power of my Unbinding that night, I would have destroyed Evan as well."

Ezelbrecht's smile was even more malicious than before. "So, you truly can feel the arcane stream with such precision that you know the anticipated results of your Unbinding without a doubt. You're an incredible wizard, Erilkaiden."

Erk frowned. "You have no need to flatter me beyond your own gain. What is it you wish, in truth?"

Ezelbrecht raised a talon to their chin. "To see your power, as I said. It's not often that even a god watches a star die."

The pirate lord sighed. "Three stars in my own universe have been extinguished, I cannot find one, and the other is dying as we speak. If I demonstrate my uncanny magic for you, will you help guide me to a solution to cure my brother?"

The eldritch dragon sneered, exposing their sharp teeth. "Fine, fool. If you show me your true power, I will point you in the direction that should help, eventually." Ezelbrecht felt Gorthran's excitement.

As the universe ceased its rotation around Erk, Ezelbrecht rushed to the edge of the hole. They reached out with their tail to hold Erk in the air. He remained unconscious for almost twelve hours. In that time, Gorthran used his divine essence to hold Erk's Black Hole in fragmentary stasis. The next time the pirate used his power, Ezelbrecht, Gorthran, and the other shards making up their essence would be able to escape their divine prison on Olvidado and return to the primary plane of existence. After over three millennia of captivity, the Dragon Father would be ready to take his place as the rightful ruler of all of existence.

However, in the decade that passed, Gorthran developed new priorities. Doctor One had been abusing his children. The scientist would be the first to pay the price for meddling.

Chapter 14
An Uncanny Alliance

"Solisberry blooms make a wonderful tea. They also enhance a wizard's connection to the arcane stream." – Marin Elitirin, *The Sacred Trees of Espa*

iranda sat on a bench at the foot of Erk's bed in the captain's quarters on *The Nebula*. Her eyes were closed, and she clutched her holy symbol in her right hand. She whispered prayers of healing fervently, even though she did not focus her spirit to her deity. Something inside her told her Invictus was walking among mortals, and that it was Lexcord answering prayers in the Sword of Justice's place. Naomi and Erk were in the bed, and August and Evan rested on lounges Erk had accumulated in his previous raids against Gelidor. The warpriest sighed contently. Though Gorthran the Dragon Father had emerged from his hiding inside Ezelbrecht on Olvidado, he seemed more concerned with the calamity currently befalling the dragons of Espa. He made several blustering threats against all mortal kind, but then he flew away from Mystalon as confoundingly as he arrived. Miranda used her enhanced size to rescue all her friends at the end of the Battle of Mystalon. She found that Sender had even incapacitated Celyth and her father with some sort of paralysis magic. They had been positioned to retrieve the solisberry branch if Naomi's initial plan failed; they did not, however, anticipate an interloper like Sender.

Fortunately, there were no fatalities among Miranda's friends. Evan's and August's wounds were lethal, but Miranda's healing power had spared them. Naomi and Erk needed significant healing, which is what Miranda had been working on for the last hour. Selasine was on the deck of the ship with Jax Slicer, Erk's first officer. In any normal series of events, Selasine would have arrested Jax last year for his crimes of piracy; instead, the corsair and the priest bonded over their love of agriculture and hunting. Jax served as the pilot of *The Nebula* if Erk was incapacitated or otherwise indisposed. Selasine represented the church on official business; Jax, however, had proven that he was more loyal to Erk than he was to the code of pirates that thrived on chaos and unjust plundering. Selasine was only ten years older than the first officer, and he had taken an elder-brotherly role in helping rehabilitate the pirate's way of thinking. Miranda was thankful for that, but she was more in awe of her adoptive father's role in Mystalon earlier that day.

Once Miranda and Yuvina saw Sender fighting with August and Evan from their vantage point outside the arboretum, they rushed to help their friends. Selasine stayed behind to comfort the people of Mystalon as Miranda's healing presence departed their company. The Battle of Beriton and the fight against Vortex the Lich had aged Selasine more than he cared to admit, and Miranda knew it. He was as stubborn as he was caring, so he insisted on continuing to fight. In Mystalon, however, he channeled the spirit of Lexcord much the way Miranda did before she joined the melee. The people of Mystalon were left with a feeling of hope for their future. The potion Arlindra had acquired from Elitirin allowed them to regrow several eolnut and yindai trees within an hour after the battle. Even the solisberry branch had grown to around twenty feet long, and the Mystalonians worked together to plant it anew.

Nevertheless, the warpriest began to worry after spending the morning with Selasine. She realized that she had taken him for granted by embarking on her own half-year adventure. She knew she needed to stay by his side no matter his course. For now, though, he could discuss animal husbandry and different crop-growing techniques with a pirate that grew up on a farm. That was the least threatening place that Miranda could think of for High Priest of Invictus, Thomas Selasine. At least for the time being.

Miranda was further surprised that Arlindra and Celyth insisted on accompanying her back to Nulodia to assist in the hunt for Farzg. They contended that his crimes of egg smuggling were partly responsible for the destruction of Mystalon, and that by destroying the supply chain, perhaps future tragedies could be prevented. They were in Naomi's dressing room, resting seriously for the first time in a week. Yuvina was also in there, but she struggled being on the open water. She might have still been on deck with a bit of seasickness, but Miranda was not sure.

Naomi's deep, rich voice cooed suddenly, "Praise the earth mother, he's alive."

Miranda's blue eyes opened wide with excitement. "Naomi!" she exclaimed.

The giantkin sat up, Erk's silk blankets falling to reveal her armor and captain's jacket. She scooped Erk into her arms and held him as he breathed, resting peacefully. "Miranda, my sweet, sweet Miranda. You've saved us all again!" she sang as she squeezed her beloved in her arms.

Tears welled in Miranda's eyes. "I'm so glad you're okay, Naomi. May the Sword of Justice rejoice with us both," she said, redirecting Naomi's praise.

"What happened out there?" the giantkin inquired, her hands protectively cupping Erk's head against her chest.

Miranda summarized the Battle of Mystalon for the pirate lady. As she recounted events, Evan stirred, sitting up and listening intently. Three Umbrals and Doctor One's fourth in command proved to be a greater threat than all of Claston's mobilized navy. Neither Naomi nor Evan could believe it. Though Miranda could not explain Sender's power, she could explain that she was able to repress it easily. She was also able to fight using a sword with confidence and acuity. She further described Sender's demonic transformation and the arrival of Gorthran. The eldritch dragon Ezelbrecht had focused all of their strength into keeping Erk's first Black Hole open so that Gorthran could emerge from Olvidado the next time Erk opened another. She didn't understand the Dragon Father's brief explanation fully, but it seemed that Erk's Black Hole opened a way through space and time.

August awoke as she concluded her summary. "Miranda," he groaned.

The warpriest turned her attention to the young man that she looked up to like an older brother. "August!" she replied, her voice becoming more musical by the moment.

He tried to sit up but had trouble moving. "I can't see so well," he complained. "Everything is pretty fuzzy."

Miranda was at his side in less than a moment. "Maybe you should continue to rest?" she suggested, holding his hands in hers.

She knelt beside him, her eyes scanning his, realizing that they had a milky glaze suggesting his vision had been significantly damaged by the injuries inflicted upon him by Sender.

August shook his head. "I can still feel where I took that hit. I know you've worked Invictus to the bone, haven't you? It's no fault of yours, Miranda. Don't you dare."

The tears in Miranda's eyes found their way down her round cheeks easily. "Please tell me you can see, at least. Something, anything," she pleaded.

August looked at her, but his gaze seemed unfocused. "Yeah, I can see you are there. It's not a problem, okay? Just give me a little more time to recover, and I'll be good as new by the time you and the high priest get done with me. Right?"

Miranda let out a deep breath, but then she turned her attention to Evan. "Hello," she greeted, feeling the immediate pressure of butterflies in her stomach. During the fight with Sender, she realized Evan had come closer to death in that moment than he did when she healed him on *The Nebula* months ago. That thought turned her memories to her time with Evan at her estate in Devitus. Evan expressed an interest in her that she wanted to reciprocate, but she wasn't sure what that meant exactly. She liked him and thought that he was handsome, impressive, and dedicated. Still, every time they interacted seemed like monumental, life-altering moments. Now, he was injured once more, and she wanted to see him healed and ready to fight again.

Evan smiled. "Miranda." His voice was calm and grateful.

"Are you—" Miranda started to ask, but Evan interrupted her.

"I'm fine, thanks to you. As always. Please, tend to August." His smile was sweet and genuine, and the butterflies swirled in Miranda's stomach again. His concern for her friend was rooted in mutual trust and love.

August chuckled, "Hey, maverick. Long time no 'see'" he teased, causing Miranda to let out an angry, incredulous screech at his ironic phrasing.

Evan laughed. "Don't take your injuries in such good humor, commander. Your beautiful sister seems to take it quite personally. I mean seriously."

Miranda stood up straight, smoothing the metal of her battlemail's long, mesh skirt with her fingers. Naomi continued to hold Erk in her arms, giving Miranda a twisted, pained smile. The warpriest placed her fingers on August's temples and closed her eyes.

She began to whisper a prayer to Invictus, and her holy symbol, the scales of justice, radiated bright white light. After a moment she opened her eyes and shook her head. "The damage is beyond Invictus, even."

August sat quietly for a moment, his emotions whirling from sadness to anger. Evan's lips were drawn up into an expression of sorrow and dread, and Naomi watched, still holding Erk. Miranda looked around for a moment and began to draw in the arcane energy in the air. It was thin here at sea, but she had eaten several solisberry blossoms to supplement her healing prayers with arcane energy. Though wizards had never used the arcane to heal did not mean it was impossible, and Miranda was a continual reminder that even the wizards of old had much to learn about the stream. As she began to shape the ether inside of her essence, she thought of her singular desire: to restore August's sight.

A purple light now shone from Miranda, enveloping her and August. The intensity caused Erk to stir as well. She realized this injury would take nearly all of her mana to restore, and she was already severely exhausted. She'd likely be unconscious for a while, but she saw it as a small price to pay. She pushed her willpower to the brink, and the arcane stream bowed to her desire. August's vision cleared quickly, giving him enough clarity and excitement that he caught Miranda in his arms as she collapsed. As expected, her hair was a very light shade of pink.

Erk suddenly shouted, "No, Miranda!" Naomi, also concerned, scooped him out of the bed as she stood up. The four Miranda had been working so long to heal now laid her in Erk's bed, placing another solisberry bloom under her tongue.

Naomi sighed deeply, "She's used a dozen of these since yesterday. I'm concerned she's overdone it again."

Erk smiled gently, looking at the warpriest asleep in his bed. She was still in her battlemail, and it was in serious need of a polish. Between that and her horribly unraveled braids, he realized she had not rested since the battle. Channeling enough arcane energy to execute the Black Hole attack had been more painful to Erk than the fall that followed. There was no way that she was not in pain herself, even if she had draconic heritage to help her bond with the magic more easily. Seven months ago, he kidnapped her to use as a pawn in a game of Xanadu. Now, she fit The Priestess piece perfectly, protecting her adjacent allies from enemy pieces. In the game, she was a piece often sacrificed, but Erk could never imagine Miranda being disposable.

After August laid Miranda in the bed, he sat back down on a lounge. He could feel Miranda's arcane energy swirling within him still. His injury was healed, but he felt like his uncanny magic was about to run wild for a few moments. He worried he would not be able to control his speed, so he remained stationary until the feeling passed. Evan placed a hand on his shoulder, "Are you alright, commander?" he inquired. August nodded.

Erk and Naomi turned, examining the paladin. Erk commented, "It seems you were under a great affliction if it required such an intense amount of mana to rectify. I am thankful that Miranda is the person she is. But we must work as a group to keep her from overdoing it moving forward."

Evan cast a glance at her, feeling an inexplicable anxiety, "What do you mean brother?"

Erk let out a sigh, causing Naomi to place a hand on his shoulder. He continued, "I just worry that somehow she will deplete the draconic gift within her further."

Evan's expression shifted from worry to excitement, "Oh, brother. You must know. Somehow, she absorbed the souls of her parents when she found them in the statues last year. I'm surprised that her capacity isn't expanding rather than contracting."

Naomi wrinkled her nose a bit, "Is that so?" she clarified, returning to stand by the bed where Miranda rested. "Maybe that's why she's become so strong in spite of what she lost. The greatest gift a parent can leave to their children is the means to overcome the hardships that they will eventually face." She touched Miranda's pink hair affectionately. "Though it seems our songbird has been pushed into more conflict than she bargained for, through no fault of her own."

August chuckled. "I used to call her that back in Devitus. 'Invictus's songbird.' Funny, that's the main thing that hasn't changed with her. She's become so strong and unbelievable, but she's still as caring and helpful as she always was."

A knock at the door startled everyone, but they were not surprised when High Priest Selasine entered the captain's quarters of *The Nebula* without invitation. He stopped abruptly with a moment of shock, finding the occupants of the room in opposite states of consciousness from when he was last here. "Well, apologies for barging in," he began.

Erk smiled broadly, "Nulestotejin. Extraordinary circumstances require a suspension of protocol. No need to apologize."

Selasine nodded, giving a small smile. "Let me guess, she made one last push with the mana to get you all awake?"

Evan shook his head. "Not quite. She went to some pretty extraordinary lengths to restore August's vision, Your Holiness."

Naomi nodded in agreement, taking a seat beside Miranda in the bed. She began to unravel what was left of the warpriest's healer braids. Selasine responded, "I owe her an apology then. She insisted that I take a break above deck, and she promised she wouldn't do any more healing until I came back." He sighed. "I knew better than to leave her alone."

August sighed. "More like it's my fault, Your Holiness. My injuries were what required such an effort."

Evan gave August a shake. "Hey, don't be hard on yourself. You'd do the same for her, and we both know it. She's going to be fine; we just need to let her rest."

Naomi nodded profusely, taking the sapphire comb that Miranda always wore with braided hair in her hand. She began to brush. "You are absolutely correct. I've given her another solisberry bloom, and now I'm going to help her groom and clean up. Because she's been fighting nonstop for gods know how long. Let's give her some space to just be herself."

Everyone but Naomi dispersed about the ship. August returned to his officer's cabin on the first deck. Selasine sat on a crate outside of Erk's cabin. Erk joined Jax on the upper deck, and Evan found sundry sailing duties to help with. He did not want to sit idly for the time being. Justin and Valarie were working the sails with Erk's crew, and Evan decided he'd join them.

As he approached, Justin waved him over. "Lord Evanthalus, welcome back aboard," the paladin greeted.

The elf grinned and picked up a length of rope, refastening the knots as he inspected it. "I should say the same to you, Justin the Watchful. You've not traveled on *The Nebula* with us in ages," he replied.

"We've missed you too, Evan," Valarie interjected with a laugh. She pulled hard on a rope as she spoke, causing her to grunt with the exertion at the end of her sentence.

Evan continued retying knots in the rope as needed. His jovial expression remained as he said, "And you as well, Valarie the Persistent. And your unseen companion," he growled, lashing the rope fiercely at a crate nearby.

A gruff voice yowled, "By the gods, Evan, you scoundrel!" After a moment, the chef of *The Nebula* materialized out of nowhere. "Always making a deal harder 'an it's gotta be!" A pungent odor also filled the air. Justin thought it smelled like old onions and garlic. The paladin knew this was the pirate that had killed him seven months ago.

"Don't whine, Shalo. You're not going to get a chance to redeem yourself lazing on deck watching the paladins work. Captain's awake."

Shalo's eyes widened. "That's good news, bosun! I guess yer right, I'll get right on it!" he said, scrambling off the crate and charging for the stairs that would lead down to the kitchen eventually.

Justin gave a soft, single chortle. Valarie narrowed her eyes with harsh prejudice as Shalo departed their company. She seemed to harbor more resentment toward the pirate than Justin did. Even if he was at peace with the present, she knew she would always be suspicious of the smelly pirate. Evan continued working the rope, adding, "I suppose the captain will call everyone for food in a couple of hours."

Justin nodded in agreement, dutifully minding the sails according to Jax's calls from the upper deck. Valarie hummed a bit before she spoke, "So does that mean everyone is alright?"

Evan nodded. "Miranda is resting now, finally. We need only return to Nulodia and perhaps find a decisive action to put this egg and Umbral business behind us."

Justin replied, "Certainly. I'm glad to hear she is resting now. She deserves that and so much more."

They all agreed silently, working on the deck together for a few moments before Evan caught sight of activity outside of Naomi's dressing room. He dismissed himself from working with the paladins and approached Celyth who had emerged from the cabin. "Good afternoon, Lady Fernith" he greeted.

She had changed from her armor into a white, cotton blouse and some leather trousers that Naomi procured from the dressing room. She gave him a casual wave. "Oh, hey, Evan." She walked over to the starboard railing close to the stairs that led to the upper deck. She climbed on a crate so she could peer through the ornate rails, "I've never been on a boat this large before. This is pretty fun." She seemed evasive.

Evan merely wanted to check on her, however. "I'm glad that you get to experience *The Nebula*, then. I trust you are well? No lingering side effects from Sender's attacks?"

He approached the railing but did not jump up to see over the side. Even though they were tall for elves, the ship's railing was high here for safety and design reasons. She responded in an unusually serious voice, "With me, sure. No lingering side effects. But Mystalon?" she scoffed as she said the name of her homeland.

Evan frowned a bit, hearing the dressing room door click behind them. He glanced behind, watching as Arlindra emerged, still dressed in her brown, leather tunic. He replied to Celyth, "I understand, then." He let the silence around them rest as Arlindra approached. Nebu was asleep in her hair as usual, but he had at least brushed it out for her and helped her freshly shave the right side.

Celyth shifted the conversation, "You know, we really do want to help you stop the trafficking of these eggs." She shuddered, remembering how it felt when she fired her bow at Sender. The way he moved seemed unreal, and, before she had time to adjust her focus, the scientist struck her with a wand of some sort. "These people are dangerous. We will probably need to take them all down. One at a time if we have to. Mystalon wrought its own fate, in a sense. But that is not a fate that the rest of the world deserves."

Arlindra gazed at her cousin, nodding in agreement. "I understand why you judge the Sages harshly, and I share your sentiment. We are glad to have crossed paths with Miranda and by extension you, Evanthalus."

He smiled. "And I'm glad you've decided to accompany us as we move against Farzg. The next blow we strike must be final." He looked back to the dressing room door. "Plus, there is the Yuvina situation," he remarked.

"Miranda is very worried for her," Celyth added.

Arlindra shook her head once. "While you were recovering, Miranda revealed Sender knew Yuvina and referred to her as one of the other doctor's experiments."

Evan tapped his chin in contemplation. "I wonder what that means, then. Hopefully we can address it on the way to Nulodia."

Celyth finally turned from the railing. "Yuvina says we should make contact with her organization in the city. She needs to make a full report, and Selasine wants to make her the organization's ambassador to the church." She smiled. "Hopefully the situation is not as dire as Mystalon's."

Evan answered, "Agreed." His gaze bounced between the

cousins. "Well, please let Yuvina know the captain is awake, and I've ordered Shalo to get a meal ready for us. Erk is going to want to welcome all of you newcomers in style, or whatever that means."

Celyth tilted her head to the side. "Well to us, Erk is the newcomer. Remind him of that, okay?"

Arlindra laughed fully for the first time in days. "Consider us diplomats of our people, nothing more."

Evan gave her a sideways grin, "You know that means he'll up the ceremony, right?"

Celyth's eyes widened. "Okay, nothing of the sort. A casual dinner will be fine, no speeches and no orations. Got it?"

Evan's grin softened, and his eyes shifted to the captain's door. "With any luck, Erk will agree."

Evan's suspicions were confirmed. Erk was planning a larger-than-necessary gathering, but it was not for dinner. Though Shalo served a meal fit for a pirate lord, it was immediately evident this was a feast to share during serious planning. The smell of food roused Miranda, who sleepily joined the others as they ate and discussed plans to pursue Farzg. The group of adventurers had grown to an impressive lot, numbering twelve in total. High Priest Thomas Selasine and his adopted daughter Miranda Hyacinth, along with Commander August Burchard, Shield Knight Justin the Watchful, and Shield Knight Valarie the Persistent represented the Church of Invictus in this ordeal. Pirate Lady Naomi and Pirate Lord Erilkaiden with his brother Evanthalus represented the pirates of Yendralia. Arlindra and Celyth Fernith represented Mystalon, and Yuvina asked to join on behalf of The Forgotten. Nebu was technically an independent entity, but he insisted twelve was an unlucky number. Arlindra and Celyth would represent his interests while he continued to nap in the ranger's hair for the foreseeable future. Unfortunately for the dracofly, Nebu's refusal to be counted left the official number at twelve, with Damil assisting in the endeavor as Selasine's partner rather than in an official church capacity. Erk asserted that twelve was a lucky number, and their collective made an impressive battalion. With the High Priest of Invictus of Nulodia as their leader, they had little worry they would be able to overwhelm Farzg. If he had rebuilt his estate far to the northeast of the capital city of the kingdom, they would travel to face him there. The waters of the north were treacherous, but an approach on land guaranteed they would have to travel through The Lichwood, a horrifying forest that inspired numerous legends and ghost stories.

They agreed a reconnaissance mission was the first priority upon returning to Nulodia. There was enough evidence to tie Farzg to the events in Mystalon, emphasizing the seriousness of the warrant issued by the Council of Four against him. Everyone further felt that pursuing Farzg should lead them to the conclusory threads that would shut down the scientists relying on the frost giantkin for his smuggling network. In the meantime, the elders of the group made it clear: for the next three days on the return voyage to Nulodia, the paladins, Miranda, and the Fernith cousins were to spend their time at sea relaxing. Miranda wanted to work with Yuvina to uncover her lost memories the following day, however, which brought up a debate of the dangers.

Yuvina, on the other hand, asserted it was necessary, and everyone needed to know if she posed a threat to them. Selasine and Erk agreed, but they cautioned Miranda to go easy on the magic. She used almost half of the newly acquired solisberry blooms healing everyone; she needed to be conservative with the rest of them. They finalized their plan to go to The Lichwood as a group, taking *The Nebula* as far as the North Timbyl region of the Alabaster Kingdom. If Farzg had rebuilt his stronghold there, he would stand no chance against the combined might of these four factions. Until their arrival in Nulodia to formalize the operation, everyone was to relax. Erk insisted that people wear casual, comfortable clothes, play games, and engage in diversions like music and dance for the next three days.

Arlindra rolled her eyes at the idea. She'd rather just nap if she was going to be relegated to a completely unproductive member of the group for a short time. She returned to the dressing room to do exactly that.

Celyth wanted to read a book that she found in Erk's cabin. She went up to the crow's nest of the mast on the upper deck since the sails filtered the sun at this time of day on their western voyage. The book was titled *Sniper's Journey*, and Erk gifted it to her permanently.

August still felt weary from his injuries, and he wanted to retire early as well. He took a book from Erk's library titled *Seven Recipes for Savory Stews at Sea*. Over dinner, Arlindra argued with her cousin that people who could cook were far more impressive than oafs that expected others to do all of the cooking. He had learned quite a few culinary tricks while hunting and preparing game with his father in his younger years, and he found the elf's love of the outdoors intriguing. He was interested in getting to know her better, and he estimated good cooking would be an excellent icebreaker.

Justin and Valarie were keen to stay with Erk and Naomi. Selasine went to the foredeck to watch the waves. Miranda stood at Erk's cabin door, watching as the remaining four prepared to play a couples' match of Xanadu. She wanted to play board games, but she wanted to follow her dad more. Yuvina accompanied her toward the door, asking, "Surely there's more to sailing than persistent illness. May I accompany you, friend?"

Miranda smiled and reached out to take the kitsune's paw in her hand. "We're going to enjoy the evening air, everyone!" she called out, her electric blue gaze connecting with the kitsune's orange and green eyes. As their palms touched, the arcane stream became visible again, providing a brilliant, gentle rain of ether.

Everyone gave her a nonchalant wave. Naomi added, "Are you sure you won't be a third team? It does add to the suspense when it's not just a two-way game."

Miranda winced. "I can literally use a tiny amount of mana and peek at the tiles. One of you has access to a river tile after three turns." Her lips twisted into a cheeky, evil grin.

Justin snarled, "Hey, yeah, no fair. She doesn't get to play now!"

Miranda giggled to herself. She didn't even look at the tiles with her magic, but she knew her statement would be enough to revoke her invitation.

Valarie nudged Justin with her elbow. "Even if you get to a river tile, there's no guarantee that you'll even have the right cards. Be nice."

The paladin looked back at the two ladies at the door. "Oh, right. Well, enjoy the evening air at sea," he mumbled as Erk shook some dice in a small cup. They rattled louder than Justin's voice.

Miranda waved another goodbye, tugging on Yuvina's paw as they emerged on the deck. Erk's crew was hard at work, and Evan had taken the helm to relieve Jax. Though the deck was massive, stretching thirty feet across and over one-hundred feet long, Selasine could still be seen clearly on the foredeck. *The Nebula* did not have a forecastle like some galleons, but the front of the ship had a slightly raised deck. It allowed for masts of three different heights, and between its flexible construction and substantial magical enhancements, the ship moved at a pace unlike any other ship in the water except for Naomi's, *The Violet Blur*.

The two young ladies approached the high priest from behind, and Miranda tried to sneak up beside him. As she did, he instinctively stuck an arm out to grab her, but he pulled both her and Yuvina close since they were still paw-in-hand together. The warpriest looked like a young noblewoman, dressed in a white cotton surcoat that would have normally been worn over some kind of mesh armor. Her hair was not braided, spilling midway down her back. Yuvina had on her leather cloak still, but she had followed orders and left her armor behind. They both plunked into the high priest, leather padding obvious beneath his ceremonial robes.

"You're dressed for war, dad," Miranda teased as she leaned into his embrace.

Yuvina gave a small smile. "I'm glad I wasn't the only one tempted to break the rule!" she added, gripping the two of them tight. She had not trusted people with Unbinding powers since her adolescence, but these two changed her opinion greatly. She was glad she had finally met somebody who could help her bring the plight of The Forgotten to the forefront of urban church priorities. She felt bad that she saw it as an opportunity, as Pulhash was not an ally of the Sword of Justice. She truly did care for Miranda and her father, however. She could see their genuine care for the people who needed them, and that drew her to them.

Selasine laughed. "That's not armor, just an old guy's clothes." He looked down at them. He and Yuvina had not spent enough time together, and he was glad Miranda could read his heart. He needed to know more about this potential victim of Farzg and the mad scientists. "Besides, I just wanted to breathe the salty air for a bit. I didn't expect an ambush!" he teased in return.

Miranda let out a deep, contented sigh. "I know. I'm just glad we're back together. I've been worried about you."

The high priest laughed heartily. "Worried about me, while you're the one off in the wilderness! Fighting shadows and trying to peel back the secrets of the universe. Tell me why I haven't restricted your adventuring clearance yet, yolasha."

She laughed again and gave him another squeeze. As she pulled away, she held firmly to Yuvina's paw. "It's because you needed to meet wonderful people like Yuvina. She came to us under suspicious circumstances, and based on the words of Sender, I think the leader of their organization has conducted some sort of ritual or experiment on her. Would it be possible to reclaim memories that seem to be lost to the void?" She spoke with confidence, and the normal melody of her voice was replaced by a serious cadence. The rhythm was as compulsory as her words.

Selasine nodded in response. "Of course. Every memory in the universe is stored in the primordial place where the gods reside." He looked at Yuvina as he spoke, noting her features and her genuine expressions. "Even if your memories were stolen by some kind of magic, they would reside there. Unfortunately, such knowledge is beyond mortals. I'm afraid unless Invictus himself can find your memories, then there is no way I know to utilize that type of knowledge."

Yuvina's nose twitched with curious desire. "Could a mortal go to the primordial place?"

Selasine's posture stiffened. "They could, but the gods of order and justice have declared that a blasphemy. The powers that flow there would destroy the minds of a simple mortal like any of us, and—"

Yuvina interrupted him, "But Miranda is definitely not just a simple mortal. She is one who could look in the primordial place, is she not?"

Selasine looked at his pupil and daughter as he spoke. "You're correct in that regard, Yuvina. But would you ask her to take such a risk?"

Miranda looked up at Selasine then over to her new friend. "But I'd gladly take that risk, modai-rin," she interjected.

He nodded in deference. "Of course, it is your decision to make. Forgive my overprotectiveness." He gave her a concerned look, genuine care in his eye. "Just remember, you're not immortal, yolasha. Dragon, human, or otherwise."

She smiled up at him. "Nothing to forgive. I would not wish to enter the primordial place without the blessing and guidance of Invictus himself!" she continued. "I am, however, willing to chase an answer by whatever means we can." Miranda squeezed Yuvina's paw gently.

Selasine looked from Miranda to the foxkin, then back to his daughter. "You've really been overdoing it, you know? I'm not the only one worried about you."

Miranda started to object, but then she laid her head against Selasine's chest. "I know. I'm sorry. Everyone was on the brink of death though, I—"

Thomas chuckled and interrupted her. "Evan found you in K'tal H'yuck with pink hair. And the fight with the assassin?"

Miranda's bottom lip quivered, and she looked up at him, "He told you about that?"

This time, he laughed. "Of course he did, darling daughter. I told you, I'm not the only person worried about you. To make matters worse, you're using prayers that priests twice your age haven't mastered." He paused a moment, looking between the two young women that were clutching him, Miranda from the front and Yuvina from the side. "I risk being blasphemous, but I think even Invictus is being reckless with you."

Miranda's jaw slacked. Yuvina, though not a cleric of Pulhash, understood what it meant to question one's god. Miranda replied, "Modai-rin." Her voice trailed off, unusually monotone. She began to think of some of the prayers she had been using, especially the healing prayers. To heal at a distance like she did against Sender taxed her body and soul greatly, but she knew it was the only option at that time. She purposefully did not use the End spell against Sender, but she thought about how close she was. She realized what her father meant. "Oh, by Invictus. I'm so sorry." She wept gently against Selasine, who gripped her tighter.

The foxkin smiled, a sadness creeping into her expression. Over dinner, she saw the great lengths Miranda went to heal her friends. Yuvina could see her exhaustion, and Miranda was already planning to spend considerable energy on helping her recover the memories of the most recent month. Based on the current conversation, she realized how much of a risk the woman was willing to take for her. She squeezed Miranda's hand as the warpriest had done to her a moment ago. "Please don't put yourself in harm's way on my account. Far too many have suffered as a result of my weakness." Miranda and Selasine both fixed their eyes on Yuvina. The foxkin did not give them time to interrupt her, continuing, "I felt something different using the magic within me when I activated the Magic Mirror against Sender. My body—no, my very soul. It ached."

Miranda's eyes widened, and Selasine closed his with a deep breath of sorrow. Miranda inquired, "You're absolutely certain you did not have any powers before the month that has left your memory?"

The kitsune nodded with finality.

Selasine added, "If what you say is true, then your very life is in danger each time you use your uncanny magic. I would not be surprised if the enemy we face has put you with us as a disposable pawn in a greater scheme. I do wonder," he said, pausing a moment. He gripped the two in his arms a little tighter. "I do wonder why they would place you in a position to become an ally rather than pit you against us with your incredible power."

The logic terrified Yuvina. She buried her snout into Selasine's robe now. She felt scared, but she did not feel alone. That comfort encouraged her, and she replied, "What have I done?" She started to cry as well, tears dampening her fur.

"Nothing that I won't undo," Miranda insisted.

Selasine sighed, resigned. She truly could not help herself. He smiled. After scolding her for overdoing it, she was ready to overdo it again. Her spirit was infinite and her kindness boundless. "Are you certain, yolasha?" he asked, his voice tired.

She looked up at Thomas with a devious smile. "I am. Because I'm Mir'thax Toi'landra, the daughter of Philotrax and Reshiria Hyacinth. Daughter of High Priest Thomas Selasine. I'm also Lady Miranda Hyacinth, Warpriest of Invictus, Judge of Hearts. And Yuvina's heart is one worth saving. That's why I'm certain."

Yuvina's tears stopped. For the first time in her life, she realized her powers did not define her, but her genuine heart gave her a value beyond any comparable magic. "Thank you, Miranda."

Doctor One slammed his fists on a steel worktable repeatedly. Diablo and Artificer stood on the other side of it, looking at him in disbelief.

The mad doctor shouted, "How!? How!? How could anyone defeat Sender!? I gave him tool after tool! I infused him with plasmatic Fuerzul! I worked for years to transmute his soul! He was a royal class of demon! A soul full of bile and deceit! This is absurd! You've all failed me!" His eyes were wide and his expression hysterical. "The solisberry tree lives!" His voice was frantic and maniacal at the same time.

Diablo, a hellspawn standing at seven feet tall with corkscrew horns extending another foot upward, towered over Doctor One. "But, sir, we—"

"DON'T you dare. Don't even try it. Farzg is becoming unresponsive as predicted. He is not a fool, and Watcher reported his musings with the assassin. He has a plan to abscond with the shard of Saraix. It matters not; his usefulness to me has run its course. I need godshards now, and I need Saraix's shard! Or I need Gorthran's shard, which might be easier to obtain." His voice calmed as he calculated a plot. His rainbow-colored eyes shimmered with rage. "Sender's failure is only a setback. I have contingencies."

Artificer added, "Sender was a cocky fool. He thought he could solve every problem by relying on his power. His fate was wrought by his own hand."

One's lips trembled with anger. "You're not wrong, Artificer, but right now, I am the only one allowed to be right. This Miranda will pay! Did you say that she is sailing with that fool Erk toward Nulodia?"

Diablo nodded. "Yes, sir! Furthermore, Watcher says Farzg is within the city, seeking to wreak havoc and 'reclaim what is his,'" the hellspawn added, his red skin glowing and contrasting with the white, artificial torchlight filling Doctor One's primary laboratory. "Though a plague of Umbrals would throw the city into chaos, their resources and response will be much swifter and more thorough than in Mystalon. Plus," he paused for a moment. "The Umbrals in Mystalon were made of entire eggs."

Doctor One slammed his fists on the table again. "I already know all of this, you imbecile!"

Diablo's eyes darted back and forth before he looked at the ground. His devilish talons needed no shoes; as a half-devil, he had incredible features that gave him an attractive face and form, but unbelievable strength and otherworldly hands, feet, horns, and bat-like wings. He wiggled the deadly nails on his feet, but he dared not employ them against Doctor One. He said nothing, allowing the doctor to continue shouting.

"Besides, the events in the city are a secondary priority. Right now, the dragon gods are our first priority. I discovered a way to turn a sentient being into arcane underflow while I visited the home of the gods. Hence the need for the Dragon Mother. Or Father." His screams calmed to his normal, maniacal raving. "I cannot accomplish my goals without one of those shards. I only need one to begin, but the sooner I acquire both, the better."

Artificer rolled his eyes. "Santiago, you haven't explained your findings. I can't help you design the equipment without," he began, but Doctor One interrupted him.

"We already have the Godhand, so there is no need for your expertise. I have seen the forbidden knowledge. Arcane underflow is the substance necessary for my transformation, and you cannot make the calculations required to create the Soul Scythe." Doctor One frowned and complained, "Santiago is a name forgotten by the past, Artificer. Leave it there."

Diablo's devilish eyes widened. He mused, "What manner of device harvests souls like the devils of war?"

Doctor One's demeanor shifted. He scowled and spoke in a low, threatening voice. "It is the beginning of a new era. If we cannot reach the stream of our own accord, then I will turn it inside out. The Soul Scythe will inject my essence with the godshards of four hundred dragons." His sinister tone made Diablo and Artificer shiver. The magical scientist explained, "By transforming my soul into arcane underflow, those godshards will be trapped from returning to the arcane stream. With my sentience intact, I will be able to wield the strength of those dragons. And with the shard of Saraix or Gorthran," he said but paused. His maniacal shouting resumed with a triumphant cadence. "I will have the tools to invert the stream!"

Doctors Two and Three stared in silence. Artificer crossed his arms. He spoke after a moment of pondering, his black pompadour hair bouncing as he processed Doctor One's words. "The creation myths speak of Genesis as the creator of the stream. The dragons are fragments of his mind. Sender's reports and your findings in the primordial place align. You would become a sentient being of arcane underflow, and the more godshards you acquire," he said, but Doctor One interrupted him again.

"If I can acquire the shards of the Dragon Mother or Father, I will be able to force the rest of the dragons into my soul by way of the vacuum left when the stream is forcibly starved. Watcher is returning for orders soon, and I will tell her to steal the shard from Farzg's vault. If that fails, time will tell if my calculations about the Dragon Father are correct." He glanced at an elaborate timepiece on his wrist.

Diablo bowed his head before he spoke. His horns tilted up with an intimidating glint in the laboratory light. Laboratory One, built in the palace at Argentum, was Doctor One's finest facility. Artificer's uncanny magic sped up the vampire's working acuity, and his undead nature allowed him to work without resting. The porcelain walls and lacrima-deum powered torches illuminated the room with a bright, white ambiance. Steel worktables were positioned around the room. The devilkin said, "I finished the psychic magic interference device. Would she also be able to put it in the city? It may further confound our enemies."

One tapped his chin, and his lips broke into an impressed smile. His voice was snippy as he said, "I knew I kept you around for a reason. Brilliant, Diablo! You are my strategist." His raving resumed. "I will provide her with the device by way of Reginald at Laboratory

Three." The worktables in the laboratory were covered with clock making tools and pieces of unfinished devices, extractors, and diffusers. The mad-elf looked at Diablo's workspace, locating the interference device. "Excellent work, pupil." He tapped his fingers together.

The laboratory quaked. Artificer frowned. "She's back."

Diablo shuddered. "The Devourer. Why have you brought her here, sir?"

Doctor One shook his head. His voice was high pitched and judgmental. "Nonsense, Aylabrax has been here for days. She has been lying in wait like a ghost in the city. A greater power approaches from above the peaks, a power she covets. My impatience was misplaced. Sender's efforts were not entirely in vain, and the Dragon Father has taken the bait."

As the three of them emerged from Doctor One's primary laboratory in the pyramidal palace of Argentum, they could make out the distinct silhouette of Gorthran hovering above.

Chapter 15
Aylabrax the Devourer

"Born in hate and shame, Aylabrax mopes among mortals, seeking to share her misery with those foolish enough to ally with her." – Lexcord's Reflections

The *Nebula* crashed through the waters of the southern Nulodian Sea, making its way toward Nulodia at breakneck speed. Erk had ordered his crew to sail day and night, creating a buzz of activity on the ship that never seemed to sleep. That morning, the weather was rainy and dull, and the air was frigid.

Miranda, Yuvina, and Celyth were hiding out of the weather in the dressing room. Erk, Selasine, and Naomi were working diligently in the captain's quarters to devise a plan to strike at Farzg's operation definitively. Since the frost giantkin had reestablished his smuggling network, it was likely he had the resources to rebuild his fortress in the northern reaches of Alabaster. If that were the case, then defeating him would prove to be difficult, as his fortress was designed with his ability to control the cold in mind. Justin and Valarie were taking the day to rest in their cabin, and August somehow convinced Shalo to let him experiment in the kitchen. As he had hoped, Arlindra, who was very particular about food, was already in the ship's kitchen preparing her own, personal meal.

August looked back and forth in the pantry, completely confused by the layout. All of the pickled and jarred rations were on the bottom shelf to protect them from the rocking of the ship in turbulent water; the paladin grasped the logic, but it still bothered him. The recipe book called for ingredients he could barely pronounce. Fortunately, though Shalo was a carefree person, he took his job in Erk's kitchen very seriously. Everything was labeled, so August was eventually able to find the spices and pickled vegetables required for the stews he studied the night before.

As he came out of the ship's pantry, he watched Arlindra as she flicked a skillet toward the countertop. Some kind of flat, bread-like substance flew out and landed perfectly on a plate she had prepared for the dish. August stared for a moment, bewildered. The ranger reached into a pouch and withdrew a handful of fresh eggs. With jars and bags in hand, he unloaded and organized his ingredients on a separate countertop. The kitchen was on the second deck, and Erk had outfitted it with incredible, boat-safe ovens and stoves. The pirate lord's noble upbringing was evident around them. It was a lengthy kitchen, stretching forty feet. The stern exit led to a ramp that went all the way to the top deck at an effortless grade. The fore exit led to a mess hall serving Erk's current crew of four hundred pirates.

In that moment, however, the kitchen was mostly empty. It was sometime after breakfast for the crew working during the day. A couple of kitchen swabs were maintaining some of the cooking equipment. The stove pipes emptied out of the side of *The Nebula*, and they were cleaned daily to prevent soot and ash from creating a fire hazard on the ship. August looked at his ingredients and then back to the flatbread that Arlindra had made. "How did you make bread without flour?" he asked.

"I didn't," she replied, curt.

August felt a little embarrassed. "Oh, it just looked fluffy and really good," he replied.

Arlindra's stoic expression twisted up into a half-smile, half-smirk. "A goha-ter'k?" she asked, using an obscure phrase in Khantongue, a language of hunters and wilderness peoples. It meant "chef" in Alabaster Common.

August's eyes lit up and he grinned. "Narbin nog'liakh." A phrase meaning, "maybe soon." He spoke Khantongue fluently thanks to so many months in his youth spent at his father's hunting lodge in the mountains north of Devitus.

The elf looked up at the human. Elves approaching five and a half feet were an impressive height, and August reflected the same characteristic in humans. At six foot three, August towered in the kitchen. Though he was not as tall as Selasine or Naomi, he was still an imposing, massive presence. Arlindra's expression became a full smirk, "So you fancy yourself a hunter and cook, but you've robbed the pantry of a robber." She tapped a pouch on her belt.

August laughed, not expecting such a comment. "Robber. He really is a robber, just on a boat. Why does that get him a cooler name? Pirate. Why is pirate cooler than robber, anyway?"

Arlindra's expression went from condescension to confusion. "Wait, what?"

August nodded enthusiastically. "Think about it. If a lawbreaker takes others' possessions on land, they get labeled a robber. Bandit is a good name, but you have to get the attention of the authorities to get called something like that."

The elf narrowed her eyes. "Aren't you the authorities?" she interrogated as she cracked the eggs into the same camping skillet she used to prepare her eolflin, a flatbread made of eolnut paste.

"Wait! You're right!" He looked around the kitchen, watching the kitchen swabs for a moment. "Maybe it's because robbers at sea need to be a robber and a sailor. So, it's like, way cooler." He looked under some shelves to find some mixing bowls. He opened a jar of pickled seaweed, Osgood potatoes, and a tin of dried garlic. He added in a couple of strips of dried bacon and some canned longbeans, a savory vegetable which thrived in the northern regions of Osgood, a human kingdom northeast of Alabaster.

Arlindra nodded, the goofy paladin's logic making sense in a humorous way. Also, his agreeable phrasing made her chuckle a bit. "Well, notoriety is its own investment," she began as he continued to scoop garlic into his dish. Her "foodsense" caused her to change what she was saying, "But if you add all of that garlic you're going to—"

August stopped adding garlic at half the tin. "Of course. The recipe said three spoons. I'm assuming that the rest of it needs to be used soon, though."

The ranger craned her head backwards. "Once it's open, it won't last long," she commented, realizing that August was learning something he'd never done before. "I thought you wanted to be a chef. Shouldn't you already know your way around a kitchen?"

The paladin grunted with a bit of shame. "I gotta be honest, listening to what you said at dinner last night made me feel like a donkey. Miranda and Justin always cooked for me and His Holiness when we were a little frontier family." He spoke with a genuine and excited tone.

Arlindra could hear the sincerity, further engaging with the paladin's growth. In fact, she realized it was probably happening in real time. "Go on," she said, listening intently.

"I teased Justin about cooking, but I realized I was an idiot about that. I used to cook all the time with my dad at the hunting lodge. Just because it's done in a kitchen doesn't mean it has to be tied to some societal expectation."

The eggs in Arlindra's skillet had fluffed enough, and she was ready to toss them on her eolflin. "Gimme that garlic, goha-ter'k."

He paused for a moment; her sudden, informal tone confused him. "This garlic?" he asked, holding up the half-emptied tin.

Arlindra rolled her eyes. "No, the other one." Her sarcasm immediately melted into humor and she began to giggle, knowing August would see how silly his question sounded in the first place.

"Oh yeah, duh." He offered her the tin nonchalantly.

She giggled harder. "You've clearly never been in a kitchen before."

His lips twisted to the side in concentration. "I mean, I wouldn't say never." He watched as Arlindra scraped her eggs into her eolflin, and she put her camping skillet by a dish sink.

She tilted her head and gave August a cheeky grin. "If you're going to learn how to cook to impress a lady, you're probably going to want to start with all of the facts."

August's cheeks turned bright red. "Facts?"

Arlindra nodded. "For starters, you should cook food that will be ready quick enough to try it. A seaweed and potato stew takes about ten hours to do it right." She winked.

His embarrassment became more evident. "Right," he said, shuffling the ingredients on the countertop. "Well, they did tell us not to work today, so," he contemplated.

Arlinda laughed. "This is true, and I can help you with that stew. But I don't think your plan will work."

August looked confused. "Why not?" He wasn't sure if she was referring to the recipe or the attempt to get to know her.

Her lips drew up into a small smile. "'Coz, goha-ter'k. I like girls. I mean, I do like food. But. You take my meaning?"

August took a moment and processed her words; then he started to laugh. The redness and shyness dissipated. "Oh! That means we have two interests in common." His smile lingered after he laughed.

She returned his happy expression. "My cousin, however, is a food-lover and very much into guys. Especially if they can fight." She winked again, showing her playful, friendly side.

He looked back to his ingredients. "Well, I'm pretty good at that already." He stood, looking at the garlic sitting on top of the seaweed and potatoes. "But seriously, I studied that recipe all night. Now I absolutely have to make the stew."

Arlindra reached under a different stove and handed him a bigger pot. "Forget the recipe, goha-ter'k. Let me give you a real cooking lesson." As August put it on the counter, she reached into another pouch and withdrew some fishing lures. "Why don't we go catch something fresh to have with the stew? Cel really loves sashimi, I used to make it for her all the time." As she finished speaking, her demeanor changed. She thought about fishing trips to the coast of the Sea of Undine with her father, uncle, and cousin. Those memories seemed too distant, especially with everything that happened in Mystalon in the last few days. "On second thought, let's try something new."

August beamed. "Very well then, teacher. Shall we still fish first?"

Arlindra's voice was calm and stoic again, "Of course, pupil." She thought of one sea animal she had never hunted, and August would be the perfect partner to help. Suddenly, she sounded as enthusiastic as he did. "We're going for a big haul!"

Between August's strength and Arlindra's expertise and magical fishing equipment, they caught a tuna whale large enough to provide Erk's crew with fresh meat for a few days.

Meanwhile, in the captain's quarters, Erk stabbed a dagger into the map on his table. He positioned it a couple of hundred miles northeast of the capital city of Alabaster. "So, his former complex was beyond The Lichwood, and it was built with a type of granite that absorbs the cold."

Naomi shuddered. She indirectly contributed to the construction of Farzg's original complex; during her time as a slave in a quarry in the Mammoth Moors, she excavated incredible amounts of granite. She had no idea where it all went. She speculated, "If Haelia and Elnis obliterated the original complex, I am willing to bet Farzg has reopened the granite mine in the moors nearby."

Erk placed a hand on Naomi's back. He looked up at her. "Are you ready to go that far north again?"

She exhaled and held her breath for a moment. Selasine looked at her with compassion, understanding her hesitation. Her brown skin shimmered in the morning light pouring through the windows of Erk's cabin. It was an impressively sized room for a ship, filling about five hundred square feet. The sturdy windows built into the back of the ship's stern were covered in ornate curtains, but the morning sun in late winter was bright right after the breakfast hour. She took a moment to take in the surroundings before replying, reminding herself that her words were real. "Of course, honeycomb. Justice must be served."

Selasine replied to Naomi, "Sword of Justice, guide our vengeance. May his holy wrath be known to those that scoff at the law."

Erk's lips twisted up as he joked, "Iria used to say that to me when I acted out. If that didn't work, then it was a binding curse."

The three of them chuckled for a moment, Iria's demeanor consistent through all their experiences. She was a bright spirit but detailed with protocol and discipline. Erk tested her limits, Naomi needed her clarity, and Selasine adored her strict but warm nature. The three of them loved her for the same reasons even though they experienced different facets of the same elf. Naomi's smile fell a bit. "Sword of Justice, guide our hand, indeed." She pulled Erk's dagger out of the map and handed it to him. "The Blur could actually sail through The Fragments. I know she's had an all-girl crew for a while, but—"

Erk interrupted her. "Where would we dock her? She shouldn't fall into evil hands, ever again." Most rumors held that *The Violet Blur* was a magical ship, and they were correct. The ship had a mind and personality of her own, and Naomi had unintentionally rescued her from the hands of a Death Pirate known as Falindeth. Though Blur had a personality, the captain could control the magic powering her sails. By stealing her from Falindeth, Naomi unwittingly became her captain and friend for thirty years, passing the title of captain on to her longtime first mate, Annaia. The human of thirty-five years had been by Naomi's side since they both escaped the quarry together. Even Annaia remembered Iria, as Naomi trusted nobody but Iria to keep Annaia when the giantkin had to be away. Annaia was only five years old the last time she saw "Miss Iria" as she called her.

Naomi let out a deep sigh. "You're right. Even if I'm ready, I couldn't risk leaving Blur in a compromised position. And if she doesn't stay, it would be a suicide mission for us." She drummed her fingertips on the table, her nails clicking in an unusual cadence.

Erk added, "And, besides. Farzg will be expecting us. He probably has been for some time. He just needs to know that we mean business."

Selasine cleared his throat before speaking, "If he has rebuilt his fortress, he will be waiting for us in his vaults. They amplify the danger of his magic. There are pipes built into the walls that give his geyser additional range. In spite of all of that, Damil nearly killed him thanks to Haelia. We were close. So close we thought he was ended." A somber tenor hummed in his words.

Erk's nose twitched with frustration, realizing his sister's life was eventually lost because Farzg's power froze his own heart. It was so frigid that Damil's sword did not pierce it. "This time, we'll thaw his deep freeze, no matter how many vaults he has. He'll know the weight of his crimes, and," he trailed off, looking around his room. "His lack of penitence, on top of his crimes."

Selasine glared hard at his own thoughts. Even though one of his eyes was covered by an eyepatch, the sharpness could be felt through the fabric that covered the permanent injury Farzg gave him twenty-five years ago. "Pay he will, nulestotejin. Do not doubt it for a moment."

Naomi chewed on her lip before speaking. "Don't pretend like it'll be any one of us."

Erk and Selasine both looked at her, then they looked to the ground. They felt the truth of her words. Selasine responded, "She has the strength and the resolve, this time. Sender proved that for us."

Erk let out a sigh. In his heart, he felt like he had turned Miranda into a vicious killer, but in reality, he had brought her along on an ordeal that strengthened her resolve in the matters of law and order. Naomi nudged him lovingly and said, "You would do so much worse than she would. If she kills Farzg, she'll be the only one who can do so in the name of justice. Me, you, His Holiness, it's vengeance for vengeance's sake."

Selasine nodded in agreement. "I would never have wished a destiny so dark as Invictus's executioner upon her. She neither wishes for nor would live with such a title."

Erk's somber expression started to lighten. "She wields my sister's sword."

The high priest nodded, and Naomi asked, "Holyfang?"

Erk's smile blended hope and malice as he replied, "Indeed."

Yuvina was lying on the bed in the dressing room. Miranda sat beside her on a padded stool. Celyth watched intently as the priestess touched the foxkin's temples with her fingertips as she did August the day before. Miranda whispered, "I forced my way inside Elyndandria's mind with the arcane stream. I'm worried it might be painful."

The kitsune's nose twitched. "I have a feeling that whatever I've done was extremely painful in the first place." She closed her eyes and cycled her breath. "Besides, Miranda. I trust you. You should be the last person I trust, especially because the stream favors you so highly. But you are a great hope for people like me, and I fear for what I've done." She licked her snout. "Whatever it takes, please."

Miranda focused on the mana inside her, funneling it through her mind. She felt more at ease using magic to extend the reach of her consciousness, and she could take her time. She adjusted the flow of ether as necessary since it was a safe situation. A cold sensation filled her body as her perception made contact with Yuvina's feelings and thoughts.

"Is that you?" the foxkin's mind pressed.

Miranda gave a psychic nod, remaining physically motionless on purpose. Yuvina smiled, leaving her eyes closed. The warpriest could feel her relief, and it was contagious. "This is so strange, Yuvina!" the priestess thought.

"I know, but it feels comforting. Please, feel free to look around."

The priestess thought a prayer to safeguard Yuvina from unintended side effects of exploring her mind, but the feeling in her heart was confident. "I worry for you, so I only pray for your safety."

Yuvina's body trembled a bit. Miranda's love and empathy were so real, and having the warpriest walk among her thoughts and memories let the kitsune glimpse into Miranda's as well. Though she trusted the priestess and her story, their connected emotions further enhanced that trust. The foxkin shed a tear as Miranda's soothing concern touched the very fabric of her soul. While Miranda was in her mind, Yuvina perceived the priestess with blue hair and red eyes, but that distortion did not distract her from their present mission.

Miranda asked Yuvina's mind, "What is the last thing you remember before your memories go blank?" In that instant, the priestess could see what Yuvina remembered. The kitsune stood in front of Seiv Everdusk, receiving compliments on her recent mission well done. He assured the foxkin her next task would be much better than reconnaissance. "That's it! He must know what happened to you!"

Yuvina whimpered a bit. "That's one reason I want to see him when we return to the city. I hope he is able to help begin filling in the gaps."

Celyth cleared her throat, the room awkwardly silent for her as Yuvina lay crying and Miranda hummed with magical discharge. It was such a dull, low sound that the elf's strong hearing could barely register it. "Your hair is still really red, Mir. You're doing okay."

Miranda whispered, "Thank you." Then, she tried to push beyond the memory with Everdusk. "Where did he send you from there?" An unseen force blocked her consciousness. She tried to force the memory open with arcane energy.

A shock went through Yuvina's mind. "Yip!" she barked, startling Celyth and Miranda.

"I'm so sorry," Miranda thought.

"The pain has already passed, I was just surprised," Yuvina replied.

Miranda smiled as she sensed the foxkin's comfort return. "Brace yourself, Yuvina," she warned as she imagined her psyche becoming as sharp as an arrow. She launched her own mind into the wall of amnesia she detected in Yuvina's memories.

Miranda found herself in a parlor with ornate, red carpet. The room was completely empty, however, with the exception of a single throne in the center of the room. The doors that should have lined the walls were gone; Miranda felt her mind was trapped here, and she didn't understand why. This memory was most certainly incomplete. On the throne sat a feminine silhouette dressed in a drab, gray robe that might have once been white. Black hair covered her face, but Miranda could feel the creature's eyes looking at her. Though it looked human, there was too much power radiating from this presence to mistake it for a mortal. "You tread in my realm, intruder. Your mind is now mine to claim. Come, feed me. Aylabrax hungers still."

Miranda's eyes narrowed, realizing Yuvina's consciousness was no longer with her. "Who are you to hide inside the mind of a mortal? Aylabrax the Devourer, an evil entity that roams the land taking that which is not hers. Many have suffered from your actions and your unholy stain is not welcome here." She gripped her holy symbol, realizing she felt tangible. It was as if her body had manifested physically in Yuvina's blocked memories, and her thoughts were hers and hers alone.

Yuvina could still sense Miranda in her mind, but it was like hearing a sound with no discernible source. She stayed calm, hoping wherever the priestess had gone, she was finding solutions. Celyth watched carefully as she took note of Miranda's hair. "You're starting to lose a little color," she whispered.

Miranda's body nodded instinctively, but her consciousness did not receive the message. She still stood about fifteen feet away from Aylabrax sitting on the throne in this psychic cage. The dark goddess's voice was raspy and sinister as she warned, "You dare bring that symbol into my profane dimension? You will not escape your destiny, child. Your powers will soon belong to me."

"Don't count on it," Miranda spat back, reaching for the mana inside her. It did not respond, however, as this microcosm of reality was the creation of a deity. It functioned on the rules outlined by her, and somehow arcane magic could not pierce her will.

Aylabrax's face was not visible, but Miranda knew the goddess was smiling. She was confident her mind was now disconnected from Yuvina's. She was engaging with an imprint of The Devourer. Without her draconic gift, she worried she would not be able to fight back effectively.

Aylabrax responded to Miranda's thoughts, "You waver with uncertainty. Good, first I will devour your hope. Despair is the best seasoning for a soul." The figure sitting on the throne stood, her posture slumped and ragged. She shambled toward Miranda with a threatening gait.

The warpriest stayed calm. If Aylabrax's powers worked here, then certainly so would Invictus's. "Sword of Justice, shield me with your mighty hands. Cover me so that evil may not touch!" Miranda's holy symbol lit up with white light that fueled a growing, lucent barrier around her.

Aylabrax stopped, and Miranda felt her sneer. The dark deity's voice was deadpan. "So, you wield the Sword with effectiveness. I was prepared for this." The goddess reached up to her hair and started to peel it away from her face. It was so dense she had to dig through the tangled mass.

Miranda felt her heart flutter with fear and anticipation. Based on her studies of the evil gods, if Aylabrax revealed her face, she was prepared to devour a person's entity completely. Their souls would be converted into power and bolster the parasitic entity's capabilities. Fortunately, Miranda realized, this was not the goddess herself, but a mere shadow. "This vile fragment might be what was interfering with Yuvina's memories," she said to herself. Miranda hoped if she could neutralize this vestige of Aylabrax, she could restore the memories. She drew her sword.

Aylabrax's face was young and beautiful. Her eyes were completely black and her skin as pale as moonlight. Her lips were also black, the dark magics fueling her existence giving her features great contrast with her skin. In fact, she was so pale she seemed to glow. On closer observation, however, the aura around her was devoid of light. The halo of darkness enveloped her corporeal representation in a six-foot radius. She taunted, "Ah, you no longer feel despair. Perhaps I should remind you of what it is like to lose hope." She began to inhale.

Miranda prayed, "Invictus, grant my blade your holy light!" A swirl of purple and white tendrils burst from the cross guard of Iria's sword.

The beautiful face and features changed into a nightmarish visage. The eyes, nose, and mouth were exaggerated, severe, and threatening. Her teeth were razor sharp, and a pattern of lines had formed, allowing Miranda to see the veins and arteries carrying dark magic pulsing through her skin. Her black eyes contained a red, glowing nucleus. Her voice was now a shrill, hissing sound. "Fool! The Sssword cannot harm me!" She ran toward Miranda in a hostile charge, but she brandished no weapon.

Aylabrax closed the short distance between them, barely giving Miranda time to react. The priestess stabbed her sword forward, causing the light granted by Invictus to swirl and clash with Aylabrax as the dark goddess charged forward. The holy and unholy collided in a glorious display of colors. A black and red aura emanated from Aylabrax now, and the purple and white from Miranda tried to push back the darkness. "Begone from this mind, Devourer!" she shouted with righteous conviction.

The goddess cackled. "You are no match for even my shadow, mortal." The hiss was now a shriek. "I will have your sssoul!"

Miranda's lip twitched. "You've got more than you bargained for, Aylabrax. I have more souls than you were prepared to face! Mother! Father! Lend me your strength!" she cried out with her soul as much as her voice.

The amount of holy energy pouring through Miranda increased. Much like the day she comforted the people of Mystalon, she shone as a beacon for her chosen god. The aura of white and purple intensified, pushing the darkness in the parlor back. Their manifestations were so bright, the room around them was no longer visible.

Aylabrax's shrieks became harsher. "You have no place here, Invictus, begone from my realm!"

Lexcord's voice echoed around them, "Miranda, destroy this abomination. Pray for the Holy Flames of Judgment. I will answer with my full fury!" The gods could reach this subspace with their powers much easier than the primary dimension. With Lexcord responding in lieu of Invictus, Miranda felt the power she needed to defeat Aylabrax surging through her.

The Devourer's appearance changed again, now into a gorgon with numerous, autonomous snakes for hair. Miranda's spirit gulped with fear; this was probably Aylabrax's true face, and she was surprised that a mere shadow could manifest such an occurrence. The evil goddess commanded, "Begone from here Sssiblingsss of Order! You cannot interfere! Thisss mortal isss mine!" She made eye contact with Miranda. "You will die now, interloper!" She inhaled through her terrifying mouth, causing Miranda's essence to begin breaking apart and pouring into the dark entity.

Miranda heard a voice calling, though it sounded far away. "Your hair! Miranda, be careful. You're running low."

Though she could not rely on her arcane gift to fight here, she relied on it to stay here. She feared what might happen if she exhausted her mana. Furthermore, the darkness was beginning to overpower the light pouring from Miranda's sword. She remained calm and thought about the words of the prayer Lexcord's voice had commanded her to use. "Righteous Order, we beseech your divine strength. We pray for your might to rain down on our enemies in condemnation. Drive out these unholy powers before us and smite them with your Holy Flames of Judgment!"

A flash of bright, white light exploded around the shadow of Aylabrax's avatar. Her voice screamed with surprise at the divine might emanating from Miranda. Whether it was Lexcord or Invictus no longer mattered; this surge of power was funneled through the strength of three souls. Miranda's essence became whole again, the prayer interrupting Aylabrax's attempt to use Devour on the priestess. "No!" the goddess cried out in a desperate tone.

Miranda then struck with her sword. The purple and white tendrils mixed with the white light burning away the dark halo from around the evil goddess's shadow. Miranda had once faced the avatar of the god of chaos, Indervill. Chaos, as it was called by most common people, was easily thwarted with a trick and the support of a nearby solisberry tree. The shadow of Aylabrax, however, was more incredible than Miranda could have predicted. The Devourer required a substantial effort to defeat. "Release your grip on Yuvina's memories! Sword of Justice, banish The Devourer from Yuvina's mind!" she shouted, her resolve radiating through the divine power bursting from her soul.

As she prayed, the light began to consume the darkness thanks to Miranda's unrelenting determination. Lexcord's attention focused on this contest of divine power; from the primordial place, she could only channel as much of her divinity through Miranda as her soul and the souls of her parents could allow. Since they were draconic godshards, they would have been able to carry the energy of Saraix or Gorthran to its full potential, but they could still serve as divine conduits to a minor degree thanks to the fact that they were souls. Fortunately for Miranda, such an anomaly allowed her to funnel just enough of Lexcord's divine might from the primordial place to this corner of Yuvina's mind.

The snakes in Aylabrax's hair stood out straight in agony as the manifestation of the evil goddess began to dissolve. "I know nothing of memoriesss, you meddling cleric! Damn you and your godsss to the Infernia! Invictusss! Lexcord! I will find you the next time you dessscend upon this realm!" She gave a final shriek as her essence dissipated.

Miranda laughed with confidence. "He's already looking for you, thoul'thanshito." She cursed the dark goddess with a phrase meaning "unholy scarecrow" in draconic.

The evil goddess lost her grip over Yuvina's mind. Both Miranda and Yuvina heard the command echo clearly as it broke. "You will acquire dragon eggs for the Devourer. It is her will, and you cannot resist. This power within you will pull the eggs through the Dark Space, and you will be destroyed alongside it. Your sacrifice is your reward."

Yuvina opened her eyes. "Pulhash, save my soul."

Miranda also opened her eyes, allowing the psychic connection between her and her friend to dissipate. "You were planted among us to steal eggs!"

Yuvina scrambled back a bit, a momentary look of fear in her eyes. "By the gods, Miranda, I didn't know," she pleaded.

Instead of a reprimand or a rebuke, Miranda flung herself into the kitsune. She squeezed her tight in her arms, nuzzling her cheek into the foxkin's fur. "I'm so sorry they did this to you. I know you would not have meant to do any of us harm. You are too kind and sweet, Yuvina. Please don't be afraid," she comforted, tears streaming down her cheeks.

Celyth sat in disbelief. "What just happened?" Her voice was confused and excited at the same time.

Miranda continued, "Whoever did experiments on Yuvina also let the dark goddess Aylabrax plant a dark command deep within her mind. That command was held by a fragment of The Devourer left behind, but I found it. The holy light of Invictus and Lexcord has freed her from her curse."

Yuvina started to sob. "How did this happen? What did I do? I only followed Everdusk's orders."

Celyth felt unusually serious and sat on the bed. "Don't fret, foxy. You're one of our friends. I can tell because you've been nothing but helpful and kind. I used to think nice people were weak, but Miranda showed me how wrong I was in that regard." She reached out to hold Yuvina's paw. "And so, I know that your kindness and desire to help are motivated from the good in your heart."

Miranda gave a deep, contented sigh. "They were going to sacrifice you to steal eggs. But what does Aylabrax want with them?"

Yuvina shook her head. "I'm not sure. I couldn't imagine."

Before Miranda could respond, *The Nebula* was wracked by the sound of cannon fire.

✦⟡✦

Gorthran descended in front of the palace at Argentum. Doctor One stood with Artificer and Diablo to greet him. As the Dragon Father's talons hit the ground, he let out a deafening roar, extending his fifteen-foot neck toward One and his cohorts. The explosive sound shook the ground and the mountains around them. The echoes caused a small, regional quake among the lower peaks of the Selian Range in the Dundoi region.

After the mountains quietened, Doctor One greeted Gorthran with excitement. "Oh good, I'm glad you took the bait! I calculated our enemies would converge upon Mystalon at the direst hour, and Black Hole would be released as a result!" He cackled with confidence. "The knowledge of the universe is incredible, and even the gods are easy enough to manipulate!"

The Dragon Father blinked. His curiosity was piqued, and he

sought information as much as vengeance. "You mean to imply *you* orchestrated my escape? You are a fool; a mortal that has overstepped its bounds. After I've wrought my divine judgment upon you, I will then take my place as the ruler of this mortal coil." He stepped forward, his body measuring eighty feet with his neck and tail extended. Though Gorthran's consciousness was in control, the gray scales of Ezelbrecht's exterior were still listless and dull outside of Olvidado. Gorthran's voice demanded, "What are you doing to my children?" Rage permeated his words.

Artificer and Diablo traded a glance. Diablo's body radiated a red, subtle light, creating sinister shadows between them. Doctor One expressed no fear in front of such a mighty entity. They planned their exit in case the scientist had overestimated his alliances and technology. As the Dragon Father waited, Doctor One's mad smile grew dark and sadistic. "Well?" Gorthran demanded.

Doctor One's voice was methodical and twisted. It sent a pulse of fear through everyone present, including the Dragon Father. "You see, Gorthran, I am turning your children into my pawns. I plan to force their godshards inside my soul. Before I do that, I will turn myself into arcane underflow with the Soul Scythe. Their shards will feed my strength. Your powers, however, interest me greatly." The normally maniacal, wild presence was gone. Only a cold, calculated evil remained. "You, Gorthran! You can call your children to you, and I will use your voice to lure them. I will consume all of your children! Magic is but a science, meant to be controlled. The divinities of this universe are no more than stars that never matured!"

Gorthran's eyes twitched with mounting anger. "You will leave my children and their eggs alone because you are going to die. You have glimpsed too many secret corners of the universe, mortal! You tamper with things you do not understand. Removing the dragons from the stream would doom Espa!" The Dragon Father inhaled, feeling the magic stir within his stomach and lungs. As an eldritch entity, he pulled from a source beyond the arcane for his power, the essence of Espa's creator.

One's eyes flickered an otherworldly, rainbow glow. "I understand perfectly well." His voice resumed its raving tenor. "I plan to do the same to your beloved sister! I'm going to invert the stream, Gorthran!"

The Dragon Father snarled. "You are a fool, mortal, and now you will pay the price for your insolence and disrespect for creation!" Without hesitation, a geyser of hot ash and flame burst from

Gorthran's mouth. As it should have smoldered over Doctor One and his underlings, the breath weapon suddenly swirled and funneled to a single point at the door of the palace of Argentum. With a look of confusion, Gorthran craned his neck up and narrowed his eyes. "Devourer," he grumbled with annoyance.

The dark goddess whisked herself from the palace toward Gorthran, floating over the ground with incredible speed. She crossed one hundred and fifty feet in only five seconds, putting herself between One and the Dragon Father. "You have finally kept a promise, One. You will be rewarded handsomely."

Gorthran backed toward the walls of the palace complex two hundred feet behind him. This area gave the Dragon Father much less room to maneuver than he expected. The architecture of the pyramidal palace, the awkwardly shaped courtyard, and the external building complex were too fragile to help with evasive techniques. Plus, after taking flight, he'd be at the mercy of her special attack without the ability to defend himself. Even using magic to aid him, he would still be more vulnerable in the air. The Selian Range was difficult to maneuver while flying, and her powers were swift. He decided to play defensively. "Back! Devourer, why are you in league with this mortal?"

Aylabrax's smile was sinister, but Gorthran could only feel it. Black hair hung over her face like a veil of evil. She sucked in a breath through her mouth, an ironic counter for a dragon god. Her attack, Devour, struggled to damage other divinities, but Gorthran was currently vulnerable. He was only shielded by five additional dragon shards. Devour tugged at the souls of those dragons, including Ezelbrecht. "Stop, wicked fiend!" Gorthran shouted, his voice echoing throughout the Selian Range.

"You should have stayed asleep on your island as you were commanded," Aylabrax retorted with her deadpan voice.

"You cannot consume the soul of a dragon! It will just return to the stream!" Gorthran warned.

"I don't care." Aylabrax's tone was so casual that it infuriated the Dragon Father.

"Damn you to the Abyss then!" Gorthran snarled, and he gave another blast of his cindering breath weapon. The power within him surged, and instead of a gradual, smoldering wave of magma and smoke, his attack manifested with the power of an exploding volcano. A molten shower of death erupted toward Aylabrax, glowing with the heat of the core of Espa.

With a swift toss of her head, Aylabrax threw her cascading, dense hair to her back. Her gorgon-like face emerged, transforming the black locks into snakes and her dark, pale visage into a golden, beautiful woman. As she did, she inhaled, causing the whole of the incredible attack to funnel into pools of black energy pouring from her mouth in dense wisps. The darkness around her flickered and became an ominous aura of evil and foreboding. The entirety of the explosion was absorbed as quickly as Gorthran generated it. Aylabrax continued to inhale, the black energy reaching toward the Dragon Father, pulling scales from his body. They crumbled into dust and scattered to the wind. Gorthran began to shrink as a result.

The Dragon Father leapt upward, hoping to escape the effects of Aylabrax's attack. Now that Aylabrax had revealed her true face, only the Dragon Father's godshard itself stood a chance at surviving. Though the godshards of each of the dragons were unique entities, their combined presence allowed Gorthran to build an intimidating and unified dragon with as much strength, size, and magical capacity as six dragons. Thanks to Gorthran's source of power beyond the arcane, he was still able to manifest his breath weapon, enhanced by the other dragons within his body. None of that, however, had prepared him to deal with The Devourer. The black energy from her mouth pursued the Dragon Father and enveloped him in the air.

Gorthran felt the magical life force of the dragons within him crumble. His draconic exterior shattered into larger, blocky fragments as he tried to ascend deep within the mountains of the Selian Range. Their essence spilled into the arcane stream rapidly, Aylabrax's Devour utterly destroying them. A large dragon with black scales and red eyes remained. The Dragon Father felt himself dragged back to the surface of Espa, the gravity of the divine Devour attack also grounding him. Furthermore, he felt the weight of ancient accords crushing his essence.

Doctor One approached Aylabrax as she stood, panting. Using Devour at such a high level of power winded her. She knew she could destroy Gorthran's avatar in its weakened, pathetic state, but she did not anticipate it requiring so much divine energy. She shook her head, causing the gorgon hair to fall back into its humanlike appearance, and her aura of darkness flickered and vanished.

Gorthran hissed, now only thirty feet long head to tail. His black scales glistened in the red light created by Diablo's presence in this dark, afflicted location. Aylabrax pointed toward the Dragon Father, and she ordered, "Now, consume!" A mist emerged from beneath her hair, prompting Gorthran to fire his personal breath weapon; instead of Ezelbrecht's volcanic breath, a simple, powerful stream of fire sprayed from his maw to the dark goddess. It was, however, neutralized and absorbed by the growing cloud of fog around her. "It is time," she stated.

A powerful, deep voice interrupted all of them. "Not on my watch, Aylabrax!" Gorthran, Aylabrax, One, Artificer, and Diablo turned to see a tall man with broad shoulders standing about five hundred feet away. He approached from the external buildings of the palace complex. His warm, brown skin glowed with his own holy aura. Black, fine, braided hair cascaded down his shoulders, twisted into tight, neat spirals. His brown eyes sparkled with righteous judgment, and he wore a suit of plate armor more impenetrable than the strongest fortress in Espa. A heavy longsword rested in his right hand, and a small, silver shield was held at the ready in his left.

"Invictusssss," Aylabrax hissed, her hair fluttering. "Damn you, fool, you've come at the worssst possssible time!" she screeched.

Doctor One began to jump up and down with excitement. "Oh! Oh! Oh-ho-ho-ho! I've truly done it! A reunion of the gods in the primary dimension! It's incredible, and I've brought this about through my careful calculations and my undeniable genius!" His voice was back to its cocky, maniacal rave. "Sword of Justice! Welcome to my game! I hope you'll play as well as The Judge," he commented, referring to the Xanadu piece named after the god. It could conquer a tile without fail, but it would also be destroyed if the dice were disagreeable.

Invictus pointed his sword at Aylabrax, and a beam of holy light burst from the tip. She teleported several feet backwards, avoiding the blast which sent dirt and rocks into the air with significant volume. As the debris showered the area, Aylabrax took another, teleporting step backwards. "Away, Ssssword," she hissed.

Gorthran flapped his wings, calling the magic within him to teleport him away, but a sudden, electrifying sensation filled his corporeal body. With a growl, he looked to Aylabrax, who was focused on Invictus. He turned his head to Invictus with fear, knowing that the young god would be quick to punish the Dragon Father for escaping his pseudo-dimension of captivity. The Sword of Justice, however, was concentrating on Aylabrax, his brown eyes sparkling with the purity of his spirit and his tempered, humble wisdom. Instead, the source was Doctor One, holding a device shaped like a large wand, but ending in the maw of a wooden dragon.

It was made of adamant, eolnut, and lacrima-deum of various types. As a result, it looked like a jewel encrusted scepter, measuring five feet long and weighing ten pounds. The dragon maw tip contained the brightest lacrima-deum, and it projected a powerful, paralyzing ray of light that surrounded Gorthran. The Dragon Father felt his mortal form stunned. "How is this possible?" he roared.

Invictus charged across the courtyard of the palace at Argentum. The magnificent architecture was beautiful in the light cast from his avatar. His braids bounced against his armor, and he thrust his sword repeatedly at the dark goddess as she ran. "Sep-tei-forma-spada!" he shouted, an incantation that generated his most famous attack: The Seven Formed Sword. Each of his thrusts were filled with a different fragment of pure energy. Astral, celestial, cosmic, solar, and lunar represented the light, universal elements. Abyssal and infernal constituted the dark side of the universe. As the god of justice and order, all energies were accessible to him. The Sep-tei-forma-spada used all seven. The attack was equally as recognizable as Aylabrax's Devour.

The blasts from The Seven Formed Sword pursued the dark goddess, prompting her to take flight. "No! My godshard! You'll leave it with the mortal!" she screeched at Invictus, who was closing in on her quickly. She reverted to her gorgon form to accelerate her escape. As she blasted through the air at incredible speed, the Sword of Justice became a comet, spiraling after her in a pocket of energy. She tried to evade the continual bursts of power pulsing from Invictus's sword, but she was too slow. A rainbow of colors converged on her, blasting her through the air. She shrieked in agony, using her dark magic to split her mortal form into twelve shadows, four of them containing the majority of her evil essence. "You can't be everywhere and all at once like I can, Sword!" she shouted.

Invictus cursed. "Damn you, Devourer. You have just assured my defeat, but you have also assured that my sister will be here within a day." He turned, his numerous braids clinking against his radiant armor. He watched as Doctor One continued to point the strange scepter at Gorthran, causing the Dragon Father to cower.

The lacrima-deum in the scepter glowed with excitement as they prodded Gorthran's mortal remnant with arcane micro-cuts. The binding magic from the strange device was especially effective. "This is blasphemous. I am a god!" he protested.

One cackled with satisfaction, "You are, but I will be soon. And you will no longer be. Unfortunately, you miscalculated your own power." The mad scientist approached the Dragon Father within inches, the radiant, paralytic tendril squeezing the beast, preventing him from moving in any capacity. "Now my ascension is prepared," he mumbled. "This is only the beginning."

"You will fail, One," Gorthran spat, unable to retaliate physically.

The elf narrowed his eyes and pressed a button on the handle of the scepter with his thumb. A magical cord burst from the maw in the tip of the device. It wrapped around Gorthran and intensified its grip immediately, sending surges of energy through him. Doctor One laughed. "You are the strongest of all your shards, but even your power is finite in this dimension. I have built this wand with one hundred godshards of your children. They will eventually exhaust and return to the arcane stream, but you!" he shouted, emphasizing the 'you' with excitement. "You will be trapped in my body of arcane underflow, and you will call the rest of your children within. We will invert the stream and bring magic back to Espa!"

The ether continued to compress the Dragon Father, forcing him to become a long, metallic, heart-shaped shard of intense pressure. It was almost a foot long, and it hovered in a bubble of magical suspension. The shard absorbed the light around it, becoming especially pronounced at the center of the dense bubble of black. The shard itself emitted a contrasting aura, glowing midnight purple. It floated compliantly into Doctor One's hand.

Invictus frowned at the scene unfolding. "Damn mortality. I must stop Aylabrax; Miranda, Thomas. Justin, August, Valarie. I'm counting on all of you. Shalo, you too, I've heard your prayers. Sister, I'm returning," he prayed, his voice reaching her in the primordial place.

Lexcord breathed a sigh of relief for her brother, and she began preparing to pursue Aylabrax's shadows across the western continent of Espa. Once Invictus reconstituted in the primordial place she would depart. It would take him only an hour to return, but his next trip to the prime dimension would be the last for a while. Only one chance remained to right the balance. The magic of interplanar travel became slower if it was employed too frequently. She could arrive within a day, however, having not been to the primary dimension in over a decade. Invictus had used his mortal avatar too frequently over the last year.

Aylabrax's shadows scattered, fleeing the palace complex from many directions. Invictus sighed with divided frustration; One was probably more dangerous than Aylabrax at this point, but he had to rely on his own surprise piece. He might have to play the role of The Judge on the Xanadu board, but Miranda would continue to play The Priestess and bolster his chances of success. Lexcord would serve as a cluster of cavalry, pursuing their enemy in multiple directions. Beams of light were already on the horizon; The Valkindra, Lexcord's elite battalion of angelic knights, were on their way to meet their Silver Maiden. The Siblings of Order began to trade places, and Aylabrax spread her shadows among the winds, descending the Selian Range in twelve separate directions.

Invictus claimed victory against Aylabrax, but in doing so, he discovered he was in a three-way match of Xanadu. One now held the upper hand as he added Gorthran's godshard to his mysterious wand. As the prime dimension began to fade from his sight, he felt a sinking weight of hopelessness. The faith of his followers would encourage him in the primordial place. He was just thankful he was able to force Aylabrax's hand quickly. The Siphoned Sisters was a technique he was not equipped to handle.

The Valkindra, however, would make short work of the Lady in Mourning's shadows. Invictus prepared himself to listen for the numerous prayers directed to his sister; though she outweighed him in followers, they were inherently equal in both power and righteousness. "Saraix, if you're out there, we need you as desperately as One needed Gorthran," he prayed.

Elyndandria felt the strange shard in her belongings pulse with power. The Dragon Mother was awakening.

Chapter 16
The Destroyer

"While steam powered ships made of metal are growing in popularity in East Espa, The Unbinding has prevented true innovation. Such ships should be powered and defended by magic. Lacrima-deum is the solution." – Santiago Eb'lin, The Tears of God

ustin and Valarie arrived on the deck as Celyth and Yuvina helped Miranda exit the dressing room. The warpriest had expended nearly all the ether within her extracting Aylabrax's command from Yuvina's memory. Smoke curled up onto the deck from the south; the port side of *The Nebula* was coated in enough of the cloud to suggest the entire gundeck had unleashed its fury. Everyone rushed to the port side to look, but Miranda's weakened condition caused her to stumble. Yuvina, feeling stronger than normal, helped the priestess as they moved to see the cause of such commotion. Miranda's heart pounded with fear, and her mana was depleted. To worsen the situation, her stores of solisberry blooms were running low thanks to her recent healing efforts. Before she could analyze the horizon, a bell began to ring on the upper deck.

Erk's voice called out, "All hands! All hands! *The Nebula* be under attack! Man your stations, at arms men!"

Selasine's voice echoed, "Faithful, to me! Report!"

Justin and Valarie shouted in unison, "Sir!" as they rushed straight up the stairs to the east.

Miranda responded, but not as sharp or disciplined. "Sir," she said, the melody in her voice empty.

Yuvina ducked under Miranda's arm and draped the warpriest over her. "Don't worry, Miranda. You've done so much for me, I won't let anything happen to you." She grunted as she pushed with all her strength, helping Miranda to walk in spite of her disorientation.

"Thanks, Yuvina," she replied, doing her best to hurry.

Yuvina felt her connection to the mana stream pulse. She realized she could increase her strength and speed as she willed, and so she did. With an impressive burst of energy, she scooped Miranda onto her back. The warpriest held on as Yuvina caught them up with Valarie and Justin in three seconds.

As they arrived at the helm where Erk, Naomi, and Selasine stood, Erk gave another round of commands, "Hard to port men! Prepare to face them head on!"

Erk turned the wheel harder than usual, reminding Miranda of the first time she arrived in Yendralia. This time, she had no idea why they were in such a hurry. *The Nebula* dipped in the water and tilted hard to the left; Yuvina and Miranda held tightly to each other, the foxkin's enhanced strength making it easier to keep her balance. Mana particles sprayed everywhere as the two clutched each other. Everyone else grabbed for rigging or railing.

Selasine shouted a prayer, "Invictus, the ever vigilant. Shroud us with the aura of your power! Give to us great foresight and greater bravery. Send us the mercy of your sister, the Silver Maiden. Grant us her fortitude and courage!" A purple mist covered *The Nebula*, and an empowering feeling of bravery flowed through everyone on board.

"Gods, what is happening?" Miranda cursed, feeling ill and agitated thanks to her exhaustion.

Naomi extended her arm as she gripped some rigging near the helm. "Hang on, loves," she shouted and used her telekinesis to pull Yuvina toward her. The foxkin crouched low, and Miranda tightened her hold on Yuvina as much as she could. They slid across the deck until Naomi could grab Yuvina's paw. They united in strength to hold onto the rigging leading up the rear mast on *The Nebula*.

Erk's voice rang out across the deck again. "Don't let us down, men! Prepare for attack!" He growled with fury and stepped away from the wheel as *The Nebula* began to correct in the water, causing the boat to lurch back to the right.

Miranda finally had a moment to check the upper deck. Selasine, Erk, and Naomi stood close to the helm, grabbing onto the rigging near the small platform that led up a single step to the wheel. Jax and Shalo were closer to the stern, gripping the railing with all their strength. Shalo disappeared as the ship rocked wildly in the water. Valarie and Justin grabbed onto some rigging closer to the stairs they had ascended a moment prior. August was nowhere to be seen, and Miranda clung to Yuvina with all her remaining vigor. Celyth had not followed them to the upper deck, and Miranda was not sure where Arlindra might be. Her heart sank more when she realized Evan was not present. Furthermore, she was not sure how long she had been inside Yuvina's mind, but the sunlight behind a densely clouded sky suggested she had been in there all day. Evening would begin within the hour. "Dad! What's going on?" she shouted as loudly as she could.

Naomi replied, "Death Pirates, darling. They're on a fancy ship unlike anything we've ever seen. They're moving through the water so fast that the cannon deck was ready to fire before Erk even knew what was happening." Naomi's eyes darted up to the sky. "On top of the fact that they also have air support."

Yuvina gave a low growl, the mana surging within her to maintain her magically enhanced strength. She knew with certainty the magic was pulling on the life essence within her now. "Can you reach Naomi, Miranda?" she asked. As the ship caught a moment of tipping back to the left, Miranda dropped from Yuvina's back, reaching for the pirate lady. Naomi grabbed Miranda and pulled her close, wrapping her arms around the priestess protectively.

"Incoming!" a voice shouted from above. It was August, causing Miranda to look upward. The paladin and Evan sailed overhead on a pair of pegasus. They charged forward to engage with a flying enemy: goblins mounted on wyverns. Though pegasus outweighed the leathery yet scaly beasts significantly, the distant-draconic relatives had more lethal tools at their disposal. Miranda cursed to herself.

Five mounted wyverns connected with August and Evan mid-air, and *The Nebula* sailed from underneath them as they engaged.

"Evan!" Miranda shouted, her strength returning slowly. She could see her pink hair hanging on the mithril breastplate of her battlemail. "August!" she panted, her heart racing. She felt helpless, her mana depleted, and her body exhausted from channeling so much divinity through her while in Yuvina's mind.

"Miranda!" Selasine's voice boomed from the helm ten feet away. "You're too weakened to be out here, get back below deck! Please, yolasha."

The warpriest shuddered, knowing his assessment was true. She cycled her breath, her heart pounding in her chest still. "I'm okay, modai-rin! I'm exhausted, but I can still pray!"

Selasine felt a similar, gnawing helplessness surge through him. "Yolasha, be careful!"

Erk's voice followed, "Miranda, don't you dare allow harm to befall you. I'm going to try and stop them. It's Falindeth."

"Falindeth?!" Miranda shouted back in surprise. She recognized that as the name of the pirate from whom Naomi rescued *The Violet Blur*.

Erk left the helm as the ship buoyed hard again. He ran down the stairs to the lower deck, relying on his well-honed agility and strength to fight the shifting of the ship in the water.

Jax activated his uncanny magic. Suddenly, *The Nebula* froze. A bubble formed around the ship, lifting it out of the water. After less than a moment, the bubble burst, dropping the ship back in the water at a complete standstill. The sudden maneuver caused the now-obvious threat approaching from the south to turn its course east in a suggested retreat. Miranda had enough time to marvel at the shimmering globe around them, though, excited to witness the "Mighty Stop" so many of the pirates had discussed before. Stalling in combat could be fatal to many ships, but *The Nebula* was magical. It would pull toward the captain's preferred port at great speed if it stalled, an enchantment that fascinated Erk even before he was the vessel's captain. Erk and Jax employed the Mighty Stop strategically.

As Miranda stood, looking around the now-still ship, she saw Erk run up to the bow over one hundred feet away. "Erk," she whispered to herself. She felt dread in her heart, but she wasn't sure why.

The crew on the upper deck recovered and united quickly. Selasine nodded to Justin and Valarie, who charged down toward the foredeck to support Erk with their extraordinary defensive capabilities. The Shield Knights were renowned for their ability to shield their fellow clergy in combat. Erk was an ally that could benefit from such coverage, his devastating supernova concentrated into small beams of light capable of burning through the hull of a ship at great distance. It was that power that granted him the courage and will to become a pirate lord in Yendralia.

Miranda glanced back to see August and Evan had forcibly dismounted one of the goblins, causing the wyvern to flee. Magic and prayers swirled in the air, but Miranda couldn't discern their nature or source. If Evan was using the clockwork weapons relying on the lacrima-deum, she understood. This felt like an ambush. She did not regret helping Yuvina, but she realized why Selasine and everyone else had warned her against expending so much energy. To be fair, however, she had not anticipated fighting the remnants of the avatar of Aylabrax while within the foxkin's mind. Yuvina's previous state was probably graver than any of them realized thanks to her suspicious arrival, memory loss, and the events in Mystalon. Still, Miranda was sure the foxkin would be safe now.

The Nebula charged through the waters again thanks to the enchantment upon the ship. As Erk thought of Yendralia, the galleon surged toward the south. The enemy ship looked strange as it glinted in the poorly lit waters of the western Sea of Undine. Flames swirled around Erk's arms as he stood on the foredeck of *The Nebula*. As the galleon came within one thousand feet of the Death Pirate ship, Erk discharged his attack. A beam of light struck the hull, but then it reflected into the sky.

"What?" the pirate lord protested as he watched his intense heat bounce elsewhere into the atmosphere.

The enemy ship sparkled in the low light of the early evening even though clouds blocked most of the light above. The ship's hull and structure had been fitted with mirrors that deflected the pirate lord's infamous attack. Erk's radiant light caused the mirrors on the hull of the ship to flash, and the reflected beam of energy burned a massive hole in the clouds. After a moment, the pirate lord ceased his attack.

The evening sun now poured through the widening opening above, and the Sea of Undine twinkled with light. Miranda gulped, recognizing the colors of the enemy ship as those of Hoxark's own Death Pirates. Though they assisted Gelidor in the Battle of Beriton, she did not initially understand their relationship to the pirates of Yendralia. Eventually she realized that most of the pirates in Espa had a purpose or crusade against some sort of corrupt, unbalanced system. Invictus allowed for rebellion against corrupt governments, so she understood. The Death Pirates, however, were evil and bent on plundering at all costs. They had no purpose beyond causing harm, and they would execute their plans with as much cruelty as possible. Furthermore, they had aligned themselves with Farzg and Gelidor, giving her reason to hate them with righteous judgment. They campaigned in the seas of West Espa from their island capital of Cassack, as Miranda learned from her time with Erk. It was easily defended much like Yendralia.

Miranda felt the flow of mana around her change. Yuvina

bounded from her place in the rigging. There were not simply five mounted wyverns in the air; another dozen descended on *The Nebula* prompting Yuvina's action. Miranda also drew her sword, her growing fear about the situation causing her exhaustion to numb. After a moment, she realized Yuvina was discharging mana that stagnated immediately, making itself available to the warpriest. It was miniscule, however, and it only served to ease Miranda's exhaustion. Nevertheless, it caused Miranda's worries about the kitsune to grow.

As Miranda whispered a protection prayer for herself, Naomi slayed a wyvern with a barrage of daggers. The goblin in the small saddle on the creature's back fell to the deck. "Don't underestimate Naomi!" the giantkin shouted as the beast died quickly thanks to the throwing daggers straight to its brain. "Miranda, arrest the assailant for questioning!" she suggested, turning her attention back to the sky. With impressive agility, the pirate lady scaled the ropes of *The Nebula*'s rigging as quickly as she could run. Recognizing her as a threat, four of the wyvern riders gave pursuit.

The goblin on the deck had drawn two short swords and bared its teeth. Goblins were usually mischievous and cunning, and their small size made them ideal for training and riding wyverns. They did not normally stay to fight once their mounts were defeated; however, this enemy had nowhere else to go. Miranda held her sword out weakly and shouted, "Stop!" Her order had conviction behind it in spite of her exhaustion.

With an evil smile, the goblin leapt into action, his swords spinning with incredible swiftness. Miranda's eyes widened with horror as she began to parry, the bladed menace closing the distance between them in an instant.

A boot suddenly came into Miranda's view as Jax kicked the goblin squarely in the side of the head. Jax was seven feet tall, an incredible height for a human. The goblin, at barely over three feet, flew across the upper deck of *The Nebula*. Miranda jumped backwards in shock, looking at the massive pirate. He had not seen her so scared since he had met her, even when she was a captive on this ship. Empathy filled his heart, and he tried to comfort the priestess. "Be careful, kid. Yer not looking so hot, ye should get below deck."

As she was about to agree with him, she noticed two wyverns had descended on Selasine near the stairs to the lower part of the main deck. She shook her head furiously at the pirate. "I can't! No! Dad!!"

she sang with overflowing anxiety. She held her sword out again and focused on the magic within it. The blade glowed, firing a bolt of holy light at one of the serpent-necked beasts.

The creature hissed and roared at the same time. It was a strange, airy sound. It was still terrifying, however, causing Miranda's heart to leap into her throat. As she was growing concerned, her dad activated his uncanny magic, providing too many targets for the wyverns to fight effectively. Before she could adjust to a feeling of ease, she turned her eyes back to the sky.

Naomi was much harder to catch than the goblins anticipated. An endless stream of daggers flowed from her, making the wyverns agitated from continual, severe slices. Just as the enemy coordinated a trap, the giantkin turned invisible. Miranda breathed a sigh of relief, hoping this would be a much more manageable battle than Mystalon.

Jax took the wheel, defending the helm against the aerial assault. Selasine slayed the second of his attackers and used a binding curse on their riders. He turned to face his daughter, "Miranda, we can handle this fight. Are you alright, yolasha?" he asked, closing the fifteen feet between them cautiously.

Though he had a blur of duplicates surrounding him, Miranda had no trouble finding the correct Selasine to reach out for. He drew her into his arms, looking up at the sky as he held her protectively. She sighed gently and replied, "I helped Yuvina. She's going to be okay, it was Aylabrax the Devourer. The evil goddess left a portion of herself inside Yuvina's memories. I destroyed that avatar."

Selasine's attention snapped down, looking at the pink hair strewn chaotically as her braids unraveled. "No wonder you're so exhausted." Yuvina rolled nearby, dodging the snapping maw of a wyvern. Her movement prompted Selasine to shield Miranda. As he did, the barb of the wyvern's tail stabbed into an exposed part of Selasine's forearm, the impact pushing him and Miranda backward.

"Nyokto!" he cursed in Khantongue, the stinger already back behind the wyvern. Because he had Miranda in his actual arms, the wyvern knew exactly where to strike. Blood spurted from the wound, and Selasine felt the venom taking effect. His arm turned numb as his blood stopped flowing. "Invictus," he gurgled as he began to feel ill. He fell to a knee, Miranda close by his side.

Yuvina growled, stomping her left foot instinctively. A surge of viscous, sticky liquid emerged from beneath her boot, coating the ground. It spread quickly, and it was harmless to Yuvina's allies. The wyvern's feet were on the deck, and its wings were draped into the liquid. It found itself stuck. With brutality in her eyes, Yuvina put a swift end to the wyvern with a rapid series of stabs to the monster's throat. The display was so terrifying the wyvern rider screamed in terror and offered immediate surrender.

Selasine started to seize, falling to both of his knees now. He kept trying to pray, but the venom was too intense. His increasingly frantic babbles worried Miranda. Finally, the high priest fell forward, prone on the deck.

Miranda used all the strength she had to turn him over. Wyvern venom was a lethal coagulant, and the warpriest had been trained well in magical and non-magical healing. She searched in her healer's bag for a serum that would quickly stop the worst effects, tipping the vial up into her dad's mouth. "I'm going back below dad; just be okay, please," she whispered, waiting for the antivenom to take effect.

Selasine's eye opened a moment later. "Blast it, a lucky strike," he complained, feeling the effects of the wyvern venom fade. He was surprised that he was struck through his illusionary magic, but it wasn't the first time it had ever happened. He did not regret shielding Miranda even though it betrayed his location. He sat up and put a hand on Miranda's shoulder. He could feel the powerful, divine aura radiating from her. Though her physical and magical states were weakened, her spiritual power was still strong in spite of her struggle against the dark goddess. "Miranda, will you pray with me?"

She nodded. "Of course," she replied, taking his hands into hers.

The high priest exhaled, finding his spiritual center. "O, gods who rest in the primordial place, we beseech those of good heart."

Miranda's eyes widened in surprise, but she repeated the line, speaking in unison with Selasine as the prayer continued. "We are beset by evil and chaos at every turn; provide us a sanctuary from harm. Surround us with your divine protection. Our strength fails us, and we are left to the mercy of darkness."

A bright, green barrier formed around Selasine and Miranda as they completed their prayer; the intent was to generate an absolute protective barrier that would only fail if they attempted to harm someone. In this state, Miranda and Selasine could heal without worrying about their own safety as much; the barriers were impenetrable to nearly every attack. Miranda had not thought of the sanctified barrier prayer because of its limitations; however, in her current condition, she realized it was perfect.

Selasine smiled at her as they stood, the green barrier of light following their movements. It was cylindrical rather than spherical like the normal protection prayers. It was an ancient prayer meant to protect medics and healers during the Dracon Wars and the Legion of Hoxark. Furthermore, they had to reach beyond Invictus for the sanctified barrier; it was a prayer so powerful it could only be summoned by priests with a strong connection to all the gods of good heart, even the ones whose names had been lost to history. "Come now, yolasha, let us help." Though the wyvern venom was neutralized, the aftereffects would leave the high priest weakened for a few hours.

Miranda nodded, and they looked around again. At least ten wyverns had fallen on the deck of *The Nebula*, and the crew was preparing to engage with the strange vessel now looming large and relatively close to Erk's ship. The experienced pirate lord and his first officer did not fall for the feigned retreat, and the Death Pirates were now trying to outmaneuver *The Nebula* for positional advantage. "Let us pray for the injured," she added, walking with her dad toward the lower deck. Jax and Yuvina had the upper deck secure, and several of Erk's men had been injured engaging with the wyverns below. Valarie, Justin, and Erk were at the front of the ship, evaluating the enemy vessel.

As Miranda and Selasine tended to the injured with healing prayers, Erk and Valarie used spyglasses to get a closer look at the approaching ship. The first round of cannon fire helped eliminate numerous wyvern riders before combat began in earnest, but Erk knew it was a diversion. The Death Pirates could close cannon distance before the crew had time to reload. The enemy was likely planning a boarding attack, as it had no obvious cannon deck. In fact, the ship continued to grow stranger by the moment.

The vessel was smaller than *The Nebula*, and the hull was wrapped in a reflective layer of adamant-quicksilver rather than common mirroring. The upper deck was a towering building, and it was enclosed in metal and glass. It towered up a full two stories over the main deck, but the ship had three masts with no rigging or sails. Death Pirates scurried about the deck, however, preparing to board *The Nebula* as soon as they were in range. The ship moved smoothly in the water. Erk scrunched his nose with frustration after a few moments of observation, "Lexcord, shield us. What kind of vessel moves with no sails and no pilot?" He frowned hard, hearing the enemies shout with excitement as the distance between the ships closed to less than one hundred yards.

Justin let out a deep sigh. "We sure haven't had much time to recover. Do you think this is Farzg retaliating for our victory in Mystalon?"

Valarie shook her head. "I'd hardly call it a victory, dear."

The paladin grimaced, adding, "That Sender character, he was working for Farzg, right? We defeated him, so it only makes sense the enemy would retaliate."

Erk shook his head. "This is bigger than Farzg, I just don't understand how yet. Perhaps it is the scientists who should be more closely investigated. We don't have time to ponder such things now, however. Prepare to engage." Erk turned to shout across the deck of *The Nebula*, the authority in his voice unquestionable. "We be boarded soon men, unleash Infernia!"

A cheer returned from Erk's crew. Selasine's prayer coursed through all of them; Invictus had poured his blessing of courage and strength into their bodies and hearts. The pirate lord turned back to face the enemy, and the flames formed around his arms again. "I might not be able to sink the vessel, but this will be hotter than Agnikyo," he said, referencing the dimension of fire. He unleashed a beam of light toward the pirates gathered on the deck of the enemy ship. Screams of agony and panic could be heard.

Justin shouted, "Captain!" and he slung his shield hard in front of Erk. The paladin noticed a flicker of mana igniting. The flash gave him just enough warning to try and block the attack with his versatile and powerful shield. His title, Justin the Watchful, was more accurate than the paladin realized. Though mithril was metal, it blocked the manifestations of mana particles with incredible sturdiness. It dampened the effects of flames, freezes, and lightning bolts.

The flash was a crackle of electricity, and it surged from the enemy ship; an assailant had waited for Erk's position, and once it was revealed, they unleashed their lethal attack.

The lightning discharged four feet in front of Justin's shield as it struck a humanoid figure that became suddenly visible. Additional arcs of electricity connected with Justin, Valarie, and Erk as they radiated from the person struck by the initial bolt. The three of them screamed in surprise, the shield and the previously unseen person seeming to have blocked most of the deadly blast. Still, the attack's ferocity exposed a primary target among the enemy.

"Justin!" Valarie called as the lightning wracked him hardest behind the unidentified victim of the full force of the first blast.

Erk was by Justin's side in an instant, pulling the shield out of his hand. The paladin took more damage than he felt, but it was not lethal. His eyes widened as he started to fall to the deck. In front of him lay Shalo, his body completely crisped by the electricity. Smoke rose from the smelly pirate's body as the connecting bolt was so powerful that it would have likely destroyed Justin through his shield.

"Restore the feeling in your faithful's body!" Valarie shouted and gripped her holy symbol, channeling the divinity of Invictus through herself to ease Justin's wounds. He felt sensation returning throughout him; somehow, the secondary arc of lightning was still enough to paralyze him. Valarie had tears in her eyes but still seemed combat aware.

"Shalo!" Justin shouted as he scrambled to stand.

Erk looked at his chef's smoldering remains. "Shalo!" he cried out, his face twisting into a furious visage. "Gods damn you, now. You bastards!" he shouted, turning his attention back to the enemy vessel. He could see the magical assailant hidden behind a mirrored wall on a balcony outside the enclosed upper deck of the otherworldly ship.

As the rage in Erk started to surge to an unbelievable level, he felt his heart race as an elven arrow pierced the throat of the lightning wielder. His eyes snapped up to the crow's nest above *The Nebula*'s main mast. Arlindra and Celyth stood far above, bows drawn and a rain of death beginning for the Death Pirates. Hope and righteousness swelled in Erk's spirit. "Hu-yozi Mystalon!" he shouted. His grief for Shalo powered his spite and anger.

Celyth shouted back, "To the Infernia with Mystalon. Long live House Fernith!"

Arlindra added in her loudest voice, "Shut up and fight, captain!"

August and Evan circled up above the four remaining wyvern riders. Evan wielded his father's longsword, an heirloom Erk had kept for him ever since they raided the palace at Claston after defeating the Usurper. It was recovered alongside many other treasures stolen by Gelidor. After the events in Mystalon, Evan abandoned the clockwork equipment they had acquired. He was now eager to shed the enemy's blood with his father's magical sword. Though it was not as powerful as Holyfang, his sister's former sword, now Miranda's, it was still quite capable of cleaving through steel with little effort.

August wielded his holy longsword blessed by a high paladin of Invictus, giving it enhancements that were particularly potent against evil enemies. Otherwise, it was functionally non-magical. Fortunately, most of the enemies of the Church of Invictus were evil in nature.

Evan shouted, "Diving!" and spurred his pegasus into a deep, downward plunge.

August returned, "Spiral!" and leaned in his saddle, pushing his mount to fly in a rapid, circular descent. As the wyvern riders took Evan's bait, August was able to pursue in his slower fall. He swiped his sword with deadly accuracy, sundering off a wyvern's tail as he caught up to one. Losing a tail caused wyverns to panic; they would regrow them, eventually, but their most efficient defense had been eliminated if they lost a tail in combat. Their survival instincts overtook their training, and August was able to send two wyverns into a frenzied retreat with his strategy. The other two continued to dive after Evan, but they were sorely outpaced. The pegasus maintained several dozen feet between herself and the leathery-winged beasts. Their serpent-like necks lashed out, snapping at the pegasus's rear hooves. As the wyrms approached striking distance, the magical, flying horse's strong hooves stomped their snouts. The surface of the ocean was about one hundred feet below, and Evan tilted his mount to begin a new ascent. The well-trained pegasus complied, making Evan's weaker experience with flying combat less noticeable. He had experience in hunting on pegasus mounts in his youth with his father, and flying seemed to come naturally to him.

One of the goblin riders demanded, "Surrender and die, elf!" but they choked as their mount hesitated and flapped upward. It had gotten another mouthful of pegasus hoof, and it was starting to panic. Unfortunately for the goblin in the saddle, August used the opportunity to strike him down, dismounting him with ease. He plunged into the ocean, and his mount fled, afraid of the pegasus' superior size.

Evan laughed, spurring his mount back up to two hundred feet, noticing *The Nebula* was about to enter boarding range with the enemy vessel. "Let's get to it, commander, no time to waste!" He clenched his legs hard, causing the pegasus to lower to the water's surface. She galloped across the top of the calm ocean below. The remaining wyvern rider drew up short and retreated. Two, well-trained pegasus were too much for a group of five wyvern riders, and there was no way it made sense to try and fight now that he was outnumbered. Besides, the bulk of his force had been stopped by *The Nebula*'s cannons; the Death Pirates would never hear from him nor his precious Bitey again.

August and Evan flew toward *The Nebula* in time to see a massive bolt of lightning strike close to the bow of the ship. "By the gods, what was that?" Evan shouted, spurring his mount faster.

"I'm not sure," August called back, following as quickly as he could.

They swung around *The Nebula*'s port side as it now sailed directly south. The Death Pirate vessel had turned north and looked to be preparing to board. "Let's give them a taste of the Infernia!" Evan shouted.

"Invictus condemn them!" August yelled in return. It was then they realized this fight would be difficult, but they would surely overcome the enemy. From further west, August and Evan could see a caravel surging through the water. It was *The Violet Blur*, Naomi's flagship captained by her closest friend, Annaia. "Evan! It's the girls!" he added once he noticed the ship.

Evan's excited laugh was audible and strong. "For *The Nebula*! For *The Violet Blur*!"

The two of them decided to attack the Death Pirates from behind just as the enemy attempted to board *The Nebula*. They could see Arlindra and Celyth in the crow's nest of Erk's ship, unleashing an initial volley of arrows just as deadly as the scattershot fired from the cannons earlier. "Hey, Evan?" August asked with excitement.

The elf looked over at August as they hovered mid-air, waiting for the opportune time to join the assault. They were close together now. "Commander?" he replied.

"Keep score. I'm going to beat that Arlindra in enemy kills."

Evan raised his eyebrow, "I didn't realize there was a competition?"

August shrugged. "I dunno, she's pretty cool. And if I bring more Death Pirates to justice than she does, I've got some ammo for our next actual competition. She's already competing, she just doesn't know it."

Evan laughed heartily again. "You really don't quit, do you commander? Alright, August. Let's do what we do best."

August's face twitched with anticipation. "For justice?"

With conviction and a smirk, Evan concluded, "This evening, *The Nebula* is the weight of justice. We are merely its backhanded slap, reminding the enemy of their frailty in the grip of chaos." When the time was right, they charged.

Naomi dropped out of the rigging, using her agility to roll harmlessly to the deck below. While invisible, the world was coated in a subtle, blue tint. Invisibility was simply covering oneself with the arcane stream to veil their physical presence. Shalo could do it naturally with his uncanny magic, but Naomi relied on the gift of a powerful ring she acquired through fighting Death Pirates and slavers over the last thirty years. It had saved her life on more than one occasion, and today, it had made fighting the wyverns above so much easier. She looked up and gave a small grin to herself.

A rain of arrows showered the wyverns and their riders with deadly efficiency. Arlindra and Celyth cut them out of the air in a mere twelve seconds of steady barrage. Both of them were capable of firing a shot in a single second, and in this evening visibility, they could mow their targets down with ease. The cousins were so effective not even a single shot went astray. "Wow," Naomi marveled, realizing why Miranda had allied herself with these cousins so easily. Not only were they strong in their hearts, but they were also more than capable with their bows. "Get 'em, girls," she encouraged quietly.

A strange sound in Naomi's mind disoriented her for a moment. Damil was trying to reach her, but his thoughts could not connect. Instead, all she heard was Erk's voice shouting about Shalo. At first, she wondered what the chef had done in the middle of a fight, but then she felt Erk's heartbreak. Shalo had been blasted by electricity, saving Justin and possibly Erk and Valarie from a chain of lightning that could have devastated even *The Nebula*. "No!" she whispered to herself. "Damil, can you hear me?"

The paladin's thoughts barely pushed through, "Umbrals in Nulodia."

Naomi wasn't sure if she had heard correctly, but just the thought of it shook her to her core. "By the gods, what's going on? This is too much." She drew daggers in each of her hands from a bandolier strapped to her thigh and rushed toward the front of the ship. As she did, she realized the Death Pirates were prepared to board. An assault of grappling hooks launched from the deck of the enemy vessel. So far, the only uncanny magic they had revealed was the lightning wielder, and she did not imagine they would last long with the Fernith cousins in the crow's nest above. "Poor Shalo," she mourned, realizing now the pirate had been waiting for such a moment. Ever since he had hurt Justin and found out how much the young paladin meant to Miranda, Shalo had been looking for a chance to redeem himself. She worried, however, that the chef's death would have been in vain if she did not move to help her current crewmates.

The crew of *The Nebula* was ready. Three hundred armed pirates awaited the barely one hundred Death Pirates as they reeled the massive galleon close to their strange, metal ship. Jax commanded from the helm, "Give 'em the radiant light men!"

Steel gang planks plunked down into the port side of *The Nebula*. The Death Pirates were well-prepared, and it made Naomi's skin crawl. They somehow had a plan for each member of their crew, and the situation began to gnaw at her. Somebody was watching them and likely had been for some time. Erk's ship-sinking light was reflected by the mirror-like coating on the enemy's strange ship. They also attacked with air support, something unique to *The Nebula* when compared to other pirate vessels. She assumed it was Farzg behind such tedious attention to detail, but at this point the enemy was far too prepared and equipped for even the slaver's resources. "Doctor One," she murmured. "By the gods. How are you watching us so closely?" she questioned out loud.

Before she could make further analyses, she realized *The Violet Blur* was approaching from the other side of the enemy vessel. She couldn't help but smile. "Annaia," she whispered.

✦❦✦

A beautiful woman of thirty-six years with blond hair and a purple bandana stood at the helm of *The Violet Blur*. The ship's voice echoed in her mind, "Death Pirates and Erk's vessel within three hundred feet. Ram?"

Annaia shook her head, and Blur felt the gesture through their telepathy. "Board. We want to take that ship while they're outclassed by Erk's men." She giggled. "It's like shopping with unlimited money! Except that the store might kill you."

Blur rolled her eyes in thought. "Annaia, you really should take this more seriously. Naomi is in grave danger!"

Annaia laughed, causing the women around her to look with concern. "Don't worry, Blur," she thought back. "Naomi's never in danger. Shoulders back, hips forward, fight!" She emulated Naomi's base fighting stance, letting go of the wheel without worry.

Blur laughed. "Right you are. Let's get us a handsome chunk of steel to sail side-by-side. Boarding! Blur boarding!" she shouted into the minds of all the relevant crew. Annaia made sure to transfer all of their recent rescues to other ships in Naomi's fleet before definitively deciding on rescuing *The Nebula* and its sailors from the Death Pirate ship. Twenty of those dangerous, metal ships currently sat outside the Isles Known for Nothing, blockading the pirate haven of Yendralia. Annaia's current mission was not on behalf of the church; Ut'wah the Magnificent had personally found *The Violet Blur* to pass on his message.

"Death Pirates from Cassack have arrived at Yendralia on strange ships. They have formed a blockade, and the Pirate Nobles are ordered to return and break it. A one hundred thousand gold coin bounty has been placed on each of the enemy vessels, and we hope you will return to claim your portion of the prize. Participation is mandatory, even for those in East Espa. Additional prizes will be awarded by Cantalus based on the order of arrival."—Noble Pirate Lord Ut'wah the Magnificent.

His words echoed in Annaia's head endlessly. "Blur, you're right. Naomi needs me! Yendralia needs us! And I need that money!" The Death Pirates were boarding *The Nebula* to great resistance, and a couple of pegasus riders descended above their ship; Annaia recognized one of them as Erk's brother, but the other was a newer face. He was clean shaven and handsome with youthful spirit and bravery. As Captain Annaia looked up into the sky, she watched as Commander August Burchard descended into the backs of the Death Pirates, cutting them down without mercy or hesitation. Her lips pursed with intrigue as she watched his finesse. Pirates retaliated with an array of uncanny magic including acid and fire sprays, necromantic drains, and paralysis inducing beams of light. Somehow, he managed to stay one step ahead of them, dodging volleys and slaying the enemy with impunity. The air, even though it was filled with dangerous electrical blasts, didn't cause the paladin to hesitate; he fought with the same kind of conviction Naomi had taught Annaia to value. It was the same trait Naomi, essentially her adoptive mother, had seen in Erk from a different angle; this paladin was the bravest man she had ever seen. He fought from such an advantageously vulnerable position that she admired his confidence, but his efficacy was beyond anything she could have imagined. It was love at first sight, and she meant to make that paladin hers. Just the way that Naomi had decided the same about Erilkaiden.

As the Death Pirates forced down their heavy gangplanks, cheers of battle erupted from both decks. Then, it became clear why the Death Pirates were willing to board while being significantly outnumbered. Miranda looked up at the main mast of the enemy vessel's deck; it began to glow with an ominous, blue light. She felt the tingle of electricity building in the air. Something was agitating the flow of mana, creating a field of unbelievable static. As swords began to clash between Erk's men and the Death Pirates, arcs of crackling electricity burst between the combatants. Miranda's eyes widened; the Death Pirates were partially insulated by thick, padded armor. They were wearing protective uniforms.

The electricity was not significantly damaging, but it was debilitating. Every parry resulted in a weaker position as the jolts inflicted enough pain for Erk's fighters to be easily overcome. The field of static enveloped the deck of *The Nebula*, and then the mast's power amplified. As Arlindra and Celyth rained down arrows, the static field interfered with their ammunition, knocking them harmlessly out of the air. Then, miniature bolts of lightning began randomly striking from the top of the enemy mast, showing bias to Erk's uninsulated crew.

Miranda's heart swirled with fear, but she knew the divine sanctuary would keep the lightning away. She was protected from all harm as long as her actions were not to harm others. She could, however, pray for protection. As she stepped up to the gangplank, she sang out, "Invictus, ground us in faith and firmament. Shield us from the fury of the Tempest!" As she prayed, a purple globe formed around the pirates closest to her, providing insulation for Erk's men as they attempted to push back the enemy. The static bolts became harmless, and the lightning from the mast was absorbed by the protection prayer.

Still, several dozen of Erk's men had been struck by the powerful bolts. Selasine slid into action, praying for the mortally injured first. As he began to heal the crew, Miranda noticed August flying around the mast of the enemy vessel. Somehow, being in the air kept her friend from being a target of the lightning. His fierce presence caused the boarding pirates enough confusion that Erk's men began to press back onto the enemy ship. Miranda then realized *The Violet Blur* was boarding from the starboard side of the Death Pirate super-ship. She smiled with confidence, realizing that they would overwhelm the enemy quickly. She prayed for more insulating protection, shielding more of Erk's crew from the magical mast on the enemy ship.

Erk suddenly bounded across the gangplank in front of Miranda. His haste and relentlessness shocked her; he bowled into a group of Death Pirates looking up to target August. They were near the main mast, and as Erk approached, lightning arced down to strike him. Just before it connected, he let out a massive burst of his uncanny magic. A miniscule but dense supernova blasted around him, cracking the mast and blasting the Death Pirates backward into the boarders from Annaia's crew.

The vessel rocked heavily in the water; Erk did not fuel his power long enough to summon Black Hole, so the destruction was minimal and focused. With a fury unlike anything Miranda had ever heard from the pirate, he shouted, "You'll pay for what you did to Shalo, Hak-koth'i!" he swore, using the worst possible curse in the elven language.

Miranda's heart leapt into her throat. "Shalo?" she called back, a sudden anxiety coursing through her. The divine sanctuary around her shimmered with green and white holy protection, which was fortunate because her focus on the battle completely dissipated. She looked to the bow of the ship where she could see Justin and Valarie hobbling down the steps to the foredeck. Justin's arm was draped over Valarie's shoulder as she helped him walk in his critically injured state. Miranda rushed toward them with concern. "Valarie! Justin!" she called out on the way.

"Miranda!" Valarie returned. "Justin has been severely wounded!" Paladins were not generally able to heal as effectively as the clerics of Invictus, and Miranda was a designated healer within the church. This was her specialty.

"Say no more," she replied as she closed in on the two, nearly tackling Justin with her charging embrace. "Restore to order what was damaged by chaos!" she shouted. A brilliant, purple light surged around them as Miranda infused the healing prayer with a dose of arcane restoration. The curative aura was so intense that it healed many members of Erk's crew as well, invigorating them with a new, fighting spirit. Miranda's hair changed from a deep pink to light coral, an indication that the mana within her was nearly extinguished. With shallow breaths, she looked up toward the bow. "Shalo? What happened to Shalo?" she pleaded, the music in her voice dissonant.

Valarie glared at Miranda with concern. "Stop! You're going to kill yourself!" Justin stood easily on his own, looking at his hands and then down to his feet. The sensation in his extremities was restored instantly with the healing burst from Miranda.

The priestess looked at Valarie with surprise. She couldn't think of anything to say, so she bounded up the stairs. On the bow she found the spot where Shalo had been struck by lightning. The intense healing energy Miranda unleashed did not affect the smoldering remains, an indication that his injuries were beyond simple healing prayers. Miranda slid onto the deck close to Shalo, tears flowing down her cheeks. Valarie was hot on her heels, however, sliding in behind Miranda and clutching her tight. She knew Miranda would not give up in spite of her limited mana.

Miranda shouted, "By the gods, listen! Restore to order what was damaged by chaos!"

Valarie squeezed Miranda harder as the priestess received no response from Invictus. "Miranda," she said gently, trying to calm her friend.

"Shalo!" Miranda cried. Though her relationship with the pirate endured significant strain upon learning Shalo had nearly killed Justin, Miranda still hoped Shalo would find redemption. "This is not how his story should end!" she pleaded with the universe out loud.

"He saved Justin and maybe Erk and me," Valarie explained, still holding onto Miranda. "He put himself between the lightning and Justin. He—" she began but Miranda interrupted.

"Is there nothing I can do?" she asked, helpless. Her face drew up into a combination of frustration and sorrow. "A life ended too early is the work of chaos! Let us set the universe to right in the Path of the Sword of Justice," she tried, reciting an advanced prayer that could restore the lives of recently departed mortals. Though her holy symbol glowed in response, Shalo's injuries were far too significant for the simple raising prayer. He was unrecoverable.

Valarie closed her eyes and laid her head on Miranda's shoulder, still embracing her from behind on the bow of *The Nebula*. Justin joined them, looking around the deck. "In a way," he started, feeling his empathy for his friend swelling. He eventually sat with Miranda and Valarie beside the charred husk that was once Shalo. "In a way, he got his wish, didn't he?"

Miranda looked at Justin, tears flowing freely. She thought back to the day Shalo kidnapped her and helped her get through the caves on the Undine Coast. His entire world changed that day, just like Miranda's. It was in that moment that Miranda recognized the impact she had on others. A year ago, Shalo was a ruthless pirate working for Erk, ready to commit horrible deeds in the name of the dread pirate. Today, he had saved Justin from a powerful ambush meant to neutralize Erk. "His wish?" she asked, her head spinning from the emotions of sudden loss and the battle on the decks below.

Valarie nodded, her head shaking Miranda's armored shoulder. "He's been following us for months, invisible. Waiting, trying to help from the shadows."

Justin let out a deep breath. "He tried to hide, but we could always smell when he became visible. He's probably helped us bring down dozens of slavers."

Miranda blinked, her tears starting to subside. She looked back at Shalo. "He promised he would make me proud," she started. A new wave of sadness overtook her, but there was significant anger growing inside her as well. Though she felt pushed to her limit after battling the shadow of an evil goddess, she knew her fight was not over. The clouds in the sky had thickened back over the hole Erk unintentionally made. Darkness descended over the three ships engaged in the western reaches of the Sea of Undine. A similar darkness began to grow in Miranda's heart.

With the ship's primary defense disabled, the Death Pirates surrendered quickly. Justin, Valarie, and August oversaw the arrest of the thirty surviving enemies. Miranda and Selasine continued to treat the injured, and Arlindra and Celyth assisted the crew in cleaning off the deck of *The Nebula*. Miranda worked on the injured without speaking anything more than the healing prayer she had been using since she became a peacekeeper under Bishop Selasine in Devitus. Erk, Evan, and Naomi congregated at the grand stairs leading into the towering structure on the strange ship. Erk looked to Naomi, reaching out to take her hand. "Another demon from the past," he commented.

The giantkin did not return her beloved's gaze. She stared at the door to the imposing structure made of metal and glass. It was a wonder to behold, but it was terrifying. Somebody had an incredible mind to create a ship so destructive and strange. She added, "Even so many years later." Her voice was forlorn and timid, uncharacteristic for her brave, strong nature. Together, she and Erk reached out to pull open the large, metal door in front of them.

Annaia looked around at the lavish party. She had just turned twenty-one, and Naomi spared no expense for the celebration. Erk was there, of course, with his creepy and quiet brother. Annaia realized this was why Naomi insisted that they remain in Yendralia for the month of The Warming instead of taking new missions. The orphan's birthday was sometime that month, though the exact day was unknown. Annaia was rescued by Naomi when she was only four years old, and together they escaped horrors unlike anything they had seen since.

"Happy birthday, beautiful!" Naomi called out, bringing the young woman's mind back to the present.

Annaia beamed with surprise; they had rented out the entire restaurant known as Chummy's Slums, an upscale establishment at the heart of Yendralia's lower district. "Naomi," was all she could reply, her green eyes full of tears of joy.

Erk clasped his hands together while everyone in the room had their eyes fixed on Annaia. The pirate lord's voice was encouraging and light as he said, "Come now, we've startled her too greatly. Please, Annaia, come in and enjoy the gathering. Shalo is hard at work in the kitchen, and a feast will soon follow." His powerful, commanding voice caused the attention to shift from her to him, giving Annaia a moment to let her tears drop.

Naomi smiled, walking from the center of the restaurant to the door where Annaia stood, quiet. Her blond hair was tied up underneath a purple bandana. She gazed up as Naomi towered over her, and Annaia reached out for her like a child. Not one year since their escape had Naomi let the girl go without a party around her birthday, but the giantkin had never rented an entire restaurant and hired her crew and consorts to make it such a big event. Annaia was speechless, and Naomi took the young woman in her arms. "What's wrong, darling?" Naomi asked, her worry evident.

Annaia shook her head and then pressed it into Naomi's chest, "Nothing's wrong, mom. I just wasn't expecting this, that's all." She shivered, feelings of gratefulness permeating her entire essence.

Naomi giggled, cupping Annaia's head in her hand, stroking her hair tenderly. "I fight so that every little girl can have the best birthday party. I hope it's not overwhelming," she began, but Annaia interrupted with a laugh.

"No, nothing of the sort. I just wish dad was still here, and Elrune," she said, remembering them vividly from the slave camp in the Mammoth Moors far to the north. The Isles Known for Nothing were far enough away that Annaia no longer shuddered when she heard the region mentioned.

Naomi's silver eyes turned sad for a moment. "I wish they were too, dear." She squeezed the girl lovingly. Meanwhile, the other attendees found refreshments and conversation so Naomi could welcome Annaia. Even Erk, Naomi's betrothed, let them have their space. He was normally pretty nosy, but as Annaia grew older, she understood why. Information was the most valuable commodity in a pirate city like Yendralia, which is why Erk insisted on staying informed.

Annaia let out a sigh. "Does this mean we've found a home? Like, for good?"

Naomi tilted her head, her silver gaze sparkling in the low light of Chummy's Slums. "What do you mean?"

Annaia released Naomi from the embrace, looking up at her. "Are we done running? From The Emissary. What if he finds us again? We would have to just run again—" she started, worry running rampant in her voice.

Naomi smiled and pressed a finger to Annaia's lips. "We're never running again. Falindeth won't take what we've built here, neither will The Emissary." She looked at the table where Erk was sitting with Evan, who was hunched over in a most uncomfortable contortion. "There are people willing to fight for us now. With us. We don't have to run."

Annaia's lips stretched thin with uncertainty. "But then, won't The Emissary just take them from us too?" she asked, a bit of heartbreak surfacing.

Naomi's eyes cut back to Annaia with grave seriousness. "That demon will never take another soul that I love. Even if I can't send it back to the Abyss myself, I'll find a priest who can."

Annaia's eyes widened, hearing the lethality in Naomi's voice. "Naomi," she whispered.

The earth giantkin nodded. "Falindeth knows where we are, and so does The Emissary. I'm certain of that. At this point, we live to our fullest and dare those bastards to threaten us." Her demeanor was always confident, but this was something new to Annaia. Naomi's sincerity and conviction now intermingled with her confidence, and there was no fear left in her. Annaia's own courage began to swell. Naomi finished, "And when they show up?"

Annaia grinned. "We'll put an end to their reign of terror."

Naomi wrapped her arm around Annaia's shoulder and walked her through the restaurant. The numerous, celebratory remarks and invitations faded to the back of their minds. Naomi was so proud of Annaia, and she didn't want her to be afraid anymore. They greeted and visited with everyone, making a casual pass through the party for courtesy's sake. The birthday girl was the excuse for the gathering, but everyone showed up for their own reasons. After fulfilling their responsibility to greet the guests, Naomi led Annaia to a table that had been specially prepared for the birthday dinner.

Erk and his brother were already seated, and Dread Pirate Lady Lascha was standing beside the table. She was an elf dressed in black robes with flowing, black hair that glinted a dark shade of blue in the right lighting. She was one of Naomi's closest allies among the pirates of Yendralia, and she was well learned in the ways of magic beyond the arcane stream. "Happy birthday, creature," the elf said, her voice cool and slow.

Annaia smiled, approaching Lascha and leaning over to exchange kisses on the cheek. "Thank you, Dread Pirate Lady Lascha," she replied.

The table was round, and Naomi, Lascha, and Annaia sat with Annaia's closest friends from Naomi's crew: Rose, a descendent of the Drakinskäld, and Hephaestia, a young orc with a penchant for setting things on fire. Lascha, Naomi, and Annaia joined everyone else and began to exchange pleasantries. The birthday celebration lasted for hours, and Erk's chef served a fantastic meal. Naomi and Annaia left one hour before midnight to return to *The Violet Blur*. Naomi insisted she had a present to give Annaia as well.

In the captain's quarters on the caravel, Naomi offered Annaia a heavy object covered in an ornate but tattered cloth. Annaia removed the fabric, finding a splendidly crafted pistol shimmering with magic. "Naomi!" she exclaimed, recognizing it as a legendary firearm.

The giantkin smiled, her silver eyes narrow. Annaia had no reason to be afraid. She was one of the best sailors in the Solar Sea, and she fought alongside Naomi hundreds of times. She was a great shot with poor quality pistols, so Naomi hunted for this famed pistol just for Annaia. "It has a name," Naomi explained.

Annaia held the pistol in her hand, feeling its weight. It was definitely well-crafted, so she asked, "What is it called?"

Naomi's smile turned bittersweet. "The Alexander," she explained.

Annaia's eyes widened. "You named it after father? It's a gun, not a ship." She spoke with a teasing, surprised tone.

Naomi shrugged. "The gunsmith that created it over a century ago gave it the name, darling. I just knew it was the perfect piece for you. I promised your father I would protect you, and with this on your hip, he's there with you in spirit."

Annaia slid it into an empty holster on her belt and gave Naomi a new embrace. "Thank you for the party, mom."

Naomi laughed, "Okay, that's twice in one day. Don't call me mom so much, it makes me feel old!" she protested.

Annaia closed her eyes, squeezing the giantkin again. "Okay, mom," she prodded, emphasizing the 'mom' with the deepest voice she could muster.

Naomi stared at the windows of her captain's quarters. "There's no need to be afraid anymore. When The Emissary and Falindeth come back into our lives, we'll have what we need to defeat them."

Annaia remained silent, their embrace lasting another half hour. It was the best birthday Annaia had ever had.

Chapter 17
Falindeth

"The Death Scythes do not stray far from Cassack, for there they possess a mysterious power. Their days of piracy ended shortly after The Unbinding, and their machinations have grown quieter." – Historian Oddawl, *Magical Calamities: Unbinding Edition*

aomi, Erk, and Evan peered down a fifteen-foot hallway. It was lit by eerie, teal runes etched into the metal walls of the ship. The corridor was narrow and low, forcing Naomi to duck a bit as they entered. At the end of that hallway were two doors, one on the left and right. Both led into a stairwell that curved around the towering structure above. Taking the path on the right, the three of them followed more glowing runes, ascending twenty feet up as they circled the tower. Massive glass panels lined the outside wall, providing an eerie overlook of the ship. They arrived at a set of double, glass doors. Through them, they could see a room full of mysterious fog.

"An Abyssal Cloud," Erk lamented. "There's no way we'll be able to use our uncanny magic in there. It's dense."

Naomi's face twisted with anger. "I feel a familiar, evil presence," she added, her voice betraying her anxiety over the situation. "Falindeth is here, but he is not alone."

Evan looked at the ground with frustration. "You two seem to know a lot more about what's going on than I do. What in the Infernia is an Abyssal Cloud?" he asked, his concern growing as he let his hand rest on the hilt of his father's sword.

Erk nodded slowly. "While you were cursed, I consulted with every healer and former wizard I could find. I learned much about the flow of the arcane during that time. An Abyssal Cloud is a pocket of stale demonic energy. It will bond to any discharge of mana, making it heavier. Metaphorically, of course." His voice trembled a bit as he continued. "Falindeth was a famous Death Pirate, a Scythe of Hoxark," he explained, indicating that the Death Pirate was a high-ranking member of the worshippers of the Lord of the Abyss. "He hasn't really been heard from since Naomi stole Blur from him. Do you remember the dispelling light spell from so many years ago?"

Evan nodded. "Of course, it was a required spell for the academies." His eyes narrowed with thought. "What does that have to do with the Abyssal Cloud?"

Erk peered through the glass doors, hoping to catch a hint as to the contents of the room. "The Abyssal Cloud is a similar magical phenomenon, but it's inert until it bonds with magic being used in the primary dimension. It converts mana to demonic energy. It's rather fascinating, but it will hamper our ability to fight with uncanny magic. Any magic will fuel the demon's most devastating powers." As he finished speaking, he approached the glass doors. He turned to his beloved and his brother. "It will dull the fires of my supernova, and it will make telekinetic movement feel much heavier. If we overcome the cloud, though, we can unleash our powers against the enemy."

Naomi gulped. She remembered the day she stole Blur from Falindeth clearly. It was only a year after she had escaped her fate as a slave, and she found herself hunted by a cambion known as Nomolos. The Church of Invictus in Alabaster worked with Naomi to isolate the demonkin. Falindeth was the one that sailed with Nomolos from Alabaster to the Waypoint Lighthouse off the western coast of the Alabaster Kingdom. There, Naomi waited as part of the ambush to destroy Nomolos and Falindeth. She shuddered as she walked through those memories, the vision of a huge, centipede-like demon materializing in her mind. "Erilkaiden," she whispered, feeling dizzy. "Elrune."

Erk's gaze softened, recognizing the distress Naomi was experiencing. "Darling?" he asked, stepping away from the door. He stood in front of Naomi, who was now looking at the ground. He did not touch her, realizing her psyche was in a sensitive place. "Are you alright?" he asked, gentleness in his tone.

Naomi let out a deep sigh, her timidness uncharacteristic.

Nomolos hunted her because she freed an ancient, powerful demon from the Legion of Hoxark. She opened its millennia-old prison under the Mammoth Moors. That demon, called The Emissary of Hoxark, wanted to use Naomi as a sacrifice in a ritual to open a gate to the Abyss. In her flight to escape Nomolos, she ended up in Yendralia with Annaia. Though she had made a great life for herself and the girl who had been with her for the last thirty years, she still froze with fear at the mention of The Emissary. She shook her head at Erk's question but then snapped her eyes at the door. "You were there with me. You saw Nomolos die with your own eyes. Both of you."

Evan gave Naomi a surprised glance. He had almost no memories from his cursed state, as Miranda's healing power erased both the physical and emotional pain he endured as a desiccated husk. He replied, "I'm afraid my accounting of events would be unreliable at best."

Erk, however, nodded affirmingly. "Blur has insisted that Falindeth would look for her. It seems that time has come. At least the worst of the pair has already been slain," he tried to comfort her.

Naomi shook her head. "I've been in the presence of such evil before, too many times. The worst of the pair was neither Nomolos nor Falindeth."

Erk's stomach dropped. "No," he cursed. "The Emissary died with Nomolos, did it not?"

Naomi continued to shake her head. "It seems that it did not. An ancient demon from the Legion of Hoxark waits in that cloud. I can feel its malice from here," she explained. "A demon from the past, indeed, honeycomb." Her expression shifted from fear to excited anger. Her rich, deep voice regained its confidence and poise. "The last mistake it will make is finding me."

Erk's eyes narrowed as his lips twisted up into an evil smile. His years as a dread pirate had given him a lust for battle, and he felt excited about facing The Emissary again. "Why don't we put it to rest then?" he prompted, reaching up to take her hands in his.

Evan drew his father's sword and a clockwork dagger from his belt. "I don't have any uncanny magic to worry about."

Naomi grimaced. "Please, fight with caution. Nomolos prevented The Emissary from taking over his physical form. Falindeth is human. There is no way there is any humanity left in him. The ship flies Falindeth's colors, but we face The Emissary."

Erk turned, drawing his own magical sword. Flames began to

swirl around his arms. "I will try to burn through as much of the Abyssal Cloud as possible with my magic. Then, you two slay the demon before it regains its strength." He seemed confident in his plan.

Naomi hesitated. "We should probably bring everyone. We will need His Holiness's prayers."

A sweet, musical, but tired voice called up from the metal stairwell behind them. "Will my prayers help?" Miranda asked as she and Yuvina came into view. After learning of Shalo's fate and tending to the injured, Yuvina warned Miranda that Erk, Naomi, and Evan had entered the mysterious tower on the enemy ship.

Evan's eyes widened, "Miranda, your hair! You're almost completely out of mana!" he exclaimed, noticing that the red tint was almost gone.

She nodded in return. "But I can still pray." She walked toward them with a confident step. Yuvina stayed a pace behind her, looking into the room behind the glass doors. Though Miranda felt physically exhausted, her determination fueled her unwillingness to bow out of the fight. Covered in the protection of divine sanctuary, she could support her allies with the power of Invictus. Not even an eldritch demon would be able to pierce the protection of the ancient prayer. "Besides, that looks dangerous," she said pointing inside the room.

Erk narrowed his eyes, but he understood the nature of divine sanctuary. "Miranda," he began.

She shook her head. "You wouldn't let me help in Mystalon, and August and Evan almost died. I'm not going to leave any of you alone, ever again!" she protested. "I know my powers are limited, but I won't lose another friend," she started, stopping just as the song in her voice broke. Shalo's death was still at the front of her mind, but she was not in any position to process that right now. "Besides, I have been practicing the banishing prayer."

Evan tilted his head forward with curiosity. "Banishing prayer?" he asked.

Miranda gave a weak smile. Naomi's lips opened with an expression of hope. The priestess continued, "A prayer that will send an otherworldly creature like a demon home. And you are correct; The Emissary would need to be banished."

Erk took a deep breath. "That prayer would be advanced even for Thomas. Are you sure you want to try it? Banishing an entity is a hostile movement. It will destroy your sanctuary."

Miranda's blue eyes narrowed with malice. "Then make sure

you've weakened it enough that I can do what needs to be done when the time comes." She drew Iria's sword out of the scabbard on her belt and offered it to Erk, who took it in his left hand with a smile. He was now wielding two magical longswords, a cumbersome but deadly combination.

"No matter what I try, I don't seem to be able to get far away from my sister's sword, do I?" Erk lamented. He swore he heard his sister's laugh while he examined the blade. Naomi inhaled in preparation, and Evan's eyes were closed as he offered lay prayers for his companions. Yuvina's whiskers trembled with anticipation. Erk looked at his allies with confidence. "Then pray, Miranda. May the Sword of Justice and the Silver Maiden shield us from the horrors within."

Miranda clutched her holy symbol and closed her eyes. "Sword of Justice, may your enervating hand sweep the enemy before us, and may your infinite grace shield us from unyielding evil." Erk recognized Enervating Shield as an advanced prayer; he gained confidence in Miranda's ability to banish a demon as everyone's body glowed with a reddish-golden aura. Since it was not fueled by mana, the Abyssal Cloud would not dampen the powerful prayer. Miranda opened her eyes and gave a nod toward the doors. Evan approached it first, and Erk joined his brother at the glass entrance.

Yuvina jumped ahead of Miranda, standing beside Naomi as the giantkin moved toward the doors gingerly. "Open it," the giantkin commanded.

The Lancethinas brothers complied, pulling the doors hard. They popped open with the sound of a vacuum releasing. The Abyssal Cloud rushed into the stairwell, coating everyone but Evan with a fine, dusty mist. Miranda recognized the particles bonding with the mana inside her. The Abyssal Cloud was the same state of stale magic she felt at Argentum. Furthermore, it reminded her of the miasma left behind by fallen Umbrals. Instead of growing heavier, however, her connection to the arcane stream reinvigorated the stale magic. Her mana supply began to recharge with incredible speed, and she felt her physical strength returning. "Oh, by Invictus, what is happening?" she cried out in a timid voice, the song comforting. Her hair was already the deep red everyone preferred to see.

Erk's grin widened. "You really are marvelous, Miranda. I believe in you." He then turned and charged into the cloud, activating his uncanny magic with no restraint. Immediately, the stagnant particles bonded with the heat from his spell, neutralizing its effects.

However, it began to disintegrate the cloud with flashes of blue light.

Evan was right behind his brother, using his well-honed fighting instincts to search for the enemy's presence. A tingle ran down his spine, and he swung his father's sword in an arc in front of him. The tip of a massive arthropodan leg became visible in the same instant, and Evan severed it from its source. "The centipede form!" he called out, remembering the demon's description from Naomi's stories since he had been healed.

Yuvina slipped inside the room, unable to see well in the Abyssal Cloud. In the gaseous arcane underflow, she could not feel her uncanny magic at all. It was a momentary relief, and she felt her life essence aching from all she had lost over the last few days. She drew her daggers, content to fight as she had learned: without magic. She then skipped across the room, using her enhanced hearing and sense of smell to locate the enemy. It smelled like rot and evil, putrid and acrid. Then, the barrage of legs came, several clusters aimed at each of her companions.

A fiery burst erupted as the sudden onslaught connected with the fighters. The Enervating Shield activated, shattering the evil form of The Emissary's massive, arthropodan legs with righteous fury. Each one was a foot around, and the ends were lethally sharp. There were over ten legs in each extended pod, causing at least one hundred legs to burn under the weight of Invictus's protection. Enervating Shield was useful in every case, but it was especially potent against evil creatures outside of their home dimensions. The Emissary shouted in agony, a human-like voice. "Naomi! It looks like you've found some powerful allies." A cackle followed as the Abyssal Cloud swirled, regenerating the demon's limbs with the demonic energy converted from Erk's magical discharge. The cloud thinned, and the teal light in the room allowed Miranda and the others to get a look around.

It was a large, circular area seventy feet in diameter. The ceiling went up another twenty-five feet, and, in the teal light reflecting through the Abyssal Cloud, they could see the figure of a massive centipede raised up in the center of the room. Its bug-like head was pressed against the ceiling. Close to the glass overlooking the deck, they saw several clusters of levers and buttons. Miranda felt her heart swirl with wonder, but she had to focus on the fight. She could play with the buttons and levers later; she needed to know what they all did.

Naomi shouted back, "And it looks like you've made a deal with your god. You will not win, Falindeth! Your return to the Abyss is near, Emissary of Hoxark!" She charged forward, swiftly hurling daggers at the shadowy form in the center of the room. They chipped at the dense carapace of the demon.

Evan used the new visual information to reformulate his strategy. Using his sharpened agility and reflexes, he began running at an angle that would allow him to flank the creature on the left. Though it had no problem attacking in every direction, splitting its focus would give each of them a better chance of survival. The next wave of attacks from the legs came as he closed in, and he nimbly ducked, rolled, and parried his way through a series of massive stabs. His swiftness caused the demon to shriek in frustration, and more pods of legs struck at him.

Miranda's heart skipped a beat. "Shield us from the onslaught of chaos, Sword of Justice. May your hand stay the enemy!" she prayed. As she did, a shimmering wall formed between Evan and The Emissary. The arthropodan legs connected with it, shattering the barrier and breaking some of themselves in the process. Fortunately, it neutralized enough attacks that Evan's Enervating Shield would be able to protect him; it activated for the second time, burning a couple of leg pods.

The demon let out a terrifying, hissing sound. As it did, it exhaled a burst of underflow particles. Erk shouted as he increased the mana flowing into his uncanny magic, causing a swirling orb of the cloud to thin around him. Miranda knew it had to be painful, so she channeled some healing energy in his direction. As she did, she infused it with a burst of arcane healing as she had done on the deck of *The Nebula* earlier.

In that moment, she felt the Abyssal Cloud surge into her to replace the expended mana. Unfortunately, the arcane healing she sent out was weakened, but it dissipated the cloud at an incredible rate.

Erk felt the warmth of Invictus's healing cover his body. The pain from activating Black Hole at full strength in an Abyssal Cloud was possibly the most agonizing sensation he had ever experienced. Inhaling an acidic cloud paled in comparison, he thought. "Thanks, Miranda!" he called out, still leaving his uncanny magic active enough to continue thinning the underflow.

Naomi closed the gap between herself and The Emissary, and Evan approached from her left. Yuvina took a wide circle around the room, forming a triangle around the demon. Their synergy divided its focus enough that they gained the upper hand. In response, its legs wiggled and retracted to serve as armor, a tactic with immediate results. As the trio attacked, they realized they were not damaging it, even with their magical weapons. Then, a gurgling sound erupted from the demon's horned centipede head. A viscous blast of sticky liquid burst from The Emissary's mandibles.

Miranda heard the sickening sound and realized Enervating Shield would not protect them from an attack of that type. "Invictus, our rock of righteousness. We strike thee in the desert when we thirst! Send your purifying rain!"

As the deadly shower splattered on Miranda's allies, the healing rain Miranda conjured purified them with a soothing shower. Instead of dissolving them, the acidic goo washed off and fizzled on the floor, corroding it. The Emissary then jutted out his numerous legs in a spinning attack, using the barbs on the arthropodan joints as a sharp, spinning tornado. All three of their Enervating Shields activated, blasting the leg pods into oblivion. Demons were truly weak against the strength of the gods of good and righteousness. Miranda smiled with excitement until the demon hissed again. It absorbed the converted underflow and regenerated anew. It expelled a new mass of dense, magically inhibiting fog from its mouth.

Miranda felt her desperation increasing. With the power to replenish the Abyssal Cloud, the demon would have an unlimited source of healing. That was, unless she could figure out a way to neutralize the underflow as he spit it out. She decided to try something different. As the three fighters within melee range of the eldritch demon tried to engage with the regenerating creature, she rushed forward as well. She focused on the mana within her; she could absorb the stale magic without healing the demon. She needed to discharge ether to absorb the underflow, however, so she decided to try a variation of Erk's uncanny magic. She focused on the essence of good deities. Her pure heart allowed her to shape the mana into holy elemental energy. As she did, the sanctuary around her shattered, brilliant green and white light creating additional strikes of lightning infused with the power of righteousness. As they struck the demon, Miranda's "Holynova" burst, which caused her to use a massive amount of mana. As she did, the Abyssal Cloud poured into the newly created void in her magical essence. Doing so reinvigorated the stale ether, allowing her sustained focus on the Holynova to then burn the demon's legs. The cycle caused Miranda to use nearly the entire cloud within only a few moments.

Using ether at such an enhanced rate, however, also caused her to quickly burn through her magic once the Abyssal Cloud was exhausted. After the inhibiting properties of the atmosphere were eliminated, her Holynova ran out of fuel. She went from rich ruby to a light shade of coral in an instant. She fell to her knees, the skirt of her battlemail rattling loudly on the metal floor of the room. Something felt wrong in her soul, like a sharp pain piercing a single, unidentified point in her existence. It came from everywhere and nowhere, but it did not incapacitate her.

The powerful attack, however, severely damaged the demon again. The Emissary shrieked in a voice that pierced the mind. "Foolish priestess! Though I lack Fuerzul, I am not helpless! I can change arcane underflow to raw power! You should have hidden behind your sanctuary longer! Now die!"

Miranda looked up and gave a devilish smile. As the sparse pods of legs connected with her, her own Enervating Shield activated. It destroyed many of the demon's remaining natural weapons. Erk was at Miranda's side a moment later, the arthropodan appendages dissolving into black miasma now that the Abyssal Cloud was cleared. "Brilliant work, Miranda!" he complimented, intensifying the fires swirling around his arms. Within a second, he cast a powerful beam of light into the center mass of The Emissary. Evan, Naomi, and Yuvina now assailed the core of the demon's body as well, causing it to lose mass to miasma.

"Noooo!" The Emissary cursed. It sprayed a new stream of arcane underflow, but the magical vacuum created by Miranda's depleted state absorbed it greedily. In response, Hoxark's chosen accelerated the output, causing an instability in the arcane stream. Miranda felt the universe around them shaking. She tried to right the flow by expending the mana, teetering on the brink of a magical coma. It vibrated that sharp pain from before and caused it to spread through her consciousness. Her life essence was scattering into the stream. Generating a new Holynova, however, made sure that every bit of Abyssal Cloud was recycled and purified.

The exertion, however, finally overcame Miranda. The world around her went dark, but her consciousness continued. After a moment, she could see the world through a blue tint, an indication she had been pushed into the arcane stream. Her friends were now destroying an almost defenseless eldritch demon. She found it further interesting that the demon somehow stored arcane underflow within its essence, like a pocket of stale magic concentrated in the bowels of a demon. The growing prevalence of arcane underflow bothered her to the core, but she could not explain why. The continual Abyssal Cloud discharging from The Emissary was concerning, but her last Holynova had done significant damage. The demon hesitated to expel more underflow.

Still, her consciousness found itself in the arcane stream. "How?" she called out into the ether.

A severe but loving voice replied, "You can thank your father for the idea. As you became more reckless out there, he began to draw in your core essence."

Philotrax laughed. It sounded like their voices were coming from everywhere. "Well, thank your mother, too. She collected more than half of your particles. You're both overachievers, and I love it."

Miranda felt her essence blink. "Uh, Mom? Dad?"

Reshiria's presence pressed against Miranda's. "Of course, darling. We've been here ever since you came into the stream before."

The mana body she formed previously was easy enough to reshape. She looked through the lens of the arcane stream, watching the demon begin to regenerate, albeit more slowly. "What do you mean? I don't have much time; I need to rejoin my friends!"

Philotrax also pressed his essence into Miranda. "Then go! But before you do, you need to know something. We have been watching you for months, and we know everything that's happening. Listen. Dragons can bond to other dragons. It is how Ezelbrecht was the face of Gorthran. While we are within you, we are within the stream. Dragon souls are vital to its health, but we also draw our power from it."

Miranda froze, realizing that she was interacting with her parents as casually as she would if she had known them for all her twenty-one years. "By Invictus, Mom! Dad!" She pressed her essence back against them in a magical embrace.

Reshiria gave a soft, caring sigh. "Oh, Mir'thax. We are sorry that we did not understand the last time you were here. As you were pulled away from us, we realized we were trapped outside the stream."

Miranda felt tears of relief swelling in her mana body. The fight was turning bad for her friends very quickly now that The Emissary realized Miranda was out of commission. A new Abyssal Cloud fumed from its mouth.

Philotrax added hurriedly, "We attached our souls to you,

Miranda. We are here for you, our memories, our power."

Miranda sensed Reshiria's affirming nod. She asked her parents, "Power? What do you mean? Fire and lightning?"

They both laughed with adoration for their daughter. Philotrax spoke, "If that's what you will it to be, precious Mir'thax Toi'landra. I mean the power of our souls."

Reshiria explained, "We are twice as much as the capacity that Gelidor stole from you, darling. You've only had to open your soul to ours!" she invited.

"How do I do that?" Miranda cried in response. "By Invictus, I love you both! So much! My soul has always been open to you!"

"Indeed, and we helped you pray against Aylabrax," Philotrax replied. "It felt strange to call out to a deity other than the Dragon Mother."

Miranda's essence filled with confidence, remembering her strength facing the dark goddess. "Is that different than your draconic powers?" she asked, a childlike innocence in her voice in spite of the calamity unfolding in the primary dimension.

Reshiria's voice answered, "It is, my beloved daughter. Though my nature is dark, my soul reached out for Invictus's strength alongside yours. I must warn you, Mir'thax. Demons are fueled by a power known as Fuerzul. This demon possesses none; he is extremely vulnerable. The runes in this room anchor the astral tunnels here. The difficulty you face while teleporting recently is likely connected. If these runes are powered by some kind of crystallized magic, the demon could siphon energy out of the astral tunnels."

Miranda glared and spat, "No wonder he's using an Abyssal Cloud, then. I have to stop this monster and protect my friends. I would gladly accept your help! Mom! Dad! I love you both! Please!" she asked.

Philotrax laughed before he replied. "The fact that you ask so kindly makes me proud to call you my daughter. Just focus on the arcane energies within us."

Reshiria added, "Unleash the strength of our souls and our combined draconic might. We, too, hold reserves of magic. Look for us when you feel your strength running out."

Their essences pressed against her again, and this time she felt them bond together. It eased that earlier pain in her existence. All of the strange occurrences over recent months were easily explained by the presence of her mother and father within her own essence.

Miranda, however, did not know their souls were bonded. She opened her focus to the godshards of her parents. With the love of a child, her soul called out to Philotrax and Reshiria. As she did, her consciousness fused back into her body, still kneeling nearby.

Miranda returned to the fight, her hair soaking with the mana reserves unleashed by her parents' godshards. It turned a deep, purple hue. She was overflowing with power to the point that her body glowed with a brilliant, indigo aura. She immediately funneled the mana through her to create a new Holynova, and, this time, the power was overwhelming. Thanks to her increased maximum capacity, she could fuel the magic behind the spell for much longer after absorbing the entirety of the demon's underflow.

Evan, Naomi, and Yuvina continued to assault the core of the demon, weakening it. Erk's radiant light diffused large swathes of the demon into black miasma. Because of their good hearts, the purifying fires of Miranda's attack did not harm them at all.

"You cannot destroy me! I am The Emissary of Hoxark! I only bring news of his return! You fools do not see the coming era of darkness!" The eldritch demon shouted as it scattered underflow particles throughout the room.

Miranda stomped her foot and shouted, "I don't think so!" She reached up and grabbed her holy symbol as she fueled more mana through herself. Between her still-burning orb of holy flame and Erk's intensifying ray of light, the Abyssal Cloud was burned up immediately. The new reserves of mana allowed Miranda to outlast The Emissary in a battle of wills. This time the complete form of the demon shattered into miasma, and Miranda prayed. "Sword of Justice, an agent of chaos has crossed the barriers between space and time to wreak havoc on the mortal coil. We beseech thee, open the void between worlds and cast this fiend back into the bowels of the universe. May orc and fae know peace, may the people rejoice as your hand descends to right what has been wronged by this aberrant presence!"

The three close to the demon scrambled backwards as a brilliant, red circle opened up underneath the scattering miasma. A vortex of wind filled the room, drawing in the smoky essence of The Emissary as it tried to disperse. The red circle manifested a physical gate underneath the wisps that now constituted the demon. The portal was a ring wrapped in tendrils with protruding, pointed bones. A mouth of flesh and death rose from the ground, and it began to inhale the miasma. The smoky cloud tried to form a new centipede body, but the energy of the banishing prayer was pulling at its very presence in the primary dimension.

"Lord of the Abyss, save me! Anchor me to this reality!" he shouted, trying to leave any fragment of himself behind. His arthropodan body began to form anew.

Miranda shook her head, giving another burst of Holynova. It disintegrated the new, much smaller avatar of The Emissary. The banishing prayer consumed the rest of the demon. As it did, the visceral form of the gate sank into the floor. It shrank rather slowly, the miasma of The Emissary swirling through the center. The demon gave a painful shout as the last of its essence was forced out of the primary dimension. The banishing gate winked out of existence as the last of The Emissary was pulled into the Abyss. The room sat quiet for a moment; nobody moved.

Naomi finally walked to where the gate was. "Is it over?" she asked, tapping the ground with her foot. The room was now well-lit by the teal runes framing the glass and metal shell of the tower.

Erk smiled as he replied, "I believe it is. Thanks to our miracle dragon." He stood slightly behind Miranda, reaching out to take her hand in his. Naomi ran the fifteen feet between them and embraced the priestess, who stood motionless, the purple hue in her hair softening back to its normal, red tones.

Evan and Yuvina beamed with pride for their friend. Evan called out, "Look at that. It's like she's more powerful than ever!"

Miranda began to cry. She sat down on the floor and crossed her legs. She pressed her face into her hands.

"Are you hurt?" Erk asked with concern.

Naomi joined her on the floor, sitting the same way as Miranda. The pirate lady speculated, "These injuries aren't physical. Perhaps it's something spiritual, like a Wailing Despair curse." Such a foul magic would slay the victim through unconquerable sorrow.

Miranda started to laugh as she cried. "I'm sad that Shalo died, but I'm so relieved. My parents really do live on in me. They're here. My mom and dad are right here with me!" She sobbed a bit but giggled.

Evan blinked, but his lips broke into a joyous smile. "Miranda," he murmured, feeling his heart race. She was willing to push herself to the limit, and he admired that. It also filled him with fear as his feelings toward her continued to grow. Her bravery and stubbornness made his heart skip beats.

Yuvina yipped a bit with excitement. "We did it! We took down a super evil demon!" She jumped toward Miranda, Naomi, and Erk, and slid next to Miranda on the floor. "I'm so proud to be your friend." She took one of Miranda's hands in her paw. As they touched, particles of ether visibly poured out. Yuvina realized the magical reaction between them depended on her own internal feelings. The first time Miranda touched her, Yuvina was afraid. Now that she wanted to comfort the priestess, the magic no longer backfired. "I'm so sorry about your friend," she added, understanding that Miranda's elation was tempered by sadness.

Erk looked to the ground. "I'm responsible for his death. I'm the one who sent him down the path that led him to kill Justin. After everything," he started, everyone looking at him intently. "After everything that happened when you were part of our crew, Miranda. You changed him. He wanted nothing more than to make up for the wrongs he did as a pirate."

Miranda's lips trembled with grief. Erk was not wrong; he was indeed the one who sent Shalo to kidnap her. Before she could reply, the pirate lord continued, "None of us would have estimated the lightning would be so powerful. Shalo's quick thinking saved all of us. You'd all be right to blame me. I know that I blame myself."

"Nonsense," a strong voice called back from the stairwell. It was High Priest Selasine. "Shalo's quick thinking saved all of us, and Invictus has acknowledged his sacrifice." Everyone that fought against The Emissary turned to see Thomas, Celyth, Arlindra, and Nebu at the glass doors.

Erk smiled. "Nulestotejin!"

Selasine cocked his head to the side. "It looks like we're a little late to the fight."

Miranda stood, and Naomi and Yuvina sprung up quickly. They helped the priestess to her feet. She looked at her adoptive father, "Modai-rin! You speak of Invictus's judgement on Shalo's soul?"

He nodded in reply. "His soul is to rest among the Heroes Departed. He is the first dread pirate to ever be given such an honor."

Erk grinned, and Evan breathed a sigh of relief. More tears dripped from Miranda's eyes. "Then he knows. He has made me proud. And he died, favored by the gods of goodness and righteousness."

Naomi looked toward the levers and buttons in the front of the room. She thought a change of subject might help to encourage the priestess. "Miranda, do you want to help me figure out how to drive this ship?"

Miranda blinked for a moment then smiled through her tears. "Of course!"

Evan laughed and bounded over to one of the panels built into a metal counter that seemed to be constructed from the same metal as the floor. "Ok, I get the urge to just push buttons, but maybe we should unboard The Neb and The Blur. Savvy?"

Erk nodded. "Brother is right. I'll get us separated, but we need to meet to discuss our next steps."

Naomi's eyes widened. "By the gods, can anyone reach Damil?"

Thomas looked around and raised his fingers to his temples. "Beloved, can you hear me?" he thought. Nothing returned. Thanks to the intensity of the battle, Selasine had not realized Damil's contact had been broken. "Nothing," he lamented.

Naomi's face drew up in anger. "I thought I heard him say 'Umbrals in Nulodia' right as the boarding began."

Selasine scowled. "We definitely have much to discuss, then. We'll decide what to do overnight. Can we weigh anchor here?"

Erk nodded. "We can. The coast is only a few miles away. Our crews need a rest anyway. We can interrogate the surviving Death Pirates before we make any decisions."

Miranda walked over to Evan and took his hands in hers. "Thanks." Then she looked to Erk and ran over to him. She tackled him with a hug. "Thank you, too. For believing in me."

The pirate laughed, and everyone else followed. Miranda inspired them, and she continued to surprise them at every turn. Her parents' power helped turn the tide of that battle, and everyone present understood the implications. Miranda had learned so much over the last six months, but now she possessed the arcane capacity to realize her wishes. Though Miranda was elated to be reconnected with her parents in a conscious, communicative way, she felt the draconic blood within her surge. Her official name was Mir'thax Toi'landra, but everyone she loved knew her by Miranda. A second person within her was waking up, reminiscent of the whispers she once heard when activating her gift. She sighed. Though the pain in her soul bothered her, she wasn't sure how to explain it to anyone else. This news would only concern Selasine, she worried. She hoped she could sort out the feelings on her own.

Farzg and Elyndandria stood in the central plaza of Nulodia between the Peacekeeper Precinct and the grand cathedral of Invictus. The soul prism Elyndandria demanded was located in a highly secure evidence room in the Peacekeeper Precinct. The elven assassin and the frost giantkin had their cloaks drawn, obscuring their faces as they watched the law enforcement headquarters with great interest. It had been a day since the two of them broke into a different evidence warehouse and used Doctor One's lacrima-deum diffuser to dispense chunks of scattered, crystalized magic. The resulting plague of Umbrals would soon commence, creating a crisis to allow them to retrieve the soul prism from the evidence locker.

Farzg let out a deep, discontented sigh. "Elyndandria," he said in his gravelly, slow voice.

"What?" she replied, curt.

She saw him shake his head beneath his cloak. "Do you want to know the reason the Church of the Sword of Justice pursues me so relentlessly?"

Her teal eyes flashed in the light of a streetlamp powered by a large, everburning candle. "Of course. The more of your secrets I learn, the more I see that I am a fool for getting mixed up with you. Please, tell me how you pissed off these people so much." Her voice was angry and impatient.

Farzg's smile chilled the already cold, winter air. "Simple. I rejected their hypocrisy and began to forge my own destiny without the aid of a god. After spurning the Sword, I found his agents on my heels at every turn. Their rigid laws and silly protocols fail in the moments of direst need." He spoke in a relieved, calm manner, something to which Elyndandria was unaccustomed. "I merely wished to prove their laws are meaningless without the brute force to enforce them. I've given them many opportunities to demonstrate their hypocrisy."

The assassin narrowed her eyes. "Are you trying to say that you used to be affiliated with these slimy peacekeepers?"

Farzg only nodded and let the air remain cold and silent around them.

After another hour of quiet, peacekeepers and their commanding officers poured out of the Peacekeeper Precinct. Farzg chuckled. His condescension was colder than his magic as he spoke, "So predictable. There's a crisis, let's run in, swords brandished. For a church of law and order, they seem swift to execute judgment with violence."

Elyndandria twisted her lips into a smirk. "You're the one who just unleashed a plague of shadow creatures on their city. Not to downplay my role in this incident, but you were the mastermind. If you hadn't allied yourself with Doctor One," she began, but the frost giantkin interrupted her.

"Then maybe your husband's soul prism would be in Cassack by now," he agreed, the sarcasm light and almost playful.

Elyndandria's eyes narrowed further, the teal irises within thin and particularly savage. "You're showing an awful lot of humility tonight, Farzg, and I don't like it. What's with you?" Her breath puffed in dense clouds thanks to the freezing air. The sounds of peacekeepers on a mission filled the city around them.

He exhaled. No condensation emerged from his lips. "For the first time in my one hundred and seventy-four years, I feel like I might have played The Executioner poorly," he explained.

The assassin pulled her cloak tighter over her face as a small unit of peacekeepers passed them in the plaza. Farzg made no additional effort to hide his obvious, well-known identity, and he was confident the simple-minded religious fanatics would only have a singular mission. As they rushed by, the frost giantkin laughed. "We could be venom hydras salivating deadly acid right in front of them, and they wouldn't even notice. Not if you give them ghosts to chase," he said, his voice amused and disgusted.

Elyndandria scowled, returning her eyes to the Peacekeeper Precinct. "Now?" she asked.

Farzg nodded and walked toward the headquarters. They walked up a small set of steps bringing them level with the city streets. A line of evergreen trees framed the perimeter of the plaza. The paths stretching through that central area were numerous, winding up and down the rolling terrain of the Nulodian coast. The entrance of the Peacekeeper Precinct awaited one thousand feet ahead. Farzg licked his dry, frozen lips. "Are you ready?" he asked.

Elyndandria nodded and withdrew a pair of daggers created by Doctor Two and provided to her by Farzg. He had no use for them, detesting the use of violent instruments. Instead of normal, metal blades, a lacrima-deum had been fashioned into a thick, jagged crystal. They were fixed into an eolnut extractor designed to give the weapons longer lifespans than the weapons powered by lacrima-deum fragments. These daggers were much more deadly and efficient than even Elyndandria's wands.

They walked toward the front doors of the Peacekeeper Precinct, the majority of the night watch called to the streets as Umbrals began to emerge around the city. As they approached the doors, a middle-aged human burst from them. He was dressed in plate mail and seemed agitated. He ran right past Farzg and Elyndandria, shouting, "If your needs are not urgent, please withdraw to your homes!"

Farzg smiled, never looking back. As he reached for the Peacekeeper Precinct's front doors, Elyndandria hissed. "Eldon."

The frost giantkin tilted his head to the right as his hand rested on the handle of the front doors. "Captain Starnes, was it?"

The paladin who passed them a moment ago stopped and turned his full attention to the strangers approaching the building in the middle of a crisis. He responded, "Yes, that's correct. Who are you? Do you have a pressing need the church should address?" He had a short salt and pepper beard, and his black hair was covered by a helmet.

Farzg let out a deep sigh. "I'm afraid it's too late for you now."

As he spoke, the paladin recognized the powerful, evil aura radiating from Farzg's presence. "By Invictus, no," the captain protested. He drew his sword, but before he could react further, a small splash of Death Geyser had impaled him. Elyndandria shivered as the temperature in the air jumped from livable to lethally cold in only an instant. Before she could complain, the air was back to freezing instead of deadly.

"What in the Infernia?" she scathed.

Farzg sighed. "One violent act now, ten less in the future."

Elyndandria rolled her eyes. "For a person who trades in violence, you sure seem to be on some kind of moral crusade."

Captain Starnes's body collapsed to the ground as the Death Geyser melted. Farzg stared down at the elven assassin, easily twice her height. "Ely, you should know by now that it's not the violence that bothers me. It's just beneath me. If I am the one killing, then my enterprise has failed."

She scoffed. "You really are an arrogant ass. I can see that you're not afraid to get your hands dirty, but I'm not sure you even appreciate your own power."

Farzg sighed again, this time a slight hint of vapor escaping his lips. "My arrogance and pride are founded in my merit, Elyndandria. Come. The evidence room is this way," he ordered, forcing open the front door. The hallway to the evidence locker was immediately to their left, and Farzg manifested his Death Geyser in the form of a shield-like dome reminiscent of protection prayers. The obstacle gave him and Elyndandria coverage to make their way to the storage area. The assassin picked the simple lock on the first door. The remaining peacekeepers, acolytes, paladins, and clerics were far too inexperienced to defrost Farzg's barrier, giving the two plenty of time for the next phase of their plan.

They stopped in front of the correct door, discerned by the plate on the front with a series of letters and numbers followed by "Farzg, Eldon." The frost giantkin cracked his knuckles as he stretched and pressed his arms out to his sides. He crouched into a low fighting stance, and the air temperature dropped.

The assassin reached into a pouch on her belt and withdrew a ring. "You really are insane," she insisted.

Farzg grinned as the elf slipped the ring onto one of her fingers. It covered her in a fiery aura that shielded her from the worst effects of the frost giantkin's signature ability. "Behold, Elyndandria. I defy the will of a god!" he shouted as he concentrated all of his energy into the cold around them. He called upon his nature as a descendant of the frost giants to make the air impossibly cold. Then, as a blessing of The Unbinding, he used his uncanny magic. A simple, but for him, lethal spell: Create Water.

Even as a young person, he could not believe the way the universe had blessed him with a natural and uncanny gift. Thanks to the frost giant blood in his veins, he could lower the temperature in the air around him to far below freezing within moments. If the temperature was low enough, the water created by his uncanny magic would immediately cause frostbite so significant that not even the gods could heal it. He focused his natural gift on the metal door standing between them and the evidence they needed to recover.

"Your power really isn't that great if all it takes is a ring to resist the temperature drop," Elyndandria taunted as he channeled all the mana he could find into his uncanny magic. The water he conjured weathered the hinges and stonework holding the door in place. The damage was so sudden the door clanged into the evidence room before the assassin had finished her remark.

Farzg gave an evil smile, relaxing from his fighting stance. "You were saying?"

She blinked for several moments before she spotted the soul prism in the room. It glowed with a bright orange light in the dark, revealing it immediately. "Ah! There it is!" she cackled.

"That's what I thought," he added. He didn't want to enter the room; the ceiling was only seven feet high. He was far too dignified to bow in the presence of a false god who could not defend Captain Starnes. Farzg was sure the man had a family and a significant life here in the city if he had attained the rank of captain at the

Peacekeeper Precinct. If Invictus was who he claimed to be, then he would find a way to reunite Starnes with his family. Farzg had bigger things to attend to than worrying about the consequences of his choices. Starnes made a choice, too, the frost giantkin reminded himself.

Elyndandria took the soul prism in her hands; it was one foot wide and deep, but two feet high. It was a red, crystalline material reminiscent of colored quartz. "Daniel! Oh, Daniel!" she cooed, holding the crystal.

Farzg stood there for a moment, letting the elf savor the reunion. He smiled, thinking he had just accomplished something resembling friendship, but he quickly realized his error. Elyndandria withdrew a different clockwork dagger, and she shredded the soul prism with its chainlike blades. Farzg craned his head backward. "What in the Infernia?" he shouted. Geysers of flame erupted from the soul prism as she devastated it with her strange knife. The ring he loaned her also absorbed the elemental energy emanating from the magical fires protecting the soul prism.

As Elyndandria destroyed the lich's safe haven, she smiled at the frost giantkin. "There. Whatever he did to our daughter has been avenged."

Farzg frowned intensely. "I could've just killed him for you!" he shouted.

Elyndandria shook her head. "Nope. Had to be me. After learning the truth, did you think I was trying to find his soul prism to save him?" she taunted.

Farzg's evil smile returned. "Oh, now I understand." He tried to lick his lips, but they were so dry and frozen that he did not feel his tongue nor his lips. "Well. While we are here, please take that journal, snow globe, and wand," he commented, pointing inside the evidence locker. The sound of panicked clergy echoed throughout the Peacekeeper Precinct.

Elyndandria looked around, the fragments of Daniel's soul prism scattered at her feet. She gathered Farzg's requested items, but then asked as she handed them to him, "Why those things? Especially the terrible decoration," she commented, looking at the snow globe.

Farzg clicked open the toy, revealing a small key. "If you want your payment for providing the girl with the shard, then you better take this." He offered it to her.

She scowled at it. "The key to the portal chest?"

Farzg nodded. "The chest is hidden in the Eastpoint Lighthouse.

You'll find the additional artifacts I promised inside, along with a few more of One's trinkets. And a letter with my final will."

Elyndandria relaxed and perched a hand on her hip. "Have you given up Farzg? Are you going to die at the hands of these church people?"

The voices of more experienced clergy shouted outside the barrier built by Farzg's magic. They were getting ready to destroy it with the Holy Flames of Judgment. The frost giantkin shook his head. "If I die, then Miranda is a goddess among mortals. Provide her with the tools necessary so that I may reap revenge on Doctor One from the grave. My soul will certainly pass into the Abyss. And there I will become a demon lord rivaling Hoxark himself."

Elyndandria glared. "You're already plotting your afterlife. That tells me everything I need to know, Eldon."

The frost giantkin smiled as he used Death Geyser to destroy the exterior wall of the Peacekeeper Precinct hallway, and they used the hole as an escape. They walked away from the evidence room; the three-clergy prayer failed utterly in the face of Farzg's incredible power. "So be it, then, assassin. Realize, then, that if I die, the threat that will follow will also compromise your future. Align yourself with the holy ones when it fits your agenda."

They waited in a beautiful gazebo in the plaza until a white scaled dragon slammed into a field across from the structure. Echo was onboard with several crates of dragon eggs tied into the saddle. Farzg and Elyndandria mounted Glacirix quickly, and the four of them retreated to Farzg's compound far in the northeast. It took them a day of flying, but Glacirix had strengthened his body since The Unbinding. He could transport fifteen soldiers plus Farzg if necessary. His dragon saddle was elaborate and balanced by engineers and artificers.

Upon their return, Echo took the eggs into the compound. Farzg bid his farewells to Elyndandria and Glacirix before they headed southeast to bring her to the Eastpoint Lighthouse. Just before they flew away, he emphasized, "They'll take more than a day to get here. Glacirix, I know it's so much to ask, but please. She is a dragon. You can help her. Do not let One get away with his plan."

Glacirix closed his beautiful, violet eyes. "Eldon. The way you speak concerns me."

The frost giantkin flailed, annoyed at the concern. "You idiots must think I'm a simple mortal! You're all underestimating me based on my preparedness! I'm not giving up, I'm just calculating odds!" he shouted, the anger in his voice causing the temperature to drop.

Elyndandria asked, "Then, why? You're so calm and accepting until we question you."

Farzg waved his hand nonchalantly as he entered his estate, his voice barely audible. "There's not even a ten percent chance that I will lose, but in case I do, I want One to know my wrath from the grave. I trust only the two of you and Echo with such a task." He realized he had more orders and returned to the door. His voice was strong and confident now. "Get on with it then, Ely. Glacirix. If this is all a waste of time, I promise I will find a way to repay you for your preparations." He wrinkled his nose a bit, causing his beard to wiggle as he spoke. "And if my calculations are incorrect, and One wins this? Do not let him win the rest. Aid the church in any way you see fit."

Elyndandria and Glacirix traded glances. The assassin replied, "Very well, then. You'll have it your way, even if you're dead. Just make sure to leave me your vault codes and all that, right?" she prodded.

Farzg turned his back to them again. "You won't need codes. Just what's in the portal chest. Take your due, Ely. And if this is the last time we meet? It's all the more fitting."

She glared. "What do you mean?"

Farzg's forced smile was emotionless. "That means One has bet the best hand. The gambler. So unpredictable."

Elyndandria rolled her eyes. "You play too many board games, Farzg. If you die, I'm taking my price from what's left here, got it?"

Farzg's emotionless face twisted up into a sinister grin. "You will indeed, Ely."

Chapter 18
The Crossroad

"And to the thirteen paradises depart the souls of heroes and common people of good hearts. Heroes Departed is an afterlife full of reminiscences and cheers for the achievements of mortals who sacrificed much to protect others." – Lexcord's *Reflections*

ll of Erk's crew was present for Shalo's funeral. The pirate lord delivered a powerful eulogy highlighting the ways Shalo's heart had turned to good in recent months. It was moving, but it felt like background noise to Miranda. There was too much going on, and she found herself trapped in her thoughts; her anxiety was escalating. Although she could feel the immense increase in her ability to store mana within her, that further worried her. On one hand, she wondered if using the increased capacity would damage her parents' godshards. On the other hand, she worried an increase in power was necessary to face Farzg and Doctor One. As Erk's crew burst into a cheer at something their captain had said, Miranda felt a nudge on her shoulder.

She turned to see Evan looking up at her with an expression of sympathy and mournfulness. Miranda couldn't hear what he said, but she embraced him from within her pocket of mental silence. If there were Umbrals in Nulodia, she knew they needed to leave right away. With her new limits, she could teleport them easily. She was not afraid of the interference in the astral tunnels. In all honesty, teleportation was one of the easier ways to bend the mana. Jax and Annaia could get the ships where they needed to be, and Miranda could get her companions where they needed to be. There was no question, and she would not take no for an answer.

Miranda started to chew on her lip. She thought she should feel sadder at Shalo's funeral, but he died a hero. Selasine's declaration that he would rest among the Heroes Departed comforted her greatly; there, his feats of bravery would be celebrated alongside other heroes who perished in the protection of others. As a result, her mind was already racing toward the next steps she needed to take to protect the dragons and faekin targeted by Doctor One. She could barely feel Evan as her thoughts held her consciousness captive. She went through the motions of walking up toward the bow of the ship where Shalo's remains were waiting to be pushed into the sea. She used her draconic magic to summon a burst of beautiful hyacinth petals. They swirled around Miranda, the casket, and Erk who was standing nearby. Evan was behind her, and her distant thoughts numbed her emotions to everything. The colorful blooms caught in the wind, showering *The Nebula* in a thick blanket of spring beauty in the heart of winter.

Erk and Evan realized Miranda's presence of thought was elsewhere. Her normally musical, joyful attitude seemed trapped behind a curtain of anxiety and doubt. They both knew she was plotting their next move, and they shared her urgency. For the sake of the crew and the companions, they needed to give Shalo a proper burial at sea. Selasine began to administer rites as Erk, Jax, Evan, and Naomi lifted the casket and tossed it over the side gracefully. The words echoed in Miranda's mind as her dad spoke in a deep, somber voice. It was the only sound that penetrated the fog in her mind. She wondered if this was a side effect of consuming the Abyssal Cloud. The memory of that sharp pain terrified the peripheries of her imagination. Her focus was nonexistent. "May the arms of justice embrace this soul, tormented by redemption. May he rest with the Heroes Departed, grant him eternal lauds for his sacrifice." Her dad's voice was present in her mind, but it seemed distant. It reminded her of Erk in Vortex's soul prism. There, she could hear his voice, but she was never sure that it was him. Her mind sighed.

The splash of the casket falling into the water was indistinguishable to Miranda. It sounded like just another wave against the hull. A tear formed as she forced herself to feel grief for the pungent pirate. He may have almost killed Justin, but he also saved Justin at the cost of his own life. Miranda was proud of him, although her heart would be sad that he did not have more time to do good. She physically sighed this time, the afternoon sun bright in her eyes. The crew began to disperse, a din of conversations breaking out. Miranda approached Selasine, and her cognizance caught up to the mental fog she felt since she woke up that morning. "We haven't much time then, do we?" she stated more than asked, but her inflection was still interrogative.

Selasine shook his head. He replied, "I fear that neither do the pirates." The high priest was worried about his betrothed, as they had not been out of mental contact for the last six months. It was magically possible to interrupt telepathic communication, but Selasine wondered how it would be feasible in the midst of The Unbinding. Such an uncanny magic would be just as rare as Damil's. He suspected the culprit was a magical device powered by lacrimadeum.

Erk saw Miranda and Selasine speaking. He and Naomi received the summons to return to Yendralia. The island was blockaded by ships similar to the one The Emissary had under his control. All of the pirate nobles needed to return. He could not accompany Miranda and Selasine to Nulodia, and he was further torn when he discovered Naomi transferred her pirate ladyship to Annaia. The giantkin wanted to stay close to Miranda; Naomi knew her immense power and protection would be necessary. She loved Erk, and she was patient with him when he walked through darkness trying to cure his brother. He now returned that same grace by understanding her protectiveness of the miracle dragon, and he felt confident they would reunite soon after.

Evan put his hand on his older brother's shoulder as the pirate lord watched the priest and priestess speaking. "At least one of us should go with them. I hear the paladins are going to accompany you to Yendralia as official representatives of the church."

Erk sighed. He had only spent seven months with his brother since he was cured of his curse. The pirate lord agreed, however, as he was protective of Miranda as well. Evan's agility and fighting proficiency would be incredible contributions toward Miranda's safety. "Fine, moshirin. You will keep her safe, even safer than I could."

Evan gave a single, somber chuckle. "Don't inflate my ego, moshirote. I am humbled to go in your stead. Look, they've noticed us. I suspect that His Holiness is explaining the circumstances."

As the Lancethinas brothers approached Miranda and Selasine, the priestess glared at Erk. "Absolutely not."

Erk raised his hands, "Woah, I promise it wasn't my decision."

Evan looked around and asked, "What do you mean, Miranda?"

She made a sour face. She didn't express such emotions often, but when she did, she was very stubborn. "Naomi can't give up her seat at the table, and you can't go back to Yendralia alone."

Selasine sighed. "I promise, the paladins will be excellent reinforcements for the pirates. This will be the second time in a year that the forces of pirates and the Church of Invictus display solidarity in the name of justice." His tone was that of a lecture, which made Miranda scowl more.

Miranda's gaze softened after a moment. "So be it. You're close enough to Yendralia that you could make it in just a week. I could get us there now, though."

Erk nodded as Naomi approached the four of them. She had taken a moment to comfort the chef of her own ship, Milda. She and Shalo were often consorts when both ships had sufficient shore leave in Yendralia. Naomi saw the look in Miranda's eyes and gave the young woman a cold, confident smile. The giantkin's voice was rich, "Come now, darling. Annaia is more than capable of sitting in my seat. She can give it back at any time. She needs the bounty for shopping money."

The warpriest's eyes widened. She realized she was probably the one being overprotective. Until Mystalon, none of them really understood the seriousness of this current threat. But now, especially after encountering the strange ship, they realized they were severely underestimating the wide reaches of Farzg's activity. If Miranda could help Selasine eliminate Farzg quickly, she could then transport them to Yendralia to help Erk and the others. She would not allow the machinations of Doctor One to destroy another homeland. The music in her voice began to return as she spoke, "I'm sorry, I'm not really being fair. I'm worried about everyone and everything."

Erk smiled as he comforted her. "And I'm worried about you. That's why I'm going to send Naomi and Evan to protect you. Since I can't really be in two places at once, I'll wait for you all to join me in Yendralia."

Miranda nodded with certainty. "Yuvina is hiding in the dressing room. She wants to return to Nulodia to question the head of her organization about her most recent mission, but she also wishes to aid us in defeating Farzg. It was his men that took her from her homeland fifteen years ago. That makes us five strong."

Naomi twisted her lips in thought. Yuvina was set free by her crew, but the earth giantkin had no recollection of meeting the kitsune over a decade ago. She was glad, however, that the foxkin found Miranda. She felt like the gods must have been assembling a crew specifically to bring down the frost giantkin.

Selasine smiled. Farzg made too many enemies to count. He suspected the frost giantkin probably regretted his alliance with Doctor One, but the criminal had no recourse but to double down on his efforts. Thomas knew every move The Frozen Death made would be calculated to be as painful for Thomas as possible. He knew Miranda would not hesitate to get them back to Nulodia, but he wanted to make sure they had a plan in place. "If there are Umbrals in Nulodia, how will we approach the situation? I certainly doubt they are as infinitely powerful as there is no solisberry tree, but they may be numerous. There were tons of lacrima-deum in the evidence warehouses." He scratched his beard and narrowed his eye. The eyepatch over his right eye crunched toward the center of his face, an expression of deep thought.

Miranda frowned. "I will use my uncanny magic to purge the city of stale magic and the manifestations of underflow." Her voice was matter of fact, her confidence brimming now that she held the power of her parents' godshards. She feared for them, but she hoped they were safe. If their essences burned up in the process, they would return to the arcane stream. That was where they belonged, anyway, as they awaited the cycle of reincarnation that happened for all dragons.

Naomi grinned. "It's a lot easier than fighting a demon, and your confidence is warranted, sweet Miranda. Just promise you won't overdo it?"

The warpriest nodded with a smile, then looked up at Thomas. "I promise, all of you. The strength I now hold inside me is enough to turn the tide of this conflict. With my Mom and Dad beside me, I have enough magic. I think I can neutralize Farzg's Death Geyser."

Selasine and Erk grimaced. They knew Farzg would target Miranda specifically for her connection to them. He had already targeted Evan, Miranda, and the cousins with an assassin, and walking into one of the criminal mastermind's traps would give him the ability to choose his victims according to his own plan. Before either of them could speak, a voice interjected, "You can count on me too. It's dangerous. I figure you need a bodyguard."

Miranda turned around, still near the bow of the ship. She saw Celyth and Arlindra standing nearby, grave expressions on their faces. Celyth was the one who spoke, and Arlindra looked at the deck. Miranda's lips twisted in thought. "And you, Arlindra?"

Her eyes snapped to Miranda's, their mutual blue gazes brimming with anxiety. The ranger's lips stretched thin as she spoke, "I wish to accompany Captain Erk and his crew to Yendralia."

Celyth rolled her eyes. "Yeah, but tell them why, cousin."

Arlindra's eyes cut across everyone present. "Mystalon owes all of you a great debt, but I see an opportunity for personal gain as well. My aid is rendered to avenge the earth mother's pain. If the Death Pirates that hold Yendralia hostage are in league with this Doctor One," she spoke with a rabid tenor. "Then their lives are forfeit and Umiaigén will wash their corpses to The Brines," she spat.

Erk deflected her anger with a compliment. "In the meantime, my vessel could use your culinary expertise. It would be a lucrative role for you."

Arlindra's eyes narrowed. "Then make sure my sous chef is the paladin. August. His cooking needs as much work as his fighting."

Miranda laughed, the first burst of emotion from her since they had awoken that morning. "August isn't a cook, though."

The ranger grinned. "While you were busy with Yuvina, he became one. And I defeated one more enemy than him in that recent battle." She reached up and tugged the collar of her tunic. "He slew sixteen, I seventeen. He thought I wouldn't be counting."

Celyth scrunched her nose. "I killed the bastard that killed the cook. And like twenty more."

Miranda's lips twisted down. It seemed horrible that her companions were celebrating the deaths of others as if there were a score to keep count. She understood, however, that each of them took their deadly responsibilities seriously. It was gruesome and sad, especially the fact that most of their enemies would choose violence and death over harmony. It wasn't the cousins' or August's fault. Nor was it her own fault that some chose evil. Sender deserved his fate. And so would Farzg, she reassured herself. She wanted to make sure that her dad had a chance to avenge his wife and daughter. Such retribution was lawful, and the warrants had been issued by the Council of Four. Farzg would pay for his crimes, she just hoped that those blinded by the frost giantkin's wealth would find the error of their ways. "Your fighting spirit is always appreciated Celyth," Miranda said. "And, Erk," she turned to the pirate lord and straightened the long skirt of her battlemail. "I promise, we will deal with the threats in the north quickly and return to aid the Yendralians. Much as you all came to our aid in the Battle of Beriton."

Erk's lips parted in gratitude. "Miranda," he whispered.

Selasine's eye sparkled with pride. Miranda had regained her poise and her music, but she added an overwhelming confidence. He had grown very close to her, Justin, and August over the course of their first year together; these last six months, however, he had sparsely seen any of them. He felt like he was experiencing fatherhood at a frustratingly accelerated pace. Still, he had known all of them since they were children in the community of Devitus, and hearing Miranda's new confidence brought comfort to his worry. Plus, she was wise, and he shared her sentiment. "Miranda, Judge of Hearts, speaks the truth. We send our Airborne Marines with you as a gesture of cooperation, and I promise the full force of the church when the paperwork makes it through." He nodded firmly. "I'll see to it that it is expedited."

Evan left his brother's side to stand beside Miranda and Selasine. The three now faced Erk and Naomi, and the Fernith cousins stood close to the port side of the bow. Erk's nose wrinkled with disappointment. "I feel like we should have a farewell feast, but such diversions would be a waste of precious moments. Lives are at stake."

Naomi scooped him up and kissed him boldly. Everyone stared at them in a moment of shock followed by adoration. Her love for the pirate lord was tangible, but Naomi was also the kind of person who loved with abundance and excess. She blamed the hate she had seen in her past for her inability to hold back her affection. She scowled at him and then embraced him. "I keep putting off the damn date. But when I get back," she warned, setting him gently on the ground. "I'm going to marry you, scoundrel." There were tears in her eyes, but her voice did not waver. She was still so collected. Miranda marveled at the giantkin's control over her emotions.

Erk laughed, kissing his beloved happily in return. He appreciated her size and strength, relaxing in her embrace. The conflict in Yendralia seemed further away as long as she was near; now that Annaia held the token of the pirate lady, however, he worried about Naomi. She was invested in Miranda in a way he didn't understand at this moment. Either that, or he suspected she harbored additional anger toward Farzg and would rather be on the mission to destroy the monster that killed his sister. He, too, wanted vengeance, but he also took his role as pirate lord with the utmost seriousness. Sending his beloved and his brother to avenge his sister felt right; after all, he knew of his sister's abhorrence to violence. He could not in good conscience reap revenge for her. Not after the tears he saw in her eyes so many years ago when her will was broken. These were the people he trusted to avenge his sister; he, in turn, would protect their pirate brethren. He finally spoke, "Promise me that you'll keep each other safe. This will not be our crossroads of departure. That's an order."

Miranda and Selasine saluted in tandem. Evan nodded, and Naomi smiled. She responded, "You can't tell me what to do honeycomb. But I do promise you I'll keep Miranda and His Holiness safe. And your sister will see justice."

Yuvina's voice joined the conversation as she ascended the stairs to the foredeck, "I hope there is room for me in this quest. I wish to help stop the slaver responsible for exposing my weakness as a pup." She came into view at the top of the stairs leading up to the bow. "And somebody with such deadly and abused uncanny magic would no doubt be an appropriate target for The Forgotten. I represent those with no uncanny magic who would rather stay powerless than see magic misused in such a way." Her voice was confident and convicted.

Miranda rushed to the kitsune and hugged her. Instead of a magical backfire, a swirl of mana wrapped around them. The priestess felt especially fond of the foxkin, her plight interesting to Miranda's magically anomalous nature. She wanted to help the kitsune recover her memories, and she was sure doing so was just. "Can I say 'see you soon' to the paladins?" she asked.

"We all should," Selasine remarked.

They headed down to the primary deck where the Airborne Marines were helping prepare *The Nebula* for the long voyage to Yendralia. The crew wasted no time after the close of Shalo's ceremony to resume their duties. Half of them, however, were now below deck, resting. A rushed, return voyage to the pirate capital could require significant stretches of night duty. Erk's crew, however, had grown in recent months. The Unbound Pirates, their obscure nickname, now resembled a crew of heroes, with individuals of all backgrounds wishing to join the crusade against evil on the high seas. Selasine shouted, "Adûnzha!"

The paladins finished tying off rigging and moving supplies, then rushed forward to salute in front of High Priest Selasine. "Sir!" they shouted in unison, August standing in front of Valarie and Justin.

Thomas's lips broke into a smile. "I hereby order you to accompany Noble Pirate Lord Erk in his journey to liberate Yendralia from the Death Pirates of Cassack. You are to exercise all church authority in your mission." He looked at the three of them and narrowed his eye in scrutiny. "You are all hereby promoted to the rank of Protector of Invictus."

Justin's salute dropped. "Your Holiness!" he protested.

Selasine raised his hand in a scolding gesture. "Justin the Watchful, you are out of line. You will pay penance by accepting this promotion and performing fifteen acts of charity."

With a momentary look of shock, Justin snapped back into salute. "Sir!" he agreed.

Valarie grinned but held her form. Protector of Invictus was a special rank given to individuals with the great burden of sheltering the innocent from violence. She had long coveted such an appointment, and many Shield Knights attained that rank through their defensive fighting style. Valarie the Protector sounded like the perfect title to her. She carefully hid her wink to Justin from His Holiness. Her boyfriend's cheeks were flushed from elation and embarrassment. He had gotten lax, but Valarie liked it.

August replied, "Honored, sir! Permission to request plan details, sir?" he followed up. Justin's eyes widened; August's petition was perfect in form and wording. He recognized the ways he had underestimated his friend's capacity for discipline, and even in their recent endeavors, he had focused too much on August's moments of bravado. The brutish paladin chased Lenis so far that Justin assumed that Commander Burchard was impetuous and undisciplined. In this moment, however, he gave full respect for those moments when August had proven his capabilities. After all, Justin was now the one with penance required for breaking form.

Selasine nodded. "Miranda, Celyth, Yuvina, Naomi, Evan, and I will return to Nulodia. We have several affairs to tend to, including possible danger with Umbrals. Arlindra, Erk, and the three of you will sail to Yendralia. Do whatever is permissible and necessary to break the Death Pirate blockade. Understood?"

The paladins saluted again, giving a unified, "Sir!"

Erk felt his excitement for the conflict building. The Death Pirates had long been a thorn in his side, and, even as a dread pirate, he found their methods sickening. Returning to Yendralia with the church on his side filled him with pride, and now that the Death Pirates were openly in league with Doctor One, he would have the support he needed to strike a decisive blow against the evil lurking to the east of the Isles Known for Nothing. He hoped they had overplayed their hand, and though their new ships were dangerous, their hearts were corrupt and their purposes evil. Erk felt confident righteousness would turn the tide of battle against them, and with the church supporting their efforts, the Death Pirates would finally meet their match. The pirate lord added, "In that case, you also need roles on the ship. You're all capable sailors and you've proven it time and again." Erk found himself standing rigid and in a pseudo-salute of his own. It felt natural when speaking to clergy of the Path of the Sword of Justice. His own sisters demanded such rigidity in him from a young age, and he currently relished the feeling. "Boson is an appropriate rank, but you'll each need something to be the boson of." He reached up and scratched his smooth chin looking at them.

The paladins turned to face Erk, holding their salute. Their left hands were pressed firmly to the hilts of their swords, and their right palms were turned up toward the sky, chest high. When they stomped to attention and replied with, "Sir!" Erk felt his spine tingle. The order and pomp made his blood rush with delight.

He pursed his lips. "Justin, Protector of Invictus. You will be the boson of surveillance."

Justin nodded and stomped, replying with only a commanding, "Sir!"

Erk smiled. "Valarie, Protector of Invictus. You shall serve as the boson of discipline, a task you'll share with my first mate." He winked. "Don't worry, the crew is more disciplined than ever. You'll get to lounge your way to Yendralia."

Valarie's lips twisted up into a thin, severe smile. "You'll find I'm not good at relaxing, Captain. Boson of ship discipline will be an honorable title, and I'll see to it that your crew is ready to face the enemy awaiting in Yendralia."

Everyone looked at Valarie with admiration. She was carefree, but she balanced her whimsy with incredible protocol. Miranda knew Valarie's promise was genuine. The priestess smiled, proud to know this incredible woman. It was clear how she'd stolen Justin's heart so easily.

Erk smiled but moved on with his appointments. "And Commander Burchard, Protector of Invictus, you will serve as the sous-chef to the interim boson of the kitchen. Arlindra."

The ranger's eyes narrowed with victory as the commander's eyes widened with surprise. Everyone else laughed but then realized Erk was serious. There was an awkward pause as everyone looked between August and Arlindra. Eventually the paladin shrugged, responding, "I see no better teacher here, anyway. Besides, I've got a lot to learn from somebody like Arlindra. And you, too, pirate." He smiled, his clean-shaven face still rugged and handsome. "Or should I say, Captain."

Miranda beamed. Seven months ago, August, Justin, and she were all just acolytes off on their first adventure. Now they were decorated members of the clergy of Invictus, and their hands had a direct role in saving lives and keeping chaos at bay. Moreover, Miranda realized her dreams were coming true. She could not have articulated them seven months ago, but she had a strange, wonderful family provided by destiny. She had no living relatives, but her mother and father were close to her heart. Selasine, her Modai-rin, Erk and Naomi, Evan, the Fernith cousins, and even Yuvina pressed upon her the importance of her own fate. She was born with an incredible power, and though she still had much to learn about Espa, she wanted to change it for the better. These people deserved a safe, happy future, and she hoped she could be instrumental in providing and protecting it. The warpriest declared with confidence and authority, "Whenever the Nulodia team is ready to depart, I am ready to teleport us there. I will aim for the sanctuary of the cathedral."

The paladins turned with a salute to Miranda. August spoke first, "Warpriest Miranda." He then broke his salute and ran over to hug her. Justin and Valarie exchanged glances. They all outranked her now, technically. It was still against protocol, but they figured neither Miranda nor Selasine would scold them for breaking the rules at such a time.

Miranda cried and giggled. Something inside her told her she would not see her friends again for a while. The thought filled her with a sadness greater than the sorrow she felt for Shalo's death. That, in turn, filled her with guilt and she cried more than she giggled. She hugged them back in return as the three wrapped themselves around her. "Don't be dramatic, the lot of you. An increase in rank is no reason to break protocol, in fact, it demands the opposite!" she chastised through her tears.

The paladins laughed together, squeezing her harder. August said, "Don't worry, Miranda, we'll see you soon." Though his voice was confident and strong, he sounded as if it were tempered by sadness.

Justin felt himself growing emotional as well, adding, "Our missions have different details, but we pursue the same goal."

Valarie caught the catechism couched in his farewell. She continued it, saying, "Though our paths stray from each other for a time, we will meet again when the Sword of Justice has righted the chaos."

Miranda's heart leapt into her throat, and August closed his eyes to prevent them from welling with tears. It was the Catechism of Departure. It was the one he knew the best, and the one kept closest to his heart. He added the next line, "May the roads we walk lead to a unified destination, order and peace."

Miranda knew the catechism as well, and she added the closing line, "As it is written, so shall it be. Such is the way of the Path of the Sword of Justice." The four of them broke apart, everyone now looking at Miranda. For the first time, she was not surprised. "Alright then. See you soon, my beloved friends." She turned to the others on the deck, their mighty group now divided in destination. "Erk," she said.

The pirate lord nodded. "Miranda," he replied.

She wrinkled her nose. "I hope you know," she began.

He nodded again. "Of course, Miranda. The path before us both is—"

She shook her head vigorously. "Not that, silly. I think your brother has a crush on me."

Everyone nearby on the deck froze. Miranda's lips curled up into a devious smile as she activated the mana within her. A blazing, white circle opened underneath the entirety of The Nebula. Evan was particularly flushed, and he tried to protest, "Miranda! What in the Infernia?"

Miranda inhaled deeply. "Think of the stuff you need if you don't have it with you!" she warned. The circle of light intensified. Her enhanced power would burn through the interference with no problem.

Selasine thought of the entire contents of his officer's cabin; he had been doing correspondence from there and couldn't risk any of it getting lost. Evan thought of his dignity but that couldn't be teleported. Instead, he hoped Miranda's magic would find the chests underneath his bed in his cabin. Naomi growled with internal fury as she didn't have time to choose outfits. Instead, she wished for her seven spare sets of magical daggers, a few armored corsets, and a hand cannon that she had been dying to use. Yuvina had all of her possessions on her, and Celyth was already packed for travel.

Arlindra gave her cousin a wave as the light began to send Celyth across the continent. "Yash-zim'nides," she shouted, a warbling sound filling the air as the teleportation intensified.

Celyth felt her world freeze. "Arli'nides!" she shouted back, hoping to get the message to her cousin in time. The suffix expressed unconditional love in elven, and it was the first time her cousin had ever voiced anything of the sort. The elven warrioress was in shock, and she saw Nebu's insect eyes poking out of the top of Arlindra's hair. The teleporting had already begun, however, and she wasn't sure if her message got through the intensifying sound of the magic around them.

Yuvina closed her eyes. She had spent so long with antagonism toward magic she felt odd subjecting herself to the magical whims of a person she had recently met. Miranda, however, seemed different from other Wielders. Her pure heart was so exposed Yuvina worried the woman's naivete would be her undoing. She speculated Miranda had sufficient power to defend that pure heart if needed, and the dragon-human changed Yuvina's opinions on people with uncanny magics. She let the sensation of the ether wash over her; it was something she found comforting, even though she experienced a twinge of pain whenever she thought of her own Unbinding power. She needed to see Everdusk. He held the clues to unlock her lost memories.

Before anyone could give their last farewells, they appeared in the sanctuary of the grand cathedral of Invictus in Nulodia. The equipment and objects they desired were transported alongside them, hitting the ground with a series of thuds. Miranda's hair did not change color; in fact, it looked more red than normal. It was already late afternoon, and the sun reflected through the stained glass of the cathedral with intense hues of yellow and gold. They shimmered on Miranda's hair as she stared at the doors of the cathedral. Evan secured the lockboxes from his cabin, and Naomi found her outfits in the pile of things that had appeared with them. Selasine put a hand on his head, realizing he'd created a bigger mess with his wish, underestimating the precision of Miranda's teleport. Yuvina and Celyth grinned with cockiness; their minimalism had prevented yet another headache.

Miranda said, "It's time to search the city." The melody in her voice was a minor key, echoing her aggressive temperament.

Selasine looked from the contents of his ship cabin to his daughter. "Yolasha, don't overdo it!" he pleaded.

She turned to him with a smile. "Getting us here didn't even use a fraction of the power of my parents. I promise, I won't overdo it." The floaty tones had returned to her voice, but it was clear the innocence of her pre-adventuring days had mixed with the confidence she had gained in her heritage.

Selasine reached to the sword underneath his robes. "I can feel we are not alone." He could see shadows moving throughout the sanctuary.

Evan and Yuvina had already taken defensive positions, weapons drawn.

Celyth was by Miranda's side in less than a second. "You asked for a bodyguard, yeah?"

Miranda giggled. "No, but I wouldn't ask for anybody else as one."

Celyth smiled. Naomi approached, standing over both of them. She grinned at Miranda. "Give 'em the Infernia. They deserve it."

Miranda pressed her fingers together and the mana swelled within her. There was so much magic swirling inside her, she felt like she could do anything. A wave of purifying, purple light emitted from her as the epicenter. Umbrals prowling in the sanctuary of Invictus's cathedral dissolved as the light washed over them. The radiance possessed a heat only the shadows could feel.

Evan looked at her with wonder. As the light and mana swirled around her, the braids pulled to the front of her face tossed wildly. The vortex of energy surrounding her caused a physical wind to pulse throughout the place of worship. It further blew the correspondence Selasine brought with him, causing him to sigh in resignation to a frustrating next few hours. Still, he knew the unfolding events were beyond even Invictus himself. He worried about his daughter, but he trusted her.

The purple light emanated from Miranda with a steady rhythm. Each wave strengthened, passing harmlessly through the walls of the cathedral. The first few were barely big enough to fill the room. As they persisted, they grew in size and intensity. Within minutes, the entire city of Nulodia was filled with a pulse of radiant, cleansing light. Miranda's thoughts coalesced on a single desire: "Purify Nulodia, Invictus. Rid this place of the Umbrals; with the might of the arcane stream and your holy righteousness, evil should know no place here." Her prayer resonated through the waves of light pulsing through the city. With each new blast of light, a new echo of the prayer filled the streets.

The omen came just in time, as well. High Paladin Erista and the Peacekeeper Precinct were stretched thin. The Umbrals began appearing approximately twenty hours ago, and Damil's telepathic communication had been abruptly disrupted about an hour before that. The faithful of Invictus began to repeat the prayer they heard echoing in the light.

In the primordial place, Invictus heard his name being called to the port city of Nulodia. His sister was currently on the surface of Espa pursuing Aylabrax's mortal form, and though he worried for her safety, he spread his divinity across his believers and those of Lexcord. This echoing of his name, however, caught his attention. Many of the prayers he had been answering were in response to a great danger in that same city, but due to the limitations of his consciousness in the primordial place, he could not cohesively connect the prayers to their threats. With Miranda's prayer captured in light, Reshiria's demanding presence, and Philotrax's charismatic request, Invictus could not help but find himself drawn to the city on that late afternoon. As the sun set over Nulodia in the primary dimension, the pulsating surges of purple light kept the city well lit. At each wave, Umbrals of many sizes were destroyed. Miranda pleaded for the might of Invictus, and so he imbued her spell with his own fury.

The light coming from Miranda radiated in all directions, even beneath the city. The vibrant energy imbued with the might of Invictus located another threat. Deep in the sewer network, a device powered by lacrima-deum cracked as the purifying waves crashed into it. As it broke, Damil's voice echoed throughout the minds of everyone in the city, "By the Sword of Justice, salvation is brought!"

Selasine's eye widened with excitement. His fingers reached up to his temples, letting another gust of wind from Miranda's light blow his papers everywhere. "Damil! My love! Are you alright?!"

A feeling of relief washed over everyone in touch with Damil. The whole of Nulodia could hear the elation in his thought, "Thomas!" he called back.

Miranda inhaled again, feeling the mana within her begin to deplete. She was powerful now, but she was not omnipotent. The waves of light should have been enough to save the city from cataclysmic threats. Any remaining Umbrals would have to be the concern of the peacekeepers. She hated to leave them with that burden, but she needed to conserve the ether within her.

Shalo opened his eyes to a panorama of gold and gray clouds. They rotated, wrapping him in a vortex stretching fifty feet in radius. "By the gods, I've went 'n done it!" he shouted. His voice echoed in this strange, ambiguous space.

A deep, powerful voice replied, "Indeed, Shalo. You have died."

The pungent pirate turned in a circle, seeing no one else. "Ay! That's my bloody trick, show yerself!" he demanded of the voice with no source.

After a moment of silence, a figure dressed in a cloak emerged from the clouds. It pulled the hood from its head, revealing an aged man with eyes that had no irises or pupils. His head was shaved, and he towered over Shalo with his presence and stature. "Fair, Shalo. I am Ahnkhetet, but many know me simply as 'Death.' I am here to guide you to your final resting place."

Shalo rolled up his sleeves and grunted. "I guess this means Miss Miranda ain't gonna bring me back, eh?"

Death laughed. "Not for lack of trying, Shalo. Your vessel has been," he began but paused, examining the pirate's soul. He found the perfect metaphor in the pirate's past. "You might say your body is 'well-done,' and no amount of sauce will 'cure the burn.'" Ahnkhetet shivered, the pirate's past mixed with many misdeeds.

"Ay, so long as the boy made it out alive, then. Please tell me, Death, did the boy make it? Did I—" he began to beg, but Ahnkhetet interrupted him.

"You made all of the difference, and Invictus has interceded on your behalf. Count yourself lucky. I am about to be very busy. A dark time waits in Espa's future. You, however, will rest in Heroes Departed."

Shalo's soul shuddered with lingering concern for the friends he left behind. They would have to face those dark times without his cooking. He accompanied Ahnkhetet to the designated paradise.

There in the Heroes Departed, legends of old looked upon Miranda's deeds. A grand feast had been prepared with ingredients unlike anything Shalo had ever seen. Though he was the chef in charge of preparations, he was also the hero of the era. Instead of a retelling of his own accomplishments, however, he demanded the heroes look upon the true heroine of his story. Miranda used the magic within her to destroy the Umbrals in Nulodia. They worried for her next challenge: The Frozen Death awaited on the other side of The Lichwood. Shalo the pirate hero and above average cook was right; this was a story worth watching. The entirety of the Heroes Departed observed from beyond the void as the girl from Devitus chased her destiny with tenacity and hope.

Interlude
Sisters at Heart

"Blood is not the true test of family. Familial bonds must be tempered through mutual struggle, and those challenges must align hearts toward a common goal." – Siblings of Order

rlindra blinked with incredulity. Her father had just ordered her to play with her cousin, Celyth. In Arlindra's mind, eleven years old was too old to play. And Celyth was a whole year older! Why would any of the adults in this formula expect a couple of young elf girls to play? They should be studying and reading together, not wasting time. Alaric repeated to his daughter, "Your uncle's election has been contested by that harpy over in the Namidan district. Uncle Evander and I have much to discuss. Please, get along with your cousin for a little while at least."

They were sitting in the parlor of Alaric's house. Modest furniture provided a cozy space for hosting a small group. Arlindra stared out the open window in the front of the parlor. This was the room where the adults in the family would stay and discuss whatever it was that had them all upset. The parlor connected to a hallway, the master bedroom, and the kitchen. Arlindra, however, was upset she was being forced to spend time with somebody way too loud. Why couldn't her older sister or mom hang out with Celyth? The adults wrongly assumed two elf girls close in age would have a lot in common. Today promised to be torture.

Arlindra spotted four individuals approaching her home, one of them the cousin in question. They had been around each other plenty; that's how she knew Celyth was obnoxious and demanded too much attention. With a grumble, Arlindra walked toward her room at the end of the hallway, waiting at the parlor's exit. Alaric and Arlindra's mother, Vanesa, looked at their daughter. Her mother gave her a weak smile as she spoke. "I know it seems like a lot, but this conversation will affect your future, too. You should get along with your cousin. The key is to find something you both like to do and share it with each other."

The girl looked at her mother and said nothing. Her father added, "You two are so close in age, you should be like sisters!" His voice was endearing and encouraging. Arlindra wrinkled her nose. "Come, now, Arlindra. Don't be like that," he insisted.

Before Arlindra could respond, company knocked at the door. Her day of peace and quiet was now ruined. Vanesa ran to the door, opening it quickly. There stood Uncle Evander and Aunt Kiriana, but there were two others. One was an old elf Arlindra knew as Wikton, and the other was her cousin, Celyth. As soon as Celyth saw Arlindra, she pushed past her Aunt Vanesa and stood face to face with Arlindra at the entrance to the hallway. She remarked, "They said it's not a meeting for kids, so I guess you can't be here."

The cousins exchanged silent stares for a moment. Celyth had purple hair pulled back into a tight ponytail. It was short because she tended to destroy her hair in her wild activities; she did not hesitate to play with fire-generating magitabs, and as a result, her mother would always have to cut off the singed ends of her hair. Her green eyes were full of excitement and hostility, expressions that made Arlindra shudder.

Celyth, however, looked at Arlindra's well-groomed, light blue hair. It came down to the middle of her back, and bangs framed her face, highlighting her blue eyes. They looked as opposite as they sounded.

The adults began to talk, but Arlindra gave a half grin to her cousin's taunt. "Guess you're kicked out too, then. They told me I have to babysit you."

Celyth scrunched her nose. "That's not possible! I am older than you! I should be the babysitter!"

Arlindra's grin widened, realizing she could get under her cousin's skin by questioning her authority. "Well, I have like four books I'm supposed to read. So, if anybody told me what to do, it would probably be to read those four books."

Celyth stomped her foot. Evander's voice escaped from the din of adult conversation as he addressed the girls, "No roughhousing, okay Celyth?"

Arlindra's smile could not spread any further; she continued teasing her cousin. "You see, they probably would prefer we read those books anyway. So, you should just try to tell me to read them already."

Celyth returned Arlindra's grin. "No roughhousing, at least in the common room. You have a big bed, and lots of room. Do you want to fight?"

Arlindra's head recoiled. "Fight? Why?"

Celyth crossed her arms. Wikton tapped her on the shoulder as he walked by. "Ah the vigor of youth. Spare some of that for the geezers like me. Maybe?" he asked. He pretended to look around the parlor, but he clued the girls into the truth. It was almost like the adults could hear every word they said, but for some reason, they didn't intervene. They had their own worries to attend to anyway, Arlindra processed.

Celyth replied, finally, "Well to see who is the strongest, of course!"

Arlindra rolled her eyes. "Why is it always the strongest and never the smartest or fastest or hungriest?"

"We *could* race, but you'd lose. I don't want to listen to crybaby losers," Celyth said.

Arlindra's eyes narrowed. "You sure you want to run all the way from here to the arboretum and back in like, ten minutes?" She gave her estimate based on her father's morning runs. He supposedly jogged all the way to the tree and back, and he claimed physical fitness was just as important as magical competence. She also heard him talk about the hair bringers when he said those things, but that further confused her. Nobody who was strong needed hair.

Celyth's eyes widened. "No way! How did you know that's how long it takes to run to the tree?"

Arlindra shrugged. "Guess we better not race. C'mon. I have books in my room."

Celyth groaned but followed her cousin. She didn't want to say it, but she loved books. "They better not be those boring fairy stories."

Arlindra groaned back. "No, they are plant books. And some fairy stories about plants."

They did not pay much attention to the detail in the house but went to the end of the hallway where Arlindra's room sat across from her older sister's. Aurora was twenty-seven and very insistent about her privacy. Arlindra dared not encroach, not even at Celyth's prodding. Celyth also knew better, however, as Aurora was equal parts scary and mean. At least, Celyth thought so.

Arlindra's room was as boring as Celyth remembered. There were a couple of bookshelves, and, as the cousins entered the room, Arlindra bounded over to one of them. She began to toss books at Celyth which the young elf interpreted as a blocking drill. Books bounced off the walls, eliciting a "What did I say about roughhousing?" from the parlor.

Celyth then dove behind the dresser, protesting, "Stop, cousin, we'll get scolded!"

Arlindra stood up straight. "All the better, maybe you'll finally read a book!"

Celyth shouted, "I like to read just as much as you! Why are you pretending like I'm some dummy?"

Arlindra froze. She responded with a quick tempo, "Well, you always want to fight, and you never read with me."

Celyth crawled under the dresser then up to her cousin's bed. "You didn't really ask about the books I read, though. You just wanted to tell me about the ones you read." She huffed, indignant.

Arlindra frowned. "I guess that's true. I just figured you wanted to fight because you couldn't read."

Her cousin stretched out her small torso on Arlindra's bed. "No, I wanted to fight because that's just what we're supposed to do, right? We're cousins, so we're supposed to fight."

Arlindra sighed. For eleven years old, she showed extraordinary wisdom. Her voice was condescending as she spoke, "Who told you that? That sounds bad, always fighting."

Celyth's eyes filled with tears. "Well, if you can beat me in a fight, I know you'll be able to beat anybody. And that way I know you'll always be safe."

Arlindra groaned. "We live in a magic society. What kind of harm will happen to us here?"

Celyth looked up with deadly anger. "There's no telling. But we better be ready to fight it."

Arlindra nodded in agreement before she realized what her cousin had said. Perhaps her rebellious spirit was not against learning and growing, but against society itself. Arlindra understood the limitations of hating the outside; her dad had told her how such attitudes were dangerous. "So do you think we'll really have to fight at every turn?"

Celyth, also wise for her age, looked at her cousin with the same incredulity that Arlindra had shown before. "Would you rather be ready for a fight that never comes, or not ready for a fight that lands in your face?"

Arlindra couldn't argue with that. Maybe her obnoxious yash-zim was smarter and cooler than she gave her credit for. "You know what fight I always lose?"

Celyth narrowed her eyes, "Don't you dare pretend like you know a dragon or something. It better be a real fight."

The blue-haired cousin sighed. "No, but mom and dad won't let me have eolnut tarts whenever I want. And we've got this great meat that dad only lets us have every once in a while."

The purple haired cousin's eyes widened. "What kind of meat?" she asked, bewildered.

Arlindra's eyes and lips narrowed. "Some kind of bear, he says. It's got the face of a bird, or something. But it's meat," she said, licking her lips in a sinister way. "Well, it tastes delicious. It makes the best sandwich."

Celyth yawned. "So does he have any of this bird-bear-face-meat laying around anywhere, or are you just going to tease me with stories of forbidden snacks?"

Arlindra raised a finger. "It doesn't come from the face—"

Celyth interrupted her. "Shh! Can you hear that? The grown-ups! They're yelling!"

Arlindra looked around her room, and they heard the words clearly. "Elitirin would kill every person in this city if she thought it would raise her station. There's no way she should have the influence she does!" It sounded like Alaric. Arlindra looked at her cousin with a pleading expression. She hated the "poly-ticks" thing her dad had been playing as long as she could remember.

Celyth groaned. "See? Adults are always fighting, even if it's not violent." She shook her fist, still sprawled out over Arlindra's bed.

Arlindra furrowed her brow. She replied, "You know, I'm pretty sure dad has a good chunk of that bird-bear meat out in the smoker. And mom baked a loaf of fresh eolnut bread this morning. There's a bit of zaligoat cheese in the preservatory. Want to go out to the woods and get some veggies to make sandwiches?"

Celyth's eyes widened. She had no idea Arlindra would be willing to break the rules. "Infernia's blessing!" she replied, a horrible swear for a twelve-year-old elf maiden.

Arlindra's grin returned. "When they start arguing like that, we can literally just go out my window."

Celyth shrugged; it seemed logical. They slipped into the Mystalonian Forest. Arlindra told her cousin about numerous plants and animals as they foraged in the loam formed by the leaves of the grand trees above. They sought flavorful peppers and savory onions which favored the rich soil. As they brought their vegetables into Arlindra's room, they put them on the bed. Celyth looked at her cousin and said, "You know, I see what you mean. Sometimes working together is better than fighting."

Arlindra rolled her eyes, as she did so frequently. "Yeah, duh. Fighting is a lot of effort. Helping each other out is like half the work."

Celyth giggled. "I wanted to fight because I was worried about you. Oh well. You're better in the woods than I expected. Where did you learn all that about the plants?"

Arlindra pointed to her bookshelf in severe disarray. "Dad made sure I had enough knowledge to explore the forest on my own. He taught me how to read. I did the rest myself."

Celyth scowled. "Well, you seem to know a lot more about food than I expected."

Arlindra grinned. "That's because I love a good snack. Now we just have to sneak out to the smoker and get the meat."

Celyth nodded. "That's an easy mission." She looked toward the slightly ajar door of Arlindra's room, and they could hear more, vivid discussion.

Evander's voice echoed down the hallway, "Mystalon has to change; the world around us is changing. We can't stay reclusive forever."

The cousins exited from Arlindra's window, but they only went to the back yard. The smoker was hot, but Arlindra knew how to manipulate the contraption to expose the prize. Celyth was impressed. They shredded off enough to make a couple of sandwiches.

They had all of the ingredients they needed except bread and cheese. There was only one place to secure such delicacies, however: the kitchen. The adults kept those precious resources secure in the magical pantry. Arlindra knew it would be arduous, but at this point, Celyth was sold on the task. Together they devised a plan. Celyth would take Arlindra's book and run through the house with it, yelling that she had taken the treasure. Arlindra would pursue her cousin, shouting about the robbery indignantly until the adults intervened. They would likely stop Celyth and hold her for questioning, and, in the meantime, Arlindra could steal the bread they needed for bird-bear sandwiches.

Celyth looked at the title of the book and read it aloud. *"Fun Fungus, Final Fungus."* She looked at her cousin. "What in the Infernia is this about?"

Arlindra blinked. "Mushrooms."

Celyth shrugged. It was an honest title, then. "Well here goes!" she said, her lips breaking into a devilish grin. She stood at Arlindra's door for a moment before shouting, "Aha! Take it back, yash-zim! You can't catch me!" As she finished her shouted taunt, she bolted down the hallway toward the parlor.

Arlindra smiled. Her cousin wasn't annoying this time; she was actually fun. She realized she needed to be in character. "Get back here with my book!" she growled, trying to sound angry. She spotted the error in their plan; the adults would see through their game.

As Celyth entered the front of the house, she saw her family and the old elf Wikton. With them, however, were two elves that Celyth had seen before but did not know their names. She froze, feeling panic and fear seize her.

Arlindra saw her cousin hesitate, slowing her pursuit. As the adults' eyes all fixed on Celyth, Arlindra slipped quietly behind her cousin into the kitchen, as it was adjacent to the parlor. As she left the room, she heard her father's voice, "Celyth?" His tone was confused.

Celyth improvised. "We heard strange voices and came to investigate!" she said, pompous.

The two strangers laughed. One had a feminine appearance, and the other androgynous. They wore brilliant, red mantles, an indication that they were members of the Congress of Sages like Alaric and her father. "You must be Celyth," the feminine elf said.

Arlindra seized the moment. She slid through the kitchen and into the pantry. The adults called it a preservatory. It kept perishable foods longer using a magitab that kept the air dry and cool. While inside, Arlindra secured an entire loaf of eolnut bread, a wheel of cheese probably made from zaligoat milk, and a bottle of sauce her dad always said was "too spicy for young elves." She was determined to know what the sauce tasted like; after all, food was her favorite thing in the world.

She bundled the ingredients under her shirt and snuck toward her room. As she slipped from the kitchen into the parlor, she heard the other of the strange elves speaking. "As you know, we strive to keep Mystalonian magic pure and sacred. Our lives revolve around the tree, which is the child of the arcane stream. Inviting outsiders would only invite the exploitation of the tree. We hope that you, Sage Evander, will understand. If Elitirin suspects wrongdoing on your part, we will not hesitate to remove you from the Congress."

Arlindra's heartbeat accelerated. That sounded like a threat against her family, and she wouldn't stand for it. She turned down the hallway, almost to her goal, but she thought she finally understood Celyth's unwavering need to fight. "The monsters are back, Celyth!" she shouted.

Celyth's eyes darted across the faces of her family members. She knew that she had no place in the current conversation, and her diversion was probably a bad idea in the end. She started to back away from the adults, catching everyone's attention anew. One of the strangers commented, "Oh, she's got a copy of Elitirin's book."

The other looked at her with scrutiny, their eyes beautiful and feminine but their facial features rigid and masculine. They spoke in a soft voice, "Tell us, Celyth, what's the book about?"

With an indignant huff, she shouted, "Mushrooms!" She turned and sprinted toward Arlindra at the end of the hallway.

Arlindra ran inside the room and slipped behind the door which opened to the inside. As Celyth barreled past, Arlindra slammed the door behind her cousin. They did not hear the adults giving pursuit, so Arlindra ran to the bed and poured the haul out of her shirt.

Celyth's eyes widened with excitement. "You stole the hot sauce too?" she asked in a voice just a little louder than need be.

Arlindra nodded furiously. "Dad never shares it. I want to know what it is," she commented, examining the label. "I don't know what these symbols mean, though." She offered the bottle to her cousin, an indication of trust.

Celyth took it and opened it immediately. She pushed her smallest finger into the bottle and gave it a try. "Infernia's blessing," she commented.

Arlindra scrunched her nose. "Hey, you were supposed to read it!"

Celyth shrugged. "I can't read those letters either, but if I had to guess, they are dwarf letters."

Arlindra looked at the bottle in her cousin's hand carefully.

"Dwarves don't come to Mystalon though."

Celyth began tearing the bread apart to make a sandwich. "Maybe they don't, but I think dad went to go see some dwarves last year." She shrugged, tearing some cheese with her fingers and stuffing it into the pocket she had formed in the bread.

Arlindra's lips pursed upward in thought. "Maybe that's why they don't want to share. It came from the outside, and they don't want us to tell the other adults. It's a secret."

Celyth stuffed some of the shredded meat into her bread as well. "Well, it's delicious. I certainly wouldn't tell anyone."

Arlindra made her own sandwich, her heart racing with excitement. She was going to try some spicy sauce from the outside world! None of the kids in school could say they did that; she knew, however, she couldn't brag about it. She added meat, cheese, and some of the peppers and onions from the forest. She probably should have washed them, but she didn't mind a little earthy flavor on her vegetables. She added the dwarven sauce to her sandwich.

Fortunately, the strangers were gone by the time Arlindra screamed in shock at the intense spice. It was the best thing she had eaten in her life, and she decided she would leave Mystalon and become a traveling chef when she grew up. From that day, Celyth and Arlindra became best friends.

Adolescence, however, challenged them with expected growing pains. After Arlindra and Celyth finished their primary education in the small school in the Galathan district, Arlindra began an apprenticeship with Wikton. She was nineteen, and Celyth had recently turned twenty. As Arlindra studied with the old elf, she learned Wikton was a druid. Though he could draw upon the earth mother for certain types of magic, he insisted he was a better wizard. He discovered many formulas for magitabs and magisalves fulfilling common, practical uses. Still, his connection with nature caught Arlindra's attention. He taught her about plants and animals in great detail. She learned how to commune with the earth mother and to draw upon her magic.

Celyth, on the other hand, opted to train as a member of the militia. Evander hoped she would pursue a magical trade, but he also saw the position as an opportunity for his rebellious daughter to learn discipline. She established a reputation as the best archer in the militia, which prompted Arlindra to adopt archery as a hobby. Though they seemed rivals, their continual competition was a relationship that fostered growth in both of them.

As Arlindra showed interest in both the earth mother and martial training, Wikton introduced her to a middle-aged elf named Harmony. She was a wilderness expert and a ranger of great repute. She had light blue hair like Arlindra, but her eyes were a vivid pink. A scar cut across her right cheek from an encounter with a bear; a single claw had gashed her face as she evaded the rest of its paw. She knew every corner of the Mystalonian Forest and understood the terrain outside of their homeland. She served as Arlindra's mentor, teaching her to track and hunt. Arlindra enjoyed hunting, but she loved cooking her quarry more. Harmony was impressed with Arlindra's culinary skills, and the older ranger shared new sources for ingredients, the bounty of the earth mother providing flavor in unexpected ways.

Their primary work in Mystalonian society was hunting meat in the countryside for distribution in the marketplace. They also foraged for ingredients to assist in the production of magitabs and magisalves. Arlindra spent a lot of time exploring the wilderness when she was not performing her official duties. The cousins persisted in these roles as they reached adulthood, but the year Celyth turned forty, things changed for the Fernith family.

One day after training, Celyth went looking for her cousin in the forest. She walked thirty minutes to the north of the city, finding herself in a dense cluster of young Mystalonian trees. She called out, "Arlindra! I know you're out here! Your dad told me you would be here!"

Her voice echoed off the trees, and her information proved accurate. Arlindra heard her cousin's impetuous shouting, and she couldn't help but smile. She scaled a Mystalonian tree and used her agility to bound through the sturdy, massive branches. She chased the sound of Celyth's voice until she could see her between trees below. She reached up and ruffled her hair, "Okay, Nebu, now!" she ordered as she jumped out of the tree.

The dracofly stirred suddenly. "Hey, woah, what in the Infernia!" he protested. As he did, a bubble of innate magic formed around them, slowing Arlindra's descent. She landed without harm.

Celyth looked up with a grin at her air-walking cousin. The dracofly showed up and started following Arlindra about a month ago. Arlindra was shocked by the animal's intelligence and demeanor, but she welcomed his aid and wisdom, nonetheless. Celyth thought it was funny that the bug was so annoying. She thought Arlindra's personality should have clashed with Nebu's, but her cousin insisted Nebu was a lot like Celyth.

The warrior flipped her hair with her left hand and asked, "Showing off more of your ranger tricks?" Her voice projected louder than necessary as Arlindra's boots connected with the ground.

"Not really my trick. That's Nebu's doing," she replied, striding up to her cousin.

Nebu poked his head out of Arlindra's wild hair. Harmony shaved her hair on the side of her sight-eye. She insisted it helped with accuracy in archery, and Arlindra began to do the same. Her light blue hair shimmered even though the canopy in this part of the forest blocked most of the sunlight. The dracofly had made its home in the other half of Arlindra's hair, turning it into a well-groomed nest. He shook one of his lizard-like fists at Celyth, shouting, "Don't you forget it either. If you fall, you know who to call. One zipping dracofly hero, right to your rescue. Just, uh, please don't fall. I don't really do well with split second decisions."

Celyth laughed. "You really are the most annoying bug in the world, aren't you?"

Arlindra's eyes widened, but Nebu retorted, "And you are the most annoying elf in the world. See if I save you from falling."

Celyth's expression went from humor to shock. "Well, if that ever happens, I'll quit calling you bug. Got it, bug?"

Arlindra rolled her eyes and reached up and stuffed Nebu into her hair. "Would you two quit? Why did you come out here, cousin? Don't you have extended training?"

Celyth shook her head. "Not today. You and me haven't fought in a little while, and I thought we should spar, but," she looked at the ground. "Dad said mom is sick, and it might be the plague. They have her quarantined."

Arlindra let go of Nebu and pressed her hands together in front of her. "Are you sure it might be the plague? How would the plague even come to Mystalon?" She focused on the power of the earth beneath her. "We need to get home quickly," she said, her voice in a panic.

Celyth raised a hand to slow her cousin. "No, don't rush. They sent me away." She looked around the forest, the dull light creating a shadowy ambiance. "I couldn't think of anyone else to turn to. Elitirin is going to blame this on dad's trip to Acero, that dwarven settlement."

Arlindra relaxed her posture. "You're right. She is going to blame your dad, but if Uncle Evander brought the plague back, why is he not ill?"

Celyth shrugged. "I don't know, it doesn't make sense."

Nebu looked over Arlindra's hair again, the insect eyes on his draconic face shimmering with sympathy. He had no sarcasm, but he offered his wisdom, "Mortals are prone to all kinds of illness. Hopefully there will be an answer. Nebu will help however he can."

Arlindra's lips drew tight. "Well, did you still want to fight?"

Celyth's eyes snapped to meet her cousin's gaze. "You betcha," she shouted and threw a punch at Arlindra's face.

The ranger evaded by turning to the side, and she grabbed her cousin's wrist. She threw her hips to flip Celyth over her back.

Celyth activated her uncanny magic, however, slowing Arlindra's reactions. She then tried to sweep Arlindra's legs with a kick, but the ranger dodged by letting go of Celyth's wrist and doing a slow but fluid backflip. As she did, Arlindra activated her own uncanny magic, and she began to blink in and out of existence. Celyth smiled. "Infernia's blessing," she hissed.

When Arlindra's hands hit the ground in her backflip, she kicked her legs out in a split motion. She twisted her momentum and went on the offensive.

Celyth rolled forward and tried to tackle Arlindra's torso, but the moment their bodies should have connected, Arlindra's presence winked out. Celyth was on the ground by the time Arlindra reappeared an instant later. She fell out of her handstand and converted her momentum into a bullrush.

She crashed into Celyth and pinned her to the ground. Though her cousin struggled, Arlindra was stronger. After a moment, Celyth accepted defeat. Arlindra smiled, but her expression melted to neutrality as she helped her cousin up. Celyth remarked, "By the solisberry, you have put on twenty pounds since we last fought."

Arlindra nodded. "The earth mother is bountiful in nutrition if you know where to look." Arlindra was quite strong, and her muscle mass was denser than Celyth's. Her diet and rugged lifestyle for the last decade had helped her bulk up.

Celyth grinned. "The stronger you get, the stronger you make me."

Arlindra shrugged. "I might be strong, but you're faster."

With a stretch, Celyth replied, "Damn right I am. Want to race home, no magic allowed? I saw you getting ready to do your cheetah sprint thing."

Her cousin's grin was shy, "Yeah. I suppose it's better exercise if we race though."

Celyth turned to face Arlindra. She hugged her cousin, saying with a tone of relief, "Dad and Uncle Alaric have been targets for so long. I'm glad you're strong enough to take care of yourself."

Arlindra squeezed her cousin. "Hey, I'm only so strong because you won't let me be weak."

Nebu poked his head up, "Well that's not—" he started.

Celyth reached up and stuffed him back into Arlindra's hair. "Don't ruin the moment, buggy."

Arlindra giggled, a rare happening. She pushed her cousin away. "I'm sure it's going to be fine, yash-zim," she used the formal word for cousin with affection.

Celyth's eyes watered, but she stretched again to interrupt her emotions. "We better get this race on. Even if mom is quarantined, everybody is going to want to eat. And when somebody gets sick, you know we have to cook everything."

Arlindra nodded, stretching as well. "I'll give you a head start."

Celyth's expression crunched, and she moved to kick her cousin. Arlindra started running toward Evander's home in the Pleidis district. "Looks like you wasted it!" she teased as she got a full hundred-foot lead.

Within the week, it became apparent Kiriana did not have the plague. Kiriana's fever had worsened, however, and her ability to move independently was depleted within the month. Her body deteriorated by the day.

To help, Mystalonian healers attempted to intervene with various formulas of yinfruit pastes. Nothing was able to cure her underlying symptoms. Some of the medicine alleviated her pain, but her body continued to worsen. Within six months, she was deathly ill; it was at that time that Vanesa, Kiriana's twin sister, also became sick with the initial symptoms that Kiriana had. Rather than endure the continual bombardment of ineffective treatment, Vanesa left Mystalon in the middle of the night, leaving behind only a note.

My dearest family, I cannot walk down the same path as my sister. I go to the edges of Espa to seek healing from the gods or some other power. Our society has failed thanks to their reclusiveness. If even one person dies as a result of pride too great to ask for help from the outside, then the rules have failed to protect us. Please do not seek me and risk your lives and stations. See my sister through to the end. I love you all,

Vanesa Fernith

Arlindra wept as she read the note. She heard her mother leave, and she could have tracked her if she wished. Instead, she prayed the earth mother would watch over her own mother while she searched for a cure for her ailment. Her aunt's condition had broken her heart enough already, and watching the Sages' unwillingness to make exceptions for seeking outside help had turned her completely against the "Mystalonian" way of life.

On the day after her forty-second birthday, Arlindra knocked on the door to her uncle's home in the Pleidis district. "Yash-zim?" she spoke into the house, opening the door after a moment of no response. "Modai-moshir?" She called for them formally, but something in her heart already knew the truth. Celyth was inconsolable, and, even though Arlindra had not seen her in person for the last twelve hours, she could feel it.

She entered the house and made her way to Kiriana's room, converted into a medical ward of sorts. It had all the tools and resources necessary to comfort Kiriana's pain. As Arlindra looked into the room, she saw her cousins, Celyth and Caelus, Celyth's younger brother of fifteen years. She also saw her Uncle Evander, and they were locked in an embrace. Arlindra knew it was true; the feeling she had in her heart was the feeling of her cousin's heart breaking. She thought back to their childhood and remembered the day she stopped hating her cousin; they'd read so many books together by now, searching for a cure for Kiriana. Arlindra winced as she pushed the door open with the toe of her boot.

Evander looked up first. "Oh, dearest yolen," he used the formal word for niece. "Come, your spirit, too, has felt the shift in the mana."

Arlindra nodded, rushing forward to embrace her cousin, wrapping her arms around her and only her. Aurora might have been her biological sister, and Aluxel might have been her older brother, but Celyth was more a sister to her than anybody else. After all, they had been fighting for thirty years. Maybe it was time to fight someone other than each other. All of their training and preparation had been to protect their loved ones, but that was of little use when the attacker was something beyond their understanding. Neither a curse nor an obvious illness; just a wasting without explanation.

Celyth sobbed. "Yash-zim'nides," she cried into her cousin's arms.

Arlindra said nothing, but she held her cousin tight. She loved her too, like a sister. Their mothers were twins, and Arlindra had imagined in her maturing years she and Celyth were twins like their mothers. Now, though, Aunt Kiriana had passed, and Vanesa had vanished weeks ago. The Sages questioned Alaric and Evander thoroughly after Vanesa disappeared, suspecting them of seeking outside help. Furthermore, they worried if a Mystalonian departed their borders without permission, they would expose the secrets of Mystalon to the outside world. Their sacred solisberry tree would be at risk. Vanesa was declared an exile, and now Kiriana was dead. Arlindra felt her heart harden with anger, but she knew it was her cousin who was already plotting some kind of revenge. Celyth rightly blamed the Sages in Elitirin's coalition for her mother's death; perhaps a cleric of some foreign god could have helped. The earth mother had prayers to ease suffering, but nothing that could cure afflictions within unless they were of a magical nature. Furthermore, there were doctors in the great cities specializing in medicine and surgery to treat internal illnesses. Arlindra stayed lost in her thoughts for the next hour until Alaric arrived.

"Moshirin," he spoke as he entered the door. He had brought the Congress of Sages. They needed to witness the pain they had needlessly inflicted on his little brother and his family. He was angry, and rightly so. He sent out a petition to the church of a goddess known as Lexcord, and they were ready to respond before Elitirin intervened. She submitted it to the Congress of Sages as evidence that Alaric was ready to consort with outsiders. Alaric denied his involvement and accused Elitirin of fraud, in which case Wikton of the Garand district and Poderdelin of the Sanguile district demanded the investigation be dismissed as "dirty politics." Elitirin always seemed to cast sinister eyes at Evander and Alaric, and they were unsure why. "Could she look on a grieving family with such disdain?" he wondered.

As the Sages congregated, Arlindra left the embrace of her family, muscled her way down the hallway, and found Elitirin with her allies Deritax and Gallily. The ranger's voice dripped with hostility as she interrogated the manabotanist, "Moondrake and Belleshade. Twisted ent root, and a little bit of unicorn dung. What is that?"

Elitirin's eyes widened in horror. "What madness? Why do you recite the recipe for a death potion?"

Arlindra shook her head. "Moondrake is toxic to elves. But in small doses it can treat unverified afflictions. Boils on the organs, they say. But Mystalon has no surgeons."

Elitirin's gaze went from shocked to anger. "You've been consulting sources from the outside, haven't you rebel child?" She spoke like a schoolteacher scolding a student, expecting a submissive response.

The wicked Sage, however, was not ready for Arlindra's defiance. "Infernia's blessing, I have!" She borrowed from Celyth's vernacular to emphasize her point. "My own mother is now suffering from the same illness, and she fled your backwards society to try and find healing. My aunt is dead, and it's at your hands. If my mother survives thanks to outside help, you should all resign and exile yourselves to the deepest pits of the Abyss."

Elitirin's judgmental gaze became one of fear. Her allies, the same two who had come to Arlindra's home nearly thirty years ago, also looked like they had seen a ghost. Though the Sages had come to show Mystalonian solidarity, Arlindra exposed their government agents for their hypocrisy. Rumor had it Elitirin was consorting with outsiders to find a way to travel through time. Such a concept was insane, Arlindra thought. It was hard to verify rumors in their secretive society, however, and she began to look for any reason to leave.

Half a year passed. In that time, the Sages that felt guilt over Kiriana's death began to entertain more technology and resources from outside their society. They invited the dwarves of Acero to trade metal for magitabs and magisalves, and the dwarves were more than polite and generous in their exchange. The Sages denied their request to send a historian to document the ways of Mystalonian society, but the general attitude toward outside influence remained positive. Elitirin's coalition also began their own relationships with outsiders, but they seemed more secretive than Alaric and Evander's economic initiatives. According to Elitirin's official reports, the outsiders utilized a magic similar to that of the Mystalonians, but its crystalized nature made it more diverse. In order to protect Mystalon and gain the technology of the outsiders, she played the role of a double agent; she promised to steal secrets for both sides, and she seemed to be fulfilling her end of the bargain well enough.

Celyth was still abrasive and obnoxious, but she had withdrawn from participating in Mystalonian society almost all together. Most people complained she was curt and rude, and Celyth insisted it was on purpose. At first people were taken aback by her shift in demeanor, and she was very vocally bitter. Anyone who questioned her antisocial attitude was quickly met by a lecture about Kiriana and their role in her death. Arlindra, however, continued to see Celyth's kindness and bravery.

Nine months after Mystalon reached a trade agreement with the dwarves of Acero, Mystalon was beset by a different type of threat. One fateful day in the month of The Festival, Arlindra and Celyth walked beneath the branches of the solisberry tree.

As they passed under a solisberry root forming an arch over a path, Arlindra caught movement in her periphery. "Cel," she hissed.

Celyth had already drawn a short bow from over her shoulder and had an arrow knocked. "I saw it too," she replied, crouching and looking in the shadows cast by the solisberry tree's towering roots.

Arlindra reached under her quiver to loosen a sheath on her back. From within, she drew a heavy, steel zweihänder. "Don't think we'll have time to shoot, cousin," she insisted, spinning behind a different, protruding root. "There!" she said pointing with her sword. She lunged toward a different root of the solisberry but stabbed only shadow.

She then realized the shadow was alive, and it scrambled to counterattack. Her mundane sword had no effect on the creature, and its shadowy paws drained her strength. It was vaguely humanoid like a draikin, but taller and elongated. She backed away quickly, and Celyth shot her arrow into the darkness pursuing Arlindra. The magitab affixed to the arrowhead caused it to burst into magical fire, which dispelled the shadow.

Arlindra fell to the ground, shivering. "By the earth mother, what was that?" she asked as an otherworldly chill penetrated her very essence.

Celyth shook her head. "I don't know yash-zim, and I've never heard of such beasts."

Arlindra waited a few moments and began searching her mind for prayers to the earth mother that might relieve her fatigue. Before she found a solution, Celyth reached inside a pouch she had hidden beneath another. "Here, try this," she said as she offered Arlindra a flask.

She did not question her cousin as she poured the vial into her mouth, the contents giving hints of mint and lavender. Within moments, her strength was restored. Arlindra stared at the vial for a moment. "Woah, can I get this in an ale?" she asked.

Celyth grinned. "It was a restorative potion, blessed by Thoradalia, Goddess of Dwarves."

Arlindra's eyes widened with shock. "It worked so easily?" she asked as she lifted her arms and wiggled her fingers, all of them feeling immensely heavy a moment ago.

Celyth looked around them. "Yeah, and I have a feeling that if I'd found something like that a while back, my mom might still be alive."

Arlindra's eyes dropped to the ground. "Oh, gods, Cel," she lamented.

"Yash-zim, don't get emotional. I might not be able to change what happened to Mom, but I sure can make sure my cousin is oh-kay-doh-kay." She drew out the sounds with a bit of whimsy, giving a giggle as she finished her silly voice. "Besides, if Elitirin had drank it, she'd be clawing her own throat out to make a point. And I'd love to watch her rip her own—"

Arlindra squirmed with discomfort, "Oh, gods, Cel, stop! That's awful!"

Celyth's eyes narrowed, and her lips curled up into an evil smile. "Well, they deserve it, don't they?" She had already lost interest in the shadow creature or its implications.

Arlindra returned the dark gaze, but her mouth twisted into a frown. "Just because they deserve it doesn't mean you have to relish in their suffering. Justice is found in balance. Find your neutral spirit, cousin, please."

Celyth rolled her eyes like Arlindra. "Of course, cousin. You know, you should be a little bit more hateful toward these bastards."

Arlindra sighed as she stood with a spinning motion from her hips and a push from her hands. "I could be, and it would be justified. But would that help anyone other than you?"

Celyth looked at the ground. "Not really, no. Hate is a heavy burden."

Arlindra nodded in agreement. "I know my mother is still alive, and perhaps that is why I can find my balance. I understand your hate, cousin. And I do not begrudge it. But." she tilted her head forward, her blue hair hiding a sleeping Nebu.

Celyth stuck her tongue between her teeth as Arlindra spoke, but then interrupted her, "I shouldn't force my feelings on you. Yash-zim'nides, I'm so sorry," she said, her voice filling with rare emotion. "I'm just glad I had a potion to help you, even though it came from the outside. And you understand me, and my position. I just wish you shared my willingness to burn this place to the ground."

Arlindra's frown deepened. "I'm sorry, but the Mystalonians have one thing correct. The solisberry tree is sacred. If true harm is to come upon them, then the tree would suffer greatly. And that is not a price I would pay, even at the expense of my own life."

Celyth's eyes widened with anger. "Infernia you will! You mean more to me than any damnable tree. Even one capable of what the solisberry is."

Arlindra's gaze softened. "Oh, cousin," she said with guilt as she realized her error.

As she often did these days, Celyth reached out and grabbed her cousin for an embrace. The introverted ranger squeezed back with all her might. There was only one person in the world who understood her, and that was Celyth. She felt like she might have been the only person in the world to understand her cousin as well.

Arlindra pushed her cousin back a bit, placing her own hands firmly on Celyth's shoulders. "Besides, that shadow creature should concern you as much as it does the Mystalonians. Your father and uncle are important members of this society. Would you see them slain, too? In some sort of revenge plot, you could very well cost our fathers their lives." She hugged Celyth again.

Celyth huffed, but then whimpered, "I know, Arli."

Arlindra held her cousin close for almost half an hour before they were beset by another shadow, which Celyth dispersed with a single shot of a magitab-infused arrow.

The cousins were not the only ones to encounter the strange, shadow creatures the Sages promptly dubbed "Umbrals." A wave of fifty of them spread throughout the city over the next week. The militia maintained extra vigilance and increased their patrols. Everyone else went about their normal lives, and Arlindra and Harmony departed on a hunting trip in the middle of that week. They were accompanied by Harmony's younger sister, Unity. The three of them rode on horses tamed from the wild stallions roaming near the city of Tanlin Falls to the west of Mystalon. The beasts were glad to help the rangers, and they returned to their wandering after each trip. The three had a successful hunt, transporting their quarry in a cart pulled by Harmony's mount. On their return, however, they found something that disturbed them greatly.

In the sparser, southwestern reaches of the Mystalonian Forest, they found a large, metal, capsule-like building. The only obvious entrance was on top through a door with a valve wheel on it. They dismounted their temporary steeds, bidding them return to the plains. The elves would carry the haul back to the city on their own. Strange tools were scattered about the area, implying construction was still underway. As the rangers investigated, Harmony was the first to comment, "Aren't we standing in territory controlled by Elitirin's family?"

Arlindra and Unity nodded together. Arlindra replied, "It seems Elitirin has expanded from manabotanist to engineer in a remarkably short time." She picked up a shovel that was made of clock parts. In the handle of the tool, there was a glowing stone. The light intensified when Arlindra focused on it, causing the blade of the shovel to vibrate. The ranger tossed the tool out of her hand in shock.

Unity, now apprenticed to her older sister, was thirty years old. She had taken the Fernith's side in the tragedy with Kiriana; as a result, she, too, had a deep distrust for Elitirin. She shared Harmony's vivid, pink eyes, but the color also extended to her hair. She shaved the right side of her head like her sister and Arlindra, too. With a grimace, she remarked, "That or she's consorting with outsiders and inviting them to Mystalon for their dirty work." She gestured toward the strange building. "That's not elven or dwarven. That's madness."

Arlindra's eyes narrowed, lingering on the strange shovel. "I wonder what my father knows of this."

Harmony gave a deep sigh, standing beside the strange building. "Something sinister is afoot; the earth mother is unsettled."

Unity returned to the cart, lifting its hitch. "We should report this to the Sages immediately."

Of one accord, they returned to the marketplace and turned their bounty over to one of the butchers there. Then, they rushed to Alaric's home in the Haerulf district. Upon their initial report, Alaric sent urgent messages to Wikton, Evander, and Shaelides. Within the hour, a quarter of the Sages of Mystalon were gathered in Alaric's home.

Arlindra finished repeating her report to the other Sages. "We did not enter the building, as we could not assess the danger. We wanted to make a report before intervening." She looked at the floor as she finished speaking. She trusted Wikton and her uncle, but Shaelides was a new member of their coalition. She was a silver haired elf standing just short of five feet, and she wore warm, white robes year-round. She was always adorned with gold and sapphire jewelry, and she wore a simple, silver tiara in her hair. Her eyes, however, were a brilliant green, and they reflected cunning and shrewdness, traits that attracted the young elf to politics. She was only ninety-five years old, making her the youngest Sage in the Congress.

Alaric replied, "As you can see, the report comes not only from Arlindra, but from Harmony and Unity as well. Requesting an inspection would not be politically motivated, as the story has been corroborated."

Shaelides smiled, her lips thin and her face angular and sharper than average. "Regardless of the veracity of their report, Elitirin will insist that it is politically motivated and attempt to retaliate."

Wikton shook his head with frustration. "After a week of dealing with Umbrals antagonizing citizens and keeping our militia overworked, I don't think the other Sages will see this as a wise use of time or resources. Especially if Elitirin has a way to hide the evidence." Everyone looked at the wise, aged druid. He stroked the thin, gray beard hanging from his chin. Elves rarely kept facial hair due to its fine, stringy nature. He continued, "If what you say is true, then she is no doubt consorting with outsiders. But we don't know what she's doing, nor if those activities could be easily concealed. Don't think Elitirin a fool."

Unity reiterated, "Again, the building was around one hundred feet long and somewhat rounded."

Wikton shook a finger as he rebutted, "Could it be easily moved? Buried? Was it magical in nature? Could it be hidden in the mana somehow?" He then straightened his robe. "Your presence there likely alerted them to your discovery, whoever 'them' may be."

Evander nodded in agreement. "Still, we could describe it as anomalous activity in that region of the forest, and the Sages will send their own agents to investigate. It could be ambiguous enough that the Sages won't be surprised if nothing is discovered."

Alaric and Shaelides smiled. Arlindra's father spoke confidently, "That way, if Elitirin is up to something, she'll be caught red handed. If nobody accuses her in the first place, nobody will think the report was politically motivated."

Arlindra's brow furrowed. "Wouldn't an ambiguous report give Elitirin time to hide her activity?" she questioned.

Wikton beamed. "And so, the report will be made for naught. Accept the futility of this avenue, friends. Arlindra is right. We need to keep this information close and get ahead of Elitirin's design. I say we offer to send agents to the outside world to seek an answer to the

Umbrals. This may give us an alternative way to identify what is coming into Mystalon from the outside." He cleared his throat. He sounded graver than normal, and it made Arlindra shudder.

Shaelides licked her lips. "I say we send your daughters, Alaric, Evander. As a gesture of solidarity." She looked around the room, making sure everyone was listening. "The most widely accepted theory is that the Umbrals are related to The Unbinding. So, let's do what Elitirin isn't brave enough to do herself."

Arlindra's heart skipped a beat. Traveling to the outside world was something she had only dreamed of. Still, the mission sounded dangerous, so she clarified, "What do you mean?"

Shaelides's smile was sinister, but it didn't feel malicious. Instead, it felt as if she knew something the others did not. "I have heard it rumored she seeks a way to reverse The Unbinding. She is seeking a metaphysical way to reach Argentum, the magical society where it all unfolded a century ago."

The other three Sages in her coalition looked to Shaelides with shock. Alaric asked with a sliver of hostility, "Where did you get such information? And was there a reason you waited to share it?"

Shaelides nodded, nonchalant. "Oh, of course, Alaric. I learned these things from Diamantra of the Eternidad district. Just this morning over tea, actually." She tilted her head to the side, glancing at the ground. "And the time to share has only now presented itself. It's a puzzle piece that I didn't know where to put."

Alaric winced internally. Shaelides was aligned in philosophy with the Fernith brothers, but she utilized different methods. "Very well, apologies for my tone. The Umbrals do present a more pressing issue, and a pilgrimage to such a magically mysterious place could benefit our society with information."

Arlindra stared at the ground. She wanted to go, but she also wanted to object. There was not a strong link between Elitirin's wishes to uncover the secrets of Argentum and sending the ranger to investigate it. Then, she realized, it was more a political move than a logical step. She frowned, looking up. "Do you really think such political posturing is necessary? The Umbrals could pose a threat to our society, and your solution is to try and get something useless before your opponent?"

Evander closed his eyes. She was right, and political posturing is what caused his wife's pain. He replied, somber, "Please, Arlindra. See the subtext of the mission. While you are out there, maybe you can find a way to stop the Umbrals. Even if you have to find an outsider to bring back with you." He opened his eyes, full of sorrow, as he continued, "By any means needed, if you can stop this crisis, please, yolen."

Arlindra's gaze softened. "Of course, uncle," she replied, informal. She realized sending them away was also a means to protect them. If the situation got worse and Alaric and Evander were blamed, violence against their families was a possible outcome. She felt helpless and angry, the same way she felt as her aunt's health deteriorated. Still, travelling to the outside could be an opportunity to reclaim control of the situation.

The Sages convened late that evening in the government building located in the northern part of the southernmost district, Behn. As reports of Umbrals continued to increase, the room became tense. The rangers gave their report in an ambiguous way as planned, prompting most of the Sages to ask Elitirin for permission to give a cursory inspection of her family's land. Then, she admitted the unthinkable: she had leased the land to outsiders wishing to graze zaligoats in that part of the forest. They were not to build any permanent structures within the forest and doing so would be a violation of their lease. She gave the Sages permission to investigate but asked for their understanding. Now that Mystalon had been entertaining outsiders, she saw this as an opportunity to acquire their currency in exchange for resources the Mystalonians sparsely used.

The Fernith brothers then voiced their proposal to send Celyth and Arlindra to investigate Argentum. Alaric's knowledge as a former wizard allowed him to explain his theory; if Umbrals were only present in Mystalon, then the threat was coming from within. The militia member and the ranger would seek the occurrence of Umbrals outside of Mystalon, and they would further seek answers to the nature of The Unbinding by investigating Argentum. Elitirin grew incensed at the mention of the magical society far to the northwest. Still, the other Sages interpreted Alaric's intent in a positive light, voting fourteen to two to send the Fernith cousins on such a quest. Though the objectives were vague, most of the Sages wanted to explore any avenue for identifying and halting the occurrence of Umbrals.

Arlindra was already prepared for such a journey; as she, her uncle, and her father went to Evander's home to discuss the mission with Celyth, they moved with swiftness. They already suspected that the Sages would find nothing incriminating thanks to Elitirin's cooperation. Arlindra's stride was much faster than her father's and uncle's, they thought she was running for a moment. Instead, they realized she moved with incredible purpose. If anyone could find answers, Arlindra was one of their greatest hopes.

As they arrived, they found Celyth already packed for a journey. She had a backpack loaded with supplies, magitabs, and food. Arlindra grinned. "Going somewhere, cousin?" she asked, meeting her just outside the front door of Evander's home.

"There's no need to explain. Nebu filled me in on all the details." She winked, and a moment later, the dracofly's eyes bulged out of Celyth's wild, purple hair.

Arlindra's eyes widened, and she reached up to her own hair, finding Nebu had left behind an illusory copy of himself there. She scrunched her face at the betrayal but was thankful for his foresight. "I had a feeling you couldn't wait to get away from here," she replied, feeling her heart race with excitement.

Celyth nodded, and she withdrew a regional map from a scroll case attached to her belt. "Argentum is supposed to be in the Dundoi region in the Selian Range, those huge mountains. Right?" she asked, impressing Arlindra with her knowledge of geography.

Alaric interrupted, "Indeed, but the journey will no doubt be treacherous. You should travel first to Acero to the northwest. You'll have to cross the river near Tanlin Falls. From Acero and beyond, you should be able to gather information related to Umbrals on the outside, as well as what Elitirin might possibly want to find at Argentum."

Celyth walked toward the main road, paved with beautiful, glowing stones. She turned to wave at her father and uncle. "I already figured that, uncle. I just hope Arli can keep up."

Arlindra joined her cousin in her swift departure. "She speaks the truth, father. Our objectives are clear to us, even if they remain hidden from others. Farewell, modai-rin and modai-moshir." Her rare use of formal elven caused the Fernith brothers to tear up. The coming months would be perilous for their daughters.

Celyth moved faster than Arlindra for the entirety of their journey.

Their first month of travel led them to a draikin settlement known as K'tal H'yuck. It was the only clear access point to the Dundoi Mountains, above which rested the magical ruins of Argentum. In the fallout of The Unbinding, the way to the ancient city had been lost. Their hunt for information led them to meet with a warpriest of the god of law and order. She was known by the draikin as "Mir'thax," but when they finally met face to face in The Copper Crescendo, the priestess was human.

"Please, to the draikin I am known as Mir'thax, which is the draconic version of my name. Call me Miranda, I insist." She was very polite, and her voice was musical. She had pretty cheeks and stunning blue eyes. Red hair had been braided to the front of her face, and she wore a resplendent, elven battlemail. The cousins quickly took an interest in the priestess's story.

Dragons from around the region had fled to the Dundoi Mountains as teams of dragon slayers armed with strange weapons began to hunt them and their eggs. Miranda was tied to the draikin here through her parents somehow, who happened to be dragons trapped as humans at the onset of The Unbinding. It became clear the young woman's friendly, determined demeanor and her growing faith would be the assets that Mystalon needed. They shared their plight with Miranda, and she swore to aid them in their endeavor. As such, Arlindra investigated ways to ascend the mountain through a massive cave network. The Unbinding rendered previous maps of the caverns obsolete, as the magical calamity drastically changed the tunnels. Old paths collapsed and new tunnels opened, creating a dangerous underground maze.

After working through the month of the Winter Solstice and a good portion of The Resting, the three found themselves high in the Dundoi Mountains. They had explored and mapped large sections of the winding paths under the mountains.

As they stepped into open air on the other side of an unmapped cavern, the sky above them was black and foggy. Their torches gave them a wide, visible range, but the mountainous terrain was treacherous and rocky. Arlindra struggled to find a safe path up the two-hundred-foot slope toward another cave. Getting back to K'tal H'yuck could prove difficult from here, Arlindra worried. She called back to her cousin and the heavily armored priestess, "Beware the loose stones." There was no clear, paved path, and the hilly, difficult slope stretched fifty feet wide. It narrowed as it approached the opening in an adjacent, spiring peak. The sides around them descended into infinite darkness below.

As Celyth followed her cousin up the path, a grassy mound crumbled beneath her feet, causing her to tumble backwards. She failed to catch her balance as she started to roll down the slope toward the side. Without hesitation, Miranda snapped her fingers in Celyth's direction, catching her in a bubble of subtle, purple light. It gently sat Celyth on the ground, laying her on her left side, looking up the slope. She hissed up, "Infernia's blessing, was that it? Your uncanny magic?"

Miranda looked down the slope with a sigh of relief. Her imitation of Jax's uncanny magic, the Mighty Stop, was the first idea she had, though she had yet to experience the pirate's power for herself. She had heard plenty of stories and knew it would be easy to duplicate with minimal mana expenditure. However, for safety's sake, she then surrounded the three of them with a similar purple aura. They found themselves nimble and light. She called out, "Hey, you should be able to fly up the slope now!"

Her words rang true; the three of them willed their bodies to the top. Celyth dusted herself off, glad she didn't injure herself in the sudden fall. "Miranda," she started, looking at the human with suspicion. "You've manifest so many different powers over the last month. I'm convinced that you are an omen of things to come."

Miranda tilted her head from side to side. "I have some kind of destiny, I am sure. I am only more sure that it would be prudent to move on into the next set of tunnels," she said, ending with a smile.

Arlindra nodded. She was impressed with Miranda's practicality. Though the priestess had a wide range of capabilities, she managed to parcel out her limited mana for the most effectiveness. Heightened senses and a magical safety net were hardly a fraction of her power, and she seemed to demonstrate extensive control. The cave entrance was ten feet high and eight feet wide, and it narrowed inside. In the light from her torch, Arlindra detected the priestess's hair had lightened in hue somewhat. The ranger assigned significance to such a change, suspecting it was tied to Miranda's limitations with the mana. Perhaps she had been too quick to assume Miranda as disciplined; it seemed that she was more practical in the sense of saving lives and preventing injury, regardless of the expense to herself. Nevertheless, Arlindra's growing trust for the priestess increased, recognizing the way using magic taxed her.

As they navigated the next tunnel, Arlindra asked, "What do you stand to gain by helping us to such a remote location, then? I have wondered about your motives since we came into partnership." She spoke in a stiff, formal tone. Miranda appreciated Arlindra's directness.

The priestess replied, "Understanding the nature of this location could be pivotal in helping restore the strength of the dragons. As it stands, there is an imbalance that justice would see corrected. Perhaps there is a clue among the ruins, or perhaps we face demons left behind from a century ago. I do not know." She smiled, her pretty cheeks reflecting the torchlight with a rich, sandy color. "I'll get us out of here quickly if we find ourselves in danger. I have to. I want to make sure you are both safe. Your city is relying on you, and I hope that we find answers up here. For all of us."

Celyth laughed. She had never considered the possibility somebody so powerful could be so honest. Growing up around politicians gave her trust issues. "You really are that selfless, aren't you?" she asked, a bit of condescension in her voice.

Miranda sighed. "Perhaps to the detriment of others. I'm terrified that I'll hurt people, whether it's through my own power or through my indecision. I refuse to hesitate to help people in need, even if that path is violent. I will never again stand idle while the innocent suffer." She shrugged her shoulders and tilted her head. "Sometimes one has to give up part of themselves for the greater good. Other times, we defend the innocent and the weak so that they do not endure the same sacrifices. I am no longer either of those, and so I have a duty."

Arlindra's curiosity was piqued by the woman's candidness. "What manner of duty?" she asked as they traversed the steep tunnel. The priestess did not give an immediate response. Miranda and Celyth followed Arlindra's path through the cave, using secure stalagmites and stalactites to move up sheer rockfaces. They even had to grapple a few areas, pulling themselves up with nothing more than a rope and the reliable, sharp grappling teeth. Miranda was exceptionally strong, impressing the cousins with her nimble movement in her heavy armor. The mithril parts were simple and light, but adamant was as heavy as it was dense. The entire, long chain skirt had to weigh thirty pounds; still, Miranda was able to ascend ropes and cliff faces, even with a clumsy tower shield strapped to her back.

As they finished scaling a rockface, Miranda sat on the ground for a moment to catch her breath. "My duty. To protect the innocent and the weak, of course." She replied as sincerely as she seemed in every other mannerism.

Arlindra looked at her cousin. Celyth shrugged. She felt the same way, and she knew Miranda had already seen through their stories.

Celyth spoke. "Well then, when we find this ancient city, what will we do if we find answers about The Unbinding as a whole, but not the Umbrals or anything else? Like, how can we go back with something that Elitirin would hate if we found it?"

Arlindra blinked. "What do you mean, cousin?" she asked with confusion.

Celyth pointed at Miranda. "I think we should take her back to Mystalon. That's probably all we need to figure out the Umbral problem."

Miranda looked around them in the cave. "I'm a little lost, myself, Arlindra," she commented. "I can go back with you at a moment's notice, I just hope you weigh the situation carefully."

Arlindra's eyes widened. "Miranda, did you say that your magical essence is replenished by the strength of the arcane stream?"

The priestess nodded, her braids bouncing off her breastplate with a thud. "Yes. It flows with richness here. I can supplement my protection prayers with arcane power. Beyond that, though, I might find myself running out of mana quickly." She sighed. "Before I understood this power, I had a huge capacity to use it. Before I knew what I had." She trembled as she spoke, her eyes dropping to the stone floor of the cave. "I lost a great deal of it. Almost ninety percent. Maybe a bit more."

Arlindra speculated Miranda's power would be nearly unlimited near the solisberry tree. Celyth was right about taking Miranda to Mystalon, but her cousin interrupted before Arlindra could continue.

Celyth's face scrunched with annoyance. "Well, is there any way to get it back? Like a way to recharge your essence?"

Miranda shook her head. "All I know is that Invictus is righteous, and I've been blessed with a gift greater than I could have ever asked for. I intend to fulfill my duty to the best of my ability."

Arlindra's lips pursed with a pleased expression. Miranda might have seemed gullible and enthusiastic, but those traits masked an emotional burden. The priestess saw the sincerity of the cousins' cause with her exceptional wisdom. She explained to them her role as a Judge of Hearts. She could see people's souls, and that gift came from a place of faith. As long as the objectives of her god were aligned with the objectives of other mortals, she would feel friendship and empathy with them. If their intentions were different, however, Miranda would sense the friction between their souls. Arlindra then smiled, adding, "You are sincere and wise for a human."

Miranda frowned. "Well, I'm a dragon, too. Not just a human.

Although my body is definitely human." She giggled. "It doesn't entirely make sense to most people."

Celyth shook her head. "Wait, so you literally meant you are a dragon?"

Nebu's head appeared above Arlindra's hair. "I told you! I smelled it on her from day one! There's no way anybody can doubt the power of my sense of smell. Dracoflies have the best noses in Espa!"

Miranda laughed as she stood, her heavy skirt rattling in the compact space of the cave. She had to bend, and even the elf cousins seemed cramped. There was, however, another rockface that needed scaling. It went up over one hundred feet. The priestess added, "Well, I'm starting to get bored with climbing like this over and over again. Can I make this faster?"

Arlindra and Celyth traded glances again. Arlindra then made eye contact with Miranda, which the priestess broke immediately, looking at the ground. "You mean, you could have teleported us up the mountain all along?"

Miranda shook her head, realizing that she had miscommunicated. Sometimes she struggled with what she meant to say, and trying to impress her new friends had led her to fail in her bravado. "Not exactly, but I can see right there. It takes a lot out of me to teleport too far, but just a step here and there reminds me of Master Zeak's power. He's one of the best fighters in K'tal H'yuck. I promise he's not just a drunk," she said with a sigh. She hoped she could recover from the miscommunication. "He taught me how to step through space and time briefly. It could help us reach Argentum, but I might need to rest by the time we get through this mountain."

Celyth frowned. "Miranda," she said with a bit of worry in her voice.

The priestess giggled. "Stop, Celyth. I've got way too many people worried about me. I have to send them letters every week or they'll send a battalion of pirates or paladins looking for me." She shuddered. "I'd hate to think of Erk's crew this far inland, or Justin and August assigned to hunt me down. And I don't know who'd make the call to send them first."

Arlindra let out a sigh of relief. Miranda was being as whimsical as Celyth. The ranger explained, "We are close to the top, anyway. Your mana should be easy to replenish, and I swear to serve as your bodyguard for as long as needed for you to recover."

Celyth tilted her head impetuously. "Excuse you? I'm the militia girl. I'm the real bodyguard."

Miranda looked above and moved her hands in quick circles in front of her. They left behind a tangible, glowing trail. She focused on the space she could see above. Light poured from her, illuminating the cramped cave with purple brilliance. After a moment, a small, magical gate opened. "Okay, hop on through," she ordered. The destination at the top was visible through the round door opened by mana.

The cousins entered the portal, taking them another hundred feet up with just a step. "Oh, Infernia's blessing," Celyth cursed with relief at the top. The light from Miranda's gateway lingered, showing them a possible exit ahead. As they walked toward it, Miranda took the lead. It was now clear in the residual light that her hair had turned pink. It reminded Arlindra of Unity's vivid hair. She sighed, contemplating the implications.

The ranger insisted, "When we get to the top here, we should take a rest."

Celyth's lips curled up with an eager rebuke, "What's wrong, cousin, can't handle the climb?"

Arlindra shook her head and gave a nod in Miranda's direction, who was nearing the exit of the cavern. "Her hair," she cautioned.

Celyth's lips drew tight, her green eyes glinting in the torchlight. "Oh," she said, her voice becoming meek and concerned.

Miranda turned to face them. "I can feel Argentum on the other side of this passage. Are you both ready?" She could feel their worry. Before they could voice their apprehension, she replied, "You two are cousins, but you grew up more like sisters, didn't you?"

They froze. Arlindra gave an affirming nod, and Celyth explained, "It's probably pretty obvious. We were born cousins, but I think we're sisters at heart."

Arlindra smiled but added nothing. They rested for a few hours just inside the exit to Argentum. Miranda regained some color in her hair, but the cousins were now among the people who worried about her as she expended mana.

After Shalo's funeral, the Fernith cousins embraced outside the dressing room of *The Nebula*, waiting to join Miranda and the others on the bow. Celyth pushed Arlindra away from her for a moment. She asked the ranger pointedly, "Are you sure? Yash-zim, are you absolutely sure?"

Her cousin nodded. "Elitirin said to start my search in the Isles Known for Nothing. Plus, in a stroke of destiny . . ." she started but trailed off. She scratched her chin before continuing, "The pirate captain. He spent so much time and money trying to cure his brother that his contacts are wide and varied. Surely, somebody would know where she went."

Celyth looked up to the bow of the ship, only minutes remaining before Miranda would decide to leave.

Arlindra waved to her cousin in the warbling light created by Miranda's massive teleport. She knew she would not see Celyth for a while, and she called out, "Yashirote'nides!" Celyth thought she heard yash-zim'nides, which prompted a moment of panic. As the teleport ended, she realized what Arlindra had said. Now, as Miranda purified the city of Nulodia with purple waves of light, she sat down on the floor in the sanctuary of the grand cathedral of Invictus and cried.

"I love you too, sister," she said out loud and in her heart.

At that moment, the bulging eyes of a dracofly emerged from her wild hair. "Uh, Celyth," he commented.

She grabbed the dracofly and gave him a violent hug. "I love you too, buggy, don't you ever forget it. And you better tell my cousin what I said!"

He buzzed up into the air, his skin shimmering between waves of purple brilliance. "I will tell her none of the sort! Do it yourself. Plus! I have orders not to leave until you make it to The Lichwood!"

Chapter 19
Loose Ends

"Justice is vengeance with extra steps. Do not suffer the oppressors another chance to lie. Reliance on a system of law dooms another group to oppression. Even if you defeat your oppressors through legal means, they will survive to ply their greed again." – Pulhash, *The Liberator*

Yuvina knocked on the nondescript door of an abandoned structure in the slummier part of Nulodia. She knew this building to be the headquarters of The Forgotten's operations within the city, and she rapped with a coded rhythm indicating her status as a member. She waited three, precise minutes then repeated the knock. After a moment, she, Miranda, Selasine, and Damil Starstorm heard several latches clicking. The door opened, revealing three, heavily armed individuals. A gnoll standing at six feet tall with forest green fur, a dwarf with countless knives strapped on his belt, and a human with an eyepatch over his left eye all began to greet Yuvina. They stopped and drew their weapons at the sight of her entourage.

Yuvina yapped, "Calm, brethren. They represent the Church of Invictus, and they are here to serve a search warrant." Selasine held up the warrant signed by High Paladin Erista. The Peacekeeper Precinct had issued an expedited warrant since Yuvina's life was in danger. Erista was shocked to learn the abandoned buildings in question were the hideout of The Forgotten, but their activity was only borderline suspicious. The church did not keep track of them due to their willingness to abide by the law.

The dwarf bellowed, "Yuvina, yer alive! Everdusk has yer name in the ears of every member, and here ye show up with Wielders."

Yuvina snarled, "Don't lecture me, Bim. I can't remember an entire month of my life and Aylabrax the Devourer planted an evil command in my mind without my knowledge. If it wasn't for these Wielders, I'd have been dead for certain."

The dwarf's cheeks flushed deep crimson in spite of his earth toned skin. "Listen here, lass, a good portion of The Forgotten feel forgotten since ye found power and up and left us. We should arrest ye and take ye for interrogation!"

At the threat, Damil touched his fingers to his temple. Miranda's eyes narrowed as she witnessed the offensive capability of his magic for the first time. He sent a scrambled, psychic message into the minds of the door guards, causing them to fall to the ground, hopelessly and needlessly covering their ears. After the incapacitating mental blow, Selasine spoke firmly, "Or perhaps we will arrest you on behalf of the Sword of Justice and interrogate you about Yuvina's missing memories. I'm sure you understand, this is a matter of saving a life, and the church is legally authorized to exercise full authority in such a matter."

The gnoll growled, "Yuuuuvinaaaa, why would you betray us?" His voice was raspy and agitated.

The kitsune bared her teeth and knelt beside him. "Do you know what it's like to have incredible power? The blessings of The Unbinding we all wished for?"

He shook his head, his paws easing from around his ear as the echoes of Damil's attack faded. "I suppose you'll tell me how it feels, then, since you've left our folds." He panted with lingering pain.

Yuvina's expression softened. "It feels terrifying. Control over the universe is something mortals should not take lightly. And what's worse is when you know every time you use that incredible gift, you bring yourself one moment closer to death." Her whiskers trembled as she spoke.

The human with the eyepatch drew ragged breaths. He was overcome with emotion. Damil's attack exposed the door guard to Yuvina's emotions, and the foxkin's terror took over his state of mind. "Bim, Thimble, please, can't you see? Just look at Yuvina! She's terrified! Her tail, her whiskers." He started to cry uncontrollably. "By Pulhash, Yuvina, I'm so sorry!"

Yuvina stood, still curling her lips in disgust. "What in the

Infernia did you do to Sal, paladin?"

Damil shook his head and replied with a gentle voice. "I've only opened his mind to the feelings of your heart. He truly weeps for you, Yuvina." His hazel eyes shimmered with sincerity, his aging face still boyish but intimidating.

Miranda stepped forward and stood over the incapacitated door guards. "In the name of Invictus, we are here to search the premises for clues to the whereabouts of Yuvina's memories. We intend to extract the information by all legally permissible means." She stomped her foot. "And Mir'thax Toi'landra comes calling on behalf of her friend Yuvina. Dragons of light still watch over mortals in the name of the Dragon Queen. Be warned, the servants of Invictus are bound by the laws of our god, but the dragons are bound only by The Unbinding."

The three looked up with terror. Distinct red and blue auras flickered around her physical presence. Two ephemeral dragons, one red and the other blue, hovered around the young woman. According to legends, dragons were so overwhelming they were surrounded by fear-inducing magic. Miranda created such an aura with the power of her parents' godshards.

The dwarf cowered harder, "By Pulhash, we're doomed!" he cried out.

Miranda neutralized her ethereal flex. She remembered her experience with dragon fear when she arrived on Olvidado for the first time. The auras of her parents were true to their form and personalities, and Miranda expressed those traits with illusions woven with mana. The warpriest sighed before saying, "Don't worry. We are only here to save Yuvina. I know that in your heart, you want the same." Her role as a Judge of Hearts permeated her words. "Please. We do not wish any harm upon The Forgotten; in fact, we are here to aid you."

Damil lowered his fingers from his temple. "There are more than fifty people here. Many minds, all of them stressed." He was tall, standing around six foot two. He still looked small next to Selasine, however, as his frame was nowhere near as broad, and his clean shaven features were delicate and handsome. "I'm afraid confrontation will result in casualties. Note the hostility from the doormen, and Yuvina's designation as a deserter. We need to find Everdusk sooner rather than later."

Selasine furrowed his brow. "Yolasha?"

Miranda frowned, and the music in her voice was a consistent, minor key. "At once, modai-rin." She looked around the 'abandoned' building. The inside was clean, and a sitting room for receiving guests opened before them. Miranda entered, finding a mirror on the wall in the sitting room. She licked her lips in anticipation as she prepared to ask the mana to do something new. Her heart skipped a beat. Like the purifying purple light, such requests had become more powerful but demanding. She remained vigilant for the safety of Reshiria's and Philotrax's souls.

Looking into the mirror, her reflection stared back as expected. Her braids looked a little frayed, but she thought she looked incredible. The blue lines painted up her cheeks gave her the appearance of a fierce warpriest on a warpath. "Sword of Justice, guide my hand," she prayed. Divine power surged through her, and her demeanor changed in the mirror. Her lips curled down with anger. She punched the mirror with her gauntleted fist. "Everdusk! You have been summoned by agents of the law!"

She funneled the might of the arcane stream into the shattered glass and meli-to'thril, a reflective layer of mithril so thin it was as brittle as dry leaves. As the pieces fell, the ether around Miranda swirled, creating a forceful, steady wind. The remnants of the mirror vibrated until the gusts surrounding Miranda lifted them up. They whirred around her, generating a low hum. The sound grew into a melody sung by a pirate on a distant shore. "Let the weary rest, those with a crusade, those with war in their hearts. Let the harmony of peace comfort their bodies and their souls. Sleep now, forgotten of the arcane. Dreams of power, dreams of pride."

Cantalus, He Who Sings at the Gate, god of the pirates, floated his voice across space and time. When Miranda smashed the mirror, Cantalus heard her magical plea. It was not a telepathic message, but a prayer sent through the pulse of the arcane stream. Her petition for The Forgotten alerted the immortal pirate of the need for a song. In order to save the lives of the downtrodden and the fearful, Cantalus composed a verse to put everyone to sleep except the one named by Miranda: Everdusk. The Guardian Dragon of Yendralia, as Cantalus called her in song these days, called out to him as one more sympathetic than Pulhash and yet one aligned in goals and philosophy. The followers of the Avenging Rider were lulled by the soothing tones of the god of pirates.

In his song, however, he taunted Miranda. "The dragon rages on, but a game she's going to miss. The Death Pirates bounty be great, and their blockade is a show. The prize money will be spent before you come to see us again, and for that, we weep." The melody sounded like a lullaby tinkling on a music box. Miranda's hand rested on her healer's bag, the song reminding her of the family heirloom specifically crafted for her.

Cantalus's voice faded. They waited for ten minutes in the sitting room. The door guards were all asleep; so was the entire operational headquarters of The Forgotten with the exception of one person: Seiv Everdusk. The elected head of the organization appeared at the top of a stairwell leading up into the complex made of adjoined, abandoned buildings. "What is the meaning of this infernal, unbreakable sleep? Who is it that calls my name through all the mirrors of this place?"

Selasine's face twitched with anger, so he cycled his breath before speaking. "Seiv Everdusk! High Priest Selasine of the Church of Invictus requests an audience with the head of The Forgotten. I wish to speak with you on a matter of life and death."

Before Selasine could finish his formal introduction, Yuvina pounced up the stairs, tackling Everdusk. "What did they do to me after the hunt at the merchant guild?" she yapped furiously. She sounded equal parts scared and angry.

"No! Yuvina, stay calm! Don't accidentally activate your powers!" Miranda called after her fox friend as she leapt, intent on violence.

Yuvina had expressed she felt her life tugged away from her when her powers activated. Miranda was disheartened to learn that she had known that since the fight in Mystalon, but she was glad Yuvina shared that with her. Miranda's voice soothed her anger, the melody dissonant enough it distracted the foxkin. She called back to the priestess, "Don't worry Miranda! I won't hurt him. He's my boss. He just has a lot to answer for right now." Her vulpine eyes connected with Everdusk's as he lay underneath her.

The head of The Forgotten's eyes filled with tears. "Gods. Pulhash be praised, you're alive. Yuvina, we've been worried about you. We left you with One, and he promised he'd help you hone your gift. We haven't heard from him or you since a week ago." He exhaled.

Yuvina snarled, but she felt Damil pressing his mind against her and Everdusk. "Do not worry, churchman. Everdusk is honest. He should know that whatever happened to me is killing me."

Miranda took a moment to evaluate her surroundings. The staircase scaled a wall to the left of the door. The stairs doubled back up to the second story directly above the sitting room. Everdusk had been standing on the walkway halfway up the stairs. As Miranda sized up the structure of the base, the head of The Forgotten replied to Yuvina's veiled, honest explanation. "Killing you? One promised it was safe and had been tested on animals, numerous times, even! He promised he would not give you power without your consent!"

Yuvina gave a sharp yowl. "Gods be damned, Everdusk. I don't know where I've been for a month until a week ago! Who in the Infernia is One? What kind of powers was I supposed to receive? Is this possible to undo?" As she confronted Everdusk, the Magic Mirror's orbs formed around her. Their lights reflected Yuvina's agitation. If nobody provoked the mirrors, they would need no mana. No lifeforce was required to reveal her power. Everdusk, however, had already seen it.

The head of The Forgotten frowned, "Yes, I've seen your power, Yuvina. Do you truly not remember my appearance at One's estate? I was there with that frost giant, Farzg, yes?"

At the mention of the slaver's name, Damil and Selasine rushed up the stairs. Miranda teleported up before them, standing over Yuvina and Everdusk, sword drawn. With authority in her voice, she interrogated, "What manner of relationship does The Forgotten have with The Frozen Death?"

Selasine winced. "Miranda, slow down!" In his experience interrogations went better without revealing relationships between parties involved. The use of Farzg's criminal designation would reveal the church's antagonism toward the slaver, though, in truth, he figured Everdusk already knew the church's disposition.

Damil gave Selasine a mental nudge, sending him a thought. "Careful. I still can't see Miranda's mind. She seems confident, though, let her work. Everdusk is vulnerable."

Selasine stopped at the top of the first stairs. Damil approached by his side, reaching over to grab Thomas's hand. They had on armored gauntlets, but the gesture was the most important part of the action.

Everdusk huffed, "We have no relationship beyond a mutual client. One, as he calls himself. Doctor One."

Miranda's eyes narrowed. "And who is that?"

Yuvina stayed perched on top of him. She looked at him with terror in her vulpine pupils. "You—You are in league with them?" she panted. "The scientists! Sender! Reginald!" she started to tremble with anger and fear.

Miranda glanced at Selasine and Damil. Her lips twisted up into a frustrated grin. "Not too fast, Yuvina. What if he doesn't know them?"

Everdusk shook his head, "The names—They, they—" he hesitated with panic.

Miranda bent down. "Please." She spoke with a compassionate melody. "We really only want to save Yuvina. If you value her life, you'll tell us everything that's happened to her since the Winter Solstice."

Yuvina's legs relaxed and she stood, towering over Everdusk. The mirror orbs around her vanished.

Everdusk blinked and nodded but remained on the ground, propping up on his elbows. "One approached us about a contract; he needed a full detail on a merchant guild trafficking dragon eggs."

Miranda inhaled a sharp breath. Selasine trusted her, giving an internal smile as she attempted to extract information without revealing purpose. She replied, "Is this some kind of secret culinary guild? Or would there be another reason to move the eggs without checking them through customs?"

Everdusk's eyes tried to find the interrogating priestess, and his mind recognized the voice. "Are you the woman who slew the shadows plaguing the city last night? The prayer and the purple light? Your voice, it reminds me of that song of hope."

Selasine and Damil both smiled as Miranda replied, "The arcane stream and the holy judgment of Invictus saved Nulodia. I was merely the hand that put those powers in their needed place." She gave a calming breath. "Please, Mister Everdusk. You've avoided my question, and that bothers me. We need your full cooperation."

Yuvina looked down at him, tears filling her eyes. "I need you to tell them, please."

Everdusk finally understood. "One seemed intent on acquiring dragon eggs, and he needed information on people trafficking them within the city. A few merchant guilds are trying to raise prices by buying them up with excessive coin. Doctor One wanted to know what uncanny magics they wielded, which is our specialty. Yuvina personally succeeded on that mission, and One was able to reach a deal with the merchants." He paused, and his clean shaven upper lip quivered in thought. "He was so impressed with our work, he showed us the way he could infuse the arcane stream into a living creature. Yuvina was our best candidate, so we sent her to meet One without pretense. He sold her on the idea, and he reported her missing a week ago. We've been looking for you everywhere." His face was torn by guilt, and his voice wavered. "I had no idea he would so willingly throw you away and sell you to the highest bidder."

Yuvina glared. "So, there was money involved beyond the recon?" she growled.

Everdusk's eyes widened. "There was a substantial payment, but you were supposed to receive a great sum as well! I would never have involved you had I realized this was an experiment, but it makes sense. He hired us to move some correspondence after we agreed to provide him with one of our top agents to try the infusion. How did he convince you?" he asked, his question genuine enough in tone.

Yuvina snarled, "I don't remember! I can't see any of it! I even let the paladin look in my mind this morning! There is nothing there!" She sounded hysterical.

Miranda's soothing voice intervened, calming the kitsune. "Everdusk. Is there any evidence that One is aligned with Aylabrax, the Devourer?"

The head of The Forgotten lay motionless for a few moments. He stuttered a bit. "I-it's hard t-to say. He was s-secretive." Yuvina's fit had unsettled him.

Miranda detected his anxiety, and his fear for Yuvina was clear. She reassured him, "We are not here to harm you. The information you're sharing could save Yuvina's life. She said she didn't have many uses of Magic Mirror left before it totally consumes her remaining life essence." The Judge of Heart's voice was calming.

Everdusk looked at Yuvina with concern. He fought through his guilt as he explained, "You worked a mission for us, the merchant guild. The one with the dragon eggs. As a result, we sent you to meet with One. He took you to his base outside of the city, up in the north; whatever he did to you there gave you an incredible power that could block the big guy's Death Geyser attack. Completely." He licked his lips, but his dry mouth made it futile. "One promised to train you to use your power. It seems he had other plans."

Selasine and Damil traded glances. The high priest stepped forward and added, "One and Farzg are aligned in some goal, but we will deal with that after we discover what happened to Yuvina. Does this One have great wealth and resources?" he asked, his voice carrying the authority of his station within the church.

Yuvina stepped backwards cautiously, allowing Everdusk to sit upright. He nodded. "Great wealth and even greater technology. He's managed to replicate dozens of spells using contraptions and the lacrima-deum he used for the infusion." He spoke honestly, putting Miranda's hostility at ease. She hated it when people dodged questions, and she could feel his forthcomingness. "He was working with Yuvina at his estate in the Ermen Moors to the north, as I mentioned. Perhaps searching there would be useful?"

Damil touched his fingers to his temple. "The magical sleep from Cantalus has started to fade. If they think we've made a hostile move, this will be a bloodbath."

The door guards began to rouse and Everdusk stood up. He inhaled and looked at Yuvina, "I could send correspondence to One, but I doubt he will respond at this point. He reported you missing under false pretenses; and, as to your question, savior of Nulodia," he continued, looking at Miranda. "I am a cleric of Pulhash, and I did not detect the sinister stain of Aylabrax on One. However, if he is in league with her, that could explain Yuvina's missing memories."

Selasine nodded in agreement. "Very few powers in this universe can erase memories without so much as even a trace. Aylabrax is on that short list." He reached up to his chest and clutched the holy symbol hanging from his neck. He felt Invictus and Lexcord had been struggling to keep the Devourer busy. He wasn't sure what was happening, but he suspected their interventions were necessary.

Miranda grimaced. She was hoping for easy answers, but as usual, this seemed to be futile. She said, "You mentioned an infusion and lacrima-deum." Her electric gaze had softened, but the music in her voice sounded hostile and uncertain. "Do you mean to say Doctor One has put lacrima-deum inside Yuvina somehow?"

Everdusk shook his head, the sounds of The Forgotten waking up throughout the base surrounding them. "I do not know the specifics, but he promised that he could bond her to the arcane using strange devices made of eolnut. He promised that the process would be painful but successful."

Bim looked up the stairs, his voice still sleepy, "They've got the boss surrounded!" he shouted.

Everdusk looked down the stairs and raised a hand. "Nonsense, Bim. These are our esteemed guests from the Church of Invictus. And our precious Yuvina has returned. You should be celebrating, not accosting them." In that moment, Everdusk realized the distrustful organization he had built was far too clandestine. If he could convince the Church of Invictus to sponsor changes in the legal system, then it would be simple enough to gain equality for The Forgotten. Trust and love had eroded all around him, and the only thing remaining was doubt and fear. He turned around to face Miranda directly. "If you are a priestess of Invictus, how is it that you summoned the pirate god, Cantalus? I heard his voice as my organization was put to sleep."

Miranda's lips pursed up into a cocky smile, an expression that shocked Selasine. The high priest looked back to Damil with confusion, but his beloved merely shrugged. The warpriest replied, "I am afraid what I know of Pulhash is little compared to what I know of Cantalus. I knew he would be sympathetic to your plight." The melody in her voice was boastful. "Thanks to the gifts I hold within myself, I can use the arcane stream to contact gods outside the primordial place. With Cantalus's song, I knew I could prevent violence between The Forgotten and the Church of Invictus." Her eyes sparkled with excitement.

Selasine's stomach dropped. Miranda was different. Very different. This was ego, and he had never once seen her express such pride and cockiness, even for something so great as reviving hundreds of injured and dead. His eye darted around nervously, and he tried to listen for the melody in her voice. She was speaking frantically, and the notes were dissonant and disconnected.

Damil picked up on Selasine's worry, inhaling a deep breath. He interrupted Miranda's explanation, asking out loud, "Dear Miranda, are you feeling alright?"

She stopped mid-sentence, and her cheeks flushed red. Her eyes widened, and she realized she had gotten carried away with a series of prideful boasts. There was a time and a place to celebrate one's achievements. She vowed to look up her penance before bedtime. "Apologies, High Paladin Emeritus, Your Holiness. My brashness is unbecoming of my station, and I will pay penance." She turned her eyes back to Everdusk, her cheeks still burning. "I just knew Cantalus would keep everyone safe. Which is what Yuvina wanted most." She still felt more of a violent impulse than she was used to, and it worried her further. Mir'thax truly was calling alongside Miranda, and she felt a duality within herself that had been growing since the events in Mystalon. That pain in her soul lingered in her memory, and she was glad it hadn't returned.

Selasine interjected, "So we know that Yuvina was with Doctor One during the missing month. That leads us no closer to answers, and Yuvina's life is still at risk." He looked at the kitsune. "Healers have no answers, either."

Members of The Forgotten had gathered around the stairs above and below. Yuvina and Everdusk stood face to face, her whiskers still trembling with anxiety. Everdusk reached out and offered to take the kitsune's paw. "Please know, Yuvina, I never would have sent you to Doctor One had I known his true intent. As far as reversing the process, I know nothing." The leader of The Forgotten looked back at Miranda, who was behind him as he faced Yuvina. "It is unlike The Forgotten to seek the aid of Wielders, but from a place of desperation, it is not unheard of. Is there anything you can do?"

Miranda felt her ego melt into fear. She was not sure what could be done, and the arcane was bonded to Yuvina, flowing through her like it did everyone with an uncanny gift. She thought of Evan, who once had an Unbinding power, but it was lost when his essence returned from within the arcane stream. Miranda healed Evan before she fully understood her draconic gifts, but she began to think about that moment. She remembered praying to the gods to no avail. Then, she called to those whispers inside her mind to heal the curse. With the ether stored within her, she reached into the stream and pulled Evan's life essence out, leaving all attachment to the arcane inside. Her eyes widened and her lips formed a round shape of wonder.

Selasine raised the eyebrow above his eyepatch, watching her demeanor revert to her normal, contemplative expression. "Yolasha, have you thought of something?"

She nodded in return, stepping beside Everdusk, looking at Yuvina. "Maybe I can save you the way I saved Evan." Her eyes filled with tears. "I'm certain that you will lose access to your new gifts, however."

Yuvina gave a simple nod. "A year ago, I would never have believed any of this was possible. Now that I have had a great power, I know it's not worth the price." She gave a small smile. "And you taught me. There is always a price."

Selasine and Damil traded adoring looks. Though Miranda was starting to express uncharacteristic behavior, her heart was still in the right place. She had such an impact on those around her, and the two of them beamed with pride. The priestess reached out to touch Yuvina's shoulder, a momentary spark of magical friction causing Everdusk to jump backward, letting go of Yuvina's paw. "What is this reaction?" he asked, confused.

Yuvina's nose twitched twice before she replied, "We don't really know." After the initial backfire of mana, the stream calmed to a steady waterfall of particles. It rained down Yuvina's left arm from where Miranda rested her hand on Yuvina's shoulder. "But whatever it is, it's because of whatever One did to me."

Miranda's lips drew tight, and she closed her eyes. She could see

Evan's desiccated husk in her arms on the deck of *The Nebula* so many months ago. "It's not a curse like Evan's condition, though. I may have more trouble severing the connection," she warned. She opened her eyes and frowned. "Trying to cut the bond to the arcane stream with more arcane energy could be dangerous to those around us. I believe the magical reaction between Yuvina and me might have deadly consequences." The music in her voice was serious and punctuated. "Perhaps we should seek answers at One's base to the north of the city as Everdusk suggested." She looked at the leader of The Forgotten. "Would you be willing to guide us there?"

Everdusk smiled as he replied, "Of course. We haven't far to go from here, anyway." He turned to his followers gathering around. "Forgotten of the arcane, hear this. Doctor One and his ilk have proven to be more dangerous than the Wielders who discriminate against us. Please cease all cooperation with their group and report any correspondence to me immediately. One will answer for his crimes." He looked at Selasine.

The high priest nodded in agreement. "Indeed, and the Church of Invictus wishes to hear in great detail the struggles of The Forgotten. May we work together to build a future so that nobody feels forgotten."

Miranda's heart skipped with excitement. Though their recent adventures had seen many hardships, they were still working hard to create a better world for everyone. She had to reign in these emotions that were starting to make her act wildly.

Everdusk gave some final orders to his lieutenants then walked to the front door of The Forgotten's headquarters. He gestured to invite the representatives of the church. He talked as they followed him. "I fear some of my recent decisions will have wider implications. I'm providing the Church of Invictus with The Forgotten's financial records. We want to help stop Doctor One. What he has done to Yuvina is inexcusable." He walked out the door and crossed his arms. "As I said, the way to his base is not far from here. We cannot hesitate. Yuvina's life is at stake."

Selasine led the others out of the building. He replied to Everdusk, "We have an expert who can review your documents for leads at the cathedral."

The leader of The Forgotten smiled and answered, "That's where my courier will take them. Come, follow me to One's base."

As he guided them to the abandoned building with the sewer access, Yuvina started to tremble. Miranda held onto the kitsune's paw, watching her new friend react instinctively to the surroundings. Yuvina explained, "This. I know I've been here before." When they descended into the sewers, she knew the way, but she didn't know why. The boat in the aqueduct also felt familiar, as did the low arch in the city wall. Miranda used her draconic gift to levitate herself, Damil, and Selasine over the structure; they were simply too big to fit through. Everdusk and Yuvina laid low in the small boat, reuniting on the other side. They floated through the Ermen Moors, arriving in the waste pond where several other crafts had been tied off and abandoned.

Everdusk pointed to the west. "This way," he instructed. They spent an hour traversing the moors before the simple building came into view.

Yuvina whimpered as they approached, the mana pouring from her and Miranda's interlocked paw and hand. "I have no real recollection, but I know this place. This is it." The evening sun cast an eerie glow over the complex.

Selasine and Damil approached the lone entrance. Damil nudged Thomas with his elbow. "Do we need a warrant?" he asked.

Selasine gave a single head shake. "Probable cause." He reached up and gripped his holy symbol. He had worn his full plate armor and painted the lines of a warpriest on his cheeks that morning. His face would have sent his enemies into panic as he prayed, "Sword of Justice, grant me the strength to bring the work of chaos to justice. Let this nightmare end for the innocent." As he spoke, his body glowed with intense, white light. It formed a silhouette around him, enhancing his physical strength and spiritual awareness. Damil took a step back, looking at Yuvina, Miranda, and Everdusk with a coy grin.

Miranda returned the paladin's smile. She knew the prayer; it was an advanced version of the regular strength-enhancing prayer usable by many clerics and paladins. Whatever waited on the other side of that door would not be ready for Selasine. "Let's go, dad!" she shouted. She let go of Yuvina's paw and drew Iria's sword from the ivory scabbard on her belt. Every time she gave the sword to Erk, he complained, but she got a comforting feeling from it in her hand. She had not replaced her tower shield, but she knew she could make her own with magic if needed.

Selasine took a ten-foot running start at the door, drawing his own sword. He barreled into it with an incredible kick, shattering the stone door frame. Before them stood a magnificent parlor that

Yuvina and Miranda both recognized. This was the room in Yuvina's memory where Aylabrax's shadow was hiding with her sinister command.

There was no avatar of a dark goddess, this time, however. Instead, the entire parlor was full of partial Umbrals swarming toward the door without hesitation. Selasine cleaved his sword in a lateral arc in front of him. As he did, he shouted, "Moonbeam!"

Miranda's eyes widened with excitement, and enthusiasm filled the music of her voice as she sang out the words to the prayer, "O, Sword of Justice, reflect the rays of your justice through this blade of mine. May the Silver Maiden cast her light across that which does wickedness and dispel their vile intent!"

Damil had heard many stories about Miranda and Selasine's previous adventure, and Miranda and Damil had difficulty ending up in the same place at the same time in spite of the fact that Selasine had adopted her. He was glad to know the mind of the dragon he contacted months before was this impressive priestess. He drew his own sword, which was on the longer side of one-handed swords. He made efficient use of the extra reach as a Pegasus Knight, and he wielded the extended blade on the ground.

Selasine's Moonbeam cut an arc of Umbrals down in front of him, but there were thousands emerging from the doors attached to the parlor. Damil and Miranda joined him in the entryway, using their unified prayer of holy Moonlight to dispel the fragmented shadows. Invictus's might held strong, allowing the clergy to make swift work of the Umbrals.

Yuvina and Everdusk joined Miranda, Damil, and Selasine in the parlor as the sun settled its way beneath the northwestern horizon. Yuvina felt an anxious anger swell within her. "I know this place, but I don't know why! This is the most terrifying feeling," she yipped in panic.

Miranda was quickly by her side, holding her friend's paw with care and love. "Don't worry, Yuvina. We are here to understand what happened."

For the most part, the rooms of the complex had been abandoned to the Umbrals which must have consumed all remaining magic in the strange building. Yuvina recognized the conservatory and the bedrooms, but it was the medical room that scared her most. "This is where it happened," she said to herself more than anyone.

As the five of them inspected the room, they found the eolnut devices Doctor One had used to bond the arcane to Yuvina. The foxkin jumped onto the examination table where she had the lacrima-deum infusion. "Here. My life became forfeit here."

Miranda gave Yuvina an encouraging glance. The priestess said, "Hey, it's not forfeit. I'm not sure what these devices did, but they look sick and dangerous," she commented, holding one in the palm of her hand. The needle-like apparatus was sharp enough to puncture skin with only a gentle press. Her imagination spiraled, and she reached into one of her pouches. She withdrew a small lacrima-deum. She pressed it into the chamber of the eolnut device and activated the spell that allowed her to see the flow of mana. She watched as the particles filtered through the device and became a liquid that funneled through the tips of the needles on the back of the device. After pooling on the ground, the liquid evaporated as the particles returned to the stream. She gave a sudden, understanding smile.

The other three were still looking for clues in the strange laboratory when Miranda started to giggle. She explained her realization to Yuvina. "Liquid magic. The Mystalonians have been doing that for a century. One's discoveries are nothing new. He injected you with liquid mana that is slowly seeping from your body back into the arcane. It doesn't have to take your life force with it, though!" she said, embracing the kitsune. A magical, fizzling aura surrounded them. "That's why we create a magical reaction; the arcane stream pools within me, and you have an artificial arcane pool within you. As you use your spells, the liquid is dissolving back into ether."

Yuvina felt a warmth fill her as Miranda's magical aura changed from a static white light to a brilliant purple glow. "Your body has been treating the mana as an illness. In the search for a cure, you've unwittingly made yourself sick!" Miranda confirmed her suspicions with her own gift, looking inside Yuvina's body with the mana. She then prayed, "Light of righteousness, Sword of Justice. What chaos has sullied, cleanse with your purity. Extract the filth from the blood, restore this body and heal this mind."

Selasine and Damil stood in disbelief as the prayer covered Yuvina in a purple mist. The cleansing prayer removed all of the lacrima-deum liquid from her body. As the particles dissipated in the halo around them, Yuvina felt her connection to the arcane dissolving. Her heart raced with simultaneous grief and relief; though she would no longer have an incredible uncanny magic, she could continue to fight by Miranda's side. She intended to do so, regardless.

Everdusk's expression lifted with relief, feeling his guilt for Yuvina's situation disappearing with the toxic ether being purged from the foxkin. Miranda held Yuvina until every drop of lacrima-deum was cleansed, and the magical backfire between them stopped. Yuvina embraced her new friend tightly in return, tears soaking the fur around her eyes. "Miranda, thank you," she whimpered, her body shaking from the release of her pent-up fear.

Before anyone could celebrate, however, a voice rang out from the door of the laboratory. "Doctor One said you might figure it out!"

Miranda's eyes opened with a harsh glare at the door. "Reginald," she hissed. She broke away from Yuvina and drew her sword anew.

"Doctor Thirteen, as you might also call me!" he replied, a cruel thorn whip in his left hand. He wore his white scholar's robes, but Miranda could still see the arcane stream. He, too, had been infused with liquid from a lacrima-deum. More than ten distinct strands of ether flowed through him. He stepped into the laboratory, prompting everyone else to draw their weapons only an instant behind Miranda.

Miranda scowled, responding first, "Would you like me to save your life and remove the ether from your blood?" The offer was sincere although the music in her voice was hostile and untrusting.

Reginald's lips broke into a wide smile. "No need for that, Mir'thax Toi'landra. Doctor One realized the body would have a reaction to the underflow after a time, which is why he spent so long with Yuvina after her infusion. He has reconfigured the devices so that the infusions are no longer lethal in the mid-range. I will have access to these powers for decades to come!" he said laughing.

Everdusk's eyes narrowed. "So, Yuvina was just an experiment, after all." His voice was full of disdain.

Reginald continued to smile, his eyes teeming with malevolence. "Yes, and her near-sacrifice has made it possible for others to share in the bounty of One's knowledge safely and effectively." He looked around the room. "Doctor One no longer needs any of you, however, and since you are the people who killed Sender, I will deal with you personally."

Miranda's gaze filled with indignation at the mention of Doctor Five. Selasine and Damil moved to flank the assailant on the left and right respectively, while Miranda, Everdusk, and Yuvina remained in front of him. Reginald laughed. "Five against me, how fitting. Perhaps I should skip from rank thirteen to rank five for destroying those who destroyed the architect of the uprooting." He cracked his whip, prompting Damil and Selasine to both utter protection prayers. An invisible orb of protection surrounded their bodies, providing defense against many types of attacks. Selasine was tempted to try the Enervating Shield Miranda used against The Emissary, but he decided it would be overkill. This "Thirteen" stood no chance against the five of them.

Miranda stepped forward, Yuvina and Everdusk on her heels. The priestess warned, "I know from experience the Doctors will not yield easily. Do not underestimate their gifts. Reginald has been infused with a lot of mana, beware!" As she spoke, she then prayed for the same protection prayer as Selasine and Damil.

Yuvina's whiskers twitched with anticipation before she made a sudden leap at Reginald. As she moved, Everdusk swept in low, withdrawing a small, razor-thin dagger. Doctor Thirteen's smile melted into a sinister glare, and he cracked his thorn-covered whip at Yuvina; the weapon was made of leather tanned from the hides of demons. The thorns appeared unnaturally sharp and deadly, but Yuvina's agility allowed her to evade. That, however, was what the enemy wanted: Yuvina's midair shift sent her directly into a bolt of lightning that blasted her across the room into the porcelain tile wall. The weight of her impact left a four-foot vertical crack.

Miranda's eyes widened in shock as she watched Reginald's attacks carefully. He used the whip as a diversion and generated a bolt of lightning without moving any other part of his body. It simply surged from him toward the point he willed. Such accuracy was unnerving, prompting Miranda to draw on the mana inside her. She activated the dispelling light, pressing her energy in Reginald's direction.

The scholar's eyes lit up with excitement, "Oh! It's time to try out Doctor One's new trick!" His voice was a taunt Miranda immediately understood. He pulled the outer layer of his scholar's robes aside, revealing several contraptions on his belt. His fingers went to one and pushed a switch. A bolt of white, searing light burst from a six-inch cube sitting on Reginald's hip. It connected with Miranda's dispel and cancelled the attack. Miranda's expression went from determined to frustrated. He was able to dispel the dispel, making it hard for her to nullify his wide array of uncanny infusions. She didn't want to push the mana too hard; its flow within the moors was thin.

Damil raised his fingers to his temple, ready to unleash a psychic barrage, but as he tried to tap into Reginald's consciousness, he was met by an unseen, dark force. His thoughts echoed in Selasine's mind. "Aylabrax! Her essence dwells within the scholar!"

Selasine activated his uncanny magic, creating a dozen, illusory duplicates of himself. He closed the distance between himself and Reginald with surprising quickness; the enhancement prayer from earlier was still active and boosting his physical prowess and agility. Doctor Thirteen tried to crack his whip horizontally through the illusions to dispel them, but the whip cracked harmlessly off the globe of protection surrounding the high priest. Unsure of how to counter, Reginald activated an uncanny infusion, causing everyone in the room to randomly change places.

Selasine's assault was interrupted as he tripped over an injured Yuvina; Reginald moved to where the kitsune had been against the far wall of the laboratory, and Damil, Everdusk, and Miranda harmlessly rotated one place clockwise, putting Miranda where Damil had been by the door. It took everyone a moment to orient themselves, and Reginald used the opportunity to reach for another contraption on his belt.

Selasine reached over to touch Yuvina, praying, "Restore to order what was damaged by chaos!" The healing energy was enough to soothe the pain of the electrical blast, but her head still swirled from all of the massive changes to her body in the last few minutes.

Miranda charged across the room as Doctor Thirteen produced a wand-like device with an entire, red, crystallized dragon egg attached to the end. It looked heavy, and Miranda targeted the obvious lacrima-deum with her sword, stabbing it toward Doctor Thirteen. A surge of holy light burst from the tip of the sword, striking the strange wand. It knocked the weapon out of Reginald's hand, but a geyser of ashy flames erupted from the tip of the device. Burning cinders started to fill the room, causing Reginald to burst into hysterical laughter. "Oh, you fool, you've knocked it from my hand in the on position. You'll inhale volcanic ash and die!" He then reached under the collar of his robes, lifting an apparatus to fit over his eyes, nose, and mouth. By then, Miranda had closed the distance between them, and she was able to neutralize the magic spilling from the lacrima-deum wand with a quick dispelling light. Doctor Thirteen was not lying; the device continued to extract the magic from the egg, generating a constant, flaming geyser of ash. Miranda could not concentrate her efforts on the device and face Reginald simultaneously.

Selasine and Yuvina stood, watching Damil and Everdusk rush to support Miranda. The volcanic wand, however, forced them to keep a healthy distance, and Miranda's bubble of dispelling light had separated them from the warpriest. As the ash and smoke became denser, they lost sight of what was happening between Doctor Thirteen and Miranda. Selasine felt his stomach drop with fear for his daughter.

Reginald slung his whip at Miranda, and she blocked the horrifying weapon by catching it. She let it flick harmlessly around the gauntlet on her left arm, and she tugged hard after it had her ensnared. Due to the unexpected shift in tactic, Reginald let out a startled yelp. His body charged with electricity as Miranda expected, giving her a chance to try something new with the mana. As the lightning bolt should have connected with her, she conjured a single magic orb. It absorbed the attack, causing it to change from white to blue.

At this point, the wand had filled the laboratory with ash and smoke. Selasine and Damil were using various prayers to shield themselves and their allies from the harmful heat and gas. Yuvina and Everdusk rushed toward the door, not having an uncanny magic to help. Selasine prayed, "Sword of Justice, shield my lungs from the toxic air of chaos and envelope me in your embrace. May the fires of evil leave no mark!" He then charged headlong into the black, billowing flames to find the device. From within the dense cloud, he could not see anything, but his protection prayers shielded him from the worst effects of the magic.

Everdusk, too, clutched his holy symbol. "There's a fight down here, Pulhash, and I need reinforcements!" In response to his prayer, humanoid figures of light formed around him. They rushed into the cindering cloud toward the far wall where Doctor Thirteen was facing off against Miranda.

Reginald frowned, recognizing the spell Miranda had duplicated using her reserves of mana. "It's impossible, that spell is too rare for a nobody like you or the fox to use!"

Miranda glared, and her lips broke into a smile. "Unfortunately, I am somebody. I'm Mir'thax Toi'landra, the daughter of Reshiria and Philotrax Hyacinth! And I am Miranda, Judge of Hearts, and I find your heart lacking in empathy and kindness!" She had pulled Reginald within striking range, and the Magic Mirror orb had neutralized the scholar's lightning attack. He tried to blast her with a prismatic ray of light. Three more orbs formed, absorbing the attack. They whirred around Miranda with excitement. Reginald's eyes widened in fear, and he barely evaded the swing the priestess targeted directly at his neck. With an agonizing groan, he tried the spatial-changing magic again, but another orb appeared and cancelled the attack.

Suddenly, the figures of light summoned by Everdusk slammed into Reginald, causing him to stumble backwards. Each one of them created a tangible force, catching Doctor Thirteen off guard. He was struck seven times, disorienting him enough that he dropped his whip. There were now five Magic Mirror orbs around Miranda, all of them growing more agitated as the incendiary cloud enveloped her. As the magic from the wand exhausted, the lacrima-deum on top shattered and disintegrated. Selasine found it in the fumes just as it ran out, but before he could analyze the situation, the hot, ashen cloud around him rushed toward a center point.

Reginald could barely see; the Vengeful Guardian prayer rattled him. By the time he regained his senses, he saw the whole of the billowing ash rushing into Miranda, causing seven more orbs to form and activate. They glowed a deep, smoky red. The orbs spun around her, clearing the room of the magical, toxic smoke and heat. The scientist reached for a contraption on his belt, but it was too late. The Magic Mirror activated, and everyone watched as the retaliatory strike obliterated the scholar where he stood. The magical explosion blew out the entire back wall of the laboratory, debris and building materials scattering everywhere in the moors outside the laboratory. No trace of Doctor Thirteen remained; the intensity of the Magic Mirror vaporized him and all of his magical accessories.

The room remained quiet for a moment as everyone stared in disbelief until Yuvina began to giggle. Everyone looked at her, Miranda turning with a bewildered expression, her lips forming their distinct round "o" shape. She asked in a quiet voice, "Are you alright, Yuvina?" Her music was calm.

Yuvina bounded across the room and took Miranda's hand in hers; there was no magical reaction this time, causing Yuvina's heart to swell with happiness. "I'm going to be alright now. I was trying to say thank you before that guy interrupted. I knew I didn't like him when we met him in Devitus."

Miranda smiled, and Selasine, Damil, and Everdusk joined them near the destroyed wall. Miranda looked out into the frigid winter night. With a small smile on her lips, she said, "I think we've tied up all of our loose ends now, for sure. Should we go back and get Evan, Naomi, and Celyth? It's time to face the cold."

Selasine gave a slow nod. "The Lichwood awaits."

Yuvina's whiskers trembled. "Miranda?" Her voice was timid.

The priestess squeezed Yuvina's paw. "Yes?"

The foxkin sounded afraid. "May I accompany you further? I do not wish to part ways. You have saved my life and given me answers to many lifelong questions. I know there is power within me, even if it's not magical in nature." As she spoke, however, her confidence built. "And I know my chance to show that strength is by your side."

Miranda's smile was uncontainable. "Of course, Yuvina!" she piped, a happy melody. She reached out and embraced the foxkin. The other three looked on in silence, gentle smiles for the happy conclusion of this part of their ordeal. The priestess pushed Yuvina back gently but held onto her by the elbows. She turned her electric blue gaze toward Everdusk. "That is, if The Forgotten wishes to be formally represented in the hunt for Farzg. Our first joint mission to stop the abuse of uncanny magics supporting oppression. I may know little of Pulhash, but I hope he would agree with such a mission."

Selasine tilted his head forward, raising an eyebrow again. A year ago, he would have never guessed she was capable of such shrewd diplomacy. Now, with his concerns about her current state growing, he was certain she was battling a growing ego within. As a Judge of Hearts, however, he trusted the Miranda he knew and loved. She would face that side of herself in her own time, and she would grow even stronger and more loving through the experience.

Everdusk gave a cordial nod. "Then so it shall be. Yuvina, your mission is to aid Miranda in any capacity you are comfortable with. Understood?"

Yuvina raised her paw and pounded the front of her left shoulder in a salute. Miranda realized The Forgotten probably had all kinds of interesting traditions and rituals, just like the Church of Invictus. She couldn't wait to ask the kitsune about all of them, hoping Yuvina would be able to share such secrets and details with her.

Instead of walking back to Nulodia, Miranda teleported everyone to the grand cathedral of Invictus so they could regroup and prepare for a journey far to the northeast. Everdusk personally handed The Forgotten's financial records to Gaius Carulus to search for clues about One's sources of funding.

✦❤✦

The Valkindra and Lexcord flew across the twelve winds of Espa in pursuit of the various shadows of Aylabrax, the duplicates created by her Siphoned Sisters attack. The spell allowed the parasitic entity to separate into as many as thirteen fragments with varying strengths.

The Valkindra, however, were twenty Celestin warriors who awakened when Lexcord's mortal avatar arrived in Espa's primary dimension. They were large, humanoid creatures with angelic, white wings. On average, they stood fifteen feet tall, and they wielded massive war hammers like their chosen goddess. They spent most of their time slumbering in their magnificent palaces in the skies far above Espa, but they were devout, powerful priestesses of Lexcord. The Silver Maiden pursued one of the remaining shadows of Aylabrax far to the north of Argentum, ending up near North Timbyl, a region northeast of Alabaster's capital city. She, along with the Valkindra, had dispatched eleven manifestations, and only one remained. As the dark goddess's duplicates were destroyed, the evil energies within returned to a different avatar. This final, continuing Aylabrax, then, had regained her full strength and would be able to use Devour relentlessly. The Valkindra returned to their rest, Lexcord's mission nearly fulfilled.

Lexcord walked to the center of a fallow field, the ground cold and life sparse. In six months, this would be a beautiful, golden display of wheat. Unless, however, the danger lurking on the other side of this place had tainted the ground with her evil presence. "Aylabrax," The Silver Maiden cursed, catching a glimpse of the dark goddess's gray robes moving into the forest beyond the field.

The temperate, cool climate of North Timbyl allowed the mortals to farm crops that thrived in colder regions. Ever since Invictus had wounded her, Aylabrax had been on the run from the Siblings of Order. If they could force her to retreat to the primordial place, One would lose his direct, divine support for a short time. It seemed, however, she was intent on fleeing to the northeast. From this region, it would take the divinities no time to reach The Lichwood. Lexcord suspected the dark goddess had learned the truth about that region from Doctor One. Still, even though Aylabrax was only a few hundred feet away from her, she knew she was chasing the shadow of a shadow. She would not have been steadily gaining ground against a fully powered Aylabrax, especially since the Valkindra helped her clean up the mess from the day before. In truth, Invictus was faster and better equipped to handle a single, powerful enemy. Lexcord realized Aylabrax was baiting her with a thirteenth, weak duplicate.

Lexcord looked far ahead as the sinister form melted into the shadows of the forest, daring the goddess of righteousness to pursue. "This is futile. We simply need to prevent her from reaching The Lichwood, then." She turned her eyes up to the sky, the blue orbs within turning green. Her silver, shoulder-length hair flailed, and she called out, "Brother! I return home! The Siphoning Sisters are unified, and you can finish this!"

The physical space around her vibrated with power and energy. Aylabrax's shadow emerged from the woods in frustration; Lexcord had not taken the bait. The goddess of truth and beauty radiated with silver luminance. The Devourer growled and dismissed the shadow puppet. She was at least twenty actual miles ahead of Lexcord, and she would not be able to use the Siphoning Sisters again for a while. She needed to consume souls to generate more of her dark, evil energy.

A moment later, Lexcord jetted into the sky, turning into a shooting star as she beamed away from the mortal coil. She returned to the primordial place. Aylabrax could see it from her real location, causing her to shudder. Invictus would come back next, and she did not want to fight the Sword of Justice again. Still, there was another great demon lurking in the mortal coil. One of Hoxark's lieutenants, The Root. An ancient demon sleeping beneath The Lichwood, cursing the ground and the trees there with its evil presence. If she could Devour it, she would add a significant sliver of power to her arsenal, allowing her to fight with the other, more martially inclined deities. She would not be bullied, and she intended to exact revenge once she consumed the essence and power of one of her mortal enemies: Hoxark.

Invictus prepared himself to return to the mortal coil, aiming to arrive at the southwestern tip of The Lichwood. He knew he would be very close to many important mortals who called upon him for strength. He hoped, for their sake, their paths would not cross and Lexcord would bless them on his behalf for another, brief time. He had to make this trip count. It would be the last time he could make a trip to the primary dimension for several months.

Chapter 20
The Lichwood

"At the end of the Legion, many ancient and powerful demons hid. Cut off from Fuerzul, they were forced to find other ways to feed on the evil in the hearts and minds of mortals." – Historian Oddawl, *Magical Calamities: Legion of Hoxark Edition*

The group heading northeast was seven strong: Miranda, Selasine, Damil, Yuvina, Celyth, Evan, and Naomi were prepared to confront Farzg in his stronghold on the other side of The Lichwood. They had prepared for a long journey, but Miranda summoned horses made of light for them to ride. They moved much swifter than ordinary horses, and their blazing speed carried the companions across the Ermen Moors, over the notorious Tumbleweed Valley, skirting the Selian Range and across the northern foothills of the Trollcrag Mountains. They crossed the Zenith Plains and the Zenith River less than six hours after their departure from Nulodia. Though they covered much ground, Miranda was disappointed she did not have time to soak in the beauty of the northern reaches of Alabaster. She did not stay sad for long, however, as she could return any time she wanted now. She only had to make sure Farzg met his final fate, and she would come back with Erk after Yendralia was safe.

They stopped for a break on the edge of the Mammoth Moors, a place that held great significance for Naomi. She gazed into the barren region, shuddering at the disturbing memories she had of this place. Though they were distant and thirty years in the past, seeing the gray, cold ground of the moors made it feel like only a week ago.

At least the demon she unwittingly unleashed from here was now safely banished to the Abyss. She let out a deep sigh, knowing her next trial would likely be something else terrifying from the past.

The group ate and freshened up next to the Zenith River. The city of Eodan shimmered on the eastern horizon, a strange city built on an island at the convergence of the Zenith River and the Shindor Channel. Its strange architecture lifted it out of the marshy edges of the swamp, and Miranda lamented that she did not have time to visit such a strange looking city. Instead, she helped the others resume their journey on the horses of light. They arrived at the edge of The Lichwood in another hour, the magical mounts allowing them to travel across great distances with little danger or effort. She could not use the mana to teleport somewhere she had never been, or if she could, she didn't know how. It seemed like a risky endeavor, anyway. The horses were safer even though they moved incredibly fast. Still, they took a substantial amount of magic to conjure for the entirety of the day, so the companions set up a camp half a mile outside the forest. Here, they hoped they would be safe from the wicked curses of The Lichwood, and they were. Miranda's mana reserves replenished by morning, and the seven prepared to enter the forest filled with unknown dangers.

Damil and Selasine traded glances as they followed the path toward the foreboding treeline. The last time they confronted Farzg, they sailed over the top of The Lichwood on pegasus back. As a result, they had to fight Farzg's faithful friend, Glacirix the Blizzard King. An especially large white and pink scaled dragon, he was vicious in his pursuit of Selasine, Damil, Iria, and Haelia. Miranda refused to fly over The Lichwood and risk confronting the dragon, even if it were a shard of Gorthran. Right now, even evil dragons needed as much mercy as possible, something Miranda concluded based on the teachings of Invictus.

As they reached the treeline, Nebu popped out of Celyth's hair. He whizzed around the group. "Well, I had no idea you'd get here so fast! And now that you are here, I can report back to Arlindra!"

Damil gave the dracofly a sly grin. "Do not fear, Nebu. Erk and the others are making great time toward Yendralia. You won't have long to go to find them."

Celyth waved and shouted, "Bye, Nebu!" She felt tears pushing against her eyes, but she fought to keep her emotion under control. She missed her cousin, and they had never been apart for this long.

Miranda's smile was weak, sensing the evil aura of The Lichwood.

It cast an ominous shadow against the sun's light as if it were reaching out for the companions. She also waved to Nebu, calling back to him, "Tell Arlindra we will see her soon!"

"You betcha!" he shouted back as his flight shifted to an upward spiral. The dracofly zipped out of sight within moments, his enhanced flight even faster than the horses made of light.

The seven created a formation emphasizing their strengths. Damil and Selasine marched in front, with Miranda, Evan, and Yuvina walking a few paces behind them. Naomi and Celyth walked further back, serving as lookouts for a wider periphery; they could send warning and retaliate against ambushes toward the front from this distance easily.

The group now faced The Lichwood, and it was terrifying to behold. The gnarled trees had ancient, tormented faces growing in their bark. They were human sized faces, and they twisted up the undead trees to form a canopy of horrors. Light could not penetrate the morbid-looking branches deep within. A clear path welcomed them, but the density of the trees grew quickly, making the road feel like a tunnel into the Abyss.

The trees also had appendages ending in horrifying hands and feet. As the group entered the treeline, Selasine lit an everburning torch, causing the hands to clench repeatedly. Though it was mid-morning, the light from the sun was hesitant to fill The Lichwood with its radiance. The torch light was bright, but the long shadows and twisted faces in the trees gave the party a feeling they were not alone. They could not see or detect an actual threat, but it felt as if the aura of the forest was dangerous enough.

As they walked, the three in the middle carried on a conversation. Yuvina commented, "There must be truly evil magic at work to twist nature into such abominable forms."

Miranda smiled, realizing the kitsune's affinity for forests, being from a place like The Tymbyrwylde. "I can feel the evil that permeates this place, but I detect no threat."

Yuvina sniffed the air, "Nor do I."

Evan shrugged and chuckled. "Well, you two just tell me when it's time, and I'll help cut the enemy down." He flanked Yuvina on the right, and Miranda was on the kitsune's left.

Yuvina's snout turned up into a smile. This place smelled like decay and filth, very similar to Sender's scent in Mystalon and The Emissary's on the Death Pirate destroyer. Though it was sinister, she could still smile because she had a different kind of faith in Miranda and her new friends. Thanks to the priestess's determination and overwhelming power, Yuvina managed to recover from her hideous mistake; however, she realized Doctor One was more dangerous than even Farzg. Whatever he did to convince her to take the infusion concerned her, but in the meantime, she smiled in the face of danger.

Selasine and Damil stopped. "The darkness is thickening ahead," Selasine cautioned.

Damil whispered, "Daylight," causing his holy symbol to radiate an aura of bright but gentle sunshine. On the path ahead, the darkness was so intense the prayer did not penetrate it. Furthermore, as the light from his holy symbol filled the area, the faces on the trees opened their eyes. Miranda's stomach lurched with anxiety. She did not even realize they were closed until holes began to open in the outer layer of bark of the disturbing trees. What was once unsettling was now absolutely terrifying.

Naomi called from behind, "What's the visibility?" She was fifty feet behind Miranda at first, closing the distance quickly.

Damil peered into the darkness and grimaced. "You'll be able to see your hand in front of your face, at least," he speculated. "Probably less than a foot, we'll be practically blind in there." His voice was calm yet commanding.

The rest of the group caught up to the high priest and high paladin. Selasine looked over the group, and then at Miranda. "Are you able to see in the darkness using your draconic gift?"

She peered into the overwhelming shadows ten feet in front of her. It looked like a tangible cloud of darkness. She shook her head, her healer braids flailing a bit. She had taken the time to give them a fresh braid that morning, and she had affixed her favorite, sapphire comb into the back of her hair. Two, blue lines went up each of her cheeks, the traditional warpriest makeup. "I cannot, and I am afraid there is likely no way forward without venturing off the path." She flexed the mana around her, generating an aura of holy light similar to the Holynova. It did not push against the darkness. Instead of channeling destructive holy energy, however, she used the light to feel the forest ahead. Peering in that direction, she murmured, "This evil is all consuming, and we must face it together." For a moment, Miranda swore the tormented faces sunk into the bark of the trees to avoid the light radiating from her. She felt a surge of confidence swell within.

Evan cracked his knuckles and shrugged. "I don't think we have to be afraid of whatever is in there. We've got the gods on our side, Invictus, Lexcord, even Saraix and Cantalus. It's terrifying, but there is no other real way. Besides, we've killed demons before, right?" His voice was excited and inspiring.

Selasine looked up, "Are you sure you don't want to fly us over? Glacirix is fierce, but he is without his breath weapon. We could outrun him easily."

Miranda felt something inside her aching to bring justice to the evil within the darkness. She shook her head again. "When you came here years ago, Dad, you weren't ready to face the evil within." She continued to stare into the impenetrable gloom, chewing on her lip as she considered the dangers beyond. They could very well be forced to enter a dimension similar to Vortex the Lich's soul prism. Or, more likely, the shadows ahead obscured the real evil hiding among the trees of The Lichwood. "I don't know what it is, but we need to face it. Together. Like Evan said." She broke her gaze away from the darkness and looked at Evan. "We have the gods. And the dragons." Her lips softened into an innocent grin, her left hand unconsciously raising to her heart.

Evan smiled, confident. Yuvina added, "I trust my senses. I smell nothing ahead that spells major change for us."

Naomi smirked. "We are all capable fighters. Whatever evil lies within should be afraid of us!" With a reckless dash, she charged forward. Her silhouette disappeared into the solid globe of darkness.

Celyth stepped forward, giving a shrug. "Naomi's right. Visibility may be poor, but we can still fight. And hopefully use our magic and prayers." She drew a magical longsword. "Let's go, Miranda!" she encouraged, running ahead.

Yuvina bounded behind them, turning to give the others a wink. "My nose never lies!" She then vanished into the overwhelming darkness, following Naomi and Celyth.

Damil and Selasine nodded. Selasine groaned. "I really am getting too old for this. Be on your guard." The two of them entered the darkness hand in hand.

The Daylight prayer vanished as well, leaving Evan and Miranda in total blackness. He laughed. "It's our turn, I guess. Stay close, okay?"

Miranda nodded, her draconic vision not letting her see past the magical, evil abyss in front of them. "Alright," she remarked, rushing toward the deep shadows. She grabbed Evan's hand to guide him in, as he likely could not see already. They ran hand in hand for a while,

Miranda calling up ahead. "Dad! Damil!"

They moved forward blindly. Evan called out, "Naomi! Celyth?" It did not echo; instead, a sudden, horrifying feeling swelled within him. It was reminiscent of speaking while his life essence was trapped in the arcane stream. His mother sacrificed her life to anchor him among the living, but his voice and personality were trapped with his consciousness on the other side of the veil.

Miranda shouted, "Yuvina? Can anyone hear me?" Her voice carried through empty space. Instead of a forest around her, she thought her voice echoed off the walls of a mountainside far away. She felt Evan's hand in hers, but after a moment it slipped. She could not see what happened in the overwhelming darkness, so she stopped. They had advanced maybe three hundred feet. "Evan?" she asked, moving forward slowly. She held her hand up to her face, barely able to see its outline. She expected to stumble into her friends thanks to the poor visibility, but she realized she was alone. She felt the mana flowing within her and the ever-watchful presence of her parents. She chewed her lip harder. Surely there was some way she could dispel this unnatural darkness around them. She scanned her memories for prayers and spells, hoping something in her parents' larger knowledge and wisdom would help her. After a moment, though, her thoughts ceased their search.

The gloom peeled back suddenly, as if the sky had been filled with black, obscuring clouds. Light rushed toward Miranda, beginning from a tiny point one thousand feet down the path in front of her. It revealed a beautiful, spring meadow. The undead trees were nowhere to be seen. Miranda's heart raced. If the evil magic of The Lichwood had created such sinister trees, she was not surprised they could also disappear so easily. She knew she was in an illusory world. Furthermore, none of her companions were nearby. She stood alone in this vibrant meadow for a moment, appreciating the warm sunlight and the colors of the flowers on the rolling hills. Then, she saw something that ended her moment of peace and caused her heart to leap into her throat.

On the path before her stood her reflection, or so she thought at first. A young woman with beautiful, deep blue hair stood before her. The reflection's locks had been braided to the front of her face like a healer of Invictus, but it was her eyes that caught Miranda off guard. Her reflection had powerful, red eyes, and their gaze teemed with hostility and fear. She wore the same battlemail as Miranda, but her warpriest paint was red instead of blue. She wore a ruby comb instead of sapphire. Miranda's nose scrunched with a moment of confusion before she approached what looked to be herself with the color of her eyes and hair swapped.

As she came within ten feet, the reflection smiled. "Hello, Miranda," she said, her own voice sounding odd to Miranda's ears. There was a melody in her words.

"Is that what I sound like?" Miranda asked, a puzzled song.

The blue-haired Miranda nodded. "Yes, but with a little less faith in the gods."

Miranda twisted her lips into a scowl. "Well, then, who are you? Are you a dark reflection of me that I have to defeat as some sort of trial?"

The other Miranda shook her head, her blue braids flailing the same way Miranda's always did when making enthusiastic gestures. "I'm actually you. Well. My name is Mir'thax."

Miranda felt her heart skip a beat. "My name is Mir'thax!" she protested in return.

Mir'thax shook her head. "Our mother chose the name. Our father humanized it so you would fit in."

Miranda blinked for a moment. "What do you mean? How do you know this?" she interrogated, the music in her voice becoming frantic and worried.

Mir'thax gave an evil smile, causing Miranda's heart to sink. She felt like she was looking into a mirror, but the vision of herself did not match what she expected to see. The reflection was acting on its own, and the situation unsettled Miranda. Mir'thax replied, "Unlike you, I've taken the time to listen to the godshards."

Miranda glared at this other manifestation of herself. "I can only listen when they speak to me. If I could, I'd spend hours with them; Mom and Dad. If you're really me, then you'd know that I'd give anything to hear their voices again outside the mana." Her voice was judgmental and incredulous.

Mir'thax sighed. "I'm not necessarily the evil within you, but I am the dragon." Her smile shifted and her eyes narrowed. It was the most terrifying expression Miranda had ever seen, and she finally understood why everyone in the Battle of Beriton was disturbed when she smiled as a dragon. It was a look of overwhelming power, putting any who see it at the mercy of the mighty wyrm smiling above them. Still, this reflection of her captured the expression in a way that helped Miranda make the connection. Mir'thax continued, "I am stronger, wiser, and I will never age. You are human. Weak.

The power that pools within you and the shards of mother and father? It pales in comparison to my power."

Miranda's glare became more severe. The song in her voice was hostile. "You're wrong. I would never start a power competition with myself. My powers are strong enough to protect modai-rin and Evan and everyone else. That's more than I could ever ask for!" She flexed the mana within her, causing the auras of her mother and father to surround her.

Mir'thax's smile became darker. "Dragons aren't affected by dragon fear." She then responded by pulling enough ether to surround herself with an unnerving aura that manifested into a tangible purple dragon.

Miranda's eyes widened as she felt the unnatural fear spread through her. She steeled herself against it, reaching deeper for more mana. "Invictus, protect your chosen!" she prayed, providing herself with as much divine courage as Mir'thax's draconic fear.

The dark manifestation of Miranda stopped smiling and relaxed her intense focus. The dragon vanished into a wisp of smoke. "You say you can protect them, but you don't even need to protect them. All this time, they've been protecting you, and you can't cope with that. Which is where I enter the formula."

Miranda's expression went from angry to fearful and confused. "What do you mean?"

Mir'thax sighed. "Even now, your friends and 'family' are facing the sins of their past. You have so few to speak of until recently, so the enchantment of The Lichwood chose me. I am the violence within you that is close to the surface now."

Miranda felt queasy. "Violence? I would never use violence if it could be avoided!"

Mir'thax started to smile again. "You could have incapacitated Sender and Reginald both, but you chose to end their lives."

Miranda shook her head in protest. "They chose their fate!"

The reflection shrugged. "Did they? Or did you? You can justify anything with the Path of the Sword of Justice. Honestly, though, it's good that you've started to listen to me more. You can't protect them without violence, now. Not anymore. Our fate is written in blood."

Miranda's thoughts returned to Maréli, the chief healer in Nulodia. The elf had warned her that her destiny was dark many months ago, but Miranda had not thought of that moment since she met Maréli. With growing concern for Selasine and the others, she asked, "What do you mean everyone else is facing the sins of their past?"

Mir'thax looked away toward one of the knolls in the meadow. "Why don't we watch and see for ourselves what kinds of trials they face? All of them are overwhelmed by guilt somehow. Their eternal crusade for justice and right is just to placate their feelings of inadequacy." Miranda bit her lip nervously as this dark manifestation spoke, prompting Mir'thax to scoff. "You're so human, it's sickening."

"You sound like Ezelbrecht. Child of Gorthran," Miranda spat in reply, feeling incensed.

Mir'thax shrugged. "The same as Reshiria. Our mother."

Miranda paused for a moment, choosing her words carefully. "And the experience of being human changed her into a beautiful soul, also full of guilt and fighting for redemption."

Mir'thax tapped her chin and tilted her head to look back at Miranda. "Could you be quiet, please? The first of your friends is about to die, destroyed by their guilt."

Miranda's eyes softened, and she hissed, "No!" Mir'thax turned her gaze back to the open air and moved her fingers. A visible stream of ether flowed from her fingertips to a point fifteen feet in front of her. Slowly, a tear in space and time opened revealing Damil and Selasine walking in thick, billowing darkness. Miranda called out, "Dad! Damil!" as she had before.

✦⟡✦

Selasine froze. "Miranda?" he called out, turning around. He swore he heard her shout for him, but he could not discern the source.

Damil also turned around in the darkness, unable to feel any other mind but Selasine's. "If she's here, she's alone. As are we," he commented, raising a hand to his temple.

The two continued to walk through the blackness, unable to see the path beneath them. Selasine had drawn a magical sword and was using the pale light emanating from the enchanted blade as a guide through the dark. It was not effective, however, and he and Damil stayed close to each other's side.

Damil hissed, "Thomas, look! A light!" Thanks to the overwhelming gloom, they were not sure from which direction the luminance originated relative to their initial path.

Selasine turned to see the light appearing a significant distance away. "Let's check it out," he suggested. As the two approached it, the darkness around them faded, revealing they were no longer in The Lichwood. They emerged in the sanctuary of the grand cathedral of Invictus in Nulodia, the same place Miranda had sent out a magical, burning light to save the city from Umbrals. All of the pews and chairs, however, had been removed, and the idol of Invictus in the front had been decapitated. The large, marble head lay at the feet of the statue.

Damil cursed, "Talirix volïs." He looked up to the pulpit in the front of the sanctuary to see a hellspawn standing there. She had warm, pink skin, and her billowing, beautiful hair sparkled orange in the dim light of the sanctuary. Two, foot-long corkscrew horns raised up from her skull, allowing her almost six-foot frame to tower over even Selasine. Her glowing red eyes were bent up with her lips as she smiled.

The hellspawn spoke with authority from the pulpit. "There they are. Arrest them!"

Selasine and Damil looked at each other, trying to understand what was happening. Thomas shouted toward the pulpit, "By the gods, Haelia? Is that you?"

Damil shook his head. "It's not, but it looks like her. There is no mind to contact!"

The doors of the sanctuary groaned as somebody pushed them open from behind. Thomas and Damil turned to search for the source of the sudden noise. The cathedral's doors were massive and required a crank to open and close like a portcullis. The person that emerged from the daylight now flooding the sanctuary caused Selasine's entire world to freeze. Before him stood a beautiful elf with jet black hair tied into the braids of a healer of Invictus. She approached the two in the center of the sanctuary, Miranda's magical sword in her hand. "Hello, loves," she spat with disdain.

Damil's eyes were full of tears, and Thomas was still frozen. The paladin replied, "This is only a nightmare conjured by The Lichwood. You are not Iria, and that is not Haelia," he said, turning to face the pulpit. The hellspawn leapt over it, stretching out her black, bat-like wings to their full fifteen-foot span. She flashed a smile, revealing sharp canine fangs. Her pointed, devilish features made her seem truly menacing.

Iria responded, "No? You don't think we are real, then? You can just disbelieve and make us go away?" she taunted, helping Thomas break free of his shock.

Selasine bellowed back, pointing his sword at this manifestation of his late wife. "Iriliandria Lancethinas, Judge of Spades, Priestess of Peace. She left that sword with her brother decades ago and died at the hands of Farzg. You are not my wife, you are a sinister being using my own memories to torment me!"

Iria's lips broke into a dark, sadistic smile, "Not your memories, Thomas. Your guilt."

The air around them warmed, causing Selasine and Damil to turn and face the manifestation of Haelia. She had surrounded herself with an immolating barrier; the closer she approached, the hotter it became. Damil prayed, "Sword of Justice, shield us from the flames of the Infernia!" A subtle, yellow glow covered the two, now standing between their fallen comrades.

Haelia yawned. "You think Thomas has guilt, you should see Damil's. Besides, it was his plan that killed me! You could have defended yourself against Farzg, Iria. Let's be fair, Damil has the most to pay for."

The high paladin stood straight and drew his sword. "You're right, Haelia. I do feel responsible for what happened to you. But I remember you with pride. You were brave to use your inherent magic to contain Elnis's Glacial Bomb. You saved thousands of lives."

Iria shrieked, something Thomas had never heard from his beloved. "And then you left me and Thomas to just pick up the pieces! You knew my cursed fate, and you left anyway!"

Damil's eyes widened, feeling the guilt and helplessness he had buried begin to resurface. Thomas interrupted, however, saying, "Nonsense. You loved Damil just the same as you did me."

Iria's cold, gray eyes darted from Damil to Selasine. "But did you always love me the same as you did him?" she hissed, a tormenting sound.

Haelia cackled. "You settled for Iria because you weren't good enough for the Pegasus Knight! Infernia's blessing, Thomas. I expected you to have more dignity than that!" She normally had a sweet, taunting voice, but in this nightmare, it was deep and raspy.

Selasine closed his eye. He pressed his hands together and inhaled. He finally understood an old catechism that was no longer commonly taught. He recited it. "From the depths of the Abyss, there is one who has sunk his tendrils deep into the flesh of the earth. Espa cries from the wound, and it festers beneath the surface. From the unending tides of evil and chaos, The Root thrives on the guilt of mortals. Walking with the Legion of Hoxark, that great demon hid himself among the dendroid, changing them into trees of death and despair." As he spoke, the images of the women began to distort. Numerous stalks, branches, and roots emerged, turning them into wretched creatures resembling the trees of The Lichwood. Selasine's visage overflowed with rage. "In the name of all that is righteous and true, back from me demon! I command you with the authority of Invictus and your true name!"

Iria and Haelia looked at each other with glances of panic as they melted into abominable forms. Iria's voice was now warped, "But Thomas! You killed me! You killed our daughter!"

Damil's face was twisted into disgust. Selasine frowned harder as there was no longer anything left of Haelia and Iria; now, two Lichwood trees stood before them. They ambled on their roots, pushing their twisted forms with an unsettling gait. They backed away from Damil and Selasine. The one that was once Haelia taunted, "Well if you want to see The Root so badly, churchman, then you asked for your fate."

As the trees moved away, they dissolved along with the illusion around them. As the sanctuary disappeared, the two stood in sheer blackness, but they were completely illuminated to one another. They stood in an infinite void, trapped outside of space and time. They waited a bit, until reality reconstituted around them so suddenly, they felt like they were moving at the speed of light.

⚜

Naomi held a throwing dagger in her left hand. She walked by moving her feet outward in semi-circles in front of her, checking that the path was free from debris. She heard a faint voice call out, "Naomi, be careful!"

She turned and responded, "Miranda?" She swore she heard the priestess, but the giantkin was not sure which direction the voice came from. "I'm here, do you need help?" she asked, peering with futility into the darkness. She stomped, trying to sense the world around her through the ground, but it yielded no answers. She was blind in this environment, but she could sometimes pick up vibrations through her connection to the earth mother. Without hearing anything else, she turned around to resume her journey through the darkness, only to find herself walking in a quarry.

The walls of the quarry towered up one hundred feet, and a ramp skirted the side of the granite mine. Naomi walked to the center and stopped. At the top of the ramp, she could see a rugged, handsome elf with green, messy hair. She turned all around, looking for some sign of the unnatural darkness that once surrounded her, but she knew she wouldn't find it. The Lichwood put her back in the quarry that had changed her life.

The elf at the top pointed at the ground beneath Naomi, "There!

It's The Emissary of Hoxark!"

Naomi's eyes cut down to the stone below her. She felt a tremor begin deep under Espa's surface; this was the vein of granite that once trapped the essence of The Emissary inside. She opened it in a small skirmish, overusing her connection to the earth mother. There was, however, no sign of the fissure she created that fateful day thirty years ago. She looked back up at the elf and said, "Elrune? Elrune, the granite is fine. We will be safe." Then her heart leapt into her throat. The love of her adolescence stood above. She started to wonder if she had been sent back in time, but as she looked up at him, everything felt out of place. She walked across the quarry, and he continued to point directly at her.

His voice called again, "The Emissary of Hoxark emerges! Please, help! Anyone!"

Naomi's eyes narrowed. Three, black apparitions formed behind Elrune, beginning as small balls of black energy and growing into three humanoid forms. One was a cambion, a half demon likely born of a succubus and elf, human, or orc. The other was the Death Pirate, Falindeth, who was consumed by The Emissary. The third was an older human she knew as Alexander, the father of Annaia.

Elrune's image shouted this time, "Please, Naomi! Save me! Save me from you!"

Naomi shook her head, "Nonsense! 'Rune, is that really you? Get Alexander and get away from there!"

Alexander shook his head slowly. "I'm so glad Annaia has had you in her life, but how long until you fail her like you failed me?" He put his hands in front of him and stepped up to the edge of the ramp which descended around the quarry in a counterclockwise direction. He was at the top, over one hundred feet between him and the ground below. "I know you were weak then; it wasn't your fault." He stepped off the side, a lethal fall.

In a panic, Naomi tried to soften the earth beneath her, but she realized doing so would release The Emissary into this strange reality. Instead, she reshaped the wall of the quarry into a softer, sliding slope, causing Alexander to slide down next to her.

She looked down at him in confusion. "What is happening? Why are the ghosts of my past all around me? Is this the evil magic of The Lichwood?"

Alexander reached out from a prone position, grabbing Naomi's leather boot. "You made her a Pirate Lady and sent her straight into danger! You're going to kill my Annaia just like you killed me!"

Naomi recoiled from the grasp. "What in the Infernia are you talking about? She's with Erk and the paladins she'll—" she started, but a voice interrupted her.

"Erilkaiden! My replacement! You really are The Emissary!" Elrune responded. "You couldn't save me because you were weak, so you replaced me! This isn't fair Naomi!"

The giantkin looked up again, her heart racing with fear. Her full lips sank into a frown. "I loved you before I knew what love was, Elrune. Erilkaiden is not your replacement, nor would he settle for being second choice. You are a beautiful part of my past, one that I wish I had never lost. Erk is my present, equally beautiful." Her voice was deep, rich, and confident. She had conquered the guilt in her heart a decade ago. She knew she would have to heal those wounds on her own before she could help Erk mend the damage in his own heart. She had already confronted these thoughts, and some of them were so uncanny and accurate to the guilt that once plagued her. However, the dark enchantments of The Lichwood had looked for guilt in Naomi's heart. Instead, it found only conquered demons that had been ultimately put to rest less than a week ago with the banishment of The Emissary. She continued her response, "And a future that spares others the way I've suffered over losing you, Elrune!"

The elf shook his head, and the cambion and pirate standing beside him reached out to lift him up underneath his arms. With a callous toss they threw Elrune into the quarry below.

Naomi's lips broke into a smile as she shattered the granite beneath her with a single stomp of her foot. Black miasma filled the entire quarry. "Besides, The Emissary is already gone! He's been banished, and that means he can't come back, not even in a vision like this." The miasma turned into a tornado of darkness, spiraling around them with incredible speed. As Elrune's body hit the shattered surface, he bounced high back into the air. Roots and vines protruded from the elf and the other three illusory people from Naomi's past.

Elrune's voice called again, "Why don't you feel guilt over me anymore Naomi? Did you ever really love me?"

Naomi's eyes glared, but her lips stayed wide in a smile. "Now, now. I don't know who you are, or what your real goal is here, but know this. Naomi doesn't let anybody tell her how to feel, not even my honeycomb on his pretty ship. If you got words for me, I suggest you take off the mask. Otherwise, you're just begging for me to rip it off you like a bad wig." She drew another dagger from a bandolier on her thigh as the faces from her past became mobile Lichwood trees. Her smile deepened. "That's what I thought. Now, you're going to pay for pretending to be Elrune and Alexander." She charged toward the trees until the ground suddenly fell out from beneath her. She, too, stood in perpetual darkness for a while until the world around her formed again with the force of being torn from a dream.

As Yuvina emerged from the darkness, she realized the light ahead of her was the burning community center of her den. She paused, soaking in the sights of the Tymbyrwylde for a moment, then her eyes narrowed. "Illusion magic of the highest degree. Likely a result of the dark power of The Lichwood," she growled to herself.

She heard a voice. "Yuvina, you're strong! I know you can do it!"

The foxkin crouched low and looked around. "Miranda? Where are you?" she asked. She could see the armored men entering the den as they did on that fateful night her brother and father were slain. She snarled. Her life had changed so much in the last fifteen years, things would not play out the same in this illusion.

She ran toward the center of the den. She did not see illusions of her brother or father there as she expected. She looked around the den, and the whole of her community had emerged from their houses to look at her with shame and judgment. Yuvina stretched out her arms and looked around at them. She could see Wise Telkut, her mother and sister, and every kitsune she knew from back then except for Aizari and Tsuyoi. "Purposefully incomplete illusions, too. Whoever is responsible for this is aiming to cause the most emotional damage."

She heard a shout from behind her as the humans entering the den attacked the kitsune. Yuvina bared her teeth. "It might not be real, but I'll never risk the life of another on a hunch!" With deadly agility, she sprang into action. As she charged toward a cluster of four armed humans, one of them holding a two-handed sword let his blade relax and held a hand up at Yuvina. A burst of wind emerged that would have been strong enough to blow Yuvina over. Instead of hitting her, however, she rolled out of the way with an agile, forward maneuver. She didn't lose a single step and continued her sprint right at the aggressor. Before he had time to respond, her teeth had already punctured his exposed throat, crushing his windpipe, beginning a slow, agonizing death. As he died, however, he became a Lichwood tree, gradually distorting into the disturbing, arboreal form.

Yuvina looked around, the taste of blood igniting her rage. She had killed numerous Wielders in her time with The Forgotten. As she continued to evade the uncanny magics of the slavers, her mind understood the lesson Miranda had taught her. Furthermore, she no longer felt guilty over her brother and father; instead, an angry bitterness lingered, and she took that frustration out on the illusions of the slavers. She fought until sixteen of the twenty of them lay strewn about the den, transforming back into undead trees.

Yuvina suspected the illusions were capable of killing her, but she was too fast and too deadly. Her life experience, her training with The Forgotten, and her time with Miranda had transformed her way of thinking drastically. Perhaps Wise Telkut was right, all along. Afterall, it was Yuvina's obstinance which created the situation that cost her brother and father their life. Trying to help with a problem incorrectly had a tendency to make a situation worse, which is how she ended up taking a lethal infusion of mana from a strange person she couldn't remember. She had power all along: swift movement, keen senses, and a determination to protect the innocent. As she slew the sixteenth slaver, she looked back to the center with a knowing smile.

There, she watched as they cut her brother and father down in front of her again, The Lichwood desperately trying to fuel her guilt. Instead, it only ignited a rage in her unlike anything she nor the evil magic in the soil here had ever seen. The mana infusions had affected and eroded her life force, and they had artificially bound her to the arcane stream. As she entered the blind rage, her fur glowed with a dull, red aura. She wasn't manipulating the stream like Wielders, but she was aware of what the mana felt like. She drew it in, enhancing her life force which had been touched by the ether. She didn't realize it, but it also made her stronger and faster. The last four slavers turned their attention moments too late. She didn't use her daggers against any of them; she eviscerated them with her bare paws. Her rage was unquenchable, and normal, rational assailants would have fled at the terrifying sight of a foxkin brutally shredding their allies with nothing but her claws.

They did not, however, flee, and Yuvina finished her rage induced killing. Once all twenty slavers had been turned into Lichwood trees, she took a few moments to recover from such an intense burning of energy. Overcoming her guilt had taken nearly losing herself to lust for power. She knew now that the only power she needed resided within her.

The other kitsune stayed gathered, looking from the edges of the den to the burning structure in the middle. Yuvina looked up into the flames, then back to the people of The Tymbyrwylde. "I was taken away from here powerless, and I've seen the pinnacle of magical strength. But none of that matters without strength of heart." She let out a deep breath. "I think I'll go back to visit, now that I've found that." As she spoke the words, free of guilt, her den dissolved until nothing was left but blackness. She could see herself fine, but she felt like she was in a strange void. Her maw curled up into a smile, and she crouched, drawing her daggers.

"I've got a feeling it's not over!" she shouted, leaping upward into the darkness. As she did, the whole of reality began to reconstitute, and she found herself flying through the air about ten feet above The Lichwood forest floor.

Celyth eventually put her sword away. She was frustrated; her cousin wasn't here to bother, and the monsters she expected to leap out from the darkness never came. She wanted to fight, but the enemy was weak or scared. As she mentally voiced her complaints, she could see a light ahead in the shroud. As she ran toward it, she heard Miranda clearly. "Cel! Be strong!"

She paused her dash, but the light continued rushing toward her. "You too, Mir," she replied. She winced as the light blew over her, placing her in a clearing in the Mystalonian Forest. "Ah, Infernia's blessing. Don't tell me we've teleported back to Mystalon!" she shouted, turning to look around her. She was alone in the clearing, and it looked to be early summer. The trees were green, and the smaller shrubs and bushes that thrived under the Mystalonian trees were covered with colorful berries and blooms. "Oh, damn. Space and time don't really matter to some people, I guess." She shrugged.

After a moment, Arlindra emerged from a thicket nearby, but she was with Vanesa. Celyth's expression contorted into confusion. "Cousin? Aunt Vanesa? What are you doing here?" she asked.

Arlindra drew her bow from her back. "I finally found my mother, so I don't need you anymore, cousin."

Celyth was ready to fire an arrow before Arlindra had one drawn. "Who are you that speaks as if you are my family, and yet so differently that I know you to be false?" She noticed her father and uncle had entered the clearing from a little to Arlindra and Vanesa's right. Celyth tilted her head. "Wait, is this possibly a reflection of what is really happening? Does this mean Aunt Vanesa is okay?"

Arlindra sighed and prepared her arrow in spite of Celyth's faster draw. "She's fine because she was brave enough to leave. I wish Aunt Kiriana had done the same. You should have tried harder to convince her. Then we'd still have our whole family together."

Celyth's eyes widened with hurt, and she lowered her bow. "We wouldn't be together at all! Our moms would both be lost to the unknown. Who knows how that would have changed our relationship?"

Kiriana's voice emerged from behind her. "Cel, does that mean you love your cousin more than you did me? Are you so ready to accept the way things are?"

Celyth turned with a devastated expression. "Hai-rin!" she shouted in disbelief. "Why would you ever say something so stupid!" she continued. "This is obviously one really twisted nightmare, and I didn't come here to fight illusions of my family talking like they've lost their minds."

Evander walked across the clearing to stand beside his wife. He spoke as he came into Celyth's vision. "You know, you could have run away too. You could have found help and brought it back. I couldn't do something like that; you know, I have to think about my role as a Sage."

Celyth's nose wrinkled as her emotions swirled. "I could have run away, but like you just said. Mister Sage, all important politician. Spare me your patronizing." Her voice was full of hurt and honesty. "It's hard to feel guilt when you know who to blame. Maybe I could have done more, but I felt like stepping outside the rules would have created more problems for us." She spat. "This is Evander's fault. Alaric. Elitirin. Especially that bitch." She raised her bow back up, pointing an arrow at Kiriana. "And the whole of Mystalon. The only person in the world I don't blame is standing behind me with an arrow trained on my back. And I trust her more than myself."

The illusory manifestations of Evander and Kiriana warped, their flesh elongating and turning into the bark of the Lichwood trees. The tormented faces were accompanied by a cacophony of similarly tortured voices. "You heroes are starting to wear my patience thin! Feed me your guilt! Let me eat your sins! You are not all blameless, it's not possible!"

As Celyth began a rapid volley of shots, the illusion of Arlindra melted into smoke. Celyth's trust for her cousin was so much greater than her internal guilt that it dispelled the deadly threat behind her.

The warrior roared at the melting, visceral figures. "It's not that I don't feel guilt, fool. It's that I've put that guilt to work doing good things. Nobody else will have to suffer like my mother did. And I'm not to blame for Mystalon, that's Elitirin. Bring her here from the afterlife if you want somebody riddled with guilt!"

As she defied The Root, reality shattered like glass, the image of the forest breaking apart and spilling into a void. The shards fell away, infinitely descending into the darkness below, but Celyth only dropped about three feet. She caught herself with an instinctive bend of her knees when she landed. She was the only thing she could see in this black, empty void. She smiled. "Yashirin'nides." As she spoke, reality reconstituted around her in a second that felt like an hour.

Evan felt the pressure of the arcane stream weighing on his life essence again. He stood motionless in the darkness until it crumbled around him, placing him in the library of Claston's royal palace. His breathing paused. "A terrible memory from the past?" he asked, not expecting anyone to hear him.

He looked around. He heard Miranda's voice and felt her hand in his for just a moment. "I think we're almost there, Evan, hurry!" she said. He tried to smile, but the curse made him incapable of expression.

Evan spoke his thoughts. "But Miranda was the one that healed me from the curse. I should be whole!" Whatever this place was, it bothered Evan that it would attack him with feelings and traumas from the past. Miranda's encouraging words reminded him of her healing touch, and he felt his body restored. His growing love for her further fueled his resolve. He would not let wicked magics undo what she had done for him.

He shouted into the library, "Alright, Gelidor. Come out, it's time to finish what we should have the night it all happened! Your curse won't work anymore because you're already dead!"

A firm, familiar voice spoke from behind him. "You're not here to face Gelidor, mu-zim." It used the word for son in formal elven.

Evan turned around, his eyes wide with shock. "Hai-rin?" he called, recognizing his mother's voice.

She stood in the doorway of the library with his father, Elian Lancethinas. "Modai-rin! What is the meaning of this? You've both left the mortal realm. Is this a dream?" he asked.

His mother shook her head and walked toward him. "No, my child. This is very real, and we have returned to reap what is ours."

His father also approached him, hostility in his step.

Evan shook his head in disbelief. "What do you mean? Reaping? What belongs to you?"

Wailindis Lancethinas stood before her son with a sinister smile. "The guilt you hold in your heart. You correctly still blame yourself for what happened to me."

Elian added in a dark, angry tone, "And you literally killed hundreds of people while you were an abominable husk! This is justice from Invictus himself."

Evan froze and stood straight. He felt his heart leap into his throat. "Mom. Dad. Why?"

The illusions of his parents stood in front of him, motionless. Wailindis finally responded, "You're the one who brought back the false lead. You led us straight into the trap, and the guilt for that eats at your conscience every time you think of me." She drew an elaborate sword. As a priestess of Invictus, she always had one ready.

Evan did not move. "You're right, mother. I certainly feel responsible for what happened that night. I even thought Erk would blame me for a while, but he moved oceans to find a cure for the curse. He stumbled into some dark places, and I was there with him every step."

His father also drew a sword, the same one that was on Evan's belt. It prompted the young elf to smile. "So, is this what Miranda feels, when she gets to speak with her parents from beyond the void? I thought I would be happier to see you both among the living again."

Elian spat, "With the crimes you've committed, you'll receive no quarter from me, son."

Evan shrugged. "If this is how I pay for my crimes, then so be it. I am accountable for my actions. My guilt is cleansed." He held his arms out to his sides.

Wailindis and Elian hesitated. His mother scolded him, "So you will just accept your judgment? You won't fight the guilt within you?"

Evan shook his head. "You are the high priestess of Invictus. If you declare my life forfeit, then the law has spoken. I have committed crimes, and I pay penance for those in every action I take and every word that I speak."

Elian drew his sword back as if he were about to stab Evan. His son watched, tears in his eyes. "Besides, how much guilt would you feel if you, father, cut down the very son your wife died to save? The same son that your other son led a century long civil war to save? Why aren't you looking for real guilt? Why are you bringing up things that have shaped me into who I am?"

Wailindis's eyes widened in anger, and Elian's sword began to break into pieces. Evan continued, "I feel more guilt than anything that I wasn't by either of my sisters' sides when they were stolen from us. I feel guilt over the burden I left on Erk's shoulders. But you know what?" He smiled as the illusion around him dissolved. "If anything, I'm guilty of being loved. Way more than I deserve. So, if you want to strike me down for such a crime, then do so."

Evan's parents distorted and shriveled into Lichwood trees. They looked visceral and fleshy until the bark hardened. He drew his father's sword from his own belt. "Besides. It was you two that taught me how to use my guilt to grow. You were the best parents an elf could have hoped for." His voice was somber, but his eyes were full of mirth. "Even though it's not really you two, I hope you're out there listening somewhere and know that I love you immensely." He then struck the Lichwood trees, shredding them as they screamed in protest. They tried to move on their roots, slithering around with a scratching sound on the crumbling stone floor.

Within a moment, the library around Evan was gone and he stood in pitch blackness. The remnants of the strange trees vanished with the environment. As he waited for what seemed like an eternity, he joked, "The arcane stream was more accommodating than this place. What kind of world is this?" As he did, the same rushing consciousness overwhelmed him, returning him to the present moment with everyone else.

Miranda let out a deep sigh of relief as the last of her friends stood safely in darkness. She then turned to Mir'thax. "Riddled with guilt? It sounds to me like I've surrounded myself with strong willed people whose desire to overcome their guilt comes from a place of power, not inadequacy."

The blue-haired priestess shook her head. "I don't understand. They're mortals. How can they overcome a being as powerful as The Root so easily? I brought you here, but The Root took them as expected."

Miranda tilted her head with a flash of anger. "Excuse me? You did this? You took me away from my friends?"

Mir'thax scowled. "We both know you're not ready to confront what happened *that* day at the obstacle course. Or how about the lives you've taken in the last week? Your justifications aren't helping us sleep at all."

Miranda's stomach dropped to The Rift, and anxiety surged in her chest. Mir'thax was right. She wasn't ready to confront those memories. She grimaced and tried to process her thoughts.

Mir'thax's expression remained harsh. "Now is not the time, anyway. I can't have an ancient demon feeding on my guilt for failing the dragons!" she shouted. "Mother, too! All of the people she hurt as a dragon, all of the horrible things she did! The Root would destroy us to get to her guilt!" Her scowl darkened further, and the red in her eyes glowed.

Miranda looked at this reflection of herself. Of course, she had negative emotions about her inability to just save the dragons outright. But she didn't feel guilty about it, did she? She started to question her emotions and realized she didn't always understand what she was feeling. As she did, she reflected on everything that had happened since she met the Fernith cousins. "A child cannot carry the sins of their parents. The law does not permit such generational guilt, as a woman who is declared guilty before trial will not be motivated to do right." Miranda's eyes softened. "Nor can an agent of justice share in the guilt of those they bring to justice." She stood tall as she turned to face Mir'thax directly, turning her attention away from the rift in space displaying her companions' ordeals.

Mir'thax's lip began to quiver with anger, a face that was extraordinarily rare for Miranda. "As I said, you would justify your violence, somehow."

With conviction, Miranda stomped the ground and saluted. She buried her guilt in the catechism. "And with those justifications, I saved others. Reginald would not have stopped until he neutralized Yuvina. Sender would have destroyed an entire solisberry tree and, along with it, a civilization! Thanks to my lack of hesitation, Mystalon has a chance to rebuild, and Yuvina and my family are safe." The music in her voice was calm, determined, and justified. "I don't like violence, and it's antithetical to who I am!" She drew Iria's sword from her belt. "But if you threaten the people I love, if you stand to harm the innocent, to exploit the weak!" The song was gone; now it was an impassioned monologue. "If anyone crosses me that way, then they had better be ready to face Mir'thax Toi'landra. I am the dragon of fire and lightning, and I come calling with the might of the arcane stream behind me. I don't like the way you look down on everyone. They've just proven they're capable of getting by without my help!"

Mir'thax's angry expression melted into one of peace. "Is that so?

Are you saying your friends don't need you?"

Miranda's eyes narrowed, and she gave her own, sweet, genuine smile. "Of course they don't need me. They can take care of themselves. I'm just glad I can be there to help keep them safe too. Honestly, watching them fight their innermost guilt makes me more confident in them than ever. It's going to take more than some illusions to make them give in to despair." She turned back to look at Evan standing in the darkness. "Any moment now, they'll all be back in The Lichwood. And I have to be there to face The Root with them."

Mir'thax shook her head. "I don't think you understand the lesson."

Miranda's lips rounded immediately, shocked. "Excuse me, but I think you didn't get the point of what I was saying. You are part of me, and I'm the outward manifestation of you. I have to ask you for help sometimes, especially when I don't think I can bring myself to do what needs to be done. You came forward and destroyed Gelidor for what he did to us. My hesitation nearly cost me you, Mir'thax. And that's a guilt neither of us needs to live with." Her eyes filled with tears of joy. "We're literally about to face another demon from the Legion of Hoxark, and here I am crying while I talk to myself."

Mir'thax's gaze softened. "You're right about one thing, Miranda." As she spoke, the spring meadow began to break apart as the other illusions had before, like glass falling into infinite darkness. "Our mother let go of her draconic pride the day we were born. You were the first human to convince her that they have the right idea. They form bonds, and the strongest and most righteous defend those weaker than themselves." As Miranda, too, found herself the only thing visible in a strange, infinitely dark dimension, Mir'thax's voice radiated from within. "And if that's the case, you're more human than mother would have imagined. And for that, I think she loves you even more."

Miranda gave a nod, clutching at her heart. "Then let us get this party started," she whispered. When she stomped her foot, the black dimension around her shattered, causing time to resume around her. They were in a well-lit clearing of The Lichwood, filled with the remnants of dozens of Lichwood trees. They had been splintered, destroyed, struck by lightning, cleaved into pieces, filled with arrows, and rendered by claws. Miranda winced for a moment. "Who used lightning?" she asked in confusion.

As she looked around, her companions were engaged with at

least a dozen, ambling Lichwood trees. The culprit was a wand of lightning Evan had hidden away among his weapons. She breathed a sigh of relief and began to collect mana from the environment. "Invictus, shower me with your grace and benevolence. Bring this demon out of hiding!" She shouted at the end of her prayer. As she did, she created a Holynova which disintegrated the dark, deadly trees. When the radius of her nova reached one hundred feet, it jetted into the air. Miranda felt the mana pulling that way, so she pushed. Her hair darkened and turned a rich, purple hue. She was drawing upon the power of her parents. Rife with mana, she pushed the Holynova further into the sky. With a burst of energy, it rocketed away, yanking a trail of ether particles with it. Lexcord heard the prayers to Invictus, and she lent her strength to Miranda's spell. Infused with copious amounts of holy elemental energy and divine strength, the trail reached deep under the surface. Everyone formed a circle around the brilliant light spiraling from the ground into the heavens.

Selasine called out, "Yolasha, what are you doing?" The energy from the combined spell and prayer made a snapping sound, and the earth beneath them trembled. After a moment, the center point of the light caused the ground to burst open. A massive, hideous demon shaped like the stump of a gnarled tree emerged, pulled by the light now soaring upward.

Damil shouted, "There! It's The Root! Wyndia! To me!" As he finished, a royal blue pegasus appeared by his side, stepping into the primary dimension through a portal that rippled like water in the air. It knelt quickly, allowing Damil to climb aboard his blessed mount. "To arms, comrades!" he ordered, old commanding habits obvious in his demeanor.

Evan laughed. "Wish I had one like that! Don't need it though!" He kept the wand in his left hand and charged at the demon, which was fifty feet tall. It had a massive, fleshy maw in the center of its trunk-like body. It sunk its tendrils into the ground, using the earth to obscure its movements as it started to lash out at Miranda and her friends.

Naomi's expression went from shock to cockiness. "Not so fast. The earth mother is really tired of your filth!" she exclaimed and jumped upward. Using her telekinesis, she boosted her jump enough that she glimpsed the top of the demon. She then angled downward as if she were diving into water, her hands in front of her in her descent. As she connected with the ground, she sunk into it like a calm lake. Her dive, however, sent out a shockwave of ripples around them. The ground became agitated, and the earth mother focused her effort on this seeping wound that had been in her side for hundreds of years at this point. The ground itself betrayed The Root, forcing its tendrils and attacks into the open.

Yuvina sniffed the air. "Just like the other demons. It is the same scent. The suffering you've caused! You will know justice!" she shouted, working herself into a new rage. Her berserk fighting made Miranda smile. She could see Yuvina's strength from the moment she met the kitsune. She would do wonderfully without magic.

Evan used blasts of lightning from his wand to keep some of the tendrils at bay, and he sliced smaller ones effortlessly with his father's sword. The Root made a deep, groaning noise, and it caused the air around them to vibrate.

Miranda glared. "Not so fast!" she shouted. She focused on the mana flowing through her and her parents' godshards. She shaped it into something new to her, a classic debuff that had hampered wizards for millennia. The monster's voice amplified, reaching a devastating volume and pitch. Miranda shouted, "Silence!"

A deafening globe settled over the clearing. All sound ceased, and it was eerie. However, the sonic attack from the demon was also nullified, causing it to writhe its massive, root-like tendrils in anger.

Damil galloped through the air swiping at viny, living branches, and Selasine charged into one of the demon's flanks. Naomi emerged from the ground and unleashed a constant barrage of her razor-sharp daggers. Celyth was providing ranged coverage to Yuvina as the kitsune raged into the demon's other flank opposite Selasine. Evan's frontal attack with air support from Damil caused the demon to begin dispersing into miasma.

With an unimpressive showing from The Root, Miranda dismissed the globe of silence. Miranda, Selasine, and Damil came together and joined hands in front of the dissipating demon. As they recited the words to the banishing prayer, the same, fleshy, spiky maw that consumed The Emissary emerged from the ground and sucked in the miasmic particles. The seven watched with disdain as the demon was banished to the Abyss. Naomi didn't need to check that the interdimensional gate closed this time; her faith in Miranda and Selasine was just as great as theirs in Invictus.

Still, all three clergy members knew it was Lexcord who answered their prayers. Their Sword of Justice was presently walking around on the mortal plane somewhere. They all echoed a prayer for his safety, too, prompting Lexcord to smile in the primordial place.

Moments after the demon was banished, the trees around them withered. The tormented faces compressed and became gnarled bark. Over the course of five minutes, the undead forest transformed into a graveyard of ancient, petrified trees. The sunlight of the late evening shone through their shriveled, stone branches. The evil permeating the soil was gone; The Lichwood would never serve as a barrier to chaos again. Miranda said out loud, "One less thing for Farzg to hide behind. How could somebody as evil as him make it through an ordeal like the ones you all faced?" she asked.

Selasine thought for a moment, perplexed that Miranda already knew of their ordeal. He, however, knew Farzg's depraved nature would have allowed him to pass by The Root without even waking the demon. "It's simple, yolasha. People like Farzg don't feel guilty for what they do."

Miranda's eyes filled with enraged, determined tears. "That's what I thought you'd say." She felt Mir'thax pulse within her. "And that's why Mir'thax will be serving his warrant in short order." She stomped and saluted, an unexpected gesture that made Selasine and Damil snap into shocked salutes of their own.

Damil reeled with a psychic realization. "Miranda! Your mind! It's you! I can see you!"

She giggled and rushed over to the older paladin, giving him a firm hug. "That's because you've been looking for Mir'thax. She's me, but only a part of me. Like. A mind of her own, but we share a soul." She turned to Selasine, her eyes still wet from the tears. "And she's where I get the strength to fight when Miranda wouldn't be capable." She lifted a cloth from inside her healer bag to wipe her eyes. "I grew up learning to hate violence. And I always will. But I can't afford to hesitate. Not when I have a critical role to play." She started to smile, her melody grateful and happy. "Thank you all for the way you look out for me. I promise, I'm looking out for you too. I'm here to help, however that's needed. You're all so strong, and I love you all."

Yuvina pounced into her new friend. She squeezed Miranda hard. Selasine and Damil also joined the embrace, holding Miranda close. Evan and Naomi smiled, but Celyth started to sob.

Miranda heard her and pushed everyone away from her, rushing to Celyth's side. She took the elf's hands in hers. "It's okay, Celyth. I meant every word I said about you, too."

Celyth cried harder. "It's not that," she said, sniffling. She was embarrassed, which only accelerated her weeping.

Selasine and Damil looked sympathetic, and Naomi moved to comfort the young elf. Evan watched Miranda's gentleness with admiration, and Yuvina tried to tackle the fighter with a hug. "What's wrong, Cel?" the kitsune growled as Celyth wrestled her to the ground and pinned her down.

Celyth looked down at Yuvina and shouted, "This is the first day I'm not going to have any food made by Arlindra in the last ten years! And I don't know why, but that sent me! Can we please just set up the damn camp and sleep over the corpses of our fallen enemies, and celebrate our victory with some boring jerky?" Her voice was frantic, but she started to laugh as she finished her emotional rant.

Miranda grinned. "Hey, Cel. I've got something for you." She reached into her healer bag and produced an object wrapped in a palm leaf.

Celyth's eyes widened. "No way!"

Miranda nodded. "She was worried you'd crave her cooking."

Celyth licked her lips while everyone watched with a smile as the elf took the leaf and unwrapped it. "A mushroom turtle," she said with glee. "It's all the mushrooms she learned about in some book we read when we were kids. The mushrooms are seasoned and baked just long enough to make them easy to chew, and she grinds them up on cheeses with herbs and dried veggies." She sounded nostalgic. Miranda, Naomi, and Yuvina giggled as the elf demolished the sandwich in just a few bites.

Selasine and Damil had already begun setting up camp. The forest looked safe enough now that the demon was gone. The seven camped in the open air of cold winter, lighting a fire, and sharing rations. Miranda and Celyth played cards for a bit, using the sweets in the rations as gambling currency. Evan even sang some songs for them. Miranda's heart felt at peace for the first time in a year, even though her greatest challenge yet awaited them on the other side of this now-petrified forest.

Chapter 21
Respite in Desolation

"To enter the forest of Mourning Despair, one must bathe in the tears of Dimittena the Weeper." – Kzar's Magical Locations and Sources of Power

Miranda's sleep was comfortable, but she became restless. She woke up, her flesh hot to the touch. She grumbled, annoyed at whatever was waking her. As she stirred, she saw only Evan, the current watch standing by the campfire. He noticed her waking, looking over with a cheeky grin. She still had a personal tent over her as she had while camping for the entire adventure. He gave her a whispered greeting, "A spring air blows, but it's still The Resting."

Miranda pushed her bedroll, sleeping bag, and tent off of her. "Are you serious? It's hotter than a day in The Flourishing out here!" she protested in a normal volumed complaint.

Evan put his finger to his lips, but Naomi was already awake looking up at the stars. She butted in, "Miranda, you're way too young for something like that!" Her voice was a powerful whisper.

Miranda winced, realizing she might have caused someone else to wake up. Evan moved toward Miranda, speaking in a soft voice. "There's definitely something strange occurring right now. As a former wizard, I can feel the mana flowing differently. I think destroying The Root might have caused something to change."

The priestess nodded, her hair unbraided and flowing freely. She was wearing one of Selasine's large, cotton shirts. It fit her easily as a night dress. She did, however, have pieces of chainmail underneath, and her sword rested nearby. She picked it up, standing to look around. The camp seemed normal enough; Celyth was awake fletching arrows, and Naomi continued to look up at the stars. Selasine and Damil slept side by side, and Yuvina was curled up close to the fire. Miranda replied, "Nobody else can feel it?" Sweat beaded her brow; to her, the heat was uncomfortable and overwhelming.

Evan shrugged. "Mana sensitivity is its own gift, or perhaps a curse in some cases," he commented, looking at her ragged state.

Her eyes narrowed. "Let's go for a walk and find the source, then," she ordered.

Naomi sat up. "Do it! I'll watch the camp!" She was on her feet before anyone could respond.

Miranda shivered with nervousness, but her body panted from the oppressive warmth in the air. "Thanks, Naomi!" she said, tying the belt with her sword around her waist and tightening it.

Evan stood still for a moment, incredulous. "Aren't you going to wear some armor?" he asked.

Miranda shrugged, nonchalant. "If it's just something changing in the mana, then what good will armor do? Besides, the best defense is a good offense, right?" She rested a hand on the hilt of the sword she inherited from Iria.

Evan smiled at her faith in his sister's sword and the optimism she exuded, even while waking up with such discomfort. "Alright, then, let's see what's going on."

Miranda brushed her hair out of her face; styling it in healer braids had trained it to fall forward. She liked it, though; it made her hair look fuller and framed her face well. She skipped alongside Evan, the temperature still blazing hot to her.

As they moved away from the camp in a spiraling direction, they could see their campsite glowing in the cold winter night. Two bright moons cast a gentle light across the remnants of The Lichwood. The petrified trees were unsettling in the dark, but they were comforting in comparison to their former, undead appearances. To Evan and Miranda, however, the air continued to warm as they walked away from the fire. Miranda's face twisted with discomfort. "At this rate, I'm going to need elemental protection prayers."

Evan nodded. "It couldn't hurt. Although, I have no idea what could be causing such an anomaly. This Lichwood place is some kind of Infernia of its own."

As Evan spoke, Miranda caught a glimpse of movement in the

moonlight. She gave a warning hiss, peering through the evening with her draconic vision. It looked like a massive mound of vines had emerged one thousand feet north of where The Root was banished. "Evan, can you see that?" she asked.

He confirmed with another nod, watching the massive, distant vines. Though it might have been difficult for a human to see in the moonlight, his elven eyesight viewed the forest in a silver twilight and purple fringes. "How could something grow so quickly? And so large?" he asked.

Miranda smiled. "At this point, I've quit asking questions about weird things. C'mon!" she insisted, reaching out to grab Evan's hand.

His heart skipped a beat as she dashed forward, and he gladly complied. This whimsical spirit was one of the things he loved about her, and he felt a surge of butterflies weighing him down as he ran behind her. By the time they neared the mound of vines, it had grown thirty feet tall and twenty feet around. They walked around it clockwise, until they found an opening on the east side. For the size of the structure, the entrance was quite small, only about two feet wide and four feet tall. The vines had grown around a stone frame, and they were rapidly expanding. "By the gods, this is amazing," Miranda cooed.

Evan smiled and squeezed her hand. It was fascinating to watch the speedy, magical plant growth, but Miranda's reaction put his heart at ease. These were the moments when her personality captured the affection of others. The young woman was often fascinated by the beauty of nature and the wonders of magic, but her reactions had been minimal since Evan reunited with her in K'tal H'yuck. This reminded him of the Miranda he sailed with in the month after The Battle of Beriton.

Miranda stepped into the vine-covered structure, looking around. She let go of Evan's hand to twist through the narrow opening. She looked around the inside, able to see without the aid of her draconic sight. She stood in front of a shimmering, stone fountain with glowing water within. It sat ten feet in front of her, the roof lower than she anticipated from the towering vines outside. She had less than a foot of clearance, meaning the space would be cramped for Selasine or August. Colorful, plush moss grew all over the stone of the fountain, giving it a comfortable, lush appearance. The pool of water collected in a carved basin, and it sat in the middle of the fountain as a bowl. Water poured from a natural-looking stone waterfall above the bowl. A miniature, stone mountain towered on the far side of the basin, and it was covered in beautiful moss, vines, and flowers.

She wondered how such a magnificent place could exist in a location as horrifying as The Lichwood. The vines that had grown throughout and over the stone structure were healthy and lively, a stark contrast to the undead trees that once stood around them. Flowers bloomed all over the vines and on the ground around the stone fountain. The myriad of colors was a spectacle beyond a vibrant rainbow, causing Miranda to pause and gasp. Her response caused Evan to reach out and touch her shoulder.

Miranda was glad Evan accompanied her away from the camp. As a former wizard, he was still sensitive to the mana even though he could no longer call upon it as a source of power. Besides, The Lichwood was no place to travel alone, even if they had defeated the demon who created the evil magics that twisted the forest. Moreover, she had grown more comfortable with Evan over the last couple of weeks. She felt safe with his watchful eyes on her, and she knew his heart was as courageous as he was handsome. Something, however, felt out of place, as if the environment were influencing her thoughts and feelings. She smiled at Evan and breathed deeply. "How can such beauty come to rise in The Lichwood? This should not be possible!" she said with a giddy melody.

Evan whispered due to his own enthralled reaction to the fascinating environment. "Miranda, the temperature? It's so warm here, are you alright?" He noted she was sweating quite a bit.

She gave a shaky nod, her unbraided hair spilling over her shoulders. "It's definitely hot here, but look!" she said, turning back to the fountain. "The inscription," she said, pointing to a smooth, circular stone just beneath the basin on the side facing the entrance. There were characters that made no sense to Evan, causing him to shake his head. Miranda continued, "It says 'Bathe, traveler, in the Pool of Effulgent Tears. Leave your burdens and guilt behind at the feet of Dimittena, The Divine Weeper. Forgive yourself, forgive your past." She cycled her breath, considering the implications of the wording here. She had never heard of a divinity by this name, but she could read the strange script with ease. She wasn't sure if it was due to her connection to the stream or her parents, but as she said earlier, she had quit questioning it. She finished translating for Evan, "Splash the tears of the goddess on your countenance. May she weep for your failings, and may you strive to grow." She shrugged as she finished reading it.

Evan chuckled gently. "Pool of Effulgent Tears? I've never heard of such a thing, and I once studied magic!"

Miranda's lips turned into a cheeky smile, "Well the goddess in this story isn't one I'm exactly familiar with, either. It seems like we've stumbled onto a magical location that has probably been lost to history for millennia! This is impossible!" she squealed with excitement.

Evan started to grin, his eyes making his expression seem sly. "Those are bold words coming from somebody who defies the laws of magic so easily," he said in his normal, confident voice. Miranda realized how that sound comforted her.

She turned to face him, still smiling. "I wonder what will happen if we splash the water on our faces like it says?"

Evan inhaled; the aroma of this place was thick with floral scents. After days of traveling in winter conditions, it was a welcome reprieve. The smell of springtime along with the intense temperature of summer reminded Evan of home, the semi-tropical environment of southeast Claston. "Wouldn't it be prudent to seek the counsel of His Holiness before engaging in such—" he started to object.

Miranda, however, interrupted him with a giggle. "Aw, Evan. I can see the aura of this place. It is welcoming and forgiving. It's like the opposite of The Root. This should be something worth trying, at least! Besides, if it's dangerous, we have the best friends in the world, right?" She looked back at Evan with a devious glance. "And I'd never put them in harm's way on purpose. If I even suspected this of being a trap, I wouldn't do it. You know that, right?" She thought back to her insistence of releasing Vortex from his soul prism months ago. She would never be that reckless again, and she trusted her instincts.

Evan's gaze softened. "You know, after the trial in the forest. I realized how to let go, something I didn't master for thirty years in the arcane stream."

She beamed, proud of her friend's growth. "And I learned that I don't have to feel like I'm the only one who can save the day. But this heat!" she protested, growing more uncomfortable by the second. Miranda's expression turned to wonder again, "By Invictus, maybe the water in the pool is what is needed to quench this infernal heat!" With that excclamation and sweat still beading hard on her face, she rushed to the pool. Evan's hand slid off her shoulder as she moved away. She cupped her hands and splashed the water all over, practically soaking her hair as it slid down into the basin. Immediately, the friction between herself and the mana eased, allowing her to feel a crisp coolness in the air. It felt like a spring day instead of the blazing heat of the summer months.

As Miranda splashed herself, Evan watched a vortex of stars begin to swirl around her. He could see her relief from the heat; he realized that it was probably the mana calling to her generating the warmth that disturbed her so greatly. "Oh, by Lexcord. No wonder," he commented.

She turned to look at him, the front of her face, nightshirt, and hair dripping with the glowing, magical water. The reacting, magical maelstrom swirled upward from her feet. It looked like the night sky enveloped her slowly, obscuring her with an enchanted darkness. However, after a moment, the vortex coalesced around the sword in the ivory scabbard on Miranda's belt.

Evan whispered, "Iriliandria."

Miranda drew the sword, watching the tiny, swirling stars surrounding the blade. She then identified the source of the heat: It was the sword! Evan felt it thanks to his sensitivity to the mana and his familial relation to Iria. When Miranda first saw the sword months ago, she could tell it was bonded to the arcane stream. Now, she felt a spiritual significance. "Iria! I can hear you!" she shouted, thrusting the blade into the water of The Pool of Effulgent Tears.

The remnants of the stars around Miranda chased the sword into the water of the mystical basin. They formed a miniature, feminine elf made of pure light. The light particles never took any color, and it reminded Miranda of the mana body she formed within the arcane stream. Still, she was never more certain. Once she saw Iria in Selasine and Damil's ordeal, she was sure she could hear the voice of the sword. Its connection to Iria's spirit could no longer be contained.

Evan choked, "Sister?" His eyes recognized her form, her braids thick and full as the healer she was.

After a minute of silence, the shimmering, tiny elf replied, "Yes, moshirin. It's me." The figure gestured an embrace, standing atop the tip of the blade in The Pool of Effulgent Tears. "Hello, Lady Hyacinth," she added after a moment.

Miranda's eyes filled with tears. She could barely remember the times she had seen Telisi and Iria at the monastery. After watching the events in The Lichwood, Miranda knew she could feel the elf's heart. "Hello, Lady Lancethinas."

The light of the foot-tall figure in the pool pulsed as it spoke in her rich, sweet voice. "Darling Miranda, I've waited so long for this moment!"

Tears flooded the sides of the priestess's eyes, rolling down her round cheeks. "I'm sorry I made you wait!" she replied in humility. She leaned against the basin of the pool, bowing her head in shame. "I should have known the holy warmth coming from this sword was your soul."

Evan tilted his head in confusion, looking from the light-image of his sister to Miranda. "But Iria left the sword with Erk long before—" he began to object.

The light figure let out a gentle but exasperated groan. "Evanthalus! Calm. I left it with our brother, but I had seen my fate long before then. I possessed Foresight. Holyfang needed to reach Miranda and my dearest Thomas. After a time, I knew Holyfang would find this water. The Pool of Effulgent Tears."

Evan looked ready to cry with frustration. "Why, sister? Is it a way for you to return to us?"

The light creature shed a brilliant wave of particles that burned like ash but generated no heat. They fizzled out in the air throughout this strange structure. "No, moshirin. It's so that I can tell Miranda to call out to me in the face of The Frozen Death."

Miranda tilted her head to her right. "And you've been present with us through your connection to Holyfang?"

The light visibly nodded. "Do you understand what I mean, Miranda? I faced him once before, and I knew he would return. My duty to Espa and my soul placed me in a most compromising predicament. I had sworn to never harm another living being when I left Claston decades before, and I nearly kept my vow. My last moment was one of violence. I entertained Farzg for an afternoon to warn him of his destiny. Even after that, Farzg forced me to protect my daughter. Please, I hope that you'll understand—" the spirit explained, but Miranda interrupted, her eyes full of tears.

"That doesn't mean you violated your vow! You did what you could. Farzg is too powerful, and the only language he speaks is violence!" Miranda replied, the music in her voice sad and frantic.

Evan's lips quivered with sorrow. "Yashirote, what is the meaning of this Pool of Effulgent Tears? What is it that keeps your thoughts in the mortal coil? Your essence and your love are here. But I know that it's not really you." His breathing became shallow. "This isn't right."

Iria's energy surged, filling the strange, botanical cavern with prismatic light. "It is me, moshirin. Do not doubt the strength of

Invictus." Iria's voice became stern. "It is a miracle from The Sword of Justice. And if it is not, there are eldritch entities reaching further than the Legion, and they too answer the prayers of those in dire need. Some of them have hearts of good." Iria paused for a moment to allow Evan and Miranda to process her words. She continued explaining in a softer voice, "As I had envisioned, leaving my sword with Erk would bring it in contact with my holy symbol over the course of years."

Miranda shook her head, "That doesn't make any sense, though, ma'am. Selasine has never shown me your holy symbol."

Iria laughed, another array of light scattering into the air. "Darling, our precious Thomas has carried only my holy symbol since I passed. His old symbol is likely tucked in a lockbox somewhere, but the one that hangs from his neck now is the one that I once carried around mine."

Evan's eyes widened, realizing he recognized Selasine's holy symbol months ago. "Oh, yashirote! If your soul is preserved, then—"

Iria interrupted him, "Sadly, moshirin, there is not enough of my essence left to bring me back to the mortal coil. When Thomas and Miranda reunited in Yendralia, I moved from the symbol into the sword. The Root's stain in this region has begun to lift, and this ancient place has resurfaced."

Miranda's eyes narrowed, still feeling a bit warm. "You knew all of this when you gave your sword to Erk?" she asked.

Iria's voice was as cryptic as her reply. "Not the details, Miranda. Only the pieces that needed to be put in their places. The gift is not always clear when it speaks to us."

Evan nodded, remembering Iria's penchant for long-term planning. "Brother should be here; His Holiness should be here, too. Damil." His voice was somber, trusting now that this was a conscious imprint of his beloved sister.

Miranda started to agree with Evan, but Iria reassured them, "Do not fret. Those goodbyes will take place at the proper time. There is something you must know, Miranda. The violence I used against Farzg was incomplete. My soul stands before you as a continuance of that violence. On my passing, Invictus gave me the Revenant's Blessing."

Miranda's eyes widened with shock, and Evan scoured his memory. Iria did not give them a chance to interrupt. "There is hope for a better future, and it lies within you, Miranda. Farzg fears you for two reasons. First, you are the culmination of a fated meeting. You are the dragon of light who must receive his most prized possession. Second, you wield the Revenant's Blessing in my sword."

Miranda stammered, "Y-your spirit carries on in the name of revenge. But of course!" she said with an excited melody. "You broke your vow in defense of an innocent person. If Aylabrax can leave her unholy stain in the mortal coil, so too can the Sword of Justice leave the means to exact justice." She paused, however, and her eyes dropped to the ground. "But what do you mean, his most prized possession? His life?" she asked.

Iria replied, "No, Miranda. I do not know what object constitutes his most prized possession, but you will move mountains and oceans to claim it for yourself."

Evan whispered, "Foresight. Your words are an omen."

The light projection scattered sizzling petals throughout the cramped space again. Iria's voice answered, "Yes, moshirin. These are the same prophecies I gave to him, and they are the ones pointing to his end. Farzg will be long dead before you claim what is yours, Miranda. A dark era awaits Espa, but you will be a beacon of light. You must first wander in the darkness to learn the way."

Miranda stared at Iria, and her lips opened into their distinct 'o' shape. Evan's gray gaze narrowed with cheek. He added, "Remember when I said she spoke in riddles?"

Iria's laughter was soothing. She replied, "Brother, it fills my spirit with joy to see you are still the same as you always were. I have missed you, and this is why I left without saying goodbye. Foresight provided me the assurance we would meet again. All I have done has been to save our world from destruction. I beg your forgiveness, moshirin."

Evan whispered, "Yashirote." He said no more, his voice stifled by his breaking heart. Tears broke the barrier of his mirth.

Miranda took a step toward Evan and embraced him as he wept. Iria continued her message while the priestess comforted her brother. "The trial before you, however, must be completed before Espa can undergo its next calamity. Without this period of darkness, Espa would perish."

Evan's sobs subsided. Miranda replied, "It's up to us to defeat Farzg before my destiny will be clear, then. If you are here as a Revenant's Blessing, then you will be the one who destroys him."

Iria's voice took a vicious tone. "As was foretold to him the day he murdered my daughter. I am entrusting you to weaken Farzg so that I can overcome him. I will come to your aid, Miranda. Just wield my sword." The blanket of stars swirled around the blade again.

Miranda reached back into the pool, touching Holyfang's hilt. "The magic flowing through this sword. It's something greater than an arcane enchantment, isn't it?"

Iria answered, "Yes, Miranda. Keep it close to you. It will be pivotal in the era of darkness ahead."

The priestess inhaled with building anxiety. "I don't know if I can face the darkness alone. Your restless spirit will depart after the Revenant's Blessing is fulfilled. Why do I have so many friends and family that are just hanging around me from the other side?" Her blue eyes widened in fear. "Am I, too, destined for a tragic fate?"

Evan looked from the glowing form of his sister to Miranda. "Nonsense!" he rebutted.

Iria's form sent another shower of light petals around the room. "Tragic? It will depend on who you ask, darling. To many, you will be remembered as a great heroine, and to others, the bane of evil and chaos. It will all depend on how you face the darkness in front of you. And this time, you are spared the burden of killing."

Miranda breathed a sigh of relief. She was resigned to call upon Mir'thax to face Farzg, but as Iria explained the plan, she felt a sense of comfort. However, a thought slowed her acceptance, "But Iria, you were sworn to nonviolence otherwise. Does your soul really seek revenge through bloodshed?"

Iria's magical form emitted a radiant burst of deep, crimson hues. The light burned red, as well. "No, dear. Do not think of this as revenge. Instead, I was chosen by Invictus to exact justice for countless lives burdened by Farzg's stain. Will you help me to that end, Miranda? You need only draw close to Farzg with my sword. I will do the rest. Do you understand?"

Evan's gaze became frantic, the red lights startling him. Miranda nodded, withdrawing the sword from the pool. The light particles that constituted Iria broke apart and wrapped around the blade. "Then our hearts are aligned, Lady Lancethinas. Together, we will bring Farzg to justice."

Iria's voice faded. "Moshirin'nides. Farewell my brother. This is not the last we will meet."

Evan pleaded, "Don't go, sister! Yoshirote'nides! I will look for your next prophecy. I know you. I know you were more ready for this than anyone. Where have you hidden your next clue?"

Miranda squeaked, "Then just say 'see you soon' Iria! Please don't say goodbye!"

Iria's voice emanated from the sword. "Yolasha. I am so glad Thomas has you, Miranda. You put his soul at ease."

Miranda stared at Holyfang with a smile. What she thought was just an incredible sword was a conduit that held the revenant spirit of her would-have-been adoptive mother. "Evan," Miranda said, looking at him with a wildness in her electric stare.

Evan stood, dumbfounded. "Goodbye, sister," he murmured. As he felt his heart breaking anew for Iria, Miranda threw herself into him, hugging him tight. He let out a surprised grunt, not even realizing she had moved. "Woah, Miranda?" he asked.

"I'm so sorry," she lamented. "I really wish I could have met her. Please," she pleaded. "We have to hurry and deal with Farzg. I'm worried about Erk."

Evan nodded, squeezing the priestess in his arms. "I know, Miranda," he comforted. She laid her head into his shoulder, still wet from the water in The Pool of Effulgent Tears.

"Thanks," she replied, looking at him. "Sometimes, it just helps to say it out loud. You're always so good at listening to me talk. I know I struggle, sometimes. Maybe most of the time."

Evan laughed but then sighed. His lips twisted into his sly grin. "Lucky for you, I spent thirty years unable to participate in a conversation. Sometimes I forget to talk back to people, but you never seem to mind it."

She shuddered to think about it. She stood up straight and replaced Holyfang in its scabbard. "I feel like we've been through so much together, but we barely know each other in sheer chronological terms."

Evan shifted his weight between his feet a couple of times. "When you put it that way, it sounds like a catechism," he teased.

She giggled, the joke diffusing her serious tone. "Back in Devitus, I said I'd try to figure this out. I know what love should look like, even what it can feel like. But I feel different inside. Like I can't help but love everyone." Evan listened to her, the music in her voice rich and emotional. She continued, "But sometimes, I feel like I need to love some people more than others. It makes me uncomfortable, but I know those feelings are true. I was afraid to tell Selasine and August and Justin how much I loved them, and right before I got the guts to do it, I thought I would never have another chance."

Evan nodded, his heart stirring. Her body language seemed different, as if she were getting ready to fight. He raised an eyebrow, looking up at her. "Miranda?" he asked, feeling speechless.

"Well, I'm not going to make the mistake of hesitating again. Not in battle, not in love." She stood tall, her cheeks flushed. "So, I think you're a handsome elf and you're really brave. And you make me laugh. And you have a good heart."

Evan chuckled and glanced at the ground. "Oh hey, you don't have to say all those things," he started to object.

Miranda shook her head, "But you know that I do. And you know that I'm honest, right? I wouldn't say it if it wasn't true."

Evan's expression changed to shock. "Right. I suppose your honesty is one of the reasons I think you're wonderful."

She smiled at him and took a deep breath. She leaned down a bit and pressed her lips against his forehead, giving him an affectionate kiss that put his shyness at ease. She then embraced him again. She asked in a small voice, "Hey, after all this is over, we should go on an adventure of our own."

Evan was still reeling from Miranda's gentle affection. "We should?" he asked.

She nodded, her head on his shoulder again. "Yeah! We'll travel to some faraway places and do some great heroic stuff!"

Evan's heart was racing. He squeezed Miranda again, "I will remain by your side as your faithful Dedicantae, and we will adventure anywhere you wish."

Miranda stood up straight, tilting her head. Her wet hair was stuck all over her face and shirt. "Dedicate who?"

Evan grinned. "Dedicantae. An elven word for faithful one. You'll have my protection, care, and presence as long as it suits you."

Miranda's eyes sparkled with adoration. "That's so romantic!" she squealed.

Evan laughed until her face practically slammed into his, giving him an awkward, uncomfortable kiss on his mouth. Before they could give mutual reactions of pain, they fell into a fit of hysterical giggling. Miranda realized that the temperature around them had fallen drastically, however, and started to shiver in her wet evening dress and armor. "Okay, Dedicantae. Let's get out of this cold."

They walked back to camp hand in hand, Miranda generating a radius of comfortable warmth. They were going to share their news about The Pool of Effulgent Tears and show the location to everyone else, but the vines and stones sank into the ground as the two departed. Miranda's eyes widened in horror, but then she realized something beyond the gods was likely responsible for bringing it to the surface in the first place. She would let the ancient site sleep, dormant beneath the surface of Espa until its duty called it to awaken again.

Naomi beamed as they returned with clasped hands. "Did you find anything to cool you off out there?" she teased with a wiggling eyebrow.

Miranda's eyes lit up, "Oh, Naomi. Behave yourself. We've got an incredible story when everyone wakes up. We've got reinforcements that we didn't even know we had."

Naomi's lips twisted into a smirk. "Then the earth mother heard your whispers correctly. Blessed Iria."

Miranda and Evan both replied with nods. Miranda said, with a determined but floaty threat, "Daybreak will bring an end to the evil that is Eldon Farzg."

❦

Aylabrax stood, staring at the petrified trees that once made up The Lichwood. Her black hair was peeled back to reveal her gorgon face. Her eyes were so black they absorbed the moonlight, burning with an evil rage. "How isss thisss possssible?" she whispered, drawing out the 's' sounds with a snakelike hiss. "The Root and The Emissssary dessstroyed by the sssame girl!"

A powerful voice called from behind her. "Do not underestimate Miranda, Aylabrax. By pitting yourself against these mortals, you've made enemies of both Lexcord and me. And to add to her incredible power, Miranda has the full weight of the arcane stream at her disposal again." As she turned, she saw a man dressed in a brilliant, glowing plate mail. He wore no helmet, revealing his black skin and handsome, brown eyes. Fine, black braids cascaded down the front of his armor. He drew a sword and taunted, "And now you have no hope to Devour The Root. I was here to see to it that you did not reach him before the mortals. I see, now, they have more ways of travel in this realm than even I do."

Aylabrax sneered. "Then I'll take my portion from your flesh, Justice!"

Invictus frowned, his broad features crunching together. "You stand no chance against me, Mourner." He raised his left hand and a beam of light burst from his palm, striking Aylabrax before she could physically react.

The darkness within her, however, swirled to absorb the light, funneling it into her Devour attack. As she spent a moment nullifying the blast of light, Invictus began a running charge at the

Lady in Mourning. "Away with you!" Invictus shouted as he thrust his sword at her mortal body.

Aylabrax smiled, spraying venom and ichor from her mouth. As she opened her jaw, it unhinged like a serpent's, revealing rows of razor sharp, hideous teeth. Her tongue flicked like a snake, and the black oozing discharge hit Invictus directly. It fizzled and crackled, knocking him backward mid-thrust. A mortal would have been dissolved by her acidic breath, but Invictus's divine power resisted the unholy magics. "Curse you, Invictusss!" she hissed. Black energy formed around her arms, creating incorporeal scythes like a mantis. "Let usss duel then!"

Invictus pulled a magical shield from his back. "Have it your way, then!" he shouted, charging forward again.

Aylabrax swung her oversized energy scythes, prompting parries from Invictus. He used his shield to block one impact, and he deflected the blade of the other with his longsword. Aylabrax unleashed another spray of liquid. It covered Invictus in a miasma generating slime. The haze swirled and swarmed, tendrils of darkness bursting from within and diving back into the smoky particles.

Invictus growled, funneling his holy divinity into the center of his being. A burst of white light blew the slime and miasma away. It spread and manifested into a collection of glowing, ethereal weapons. Everything from daggers and swords to long spears and glaives made up a shining arsenal of one hundred weapons. They radiated with Invictus's strength and conviction. Justice embodied unleashed his ultimate smite. "May the light of the universe judge your wickedness! Face the Wrath of One Hundred Confessors!"

The weapons sailed at Aylabrax with incredible velocity, and as they impacted her, she unleashed another Devour. She found, however, she could not neutralize such a powerful discharge with a single attack, and a quarter of the glowing arms crashed into her unholy, mortal form. The force was immense, causing Aylabrax to fly five hundred feet across the countryside, crashing into a tree. The density of her gorgon form shattered the tree, raining branches and splinters in an arc behind the dark goddess. She leapt to her feet and sprinted toward Invictus.

He stopped, watching her cover the distance in mere seconds, preparing a counter to her reckless charge. As she came within engagement range, however, her avatar split into two, running forms. The additional attacker's scythes radiated the same, deadly energy of the other's, though the power now only seemed half as strong between the two. Invictus smiled; she could not use the Siphoning Sisters to its full effect thanks to Lexcord and the Valkindra. Still, even a single duplicate required Aylabrax to split her strength and divinity. It was amazing to him Miranda had cleansed a shard of this evil goddess's divinity from Yuvina's mind. "I smite you, wickedness!" he shouted, swinging his sword in an unexpected arc in front of him.

A beam of energy cut through the air, blasting Aylabrax and her duplicate. The slicing light caused black, murky essence to spill profusely from the Lady in Mourning. She resorbed her duplicate to stop the bleeding, but the energy in the scythes remained lowered. Invictus had struck a decisive blow. She spoke her following complaint in a deadpan, annoyed voice. "How has this endeavor yielded nothing? Doctor One showed much promise, but now I cannot touch his essence. The lacrima-deum yield me no power, and now even the great demons uncovered by his research have been banished. I blame you, Sword of Justice." Her sudden lack of emotion was unsettling.

Invictus nodded, triumphant. "My sister deserves as much blame as I do. Together, we have thwarted a cataclysm at your hands. I trust the mortals will deal with this Doctor One with me guiding them from the primordial place. However," he paused, giving her a long threatening stare.

Aylabrax spat, then interrupted the god of law and order. "Spare me your monologue, hero. At this point, you'll keep chasing me no matter where I go. I might as well return to the primordial place for a time where I can scheme and bless my followers with my unholy affection."

Invictus shuddered. The Mourning Dusk would be active again in a time of calamity. Still, he felt his mortal form's elation. He had successfully prevented Aylabrax's machinations from materializing. He stared at her as she gathered the divinity necessary to return to the primordial place. He did not want to risk a fight to the death with her; she had many, ancient curses dwelling within her that would only be revealed were she greatly wounded. He and Lexcord knew her undetermined, slothful nature would be a more effective target. Thankfully, their plan had succeeded.

As Aylabrax burst into the sky in a rocket of black energy, five ghost-like duplicates of the Lady in Mourning spread out in a circle from her point of departure. Before Invictus could respond, they dispersed at frightening speed in different directions. They could move through solid matter with no effort, and within moments, they were scattered to the winds. Invictus knew that those duplicates would roam the land, absorbing unsuspecting souls to feed Aylabrax upon her return. He would notify the church that Aylabrax left five Gleaners, soul-harvesting fragments of significant danger. He could commune with the Council of Four from the primordial place but getting back to the mortal realm would take a little longer if he needed to return. He had already visited three times within a year, and each visit would require more time to arrive. There was a ritual the church could use to summon him in the direst circumstances, but he would strive to prevent such disaster from the primordial place through his faithful.

"On my way, sister," he said with a nod. Following Aylabrax, he charged the divinity within him and burst through the sky in a beam of light. As he moved beyond the stars and distant worlds, he crashed into an ethereal barrier that rippled like a calm lake disturbed by a stone being dropped within. As his consciousness sank into the primordial place, he felt the urgent pull of his followers' prayers. He immediately returned to his work of protecting his and his sister's faithful.

Chapter 22
Company Comes Knocking

*"The clergy of Invictus must never rely on evil, debased powers.
As such, all sources of evil magic are explicitly forbidden." –
Vexilatus*, Chapter Thirty-One

*M*iranda marched in front. Selasine and Damil were behind her. Evan, Naomi, Yuvina, and Celyth kept pace following them. As the seven emerged from The Lichwood's petrified remains, Farzg's elite troops charged down the desolate hills of this northern peninsula. Each hill had a mansion housing fifty soldiers. In total, Farzg had the capacity to support three hundred bodyguards close to his estate. The henchmen on the frost giantkin's grounds were the most powerful and dedicated to Farzg's agenda. They served as his enforcers and protectors, but their numbers were presently thin. Many of them had been recently arrested or killed in their contests with the Church of Invictus. Those left behind charged with a roar of vengeance down the hills, attempting to overwhelm the seven.

Miranda frowned and put her hands out to her sides. A large, translucent, purple bubble formed around the party. It had a three-hundred-foot diameter, following Miranda as the center point as she walked toward the front gates of Farzg's estate. As Farzg's elite troops ran into it, they found themselves trapped in a smaller, denser, personal bubble. They floated in the air one foot off the ground and remained motionless. Even as Miranda moved away, the soldiers stayed trapped in their own bubbles.

Those with the strength to resist the spell found themselves quickly overwhelmed by the other six. Yuvina's agility allowed her to cover the group's flanks, and Naomi and Celyth could target enemies from anywhere inside Miranda's gentle globe. Evan provided Miranda cover, deflecting any swift attackers from her central, protective point. Selasine and Damil supplemented the group with strength and speed enhancing prayers and fierce sword fighting. Naomi also kept the ground beneath the enemy unstable. Those troops caught in the bubbles found themselves suspended indefinitely. They felt no need to struggle, however, as their elastic prisons provided a magical comfort that broke their will to fight. Farzg, on the other hand, would slay them for their failures. In that moment, Farzg's own troops began to wish for his demise.

Miranda's heart beamed, and her body glowed with the golden aura indicating she was overflowing with ether. Her creative spell had greatly reduced the violence necessary to reach the main structure of Farzg's estate. The bubble was her own idea, loving the way soapy and shimmering water looked, floating full of air. The way they popped with a splash startled her, but she made sure the magical bubbles would not harm the victims of the spell. Mir'thax was right. She had been so singularly focused that she stopped looking for creative ways to minimize casualties. Now, the warpriest walked a path truer to her heart. She could call on Mir'thax as she needed, but now was not that time.

The seven covered the last mile and a half between The Lichwood and the walls of Farzg's primary compound in an hour of fighting Farzg's elite troops. The central building of the complex spired up, shaped like an icicle made of granite. The walls of stone resembled packed snow. Miranda admired the beautiful and cold appearance of the grounds. The fortifications were punctuated with towers made of white granite like the central building of the estate. As they neared, Miranda could see the center building was an elaborate mansion with frost giant architecture. The central gate was elaborate, also made of the snowy stone. A heavy, iron portcullis blocked their entry, but Miranda had to maintain the protective bubble until they entered the complex. Many of the troops on the outside would be susceptible to a weak, neutralizing spell, but on the inside, Farzg's generals awaited. They would require much more effort than the gentle bubble.

Evan and Yuvina scrambled toward the wall, and Naomi lifted ramps of earth to make their ascent easier. As the two of them moved up to the top of the wall, an ambush of soldiers burst from the adjacent towers. The agile fighters wasted no time jumping down the other side and using their combined strength to operate the winch on their side of the gate. The soldiers looked down the fifteen-foot drop, impressed with the interlopers' athleticism. Farzg's troops moved to confront them, but the stairs to the courtyard were within Miranda's bubble. As they entered her spell, soothing bubbles trapped the weakest willed.

Miranda's lips were pursed into an excited smile, and Evan returned it as he raised the portcullis with Yuvina. Naomi flattened the ramps. Selasine and Damil charged through the gate, shouting prayers as two, ten-foot statues near the elaborate front doors of the mansion came to life. One wielded a large stone axe, and the other an impossibly heavy zweihänder also made of stone. Evan and Yuvina took no time to breathe, rushing into the courtyard to aid the clergymen against the constructs. Celyth and Naomi stopped outside of the range of the guardians' heavy weapons, providing support at a greater distance.

Damil was quicker than Selasine, and he dove directly into the knee of the axe-wielding statue with his longsword. He felt the force of the axe slamming into the ground behind him. The statue had no mind to understand its mistake. Yuvina leapt onto the massive, stone blade, running up the shaft of the axe and the arm of the mindless creature. As she reached the top of the broad construct, she towered over its head. She worked herself up into a frenzy of frustration, pawing harmlessly at the stone. Her mind and body entered an enraged state, however, and she drew her daggers. She chipped at the guardian relentlessly, the sound of magical metal on stone reverberating throughout the courtyard. She chiseled the construct's head into nothing. To complicate matters for the golem, Damil had severely compromised the stone of its knee, causing its left leg to crumble after a few moments. As the axe-wielding statue broke apart into large, unanimated stones, the one with the sword also shattered.

Yuvina and Damil looked to see Selasine use an incredible whirlwind blow between the legs of the tall construct, and Evan used his agility and strength to kick the torso of the guardian backwards. Their overwhelming force obliterated the magics propelling the creatures, causing the remainder of Farzg's troops to freeze in fear. This group looked affiliated with the church giving them so much grief in recent months. The ease with which they destroyed Farzg's guardian golems instilled enough fear to keep remaining troops at bay.

As Miranda joined the others in the courtyard, she dismissed the magical bubble. It popped with a liquidy echo. Those previously trapped by the bubbles were also released, but they were no longer willing to fight such powerful invaders. She examined the beautiful estate. The walls and portcullis gave it a militaristic feel, but the courtyard inside was exquisite. A single, paved path led from the gate to the front door of the mansion. The door was fifteen feet tall, and the front parlor behind it raised up thirty feet high. Large, stained-glass windows covered the front of the complex, glowing a variety of colors in the mid-morning light. Their panes met in lancet arches, and the complex within looked like it could have easily been tens of thousands of square feet. Miranda could see a music room through one of the windows, causing her heart to skip. Why would anyone as evil as Farzg have time for music, she wondered.

Everyone regrouped behind Selasine as he approached the massive front door. Breaking protocol, he did not knock and identify himself. Instead, a white light swirled around him, borrowing the strength of Invictus. He charged forward, giving the door a brutal kick. The dense, wooden doors shattered beneath the weight of his divine might. He called out to the empty parlor, "Company comes knocking, Farzg!"

His voice echoed off the walls of the elaborate sitting room. It was filled with opulent furniture, and massive tapestries and paintings adorned the walls. A rounded staircase wrapped around a central, semi-circular balcony midway up. Additional stairs led to the second floor, providing access to various doors and hallways fifteen feet above the sitting room. The companions entered the mansion from the main door on the south side, and two, large hallways extended to the immediate left and right from the parlor on the ground floor. The otherwise round room had no obvious exits beyond the front door.

Evan stepped forward, looking around. "Which way?" he asked, looking back at Selasine and Damil. "It could take hours to search a place like this."

Damil gave Evan a smile. "As with so many things involving Farzg, the obvious answer is the wrong one." He stepped forward to the raised, round wall on the ground level in between the rising, circular stairs. The wall up to the mid-level balcony overlooking the sitting room was ten feet high, providing enough space for Farzg if needed. The paladin pointed to a decorated bookshelf built into the wall of the raised platform. "You might have to reach it, darling," he said to Thomas.

The high priest nodded, approaching the bookshelf. "Everyone, stay close."

Yuvina, still panting with fatigue from her enraged state, slid next to Selasine, her eyes fixed on the bookshelf. "Sir!" she yipped.

Evan, Naomi, and Celyth stood behind Selasine and Yuvina, and Miranda and Damil stood next to the bookshelf on the right side. The high priest walked up to the bookshelf and reached onto a shelf just above everyone else's reach. He fumbled for a moment, but then his expression fell. "It's gone," he complained.

Damil's eyes widened. "So, he's made it harder to get in. It looks like he's not the only one who learned a lesson last time we fought."

Celyth's eyes narrowed as she caught movement emerging from the rooms on the second floor. "Hey, uh, I think we have an issue," she commented.

Everyone else followed her eyes; swarms of partial Umbrals spilled from all over the front of Farzg's mansion. "Talirix volïs," Selasine cursed. "They're just here to slow us down. I guarantee Farzg does not expect this ambush to wipe us out."

Naomi growled, hurling a barrage of daggers at the Umbrals falling over the railing of the second floor. "Well, figure out how to get access, or we might be here for a while wasting energy."

Evan drew his father's sword and Yuvina withdrew her daggers from inside her cloak. "I think we can handle a few shadows, savvy?" Evan encouraged.

Miranda's brow furrowed. She inhaled, feeling the mana in the air. There was a lot of stagnant energy nearby. Lacrima-deum had been purposefully burned to create weak, partial Umbrals. "Just like in Nulodia!" she exclaimed. She turned her blue gaze from the balcony above to the bookshelf. "Hey, Modai-rin?" she piped.

"Yes, yolasha?" he asked, turning to her.

"Move!" she ordered. She pointed her gauntlet-covered hands at the bookshelf.

Selasine's eye widened in shock, and he slid out of the way, drawing his sword to deal with Umbrals now pouring in from every direction above.

A burst of purple, searing energy emerged from Miranda's hands with incredible force. Between the heat and the impact, the shelf shattered. It had a reinforced, steel frame behind it, and Miranda's destructive spell superheated the metal. As she focused on the mana, her hair changed from red to deep purple, signifying she was using the mana reserves held within her thanks to her parents. The superheated steel shattered in a burst of cindering, hot shards. The mana-charged particles dispelled some of the Umbrals as they scattered through the air.

Behind the bookshelf, Miranda had revealed a hallway carved with a different snowy stone than the walls outside. "Quickly, inside!" she called. Her allies withdrew into the tunnel, and she activated a Holynova to burn the nearest, closing Umbrals into dissipated mana. As they started to move down the hallway as a group, Miranda turned and made the gesture of an 'x' in the air. Two electrifying beams of yellow light appeared over the entrance to the secret tunnel. As Umbrals moved through it, they were incinerated. Miranda stood about fifteen feet away from the door, baiting the Umbrals through. Countless shadows tried to pour through the entrance, but as they did, they returned to the mana. Miranda stayed close, absorbing the remaining, stagnant ether. After a few moments, her hair returned to its normal shade of red. Everyone stared at her.

Celyth commented, "Were you, like, snacking on Umbrals just now?"

Naomi's brows shot up, and her silver eyes demonstrated disgust. "Ew! How do you snack on a shadow?"

Yuvina's whiskers twitched, joining in, "It can't be helped. She needs lots of mana to grow up strong, like me!" she said, a teasing yap behind her words.

Miranda smiled. "Yes, I was having a mana snack." Then, her eyes narrowed, and her grin became sinister. "And you're lucky I'm not the kind of dragon that snacks on adventurers."

Everyone paused for a moment, but a wave of laughter followed. Selasine brought their attention back to the mission, "Alright. Beware of traps. I'm sure this tunnel is designed to collapse or worse." He gripped the holy symbol around his neck. "Daylight," he prayed, causing it to illuminate.

"Traps? Hah!" Naomi replied. "S'cuse me, lovelies. Let me see what I can do."

The earth giantkin led them down the hallway, disabling various mechanical and magical traps built into the impossibly long tunnel. "Every pirate's a locksmith, but not every locksmith is a pirate," she commented as she jammed and disabled a pressure plate. Later, she opened a slat in the stone wall with her earth giantkin gift and cut some weights on a pulley built into an alternative, thin shaft on the other side. "Every pirate's an engineer, but not every engineer is a pirate." She had a similar saying for almost every trap, until she started to come across redundant traps. By the sixth tripwire, she groaned, "Hunters don't usually become pirates anyway. But every pirate is a hunter. By the gods, why so many traps?"

Miranda's lips stayed twisted into a smile. Now that she had rekindled her trust for the people around her, she was having fun. The constant, pressing fear had eased. If she had this kind of composure in Mystalon, perhaps she could have intervened against Sender sooner. She looked to Evan, who stayed close by her side the entire morning. He gave her a confident grin. For some reason, Miranda felt it hard to look at him today. She felt shy but could not articulate why. She gave him a sweet shrug and averted her eyes to Naomi working on another trap.

After about an hour and a half of slow, cautious movement, they had progressed fifty feet into the tunnel. Naomi finally complained, "Okay, how in the Infernia does this guy get in and out of his own damn house?" She was on her knees in the process of slamming a stone wedge under a pressure plate.

Selasine laughed. "He makes the air around him too cold. It probably changes the properties of the snowstone enough to deactivate the traps."

Miranda shook her head. "I can do that!" she offered.

Damil shook his head. "Not wise. The temperature required would likely be lower than anything we could survive for very long without exhausting resources of our own."

Celyth shivered, already chilly in the winter air further cooled by the snowstone. "We're trading off time for our other resources then?"

Selasine nodded, grim. "Unfortunately, yes. Farzg is surely aware of our arrival and will do one of two things. If he has nothing of value here, he will retreat. If, however, he has something he values here more than his own life, then he will stay and fight. Back then, he fought to protect his family and accumulated wealth. Now, I do not know what Farzg values." He let out a sigh. Miranda stepped up to him and gave him a hug.

She looked up at him and replied, "Maybe at this point, it's pride. But he's here. I can feel his evil."

Damil placed a hand on Miranda's shoulder. He smiled at Thomas, then down to the young woman who had her arms thrown around the high priest. "Your offer to help is greatly appreciated." His voice was much softer than Selasine's, but it felt authoritative and protective, nonetheless.

Miranda looked into his hazel eyes for a moment before averting her gaze. She replied, "We are in this together, so I want to help however is needed."

Naomi stood in frustration. "Everybody, hold on a second." She stomped with her right foot, sending a shockwave forward through the hewn snowstone. As it rippled down the long corridor, the party watched as numerous traps activated, including collapsing ceilings, blasts of fire, lightning, and ice, spike traps, log traps, and even crossbows rigged to fire through small slats in the walls. A moment of silence hung over the group after the rumbling in the stone ceased and the traps ran their course.

Evan started to laugh hysterically. Yuvina's whiskers twitched, and Celyth perched a hand on her hip. Miranda, Selasine, and Damil peered down the tunnel, dumbfounded. Naomi shrugged, "Nobody ruins Naomi's day!" she shouted down the now, wrecked corridor. She walked forward confidently, using her affinity with earth and stone to reconstruct impassable sections. Within ten minutes, they progressed down the remainder of the two-hundred-foot tunnel. As the speed of their progress increased, Miranda noticed the tunnel was also sloped upward. By the end, they were on the second floor of the mansion.

The tunnel emerged into a well-furnished hallway. There was no door on this end, but the hallway before them split three ways: to the left, right, and forward. The mansion was even more opulent here; the paintings that lined the walls were dozens of feet wide and ten feet tall. A series of colorful, decorative silks had been strung up over the walls, giving their black paint some contrast. The accents of the building were painted red, creating a sinister feeling. The hallways were at least fifteen feet wide, capturing the massive nature of the architecture. The floor was paved snowstone, however, a bright change from the dark on the walls and ceilings. The floor reflected the light well, making it easy to see far down the hallways.

The halls to the left and right at this juncture led to the living quarters of Farzg's closest consorts. The door at the end of the hallway directly in front of them, however, would lead to Farzg's study. His library and part of his artifact collection would be above, but his personal living space was under the study. A dozen suits of armor holding various weapons lined this hallway on each side. They were made for the descendants of frost giants, so they stood eight and a half feet tall. Selasine pointed forward. "This way!" As they got halfway down the hallway, the sound of metal grinding on metal echoed throughout.

Damil shouted, "We're not in the clear, though!" As the seven looked around the hallway, the suits of armor began to animate. Selasine and Damil ran forward, smacking a suit viciously with their magical swords. The ferocity of their blows destroyed the magic activating the armor. Celyth and Naomi had allowed the group to move forward, putting some distance between them. When the armor began to come alive, they retreated to the entrance of the secret tunnel.

Miranda closed her eyes and prayed, "Sword of Justice! Shield us from the blows of the enemy!" Her prayer was simplified but effective. All of her allies gained the protective barriers usually reserved for the faithful of Invictus.

The prayer activated just in time. As Evan made an agile roll to dodge one armor's sudden attack, another suit charged down the hallway and attempted to collide with the elf mid-maneuver. It crashed into the barrier, however, causing the divine protection to shatter. The impact shredded the suit of armor into husks of busted metal. Evan shouted, "Thanks, Invictus!" as he dove into another roll. He swung his father's sword low, cleaving the feet off another suit of armor. "And thank you, Miranda!"

Celyth stood back, watching the twenty remaining suits close into the brawl in the center of the hallway. Naomi hurled daggers into the melee with telekinesis, puncturing the breastplate and chainmail of a nearby suit trying to engage her allies. Celyth fired her bow, striking one suit six times in six seconds. The arrows delivered electrically enhanced magitabs, and the resulting shocks deactivated the magic animating the armor. She fired on another, the magitabs enhancing her deadly shot. She began to mow them down from behind, prompting Naomi to throw daggers faster. The giantkin grinned, "You're a pretty good shot, you know."

Celyth smirked. "Yeah, I know. You're not too bad, yourself. I'm still going to get more kills than Arlindra would have."

Naomi's gaze snapped from the enemy to Celyth. "If you're ready to be a real heroine, then you better keep up with me." She then looked back to the suits of armor swinging wildly in the middle of the hallway ahead. She could see Selasine and Damil parrying numerous blows while Evan and Yuvina nimbly evaded them. They disabled the enemy with various attacks. Miranda stood in the center, fervently praying to Invictus for enhancement prayers. "That beautiful warpriest. Hey! Miranda! Let me have some of that energy!" she shouted, running forward.

Celyth's eyes widened with a moment of shock, but then she locked onto another target, puncturing it and the magic moving it in a single volley.

As Naomi dove into the melee brandishing her daggers, she felt her strength and agility boosted by Miranda's prayers. She somersaulted into the air hurling daggers as she spun. Her accuracy and strength were incredible, and as she threw her weapons, they returned safely to the bandolier on her thigh. She slung twenty daggers, disabling six suits of armor in her rain of knives. She landed gracefully, rolling forward behind another one.

Before she could strike, Yuvina barreled into it from the side, knocking it into an adjacent suit of armor. The kitsune was bleeding from a slash across her snout, but she seemed incapable of feeling pain in her enraged state. The metal of the armor bent beneath her bare paws, and she crushed the first suit into the second until they both deactivated, the pieces falling harmlessly to the floor.

Selasine and Damil had cut a swathe through the animated armor, fighting at each other's side with ease. They complimented each other's tactics, and Damil's connection to Thomas's mind allowed them to act as a single unit in real time. Evan used his sword to pierce the breastplate of an armor Yuvina had knocked over in her wild rage. By the time he could reassess the battlefield, two dozen suits of guardian armors had been destroyed. Miranda tended to Yuvina's wounds, the kitsune snarling at Miranda until her fury subsided.

Naomi peered at the door at the end of the hallway. "So, he's in there?"

Miranda's healing prayers helped Yuvina make a quick, full recovery. The kitsune joined Naomi, fifteen feet away from the door to Farzg's study. She let out a deep, angry whine. "He can't hide anymore!"

Selasine and Damil stepped around Naomi and Yuvina, approaching the door. Miranda and Evan stood behind them, and Celyth joined them close to the single door, which stood five feet wide and ten feet tall. It was beautiful, carved wood, which made Miranda sad. She was sure that they were about to destroy the door.

Before Selasine could kick, however, the door handle clicked, and it opened inward. Inside, the seven saw a magnificent, massive library open before them. Bookshelves lined the walls, full of scrolls, artifacts, and tomes. Maps, tapestries, and paintings hung on the walls in between the towering, heavy shelves. On the far left and right sides of the room were spiraling metal staircases that went upward to the balconies and shelves above. In the center before them, however, was a large desk with an ornate chair behind it. It was one hundred feet away from the door. A gnoll with black fur wearing a deep, green plate mail sat in the chair. As the group spilled into the library, everyone but Damil and Selasine fanned along the walls.

Echo stood and stretched his arms wide. "The paladin and the priest return! The two men of justice that taught me almost as much as His Majesty!"

Selasine spat, "Echo. It's a surprise to see you again, to say the least." His eye narrowed, and he brandished his magical sword. He activated his uncanny magic, creating numerous, illusory copies of himself.

Damil, too, drew his blade. The gnoll stood, leaving his arms stretched out. "What, no hug? Come now! I have much to thank you for!"

Selasine called to the others along the wall. "Don't bother with keeping a distance! His uncanny magic is overwhelming!" As he spoke, he rushed toward the desk.

Echo jumped onto it, leaving his arms outstretched. "Behold, then! Stardust, ignite!" A massive gust of wind filled the library. Papers and scrolls swirled about, showing the wind had no logic or consistent direction. Before Selasine could close the gap between himself and Echo, the attack began. Tiny, burning meteors began to materialize, falling from numerous points throughout the room. As they collided with Selasine's duplicates, they fizzled out of existence along with the illusions.

Damil paused to pray, "Sword of Justice, cover us with your shield!" As he gripped his holy symbol, it flashed white, and energy barriers formed above himself, Selasine, and Yuvina. The kitsune had closed the distance between herself along the wall and the gnoll standing on the desk. The barrier above her shielded her from at least seven meteorites, flashing brightly when each one collided with the protection prayer.

Celyth, Naomi, and Evan, however, had taken defensive positions, blocking and parrying the bursts of energy that were becoming too numerous to count. Celyth had drawn her sword, and Naomi had created a telekinetic barrier of knives around herself. The magic in the daggers deflected dozens of stardust fragments as they tried to pelt her. Evan was struggling to parry with his father's larger sword, so he opted to use a couple of clockwork daggers he still had tucked away.

Miranda watched as her allies struggled to deal with the gnoll's uncanny magic. She frowned, praying for her own energy barrier. It blocked the meteorites with ease, but it did not help her allies' positions. She started to move toward the desk in the center of the long library. The first floor was flat, and four spiring columns rose up to the roof fifty feet above. They were spaced out as the corners of an interior square containing the desk. Miranda chewed on her lip for a moment, deciding. As Damil's prayer began to crack, Yuvina had engaged the gnoll in hand-to-hand combat. Stardust continued to spray, however, making the library impossible to navigate.

Yuvina swiped at Echo's face, yapping wildly in her rage. A sword materialized directly in Echo's hand forcing Yuvina to evade with a backflip. The brilliant, ethereal blade left a trail of sparkles behind his swipe. "Behold, The Acheron's Fury!" he taunted. Yuvina barked at the gnoll, looking for an opening.

Miranda frowned again. She could tell Stardust would overpower them, and it would be difficult to maintain the prayers that could protect the entire group. She condensed the mana inside her. She didn't have to kill Echo to make the attack stop, but she suspected she needed to incapacitate him. She took a deep breath, the exhale forming a dense cloud in the cold of Farzg's mansion. A beam of brilliant, purple light shone from her in every direction, but then it all focused onto Echo as a single target about twenty feet in front of Miranda. He stood atop the large desk, keeping Yuvina at bay with his magical sword. As the purple light connected with him, he looked around in a panic for the source.

Yuvina froze, then gave a devious grin. "Goodnight, gnoll," she yipped.

Echo looked from the foxkin to the priestess who had trained the light on him. "Nonsense, I'll slay you where you stand!" he shouted, moving incredibly fast as he pounced from the desk toward Miranda. Damil and Selasine were parrying meteorites, trying to engage Echo, but the blasts of energy made it difficult for them to move effectively without dropping their defenses. Miranda's lips shifted into a sad smile as the attacker sailed toward her, airborne.

As he came within swinging distance, the light buzzed, and a brilliant, white pulse surged through the beam. It exploded on contact with Echo, and Miranda's hair turned purple again. Echo flew across the library, crashing into a bookshelf. The impact knocked him out instantly, causing the Stardust to cease. Yuvina chased the gnoll across the room, looking back to the others. "He's alive. What do we do?"

Damil approached, raising his fingers to his temples. "I can search his memories to find out if Farzg is below," he commented.

Miranda interrupted. "That won't be necessary, Damil!" she said with a sweet melody. "I can feel his cold from here."

Everyone turned to see her standing beside a trapdoor behind the desk. It opened as a side effect of the intense energy Miranda shed to disable Echo. Selasine smiled. "It looks like he didn't change one detail," the high priest said. He then turned his eye back to Echo. "He has numerous warrants. We will deal with him when we emerge from below. Damil?" he prompted.

The telepath nodded, touching his hand to his temple. He closed his eyes, focusing on the gnoll's state of mind. With a powerful, psychic suggestion, Echo's body was lulled into a comforting, restful sleep. The paladin turned to face the others. "He'll sleep for an entire day now."

Miranda smiled, stepping off the side of the trap door. Instead of using the ladder, she floated down using magic similar to Nebu's Feather Step. The entrance was a wide, ten-foot square. There was a ladder on the north and south sides, built into the snowstone. The area went down twenty feet, however, making it seem narrower than it was. At the bottom, there was a vault door with a valve wheel on the west side. Miranda's friends climbed down as she inspected the door. She chimed, "It's going to get really cold from here, isn't it?"

Selasine reached over to touch her arm. "Do you have any solisberry blooms left?"

She nodded; Naomi had given her a handful more after recovering from the events in Mystalon. She reached into her pouch and placed a few underneath her tongue.

Celyth prepared her bow. "Alright, Mir. Let's get the dirty work out of the way."

Yuvina growled but didn't speak. She had her eyes trained on the door, and her legs were poised to pounce. Damil smiled, watching Miranda's hair shift from purple to red. "Perhaps we should take a moment to pray," he suggested.

Selasine and Miranda nodded in agreement. They joined hands, reciting, "Sword of Justice, may your enervating hand sweep the enemy before us, and may your infinite grace shield us from the horrors of chaos." As they did, a bright, red aura formed around all of them.

Miranda breathed deeply. "I'll keep a bubble of livable temperature active around us. It may take a lot of mana to counteract Farzg's magic, and I've never felt his will pressed against mine. Let's make sure to handle our work quickly, okay?" She smiled, focusing on the concentration of mana now overflowing from her essence. The golden aura returned.

Evan placed his hand in hers. "I'll keep you safe!" he promised.

Miranda gave him a gentle smile. "Same," she replied.

Naomi grinned, but then her silver eyes fixed on the valve on the door. "Let's give it a twist then? It's probably frozen from the inside." She approached the door, tugging on the valve. "Solid. I need honeycomb's warm sunlight," she said, her voice pouty.

Selasine, Damil, and Evan approached. The wheel was about ten feet in diameter. The door was a little larger, and it was made of a metal that looked perpetually cold. As they tugged on it, they could tell the frozen pressure behind it would make it impossible to open.

Selasine scratched his chin. "Haelia opened this last time." He looked at Miranda, who gave him a knowing nod.

Miranda held her arms out to her sides, and she imagined the warmth she felt at The Pool of Effulgent Tears the night before. She closed her eyes, thinking of the sun and the spring meadow created by Mir'thax in The Lichwood. The room around them warmed, causing the snowstone to glisten with an icy sheen. After a few moments, she opened her eyes, and a steady beam of sunlight poured from them. She stared at the center of the wheel, and steam radiated from the top. The heat was so intense that the ice was sublimating rather than melting. The four at the valve wheel gripped it again, turning it with all their might. Thanks to the sunlight from Miranda's magic, they managed to give it a full turn, causing the domed door to open. A large, ornate entrance led into a royal court. It ran one hundred feet from south to north, and at the end was a door leading to Farzg's private quarters. Pillars of snowstone ran along the walls. The room was thirty feet wide, and the columns were spaced ten feet apart, forming a beautiful colonnade.

At the far end, before the door to Farzg's room, stairs raised up to a dais with a single throne sat upon it. The dais was only five feet up, and the stairs continued upward another five feet behind the throne. Seated on the throne was a large, bearded frost giantkin with shimmering, unsettling purple eyes. He cast a long, judgmental glare across the court. "How dare you, Thomas!"

Thomas and Damil entered first, standing next to the first pillars of the colonnade. The high priest replied, "What? How dare I come uninvited to your home with the intent of committing violence? Or is that a privilege that only The Frozen Death may exercise?" His voice made Miranda wince. She had never heard such hostility from Selasine, but she breathed a sigh of relief. She knew Farzg deserved it, and she suspected Selasine was showing significant restraint.

Damil stepped forward and added, "Your journey is over, Farzg. Your life is forfeit, and your empire will be dismantled mere hours after your death is confirmed publicly." He drew his sword.

The frost giantkin rolled his eyes. He could see Miranda was the source of warmth surrounding the group this time. "Well, when you put it that way," he retorted, standing from his throne. "I don't guess I should be surprised. I've been waiting for this since I unleashed the Infernia in Nulodia."

Yuvina stepped forward, her growl growing more impatient. Celyth had arrows ready to fire and her bow trained on Farzg. Naomi's eyes were narrow, hateful slits. "This is the bastard? The notorious Farzg?" she asked.

Evan's face, too, was full of raw anger. "My sister. You'll pay for what you did to my sister and my niece!" He drew his father's sword.

Farzg sighed. "Come, now, Master Lancethinas. I spared you the assassin trying again! You could just walk away, and we could call our debt even."

Evan's gray eyes shimmered with unbridled vengeance. "I'd fight a thousand, second-rate bounty hunters just to make sure you get exactly what you deserve!"

Miranda stepped forward, the radius of her warmth protecting them from the subzero temperature of the room around them. The pillars looked slick anywhere Miranda's zone of heat reached. The floor here was also made of snowstone, and it became clear that keeping the room warm would be hazardous. Selasine and Damil struggled to maintain their balance on the slippery, warmed surface. Farzg smiled and jeered, "I've done some remodeling since you last visited. I hope you like the changes!" He held his arms out to his sides.

Damil nodded. "Here it comes."

Selasine gripped his holy symbol. "Invictus, we trust in you." The seven continued to approach in spite of Farzg's warning stance.

The frost giantkin sighed with antagonism. "Usually people hesitate when I do this."

Celyth shouted back, "Maybe that's because they can smell your bad breath!"

Farzg frowned. "What a terrible choice for last words." His disdain was palpable.

Thanks to Miranda's magic, none of them could feel the air temperature become lethally low. That, however, did not stop Farzg from charging up his Death Geyser and unleashing its full fury toward them.

As the tip of one of the massive icicles would have stabbed Selasine, the Enervating Shield activated. As the other six would have been impacted, their shields also exploded with the fury of the god of justice. An intense, retaliatory flame jetted toward Farzg from all seven of the heroes. Shards of ice and glacier burst throughout the room, shaking the foundation of Farzg's entire estate. The fallout from the counter prayer obscured the room. Seven Enervating Shields was more than enough to neutralize Farzg's first Death Geyser.

Selasine's voice called through the misty, icy fog, "Quickly! We have to get Miranda close, or he will have time for another assault!"

The seven rushed forward, keeping close to Miranda. Selasine and Damil helped her maintain her balance, and they moved as quickly as they could across the slippery snowstone. The poor visibility, however, prompted Miranda to ask, "Where did he go?"

Naomi gave a telekinetic push through the environment, forcing the obscuring debris down the court. As the light caught up to the clearing glacier fragments, Farzg was no longer at the throne. "Maldith!" Naomi cursed.

Yuvina scrambled along the edge of Miranda's barrier of warmth, looking frantically for a sign of the frost giantkin. She sniffed the air, her eyes widening with realization. "Behind us!" she warned, her voice high pitched and frantic.

Miranda turned around. Farzg used the cover to ambush the companions. Celyth and Evan were the closest to his new position, about thirty feet outside of Miranda's warmth barrier. His arms were already extended, however, and the deathly cold had already filled the air outside the bubble. "Blast!" Evan shouted, scrambling backward to evade but slipping on the slick snowstone. Naomi hurled a dagger, but the cold depleted its momentum before it reached Farzg.

With a sour face, the frost giantkin lamented, "Doctor One has taken a great interest in you, Miranda. By eliminating you, I actually think I am making the world a safer place. Isn't that a good reason for my violence?"

Miranda closed her eyes and began to force the mana through her at an accelerated rate. Her globe of survivable air expanded greatly, the sudden warming causing the room to fill with fog. As her hair turned purple in the steamy throne room, she rotated everyone's positions with a chaotic pulse of the ether. She wanted to use Reginald's trick to force Farzg closer to her.

"Confound it!" she heard Farzg curse from behind her.

Everyone, however, was disoriented by their new positions. Yuvina appeared by Miranda's side in the foggy, warm air. "I can smell him. He's so cold!" she yipped, bouncing into the billowing cloud around them.

"Away!" Miranda heard, assuming the deep, condescending voice was Farzg. She finally felt Farzg's will press against hers, and the entire cosmos froze. She tried to see the world through the eyes of the arcane stream. An immense energy dammed behind a floodgate was beginning to open. She could feel his looming, dooming presence hanging over her with this vision. In order to prevent his attack, she would need to unleash just as much ether, opening the floodgates behind her own, stored energy. For anyone to have a chance at surviving, she knew she had to. She had the solisberry leaves under her tongue, and they were supplying her with an abundance of extra ether.

Farzg forced the air temperature down from within Miranda's protective bubble. This caused the environment to spark with a reaction in the mana, crackles of lighting and wind whisking away the fog and revealing everyone's positions. Farzg was directly in the middle with Yuvina closest to him, only five feet away. Selasine and Evan were ten feet to his north, and Celyth found herself about twenty feet to Farzg's south, next to Damil. Naomi ended up next to a pillar near the end of the colonnade, Celyth's former position. Miranda had changed places with Farzg, putting herself fifty feet to his south, the closest side to the door from which they entered.

The frost giantkin laughed. "You're going to try and match me in power, Miranda?" His voice was a jeer, and he lowered himself into a deep fighting stance. As he did, Miranda felt the air freezing critically fast.

"No!" she shouted in reply, accelerating the heat generated by the mana flowing through her. Her hair turned purple in an instant, and it glowed with an electric and fiery aura. She pressed her will harder against Farzg, keeping the air too warm for his Death Geyser. His otherworldly eyes narrowed, and he pushed harder. Miranda shouted from the exertion, not having anticipated the pain possible in a battle of arcane wills. The elemental nebula expanded from her hair to her entire body, the golden aura returning. "Invictus, give me strength!" she prayed, imbuing their interlocked wills with a dose of holy fury.

A crackling sound filled the room, and a bright flash exploded from Miranda and Farzg. They were blown in opposite directions. Miranda crashed into the door to the vault, and Farzg against the door of his personal quarters behind the throne. With Miranda so far away, the temperature became immediately unbearable for her allies.

Selasine prayed, "Sword of Justice, shelter us from the storm! Protect us from the cold and the sun, may our exposure be forgiven and our travels safe." A blanket of divine warmth wrapped around them, but it did not nullify the fast-acting effects of the magic. Yuvina fell to the ground, shivering profusely. Celyth's fingers became numb, making it impossible for her to fire her bow. Naomi shuddered, resisting a good portion of the magical cold. Evan had fallen to a knee, his breath creating a heated, steamy cloud around him. Selasine and Damil stood, confident. They had prayers deep within protecting them specifically from Farzg. They would be able to fight in the impossible cold, but it would still damage their bodies over time.

Miranda and Farzg stood, and the priestess scrambled forward to extend her protective warmth to her friends. As she did, she started to slide on the slick floor beneath her. She relied on her growing battle instincts. Instead of a clumsy, forward fall, she diverted some mana to her boots, affixing a single, magical blade to the bottoms. She leaned her weight forward and caught herself with a swaying motion in her knees and hips. Farzg's eyes widened in disbelief as Miranda skated across his throne room, the snowstone now slick and perfect for the magical blades under her feet. She cleared fifty feet to the center of the room in seconds, a comforting wave of warmth dispelling the deadly cold around her allies. However, she continued sailing toward The Frozen Death, a fierce look of judgment in her eyes. In a moment of panic, Farzg could not think of a witty line or a counter, so he dove into his private chambers behind him.

In his first moment of desperation in decades, he threw open the trapdoor to his vault. He slid down the icy ladder, crashing twenty further feet below his underground living space. Even with the dragon on their side, there would be no way the girl could claim the advantage in his vault. The room was smaller, but he could endure a contest of wills much longer than she could. She was weak; he felt her spirit, but it was not alone. At first, he assumed that it was her divinity, Invictus. He had felt similar pressure before in the past from priests like Selasine. However, on closer examination of the girl's aura, he saw a ghost. It was Iriliandria. Her prophecies were now fulfilled. This was his last chance to defy the will of the universe. He would stop Doctor One and save Espa after killing the girl and his own rivals. Foresight was not absolute. This victory was not about survival. It was the last point in his argument. He had already sent Elyndandria the tools she needed to play against Doctor One in his stead. He, however, intended to stand against the Revenant's Blessing. Today, he would defy the will of a god.

Miranda moved up the steps to Farzg's throne and personal chambers with ease, converting the blades on her boots to climbing spikes, giving her extra traction on the slick snowstone. She glimpsed the frost giantkin jumping down into another, opened trapdoor. "This guy has a complex," she muttered to herself, mocking the supposed fearlessness of the criminal mastermind.

"Miranda, slow down!" Evan cautioned, sliding his way up the steps. She nodded, watching through the curtain of Farzg's bedroom. A single, plush bed was in the center, and the trapdoor took up the entire right side of the small, square room, only about fifteen feet. The rest of the space was cluttered with jewelry, dressers, clothing of all kinds, mirrors, and chests.

She replied, "Take your time, everyone, he's cornered." Her voice was calm and the music slow.

Selasine and Damil reached the top, their experience making the icy floors less dangerous for them. Naomi, Celyth, Evan, and Yuvina gathered with Miranda outside. Selasine frowned. "I hoped he wouldn't make it into his vault."

Miranda gave her dad a peculiar look. "The one with the pipes?"

Damil and Selasine both nodded. The paladin replied, "Yes, he can funnel his Death Geyser into them and attack from any angle. It's where Thomas was severely injured," he explained.

Thomas raised a hand to his right eye. "It was just a scratch," he insisted.

Miranda shook her head. "I'll go in first. I'm going to fill the room with Infernal Flames."

Selasine and Damil's heads cocked backward in shock. Selasine objected, "Miranda, there's no way there's enough darkness in you to do such a spell, even if you have control of the mana. Your Holynova is a reflection—" he explained, but she interrupted.

"Modai-rin, please. Do not worry. There is darkness in everyone, even if it is just a little bit. Mine is selfish and overprotective. I love you all so much, I can't risk losing you like I lost Shalo. Seeing how you all mourned for your lost loved ones in The Lichwood. I know that's not my destiny. That darkness, though? It's not always evil. Sometimes it's just selfish." She smiled. "Give me a minute and charge in. It's probably going to take me a moment to recover."

Damil stuttered a bit as he objected. "Miranda, do you even know what the Infernal Flames are?! They are evil compressed into fire! It would require true, unbridled evil to create such unholy embers."

She nodded as she walked into Farzg's quarters and stood by the trapdoor. "Dad told me about Haelia, and how she used the darkness within her to conjure flames with otherworldly heat." She paused, looking at Damil and Selasine. "Plus, it's not my darkness at work, here. Philotrax was a dragon of fire magic. Reshiria was a dragon with a dark heart. I have everything I need and then some! So, I've got an idea, and I'm going to try it." She smiled and stepped off the side of the trapdoor opening without fear. Evan was over the side in an instant, climbing down.

He met her at the bottom, sliding down the icy ladder, gently using the tips of his boots as a braking substitute. He landed with a solid bounce, reaching up to take Miranda's hand in his as she floated down to the bottom. She shook her head. "Can't protect me if you break your neck trying to keep up with me." She closed her eyes and huffed.

This time, he kissed her on the forehead, causing her eyes to open with wonder, a warm feeling spreading through her fingers, toes, and stomach. "Oh, jeez. Evan!" she teased. She shuddered, though. She liked how it felt in this moment, and it comforted her. "Remember, give me one whole minute. That should be all I need, okay? And it will keep you all safe." She squeezed his hand tight, before turning toward the new, valved door. She glared, and used a simple, earth moving spell like Naomi to pry the frame from around the massive dome. It nearly fell on top of her and Evan. A small, ten-foot tunnel led into a pressurized vault, full of gold, gems, treasures, and certain death. Her friends descended, Selasine the first one down the ladder.

"Yolasha," he commanded.

"Modai-rin," she saluted.

"You've got one minute. Understood? I'm still not certain about the Infernal Flames, but you are correct about Haelia. She was a devilkin. The Sword of Justice wields the Seven Formed Sword, and it uses the power of demons and devils both. Be cautious, yolasha."

She saluted again. "Sir!" She drew on the mana, her rich, purple hair crackling with energy. She walked into the tunnel, feeling the air around her drop from freezing to abysmal cold as she stood in the doorway to the vault. She inhaled, funneling enough mana into herself to keep her body warm. It required much less mana to protect herself than the environment around her. As she entered the vault, she saw Farzg, standing on a dais near yet another vault door with a pressure valve. His arms were extended to his sides, and he had prepared a Death Geyser ambush.

The vault was disorganized, with treasure strewn haphazardly about. The piles of coins were four and five feet high. A clear path cut through the treasure to the other door, but the snowstone below would make utilizing it dangerous. The real threat, however, was the pipes built into the walls of this strange vault. Structures shaped like silver, metallic, trumpet bells protruded from the walls, creating an opening to an unseen network of pipes behind the stone of the architecture here. Miranda did not recognize the metal, but she understood their purpose: Farzg could push the energy of his Death Geyser through those pipes before its glacial burst. He would use them to make his attacks unpredictable, a tactic he relied on only in desperate circumstances.

Farzg made his first attack with the new strategy, and his Death Geyser extended from his fists as a magical, lightning-quick stream of energy. They flowed into the two pipes closest to Farzg, creating a crackling sound all throughout the vault. An instant later, crystalline, glacial masses erupted from two pipes above the entry door. Miranda's first instinct was a dispelling light that erupted with an arcane force matching Farzg's output. The Death Geyser was completely canceled.

"How in the Infernia did you do that, priestess?" the frost giantkin shouted with surprise.

Miranda ignored his question and spat, "Okay, Mir'thax. Unleash the Infernal Flames, the fires fueled by that which is impure. Reshiria! Mother! Lend us your darkness!" As she called out, an electrical aura wrapped around her body, and it took the shape of a massive, blue dragon. It filled the whole of Farzg's vault, and as it became denser, a dragon's roar boomed from within, prompting Miranda's allies to crowd the door.

They watched as a shower of unholy flames filled the room, billowing with incredible heat. As the smoke from the initial barrage cleared, only a small area around Farzg remained untouched by the increased temperature. The interior of the vault began to thaw, the snowstone glistening with condensation. The Infernal Flames manifested as black orbs of energy filled with a purple flame. Fifty pools of ethereal, mystical fire bubbled throughout the vault, forming spherical embers that defied logic. Some of them floated in the air, some of them cindered on top of piles of treasure. Adjacent coins melted and formed molten pools suspending the Infernal Flames. They served as unbelievable, otherworldly sources of heat. If it weren't for the cold coming from Farzg, the heat would have killed everyone. Instead, the small orbs of fire created warmth that balanced the temperature in the room.

"Come then, clergy of the Sword of Justice. May you serve your hypocritical definition of justice on a silver platter. I'm waiting for you, Thomas! Damil!" His violet, shimmering eyes locked with Miranda's who did not break her gaze, her expression enraged. "Oh, Miranda. You better not waste this opportunity. You might survive, but I guarantee your friends will not." He cackled with self-satisfaction as he generated a new burst of cold. His stance was even deeper than before, fighting the impossible warmth of the scattered Infernal Flames.

Miranda was thankful she had the moments she did with Mir'thax. Darkness within was nothing to be ashamed of, and learning one's weaknesses was critical to staying on a path of growth. Her mother's evil heart had changed so greatly, but there was still enough darkness within to generate the Infernal Flames with incredible efficacy. Miranda sighed with relief. The orbs of dark, otherworldly heat kept the room warm enough for her allies to enter and begin their assault against the frost giantkin.

Evan and Yuvina charged in first, splitting along the sides of the round vault. The chests and piles of coins made it easy enough to find a winding path toward their target, and as they sprinted, Farzg blasted a Death Geyser into the pipes. As the glacial eruption burst from several pipes at once, they found themselves disoriented from being forced to make last second evades. Yuvina yapped in frustration, and Evan gave a steady "Woahhh," as he slid to a stop in a valley between coin heaps. The vault was about two hundred feet in diameter, giving them plenty of space to maneuver through the treasure and wealth within while avoiding the Infernal Flames.

Naomi and Celyth entered next, taking a direct route across the room. They dodged the molten orbs of Infernal Flames as well. As they moved, they sent a steady barrage of ranged attacks at the slaver. Naomi cursed him in her mind for each life she knew was personally affected by his nefarious crimes. Celyth, however, was excited; she felt like she hadn't faced a worthy opponent in months. She could tell that Farzg was many times more dangerous than even the Umbrals in Mystalon, and she was excited to be a part of the team that took down such an incredible opponent. Unless Arlindra managed to defeat some incredibly powerful Death Pirate before Celyth could get there, Celyth would definitely have bragging rights for quite some time. "Down with you, smelly breathed criminal" she taunted as she unleashed another barrage of arrows.

Another surge of geyser erupted from Farzg's hands, and Miranda realized his intent. The ice erupted from pipes closer to Farzg, crushing the ranged assault, but the tips of the geysers were pointed at the globes of Infernal Flames around the room. As the unholy fire melted the Death Geyser, they shrank. Miranda's eyes widened with horror. It wouldn't take the slaver long to turn the battle in his favor if he could extinguish the Infernal Flames. "Dad! Damil!" she shouted.

The high priest and the high paladin came charging last, Selasine's mirages around him, and a powerful protection prayer from Damil cupping them in the loving hands of Invictus. As the Death Geyser burst all around them, the protection prayer shattered, but the glacial mass still targeted spheres of magical, dark flames. The temperature in the room started to decrease, and Farzg was unrelenting. Another burst of Death Geyser erupted, targeting only orbs of insane heat around the room. Miranda could not use the Infernal Flames again with her allies in the vault. It would destroy them as surely as Farzg's assault. The purple tone in her hair had lightened to a mauve color. She used a massive amount of mana to conjure the flames, pulling deeply from the reserves unleashed by her parents. Miranda drew Iria's sword, and she joined Damil and Selasine as they advanced.

Another wave of Death Geyser blew through the pipes above them as they charged over piles of coins and dodged pools of supernatural fire. Selasine and Damil cut hard to the left and right respectively, leaving Miranda on a direct approach. Farzg stood thirty feet in front of her as she thought she could see the opening she needed. She would bait him by refusing to evade a Death Geyser and using a dispelling light to cancel it and get herself within striking distance.

As she came within ten feet of him, the burst she was expecting blasted from overhead. She activated the mana within her, but she had underestimated the decreasing temperature in the room. The Death Geyser was much stronger than before, and it struck her in the chest. It sent her flying, the battlemail absorbing almost half the impact. She dropped Iria's sword, which landed close to Selasine. He stopped to pick it up, holding it in his hand for the first time with hostile intent.

Evan and Yuvina had recovered from their sudden stop and were carefully approaching Farzg's flanks. Thanks to the full-frontal assault of the clergy, they were able to draw within ten feet of the frost giantkin. Once they arrived, however, they found themselves lost. The cold around Farzg created an aura of chill impossible to penetrate, even with magical weapons. They felt the cold around him growing as the Death Geyser targeted the Infernal Flames with burst after burst. Naomi caught up to Evan on Farzg's right and Celyth joined Yuvina on his left.

"Ranged attacks are useless, and we can't get close enough to stab the coward," Naomi growled.

Evan looked around. "Is there any way we can keep those unholy flames going? They're the only thing keeping us alive at this point."

Yuvina shrugged, but Celyth nodded. With an unexpected sprint, she moved from relative coverage at Farzg's flanks toward the center of the room. She took some arrows with cloth soaked in oil affixed at the base of the arrowhead. As she neared a sphere of dying Infernal Flame, she dipped three arrowheads in the heat. They caught on fire with a flickering, black flame, and Celyth raised her bow. She shot them directly at Farzg.

His eyes widened in shock, and he had to physically evade the attack. The Infernal Flames would have cut his Death Geyser and possibly punctured his frozen skin. His leaning contortion reverted to a deep fighting stance with a single stomp. "Oh, young lady. You just made an enemy you didn't have before!" Instead of spraying the Death Geyser through the pipes, he thrust it at her, only twenty feet away.

Celyth tried to dodge, but she was too slow. Naomi, however, dove across the room, blasting Celyth with a telekinetic push. It shattered the Death Geyser about to connect with the warrior, and it shielded Naomi from the additional mounds of glacier jutting up in her direction as Farzg continued to channel mana into his attack. The concussion knocked them both down, and the snowstone was dangerously cold. Their bodies went numb on impact.

Miranda forced warmth into the environment as she had done earlier, but she felt the extreme pull on the ether within her. Her hair was already a vivid lilac. It eased Naomi and Celyth's chill, but the Death Geyser impacted them enough to deplete their physical energy. Combined with the cold, they would have been doomed within moments. Miranda warmed the air enough to restore their senses.

Farzg shouted, "The Infernal Flames and the Sword of Justice are no match for me! Na'agamlor bought his way into godhood, but I will fight my way there!"

Damil cursed back, "The Infernia you will, Farzg! Fist of Justice, smite my enemy!" he continued, charging forward a few steps and hurling his sword at the frost giantkin from about fifteen feet away. A yellow, magical aura shaped like a fist surrounded the paladin's sword. Farzg wavered, raising his arms to block it, but also conjuring a close shield of ice. It was the second time Miranda caught the slaver changing his strategy mid-fight.

Selasine, wielding Iria's blade, moved within striking distance, but the shield of ice Farzg created to defend himself against Damil's attack shattered. The force blew Selasine to the ground. Damil slipped on the snowstone, crawling backwards to avoid a barrage of icicles spraying from Farzg. Selasine looked to have lost consciousness after the impact. Miranda's expression soured, and she tried to close the distance between herself and Farzg again.

As Farzg prepared his Death Geyser, Yuvina and Evan attempted to divert his blast by running from their newer hiding places among the treasure. He indulged their diversion, splitting his focus among many of the pipes, and the fractalizing Death Geyser trapped them. The infinite cold within knocked them both out on contact, even though the remaining Infernal Flames melted the death-inducing ice.

Miranda gritted her teeth. As her allies lay unconscious or vulnerable around her, she realized the Infernal Flames no longer had the capacity to sustain a survivable air temperature for anyone but Farzg and herself. She had to end this fight quickly or the results would be tragic. She looked at Farzg with resolve in her piercing blue eyes. Her braids swirled in the wind generated by Farzg's magic. She felt the souls of Reshiria and Philotrax vibrate within her. She shouted, "May the Sword of Justice see your end!"

Farzg's smile turned more sadistic. "You are the Sword of Justice, and yet here I stand." He held his pose with his arms stuck directly out to his sides, the stance necessary to continue generating the cold for the Death Geyser. His water conjuration uncanny magic shot out of his hands. It went up into the pipes that made this vault so dangerous. As the geyser should have crushed Miranda, she appeared behind him.

"Sender gives you his regards," she taunted as she elbowed him in the back, piercing him with the sapphire blades on her gauntlets. He growled with anger as they sunk into his frozen flesh. It didn't hurt; it just complicated his strategy. He had to get her back in front of him for a direct hit.

A burst of light interrupted their exchange. Selasine had opened his eye, and he used a surge of holy light from Iria's sword to stun Farzg much like Miranda had tried against Vortex the Lich. As the light connected with Farzg's body, Selasine tossed the sword into the air toward Miranda, but his weakened condition reduced the accuracy of his throw.

Miranda swore, "Infernia's blessing." She funneled a swirl of ether to make sure she could catch the sword, changing its direction just inches. "Iriliandria. This is where you do what you promised."

Farzg forced another gust of cold from his body, trying to turn. The bladed gauntlet stayed buried, yanking Miranda behind the frost giantkin. The additional burst of energy caused Miranda's hair to swirl in her face, the healer braids whipping her hard against her cheeks. The geyser extinguished the last of the Infernal Flames burning in the vault. She shouted with determination. Farzg bellowed, "Die, priestess. You're weaker than the raven. Your adventure ends here."

Mir'thax's instincts pulsed. "Not a chance, slaver. You will face justice, and you will know death." She thought hard about the simple spell she used against Sender just a couple of weeks ago. The dispelling light Erk mastered on the day his king was assassinated was able to bring down one of the strongest enemies Miranda had faced up to this point. She had dissolved three solisberry blossoms under her tongue already. She held Iria's sword firmly in her right hand, struggling to reach into a pouch with blade in hand. She snatched three solisberry blooms and tilted the hilt of her sword. She put the blossoms in her mouth. She was not going to risk running out of mana thanks to the efforts of a person as evil and callous as Farzg. "Please, Iria. It's time!"

She knew the dispelling light would neutralize the Death Geyser if she funneled enough mana into it. She decided to try to use it to defrost Farzg's body as well.

Philotrax's voice spoke to Miranda's heart. "Do not hesitate, my daughter."

Reshiria's malice surged within her. "Be strong, Mir'thax. Unleash the fury of the dragons on this murderer."

Her blue eyes flashed with wrath. She spoke with righteous conviction so powerful the room shook. "Eldon Farzg! For your crimes against the universe, your sentence will be carried out henceforth. Do you have any last words?"

"No," he replied. "Because I will never die." As he spoke, another surge of arctic death washed throughout the vault. As the geyser exploded from the pipes, Miranda used Sender's one-second advantage to move out of the trajectory again. In that second, she ripped the sapphire blades out of the slaver's back and spun back to the front of her enemy. She now stood face to face with him a mere two feet away.

Miranda looked at him with contempt. She funneled the simple, steady dispelling light at Farzg's body. It worked.

The following Death Geyser was neutralized by Miranda's focus before it reached the pipes. She realized while fighting Sender she could power the dispelling light as much as she needed to while fighting, and that gave her a significant advantage over enemies who relied too heavily on their uncanny or natural magics. Farzg's magic, however, was more powerful than Sender's, and it required Miranda to expel a significant amount of ether to dissolve the frost giantkin's most deadly assaults.

In that moment, after almost a century of invincibility, the criminal mastermind felt fear. Iria's final prediction unfolded before him. He could detect her spirit swelling within the sword in Miranda's hand. He also overestimated the value of his new ally, Doctor One. The mad-elf had betrayed him by allowing the church to close in on him. It was just as well. If the young woman delivered the Revenant's Blessing, Elyndandria had the shard. Doctor One would know Farzg's retribution from beyond the grave. If Saraix demanded a dragon of light, she would first journey in the company of darkness. The dispel unnerved him. "What? How! My magic!" he shouted in anger, intensifying his focus. Swirls of glacial mass surrounded his body.

Miranda increased the flow of mana into the dispel. She had to. Farzg's Death Geyser grew in strength. As she accelerated the flow, she was expending more mana than she was absorbing, even with the solisberry blooms in her mouth. She could not feel beneath her tongue as the leaves irritated her just enough, but they helped sustain the ether flowing through her. Her hair hovered at a shade of pastel purple for a while, but as the mana in the blooms dissolved, it lightened rapidly. She was only two feet away from the frost giantkin, and she pushed her body forward with every ounce of physical and magical force she could. The Death Geyser wrapped around a cone of dispelling light, casting off to Miranda's sides harmlessly. "You won't win, Farzg," she warned.

"It doesn't matter, foolish dragon. If you kill me, you prove you are capable of fixing this world. Which, you realize, is impossible. Control over the universe is using the power that you are blessed with, and fortunately I am very blessed. I am more blessed than you, even. A child of dragons trapped in mortal forms thanks to The Unbinding!" He started to laugh maniacally, his purple eyes and skin radiant in the light reflecting from the glistening snowstone vault walls.

Miranda thought it was ironic. The evil frost giantkin shrouded himself in the color of her god. "Let it end here. Sword of Justice, it pains us that a life must be lost for justice to be served, but this criminal has wreaked havoc and chaos upon Espa in proportions so great that even Invictus himself could be called to deal with him." She held Iria's sword at a point toward Farzg's unarmored chest. "May this lawbreaker know justice!"

Farzg increased his power output so much he felt his heart freezing. This was the same feeling as decades prior when Damil Starstorm had stabbed the slaver through the chest. Though blood burst from the wound, Farzg's heart was spared, and the mastermind lived to make his bold return. That, however, would no longer work. As Miranda approached the slaver, her dispelling light kept his Death Geyser at bay. "Miranda!" he shrieked. "How is this possible?" The canceling energy of her dispel thawed Farzg's organs as well.

Her hair had turned bright pink. She responded with a catechism as she stabbed Iria's sword viciously into his chest. As she stood within only a foot of him, he left his arms out to his side, attempting to funnel the mana through his own life essence in a last-ditch attempt at stopping the warpriest. "You're spent! Now die!" he screamed. He gave one last burst as Miranda's sword pierced his heart.

The air around Miranda and Farzg stood still instantly. "Know your end, slaver," he heard, but as he searched for his killer, an elf with black hair braided to the front of her face stood before him. "Murderer. You came to my home with intent to harm. You killed my daughter with your cruel ego. You put my husband through hardship unknown, but you did not succeed. No, you have failed in every sense of the word." Holyfang released a burst of holy energy directly into his heart. Now, Farzg could only see Iriliandria Lancethinas Selasine standing before him with her holy sword plunged into his chest.

Miranda felt the spirit of the elf speaking through her, and it felt like a kindred soul she had met long ago. Philotrax and Reshiria both loved Iria, and together, they poured out their wrath through the young woman who loved them all so much. Miranda's love kept their essences alive, as if she was using the arcane stream to give them voice and locus.

Farzg shouted, "You fool! You cannot bring back the long dead!" His body had stopped responding; it was his soul that protested. The world darkened, and for the first time in over a century, the giantkin felt warmth. As he began to die, his pupils dilated. He saw Miranda clearly as she delivered the killing stab. The sword that plunged into his heart belonged to the very elf that orchestrated his demise. "Is that how it is then? She comes back through you? And yet you still don't see the enemy before you. Clever Miranda. Give your parents my condescending reg—" his soul choked as it felt pity pouring from Miranda. Killing him had turned him back to human enough to feel empathy for his dying breaths. "No! It can't end!" His soul hung in the twilight between life and death, awaiting the arrival of Ahnkhetet.

Miranda swallowed hard. "Justice has been served, and the souls of Iria and Telisi can rest with the destruction of this demon. May his soul miss the Abyss and rot forever underneath the primordial place." As she finished speaking, she felt cold and exposed. She looked down to see a wall of jagged Death Geyser between herself and Farzg's still-standing corpse. The attack had pushed her ten feet backward and five feet into the air, and the vicious glacial mass punctured the breastplate and skirt of her battlemail to pierce her body. She was impaled at multiple points on the small ridge of deadly ice. She could see strands of her white hair blowing in the unstable wind of Farzg's vault. The blood trickling from the side of her mouth tickled a bit, but she understood. The frostbite was already spreading through her physical form, and it hurt worse than any of her previous injuries. She could not, however, scream or respond. As her eyes grew heavy with exhaustion, she took a deep breath and sent a surge of warmth throughout the vault. She wasn't sure where the magic came from; her mana was exhausted. That piercing pain in her soul snapped, and her very essence burned with agony.

Evan began to wake up, shouting, "Miranda! Miranda, no!" He scrambled to his feet as she slumped on the spikes of ice and Farzg's thawed body fell to the ground. Evan felt his physical faculties returning as the air in the room became tolerable. Miranda had expended so much ether neutralizing Farzg's attacks, and she used the last of the solisberry blooms to maintain the mana necessary to do so. Though she was falling unconscious, she detected Evan's pulse accelerating from across the room. He rushed toward her. "I'm here! I'm here to protect you!" he shouted.

The world turned black, but Miranda could see so many lights in her hazy vision. It was all of the souls lost at the hands of Farzg. Iria was there. Before Miranda's consciousness ended, she overheard a conversation.

Iria's voice said, "Your crimes have been adjudicated, and your sentence has been carried out. All has come to pass as I promised. Have you prepared your estate for what is to come?"

Farzg still disputed his fate. "This cannot be, Iria. Espa's future is dark indeed if I am but the second of countless evils she will face."

Miranda tried to speak, but her essence had no strength.

Iria replied, "I spoke only truths that day. Where is my daughter?"

Farzg's consciousness assured Iria, "With Elyndandria as promised. The shard as well."

No other sound echoed through Miranda's mind as the exertion from fighting Farzg and her injuries overtook her. The fight was finally over. She only hoped that her dad and her Dedicantae would care for her until she recovered.

Chapter 23
A Voyage Home

"Umiaigén struck The Intangible with her great trident, shattering the demon. Her corpse, scattered to the oceans, created cursed pools now known as Shadow Reefs. They offer dangerous but expedient travel in the waters of Espa." – Kzar's Magical Locations and Sources of Power

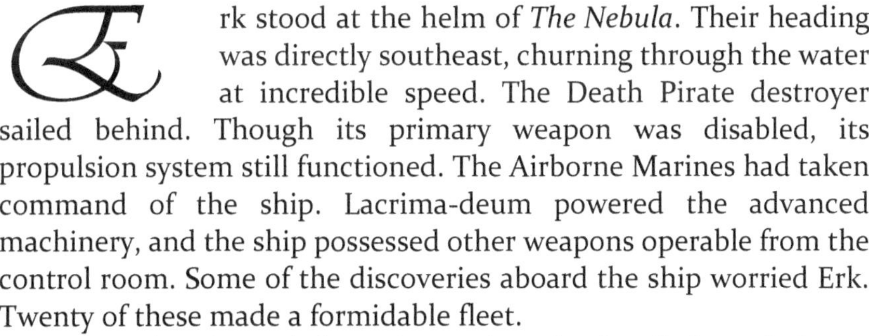rk stood at the helm of *The Nebula*. Their heading was directly southeast, churning through the water at incredible speed. The Death Pirate destroyer sailed behind. Though its primary weapon was disabled, its propulsion system still functioned. The Airborne Marines had taken command of the ship. Lacrima-deum powered the advanced machinery, and the ship possessed other weapons operable from the control room. Some of the discoveries aboard the ship worried Erk. Twenty of these made a formidable fleet.

The Violet Blur sailed on the starboard side of *The Nebula*. Its purple, triangular sails created a colorful contrast to the dark thoughts running through Erk's mind. The Death Pirates blockading Yendralia promised to put up a fierce fight. That morning, Erk received word from Ut'wah that all six of the absent Pirate Nobles of Yendralia were converging on the archipelago. Simón de la Costa Estrella, Lilith Demonborne Orestia, Cael Tempest of the Solar Sea, Ut'wah the Magnificent, Annaia Alexandria, and Erk himself would be arriving within four days. Lascha and Oorzgo were still in port, awaiting external pressure to help break the blockade.

As he contemplated the upcoming conflict, a buzzing sound caught the pirate lord's attention. His eyes scanned the horizons, and he caught a glint of light to the north. The growing buzz also drew attention from the crew members of *The Nebula*. Erk's eyes narrowed, but his gaze softened when he recognized the source.

Nebu focused his trajectory on Arlindra's location. The glint was the evening sun flashing on the draconic creature's insect wings, and the buzzing sound was magically enhanced for no other reason than to garner attention. The tiny beast zipped around *The Nebula*'s entirety, lowering his speed. As he gained control over his momentum, he spiraled up the main mast, then dove to land on the wheel of the ship.

"Nebu reporting for duty, captain!" he shouted, imitating the paladins' salute.

With a twisted smile, Erk left his hands firmly on the wheel. "Touchin' the wheel while the captain's drivin' is cause for a lashin'!" he teased, speaking with an intentional accent.

The dracofly flitted his wings and lifted to hover above the wheel. "Fine, I won't touch it! Besides, I don't have much to report. They made it to The Lichwood. Big surprise."

Erk laughed, having already received a report from Damil. "Arlindra is below deck, presumably in the kitchen." He sighed, his emotions still aching with loss. Shalo was impossible to replace, and he had spent so many years in a ship kitchen that the smell never washed off his person. Arlindra's recipes were too good, in a sense. Erk figured he should appreciate the fine dining while it had fallen into his lap. Nevertheless, he missed the mediocre fare.

Nebu shook his head. "I know where she is. I just wanted to hang out with you, since you're the captain. Like, you're Arlindra's boss. And I'm like Arlindra's boss. We have something in common! I just figured we could bond over our mutual employment of a specific—" he continued, but a voice interrupted him.

"Is that so, Nebu?" The stoic tone caused the dragon-bodied creature's insect eyes to bulge further.

"Arlindra!" he shouted with joy, dancing a spiral across the upper deck of the ship to meet his master as she stood at the top of the steps from below. He landed in her hair, wrapping himself within. After he felt comfortable, he popped his head out. "Finally, home! By the gods, it's freezing out there!"

She looked up, crossing her eyes a bit. "I thought you were going to talk about bossing me around a little bit more, yes?"

Nebu shook his head furiously. "It was a joke! I'd never boss you!" he whined.

Arlindra laughed. "Take it easy, buggy," she warned, using his hated nickname. He figured it was fair, curled up into her hair, and took a well-needed rest.

Erk looked to the ranger. "News from the kitchen?" he asked.

Arlindra paused, nodding her head briefly. "Tonight's meal is nearly ready," she replied, her voice uncharacteristically timid. She walked toward the helm, her eyes fixed on Erk. The pirate lord had turned to face her, his gray eyes scrutinizing her every step. "I also wanted to ask if I could meet with you to discuss a specific matter."

The pirate lord's eyes widened with curiosity. The ranger was notorious for her aloof nature, and her stern command of the kitchen kept it running more efficiently than ever. Erk had yet to see Arlindra's vulnerable side, however, and it intrigued him. "There's no better time than the present, Lady Fernith. Please, speak your heart and your mind." He thought about the moment he met Arlindra in Mystalon. He was impressed with her directness, then and now.

"A little more than a year ago, my mother left Mystalon to seek healing on the outside. We have heard nothing from her in that time. Before Elitirin died," she began but hesitated. Her voice started to waver, and she regained her composure before continuing. "Elitirin told me that she'd last heard from my mother in the Isles Known for Nothing. I hoped, with your network in that region, I might find where my mother has gone."

Erk contemplated her request in silence. The waves splashed against the hull, and the sounds of a ship at work filled the awkwardness. After a moment, Erk remarked, "Without a doubt, Arlindra. When we make port, we will seek out Cardinal Honesty. She is my most trusted medical advisor in Yendralia. If your mother sought healing while she was in the Isles Known for Nothing, then Cardinal Honesty would know."

The ranger blinked for a moment. "Her name is a little direct."

Erk laughed. "She chose a common name; she's piscedian. I am certain that her true name would be impossible for those of us without gills to pronounce."

Arlindra's head tilted to the side as she clarified, "Piscedian? The people of Buenmar?" she asked, referring to the aquatic capital of Central Espa. Five thousand miles of water separated West and East Espa, and numerous peoples lived on the seabed in between. Buenmar was the largest urban center of the Shindor Ocean.

The pirate lord nodded. "Indeed, chef." His voice was calm as he explained, "She is a high priestess of the goddess of the seas, Umiaigén. Her knowledge of both healing and the oceans is beyond compare." His face turned up into an encouraging smile. "As I said, she'll be able to inform you of any special cases reaching the Isles Known for Nothing. Whatever it takes, I will aid you in your quest to find your mother. I also believe she can aid us with the lightning wielder's journal. We need to know what he was doing to The Emissary."

Arlindra twisted her mouth uncomfortably. "Right," she responded, curt.

Erk bowed humbly and lifted the black tricorn hat off his head. His golden locks spilled forward. "I could offer a reward of one million gold coins for tips leading to your mother's whereabouts—" he began, but Arlindra interrupted him.

"Nonsense, captain. Such a promise on my behalf would be absurd, and there's no reason you should offer something in my place. I would never wish to burden you so." As she spoke, Erk stood and replaced the hat on his head. The ranger tried to continue, "I don't know much about outsider currency, but a million sounds like way too much. The bounties for the Death Pirate vessels is only a tenth of that!"

Erk laughed. "I have more than ten million gold coins onboard *The Nebula* right now! Lady Fernith, your mission means the world to me, especially because Miranda cares for you deeply. That means I do too. The bounties for the Death Pirates are merely a gesture to foster competition. A million? I spent hundreds of times more seeking a cure for Evan." His smile faded. "Trust me. We have to make the amount believable for my station, otherwise we'll get many false leads. The amount is high enough that people in Yendralia will know it's sincerely me. I don't seek information worth less than one million gold coins in value." He gave her a sly grin. "After all, a pirate's most precious commodity is information."

Arlindra blinked with disbelief. She felt discomfort and gratitude, but she trusted Erk's experience. "Very well, captain," she replied. She realized that the pirate would not accept no for an answer. "Your assistance is appreciated. I must see to the kitchen; your cooks are mediocre on their best days."

Erk laughed. "That's because Shalo was a mediocre chef. Arlindra, your service in my kitchen should be a labor of passion, not an obligation that causes you stress."

Arlindra narrowed her eyes with a mischievous smile. "I thought you were impeccable in your evaluations of others, like Miranda. She seems to think so."

Erk's lips twisted up into a sinister smile. "I want you to think of me as a friend, but I am a dangerous friend. While I cannot peer into another's heart like Miranda, I like to think I can understand the actions of others like my sister. She was a Judge of Spades, you know."

Arlindra shook her head, jostling Nebu and prompting him to snore. "I know what Judge of Hearts means, but I've never heard of a Judge of Spades," she said, leaving a pause for Erk to explain.

The pirate lord's eyes sparkled in the evening sun, "My sister always knew how to explain the outcomes of my actions. It's something that mystified me when I was young, but then I came to understand her wisdom. Perks and prices, actions and consequences." He let go of the wheel to straighten his hat after an unexpected gust blew over *The Nebula*. "I can see that the rigid discipline of your trade and the social hierarchy of Mystalon influence the pride you take in your work. Dinner must be impeccable, but why?"

Arlindra's lips rounded in shock. She rebuffed the captain, "Because I won't accept less than my best! I often dreamed of working as a chef outside Mystalon, and this is my chance. But I know this can't last forever. There's too much at stake in the wider conflict."

Erk crossed his arms, which brought Nebu's attention from slumber to bug eyes fixed on the wheel of the ship. "Then that's all the reason I need, Arlindra. Just so there is no pretense. I wish to aid you in the search for your mother, and in the meantime," he paused, locking eyes with the beast in Arlindra's hair. The captain's smile caused Nebu to grin. "As long as you are happy working in my kitchen, then I will enjoy your cooking until we return to Yendralia."

"Thank you, captain," she replied as Nebu zipped out of her hair and stood on the wheel of the ship, triumphant.

Erk glared at Nebu in spite of his otherwise happy expression.

The dracofly shook a fist, "Hey, you ain't touchin' it right now!"

Pirate Lord Erk smirked as he replied, "Good point, buggy."

The ranger gave a hearty laugh, feeling her tension around Erk ease. Dinner was better than Arlindra could have hoped, serving fried krakenten and salted plum stew to the captain and his officers.

Late the next day, Erk received another report from Damil.

"Farzg is dead. Iria and Telisi are avenged. Justice has been served."

Erk's expression was blank. He expected to feel elation, but instead a profound sadness crept throughout him. Iriliandria would scold him for such vindictive thoughts; however, as the report continued, his countenance sank further.

"Invictus himself imbued Iria with the Revenant's Blessing. Once Miranda was close enough, your amazing sister's spirit destroyed the slaver where he stood."

Erk breathed a sigh of relief. "And Miranda? Was she wielding my sister's blade? I'm assuming that was where the Revenant's Blessing was imprinted."

Damil's thoughts paused. "How did you know?"

Erk replied, "I knew from the day I met His Holiness that he carried my sister's holy symbol. It was forged in the same style as that of my mother's." He smiled, and it could be felt through the telepathy. "I only needed to know why. Upon learning, I trusted that all had happened according to my sister's vision."

There was another pause. "You're definitely Iria's brother," Damil thought back, an endearing sentiment.

Erk's smile softened. "I only hope to be remembered as such."

Damil's telepathy communicated a shift in tone. "We're almost to Eodan. Erk, Farzg is dead, but we're losing Miranda."

Erk's anxiety overflowed, and he started to tremble. "Losing her? Was she injured? Damil—" he pleaded.

The old paladin felt how worried Erk became at the news. He replied, "She used her draconic gift to neutralize and thaw Farzg. As she moved into place with Iria's sword, she had to let her guard down. She was hit point blank by Death Geyser."

The pirate lord swallowed hard, his thoughts begging for Damil to continue.

"Glacirix, Farzg's dragon, was supposed to fly us to the Eastpoint Lighthouse. Apparently, Farzg had a huge plan in place in case of his death. We're not really interested in playing his games. I managed to contact Maréli. She's in Eodan with Carulus for some reason, but she should be able to help Miranda recover," Damil's thoughts returned. "The dragon is taking us there instead."

Erk felt his worry subside. Maréli was the premier healer in Alabaster. "Thank Lexcord," he replied, his gasp of relief evident.

Damil's concern, however, continued to come through his words. "Farzg sent an assassin to the Eastpoint Lighthouse with an artifact that should belong to Miranda. We are not sure what it is, but the dragon suggested it could be more effective in healing Miranda. Thomas, Evan, and I agreed it's too risky to trust Farzg's plan."

Erk's mind shifted quickly, "Oh, and the others? How is my brother? My betrothed?"

A wave of calm emotion came through Damil's telepathy. Naomi's thoughts entered the conversation. "We're all fine honeycomb. Well, everyone but our precious Miranda. It's bad, Erk. Her armor is in shambles, and her wounds are too many to count. Maréli is her only hope."

Erk frowned. "I'll make a report to the others right away," he lamented. "Oh, by the gods. Naomi, please keep her close and safe."

Her determination preceded her thoughts. "I will, my love."

Before the telepathy broke, Erk added, "I have something to report as well. We've learned a lot about the destroyers. The Emissary was feeding off the underflow produced by the lacrima-deum powering the ship. The technology is sophisticated beyond imagination. There's some kind of container in the engine room. I suspect that it traps the underflow, which is why there are no Umbrals on the ship. The lacrima-deum don't look like dragon eggs, either. Well, exclusively. They're huge, blue chunks of some crystal."

Damil's heart raced, and his tension pervaded the telepathy. "Apologies. I'm unused to flying in such a manner. Please, continue."

Naomi's mind lingered, savoring Erk's presence. The pirate lord continued, "As it turns out, that hak-koth that killed Shalo worked for these scientists, not the Death Pirates."

A light feeling fluttered through the mental connection as Glacirix descended. Damil replied, "This is concerning. Fill me in. I'll debrief Thomas once we get Miranda to safety."

"I can't make sense out of the bastard's writing. He uses a script I don't know. I plan to take it to a friend of mine in Yendralia as soon as we get home."

Naomi interrupted, "Oh, Erilkaiden." Their mutual, building worry circulated through their thoughts and intensified. "This sounds dangerous. Please, break that blockade and get my sweet Annaia to her rightful place. Okay?"

Erk replied, "We have to know what we're up against. I'm glad these guys keep meticulous records."

Damil's exhaustion mixed with his mounting worries. The distance exacerbated the fatigue resulting from using his uncanny magic. Erk hugged them through his thoughts, and he worried for

Miranda. He dismissed them, "Please, Damil. Get our Miranda to safety, alright? We'll get rid of these Death Pirates, and then we'll be on our way as soon as the drama here cools. Naomi'nides, my love."

"Honeycomb," she pushed back a moment too late.

Erk shared the news of Miranda with his officers and the paladins after he received it from Damil and Naomi. When *The Nebula* and *The Violet Blur* were only a day away from Yendralia, Erk received another report.

Damil's thoughts sounded faint, and something interfered with the clarity of communication. "Miranda is stable now. The frostbite really went through her body, and the scars keep glowing with a golden aura. It's odd, but she's breathing and seems to be dreaming. Her hair is still white."

Erk replied, "We'll be engaging the Death Pirates tomorrow. We have a plan to use the enemy's ship against them. The paladins have figured out how to operate it. August is sharp, and Justin is a genius. Valarie outdoes them both. Thomas has raised some fine, spirited warriors. I'll pass on the news of Miranda. They'll be glad to hear she's stable."

Later that night, Justin sat on the edge of the bed in his officer's cabin on the Death Pirate destroyer. He rubbed his fingertips on his temples, prompting Valarie to ask, "What's wrong, paladin?"

His shoulders heaved for a moment. "I feel like something big is happening, something bigger than just what's going on around us."

Valarie moved from sitting in the bed to the edge with Justin. They were dressed in soft cotton robes. The destroyer did not rock in the water as *The Nebula*, and the steady ship did not help them sleep. "I feel nothing out of the ordinary, darling. Just the normal pre-battle jitters. Want to talk about it?"

Justin closed his eyes and began to tremble. "I should see nothing right now, but the clouds are there. The gray clouds, like after I died," he explained.

Valarie leaned against him and reached out to hold his hand. "Do you feel ill?"

He shook his head and opened his eyes. "No," he replied, his voice gentle. "I feel like I can remember more of what happened before His Holiness brought me back with the will of Invictus. There was an entity present, a man." His body trembled. "Death. Ahnkhetet was waiting for me in that place. I can't remember his face, but I feel his presence growing ever stronger in the corners of my mind."

Valarie twisted her lips in thought. "Ahnkhetet? Many theologians theorize his purpose was completed after the Legion of Hoxark era concluded." She gently squeezed his fingers between hers. "Did he speak to you?"

Justin closed his eyes again. "Not that I remember, but I also worry my mind is adding things that weren't there. I just can't explain why it took almost a year for these feelings to resurface."

She smiled, her severe features softening in the low light of the evening candle. "We've had a busy year. Our friend nearly died facing great evil. It's unpleasant to think about dying. We're fighting pirates on ships just like these tomorrow. Take your pick, paladin."

He sighed again but then laughed. He opened his eyes, his green gaze meeting Valarie's. "What you say is logical, and I agree. I just feel like something strange is happening in the primordial place. Tonight, when I seek the presence of Invictus, I find only this vision of Death. I worry for even the gods."

Valarie ran her finger tips up his arm, put her arm around him at the waist, and squeezed him. "The upcoming conflict against the Death Pirates might have something to do with it, too. I can't answer the question of what's perplexing you, handsome, but I won't let you go through it alone."

Justin's smile was short-lived. "You're amazing, Valarie. Thank you. I suppose I should worry more about Miranda's health. The visions will sort themselves, I assume. For a moment, I was worried I had somehow cheated Death, and he was returning to claim what Invictus pulled from his grasp."

Valarie pushed Justin with her shoulder. "Death isn't a businessman, is he? I can't imagine he would even recognize you. You were there for such a short time. Besides, if he thinks you're the one that got away, he'll have to take me out of the formula before he can try again."

His smile returned, Valarie's words and the humming of the lacrima-deum powered ship comforting him enough. "Shall we try and rest then?"

She smirked. "Big day tomorrow. I need shopping money."

Justin nodded, the terrifying visions behind his eyes easing. His mind wandered from the past to the future. "I know! After we break the blockade, Cantalus owes us a personal tour. I'll make him tell us about the most romantic places in town, too. He owes us that much."

Valarie stuck her tongue between her teeth, and her skin flushed with emotion. "Actually, and this might be a little presumptive on my part, but," she added, her voice unusually timid. "Well, what would you think about a pirate wedding?"

Justin blinked for a moment. "But Naomi is with Miranda!"

Valarie glared through her smile. "I obviously wouldn't want to hold a ceremony without them both!" Her voice took on a tenor similar to the way she spoke as a combat instructor.

Justin's jaw slacked. "Not a church wedding? Wouldn't that violate protocol?"

Valarie gave him an endearing gaze and pursed her lips a bit. "What happened to my bad-boy paladin with penance to pay for breaking protocol?"

Justin's bewilderment shifted to amazement. They spent the night discussing wedding details that blended pirate and Invictian customs. Justin eventually dozed off, and Valarie watched him sleep until she joined him.

Cantalus stood at the end of a dock in Yendralia. A ukulele was sheathed on his hip alongside Belladonna and Gourmand. His sentient daggers sang a warning keeping the Death Pirates at bay. As *The Nebula* and *The Violet Blur* came into view on the horizon he hummed and sang, "The dead await on ships colored slate. Great evil and darker power, and a truth as old as the phoenix tower." The song echoed throughout the Isles Known for Nothing.

Erk, however, stood on the bow of his ship. Yendralia and the Isles Known for Nothing were barely visible in the distance. He looked toward the east through a spyglass, recognizing the flags of a small fleet on that horizon. "It's Simón and Lilith." He turned to face south. "Four enemy ships in sight from here. Just as shiny as our commandeered beauty." He lowered his spyglass and sighed. "I wish they had a penchant for communication. There is no plan, and that bothers me. We know what the ships can do. I hope they got the warnings."

Arlindra stood behind him, also observing through a spyglass. She peered to the west. "What about those?" she asked, spotting ships on the horizon.

Erk's expression was determined, and he answered without looking. "That's Ut'wah and Cael. I heard they went to stop a Death Pirate raid on Tibot and Tobit. At least Ut'wah sends messages. There's been a spike of Death Pirate activity since the destroyer attacked us." He turned around to face the stern. The captured destroyer kept pace with *The Nebula*, and Justin had taken to piloting the ship. Valarie figured out the lacrima-deum powered weapon systems. Erk frowned as he added, "They're executing a plan. I don't know what that plan is, but I know it's there. The greatest evils are the most carefully planned."

The ranger smirked and joined the captain in examining the destroyer. She replied, "And the most tragic evils are committed in ignorance. I know you envy their planning, but there is a lesson the forest can teach you." Her voice resonated a wise, patient tone. "Improvising in the wilderness is necessary for survival. Our objective is clear. Your crew is well trained. We've got one of their ships on our side. We know their strengths." She gave a dark smile. "And we know their weaknesses."

Erk tilted his head with perplexion. "The Emissary was not using their ship to its fullest potential. We were unfortunate in some fortunate ways." He sighed, feeling a burning call for revenge. "You're right, Arlindra. We will accost them without warning. We know what to expect." He tipped his hat up now that he faced away from the sun. "And we have *The Violet Blur*. The enemy is well prepared. We must devise counters for counters."

Arlindra faced south again. She lifted the spyglass, but an explosion rocked the eastern horizon. She snapped her attention to the ships belonging to Simón and Lilith. Erk tilted his hat down as he turned toward the sun rising from the southeast. He explained, "It's already starting. Simón's uncanny magic. Rebuke of Stars. He can cause reality to, uh. Essentially explode. That includes the water."

Arlindra's eyes widened with surprise. "Such a thing is possible? To cause reality to combust? No wonder he's fierce on the seas."

Erk grimaced and ran his fingers along his collar. "The metal hulls might require more concentration, but make no mistake. He is our greatest rival in this little competition. His crusade is against the Empire of Gabah and their expansionism in East Espa. He primarily targets military vessels outside of treaty zones." His face wiggled with growing intensity. He wore a suit of elaborate, red leather armor instead of his captain's garb. "We'll destroy the enemy ships with a little reflected sunlight." The fire on his arms looked especially plasmatic and hot. "If anyone survives, we'll board and overwhelm them." His blaze dripped lapping, dense tongues of heat. "This armor. Do you recognize it?"

Arlindra narrowed her eyes. "My father had a similar suit."

The captain replied, "A gift that I could not refuse. He said the Umbrals left it intact in your home. He's not sure why, but he gave it to me as we departed Mystalon. Its enchantment enhances my uncanny gift. The Radiant will fight for justice, and evil will cower from the sun." He smiled, and his expression was somewhat draconic. He continued, "If Simón is nearing engagement range, we are already working at a disadvantage. He probably took the Shadow Reef to return from La Costa Estrella."

Arlindra grimaced. Her geographic knowledge of East Espa was weak. "What in the Infernia is the Shadow Reef?" she asked, her voice insistent, confident, but respectful.

The pirate lord furrowed his brow and put his spyglass in a pouch on his belt. "Legend says it's the corpse of an ancient demon. All I know is you can pay a member of the Southern Cross a million gold coins for a one-day trip to almost any major port in Espa. Almost." He soaked in the sound of the ocean crashing beneath them. His voice was somber as he said, "Too bad there's not a Shadow Reef near Eodan."

"Miranda," Arlindra whispered. She looked behind her to the primary deck, observing Erk's crew as they prepared for battle by servicing their weapons and firearms. She reassured the captain, "She's in good hands. She would chastise us for worrying over her when Yendralia is in danger."

Erk laughed. "Yes, Lady Fernith. Although, I assure you, Yendralia is under no true threat. This battle will be over by daybreak tomorrow."

Arlindra kept her spyglass handy, watching their approaching allies and awaiting enemies. "Be that as it may, sir. I have my own reasons for reaching Yendralia. Anyone standing between that objective and me will feel nature's sting." She reached up to her hair and shook Nebu awake.

The dracofly stretched and popped up over the top of his blue nest. He asked, "Is it time?"

Arlindra nodded and answered, "Engagement range by sunset. We could use a little recon. Would you scope it out for us?"

Erk smiled as Nebu's wings buzzed. The dracofly lifted into the air and replied, "You got it, Arli!"

Arlindra put her spyglass away. "You're the only eyes I need now," she said with gratitude to her companion.

Nebu snarked, "Well you better see to it your 'eyes' are properly fed! I demand fresh beef!" He whizzed into the air, leaving his dramatic buzz silent for a stealthy mission. He whooshed away.

Arlindra grumbled, "We're on a ship, buggy. Fresh beef. What a dramatic creature."

Erk chuckled and replied, "Perhaps he can enjoy such delicacies once we make port. Consider it a reward for his efforts."

As their banter quietened, they stared to the south in silence. The battle weighed over them and kept them in their thoughts while they waited for Nebu's return.

Chapter 24
An Uncertain Future

"The most dangerous evil is the one who crusades against harmony in the name of selfishness." – Lexcord's *Reflections*

igh in the Dundoi Mountains, in the former palace of Argentum, Doctor One, Artificer, and Diablo gathered crystalized draconic godshards. One was able to secure Gorthran's immortal core using the bizarre wand powered by four hundred of those divine pieces. Now that he had it, his ascendance could begin. Though he exuded the persona of a wild and eccentric scientist, a cruel genius resided underneath.

Doctor One held the clockwork scepter in his hand which now contained the essence of Gorthran. The godshard rested in the tip, its evil nature obscuring the light around it. He murmured as he admired his work, "They should have listened to me years ago when I told them what was possible through crystalized magic." He could feel the power coursing through the device. "The Manus-Deum. The Godhand."

In truth, he began working on this project long before The Unbinding. His theories of lacrima-deum began in pursuit of wealth and fame. By making magic readily accessible to people who were not wizards, he once thought Espa could build a prosperous, equal society. He studied magic at Breckinshore Ridge Magic Academy on the eastern continent. He mastered the advanced wizard threshold before age twenty-five. He was the youngest wizard to attain archwizard status in Breckinshore Ridge's history at fifty-six. He discovered the dissolution process of arcane underflow reactions, the transmutable properties of arcane particles in various states, and the existence of volatile spindles in the flow of magic constituting draconic souls. Then, he looked into the Eye of the Stream and learned truths and secrets older than the gods. Diablo interrupted his thoughts. "The royalty of the Infernia will cower before you."

Artificer added, "Two hundred years of research and experiments. Thousands of failures, millions in coin spent, and countless lives lost in the name of progress. Even my own. I had my doubts, Santiago, but you've proven me wrong."

Doctor One's eyes snapped to Doctor Two. "You dare call me that?" he hissed.

Artificer gave a sadistic smile, "Just the name of the wizard that made a promise to me the day I was cursed with this undeath."

The scientist's gaze softened, but a look of disgust remained. "You've served me loyally all this time. Your presence is a continual reminder of where this all began!" His voice was loud and enthusiastic. "Do you want me to cure the curse of vampirism with the power of arcane underflow? Would you like to see the sun again?"

Artificer shrugged. "Not until the time is right, old friend." His normally subversive, sarcastic behavior was masked under an obvious, building anxiety. "There is still much work to be done. I must remain a vampire for now."

Diablo cut his eyes between the two. Though Doctor One and Artificer were former peers at the academy, Diablo was a former student of Doctor One's. Their remaining associates had been students of the archwizard at some point, and they left the Breckinshore Ridge Magic Academy a few decades after Doctor One was censured for his publication, *The Tears of God*. Their support from other faculty and students crumbled after The Unbinding, and attempting to create lacrima-deum according to the academy's rules proved impossible. The devilkin watched the exchange but would not speak.

One's lips curled up into his maniacal grin. "Suit yourself. Once I connect the Godhand to the Soul Scythe, I can grant your wish after the transformation is complete."

The malicious, brooding sparkle in Artificer's eyes returned. "The Soul Scythe? Our final creation as friends," he remarked, his voice calm.

Doctor One jumped with excitement. "Oh, yes! I will be hungry when the transformation is complete. I am ready. There is no more need to stall! Bring these godshards," he ordered, gesturing to a pair of crates overflowing with the hearts extracted from lacrima-deum. They radiated light in various colors and possessed unique shapes.

One led them to another room in the laboratory of the palace. Before them sat the Soul Scythe. It was a five-foot tall eolnut exoskeleton, perfectly sized for an elf. Numerous needles and barbs protruded inward, resembling a nightmarish acupuncture device. A three-foot conduit hanging off the back would allow Doctor One to attach the scepter now containing Gorthran's godshard to the back of the contraption like a tail. "I will transform myself into sentient arcane underflow. This is the solution I found in the primordial place. My mind will survive the process, and I am assured of my success. The godshards will serve as reserves of power to wield as the Umbrals of great strength do."

Diablo smiled as he looked at the device, commenting, "This is going to be a painful experience."

One nodded in agreement. "Only temporarily," he replied, distracted. He held the wand in his hand, admiring Gorthran's shard in the tip. One's lips broke into a smile as he thought back to the publication of his text, *The Tears of God*. In it, he detailed the process of turning dragon eggs into lacrima-deum. The other wizards at the academy feared his ideas because they thought it would make wizarding obsolete. Furthermore, they worried extracting dragon souls would wreak havoc on the arcane stream. Fortunately, Dalyn Tyrdrac took care of that for Doctor One. Now, it made even more sense to remove the dragons from the stream. Since magic was fundamentally broken, Doctor One intended to revive it in a creative way. "Once I become arcane underflow, I will not experience pain."

Artificer placed his crate of godshards in front of the terrifying harness. It was on a raised platform connected to numerous eolnut circuits running along the floor and along the walls of the laboratory. Following the wires led to several lacrima-deum extractors constructed at specific intervals along the apparatus. The extractors were prepared with crystalized magic to power the process. Doctor One explained, "Sender was truly remarkable. The near-destruction of the solisberry in Mystalon has settled the Eye of the Stream over Argentum." His voice was unusually calm. "The transformation should allow me to return there."

Diablo's brow furrowed. "The Eye of the Stream?" he asked, confused.

Artificer turned from his crate to cast an impatient glance at

Diablo. "Shortly before The Unbinding, Santiago forcibly harnessed the Eye of the Stream. If our theories are correct, that space is what was left of Genesis after he broke himself into the Dragon Queen and Dragon King."

One's smile became more severe. "I alone know the truth. I want him close by to witness my ascension. Today, I will forcibly make the shard of Gorthran part of myself." His voice was methodical and sadistic, a shift from his normal, maniacal tone.

Diablo set his crate of shards next to the other. "What will you do with the Eye of the Arcane, then?"

Doctor One affixed the wand to the conduit in the tail of the Soul Scythe. As he did, the entire exoskeleton began to hum with power. Doctor One's smile was ambitious. Everything he had theorized, written, and experimented led to this moment. The ideas that ruined his career would now see him ascend to a power even liches and wizards of old could only imagine. He responded to Diablo's question, "Once I've accumulated the entirety of the dragons, I will invert the arcane stream. The process must begin at the Eye of the Arcane."

Before the devilkin could respond, the door of the laboratory opened, and a person entered. She was a cambion, a half-demon, half-elven beauty standing at six feet tall. She had bright, yellow hair, and two jagged horns protruded from the front of her skull. Her red eyes teemed with a dark aura, and she smiled as she approached Doctor One and the others in the center of the laboratory. Doctor One began to jump with excitement again, "At last! Doctor Seven returns!" His usual, maniacal tone was back. "Watcher has returned! And I trust you bring good news and gifts?"

Watcher tilted her head forward, her evil smile growing wider. Her canine teeth were sharp, giving her an appropriate, demonic countenance masked by angular, elven beauty. "Farzg is dead, but I am in pursuit of the shard. I thought I would stop by and update you all." Her voice was cool and otherworldly. "Farzg removed it from his vault days ago, it seems." She shrugged. "He gave it to the assassin. She has the shard and is at the Eastpoint Lighthouse. I plan to kill the girl, then I will go to the lighthouse to reclaim the last piece of the puzzle."

One's eyes bulged as he felt a surge of anger. "Are you certain about the shard? According to my calculations, Farzg acquired the shard without fully understanding what he had! Such a development could jeopardize my immediate plans."

The cambion gave a single nod. "Absolutely, teacher. I will have it in my possession by the end of the month. The church imbeciles flew away on the white dragon. The dragon girl was severely injured facing the frost giant, and I will extinguish her lingering soul. I could see her wandering between dimensions." Her smile became more sinister. "I have also seen the elf that now carries the shard, and I will watch her until I find a moment to take it. She is deadly, but I am more cunning."

The scientist cycled his breath, calming himself. "We cannot build the second Godhand for the dragons born of the Dragon Mother without that shard." His mouth trembled, enraged. "At this point, however, I have no choice but to continue with the transformation." He turned his gaze to the Soul Scythe. "I will have to acquire it for myself if you fail!" he shouted, his voice wild and angry. "No matter what transpires, I will eventually fuse with Saraix and the dragons of light. Once I trap all of the dragons within my underflow, I will invert the arcane stream. In doing so, I will replace Genesis as the source of magic. Do not fail me as Doctor Five did. I will need that shard to speed along our plans once my transformation is complete!"

Artificer smiled, showing his vampiric fangs. "I've never seen you so ready to accept failure, Santiago."

One turned his gaze to his old friend, the rainbows in his eyes shimmering. "That's because the most important pieces are all here. I correctly calculated the intervention of the gods. I correctly calculated Farzg's feud with the church would hail the return of the demons. I predict the ensuing war between the pirates will keep interlopers occupied until it is too late. Out of all of the successes here, most of them belong and will belong to me!" He spoke quickly and his cheeks flushed red. His hair wiggled as he spoke, and his voice was full of ego. "And, thanks to my planning, these are not failures. Merely setbacks. As always, I will clean up the mess my subordinates leave behind."

Diablo nodded in agreement. "It will take significant time for Doctor One to undergo the metamorphosis. We can advance the rest of the agenda once the Soul Scythe is active!" He sounded excited.

A shrill, stuffy voice added to the conversation. "While failure is the most humbling teacher, I have avoided her wicked rod of instruction this time, yes!" An elderly elf appeared in the door. She stood at a hunched four foot four, and her gray hair fell down her back in frazzled waves. She wore a white, protective coat and carried a cane in her left hand.

She hobbled into the room, prompting Doctor One to jump again. He spoke as if he had not been angry only a moment ago. "Does that mean Cassack was a success, Doctor Eleven?"

The old elf entered, struggling to look forward. "The Death Pirates and Yendralians will be in open war within days. The death of Farzg will offset the balance, and the Scythes of Hoxark will reassemble the Altar of Balthazar! This will certainly keep the world distracted!" she cackled, shuffling forward with her cane tapping the floor. As she neared the others, her body changed, prompting smiles from everyone present except Artificer. Her uncanny magic was a powerful shapeshifting spell allowing her to transform into almost any kind of creature. Her core form, however, was a young elf of around one hundred and sixty years.

After she returned to normal, Artificer groaned, "Why the old lady?"

Doctor Eleven shrugged. "I heard you speak of failure, and I decided to be old and wise. With Artificer's plans and the Death Pirate's resources, we built the lacrima-deum powered ships. There were barely enough crystalized demons to fuel them." Her younger face was long and sharp with thin lips and a pointed nose. Her burgundy hair was frayed and unkempt. She was incredibly average by all accounts. Before The Unbinding, she was one of One's most promising students, and she followed him from the academy with hopes that his ideas would help her expand her ability to shapeshift. "We lost The Emissary after Mystalon. The Death Pirates failed to deliver all of the demons. The flying ships will give the Death Pirates an unexpected edge if they can power them."

Doctor One let out a nervous but content sigh. "Excellent. The more prolonged that conflict, the more distracted our enemies. The demons will return, and the seals will be broken! The death of Farzg was the last piece I needed in place to offset the balance! Now that we have assembled, I should begin the process." He withdrew a syringe from inside his lab coat and showed it to his entourage. "I shall never again need to rely on painful, weak flesh. And you, my loyal scientists and entrepreneurs, will walk with me as we usher in a new era. The stream will walk among mortals as a living, breathing entity!"

Artificer closed his eyes. "What shall your ascended name be?"

Diablo, Watcher, and Infiltrator, as Doctor Eleven was also known, looked to their leader intently. They gathered close to the

Soul Scythe.

Doctor One pressed the needle into his arm and injected himself with the medication. "I've already chosen that by usurping the eldritch fabled deity, Genesis. You will know me as Neogenesis. My appearance will also change once I become underflow." He closed his eyes and stepped adjacent to the apparatus.

Artificer continued, "Then, this is goodbye Santiago." He looked at the ground.

Diablo smiled. Artificer was always so rude and combative to the devilkin, and seeing the vampire downtrodden felt equalizing.

Watcher stared with her evil grin, and Infiltrator looked bored. One looked at the Godhand, observing the power of Gorthran cycling through it. The divine essence flowed within, filling the wand with red light. The exoskeleton was separated into two elf-shaped halves. Doctor One would need to fit himself between the front half and the back half, and Diablo and Artificer were to press the halves together, puncturing Doctor One all over with the eolnut needles. "I am ready," he remarked, stepping into the device. He positioned his arms and legs correctly. He expected to feel one hundred and seventy-seven precise pricks. All of them would miss his vital organs, but they would press against them. Some would prick his nerves, preventing pain in his extremities. The medication was a sedative to keep him calm but lucid. There would be no test run. He had faith in his own genius and calculations. "Now!" he ordered.

Artificer stood in front of him and Diablo behind. Giving each other a nod, they forcefully pressed the exoskeleton together, piercing Doctor One's body. The eolnut barbs reacted to the pressure by funneling stagnant mana into him. After the initial, minimally painful series of stabs, the scientist could feel the empty magic mixing into his blood.

"Santiago?" Artificer asked, looking between the bands of wood that made up the device.

"Yes, I'm fine," he replied. "I can feel the underflow!"

Diablo's smile was wide. Watcher walked to the side of the harness where the eolnut wiring was connected to the Soul Scythe. "Shall I?" she asked, looking at the exoskeleton.

"Do it!" Doctor One ordered. Watcher reached to the harness and flicked a small switch. The entire machine began to hum even louder. A black aura surrounded Doctor One. His entourage stepped away from the platform, watching as the aura grew, creating an intense orb of blackness. The switch activated a lacrima-deum powered device Doctor One had prepared in a lower part of the palace. It was in the same room where Dalyn Tyrdrac entered the stream; that tear in the fabric of space and time was still there, floating in the center of a shattered solisberry trunk. It was the ultimate arcane underflow reaction, and One thought it was marvelous. By flicking that switch, Watcher emptied one hundred complete lacrima-deum into the remnants of that tree, the very opening of The Unbinding. The resulting power output overcharged the eolnut wiring attached to the Soul Scythe. If Doctor One's calculations were correct, it would force a transmutative effect.

Santiago closed his eyes as the metamorphosis began. He couldn't see in the aura of darkness around him anyway. His life flashed through his mind as stale magic pumped through his veins and reshaped his soul with the arcane underflow created by hundreds of dragon eggs. As his essence transformed, it siphoned the four hundred godshards in the Godhand. This was the moment Santiago was born for. He specialized in transmutation magic as a wizard, and his genius and talent were undeniable. His ascendance was earned.

As the godshards merged with Doctor One's soul, his consciousness began to fade. In the remnants of his cognizance, he felt the immense pressure of Gorthran adjacent to his mind. The Dragon Father warned him, "You do not understand the mistake you are making, mortal. Cease this endeavor and release my children to the stream!"

Santiago would have smiled, but he knew his body was no more. His thoughts surged with malice as he spoke to the creator of Espa instead of Gorthran. "I have seen you, Genesis. Your mind is shattered and scattered, but I will reunite your children. I will end your suffering. I will bleed you dry to form my body of arcane underflow, and I will control the magic of Espa. I am Neogenesis. I will invert the stream." After his response, reality went blank for Doctor One and Gorthran.

The hum emanating from the Soul Scythe intensified. Electricity and fire popped from the eolnut circuitry connected to Doctor One's apparatus. The entire laboratory shook. Artificer covered his ears, and Diablo protected himself with a conjured barrier. Infiltrator transformed into an earth giant, allowing her to absorb the deep, sonic waves as energy rather than pain. Watcher stepped into an adjacent dimension, her uncanny gift the ability to jump between planes at will. She watched from the layer of reality known as

Duskveil, the world of dreams. She could see the primary dimension and watch the dreams of sleeping entities from here.

The volatility increased until they were certain Doctor One had doomed them. Just as the walls of the palace began to crack, the generator downstairs exploded. The Unbinding consumed the lacrima-deum with extraordinary power output. The sounds climaxed with the boom from underneath them, fragments of the floor below shattering and scattering throughout the laboratory. As the generator died, the circuitry's humming ceased. The room filled with smoke quickly, but it did not affect Artificer or Diablo. Infiltrator changed into an Eviscervine. She could absorb the noxious fumes in that form. Watcher was safe, observing from Duskveil.

As the smoke cleared, a massive egg rested on the dais. It was five feet tall and covered in black scales. It absorbed the light in the air around it, much like the godshard of Gorthran. It rhythmically pulsed red.

Dust hung in the air from the compromised structure around them. Artificer stepped up to the egg, pressing his fingers against it. "Santiago is gone, but he will return as Neogenesis after some time. We have much work to do in the meantime," he suggested.

Diablo stepped close to the dais, dropping to both of his knees. "Power incarnate! But trapped within a shell. May the transformation bring about our dreams," he praised from the ground.

Infiltrator resumed her regular form, also approaching. "I had faith in your science, teacher. Magic is ours!" She marveled at the egg sitting where Doctor One was moments ago.

Watcher returned from Duskveil, the gate between dimensions rippling around her as if the air were water. "Did it work? Doctor One?"

The shell emanated a burst of prismatic light, but the room remained silent.

The four of them exchanged knowing glances. Neogenesis's plan would see him become the most powerful entity in all of Espa: the inversion of magic itself. Artificer, Diablo, Watcher, and Infiltrator planned to do whatever was necessary to see their mentor's plans come to fruition. That night, they began individual pursuits that would promote their ambitions in the impending chaos caused by Farzg's death and the war between the pirates of West Espa.

Miranda felt the hand in hers before she could see it. She squeezed it tightly, realizing it was Selasine's. Her body inhaled chilly air, prompting her to breathe deeply and peacefully. "Hey, dad," she murmured.

As she sat up and opened her eyes, however, the world around her was infinite emptiness. It reminded her of the strange in-between dimensions her companions passed through before facing The Root.

"They can't hear us, right now," her own, musical voice responded.

Miranda closed her eyes and smiled. "That's okay, Mir'thax. I can hear you." She turned her torso to look around, finding the color-swapped version of herself. Miranda's subconscious approached from the blackness around them and sat beside her consciousness.

"At least you're decent company," Mir'thax commented and leaned her head on Miranda's shoulder as they sat side by side. They were dressed in the large, white shirt they acquired from Selasine, Miranda's default nightdress.

The priestess exhaled and cycled her breath ten times before responding. "So, we're not out of mana, are we?"

Mir'thax shook her head. "No, it's different this time. I think you just pushed our body and soul way too hard."

Miranda leaned her head against Mir'thax's. "Do you think I would have done better as a dragon?"

Mir'thax lifted her head and looked at Miranda. Their red and blue orbs searched each other's gazes. "But you did this as a dragon! Without mom's darkness and dad's knowledge of fire magic, we never would have been able to conjure the Infernal Flames."

Miranda blinked for a moment, holding her breath. Actually, she felt like she would not be able to breathe if she wanted to. Her chest radiated with pain for a few moments, but a muffled voice echoed around them. "Restore to order what was damaged by chaos!" it shouted, but neither of them could identify the source.

The feeling passed after a moment, however, and Miranda continued, "You mean, a dragon trapped in a human's body?"

Mir'thax giggled. "Regardless of what your exterior looks like, I'm always in here. You are as much a dragon as a human. Don't forget that, Miranda. Ever."

Miranda smiled at herself. She was kind of pretty with blue hair, she thought. "Don't ever let me forget."

They sat in silence for a little while. Every so often, Miranda could hear Selasine's voice, but the words were muffled. Evan's voice came through louder and more clearly, however, "Do you think the frostbite is spreading?"

Miranda's lips pursed with wonder. "Wait, we're dying, aren't we?"

Mir'thax lifted her head up. "Right now? Definitely." She paused and let out a deep breath. "Probably not on their watch, though. Dad especially. Evan, too, but there isn't as much for him to do."

Another, gentler voice echoed through the dark space. "But can she fly? The dragon speaks sincerely."

Miranda frowned. "It seems more serious than I anticipated. Where would we be flying? Are they talking about Glacirix?"

Mir'thax giggled, "Of course it's way serious. I can't really answer the other questions any better than you can though," the draconic reflection of Miranda explained. "You were exposed to the full force of a Death Geyser more than once facing off against Farzg. We thawed his body with the dispel, but the price was exposing ourselves to his attack."

Miranda blinked for a moment, reflecting. "I guess that makes the most sense." She shrugged. "What sort of treatments exist for that sort of injury anyway?"

Mir'thax waved her hand over her right eye. "Bishop Selasine's scar. There is no real treatment, I guess." She thought for a moment, though, trying to remember Maréli's teachings.

Miranda's head nodded until she realized what Mir'thax said. "Wait, he hasn't been a bishop in a while! Where did that come from?"

Mir'thax sighed. "I'm not sure. But it's a little fuzzy in here, and our life is flashing before our eyes. They say that's what happens when you're close to death."

Miranda let out a deep, disappointed breath. "We have to live, then. Farzg will not cause another tragedy. Do we still have mana within us?"

Mir'thax nodded. "More than enough to level the solisberry tree one hundred times over if we wanted."

Miranda raised an eyebrow at her subconscious. "I'd never hurt a solisberry tree, though!"

Mir'thax continued to nod. "Good. Don't hurt yourself either. If you try to do any magic right now, even from in here, you might undo everything that your friends have done to repair the damage Farzg did to you." She twisted her lips with anger. "For once, I guess human emotion will pay off. It's a little scary to be right here. I'm a dragon. I'm supposed to cycle through the arcane over and over again." She started to cry.

Miranda's heart leapt into her throat. She realized the dragon inside her wasn't really that different from her human self. They had the same emotions but different outlooks. Mir'thax appreciated and knew her own strength; Miranda, however, was always afraid to accept her gift and its implications. After delivering Farzg to the hands of Revenant's Blessing, killing Sender, Reginald, and Gelidor, she decided her burden was unduly shared. Mir'thax didn't want to be any more violent than she did; but the dragon inside was willing to do what was necessary to protect others. Miranda felt too weak, but Mir'thax was her resolve.

Nevertheless, the priestess grimaced with impatience. Human emotion: a fear of dying, of a limited place in the universe. That was scarier than Miranda ever contemplated before this moment. She found her words, responding, "You're right." She looked down into the blackness beneath her, and it made her dizzy. "I guess we're stuck here for a little longer, then."

As they sat in silence for a few more minutes, they could hear Selasine again. This time his voice was crystal clear. "Yolasha'nides. Please, stay with us Miranda."

"Dad!" she called back to the darkness.

Mir'thax sat up. "I already told you, though!"

Miranda gave her subconscious a mischievous grin as the echoing voice changed from somber to elation. "She squeezed my hand! Without a doubt!"

Mir'thax glared. "No fair."

Miranda's eyes softened, and she reached over to hold Mir'thax's hand. "It's your hand too, weirdo."

Mir'thax's lips curled into a smirk. "You're so mean to yourself sometimes. Do you really think we're weirdos?"

Miranda smiled as she replied, "Yeah, we are. We're caught in a struggle between life and death, arguing about whether or not we're strange. I'd say that we are definitely weird, just based on that fact alone."

The draconic reflection squeezed Miranda's hand. "Can't argue with that."

They sat quietly again for what seemed like an hour, maybe longer. Time made little sense outside the primary dimension, and Miranda had experienced something like this before when she was trapped in the arcane stream. "It's way more boring here, though," she said to herself. After a moment, a wave of painful cold surged through her essence. "And cold," she complained as she shivered incessantly.

Mir'thax gave a lethargic, aloof nod. "Yep."

Miranda sighed. "It's making me sleepy. Can I just take a nap?"

Mir'thax shook her head then rested it on Miranda's shoulder again. "Well, if we go to sleep here, we probably won't ever wake up."

The warpriest blinked with heavy eyelids. She stayed with herself in silence for a bit longer. The more time she spent with Mir'thax, the closer their hearts felt. "Hey, Mir'thax?" she asked, trying to keep her subconscious awake. It felt like hours passed in the darkness. "Hey, wake up. Me. Mir'thax." The reflection did not respond. Miranda wrinkled her nose in frustration, "Dammit, you dumb dragon, wake up!" she shouted.

"Hm?" Mir'thax responded, exhausted.

"Do you remember when you came to fight Gelidor? And we were stronger than anybody ever knew we were?" She giggled. "I think we scared dad. I mean, we did almost die that time, too."

Mir'thax lifted her head up and gave a zesty laugh. "Infernia's blessing, we really are the reason he has gray hair now."

A gust of cold wind interrupted their conversation. A radiant, blue light filled the dimension. Miranda and Mir'thax looked for the source, finding a beautiful, human woman with deep blue hair. Her eyes sparkled the same, electric blue as Miranda's. The young priestess and her subconscious shouted simultaneously, "Mother?!"

Reshiria gave a solemn nod. "I've finally found you, Miranda," she replied, her voice cold.

Miranda stood as did Mir'thax. "Why are you here, mom?" they asked together, their voices elated.

A red flash also filled the dimension, and Philotrax's human form appeared in the blackness as well. They were the only four entities now visible in the dimension, an empty plane of purple light. Philotrax responded, "You've nearly died, Mir'thax. We came to find you and stay with you until your body is ready to continue. Things are dire, and your friends are worried for you."

A loud voice pressed through the darkness. "Don't leave me, friend. I need your guidance," it growled.

"Yuvina," Miranda murmured, looking around above her in the darkness. She turned her attention to her mother and father, who approached from in front of where she stood with her color-swapped self. "I didn't mean to worry anyone," she began to explain.

Reshiria rushed forward and embraced her daughter. "You've overcome a grave challenge, Miranda. I'm so proud of you. Please, hang on to life. We knew you were special the moment you were born, but we did not understand Iria's warnings about your destiny." She changed her form into that of a majestic, blue dragon. The transformation was instantaneous, accompanied only by a burst of blue light. "Your companions have found a place to help your body heal. You only have to hold on."

Philotrax continued, "I would have dreaded a confrontation with Farzg, even as a dragon of fire. My daughter, you are incredible."

Miranda's eyes filled with tears as Philotrax approached her and embraced her. A moment later, he too assumed his draconic form. Miranda looked up at them with adoration, but her heart swirled with mixed emotions. "Dad! Mom!" she replied, shouting up to their massive presences. "I won't let go, I promise! I'll face whatever is next, and I hope you can be born again one day! We can all be together then! You can meet all of the people that have helped me along the way. I can tell you about everything that's happened— Please, help me hold on!"

Reshiria lowered her head and pressed it gently into Miranda. "That's the spirit, daughter. We are here with you. Until the moment you awaken."

Philotrax also lowered his head and nuzzled Miranda and Mir'thax, pressing them together.

Mir'thax asked, "How long will that take?"

Philotrax sighed. "It's hard to say, Miranda."

Hours of silence passed as they embraced. The dragons straightened their necks without warning, leaving Miranda standing alone in the darkness. Mir'thax disappeared, but the priestess did not notice.

Miranda looked down, seeing a single point of light almost an infinity away. "Okay, I feel like it's been like a day or two since we basically died, right?" she asked.

Mir'thax's voice replied. "Probably longer. It sounds like they don't expect us back anytime soon. The voices are fading."

Miranda looked up at her mom and dad. "This place is really weird. How do I get to the light?" she asked. She then looked for Mir'thax but found she was alone. "Well," Miranda scoffed in protest. "I didn't give myself permission to leave this conversation with myself. Hey Mir'thax!" she shouted into the darkness.

She waited a moment and smiled. "Duh, you're not out there. You're in here." She looked at Reshiria and Philotrax again as their appearances began to break apart like glass. After they shattered and vanished, she continued, "You're in here with mom and dad. We're all together already." She reached up and rested her hand over her heart. She looked back down at the point of light far below. "Oh gods, the looks on their faces when I suddenly wake up. I should reenact what happened at the solisberry tree at the top of the Astral Spire." She giggled. "Alright, here goes."

She flexed the mana within her essence, hoping to force the cursed damage of Farzg's Death Geyser to finally finish fading. As she did, the light moved toward her at a quickening pace, washing over her in a blinding rush.

Epilogue

ichard the Gambler had a smile on his lips as he knelt down to scoop up an amulet. "The Heart of Ultria," he murmured. He picked up the cursed object from the floor of the seabed. Thanks to Na'agamlor, he could breathe underwater. It was just one of the many gifts granted him by the Counselor of the Corrupt. The gambler wasn't sure who or what Na'agamlor paid, but the power was permanent. He stared at the amulet for a moment before turning his gaze upward to the infinite, dim sea above him. He stood deep in the Bay of Beriton, retrieving the object that had granted Gelidor the ability to curse others. The Heart of Ultria was a relic left from the Legion of Hoxark, and it was a fraction of the heart of a dark goddess. She disappeared at the conclusion of that calamity.

He looked up into the aquatic abyss and released a lung full of bubbles. The little trinket in his hand allowed Na'agamlor to siphon the entire wealth of the Kingdom of Claston into his own coffers. Gelidor sold his kingdom to usurp his brother. The thought caused Richard's smile to widen. He knew very well the sacrifices necessary to accumulate untold wealth and power. The Heart of Ultria had consumed the usurping fool's soul, after all.

A gruff voice interrupted Richard's contemplation. "I see you found what you were looking for," it chided.

Richard turned to see Admiral Xenk, a military commander of the tiburon people who inhabited the seabed of the Solar Sea. "Only half the puzzle," Richard replied, his voice projecting in the water as if he had gills. "Can you feel the overwhelming evil here?" he asked, a sadistic smile lingering on his lips.

Xenk stood eight feet tall, and he had the arms, legs, and torso of a humanoid. Only his head appeared completely shark-like in nature, and he resembled a tiger shark with a wide, fanged snout. His nostrils were spread out on ridges, and his black eyes rested on the sides of his head so he could see in a perfect sphere in the water. A long dorsal fin ran down his back, and he also had fins on his elbows. A tail protruded from the small of his back, also ending in a fin. He responded, "Remora does not rule this seabed. What greater darkness could there be?"

The gambler let out a boisterous laugh that echoed in the ocean around him. "A great evil was slain in this very spot, friend," he said, his lips persisting in a reckless smile. "Gelidor dropped the trinket, and I found it a convenient time to come see the corpse." Richard looked at the vast, sandy expanse around them. He pointed to a distant ring of massive, jagged ridges with damaged peaks. "Come with me."

Richard led Xenk two miles away from the center of the bay. As they neared the formation, the tiburon frowned. "Remora's unholy delight. I can feel the darkness you spoke of before!" he said with a bellowing laugh.

Richard grinned and held up his hands. "Don't fear the darkness, friend. Your agenda coincides with my most important client's." He wore ten rings, each finger and both thumbs adorned in a different hue. "There is work to be done. I hold the Corona of Grunax, and I will use it to shake things up a little." He chuckled, glancing at the tiburon. "Are you ready to draw a card?"

Xenk's dark eyes glinted. "What is this darkness that I feel but cannot see?" The tiburon leader shuddered. His eyes focused on Richard's rings. The Corona of Grunax was once a singular crown decorated by ten gems of incredible power. After Grunax was slain during the Legion of Hoxark, his crown was melted and the gems dispersed into ten separate rings. Each one possessed a single, horrifying power. Only someone with a trade network as far reaching as Na'agamlor could have possibly reunited the rings. "The merchant has left a lot of trinkets in his wake," Xenk growled. His black eyes moved from Richard's rings to the amulet in the gambler's hand. "The Corona of Grunax and the Heart of Ultria in the same hands. It's hard to believe the amulet you now hold is the object responsible for Gelidor's revolution."

Richard's smile became more sinister. "The Heart of Ultria allows one to speak a curse that will grant the wielder's wishes. Gelidor only used it to kill in a very unimaginative way. It can be used to manipulate mortals much more effectively." His eyes drifted from the tiburon to the amulet now draped around his hand. "The problem rests in the dark nature of this artifact. Every time you wish upon it, Ultria feeds on your soul."

The shark-man's unblinking expression remained stoic. "How did Gelidor use it to curse so many, then? And why would you seek such a terrible fate?"

Richard ran his fingers through his dusty blond hair which was waving upward in the water. His brown eyes radiated avarice, and the tones of his brown skin were muted in the soft light of the depths. "By the time Gelidor was killed, his soul had long been traded to satiate his lust for power. I don't intend to use the amulet, but I will trade it to the right buyer." He looked at Xenk and winked. "Otherwise, it'll just accumulate dust in my collection."

Xenk's teeth chattered until Richard pointed at the top of the undersea ridge. The gambler explained, "To answer your question about the darkness, though. Here lies part of the corpse of The Intangible, one of Hoxark's most powerful demons. She was slain during the Legion of Hoxark by your favorite fish."

The tiburon looked at the peaks then the rubble below. The area lacked signs of life, creating an ambience of isolation. "Remora's sister? Umiaigén? May she be swept to the Brines. What precious warrior was slain here, and why am I unable to see her?"

Richard raised his right hand, and the teal gemstone on his middle finger flashed. The bottom of the bay lit up for an instant, but Xenk saw nothing out of the ordinary. Richard pushed his will through the ring, and a loud grinding sound filled the water around them. Impressions forming in the sand suggested Richard began to push a massive skeleton, a ribcage pattern raking its way through the silty ground in the center of the circular ridge. The rocky formation around them vibrated, and chunks of stone broke and fell to the base of the ridge. The teal light faded, and a massive weight around them shook the water and ground.

The displaced water pushed Richard and Xenk far away from the ridge. The gambler floated in the water, watching the ridge with patience.

Xenk marveled in silence. Though he could not see what

happened, he felt it was important to his soldiers. He used his fins to stabilize his body, swimming to stay close to Richard.

After five minutes, Richard lowered himself to the seabed. A shambling, black silhouette emerged from the nearby base of the rocks. It moved toward him and the tiburon at a sluggish pace. Richard pointed at it, explaining, "I think he got stuck."

The figure walked up to them without hesitation. It resembled an amorphous conglomeration of black rocks. The stones shifted throughout the creature's body, diving beneath the skin only to be replaced by another of similar size. It looked like a six-foot roiling pillar. Before Xenk could address the situation, the creature spoke. Its voice sounded foreign to Xenk, but Richard thought it sounded like a circus announcer. "Wow! How long have I been down here, and who do I have to thank for getting out?" The creature paused, laughed, and continued, "I've been really really bored! I want to take it out on some mortals."

Richard's lips curled into a persuasive smile. His voice changed to the tone of a salesman. "You can thank Luca of the Death Scythes of Hoxark for your freedom. She contracted me to push The Intangible's skeleton off of you. She's pretty sure there's big things coming up for you and your demon buddies."

The creature's strange, bubbly body continued shifting until the pillar grew arms and a discernible head. The bottom of its body remained a churning, formless dark substance. As the creature's features solidified, it replied, "Wait—Wait, so you are strong enough to pick up that old bag of bones?" The monster's laughter vibrated the seabed, and its voice carried well in the water. Xenk couldn't smell a fish for over a mile.

Richard held up his hands, wiggling his fingers to emphasize the relics on his digits.

The roiling pillar gave another jovial, quake-inducing laugh. The fit lasted for a minute. As the cackling subsided, it resumed its questioning. "The Corona of Grunax! I have no idea who you are, but I like you. What can I call my savior?"

The gambler's sinister smile returned. "Richard Terr, Na'agamlor's Ace." His sleight of hand impressed the monster as a playing card flashed in and out of sight. He twirled it around his fingers. "And you, The Adversary, are one of the four surviving Heptakhi. Your comrades in Cassack await you."

Xenk's eyes bulged in disbelief. "H-heptakhi!?" he stuttered.

The Adversary's bubbling body shifted, and the sculpted head peered at the tiburon with an unsettling posture. Though it resembled a head, it had no discernible eyes or mouth. The maniacal voice replied, "Nah. Never gave that title much stock. I just want to burn stuff! I can't though. I spent like a thousand years trying to burn Brisa's corpse, but I could never get her bones to melt. The worst part is, I can't even see how close I got!"

Richard rolled his head from side to side, lowering all but the pinky on his left hand. The ring upon it shone vivid pink, allowing him to view the planes and dimensions adjacent to Espa's reality. It further gave him the ability to see through illusions like invisibility with no effort other than a thought to the ring. He could see the bones, but he couldn't share the benefits of Piercing Sight with his companions. He answered The Adversary's lamentation, "Fear not, demon. If Hoxark had not been banished, you would have melted the skeleton eventually. I wouldn't say you made it halfway, but the bones resemble candles. Plus, it's only half of her ribcage. I think the other half got skewered off toward the Isles Known for Nothing."

Xenk tried to join the conversation. "Ah, the Shadow Reef! Yes!"

The pillar of black flashed red for a second. He ignored Xenk and replied to the gambler. "I need Fuerzul if I'm going to blow anything up! I ran out of juice a long time ago, but I'm glad to know you can see my progress. Lemme tell ya, it's really boring being trapped under your girlfriend's bones. We went from trying to kill each other daily to her weighing me down and leaving me abandoned here. After Hoxark left, I used up the last of my Fuerzul trying to BURN what was left of her, and after I ran out? Well. I started counting the grains of sand on the floor of the seabed. Was a good show up top a while back, though."

Richard smirked. "The Battle of Beriton." He held up The Heart of Ultria.

Two, distinct red eyes formed in the sides of The Adversary's head. Bubbles escaped from Xenk's gills as the tiburon gasped at the change. The demon replied, "No surprise, the deities of old still meddle in the affairs of mortals."

The gambler shrugged. "Eh! Mostly just mortals using what's left of the old gods to take their piece. Like me." He winked. "I've gotta go back to Claston and fetch something of great value."

The Adversary also formed a red, lava-like mouth. The water around it steamed. His words, however, echoed clearly in the aquatic ambience. "Is there any Fuerzul there? I need evil souls. I can take them myself if I have to!"

Richard gave a long, incredulous stare at The Adversary. "Give it a week. Hang out with Xenk here. It's the first day of The Warming. I'm sure you'll find *plenty* of Fuerzul straight from the source starting today."

The Adversary's broiling mouth sank into a frown. "I've been here waiting for Hoxark for who knows how long?! I don't want to stay anymore!" The heat boiled the water around the demon's head in spite of their depth.

Richard's eyes narrowed, his smile returned, and his voice resumed the tone of a salesman. "The barriers between dimensions are getting weak. A former client of my master's has been working on getting Na'agamlor to the primordial place. That means energy from the Abyss will flow freely soon. Follow?"

The Adversary's heat calmed and the water around him fizzled with residual bubbles. "How close are the nearest mortals?"

Richard pointed north in the water. "A few miles, but don't worry about them yet. The tiburon are planning an invasion. You probably want to help, because I'm going to take something from the palace of Claston while everyone is worried about the port. Gelidor generated a lot of Fuerzul while he was destroying his kingdom, and with Hoxark's return imminent, it's time to rebuild the Altar of Balthazar."

The demon appeared to sit down on the seabed despite a lack of legs. He replied. "Fine. I can wait a few more days for a little fun. Besides, even if you're a liar, I'm still free!" The glowing, red mouth turned up into a smile. "For all your good deeds, I'll tell you something, Richard. My name is Petro. The Adversary is just what Hoxark started calling me after he watched mortals try to douse my flames with water. Talk about stupid!"

Richard rolled his eyes and chuckled. "Your name? I agree, it's absurd." The demon's red features tightened in shock, but Richard kept talking. "Just follow the shark here, he'll help you find a way to apply your talents." The gambler winked again.

Xenk felt his heart lift with excitement. Richard just connected him with one of the most ancient, powerful demons in all of Espa. Xenk knew what needed to be done.

After some inconsequential remarks of departure, the gambler left The Adversary with Xenk. Richard walked ashore and used one of his rings to fly to the top of the mountains before him. He looked down at Beriton with a scrutinizing stare. "Twenty to one favoring the demon. No, fifty to one." He frowned and snarled with disgust. "I hate to bet on Miranda Hyacinth, but I can't pass up odds like that on a proven underdog. I'm going to be richer than my boss by the end of this. Fifty million in my pocket when Farzg died. I think I'll raise the ante before the next hand. You better get to the primordial place soon, Max. I'm tired of keeping up with this bothersome priestess for you."

GLOSSARY
AND
LITURGY

GLOSSARY

Old Common

adûnzha - attention
mahalàkhas – praise and blessings
talirix volïs - unhallowed chaos

Elven

Eba-zim - Cousin, ungendered
Hai-rin - Mother, formal (Hai-n, informal)
Hai-yashir - Aunt
Modai-moshir - Uncle
Modai-rin - Father, formal (Modai-n, informal)
Molen - Nephew
Moshirin - Little brother, formal (Moshi'n, informal)
Moshirote - Little brother, formal (Moshte, informal)
Mosh-zim - Cousin, male
Mu-zim - Son, formal. (Muz, informal)
Nen'li - Friend
Nes'ni - Come here.
Nulestotejin - Brother-in-law
Yashirin - Little sister, formal (Yashi'n, informal)
Yashirote - Big sister, formal (Yashte, informal)
Yash-zim - Cousin, female
Yolasha - Daughter, formal (Yoli, informal)
Yolen - Niece
Yulesta - Wife, formal (Yula, informal)
Yulestotejin - Sister-in-law

Suffix - 'thi: Plural marker. For example, moshirin'thi = Little brothers (formal).
Suffix - 'nides: Expression of unconditional love. Example: Moshirin'nides = I love you, little brother.

<u>LITURGY</u>

Each faith is sorted in order of appearance. Not all functional prayers are contained in the liturgical records.

ß – Denotes a basic prayer
Σ – Denotes an advanced prayer
Ω – Denotes a significantly advanced prayer

INVICTUS

Catechism of Vigilance Σ

Evil never sleeps, and chaos gnaws at the heels of society. The righteous must be ever vigilant. Those who treasure order and justice will stay the bite, and may we serve the Sword of Justice and the Silver Maiden with humble hearts and actions worthy of praise.

Orb of Protection Prayer Σ

Invictus, with your wisdom and patience, you are like an unyielding rock in the tides of time. Surround us with your protection and ward away chaos.

Prayer of Healing ß

Restore to order what was damaged by chaos.

Prayer of Divination ß

Sword of Justice, guide my eyes to the truth.

Prayer of Safe Passage

Sword of Justice, protect us from harm and lead us to safety.

Prayer of Daylight Σ

Sword of Justice, pour out your light and righteousness. Push back the darkness with your holy daylight.

Prayer of Divine Empowerment Σ

Sword of Justice, I beseech your might. Lend me the strength of your arms, the swiftness of your feet, the sharpness of your mind, and the protection of your shield.

Curse of Binding Σ

Reality is composed of beautiful form imposed by creators of order. As we weave this tapestry of life, the threads of disorder threaten to ruin the stitching of the faithful. Bind that which sews chaos!

Catechism of Meeting Again ß

The Sword of Justice smiles on this reunion. May we follow the Path of the Sword of Justice with righteousness and humility.

Catechism of the Traveler ß

May the Sword of Justice guide your path. Set out with order in your steps and righteousness in your hearts. May Invictus shine his holy light upon you and pour out his judgement in abundance. Our steps forward bring the future, but our footprints are the evidence of our deeds. Silver Maiden, guide our hearts; Sword of Justice, guide our hands. Together we depart, and together we shall return.

Flame Smite Σ

Sword of Justice, hear my voice. Your faithful are at the mercy of the unjust. Surround the enemy with your holy fire. Rain down your judgment.

Nullifying Barrier Σ

"Sword of Justice, we seek refuge behind your shield! A great calamity befalls the faithful. Disinherit the legacy of the wicked!"

Prayer of Destructive Containment Σ

Sword of Justice, contain the wrath of our enemies!

Healer's Catechism #3 ß

On this day, we face great calamity. Justice has been wounded and order bleeds at the hands of chaos. In these days, may the hands of Invictus heal the wounds. Now is not the time for more bloodshed, but for mending.

Catechism of Grief ß

We are bereft, Sword of Justice. Though Invictus is mighty, the destiny of mortals reaches beyond the sands of time. From creation to end, comfort our hearts, rest our minds. May we walk the Path of the Sword of Justice with solemnity and humility.

Empowered Breath of Salvation Ω

May the healing hand of the Sword of Justice bind the wounds caused by the hands of evil. We face a great peril this day, and we beg the Sword of Justice to pour out his mercy with abundance.

Resistance to Evil Divinity Σ

Sword of Justice, shield me with your mighty hands. Cover me so that evil may not touch!

Holy Flames of Judgment Ω

Righteous Order, we beseech your divine strength. We pray for your might to rain down on our enemies in condemnation. Drive out these unholy powers before us and smite them with your Holy Flames of Judgment.

Mass Blessing Σ

Invictus, the ever vigilant. Shroud us with the aura of your power! Give to us great foresight and greater bravery. Send us the mercy of your sister, the Silver Maiden. Grant us her fortitude and courage.

Cure Paralysis Σ

Restore the feeling in your faithful's body.

Elemental Protection: Lightning and Air ß

Invictus, ground us in faith and firmament. Shield us from the fury of the Tempest

Enervating Shield Ω

Sword of Justice, may your enervating hand sweep the enemy before us, and may your infinite grace shield us from unyielding evil.

Intercepting Shield Σ

Shield us from the onslaught of chaos, Sword of Justice. May your hand stay the enemy.

Purifying Rain Σ

Invictus, our rock of righteousness. We strike thee in the desert when we thirst! Send your purifying rain!

Banishing Prayer Ω

Sword of Justice, an agent of chaos has crossed the barriers between space and time to wreak havoc on the mortal coil. We beseech thee, open the void between worlds and cast this fiend back into the bowels of the universe. May orc and fae know peace, may the people rejoice as your hand descends to right what has been wronged by this aberrant presence

Catechism of Redeemed Death ß

May the arms of justice embrace this soul, tormented by redemption. May he rest with the Heroes Departed, grant him eternal lauds for his sacrifice.

Catechism of Departure ß

Our missions have different details, but we pursue the same goal. Though our paths stray from each other for a time, we will meet again when the Sword of Justice has righted the chaos. May the roads we walk lead to a unified destination, order and peace. As it is written, so shall it be. Such is the way of the Path of the Sword of Justice.

Prayer of Divine Empowerment #3 Σ

Sword of Justice, grant me the strength to bring the work of chaos to justice. Let this nightmare end for the innocent.

Moonbeam Σ

O, Sword of Justice, reflect the rays of your justice through this blade of mine. May the Silver Maiden cast her light across that which does wickedness and dispel their vile intent.

Prayer of Cleansing ß

Light of righteousness, Sword of Justice. What chaos has sullied, cleanse with your purity. Extract the filth from the blood, restore this body and heal this mind

Protection from Toxic Fumes ß

Sword of Justice, shield my lungs from the toxic air of chaos and envelope me in your embrace. May the fires of evil leave no mark!

Protection from Infernal Power Σ
Sword of Justice, shield us from the flames of the Infernia!

***Vexilatus* – Demonic Roster Appendix VI The Lieutenants**
From the depths of the Abyss, there is one who has sunk his tendrils deep into the flesh of the earth. Espa cries from the wound, and it festers beneath the surface. From the unending tides of evil and chaos, The Root thrives on the guilt of mortals. Walking with the Legion of Hoxark, that great demon hid himself among the dendroid, changing them into trees of death and despair.

Miranda's Demonic Wither Ω
Invictus, shower me with your grace and benevolence. Bring this demon out of hiding!

Protection from Natural Elements ß
Sword of Justice, shelter us from the storm! Protect us from the cold and the sun, may our exposure be forgiven and our travels safe.

Smiting Fist Σ
Fist of Justice, smite my enemy.

PULHASH

Protection Prayer Σ
Only fools leave the house without a shield. Help me, mighty avenger!

Vengeful Guardian Σ
There's a fight down here, Pulhash, and I need reinforcements!

HOXARK

Conjure – Metamorphosis Ω
Ak'hnashin

OTHER

Divine Sanctuary Ω
O, gods who rest in the primordial place, we beseech those of good heart. We are beset by evil and chaos at every turn; provide us a sanctuary from harm. Surround us with your divine protection. Our strength fails us, and we are left to the mercy of darkness.

Espa Historical Timeline

THE RIFTING

A great calamity preceded Espa's modern reality. The destruction of the planet's southern hemisphere marked the end of a different world. As Genesis holds the world together with the arcane stream, life evolves quickly. The nightmares of the planet's savior corrupt some of that life, giving birth to monstrous gods and beasts. To prevent the nightmares, Genesis subdued his consciousness by breaking it into the dragon gods.

THE AGE OF AWAKENING – 1000 YEARS

The explosion of life following The Rifting led to a cycle of conflict and growth. Dragons, the fragmented consciousness of Genesis, watched mortality grow in periods of Universal Harmony. As the great beings created from Genesis's nightmares caused waves of conflict through violence and intrigue, mortals responded with varying degrees of resilience. The dragons of light aided mortals, but the dragons of darkness resented them. The end of this era was marked when Solem Dragonslayer defeated Gorthran, sending the Dragon Father into the arcane stream for the first time.

THE DRACON WARS – 1000 YEARS

The dragons of light and darkness turned on each other with great violence following Gorthran's defeat. From the stream, the Dragon Father directed his children to terrorize mortals wherever and whenever they could. Their devastation was widespread, and Saraix the Dragon Mother was slain in the conflict. From the stream, she transformed her children into the Drakinskäld. They lived among mortals and aided them against the dragons of darkness. Their numbers and resistance to draconic magic made a great difference, but Genesis's mind became too fragmented. As the dragons of light triumphed, the consciousness of the stream awoke, reunifying the dragons for a brief time. He banished the core of his happy memories to Escondido and the core of his dark memories to Olvidado. Once there, those entities began devising schemes anew.

THE REBUILDING – 1000 YEARS

The Drakinskäld disappeared at the end of The Dracon Wars, but the Draikin emerged from the depths of Espa's underworld. Though dwarves, elves, humans, orcs, and the many peoples of Espa had existed together for two thousand years in some respects, they had to relearn each other's customs and cultures. The prosperity of this time was shadowed by the great conflicts between the elder gods, eager to fill the power vacuum left by the dragon gods.

THE LEGION OF HOXARK – 1000 YEARS

Legends describe the arrival of two comets marking the end of The Rebuilding. One of the two comets crashed into the nebulous, roiling Rift that replaced the planet's southern hemisphere. Upon that comet rode Hoxark, The Wanton Decay. Espa's planetary distress and hasty evolution made the perfect breeding ground for Hoxark's demonic powers. He turned the darkest actions of mortals into otherworldly power, and thus the demons of Espa were born. The remainder of the old gods banded together, but many of them were slain in the conflict. They passed their powers and domains on to great mortals like Invictus and Lexcord.

EPOCH OF NOVO DEUM – 1000 YEARS

Hoxark was banished to the Abyss by a coalition of Lexcord, Umiaigén, Gaiater the earth mother, Pulhash, and Wurfaxt. These newer gods formed a pact of mutual protection, establishing the clerical organization of the Southern Cross. They also established the Treaty of Souls, a guarantee that gods would only intervene with mortals from the primordial place. In exchange, the gods could exist in a safe place away from power hungry mortals and focus on their divine affairs. During this time period, the Empire of Gabah rose to a pinnacle of power, conquering most of the eastern continent with their industrial might.

The Unbinding revealed a great weakness in magic itself: something in the primary dimension can affect the whole of the arcane. Santiago Eb'lin's research focused on Espa's creation myths, finding some truth to the story of Gensis. As the dragon godshards empower his creations, magic weakens around Espa. The crisis is escalating as Espa's leaders covet the mad-elf's inventions.

PLACE AND CHARACTER PROFILES

Illustration: J. Neff. Oil Pastel on Canvas.

Nulodia is known as the "port capital" of the Alabaster Kingdom. A bustling hub of commerce, it is home to several hundred thousand people including the suburbs that stretch far outside the original city walls. Located on the Starlock Delta, swathes of farmland intersperse throughout the city. Boasting a working sewage system, running water for most homes inside the city walls, and a robust market, Nulodia sees thousands of travelers on a daily basis. The viscount, Royce Alabaster, is practically a despot. He funds the church generously to keep the city safe, but he expects church leadership to be impeccable and deferent to the crown. He has steered clear of the cathedral since High Priest Selasine replaced Carulus. Factories operated by steam and uncanny magic are becoming more common.

Miranda stayed for two weeks in Nulodia to train with Justin and Valarie on the art of using a shield. She had dinner with Erk and Evan during that time. Evan was frustratingly quiet. Shortly after, he hinted about his growing feelings for Miranda to Erk and Naomi. Erk arranged them a dinner alone together on her next visit to the city.

MYSTALON

Illustration: J. Neff, Graphite on Paper

The reclusive nature of Mystalon has kept much of their society's magical technology secret since The Unbinding. The founders of Mystalon left Claston four hundred years before the Clastonian Civil War began. They were the most distrustful members of the traditionalists, and they established the Mystalonian Republic to maintain their chokehold on their rejection of all things non-elven. They relied on the solisberry tree to enhance their wizards' power, and they maintained independence throughout numerous wars, uprisings, and incursions. Though their society rejected outside influence, a few members of the Congress of Sages have succumbed to the temptation of foreign influence and wealth on more than one occasion.

Illustration: J. Neff. Digital, Clip Studio Paint.

Kzar's *Magical Locations and Sources of Power* is the only tome known to document The Pool of Effulgent Tears. The goddess known as Dimittena the Weeper created it during The Age of Awakening, and she disappeared near the end of that era. Kzar wrote:

The Pool of Effulgent Tears is the consistent name of a mysterious location that foretells calamity. Great figures, heroes, and power seekers have made passing references to it in their memoires, journals, or orations. Consider Galathus Newl of The Age of Awakening, Celeste Skyborne and Gostra Mathas of The Dracon Wars, and Copernicus Vesper of The Legion of Hoxark. They describe a visit to a place they call The Pool of Effulgent Tears, a name too specific to be coincidental. Though a natural wonder to behold, great calamity befell its visitors the following day. Newl was eaten by the very dragon he swore to destroy, Celeste's daughter was slain as they struggled against the dragons of darkness, Gostra's village was destroyed in a raid, and Copernicus's tea was poisoned with mercury. Beware The Pool of Effulgent Tears, as each of these events primed a major conflict of continental scale.

THE LICHWOOD

Illustration: J. Neff, Digital, Clip Studio Paint

The Lichwood was formerly known as Dendraos, but the civilization of tree people was destroyed by The Root during the Legion of Hoxark. The cursed location has inspired numerous ghost stories. Farzg chose the peninsula on the north side for his estate. The Root fears the frost giantkin's immense power, and Farzg permits The Root to remain in close proximity in spite of the demon's aura of despair and decay. The Lichwood is visible from sixty miles away as the elevation increases in the Timbyl region. The undead trees are a blight on the horizon in most descriptions.

THE HYACINTH ESTATE

Illustration: J. Neff, Digital, Clip Studio Paint

Built in Novo Deum 980, the Hyacinth estate is the only noble manor in Devitus. Baron Alan Duchenes resided in the keep at the center of Devitus when Philotrax and Reshiria arrived. Philotrax purchased the title of "Lord and Lady Hyacinth" for his family, and the Baron deeded the estate to the Hyacinths. The last million coins from Philotrax's dragon hoard were used to renovate public buildings in the sleepy frontier town.

MIRANDA HYACINTH

Illustration: J. Neff, Clip Studio Paint

On Miranda's 21st birthday, she was in K'tal H'yuck. She celebrated with Master Zeak, Arlindra, Celyth, and Casandra Moon Lotus. The cousins revealed their desire to reach Argentum. Miranda demanded the cousins allow her to help as a birthday present. Zeak helped Miranda identify the correct tunnels, warning her, "Once you find that place, things are going to get complicated. I can't help you after that. I've got a mission of my own."

ARLINDRA FERNITH

Birthday: Vernal Equinox 9

Illustration: J. Neff, Clip Studio Paint

Arlindra loves hunting and cooking. Her older sister, Aurora, works for their father as a legal clerk. Her older brother, Aluxel, is a magitab artisan. After Vanesa's disappearance, Arlindra grew closer to her cousin than siblings. She enjoys being a ranger for the isolation it provides, but she is a friendly person deep down. She is slow to give her trust, but she is a loyal friend. As a result of her experiences with Celyth, Nebu, and Miranda, Arlindra begins to trust others. She has begun to extend that trust to Erk and August.

CELYTH FERNITH

Birthday: Warming 11

Illustration: J. Neff, Clip Studio Paint

Celyth is competitive and enthusiastic. Her low tolerance for nonsensical social expectations earned her a reputation in Mystalon as rude and uncouth. She, however, laughs and says that she's "too busy honing my talent to worry what do-nothings think of me." In spite of her abrasiveness, many Mystalonians look up to Evander's rebellious daughter. The only person in Mystalon who can compete with Celyth's archery skills is her cousin, Arlindra.

YUVINA OF THE TYMBYRWYLDE

Birthday: Festival 31

Yuvina's trauma and distrust of magic are intertwined, and she has relentlessly pursued arcane knowledge since she joined The Forgotten. Her obsession has consumed her life for over a decade; she has no hobbies beyond subterfuge and fighting Wielders.

VALARIE TERR

Birthday: Harvesting 6

Valarie ran away from home after her father tried to force her into a transactional marriage. She joined the church to follow in her mother's footsteps, as her father said it was the church that tore her mother away from the family. Valarie always suspected that her father was dishonest about what happened to her mother.

MARIN ELITIRIN

Birthday: Summer Solstice 17

Marin is one of Espa's premier manabotanists, and she secretly published papers at the University of Alabaster and the Breckinshore Ridge Magic Academy. Her early research with mushrooms and mold led to the discovery of medical antibiotics in East Espa. Her work, *The Sacred Trees of Espa*, is the standard textbook for arborists and manabotanists at Breckinshore Ridge. Nobody in Mystalon is aware, however, as nobody has left Mystalon for schooling in four hundred years.

About the Author

As a young person, Jory's favorite class in school was history. He could probably blame it on the video game *Age of Empires*, the Greek mythology focused serials *Xena* and *Hercules* of the 90s, or the really cool projects his history teachers made him do. In those early days, he dreamed of creating his own world.

He attained his master's degree in history in 2009. By that time, he had been world building with his former college roommate, Ashley, for almost five years. They were inspired by *Avatar: The Last Airbender*, Dungeons and Dragons 3.5, and the tons of stories and histories they read together for class. They took a creative writing class together, and Ashley's wild imagination worked well with Jory's detailed settings. Through those collaborations, Espa was born. (The world didn't have a name until *Unbound Chaos* was released in 2023).

Jory finished his PhD in 2021. He began writing fiction with the discipline learned from his academic studies. He has slowly found his voice, and he is more optimistic than ever about Espa's future. He has grown alongside Miranda; the lessons learned from trying to do the right thing the wrong way are embodied in this narrative. He is grateful for everyone who has been a part of his journey.

By day, Jory works as an educator teaching art, social studies, and Spanish. In his free time, he indulges his creative pursuits. With a balanced pursuit of illustrating and writing, he has grown both skills together. As an autistic adult and educator, he has made Espa his life-long "special interest." His wife, Janell, has worked diligently by his side to make Espa a reality. Her feedback and advice have shaped Jory's creative journey.

The Unbound Verse Community

Our social media direction is undergoing renovations. We are moving Jory's communication to Substack! This will give him greater control over the impact of his engagement with social media, and it will concentrate both his art and newsletters in the same place. Furthermore, with the advent of the Unbinding Chronicles website (under development), there will be TTRPG resources and maps for players and game masters.

Substack: joryneff.substack.com

Check the LinkTree for the most recent Discord link!

Instagram: @J_Neff_Artexperiments

Email: author.unbindingchronicles@gmail.com

Scan the QR Code for my LinkTree!

So much heartfelt thanks to the cover artist, Emily Verkamp, and illustrator Aesthetically Inked. Check out their socials for more of their creative projects:

Emily Verkamp	Aesthetically Inked
Insta: @emiv_photography	Insta: @aesthetically.inkedd

Website:

emilyverkamp.weebly.com

www.ingramcontent.com/pod-product-compliance
Lightning Source LLC
Chambersburg PA
CBHW070259310726
48976CB00005B/1491